ENA OF ILBREA

THE FOUR BOOK SAGA

MEGAN O'RUSSELL

Ink Worlds Press

Ena of Ilbrea: The Four Book Saga

Copyright © 2020, Megan O'Russell

Cover Art by MiblArt (https://miblart.com/)

Editing by Christopher Russell

Interior Design by Christopher Russell

Printed in the United States of America

WHITE MOUNTAINS
Royal Palace
Map Master's Palace
BARRENS
Ilara
Arion Sea
Barrens Bay
Frason's Glenn
Harane
Ian Lioche
ILBREA
Ian Mithe
Ruthir Mountain
Mountain Road
Ian Ayres
Southern Citadel
Pamerane

EMBER AND STONE

BOOK ONE

To the ones who have survived the flames.
You are strong enough to topple kingdoms.

1

The crack of the whip sent the birds scattering into the sky. They cawed their displeasure at the violence of the men below as they flew over the village and to the mountains beyond.

The whip cracked again.

Aaron did well. He didn't start to moan until the fourth lash. By the seventh, he screamed in earnest.

No one had given him a belt to bite down on. There hadn't been time when the soldiers hauled him from his house and tied him to the post in the square.

I clutched the little wooden box of salve hidden in my pocket, letting the corners bite deep into my palm.

The soldier passed forty lashes, not caring that Aaron's back had already turned to pulp.

I squeezed my way to the back of the crowd, unwilling to watch Aaron's blood stain the packed dirt.

Behind the rest of the villagers, children cowered in their mother's skirts, hiding from the horrors the Guilds' soldiers brought with them.

I didn't know how many strokes Aaron had been sentenced to. I didn't want to know. I made myself stop counting how many times the whip sliced his back.

Bida, Aaron's wife, wept on the edge of the crowd. When his screams stopped, hers grew louder.

The women around Bida held her back, keeping her out of reach of the soldiers.

My stomach stung with the urge to offer comfort as she watched her husband being beaten by the men in black uniforms. But, with the salve tucked in my pocket, hiding in the back was safest.

I couldn't give Bida the box unless Aaron survived. Spring hadn't fully arrived, and the plants Lily needed to make more salves still hadn't bloomed. The tiny portion of the stuff hidden in my pocket was worth more than someone's life, especially if that person wasn't going to survive even with Lily's help.

Lily's orders had been clear—wait and see if Aaron made it through. Give Bida the salve if he did. If he didn't, come back home and hide the wooden box under the floorboards for the next poor soul who might need it.

Aaron fell to the ground. Blood leaked from a gash under his arm.

The soldier raised his whip again.

I sank farther into the shadows, trying to comfort myself with the beautiful lie that I could never be tied to the post in the village square, though I knew the salve clutched in my hand would see me whipped at the post as quickly as whatever offense the soldiers had decided Aaron had committed.

When my fingers had gone numb from gripping the box, the soldier stopped brandishing his whip and turned to face the crowd.

"We did not come here to torment you," the soldier said. "We came here to protect Ilbrea. We came here to protect the Guilds. We are here to provide peace to all the people of this great country. This man committed a crime, and he has been punished. Do not think me cruel for upholding the law." He wrapped the bloody whip around his hand and led the other nine soldiers out of the square.

Ten soldiers. It had only taken ten of them to walk into our village and drag Aaron from his home. Ten men to tie him to the post and leave us all helpless as they beat a man who'd lived among us all his life.

The soldiers disappeared, and the crowd shifted in toward Aaron. I couldn't hear him crying or moaning over the angry mutters of the crowd.

His wife knelt by his side, wailing.

I wound my way forward, ignoring the stench of fear that surrounded the villagers.

Aaron lay on the ground, his hands still tied around the post. His back had been flayed open by the whip. His flesh looked more like something for a butcher to deal with than an illegal healer like me.

I knelt by his side, pressing my fingers to his neck to feel for a pulse.

Nothing.

I wiped my fingers on the cleanest part of Aaron's shirt I could find and weaved my way back out of the crowd, still clutching the box of salve in my hand.

Carrion birds gathered on the rooftops near the square, scenting the fresh blood in the air. They didn't know Aaron wouldn't be food for them. The villagers of Harane had yet to fall so low as to leave our own out as a feast for the birds.

There was no joy in the spring sun as I walked toward Lily's house on the eastern edge of the village.

I passed by the tavern, which had already filled with men who didn't mind we hadn't reached midday. I didn't blame them for hiding in there. If they could find somewhere away from the torment of the soldiers, better on them for seizing it. I only hoped there weren't any soldiers laughing inside the tavern's walls.

I followed the familiar path home. Along our one, wide dirt road, past the few shops Harane had to offer, to the edge of the village where only fields and pastures stood between us and the forest that reached up the eastern mountains' slopes.

It didn't take long to reach the worn wooden house with the one giant tree towering out front. It didn't take long to reach anywhere in the tiny village of Harane.

Part of me hated knowing every person who lived nearby. Part of me wished the village were smaller. Then maybe we'd fall off the Guilds' maps entirely.

As it was, the Guilds only came when they wanted to collect our taxes, to steal our men to fight their wars, or to find some other sick pleasure in inflicting agony on people who wanted nothing more than to survive. Or if their business brought them far enough south on the mountain road they had to pass through our home on their way to torment someone else.

I allowed myself a moment to breathe before facing Lily. I blinked away the images of Aaron covered in blood and shoved them into a dark corner with the rest of the wretched things it was better not to ponder.

Lily barely glanced up as I swung open the gate and stepped into the back garden. Dirt covered her hands and skirt. Her shoulders were hunched from the hours spent planting our summer garden. She never allowed me to help with the task. Everything had to be carefully planned, keeping the vegetables toward the outermost edges. Hiding the plants she could be hanged for in the center, where soldiers were less likely to spot the things she grew to protect the people of our village. The people the soldiers were so eager to hurt.

"Did he make it?" Lily stretched her shoulders back and brushed the dirt off her weathered hands.

I held the wooden box out as my response. Blood stained the corners. It wasn't Aaron's blood. It was mine. Cuts marked my hand where I'd squeezed the box too tightly.

Lily glared at my palm. "You'd better go in and wrap your hand. If you let it get infected, I'll have to treat you with the salve, and you know we're running out."

I tucked the box back into my pocket and went inside, not bothering to argue that I could heal from a tiny cut. I didn't want to look into Lily's wrinkled face and see the glimmer of pity in her eyes.

The inside of the house smelled of herbs and dried flowers. Their familiar scent did nothing to drive the stench of blood and fear from my nose.

A pot hung over the stove, waiting with whatever Lily had made for breakfast.

My stomach churned at the thought of eating. I needed to get out. Out of the village, away from the soldiers.

I pulled up the loose floorboard by the stove and tucked the salve in between the other boxes, tins, and vials. I grabbed my bag off the long, wooden table and shoved a piece of bread and a waterskin into it for later. I didn't bother grabbing a coat or shawl. I didn't care about getting cold.

I have to get out.

I was back through the door and in the garden a minute later. Lily didn't even look up from her work. "If you're running into the forest, you had better come back with something good."

"I will," I said. "I'll bring you back all sorts of wonderful things. Just make sure you save some dinner for me."

I didn't need to ask her to save me food. In all the years I'd lived with her, Lily had never let me go hungry. But she was afraid I would run away into the forest and never return. Or maybe it was me that feared I might disappear into the trees and never come back. Either way, I felt myself relax as I stepped out of the garden and turned my feet toward the forest.

2

The mountains rose up beyond the edge of the trees, fierce towers I could never hope to climb. No one else from the village would ever even dream of trying such a thing.

The soldiers wouldn't enter the woods. The villagers rarely dared to go near them. The forest was where darkness and solitude lay. A quiet place where the violence of the village couldn't follow me.

I skirted farmers' fields and picked my way through the pastures. No one bothered me as I climbed over the fences they built to keep in their scarce amounts of sheep and cows.

No one kept much livestock. They couldn't afford it in the first place. And besides, if the soldiers saw that one farmer had too many animals, they would take the beasts as taxes. Safer to be poor. Better for your belly to go empty than for the soldiers to think you had something to give.

I moved faster as I got past the last of the farmhouses and beyond the reach of the stench of animal dung.

When I was a very little girl, my brother had told me that the woods were ruled by ghosts. That none of the villagers dared to cut down the trees or venture into their shelter for fear of being taken by the dead and given a worse fate than even the Guilds could provide.

I'd never been afraid of ghosts, and I'd wandered through the woods often enough to be certain that no spirits roamed the eastern mountains.

When I first started going into the forest, I convinced myself I was braver than everyone else in Harane. I was an adventurer, and they were cowards.

Maybe I just knew better. Maybe I knew that no matter what ghosts did, they could never match the horrors men inflict on each other. What I'd seen them do to each other.

By the time I was a hundred feet into the trees, I could no longer see the village behind me. I couldn't smell anything but the fresh scent of damp earth as the little plants fought for survival in the fertile spring ground. I knew my way through the woods well enough I didn't need to bother worrying about which direction to go. It was more a question of which direction I wanted to chase the gentle wind.

I could go and find fungi for Lily to make into something useful, or I could climb. If I went quickly, I would have time to climb and still be able to find something worth Lily getting herself hanged for.

Smiling to myself, I headed due east toward the steepest part of the mountains near our village. Dirt soon covered the hem of my skirt, and mud squelched beneath my shoes, creeping in through the cracked leather of the soles. I didn't mind so much. What the cold could do to me was nothing more than a refreshing chance to prove I was still alive. Life existed outside the village, and there was beauty beyond our battered walls.

Bits of green peeked through the brown of the trees as new buds forced their way out of the branches.

I stopped, staring up at the sky, marveling at the beauty hidden within our woods.

Birds chirped overhead. Not the angry cawing of birds of death, but the beautiful songs of lovebirds who had nothing more to worry about than tipping their wings up toward the sky.

A gray and blue bird burst from a tree, carrying his song deeper into the forest.

A stream gurgled to one side of me. The snap of breaking branches came from the other. I didn't change my pace as the crackling came closer.

I headed south to a steeper slope where I had to use my hands to pull myself up the rocks.

I moved faster, outpacing the one who lumbered through the trees behind me. A rock face cut through the forest, blocking my path. I dug my fingers into the cracks in the stone, pulling myself up. Careful to keep my legs from being tangled in my skirt, I found purchase on the rock with the soft toes of my boots. In a few quick movements, I pushed myself up over the top of the ledge. I leapt to my feet and ran to the nearest tree, climbing up to the highest thick branch.

I sat silently on my perch, waiting to see what sounds would come from below.

A rustle came from the base of the rock, followed by a long string of inventive curses.

I bit my lips together, not allowing myself to call out.

The cursing came again.

"Of all the slitching, vile—" the voice from below growled.

I leaned back against the tree, closing my eyes, reveling in my last few moments of solitude. Those hints of freedom were what I loved most about being able to climb. Going up a tree, out of reach of the things that would catch me.

"Ena," the voice called. "Ena."

I didn't answer.

"Ena, are you going to leave me down here?"

My lips curved into a smile as I bit back my laughter. "I didn't ask you to follow me. You can just go back the way you came."

"I don't want to go back," he said. "Let me come up. At least show me how you did it."

"If you want to chase me, you'd better learn to climb."

I let him struggle for a few more minutes until he threatened to find a pick and crack through the rock wall. I glanced down to find him three feet off the ground, his face bright red as he tried to climb.

"Jump down," I said, not wanting him to fall and break something. I could have hauled him back to the village, but I didn't fancy the effort.

"Help me get up," he said.

"Go south a bit. You'll find an easier path."

I listened to the sounds of him stomping off through the trees, enjoying the bark against my skin as I waited for him to find the way up.

It only took him a few minutes to loop back around to stand under my perch.

Looking at Cal stole my will to flee. His blond hair glistened in the sun. He shaded his bright blue eyes as he gazed up at me.

"Are you happy now?" he said. "I'm covered in dirt."

"If you wanted to be clean, you shouldn't have come into the woods. I never ask you to follow me."

"It would have been wrong of me not to. You shouldn't be coming out here by yourself."

I didn't let it bother me that he thought it was too dangerous for me to be alone in the woods. It was nice to have someone worry about me. Even if he was worried about ghosts that didn't exist.

"What do you think you'd be able to do to help me anyway?" I said.

He stared up at me, hurt twisting his perfect brow.

Cal looked like a god, or something made at the will of the Guilds themselves. His chiseled jaw held an allure to it, the rough stubble on his cheeks luring my fingers to touch its texture.

I twisted around on my seat and dropped down to the ground, reveling in his gasp as I fell.

"You really need to get more used to the woods," I said. "It's a good place to hide."

"What would I have to hide from?" Cal's eyes twinkled, offering a hint of teasing that drew me toward him.

I touched the stubble on his chin, tracing the line of his jaw.

"There are plenty of things to hide from, fool." I turned to tramp farther into the woods.

"Ena," he called after me, "you shouldn't be going so far from home."

"Then don't follow me. Go back." I knew he would follow.

I had known when I passed by his window in the tavern on my way through the village. He always wanted to be near me. That was the beauty of Cal.

I veered closer to the stream.

Cal kept up, though he despised getting his boots muddy.

I always chose the more difficult path to make sure he knew I could outpace him. It was part of our game on those trips into the forest.

I leapt across the stream to a patch of fresh moss just beginning to take advantage of spring.

"Ena." Cal jumped the water and sank down onto the moss I had sought.

I shoved him off of the green and into the dirt.

He growled.

I didn't bother trying to hide my smile. I pulled out tufts of the green moss, tucking them into my bag for Lily.

"If you don't want me to follow you," Cal said, "you can tell me not to whenever you like."

"The forest doesn't belong to me, Cal. You can go where you choose."

He grabbed both my hands and tugged me toward him. I tipped onto him and he shifted, letting me fall onto my back. I caught a glimpse of the sun peering down through the new buds of emerald leaves, and then he was kissing me.

His taste of honey and something a bit deeper filled me. And I forgot about whips and Lily and men bleeding and soldiers coming to kill us.

There was nothing but Cal and me. And the day became beautiful.

3

I let Cal follow me up and down the mountain for hours. Cal filled the silence with news of everyone in the village. His family owned the tavern, so all news, both the happy and the terrible, passed through the walls of his home. He didn't know what the people were saying about Aaron yet. He'd followed me before anyone had grown drunk enough to loose their tongue.

"Les had better be careful, or he's going to be on the hunt for a new wife," Cal laughed.

I forced a chuckle. I hadn't been paying close enough attention to hear what Les had done this time.

I cut through a dense patch of bushes, trying to find where treasures would grow when summer neared. I didn't mind the twigs clawing at me or the mud clinging to my clothes.

Cal didn't mention his displeasure at being dirty. He was too content being with me.

I let him hold my hand, savoring the feel of his skin against mine. His warmth burned away the rest of the fear the soldiers had left lodged near my lungs.

Cal pulled me close to his side, winding his arm around my waist.

"I can't go home without proper goodies for Lily." I wriggled free from Cal's grasp.

I followed a game trail farther up the mountain, searching for evergreens whose new buds could help cure the stomach ills that always floated around the village in the spring. By the time the peak of the afternoon passed, I had enough in my bag to please Lily and had spent enough time climbing to give myself a hope of sleeping that night. I turned west, beginning the long trek home.

"We don't have to go back." Cal laced his fingers through mine.

"You think you'd survive in the woods?"

"With you by my side?" His hands moved to my waist. He held me close, swaying in time to music neither of us could hear. He pressed his lips to my forehead. "I think we could stay out here forever." He kissed my nose and cheeks before his lips finally found mine.

My heart raced as he pulled me closer, pressing my body against his.

"Cal"—I pulled an inch away, letting the cool air blow between us—"we have to get back. Lily won't be happy if I'm out too long."

"What'll she do? Scowl at you?"

"Kick me out, more like." I started back down the mountainside. "I don't fancy sleeping in the mud."

I'd lived with Lily for more than half my life, but that didn't make the old healer obligated to keep me a day longer than she wanted to.

Cal caught me in his arms, twisted me toward him, and held me tighter. He brushed his lips against mine. His tongue teased my mouth, luring me deeper into the kiss.

I sank into his arms, reveling in the feel of his hard muscles against me.

He ran his fingers along my sides, sending shivers up my spine.

I sighed as his lips found my neck and trailed out to my shoulder.

"We have to go," I murmured.

Cal wound his fingers through mine. "Let's hide in the wood forever."

"Cal—"

"I love you, Ena." A glimmer of pure bliss lit his eyes.

"I'm going," I said. "Come with me or find your own way back."

Cal pressed his lips to my forehead. "Lead the way."

If I hadn't known him so well, I might not have heard the hint of hurt in his voice.

I didn't want to hurt Cal, but I didn't have anything of myself to offer him. It was easy for Cal to declare his love. He had a solid roof, a business to inherit, a family who cared for him. I was nothing but an orphan inker kept from sleeping in the mud by the goodwill of an ornery old woman.

Cal followed me silently down the slope of the mountain.

I stopped by a fallen tree. The stench of its rot cut through the scent of spring.

"You're the best part of the village." The words tumbled out of my mouth before I'd thought through them.

"I guess that's something. Better than anyone else has gotten out of you."

"Better than they ever will."

His boots thumped on the ground as he ran a few steps to catch up to me. I didn't fight him as he laced his fingers through mine and pressed his lips to my temple. I didn't slow my pace as I started walking again either.

I hadn't been lying—we needed to be heading back to the village. As much as I loved the woods, I didn't fancy being in the trees at night.

The villagers and soldiers might have avoided the forest and mountains because of ghost stories, but their foolishness didn't make the woods entirely safe. I could hear the howls of the wolves at night from Lily's loft where I slept. And farm animals had been lost to creatures far larger than wolves. I didn't fancy having to hide up a tree, shivering as I waited for the dawn. I didn't know if Cal would be able to make it high enough in a tree to be safe.

I let my mind wander as we reached the gentler slopes toward the base of the mountain, wondering over all the terrifying animals that could be hiding just out of sight. Dug into a den that reached below our feet. Hiding in the brush where I couldn't spot them.

A shiver of something ran up my spine.

"You should have brought something warmer." Cal let go of my hand to take off his coat.

"I'm fine." I searched the shadows, trying to find whatever trick of the forest had set my nerves on edge.

Trees rustled to the south, the sound too large to be a bird and too gentle to be death speeding toward us.

I stopped, tugging on Cal's hand to keep him beside me, and reached for the thin knife I kept tucked in my bag.

Cal stepped in front of me as the rustling came closer.

My breath hitched in my chest. I wanted to climb the nearest tree but couldn't leave Cal alone on the ground. My hand trembled as I gripped the hilt of my blade tighter.

"Are you going to try and stab me?" a voice called out. "I don't think it would do you much good."

I would have known that voice after a hundred years.

I gripped my knife tighter, fighting the urge to throw it at my brother's face as he stepped out from between the trees.

"Emmet." Cal stretched a hand toward my brother as a man with black hair and dark eyes stepped out of the shadows beside Emmet.

I took Cal's arm, keeping him close to me.

"Ena"—my brother gave a nod—"Cal."

"What are you doing here?" I asked before Cal could say something more polite.

My brother shrugged. His shoulders were wide from his work as a blacksmith. The familiarity of his face—his bright blue eyes, deep brown hair, and pale skin—tugged at my heart. He looked so much like my mother had. She'd given the same coloring to both of us.

But the hard line of his jaw, which became more defined as he turned to the other man, that Emmet had inherited from our father.

The black-haired man gave my brother a nod.

"I found out you'd gone to the woods, and I decided to check on you," Emmet said.

"How did you find me?" I asked at the same moment Cal said, "We were just heading back."

"You should go then," Emmet said. "I can make sure Ena gets home safe."

"I'd rather—" Cal began.

"I think you've spent enough time in the woods with my little sister." Emmet pointed down the slope. "Keep heading that way, you'll find the village soon enough."

The man next to my brother bit back a smile.

Pink crept up Cal's neck.

"It's fine." I laid a hand on his arm. "Go."

Cal turned to me, locking eyes with me for a moment before kissing the back of my hand. "I'll see you tomorrow." He didn't look back at my brother before striding away.

I glared at Emmet as Cal's footsteps faded.

A new scar marred Emmet's left cheek. His hands had taken more damage since the last time I'd seen him as well.

"You shouldn't be alone with him in the woods," Emmet said when the sounds of Cal's footsteps had vanished.

"And you shouldn't be following me."

"I wanted to be sure you were safe," Emmet said. "A man was killed in the village today, did you not hear?"

"I saw it." I tucked my knife into my bag. "I watched the soldiers whip Aaron to death. But I don't see any soldiers around here, so I think I'll be just fine."

The man gave a low laugh.

"Who are you?" I asked.

"A friend," he said. He looked to be the same as age as my brother, only a couple of years older than Cal and me. If I hadn't been so angry, I might have thought him handsome, but there was something in the way he stood so still while I glared daggers at him that made me wish I hadn't put my knife back into my bag.

"You should get back to the village," Emmet said. "The mountains aren't a safe place to wander."

I turned and climbed farther up the mountain, not caring that he was right.

"Ena." Emmet's footfalls thundered up behind me. "You should get back to Lily." He grabbed my arm, whipping me around.

"Don't tell me where I should be." I wrenched my arm free.

"Then don't be a fool. Get yourself home. You don't belong out here."

"I had Cal with me."

"Being alone with him in the woods is a fool of a choice, too. You've got to think, Ena."

"Don't pretend you care!"

A bird screeched his anger at my shout.

"Ena—"

"You don't get to show up here, follow me into the woods, and try to tell me what to do." My voice shook as I fought to keep from scratching my brother's damned eyes out. "Once a year—once a gods' forsaken year—you show up in Harane. You don't get to pretend to care where I go or who I'm with."

Emmet's brow creased. "I do care. I make it back as often as I'm allowed."

"Liar." The word rumbled in my throat. "The only reason you haven't come back is because you don't want to."

A stick cracked as the black-haired man stepped closer.

"Where have you been, brother?" I'd been saving the question for nearly a year. Holding it in, saying it over and over again in my head as I imagined myself screaming it at Emmet. In all the times I'd thought through it, I'd never pictured him drawing his shoulders defiantly back.

"I've got to work for the blacksmith," Emmet said. "I've finished my apprenticeship, but I've got to pay—"

"You're a damned chivving liar."

"What would I be lying about?" Emmet asked.

"I went to Nantic," I said, "caught a ride in a cart to get to you."

"What?" Emmet said.

"Found the smith where you were supposed to be." I stepped forward, shoving Emmet in the chest. "Two years? Two years since you ran from the blacksmith's, and you've been lying to me."

Emmet's face paled.

"I went to find you, and you weren't there! I was lucky Lily even took me back after I left like that."

Emmet caught my hands. "Why did you go looking for me?"

"You don't get to care. You don't get to lie to me and pretend to care."

Emmet's stone face faltered for the first time. "I do care, Ena. I've come to visit because I care."

"Stopping in once a year doesn't make you a decent brother." I tore my hands free, feeling the bruises growing where he'd gripped my fingers. "You left me here. I didn't even know how to find you. I didn't know if you'd ever come back."

"I had to. I'm sorry, but what I'm doing is more important than being a blacksmith."

"How?"

Emmet looked up to the sky. "It is. You just have to believe that it is."

"And it's more important than I am?" I stared at my brother, waiting for him to crack and tell me there was nothing in all of Ilbrea more important than his only living blood relation.

"It's more important than all of us," Emmet said. "I'm sorry if I can't be the brother you need me to be, but my work has to be done."

"Why?"

"Because there has to be more to this chivving mess of a world than waiting for the Guilds to kill us." Wrinkles creased Emmet's brow. "I can't spend my life waiting to die."

The black-haired man placed a hand on my brother's shoulder. "She should get back to the village."

"Right." Emmet nodded.

I stared at the dark-haired man, wishing he would fade back into the shadows and disappear.

"Then let me help you," I said.

"What?"

"If you have work that's so important, let me help you. I'm not the little girl you left behind in Harane. Wherever it is you've been hiding, take me with you. We're blood, Emmet. I should be with you."

"No." Emmet shook his head. His hair flung around his face. "You belong here."

"I belong with the only family I have." I stepped forward, tipping my chin up to meet his gaze. "I'm not a child. I can help. Let me come with you."

"You can't." Emmet stepped away from me. "You've got to stay with Lily. You're safer here, Ena."

"You're a chivving fool if you believe that."

"It's true. You have to stay in Harane. I have to keep you safe."

"See you next year, brother." I stormed past him and back down the mountain.

He didn't follow.

14

4

I've never believed in peaceful lives and beautiful tales. Those are no truer than ghost stories. Both are lies we tell ourselves to make the pain we suffer a little less real.

Happiness doesn't swoop in and save us when everything turns dark and bloody. And men do far worse to each other than monsters could ever manage.

Even the men who aren't demons, the ones you should be able to trust when the worst storm comes, they'll hurt you as well.

At the end of the tale, there is nothing left but pain and forcing yourself to survive.

5

The ink stained my fingers, leaving them a bright blue. The color was pretty, I'd done my job well, but against the dull brown of the workshop, the hue seemed obscene. There was nothing in Harane to match the pigment's brightness.

But Lily had asked me to make the color, preparing for the merchants who would come all the way down from the capital, Ilara, seeking inks as summer neared.

It should have been Lily inside grinding up leaves and berries to make the inks that were her living, but she was too busy with her other work. Work that would see her hanged by the soldiers.

A cough had swept through the village, and no one in Harane could afford the gold demanded by the Guilds' healer. It was left to Lily to see to the children so far gone with fever they couldn't hold their heads up anymore.

She'd sneak her herbs into the houses of the desperate, treating the ill with whatever she could grow in her garden and the things I could forage in the woods. Lily rarely brought me with her when she tended to the sick and wounded. Only when there was something she wanted me to learn, or too many desperate people for her to handle on her own. I don't know if she kept me away out of fear or mercy, but either way, it ended up the same.

Lily would leave a written list of inks for me to blend and give spoken orders of what tonics and salves she needed made. I'd sit in the house, letting it fill with enough steam to clog my lungs as I made vials of ink in one set of bowls and healing things in another, all on the one worn, wooden table. I think Lily believed any Guilded soldier sent to her home wouldn't have the sense to know which flowers had been chosen for their ability to fight fever and which had been selected for their pigment. She was probably right.

Whatever her reasoning might have been, the rains hadn't stopped in the three days since I'd left my brother in the forest, and I was trapped with a mortar and pestle, grinding sweet smelling leaves until I couldn't move my fingers anymore as the storm finally drifted east over the mountains.

I left the pulpy mixture of the ink to sit. It would be hours before the stuff would be ready to be carefully strained and then poured into a glass jar to be sold.

Sun peeked in through the windows as I moved on to grinding roots for Lily's remedies. The pungent smell tickled my nose as I worked my way through one knot and then another.

A tap on the door, so light I almost thought the rain had come back, pulled me out of the monotonous motion. I froze with the pestle still in my hand, listening for sounds outside.

The tapping came again.

I gave a quiet curse before calling, "Lily's out, but I'll be with you in one moment," as I pulled down the tray that hid under the tabletop. I set the roots, leaves, mortar and pestle, and vial of oil on the tray and fixed it back under the table as quickly as I could without risking any noise.

I untied the top of my bodice, shaking the laces loose and grabbing both strings in one hand as I opened the door.

"So sorry." I tied my bodice closed over my shift. "I must have drifted off."

I looked up to find, not a soldier come to drag me out for whipping, but Karin, who gave me a scathing look as she slipped past into the workshop.

"Fell asleep?" Karin circled the long table where I'd hidden the tray before peeping through the curtain that blocked off the bit of the first floor where Lily slept.

"The storm made me sleepy." I ran my fingers through my hair, leaving smudges of blue behind that would drive me mad trying to wash out later.

"And there's no one else here?" Karin's eyes twinkled as she stopped at the ladder that led to the loft where I slept. "No one who might make you forget to work?"

If I hadn't known Karin since before either of us could walk, I would have grabbed her skirts and torn her from the ladder as she climbed up like she owned the chivving shop. But Karin meant no harm, and stopping her search would only make the rumors that I'd had a man in the house keeping me from answering the door fly through the village faster.

I could have told her the truth. I had been busy working on illegal remedies for Lily and was afraid a soldier had come to the door. And I'd rather be accused of sleeping on the job than hanged for helping an unguilded healer offer remedies. But then Karin would be obligated to turn me in or risk punishment from the soldiers herself.

I leaned against the table, tracing the outline of a purple ink stain, listening to the sounds of Karin checking under my cot and opening my trunk that wouldn't have been large enough to hide Cal anyway.

"You really are the most boring person who's ever lived." Karin carefully lifted her skirts to come back down the ladder.

"I'm sure I am." I took a box of charcoal and dumped a few bits into a fresh mortar. "So you might as well scoot back to more interesting company and leave me to my work."

"Don't you dare start on something that's going to make so much of a mess." Karin snatched the charcoal-filled mortar out of my reach. She stared at me, a glimmer of delight playing in the corners of her eyes.

I knew she wanted me to ask why she'd come and what I'd need clean hands for. The bit of obstinance that curled in my stomach wasn't as strong as the part of me that wanted something interesting to be happening after all the rain. Even if it was only Handor and Shilv fighting over whose sheep were harassing whose again.

"What is it, you fairy of a biddy?"

"Only the best, most delightful news." Karin took my shoulders, steering me to the pump sink in the corner. She worked the handle while she spoke. "Well, after word came south on the road that the map makers with a load of their soldiers were coming our way—"

"What?" I froze, a brick of harsh soap clutched in my hand.

"There's a whole pack of Guilded heading our way. How have you not heard?"

"I've been inside working." I scrubbed at the blue and black on my hands. "Some of us have things we actually have to get done."

"You should admit the real problem is you never bothering to talk to people besides Cal and Lily. You should try making friends, Ena. It would be good for you."

"Yes, fine." I snatched the pot of oily cream from the shelf. "What about the soldiers?"

"Right." Karin leaned in. "So, word comes down the road that there's a whole caravan of paun Guilded headed our way. Cal's parents are head over heels planning to have all the fancy folks at the tavern, the farmers have started trying to hide their stock so it can't be counted, and"—she paused, near shuddering with glee—"Henry Tilly took his horse and disappeared for two days."

"What?" I wiped the cream and the rest of the color from my fingers with a rag. "Did the soldiers get him?"

"No." Karin laughed. "He rode north, all the way to Nantic."

"Toward the paun caravan? Who in their right mind would do such a thing?"

Karin took my elbow and led me to a seat at the table. She pushed aside the curtain to Lily's room and snatched up Lily's hairbrush.

"Nantic is a much bigger place than Harane." Karin shook my hair free from its braid. "So many things to offer that we don't have in our tiny little village."

"Like people who tell stories that actually make sense?"

Karin dragged the brush roughly through my hair in retaliation. "Like a scribe."

"What?"

"A Guilded scribe. One who can offer all the official forms the Guilds force us to use for every little thing we do. Like buying land, being buried…getting married."

"Henry is getting married?" I spun around wide-eyed. "To you?"

"Oh gods no, not me!" Karin screwed up her face. "I'd never marry him. His left eye's bigger than his right."

"Who is he marrying then?" I knelt on the chair, gripping the back.

"Malda!" Karin clapped a hand over her mouth.

"What?"

"Henry found out the soldiers, and map makers, and entire fleet of paun were on their way and raced through the night all thirty miles up to Nantic to get marriage papers from the Guilds' scribe." Karin twirled the brush through the air. "And do you know why?"

"Love, I suppose."

"She's pregnant. That little mouse Malda is pregnant and more than just a little. Gods, now that I know, it's impossible not to see how her belly's grown."

"Henry's a slitching fool." I dragged my fingers through my hair.

Karin grabbed my shoulders, making me face front in the chair again.

18

"A fool he is," Karin said, "but at least he cares for Malda enough not to risk the paun catching her pregnant without a husband. If those soldiers found her out, she'd be taken and sent to give birth on Ian Ayres in the middle of the sea. No one ever comes back from that place."

A chill shook my spine, but Karin kept talking.

"Henry brought coin to Nantic to pay the scribe, but the scribe told him he'd have to wait seven months for marriage papers."

"Seven months?" I tried to turn again, but Karin whacked me on the head with the brush.

"By which time there will be a new little screaming Henry or Malda in this world. Henry had to give the scribe his horse to get the papers and spent the last two days trudging back through the rain."

"Is he all right?" My eyes darted toward the tray hidden under the table. That long in the cold rain, and it was only a matter of time before Lily had to darken his door.

"He's in the tavern right now having a warm frie to cheer him for his wedding this afternoon." Karin twisted my hair. "They're laying hay out in the square to make a space for it. The whole thing will be done long before the sun sets, so Malda will be a married woman before the Guilds can set eyes on her ever-expanding belly."

"This afternoon? Today?" I asked.

"Yes, Ena. That is how days usually go. The whole village will be turning up for this wedding, so you need to look like a proper lady, and I need just a little bit of your magic to give me a wonderful spring blush." Karin scraped my scalp with pins.

"What for? Even if they put down enough hay to feed the horses for a season, we'll all still end up covered in mud."

"Because," Karin said, stepping in front of me and pointing a finger at my nose, "nothing makes a man consider the fact that marriage is inevitable more than a wedding. Henry panicking could be our chance to snatch a prize worth having."

Heat shot up to my cheeks.

"No." I stood, not meeting Karin's eyes as I stalked to the corner where the few small tubs of powders and paints for women's faces were kept. "You dab as much pink on your cheeks as you like, but I'll have none of it on me. I'm too young to be worrying about marriage."

"But is Cal?" That awful twinkle sprang back into Karin's eyes.

"Paint your face, you wretch." I tossed her a tin.

6

It took more than an hour for Karin to paint her face to a marriageable hue, riffle through the few clothes I owned to choose what she wanted me to wear, and give up on the idea of her painting my cheeks as well.

She'd just finished tightening the laces on my bodice to display enough of my breasts to be considered obscene, when Lily stepped in through the garden door, basket over her arm and mud clinging to her boots.

Lily stared from Karin to me. "So, you've already heard the joyous news."

"I told her." Karin gave my bodice laces one more tug. "Had to get her ready for the wedding, didn't I?"

"What's to be gotten ready for?" Lily set her basket on the table. "Put your breasts away, Ena. You're pretty enough to get into plenty of trouble without two beacons poking out the front of your dress."

"They're not poking out." I glanced down, making sure there wasn't more showing than I'd thought.

Lily unloaded the goods from her basket. "There is a fine line between the kind of beauty gods bless you with, and the kind given by the shadows to bring trouble into your life. You, Ena Ryeland, are balancing on the edge of beauty becoming a curse. So, tuck your tits back in your top before someone you don't fancy decides they have a right to the body you were born with."

"Yes, Lily." My face burned red.

Karin slapped my hands away as I tried to loosen my bodice. She grabbed the pale blue fabric of my shift instead, giving it a tug to cover more of my chest.

"Help me get these things put away so we don't miss the wedding." Lily went to her bedroom, leaving a trail of muddy boot prints behind. "We need to bring something for the bride and groom. I would say they should be gifted a lick of common sense, but it seems they threw that away five months ago when a roll in the hay seemed worth risking a life for."

Karin turned to me, her eyebrows creeping up her forehead. "I'll see you there," she mouthed before dodging out the door.

"Is that girl gone?" Lily asked.

"Yes, Lily." I examined the goods Lily had brought home with her. A fair number of eggs, two loaves of seed bread, a bottle of chamb, and a skein of thick spun wool. "You saw that many today?"

"Bad stomach, an awful cough, and had to stitch up the side of Les's head."

"What happened to Les's head?" I tucked the eggs into the shallow basket by the iron stove and wrapped the bread in a cloth.

"If you ask Les, he knocked his head in the barn." Lily stalked back out of her bedroom, a clean dress on, mud still clinging to her boots. "If you look at the manic glint in his wife's eyes, she finally got sick of the slitch and smacked him upside the head hard enough to draw blood."

"What did Les do to make her so mad?"

"Damned if I know what he's done this time." Lily pumped the sink to scrub her hands. "That boy was born stupid, and he didn't get much better once he learned to talk."

"Fair enough." I took over pumping the giant metal handle.

Lily methodically washed the skin around her nails in the cold water. "The map maker's party is coming through. Should be here tomorrow from the sounds of it."

"Karin said as much."

"Map makers always come with a pack of soldiers. Who knows how big the company will be?"

"Either way, they should be through pretty quick." I passed Lily a cloth to dry her hands on. "They aren't coming to Harane on purpose. They're only taking the mountain road to get someplace else."

Lily nodded silently for a moment. "I don't want you in the village tomorrow. Head out to the mountains in the morning."

"It's been raining for days. There won't be anything for me to bring back but mud."

"Then bring back some mud." Lily took my face in her hands. "I don't want you around when the paun come through. I won't have it on my head when that pretty face of yours becomes a curse."

A knot of something like dread closed around my stomach. "I'll just stay inside and out of sight."

"You'll get to the mountains and thank me for it." She squeezed my face tighter.

I stared into her steel gray eyes.

"Do you hear me, girl?"

"Yes, ma'am."

"Good." She let go of my face. "Now, what in this chivving mess should we give the idiots getting married this afternoon?"

"Something for a chest rattle." I pulled up the loose floorboard that housed all of Lily's illegal goods. "If Karin is right, Henry will need it in a few days if he doesn't already."

"Fine. Give it to his mother so the fool doesn't go losing it."

"Yes, Lily." I pulled out one of the little wooden boxes that held the thick paste.

"Out you get then." Lily grabbed the broom from near the woodstove. "Go celebrate the panic caused by young lust."

I managed to pull my coat on before she spoke again.

21

"And let this be a lesson to you, Ena. Give yourself to a man with no sense, and you'll end up getting married on a godsforsaken muddy day to a fool who no longer owns a horse."

I darted out the door before Lily could say anything else. I cared for the old lady, even if she was harsh and a little strange. She swore worse than a Guilded sailor just as easily as she whispered comfort to the dying.

No one in Harane could blame Lily for her rough edges. Nigh on all of us owed our lives to her for something or other, and the few who'd been lucky enough never to need Lily's help would have been awfully lonely living at the foot of the mountains with the rest of us dead.

Mud soaked my boots before I'd made it through the garden and to the road. I lifted my hem as I leapt over the worst of the puddles, though I knew there was no hope of my skirt making it through the day unscathed.

The air in the village tasted different than it had a few days ago, and not just from the rain. The stink of despair had fled, replaced by a dancing breeze of hope.

It was true enough that Henry and Malda were only getting married to escape the wrath of the Guilds. If the lords far away in Ilara hadn't passed a law banning children being born outside marriage, then Shilv wouldn't have been carrying hay to the square.

Malda wouldn't have had to fear being snatched up by soldiers, loaded onto a ship, and sent out to the isle of Ian Ayres to give birth. Henry wouldn't have had to give up his horse. I wouldn't have been dodging puddles with salve in my coat pocket. And the whole village would have had endless hours of entertainment for the next few months wondering if Malda was carrying a child or had only taken too strongly to sweet summer cakes.

But the Guilds ruled Ilbrea with their shining, golden fist. If they said women carrying babies out of wedlock were to be taken, there was nothing we could do to fight the paun. Just like we couldn't stop them from whipping Aaron to death. In the whole land of Ilbrea, there was nothing unguilded rotta like us could do but try and avoid the Guilds' notice and hope they weren't bored enough to come after us anyway.

I'd gotten so lost in wondering what would have happened to Malda and her baby if Henry hadn't had a horse to offer, I walked right past the tavern.

"Ena!" Cal called out the kitchen window, waving a flour-covered rag, which left a puff of white floating in the air.

"Don't hang out the window," Cal's father shouted. "If you want to talk to the girl, bring her inside like a civilized man."

Cal bit back his smile. "Miss Ryeland, would you grace us with your presence in our humble kitchen?"

"Why thank you." I gave as deep a curtsy as I could manage without sinking my hem deep into the mud and headed back up the street to the tavern door.

Harane didn't have many businesses that would interest travelers, and everything that might appeal, aside from Lily's ink shop, had been packed into the very center of the village. The tavern, cobbler, stables, tannery, and smith had all been built close together with narrow alleys running between them, as though whoever had laid the foundations had thought Harane would become a town or even a city someday.

That person had been wrong.

Harane was nothing but a tract of fertile farmland situated thirty miles south of Nantic and twenty-nine miles north of Hareford on the Guild-approved road that ran as close to the mountains as travelers dared to get. The only reason the tavern managed to fill its aged, wooden tables every night was the travelers who needed a place to stop between Nantic and Hareford, and the village men, like Les, who were too afraid of their wives to go home.

The tables in the tavern only had a smattering of people since the travelers hadn't arrived for the night and the village folk were getting ready for the surprise wedding.

"Ena." Cal waved me in through the kitchen door.

The scent of baking pastries, roasting meat, and fresh poured frie warmed my face before I even neared the wide fireplace and big iron oven.

"I take it you heard?" Cal raised an eyebrow at my hair.

I ran my fingers along the delicate twists Karin promised would win me a husband, blushing to the roots of my hair as I met Cal's gaze. "Karin insisted."

"Careful of the hot." Cal's mother pulled a tray of sweet rolls from the oven. The tops had been crusted to a shining brown.

"Those are beautiful." I leaned in to sniff. "I didn't think you'd spend the time on a last minute wedding."

Cal's mother tsked. "I'm making three loaves of bread for the wedding. One for each of them."

I coughed a laugh.

"The rolls are for the Guilded coming through," she said. "I only hope it's true they're coming tomorrow. If not, the lot will go stale. But if I wait to start until they arrive, I won't be able to make enough to sell." She worried her wrinkled lips together. "I've already had the rooms upstairs cleaned, and Cal's pulled fresh barrels of frie and chamb. I only hope it's enough."

"Does it matter?" I leaned against the edge of the table. "It's a caravan of paun. If you don't have enough for them, they'll just have to stay in their camp where they belong and move on south all the faster."

"We need their business," Cal's father said. "A day with the caravan will be more coin than we'll see for the rest of the summer. The gods smiled on us when they sent the map makers down the mountain road."

"Right." I felt my mouth curve into a smile even as a horrible cold tingled down my neck and surrounded the dread in my stomach. "I'm very happy for you."

"Is there anything else you need me for?" Cal asked.

"Go." His mother shooed him toward the door. "But if anyone dares say something snide about your father and me not coming to the square, tell them not to darken the tavern door for a month. I don't care how thirsty they are for frie."

"Yes, mother." Cal kissed his mother's cheek and took a basket from near the stove.

"Someday soon, there will be a wedding worth leaving work undone for," Cal's mother said. "This is not that day."

I bit my lips together and let Cal put a hand on my waist, guiding me back out into the main room of the tavern.

"Honestly," Cal said in a low voice as soon as the kitchen door shut behind us, "it's probably better my parents not come."

"Why?" I whispered.

"Poor Henry has to stand in front of everyone, with the whole village knowing full well what a slitch he was to let Malda hang for so long. Imagine adding my mother's glare to that weight."

I laughed, and the cold and dread around my stomach vanished with a tiny pop of joy.

7

I'll never know how they managed to find enough hay to coat the mud in the square. Not that the square was large, or even properly a square.

On the northern end of the village, someone, a very long time ago, had surrounded a square of land with heavy stones. No one had moved the stones or stolen them to build for fear of angering some unknown spirit. So, the rocks as big as my torso lay undisturbed, and the people of Harane gathered within them whenever the need arose.

Most often, the need came from the soldiers issuing Guild decrees or doling out punishment. But we used the square for things like weddings and summer celebrations as well. I don't know if people thought there was some good to be gained from gathering within the stones, or if it was pure stubbornness in not letting the Guilds steal the square and make it an awful place where none of the villagers dared tread.

Either way ended with Henry and Malda standing side by side in front of a horde of people.

Tomin had become the eldest in the village after a lung infection took a few of the older folks during the winter, so it was his place to stand with Henry and Malda to perform the wedding.

"And in the bonds of marriage, do you swear to protect your other half?" Tomin said. "Through winter and drought? Through flood and famine?"

"I do," Henry and Malda said together.

Henry's face was pale, whether from fright of being married or exhaustion from walking back from Nantic, I couldn't tell.

Tomin reached into his pocket and pulled out a filthy rag. "Hands please."

Malda and Henry both held up their right palms.

Tomin unfolded the rag and patted the clump of dirt within it flat. "Hard to find anything dry."

The villagers chuckled, and Tomin gave a gap-toothed grin.

"From the dirt we all have come." Tomin sprinkled dirt onto Malda's palm. "And to the dirt we all must go." He sprinkled dirt onto Henry's palm. "May your journey in between be sweeter for standing by each other's side."

Together, Henry and Malda tipped their hands, letting the dirt tumble onto the muddy hay at their feet.

"Your lives are one," Tomin said. "Live them well!"

The crowd cheered.

Malda threw her arms around Henry's neck and kissed him.

The children winced and whined—the rest of us clapped and hollered.

Before Malda had stopped kissing Henry, someone began playing a fiddle. A drum joined a moment later, and Henry took Malda's hands, dragging her to the center of the square to dance.

I laughed at the look of pure horror on Malda's face. An arm snaked around my waist.

"Are you going to look as petrified when I make you dance?" Cal whispered in my ear.

"I don't think you could make me do anything." I twisted out of his grip and darted toward the center of the square where everyone had picked up on the dance.

Cal raced to my side, taking me in his arms before anyone else could have the chance. We spun and bounced in time with the music as the hay beneath our feet was eaten entirely by the mud.

Cal lifted me and twirled me under his arm until my heart beat so fast I thought it might race out of my chest. His laughter rang in my ears. The bright joy that lit his eyes sent my soul soaring up high above the clouds.

Then Henry's father wheeled out a barrel of frie. The crowd shifted toward the drink.

And the whipping post was there, waiting at the back of the celebration.

There was no blood on the ground, the rain had washed it all away, but dark stains mottled the post. The wood had been worn down in places where the soldiers' victims had strained against their bonds.

My feet lost the feel of the dance, and I swayed, staring at the bloody monument to all the damage the Guilds had done.

"Ena?" Cal took my waist in his hands. "Are you all right?"

"Tired." I nodded. "I'm just tired."

"Come on." He led me to the side of the square where Henry's father doled out frie in borrowed cups. I stood on the edge of the crowd while Cal dove between people to snatch each of us a drink. He emerged a moment later, his hair rumpled, but clasping a cup in each hand. "Here."

I took the cup and sipped the frie. The drink burned a path down my throat, past my lungs, and into my stomach, but didn't make me feel any better.

Cal laced his fingers through mine and led me to the south side of the square. We sat on one of the largest of the boundary stones, watching the dancers spin round and round.

"It's a nice wedding," Cal said. "And Henry's family seems happy to be getting Malda."

"They do." I took another sip of frie, trying to burn away the taste of sick in my mouth.

"Malda grew up on a farm, so she won't have trouble getting used to the labor Henry's land will require."

"She's a strong girl," I said. "They'll do well together."

"We'd do well together." Cal leaned in close. "Better than them. I could provide for you better than Henry ever—"

"I have my own work." I tightened my grip on my cup.

"And you could work with Lily if you wanted," Cal said. "But you wouldn't have to. I'm going to inherit the tavern. It's a good income, Ena."

"Don't, Cal. Please don't."

"I know we're young." Cal knelt in the mud in front of me, making it impossible for me to look away from his beautiful eyes. "And I'm not saying we should get married soon. We could wait until next summer, give Lily some time to get used to the idea of you moving to the tavern."

"I couldn't." The truth of the words tore at my chest. "I can't."

"She'll make do on her own."

"I can't live in the tavern. I can't be married to a man who makes his coin from soldiers."

"Ena—"

"The soldiers coming is good for your family, but to me it only means death. I couldn't smile at them and serve them. They are monsters. Your family makes their living feeding the monsters who slaughter us."

The glimmer of light in Cal's eyes faded. I could still see the post over his shoulder, coming in and out of view as the people danced where they had stood to watch Aaron murdered only a few days before.

"You are everything bright and wonderful, Cal. But I could never be your wife."

I stood up, set my cup down on the rock, and walked out of the square. I didn't look back. Cal didn't follow.

8

The night is pitch black, and I am racing down the road.

The thundering of the horse's hooves doesn't cover the pounding of my heart. I search for a glimmer of light up ahead, but there's nothing.

Only endless night.

I keep riding until fear finally wakes me.

9

I left for the woods at dawn the next morning. I'd heard Lily come in after the wedding but stayed silently huddled under my blankets. I didn't want to talk to her. Didn't want her to stare at me with her steel gray eyes and know she felt sorry for me—even though she'd never say it.

After a night spent trapped in a horrible dream, I still didn't want to see her. I slipped out of the house when the sun finally rose and fled for the safety of the forest.

The trees didn't ask what kind of a foolish girl would turn down the best marriage Harane had to offer. The birds didn't call me a hypocrite for making inks to be sent to Ilara where only the gods knew if Guilded paun would be using them. The rotting leaves squishing under my feet didn't say there could be no hope of joy for an orphan girl incapable of loving anyone.

I made it higher in the mountains that day than I ever had before. I stuffed every chivving leaf and lichen into my bag that had a chance of making Lily happy and took pleasure in the pain its growing weight caused me.

Better now than later. I tried to comfort myself. *Better for Cal to know you could never live in his tavern now, before Karin chooses a husband.*

The thought of Karin lying in Cal's arms made me scream loud enough to send a flock of birds scattering to the sky. But it didn't change anything. Cal belonged in the tavern with his family. I could never live with being glad the Guilds were coming.

Simple as that.

When I'd finally gotten tired enough that climbing back down the mountain would be painful, I turned around and headed home.

By the time I made it out of the forest, my legs shook so badly I wasn't sure I would be able to climb over the fences to get back to Lily's. I took a deep breath to steady myself. There was something more in the wind than the usual scent of animal dung and trees.

I took another breath, trying to find what the stench might be. My gaze caught on something on the horizon, a pillar of smoke rising from the northern side of the village.

Taking off at a run, I headed toward the flames, ignoring the trembling in my legs that threatened to send me face first into the dirt.

The smoke wasn't from the very northern edge of the village, and it was back from the main road, off toward the farms on the western side of Harane. I scrambled over fences, dodging around terrified livestock that had scented the fire and knew they had no chance of escaping their pens.

I didn't hear the screams until I neared the road.

A man crying out in agony.

I stopped behind Shilv's house, teetering between running to get Lily to help whoever had been hurt badly enough to make that sort of noise, and being afraid of leaving someone to die alone.

The man screamed again, and I ran forward, toward the sound.

"What…" My question faded away as I saw why Shilv had been screaming.

Five Guilded soldiers in black uniforms stood in a line, staring down at Shilv who clutched the bloody stump of his arm to his chest. Shilv's wife Ester knelt ten feet away, sobbing as she stared at her husband.

I stood frozen for a moment before instinct took over.

And I ran.

Around the side of the house, leaping over the fence and tearing through the pasture without looking to see if any of the soldiers had followed me.

My breath hitched in my chest as I ran. Shilv had been toying with the Guilds for years, hiding his livestock when the scribes came to do their tax accounting.

A hand for the money Shilv owed. If Lily could take care of the wound and make sure no infection set in, Shilv wouldn't be too bad off. His wife was strong. They'd find a way to make do.

I looped back out to the road, heading toward the fire. I pressed my back to a house to peer down the road before venturing into the open.

Shilv's screams had faded, and there was no blood here. But there were soldiers. A pack of soldiers moving down the road with some purpose I didn't understand. They kicked in the door of a house. I ran across the street while they weren't looking and dove into the shadows of a stable.

The horse kicked against the wall, fighting to break free. The banging shook my ears as I ran to the western end of the stable.

I didn't have to go farther than that.

Flames shot up from the Tillys' house. The whole place had been eaten by the inferno. Two figures lay bloody and bare across the walkway. Henry's unmoving back bore the marks of a terrible whipping. His father's chest had been cut open by something sharper. Both of them were dead.

I bit my lips together until they bled as I swallowed my scream.

I didn't know where Malda was. If they'd left her in the house, there was nothing I could do for her. Nothing even Lily could do for her.

"Lily."

A fear like I hadn't known in nine years seized my lungs, choking the air out of me. I ran south, along the backs of the houses, racing toward home.

Lily was smart. She hid the things the Guilds had banned. She only treated people she knew she could trust. The villagers loved her. They would sooner let themselves be whipped than turn Lily in to the Guilds.

Soldiers had gathered behind Les's house. I ducked between buildings and toward the main road before I could see what might have become of Les and his angry wife.

I made it all the way to the side of the tannery.

If I cut between the tavern and the public stables, then looped behind the houses, I'd reach home in a few minutes. I had to warn Lily, make sure she had everything hidden.

I leaned out to check up and down the street. Pain cut through my head as someone grabbed my hair and tossed me to the ground.

The dirt flying into my mouth cut off my scream.

"Who is this sneaking around?" a man said.

I pushed myself to my knees. A kick to the ribs sent me back to the ground.

"Get her up," a second voice said.

A hand grabbed the back of my coat, hauling me to my feet.

Screams came from the south end of the village as a new pillar of smoke drifted toward the sky.

"What's your name?" A soldier leaned close to my face.

I wanted to scratch his leering eyes out, but another soldier had pinned my arms behind my back.

"Your name." The soldier took my chin in his hand.

"Ena." I spat the dirt out of my mouth, letting it land on his fingers. "Ena Ryeland."

"Ryeland isn't a land owner here." A man in white scribes robes stepped forward.

"I don't own land," I said. "I'm a worker, that's all. Now let me go."

Laughter came from behind me.

I glanced back. There were six other men in black uniforms. I tried to yank my arms free.

"What kind of work would a pretty little thing like you be doing?" The soldier trailed a finger down my neck.

"Don't touch me." I kicked back, catching the man who held me in the shin.

The soldier stepped closer to me, pinning me between him and the one I'd kicked.

"You have attacked a soldier of the Guilds of Ilbrea." He wrapped a hand around my throat, cutting off my air. "You just made a terrible mistake."

"Gentlemen!" Cal's voice shouted from across the road. "Come have a drink!"

"We're busy here." The man behind me pressed his hips to my back.

I coughed as I tried to pull in air past the pain squeezing my throat.

"I can promise each of you, you'd rather have some frie and roasted lamb than mess with that." Cal laughed. "Come in. Drinks are on the house, and you can forget that little street scum ever bothered you."

None of the soldiers moved.

"You're here to uphold the laws of our great country." Cal beckoned them toward the door. "You are doing all of us a service by clearing the law breakers out of our village. Come, let me give you a good meal as a token of thanks. I promise the frie we have is the best you'll find south of Ilara."

The soldier in front of me stepped away. He let go of my throat, and the world swayed as I gulped down air. "One this pretty must be diseased anyway. Let's go, lads."

The man holding my arms threw me back down into the dirt.

"I have chamb, too, if any of you prefer," Cal said. "Six years old. I'm told the grape harvest was perfect that season."

Cal led the soldiers into the tavern.

I pushed myself to my feet before the last of them disappeared and ran back between the buildings. I'd made it past the smith's when footsteps pounded up behind me and a hand slammed me into the rough clapboard.

"Do you think I'm that much of an idiot, girl?" The man's breath touched my neck. He leaned into me, pressing his stiffness against my back. "I will not be disrespected by a filthy little rotta."

"Please don't." I tried to reach into my bag, for the knife tucked under the layers of foraged things.

He grabbed my wrist, twisting my arm with one hand and snaking my skirt up my leg with the other.

"Don't do this." I wanted to scream for help, but helping me would be a death sentence.

"Rotta need to learn their—"

A grunt, a rasp, and a gurgle cut through the man's words.

I turned in time to see a spray of red fly from the soldier's throat as he toppled to the ground.

"We need to go." A hand seized mine, dragging me away from the dying soldier.

I looked to the one who had saved me. Black curling hair and deep brown eyes—the man who'd been with my brother in the woods dragged me away.

1 0

"Emmet." That was the first word I managed to say. "Where's Emmet?"

"South. Far away from here." The black-haired man kept my hand held tightly in his.

His skin was clean. His hand hadn't been covered in the blood that had sprayed the dirt alley.

"Why are you here?" I asked.

"Are you angry I saved you?" He pressed me into the shadows as he peered around the side of Handor's shed.

"No."

"Then it should be enough that I'm here. We need to get to the woods."

"I can't." I yanked my hand from his grasp.

"If you stay here, they'll kill you. The soldiers watched that man follow you, and now that man is dead."

"I can't just leave. I have to get to Lily. If the soldiers are going after people, I have to warn her."

The man closed his eyes for a moment. "Where's her home?"

"Southeast end of the village," I said. "I can get there on my own."

"You're not leaving my sight." He grabbed my elbow, steering me to the trees between homes. "Is Lily fit enough to travel?"

"She's old but she's not decrepit."

"It'll be easier for us to stay alive if I don't have to carry anyone." He didn't offer any explanation as he took off running behind the houses.

I didn't ask for one.

"It's across from the next house," I said as the towering tree that stood in front of Lily's worn, wooden home came into view. Smoke rose from behind the barren branches.

I ran faster, outpacing the black-haired man.

My heart thundered in my ears. The pounding of faraway hooves rattled away all reasonable thought.

The man caught me around the waist, keeping me in the cover of the shadows. I didn't need to go any closer.

The soldiers had displayed her out front by the road. Her gray hair drifted with the breeze as the rope around her neck twisted. Flames cut through the roof of Lily's home, their brightness outlining her shape, as though her death would set the whole world to blazing.

11

The man kept his grip around my waist as we ran away from Lily's house. He darted between buildings and sprinted for long stretches. I made it up and over the fences on my own. I don't know how. I couldn't feel anything. Not the pain in my limbs. Not the terrible, silent scream that echoed in my chest.

I had gone numb. Completely and totally numb.

The man spoke words. Instructions for when to run, and when to lie down in the grass and hide.

I must've done as he said. We made it to the cover of the trees alive.

The stench of the smoke had broken through the scent of the forest. Or maybe it only clung to me.

"We need to keep moving." He grabbed my arm again, steering me farther into the woods.

"Moving?" The word felt heavy in my mouth.

"I can't be sure the soldiers didn't see us coming this way," he said. "The farther we get from Harane, the better off we'll be."

"But I can't just leave." I shook free of his grip. "I'll hide here until they all move on."

"And then what?" He had a cut on his forehead. I didn't know how he had gotten it. "You can't go back there. I killed that soldier—the soldier who left his friends to follow you. They'll blame his murder on you. Harane isn't safe for you, not now, not ever again. We have to keep moving."

"But I can't just leave. The soldiers might not"—a sharp pain pummeled my chest—"the soldiers can't have killed everyone."

"Probably not." He grabbed my arm, dragging me into the forest.

"What does that mean?"

"If people cooperated and didn't fight back, they might still be alive." He stopped at a thick patch of brambles.

"Karin might need help," I said. "Cal is still back there."

He dug a heavy pack out of the brambles, swinging it onto his back before turning to me. "Cal is the boy from the woods?"

I nodded.

He looked up into the trees. "Will he follow you?"

"What?"

"If we wait until dark, I can try to go back for him. If I tell him you're waiting in the woods, will he come?"

"I…" I wasn't sure if Cal would come. If he would hear I had lost the little shred of a life I had been clinging to for so long and come running to my side, ready to abandon everything he had ever known. "I don't want him to. He has a family and a home in the village."

A wrinkle formed between the man's dark eyebrows. "Then there's nothing for us to do but leave. You can't go back to Harane. I'm sorry."

"But where am I supposed to go?" I said. "I could go to Nantic or Hareford, but I don't have any coin. I can work—"

"You can't go anywhere along the mountain road." He reached toward me. "It'll be the same soldiers patrolling."

The trees twisted and swayed around me.

He took my hand, and somehow I managed to make my feet move.

To get farther away than Nantic or Hareford would take days. To get anywhere off the mountain road I would need a map, and food, and money.

"Where am I supposed to go?" A hollow, childish fear settled in my chest.

"I'll take you to your brother."

"South?"

"No." He paused for a moment, staring up at the steep mountain ahead of us. "I'll take you where he's supposed to meet me. You'll be safe there until you can figure out where you want to go."

The light faded from the sky, but he kept moving farther up the mountain. My legs screamed their protest at being asked to climb even more. Part of me wanted to lie down and wait for the forest to eat me whole. More of me wanted to run as far away as the land reached, beyond even the power of the Guilds.

"Why?" I asked when I couldn't bear to swallow the question any longer.

It took a moment for the man to speak. "Why what?"

"Why Harane? Why did the soldiers decide to come after our village? Weren't they satisfied with the damage they'd already done?"

"I don't know if a Guilded soldier is capable of feeling satisfied until a town and all its people are nothing more than ash." He stopped next to a wide boulder. Moss covered the stone, hiding most of its rough texture. He trailed his fingers along the bare patches of rock. "The whisper I heard on the wind said some fool traded a horse for marriage papers. No reason but hiding a baby to be that desperate for a scribe's help. Even the paun scum from Ilara were smart enough to know that. Made them wonder who else might be breaking the laws in Harane."

"Henry." I dug my fingers into my hair. The grit of dirt and soot covered my scalp. "All of this happened because of Henry."

"That's not true." He patted the boulder and started climbing again. "He might have been wrong not to take better care of the girl carrying his child, he might have been a slitching fool for trading his horse and thinking the scribe wouldn't know why, but the death, the blood—that's on the Guilds. They're the ones who are determined to destroy us. Everything else is just reasons the Guilds tell themselves they have a right to slaughter the tilk."

Tilk.

I hadn't even thought the word in forever. The Guilded never used the kind term for common folk. They called us rotta instead. I'd started thinking it, too. Like I believed we were disposable rodents who deserved to be exterminated for contaminating the Guilds' perfect kingdom.

"Do you think they'll leave any of the village standing?" I asked.

"Maybe. It would be a long ride from Nantic to Hareford otherwise."

I had more questions, but I couldn't bring myself to ask them. My soul had grown too heavy to bear another word of pain.

The twilight chill tickled the back of my neck. The sounds of the forest waking up for the night carried through the shadows.

I wanted to say we needed to stop, climb high in a tree and hope we made it until morning. But he kept walking, and I didn't know if letting the animals kill me would be the kinder fate.

He took my hand as he cut sideways along the edge of a rise, as though he were afraid I would tumble off the slope or run back to the village if given the chance.

I ducked my head as bats chittered above us. A gaping darkness grew from the mountainside, blocking our path.

I took a quick step to walk nearer to him. My free hand fumbled, digging into my bag for my knife.

"It's all right." He let go of my hand and stepped into the darkness in the mountain.

I held my breath, waiting for the sounds of some animal tearing him apart.

A tiny spark broke through the black. Then a deep blue light glowed in the cave.

He stood in the middle of the hollow, holding a blue light in his hand, searching each of the stone corners.

"Nothing's been sleeping here for a while." He waved me toward him. "We'll be safe here for the night."

Giving one last glance to the woods behind me, I stepped into the shelter of the cave.

It wasn't large—it only cut about ten feet back—and wasn't wide enough for me to spread my arms out. There were no loose stones on the ground, though aging sticks had been piled in the back where something had once made its bed.

He set the blue light down in the center of the cave before shrugging out of his pack. "You should eat something before you sleep."

"I'm not hungry." I knelt next to the blue light.

It wasn't a lantern with colored glass as I'd thought, but a stone formed of bright blue crystals that seemed to have trapped the spark of a fire deep within itself.

"What is this?" I reached out to poke the stone, expecting him to tell me to stop. But he only watched as my finger grazed the cool surface of the rock.

"A lae stone." He pulled a set of six black rocks from his bag.

"Won't the soldiers be able to see all that light?" I trailed my fingers over the sharp ridges of the lae stone.

"These don't light up." He laid the six stones out along the mouth of the cave.

"Then what are they for?"

"Protecting us." He eyed the line of stones before turning back to his pack.

"What do you mean?"

He didn't speak until he'd unfastened the bedroll from his bag, pulled out a packet of dried meat, and forced a piece into my hand.

"Do you know the ghost stories that keep people out of the mountains?" He leaned against the wall of the cave.

"Sure." I shivered. The cold of the night seeped into my bones now that the heat of the climb had left me. "Everyone knows the stories, even the paun."

"Well, the ghosts that haunt these mountains aren't dead," he said. "I should know. I'm one of them."

I sat against the cave wall opposite him, pressing my back to the cold, damp rock.

"There's magic in these mountains, Ena." He pointed to the stones. "These hold a tiny piece of it."

"You're mad."

"No. I'm a Black Blood."

"No." I shook my head. "No. Black Bloods are a legend. Magic doesn't exist outside the Guilds' control. The sorcerers in Ilara hoard all the magic in Ilbrea."

"Your brother said almost exactly the same thing." A hint of a smile caught in the corners of his eyes.

"My brother does not have a speck of magic in him."

"He doesn't. But he saved my life, and he's joined my family. Which makes you my family as well."

"I don't understand." I looked toward the night beyond the opening of the cave. I had trapped myself in the forest with a madman.

I have nowhere else to go.

"You don't have to understand," he said. "I owe your brother a debt. I heard the Guilds had decided to raid Harane and there was no way Emmet could have gotten to you in time. So I came for you myself."

"You came to the village for me?" The weight of his words sank into my stomach, pulling my gaze back from the open air.

"I promised your brother you would be protected." A hint of worry flitted through his dark eyes. A wrinkle that had no place on the face of one so young creased his brow. "I'm sorry I made it so you can't go back. It wasn't my intention."

"You saved me. I can't be anything but grateful for that." I wrapped my arms around myself, trying to stop my shivering.

"Here." He untied the bedroll, laying the thin pad and heavy wool blanket out on the ground. "You should get some sleep."

"You've just said there's magic outside the Guilds' control and you want me to sleep? With a fancy, glowing, blue stone and six rocks as protection?"

"We've got a long journey ahead of us. You'll have plenty of time to figure out if you think the Black Bloods are real."

I didn't move. "Where are we going to meet my brother?"

"Farther into the mountains. No point in telling you where, you'd never be able to find it."

"Right." I crawled over to the bedroll. The cold ached in my hands. "Can we start a fire?"

"Not safe." He leaned his head back against the stone wall. "Not with the chance of soldiers trying to find us."

"Are you keeping watch?" I untied my dirt-caked boots.

"No need. The stones will protect us."

"Do you have another set of blankets?" I crawled under the heavy wool, grateful for the weight of it even though the air had left the material chilled.

"I was supposed to be traveling alone."

"You should share with me." I pulled the blanket up to my chin.

"I'll be fine."

"If you die of cold, I won't be able to find my brother."

He gave a smile that only moved one corner of his mouth. "I'm not sure which Emmet will do first," he said as he untied his boots, "thank me for saving you, or murder me for dragging you through the mountains."

"I've no idea. I don't really know him."

I turned away as he crawled under the blanket. Even through my coat, I could feel the heat of him. It made the cave seem less like a tomb.

The blue light blinked out, leaving us in darkness.

I took a shuddering breath. "I don't know your name."

"Liam." His breath whispered on the back of my neck.

"I have nightmares, Liam. I'm sorry if they wake you."

12

The night stretched in front of me. Endless blackness I would never be strong enough to defeat. The pounding of hooves battered my ears, but there was a new sound.

Screaming.

A terrible, painful shriek.

I knew someone was dying. I could hear it. The awful resigned fear of a horrible end to a tortured life. I strained my eyes, trying to see into the darkness, searching for the one whose life would soon end. I couldn't let them die alone. I couldn't let their legacy be nothing more than ashes and blood.

But the blackness surrounded me, and the racing horse carried me onward, deeper into the dark.

The screams fell silent.

"Ena," a voice called. "Ena, wake up."

I opened my eyes to a darkness that was not pitch black. Faint hints of the moon and stars peered into the cave.

"Ena?" Liam had a hand on my shoulder. He'd shaken me awake. "Are you all right?"

I blinked up at him, needing to be sure this wasn't just a horrible new trick the years old nightmare had learned. I took a deep breath. The blanket that covered me stank of damp and dirt.

"I'm fine," I said. "I told you I have nightmares."

"You did." Liam laid his head down on his arm. "You're safe here. I won't let anyone hurt you."

I turned back toward the stone wall and stared at the cracks, trying to memorize as much of the pattern as the dim light would allow me to see. I dug my nails into my palms, trying to keep myself awake.

But the world had asked too much of me that day, and sleep swallowed me.

The nightmare didn't come again.

1 3

We woke at the first hint of dawn. I rolled the blankets back up while Liam packed his stones away. In the early morning sun, there was nothing remarkable about the rocks. They were all dark stone, so black they almost looked like the obsidian I'd seen in some of the fancy traders' carts. There were no markings on their surfaces, no spark glowing within like the lae stone.

When the few things were packed up, Liam stood outside the cave, staring east toward Harane for a long time.

I followed his gaze.

Even as high as we'd climbed, the trees still blocked our view of the land beyond the forest.

I knew Harane was down there somewhere. Whether it was still on fire, already reduced to ash, or if the ones who had survived the soldiers' terror were waking up to another day as though nothing had happened, I didn't know. I would never know.

I hoped some of them were still alive. I hoped someone would be kind to Lily and give her a proper funeral in thanks for all she had done for the villagers. But they were a part of a life I could never return to.

I said a silent thanks and farewell to Lily, who had scooped a crying child out of the mud and given her a home.

I sent a wish to Karin that she would survive and find a husband who would protect her.

I asked for forgiveness from Cal. The boy who made me laugh and forget the darkness. The boy I'd very nearly loved. The boy who would grieve for me.

I held them all close to my heart and tossed their memories into the wind, where they could fly free and far away from whatever journey lay ahead of me.

Liam turned and started up the mountain.

I followed him without looking back.

We climbed in silence for a long while. Liam would stop every so often and look back as though wanting to be sure I could keep up. I'd stare back at him, munching on the dried meat I was finally hungry enough to eat, then he'd climb again.

I picked through my bag as we went, tossing the things I'd gathered for Lily away from our trail.

"What are you doing?" Liam asked after a root clump I'd pitched hit the ground hard enough to make a sound.

"Lightening my bag." I tossed another root ball onto a mound of rocks that had slid down the mountainside. "I don't think the soldiers will follow our trail because of it, do you?"

"I don't think any of them would be brave enough to climb this far into the eastern mountains, no matter whose throat I slit."

"Then keep going." I shooed him onward. "If this journey is going to take as long as you said, it's best for us to make good time."

I pitched a clump of lichen aside.

"You use that in ink making?" Liam crossed his arms, decidedly not climbing the mountain.

"No, for Lily's other business."

He stared at me for a moment.

"Healing," I said.

"Healing?" Liam wrinkled his brow. "Emmet never mentioned Lily being a healer."

"I'm not sure he knew. Since he only showed up once a year, it was hard to be sure I told him all the good stories about learning how to stitch skin back together, being vomited on by half the village, and hoping I didn't get hanged by the Guilds for it." I clenched my jaw, refusing to let my mind slip back to seeing Lily hanging from the tree. "Lily helped everyone in Harane who couldn't afford to pay the Guilded healer or was too sick to make it all the way to Nantic. I gathered this lot for her from the woods, but"—I pulled a handful of moss from my bag and tossed it aside—"no point in lugging all this through the mountains."

Liam started up the slope again, moving more slowly, as though inviting me to walk by his side.

I kept my pace even, not catching up to him until we'd reached a new twist in the rise.

"She shouldn't have gotten you involved in healing," Liam said without looking at me.

"I lived in her house. If a soldier had lifted the wrong floorboard, they would have executed me whether I had ever been useful or not. If the Guilds are going to murder me, I'd rather have it be for something worth dying for."

It took me a few minutes' walking to notice Liam had shortened his steps to match my own, smaller stride. I wanted to run up the mountain out of spite, but my muscles ached with every step.

"You should have told him," Liam said. "If Emmet had known Lily was getting you involved in something dangerous—"

"He'd have found another place to abandon me?" I took a deep breath, willing the scent of the forest to bring the comfort it always had. "Lily was closer to family than my brother. I wouldn't have left her to go to some stranger's house if he'd bothered to try and make me."

A stranger's house was where I'd have to go. If I could find someone to take me. An inker or a healer who needed an extra hand. I could clean, too, cook a bit, though nothing wonderful. I'd have to find work, find something useful to do. If I couldn't, I'd have to find a man to marry who could pay my way. I was young, but I'd seen girls wed well before my age. It was either that or end up a whore.

"Emmet will find a place for you," Liam said, like he'd read the fears in my mind. For all I knew, he could have. "He's been to plenty of places off the mountain road. He'll help get you settled someplace safe."

"I don't want my brother's help. I don't need him."

"I never said you did." Liam looked sideways at me, a hint of pity playing in his dark eyes.

"And I don't feel bad for not telling him about Lily." A fist of anger wrapped around my gut. "It's none of his business to begin with. And if we're worrying about keeping secrets, my brother running around with a man who keeps magic rocks in his pack is a bit worse than me shoving lichen in some wounds."

Liam's face turned to stone. For a moment I thought he'd shout. I wanted him to.

"Of course, maybe my brother's plain lost his mind. He ran from a fine life as a smith to follow a madman with a bag full of rocks through the mountains." I untied my rag of evergreen buds and scattered them across our path.

"You're following the same man through the mountains," Liam said.

"I didn't have much of a choice."

"And the *rocks* in my bag protected us last night."

"Because of your magic?" I tossed a mushroom at his boot. "Magic the Guilds haven't claimed?"

The muscles on the sides of his neck finally started to tense. "The Guilds can't use the kind of magic that runs in my blood."

"I really have followed a madman."

"Worse, you've followed a Black Blood." He stopped and turned to face me.

"A children's story." I stepped nearer to him, tipping my chin up so I could glare into his eyes.

"Tilk whisper of my people, but that doesn't make us any less real."

"Ghosts of bandits rampaging through the mountains, slaughtering anyone fool enough to cross them? We have enough monsters in Ilbrea without scary stories coming true."

"I'm not a monster. And my people are not bandits." He stepped forward, leaving only enough space between us for my bag on my hip. "There is plenty of blood on my hands. I've killed more men than I care to count, but it's either that or hide in the woods and wait for the Guilds to slaughter every last tilk. If fighting for an Ilbrea free from the Guilds makes you think I'm a monster, so be it."

"Fighting against the Guilds." All the air had left the mountainside. The echo of his words muffled the birdcalls in my ears. "That's where my brother has been? Not whoring his way through the countryside or being a back alley thief?"

"He found out what the Black Bloods are working toward. He chose to join our cause."

"Cause?" Sound and air popped back into existence as I shouted at him. "Like you think you could do any good? Like you're actually going to rebel against the Guilds."

"We are. We are standing at the dawn of a new age of freedom. Our rebellion—"

"Rebellion is not possible!" I paced in angry circles between the trees. "Fighting the

Guilds isn't possible. How many thousands of soldiers do they have? How many sorcerers? All standing against the Guilds does is make you a volunteer for execution."

"Freedom is only impossible until someone has won it."

"So you and my brother are just going to march into Ilara and demand the Guilds stop tormenting us?"

"Eventually, yes." Blazing determination shone in his eyes.

He meant it.

It was the most terrifying thing I'd ever seen. Not because I was afraid of him. It was the idea of hope that scared me down to my very soul.

I laughed loudly, dimming the fierceness in his eyes.

"I suppose that's what you've been using my brother for, making you swords for your battle." I clapped a hand to my chest. "My apologies, Lord Black Blood, you don't need a sword. You've got magic rocks to guard you."

He stayed silent for a moment, then picked up the mushroom I'd chucked at his feet. "We do have stones to guard us. We have people and plans, weapons, and the will to bring down the Guilds forever. You don't have to believe me, not about the Black Bloods, or the magic, or the end of Ilbrea as we know it.

"But I'd have thought better of you, Ena. A girl who climbs into mountains known to kill and comes out alive with the means to save others—if she can't believe in the hope for a better tomorrow, then maybe we are all damned to burn." He tucked the mushroom back into my bag. "You should hold onto that. People outside of Harane get sick. Someone might need this where we're going."

"And where would that be?" I ran to catch up to him as he strode up the mountain. "Further into your fairytale?"

"We're going to a place guarded by stone, where the people who fight against the Guilds have made their home."

"What if I say no?" I dodged in front of him, blocking his path. "What if I refuse to indulge a lunatic in his madness?"

Liam stared at me. I waited for him to shout. He pointed behind him. "The mountain road is that way. If you want to avoid soldiers who might recognize you, I'd head north, away from the map makers' party. Get as close to the coast as you can, and hope fate favors you and allows you to stay hidden. Having to explain to your brother that you walked away from me in the woods won't be pleasant, but I won't force you to come with me."

Part of me wanted to turn and head west. Forge out into the mountains, and if an animal decided to eat me, so be it.

Part of me still wishes I'd turned and walked away.

But I didn't.

Liam nodded and started climbing the damned mountain again.

I followed him.

I tied the flap of my bag shut to keep the rest of the things I'd collected for Lily safe.

I stared at the mound of lumps in the bottom of his pack where he'd stowed the stones. I pictured myself slitting the bag open, stealing the stones, and pelting Liam's head with them. Safer to imagine that than to even begin to let myself think he could be telling the truth.

The top of the rise peeked through the trees with a wonderful glimmer of sunlight promising my legs flat ground to walk on. Gritting my teeth against the pain, I sprinted up the last bit of the mountain. Rocks took over the very edge of the slope, marking the end of the forest's reign. I burst out of the trees and into the sunshine.

There was no glorious meadow waiting for us at the top of the mountain. Only more mountains reaching as far as the land would allow me to see.

The beast we'd climbed was nothing more than a foothill to its fearsome brothers, who soared so high, trees stopped growing far before their summits. I thought I knew how deep the mountains ran, but I had never seen a full view of them, never once understood the terrifying vastness of the land.

Liam stopped next to me, scanned the mountains, took a deep breath, and headed north.

Toward a place the Guilds' map makers had never laid out for the world to know.

I stepped forward as far as I could on the eastern edge of the rise. The ground crackled beneath my feet like it might give way and toss me over the side of the mountain. I leapt back from the rocks, onto the ground softened by the dirt of the forest.

Liam stood a hundred feet away, waiting at the curve where one ridge descended to the next. He watched me as I looked back out over the mountains I'd never seen on any map. The enormity of it threatened to swallow me whole.

For a moment, I was a little girl staring into the endless black, terrified she'd be lost forever.

I felt Liam staring at me.

I turned away from the cliff to follow him.

He waited while I caught up to him, gave me a nod, and kept walking.

14

A long time ago, before the Guilds came to power in Ilbrea, there was a mother and a baby and a terrible storm.

The wind raged and howled. The rain came down so hard, no man could see the path in front of him. But the mother had been gifted with magic. She could form her own lightning, burn with her own fire—she had no reason to fear what the ungifted hid from. She ventured out into the storm with her baby, refusing to let the skies dictate her path.

The gods saw the mother and knew she thought herself stronger than the might of their storm. So they brought more rain, flooding valleys and upending forests until the mother's magic began to wane.

Exhausted and afraid, she lost her way, and had no hope of finding a safe haven from the storm. She clutched her baby in her arms, and begged the gods for forgiveness.

The gods do not forgive, and the storm raged on.

She scaled the summit at the heart of the mountains, climbing ever upward as strength abandoned her limbs, searching for a place she could shelter her child. A wide boulder was the slim hope the mountain granted, offering relief from the wind but not the pounding rain.

Lightning split the sky, and her baby wailed in her arms. The gods would not grant her child mercy, so the mother begged the mountain itself. Offered everything she had, everything she was, if the mountain would shield her child from the wrath of the gods.

She lay her hand on the great boulder, and poured out every ounce of magic she had, filling the black rocks far below with a power never meant to live in stone.

The eastern mountains are one, and separate. A vast range ruled over by one mighty summit no mortal could conquer. But the magic stirred the great one, and she bade the smaller peaks obey her. The mountain opened, granting the child shelter, as the mother was washed away by the gods' storm.

The child grew within the mountain, raised by the magic its mother had infused into the stone.

The child became a part of the mountain, and the mountain a part of the child. The mountain had bargained for the safety of the babe to gain magic. The mountain didn't know the mother's magic would change the shape of its stones, and make the mountain feel. For the heart of the mountain, where the baby found shelter, grew to love the child. To cherish each beat of its heart that echoed through the caverns and rocks.

But even young raised by magic grow up.

When the child was grown, the mountain opened its gates and let the person it loved walk out into world. But the mountain gave the one it had raised a promise—those who shared the child's blood would be marked as beloved of the mountain, and would always find safety in its embrace.

The child found a partner and had children. And those children had children. And each of those children carried the mark of the mountain in their blood.

And then the child raised in stone died.

The mountain mourned, and feared it would never again have anyone to love.

So the mountain sent a cry out on the wind, calling all the children who carried its mark in their blood home.

The generations of children felt the cry, felt the black stone in their blood calling them back to the heart of the mountain. So they ventured deep into the mountains where no one else dared go.

The mountain sheltered them from the outside world, killing all who would threaten the ones who carry the black stone in their blood. And the beloved children only left their sanctuary to slaughter those who dared to threaten the mountains they'd claimed as their own.

15

The day after the Guilds murdered Lily, I followed the madman Liam through the mountains, heading toward a place where impossible people believed in impossible things.

We didn't speak much the rest of that day, only an offer of food, and a warning of slippery ground. He found another cave for us to sleep in and surrounded the opening with his black stones. He crawled under the blanket beside me without protest.

The nightmare came. The endless black and the pounding of hooves. A gentle voice pulled me from the dream before the screaming began.

I woke to the weight of Liam's arm draped over me. I fell back asleep before I could wonder if he was awake.

1 6

My legs had never been so sore in my life.

We started the morning climbing up and over the ridge of a mountain. I looked at the long downhill waiting for us and felt a foolish sense of relief. Then I started down and realized what an idiot I'd been.

Liam kept to a pace I could match. I tried to tell myself his legs were dying, too, but I knew he was probably trying to be kind.

I had things I wanted to know—how exactly my brother had saved Liam and gotten involved in this fool's rebellion, what the hell kind of good he thought he was going to be able to do throwing stones against a giant like the Guilds, how much longer we'd have to walk—but I was too stubborn to break the silence. I didn't know if he was too stubborn to speak or just enjoyed hearing only our footsteps for hours on end.

It didn't matter much either way. I just kept tromping up and down mountains, refusing to hint at the pain that made my legs tremble.

The sun had moved past midday when Liam finally spoke more than five words at a time.

"We should get some more water." He didn't actually address me, or look at me. For all it mattered, he could have been speaking to the stones in his pack.

"We need water and more food," I said. "Unless you've got more dried meat stashed in your pack, or we'll be getting wherever we're going soon."

"I'll get us some fish."

"Fish from…" The sounds of flowing water stole my will to speak.

We rounded the corner, and a wide, shallow river blocked our path.

I opened my mouth to ask how he'd known we were close to water, before swallowing the question.

Liam shrugged out of his pack by the side of the river.

I fished the empty waterskin from my bag and knelt by the bank. I hadn't realized how thirsty I was until water was within reach. I uncorked the skin and dipped it into the wonderfully cold river.

The chill of it raised goose bumps on my flesh. I downed half the skin before sitting and unlacing my boots.

"We're not crossing through," Liam said as I set my boots aside.

"I didn't say we were." I stripped off my stockings. Deep purple bruises marked my feet and legs. I laid my stockings out next to my boots.

"Then what are you doing?"

"Catching fish between my toes."

His brow furrowed as I rolled my skirt up past my knees.

I dipped my feet into the freezing water and didn't bother biting back my moan of joy as the cold dulled my pain. A fish twice the size of my hand swam past my ankles.

"Hmm, too big for my toes. I guess you'll have to use your magic on the fish."

Liam pulled out each of his three waterskins and began filling them one by one.

"I don't know much about magic. We've never had a sorcerer visit Harane." I kicked my feet through the river. "Maybe you could form a spear of water to skewer us a meal. Or make the river solid and trap the fish where they swim."

He splashed water on his face.

"You could tell them about your rebellion and see if they'll jump up on land," I offered. "See if they're willing to sacrifice themselves to a worthy cause."

He crouched down next to the stream, running his fingers through the dirt as though searching for something.

"If you can't catch a fish, I'll find us something to eat." I scanned the plants around us—some trees, a few low-lying bushes, plenty of scrub and grass growing along the ground. "I can't promise it'll taste very nice, but—"

A sharp buzz cut through my words as a stone streaked out of Liam's hand and shot into the water. A moment later, a fish bobbed to the surface.

Liam leaned over the river and snatched the fish out of the current. He held the lifeless fish up, flipping it one way and then the other before laying it on the ground.

"What was that?" I dug my fingers into the dirt.

"Fishing." He shot another stone toward the river.

I pulled my feet from the water and dragged my stockings back on, not caring that my feet weren't dry.

Liam lifted another slain fish from the river.

"How did you do that?" I yanked on my boots.

He gave a half smile and laid the second fish next to the first.

"Was that magic?" I asked.

"Of course not." Liam pulled the knife from his belt. "I have it on good authority that magic only exists under the control of the Sorcerers Guild."

"Well, clearly I was wrong." I stood and inched my way toward him. "Unless you are from the Sorcerers Guild and are wasting a massive amount of effort tormenting me."

He started to clean the fish, like he hadn't done anything strange.

"You can't clean them with magic?" I asked.

"Some could. But that's not the sort of gift I was given."

He didn't look up. I desperately wanted him to. I wanted to look into his dark eyes and search for something I hadn't noticed before, any hint that he belonged to a world so different from the one in which I'd lived my life.

"What sort of gift were you given?" I asked.

"I'm a trueborn Black Blood."

"So you've said."

"That is my gift." With a flick of his finger, the killing stones flew out of both the fish and landed in the water with a plop, plop.

"What does *trueborn Black Blood* mean?" I knelt beside him.

"I'm a keeper of the pact." He looked up at the mountains. "I work with stone magic."

"So flying stones and the rocks that guard us?"

"Close enough."

"And that's all?"

His gaze met mine. There was no hint of magic in his dark eyes, just a touch of laughter. "I wasn't given the sort of gifts the Sorcerers Guild prizes."

"It doesn't matter. They'd still take you, lock you in their tower in Ilara and make you move stones for them."

"I know." He started cleaning the second fish. "They've taken some of the Black Bloods before, tried to take even more. The beasts hoard magic, and what's not under their control, they'll stop at nothing to destroy. We save as many as we can, get them out of reach of the Guilds."

"Aren't we already out of reach of the Guilds? All of Ilbrea could have fallen into the sea and we'd have no way of knowing."

"We keep the Black Blood children with strong magic hidden from the Guilds," Liam said. "It's the tilk children we have to rescue. Show one hint of magic, and the Guilds will snatch a child from their mother's arms to lock them in the Sorcerers Tower in Ilara."

A shiver shot up my spine.

"Some want to go," Liam said. "Safety, prestige—the Guilds paint a beautiful picture of what they offer. We don't fight that. They can go if they like. But the children who see joining the Sorcerers Guild for what it really is—captivity, being forced to fight against your own people if the order comes down from the Guilds. The ones who would rather die than be taken to the stone tower, we get as many of them out as we can find."

"How?"

"Carefully." He rinsed his hands in the water. "I'll go get some wood for a fire."

He walked off into the trees, leaving me sitting next to the two dead fish.

"Magic," I whispered to the river. I'd seen it. I couldn't deny it. "I'm following a madman with magic."

I dug into the very bottom of my bag, pulled out the bits of moss that were left behind, and made a little bundle by the riverbank. I searched the ground near the fish for twigs and sticks to start a fire.

"Magic." I leaned the twigs against the moss. "What has my chivving slitch of a brother gotten himself into?"

I waited until I heard his footsteps coming back to strike the flint and light the fire.

"Hungry?" Liam laid his armful of wood by the flames.

"I've been tromping up and down mountains. Yes, I'm hungry."

A laugh rumbled in Liam's chest. Not a bursting laugh, or a true cough of joy, but I liked the sound. It was good to know someone could laugh after slitting a monster's throat.

I built the fire up while he skewered the fish. Birds I didn't recognize circled overhead as we ate our meal. They were larger than the kinds that searched for carrion on the western edge of the mountains. I ate my fish as quickly as I could without risking swallowing bones.

"We'll have to find shelter earlier tonight," Liam said.

I rinsed my hands in the river, and took one last, long drink.

"I can walk as far as you can," I said.

"It's not that." Liam pointed northeast along the edge of the river. "Shelter is hard to find in some parts of the mountains, and there are things I'll not risk meeting after dark."

"But you're a Black Blood." I slung my bag across my shoulder. "The mountains will protect you."

"Some myths really are myths." He reached down and took my hand, helping me to my feet. "And some myths are too real for my liking."

"What's that supposed to mean?" I stayed close to his side as he headed north, suddenly afraid one of the birds high above would swoop down and try to carry me away in its great talons.

"Nothing. It doesn't mean anything at all." The tension in his shoulders told a different tale.

"Did you grow up here?" I asked. "In the mountains?"

He didn't answer until we'd cut around a bow in the river. "I was raised like a Black Blood."

"I don't know what that means."

"Does it matter?" He climbed to the top of a mound of rocks and reached down to help me follow.

I ignored his hand as I climbed. "It matters to me."

"Why?"

"Because if a fool like you managed to survive childhood in these mountains, I'd be less afraid of birds swooping down to carry me off." I jumped down on the far side of the rocks. My legs screamed their hatred of me.

"I grew up in the mountains farther east than where we're going." He stood on top of the rocks, gazing east. "There are beasts that will carry off children if you give them the chance, but it's still safer than being near the soldiers."

"So"—I looked up to the birds still circling above us—"you're saying one of those beasts could come down and snatch me?"

"If they got hungry enough." He jumped down from the rocks and landed next to me with a thump that shook my nerves. "But they prefer their food to be decaying before they taste it. Don't die and they'll probably leave you well enough alone."

He gave me another of his half smiles and strode off up the river.

"I hope he knows he's not funny," I muttered to myself.

One of the great birds cawed overhead, and I ran to catch up to Liam, hating myself for acting like such a coward.

We followed the stream for hours. I gathered berries and edible sprouts, tucking them into my bag for later. There were plants I'd never seen before. I wanted to stop and examine them, see what use they could be, but Liam's constant plodding forward kept me from pausing. The way he moved, the way his gaze darted between the peaks on either side of us, made me afraid to linger.

When the sun had started to drop toward the west, the path ahead of us opened up into a wide valley. Scrub bushes and grass covered the flat terrain. The mountains to the east and west of the valley were formed of steep rock with no hint of plants clinging to their sides.

I turned to the path behind us. There weren't the towering woods of the slopes near Harane, but there were proper trees. Then the valley began, and it was like the trees were too frightened to grow on the open ground.

"Where are the trees?"

Liam gnawed on the insides of his lips. "They don't grow in the Blood Valley."

"I can see that."

"We could wait here for the night," he said.

"And if we do?"

"We'll be stuck sleeping in the valley tomorrow night. It takes more than a day to cross. I hate taking you on this path."

"Probably could have avoided it if you hadn't come south to help me."

"There are easier paths to where we're going." Liam looked up to the graying sky.

The birds that had been following us for hours had abandoned their chase.

"Bit late to go back now." I walked past him, out into the valley. A chill nipped at the base of my neck, like a frozen noose ready to tighten.

I waited for him to pull me back or for the ground to swallow me whole.

"We should be able to get a mile or two in before we have to stop for the night." He stepped past me and into the scrubland.

17

The sharp snap of thin branches came with every step. The flatness of the valley was a relief, but I'd never been so glad to be wearing a long skirt in my life. At least the thick folds of the material offered a bit of protection from the twigs constantly jabbing at my legs. And at least the pain of the poking distracted me from the valley.

There was nothing truly frightening about the valley. The ground held firm, the wind smelled of new spring growth. But I couldn't get rid of the chill on my neck.

As the sun crept farther down, Liam began gathering wood as we walked, picking up the thickest of the branches that had fallen from the low bushes.

"Does this mean we'll get to have a fire tonight?" I gathered a handful of twigs and tucked them into my bag.

"We'll need one." He pointed east to a boulder that stuck out of the mountainside. "Ena, you're very brave."

"Am I?" I snatched up every twig I could find as we headed toward the boulder.

"You know you are. If you weren't, you wouldn't still be alive." He shook his head.

I wanted so badly to know what thoughts were rattling around in his head hard enough he had to shake them into order, to hold his face in my hands and stare into his eyes until I'd gotten one complete truth out of him.

"What's coming tonight," he said, "I'm sorry you have to witness it, and I swear I will keep you safe."

"Safe from what?"

He stopped in front of the boulder. The brush had been pulled up along the face of the rock, as though some other travelers had sought the same, poor refuge.

"The Blood Valley isn't a pleasant place." Liam laid down his firewood and took off his pack.

"I figured as much from the name." I added my wood to his pile.

He pulled out the stones and surrounded us, making a wide circle with the boulder at our backs.

"Are monsters going to come for us when night falls?" I forced out a laugh.

Liam looked up toward me. There was no smile playing on the corner of his lips. "The monsters don't come until well after dark."

"Huh." I knelt beside the firewood. "We've got some time then."

"Most don't mean any harm." Liam sat beside me, sorting through the wood as though rationing our supply. "I'm not even sure they can think."

"Does it matter if they can think if they're trying to kill us?" I pulled the flint from my bag.

"Don't light the fire yet. Better to save the wood."

"For when the monsters come." I set the stones down next to the frame of twigs he'd built.

He leaned against the boulder, staring out over the valley. "If you believe the legends, this place used to be the most beautiful land in the eastern mountains. A valley of flowers and trees, some even say a stream ran through the center."

"What happened?" I sat by his side, watching the light around us fade.

"People settled here."

"And they tore up the trees and trampled the flowers?"

"No. They lived peacefully, until they were attacked. One dark night, strangers came into the valley from the north and the south, trapping the valley folk."

"The Guilds?"

"I don't think so, but I can't say for certain. The invaders brought true monsters, things I don't think exist outside the mountains."

I pulled my coat closer around me.

"The valley folk were penned in. They had no chance of escaping," Liam said. "When morning came, the valley floor had been stained red with blood. They say the trees and flowers died before the next sunset."

"That's a terrible story."

"It's not a story," Liam said. "All of it's true."

"How do you know?"

"I've seen it." He untied the bedroll from his bag, shook the blanket free, and handed it to me. "I need you to trust me, Ena. Whatever you see, whatever comes for us, you have to stay here."

"Is this meant to be a joke?" I knew it wasn't, but I couldn't give up that last sliver of hope.

Liam touched my cheek. His fingers were warm against my chill skin. And despite their calluses, and the blood he'd spilt, there was tenderness as he brushed back the hair that had fallen free from my braid. "I won't let them hurt you. I need you to believe that."

My heart thundered in my chest, but I only nodded.

He stayed looking into my eyes for one more breath before turning away and picking up my flint to start the fire.

A tiny pang sliced through my lungs, and the chill of the night tripled without his touch.

As the last of the sun faded from the valley, our fire crackled to life.

A shiver shook me to my teeth.

"You should wrap up," Liam said.

I tucked half the blanket around me, and held up the rest for him.

"I'll be fine," he said.

I didn't move.

He poked at the fire, keeping the wood from tumbling apart, then sat beside me and took his half of the blanket.

We sat in silence as the darkness came in full. I hadn't realized how much comfort the caves had offered. Sitting with the boulder at our backs and the stones in front of us seemed like a fool's way of begging to die.

The first sound that carried on the night wind was laughter, a cheerful chorus of it, as though someone had just told an excellent joke on their way out of a tavern.

I would have wondered what the joke was if Liam hadn't tensed beside me.

The hum of distant music filled the air as a fiddler struck up a fresh tune.

I leaned close to Liam's ear to whisper, "Are there people out there?"

"Not anymore."

Voices spoke not twenty feet away.

I squinted, peering into the darkness toward the noise, but I couldn't see anyone.

"Mama, mama!" The child's voice traveled in front of us as though he were running to his mother's arms.

I glanced to Liam. Pained lines creased his brow.

"How often have you come through the Blood Valley?" I asked.

"Twice," Liam said, "but I sheltered farther on. I've never heard these echoes before."

"I'll not stay in the dark with you," a female giggled. "I don't care if you're handsome. That only makes you more of a rogue."

"If you don't want to sneak away with me, I'll find someone who does," a man said.

"You wouldn't dare." The laughter left the woman's voice. "How could you even threaten such a thing?"

A wisp of a shadow fluttered through the darkness.

"Tamin," the woman shouted. "Don't you dare walk away from me. Tamin!"

The music changed, and voices joined the tune. The happy song settled a stone of dread in the pit of my stomach.

I gasped as a figure appeared in the distance, walking briskly as though following a long lost road. The man wore a light shirt with no coat to protect him against the night chill. The feeble light of the lantern he held in front of him flickered with a wind I could not feel.

"What is he?" I whispered.

"A ghost," Liam said, "or maybe he's only the valley remembering."

The man weaved across the valley and faded from view.

More voices came from distant wisps of shadow, patches of the night that seemed to solidify, swirling around a life that was meant to be led. They moved about in a group near where the music seemed to play. The way they shifted in the night changed with each new song, as though the darkness danced to the long dead tune.

It wasn't until my hands began to cramp from clutching the blanket that another solid form appeared—a girl my age leading a boy away from the other shadows.

They ran silently through the night until he caught her around the middle and pressed his lips to her neck. She twisted in his arms and kissed him, twining her fingers through his dark hair.

56

It seemed like an intrusion to stay so near them as his fingers found the edge of her blouse and traveled up the bare skin of her back.

A crack cut through the air.

The sound wasn't loud or terrifying, no worse than a branch breaking off a tree, but Liam sat up straight as though preparing to run.

"They're coming."

My breath hitched in my chest. The young pair were still kissing, unaware of the danger preparing to end their lives.

"They need to run," my words came out as a strangled whisper. "We have to tell them to run."

I let go of the blanket, but Liam took my hand before I could try to stand.

"It's too late," Liam said.

Another, louder crack cut through the night.

The young couple finally noticed something was wrong. The boy stepped in front of the girl as though trying to shield her, but there was no way for him to know from which direction the danger came.

A scream carried from the southern side of the valley.

Before I could try to see if the one screaming had taken form, a wail sounded from the north.

"We have to get inside." The boy grabbed the girl's hand, dragging her toward the center of the valley to some safety I couldn't see.

A third crack shook the ground beneath us. I held tightly to Liam's hand.

"I won't let them hurt you." Liam spoke over the terrible screams that rent the night.

A great blackness tore up from the ground, sweeping through the fleeing wisps, seizing them and dragging them below the earth.

"What kind of a monster lives below the ground?" I asked.

"I don't know."

A band of solid figures charged into view, their shining weapons raised. For a moment, I thought they had come to slay the beasts that attacked from below. Then one of the men buried his blade in a shadow. The shadow screamed and became a woman with blood dripping down her chest.

My muscles tensed, ready to run out into the darkness to help the woman. The man stabbed again, and she fell to the ground and lay still as deep red stained the dirt around her.

"Please no!" a man shouted. He ran not thirty feet in front of us, fleeing from two men chasing after him, swords ready to kill.

A tentacle of darkness writhed up from the ground and seized the fleeing man around the stomach. His cry of pain and terror echoed in my ears.

"Run! Everyone run!" a fool called into the night.

Dozens of people took shape, fleeing from their attackers. An arrow caught an old man in the back before he had taken two steps.

"Run," I whispered. "Please run."

Liam laced his fingers through mine, offering the only comfort he could.

The boy and girl who had cared for nothing but each other's flesh such a short while before were both slain by swords. He was stabbed through the chest. Her head was taken clean off.

Bile shot up into my throat.

A shriek carried from high overhead, and the pitch of the terror on the valley floor changed. A great bird soared through the darkness, picking up people and tossing them aside, grabbing a woman in its sharp beak and cracking through her spine before swallowing her whole.

The high scream of a child cut through the ringing in my ears.

The bird heard the noise as well and dove toward the sound.

"No!" I leapt to my feet, desperate to save the child from the vicious beast.

"Ena!"

I stepped forward, and the night around me changed. The stench of blood and fear filled the air. There weren't dozens of shapes running through the slaughter, but hundreds.

"Leave them alone!"

The attackers turned toward my shout.

Liam seized me around the waist, dragging me back.

"No." I fought against his grip as the scent of blood disappeared. "I have to help them!"

"It's too late, Ena." He kept his arms wrapped tightly around me. "They're already dead."

A tendril of darkness lashed up from the earth, snaking closer, swaying back and forth as though scenting the air.

"Can it see us?" I asked.

"You stepped outside the stones," Liam said. "They all can."

The great bird spiraled through the sky and dove straight toward us.

18

A scream tore from my throat as the bird opened its talons, reaching for us. But the shouts of the attackers and the shriek of the bird drowned out the sound.

I tried to think of a way to escape, but Liam kept me pinned to his side, one arm wrapped around my waist, the other shielding my head as the talons stretched toward us.

A hum that shook my bones and a blazing blue light burst from the six stones Liam had laid on the ground. The bird's talons scraped against the glow but could not reach our flesh.

The men attacked our sanctuary, but the stones blocked their swords. The tendrils of shadow whipped through the darkness, cracking up from the ground as though determined to swallow our barrier.

"I'm sorry," I said. I don't know if Liam heard me.

A scream in the distance dragged the bird's attention from us. It soared up and over the valley. Cries of terror echoed in the monster's wake.

The men turned their backs on us, ready to slaughter the innocents who didn't have magic to protect them.

Liam didn't let me go. I think he was afraid I would run toward the ones screaming in pain. I wanted to. Every bit of me ached to. But he held me tight, and what chance did I have fighting against a giant beast?

The screams of the dying valley folk dimmed as time wore on. There were fewer of them left to cry, and their defiance had abandoned them.

The fire at our feet flickered feebly.

I looked to our pile of unburnt wood. I didn't want the fire to die, but I didn't know if I could keep from running if Liam loosened his grip on me.

"Let me in," a voice whispered from the darkness. A little girl crouched in front of the rocks. Tears and blood stained her face. "Please let me in before they find me."

"We can't," Liam said.

"We can't leave her out there." I broke free of his grip.

"Ena, she's not real. She hasn't been for a very long time."

I knelt next to the stones, inches from the girl.

"Please," the girl said, staring into my eyes, "I don't want to be alone."

"You can't go out there." Liam knelt beside me, locking his arm around my waist. "The monsters would add you to the tally of their dead, but you won't be able to save her."

A ball of grief pressed into my throat. "It's all right, littleling. You're not alone, I'm right here with you."

"They're coming." A sob shook the child's chest.

"I know," I said, "but you are brave, and you are strong."

"Don't let them find me."

"I…" I had no words of comfort to offer.

The clang of swords came closer.

"I'm right here," I said. "I will not leave you."

Liam took my hand, anchoring me to a world away from ghosts as the men found the child.

"No!" She tried to run, but the men were too quick.

One caught her by the arm and spun her around, shoving his blade into her stomach as though her death meant nothing.

The world tilted.

He dragged her back and dropped her next to the safety of our stones. He laughed as he walked away.

The child lay gasping on the ground, fighting for air that would only prolong her pain.

"It's all right," I said. "Just close your eyes and everything will be better. No one can hurt you, not anymore."

My whole body shook as I watched the little girl take her last few breaths.

Her eyes fluttered closed, and she faded into darkness.

Liam lifted me away from the stones, back to the boulder. He laid more wood on the embers of our fire.

"When will it end?" I asked.

"Not for a while." He draped the blanket over me and sat next to me.

A fresh wave of screams came from farther north in the valley.

He wrapped his arms around me, and I leaned into his warmth, waiting for the battle to end.

I don't know how long it took for the valley to finally fall silent. The human screams stopped first, then the bird vanished, and then the ground stopped shaking. Sometime before dawn, I drifted to sleep.

The sun on my face woke me the next morning. I kept my eyes shut.

If Liam had been wrong, if it wasn't ghosts we had been forced to witness being murdered, but real, living people, then I'd sat in safety and let them all be killed. If hundreds of people had been slaughtered right in front of us, then the valley floor would be coated in blood.

The weight of Liam's arm around my shoulder changed. I could tell from the pace of his breathing that he was awake.

This is the world, Ena. Bloody or not, it's all there is.

I took a deep breath and opened my eyes.

A vast valley of low scrubland shone gold and green in the dawn light. I gave a shaky exhale, burying the fear and grief down far enough they couldn't break me.

"Are you all right?" Liam asked.

"Yes." I pulled the string from the bottom of my braid and shook my hair free. "We'll be out of here before dark?"

"Unless disaster hits." Liam's gaze kept darting back to me as he rolled up the blanket. "I'm sorry you had to see that. I didn't—"

"I'm fine." I ran my fingers through my hair and wove it into a fresh braid. "I just don't understand why. Of all the terrible things that have happened in this world, why does this keep coming back? Why should these people continue to suffer in death?"

"The mountains have magic all their own. Some even say the mountains have a heart that feels and loves." Liam picked up the stones that had protected us from the monsters, both men and beasts. "Maybe the mountains don't want us to forget how evil the world can be."

"I didn't know that was a thing people forgot."

"Ena, I…" His voice trailed away. He slung his pack onto his back. "I only wanted to help you. I'm sorry if any of this makes your nightmares worse."

I stomped out the last embers of our fire. "Don't worry. The nightmare came long before I met you."

He waited while I draped my bag over my shoulder. Then we walked to the center of the valley and headed north.

There wasn't a trace of blood on the ground.

19

We found shelter under an outcropping of rocks that night. I was so tired I fell asleep before Liam climbed under the blanket behind me.

I slept through the whole night without a single dream. I woke in the morning to find I'd turned in my sleep. My cheek rested on Liam's chest, and he held me tight, as though even in sleep he wanted to protect me from the ghosts of long ago torment.

20

"This place we're going," I said as I trailed my fingers along the bark of the trees, "what sort of place is it?"

"What do you mean?" There was a hint of a smile in Liam's voice.

I wanted to dash in front of him to see if the smile had actually made it all the way to his face. Instead, I tipped my head back to stare at the treetops. We'd left the scrublands behind, and trees had taken over the mountainside again.

The forest we'd spent the afternoon trudging through wasn't made of the harsh sort of trees that had clung to the other slopes we'd traveled. These trunks were thick and healthy, with hordes of bright green buds waiting to burst through. The soil beneath our boots held a strong scent of fertility, as though the mountain herself bade the plants to grow.

"Are we going to a village?" I asked. "Is that where we're meeting my brother?"

"There aren't villages in the mountains. Villages need roads for people to reach them."

"A settlement then?" I stopped beside a low patch of berries, kneeling down to touch the waxy leaves.

"I suppose?" Liam leaned against a tree. "It's our encampment for the warm months."

"Encampment?" I picked one of the nubs that would become a berry, crushing the hard knot between my fingers. "Right."

"What were you hoping for? A grand set of caves?"

I heard the smile again and glanced up to find a beautiful glimmer in his dark eyes.

"If you want to know the truth, I was hoping for someplace I might be able to take a bath and wash my clothes." I wiped the sour-scented pulp from my fingers onto a tree. "There's enough mud on my skirts to plant a thriving garden."

Liam stepped forward, raising his hand.

I froze, not even remembering how to breathe, as he wiped his thumb across my cheek. "I'll make sure you get the chance to wash your face, too."

Heat rose up my neck and flared into my cheeks. Days in the mountains, of course I looked like a child come in from playing in the mud.

He brushed something away from my other cheek and stepped back.

I missed the warmth of his hand on my skin. An odd knot twisted the place where my lungs and stomach met.

"We'll find you a new pair of boots as well," Liam said. "A dozen more miles in yours and you might as well be barefoot."

I swallowed the sound I had meant to be a laugh.

"You'll be comfortable enough. I promise." He turned and started weaving through the trees again, heading east.

You're a filthy little waif he saved because he made your brother a promise, Ena Ryeland.

Yelling at myself in my mind didn't lessen my want for him to turn around and touch me again.

Don't be a chivving fool.

I ripped the knot from between my lungs and stomach, and packed it away with all the other things I refused to feel.

The dark space where I shoved the things I didn't want to face was bottomless. Like the sacks of the demons who come to steal naughty children in the dead of winter. A massive void that could fit all the horrors I wished to shove inside it. The seams never tore. The fabric never protested the weight.

So I shoved more and more darkness inside, hiding from the danger, one cast away thought at a time.

"Will my brother be there already?" I quickened my pace to catch up.

"I doubt it. Even with our having to take the long way, and even if his work had gone better than we'd hoped, I can't imagine he'll have beat us back."

"Long way? Did you say *long way?*"

Liam stopped and rubbed his hands over the dark scruff that had grown on his chin. "I couldn't keep you close to the mountain road. Not with the chance of Guilded soldiers wanting to see you in a noose. We had to go into the mountains, and once you dive that deep into the range, there are few paths men can survive."

"But you're a trueborn Black Blood. You can use stone magic."

"How do you think I know which ways a man can survive? We'll be to the encampment soon, and once Emmet arrives and we figure out where the best place for you is, I'll do what I can to make sure the journey out of the mountains is an easier one."

I bit my lips together for a moment, letting the things I wanted to say fade away.

"I needed new boots anyway," I said.

Liam shook his head. When he started to walk, he didn't move as quickly as before. Not like he wanted to be sure I could catch up, more as though he were searching for something.

I scanned the forest around us, trying to spot whatever it was he might be looking for.

Birds filled the trees in greater numbers than we'd seen farther east in the mountains. Small animals scurried through the woods as well, rustling the decay of last autumn's leaves in their wake. Moss clung to the northern side of the trees, though none that I saw would be useful in healing. Lichen grew in a patch by the side of a great boulder made of dark stone.

It struck me as strange that the moss and such hadn't seen fit to grow on the stone's surface.

The base of the boulder dug into the ground, hiding its edge from view. I pictured the stone reaching all the way down to the root of the mountains, touching the heart that had cared for the ill-fated woman and her stone-raised babe.

"Ena"—Liam stepped back to walk by my side—"I think you should take my arm."

"What for?" I asked even as I rested my hand on his elbow. "You think after our days of climbing, this gentle stroll will drop me?"

"No." Liam slowed his pace again. "But the first time feeling it can be shocking to some."

I didn't have the chance to open my mouth to ask what under the sky he was talking about.

It started like a bright flash of heat in the front of my ribs and tip of my nose. I flinched, shying away from the unnatural warmth, but Liam placed his hand on mine, guiding me forward.

"Trust me, Ena."

I let my body lean farther into the heat and found the warmth didn't burn. The feeling was less like a fire trying to sear my skin away and more like the bright burning of wanting something with my whole being. The utter joy and pain of longing filling my entire soul, and knowing that desire might burn away everything I was, and not having enough thought left beyond the wanting to care.

Liam led me forward, and the feeling ate me whole. I gasped and swayed on the spot.

"Just a little farther and you're through." Liam wrapped his arm around my waist, holding me close to his side.

We took two more steps, and the feeling faded, leaving me bereft and empty.

"Are you all right?" A hint of worry wrinkled Liam's brow.

"What was that?" I said, thankful my voice came out strong and not as hollow as I felt.

"A much larger version of the stones that protected us on our journey." He pointed back over my shoulder.

A second black boulder, free of moss and lichen, hid between the trees. If I squinted through the forest, I could see another stone poking up in the distance.

"Liam?" a voice called.

The shock of it sent me reaching for the knife in my bag.

"It's all right," Liam said softly before raising his voice. "It's me."

The branches of a tree to our left rustled and groaned as a man climbed down from a perch high above.

"You're late." The man beamed at Liam, striding over to give him a clap on the back before even bothering to look toward me. "And you've found a stray."

I tipped my chin up and met the man's laughing gaze without a hint of mirth.

"This is Ena Ryeland." Liam stepped away from me, giving a little nod in my direction. "Emmet's sister."

The man looked from Liam to me as though trying to see what part of the joke he'd missed out on. "She's not." He shook his head, sending his sandy brown hair flying around his face. "She can't be."

"I am." I shot the man a glare. He wasn't much taller than me, and though I'm sure he was cleaner than I was, the only reasons I could see for being the slightest bit polite to the man were the two long knives dangling from his belt. I crossed my arms and stepped toward him. "Is my brother here?"

"No," the man said, "haven't heard a chirp of him. Oh, Emmet's not going to like this."

"There weren't any other options," Liam said. "Sal, run on to camp and have them toss up a tent for Ena. Get Cati on finding her some fresh clothes and a bath."

Sal nodded, narrowing his eyes at me. "Emmet is not going to like this." He turned and ran into the trees.

"Sal," Liam called after him.

Sal turned, his face brightening as though Liam might tell him my existence had actually been a joke.

"Put her tent next to mine."

Sal shook his head, flattening his mouth into one long line. "Whatever you say, Liam."

"I'll make sure you get a good meal, too." Liam gave me a nod.

"Right, thanks."

I followed him through the trees in the direction Sal had fled.

The air beyond the stones tasted different than it had on the outside of whatever magic the boulders created.

It was something beyond the scent of smoking meat that drifted through the trees. More like a tang of vibrancy. Like the flavor of that one precious day when spring is done with its hard labor and decides to flourish into full summer bloom had been bottled, and the perfume of it had been misted through the trees.

Voices carried through the woods, more than just Sal and Cati. Dozens of voices.

My shoulders tensed as a cluster of tents came into view. All of the tents were large, big enough to fit an entire shop. Behind a cook fire, one wide tent had the flaps tied open, so the five people sitting inside laboring over food at a long table could stare at me as Liam led me past.

The number of actual living people in the camp sent my heart skipping at an irregular beat, ricocheting against my ribs, though I wasn't sure why.

Liam nodded and waved to the people we passed, but he didn't stop to answer their questions.

Where had he been, had he been attacked…who was I?

No one seemed angry their questions weren't being answered. They just turned back to their business while staring at me out of the corners of their eyes.

"Are you in charge?" I whispered as Liam led me past the last tent.

"How do you mean?" Liam turned down a worn path toward a clearing in the trees.

"You know damn well what I mean."

"Then yes."

The dirt in the clearing had been packed down as though trampled by hundreds of angry feet. Halved logs and carved stumps surrounded the space, as though spectators had enjoyed whatever sport had driven even the slightest hint of growth from the ground.

We passed by a chair wide enough to fit two, with a soaring bird carved into the back. I wondered for a moment how they had found a tree large enough to create such a thing.

Magic.

Prickles tingled the back of my neck.

On the far side of the clearing waited another batch of tents, larger than the first. A path cut through the center of them, with smaller trails leading off to the back rows where the tents seemed barely large enough to fit a cot.

A few men and women poked their heads out to gape at me as we passed.

I tucked the hair that had pulled free from my braid behind my ears and kept my head held high. I couldn't stop them from worrying that Emmet's sister had been brought to the camp, but I wouldn't have them murmuring that she had shown up looking like a filthy, chivving coward.

We stopped in front of the largest tent in this area.

A girl waited next to it, her arms crossed as she stared between Liam and me. Her hair was cut short so it rested above her shoulders. She wore a shirt and bodice, and pants like a man. The hilt of a knife poked out of the top of her boot. But it was the way she watched us, like she wasn't staring at the filth on my clothes but instead thinking of how best to gut me, that made me like the girl.

"Cati." Liam nodded.

"You've been gone a while." Cati tipped her head as she examined me. "She does look like him."

"Makes sense, I suppose," I said.

"Speaks like him, too," Cati said.

I started to say she was wrong before swallowing the words for fear my speaking might prove her right.

"I'll get her cleaned up," Cati said. "Rothford wants to meet with you, and I'm sure there's a dozen other things need doing. If you get started now, you might get to sleep tonight."

Liam shut his eyes for a moment before nodding and shrugging out of his pack. "Thanks, Cati."

"This way." Cati started down another path, leading me away from the tents. I followed her, not giving in to the temptation to look back at Liam. "We'll get you washed and work on some decent clothes for you."

"Thanks."

"Glad to," Cati said. "What kind of terrible would we be if we weren't kind to someone who came up the mountain road to get to us?"

"We didn't come up the road," I said. "We cut east and came north through the mountains."

"What?" Cati whipped around and studied me again, taking in everything from my worn boots to my filthy face.

"It's a bit of a story." I shrugged. "Liam thinks the soldiers might want me hanged."

Cati stayed silent for a moment before tipping her head back and laughing. "I think I might like you."

She beckoned me on through the trees to a mound of rocks sticking out of a cliff.

"Honestly," Cati said, "I've told Emmet he should bring you here more than once. Gods, he'll be furious. I can't wait till he gets back."

She stepped between the stones and out of sight. I took a deep breath before following her, expecting the burning to flare in my chest again, but a humid warmth and the sound of flowing water greeted me instead.

Two lae stones hung from the ceiling of the cave, casting their glow on the pool beneath. A crack in the rock wall fed water into the bath. The overflow from the current surged over the edge and into the darkness on the far side.

Cati fished in one of the dozen alcoves carved into the wall and pulled out a basket of soap that smelled as fresh as summer flowers. "Give yourself a good scrub, and I'll be back with some clean clothes."

She pressed the soap into my hand and left me alone in the cave.

21

I lay in the pool, trying not to wonder at how the water had been heated. It might have come from a fire burning far beneath the ground. Or, there was the far more terrifying option—I was sitting in a bath warmed by magic. In a camp protected by magic. After following a man whose blood held magic.

I scrubbed my hair with the sweet-smelling soap, digging my fingers into my scalp hard enough to hurt.

If Karin had been here, she'd have been positively giddy at being surrounded by magic. *Karin wouldn't have made it through the mountains.*

It wasn't a pretty thought, but I couldn't come up with a way to tell myself it wasn't true.

My eyes stung with missing Harane and all the people there. Or who had once been there.

I ducked beneath the water, rinsing the suds out of my hair. I stayed under for a moment, letting the faint rumble of the water entering and leaving the pool drown out the thoughts of wounds I couldn't mend.

Warmed by magic or not, I couldn't help but be grateful for the bath. I scrubbed my face hard before coming up for air.

"You all right?" Cati stood at the edge of the pool, looking down at me.

I brushed aside the instinct to cover my nakedness and met her gaze. "I'm halfway to clean, so things are looking up."

"Good." She stared at me for another moment before moving to a pile of clothes set at the side of the cave. "We don't usually get unexpected guests in the camp, so we don't keep many extra clothes on hand. Lucky for you, when I said I needed things for Emmet's sister, a few of the women volunteered their wardrobe."

"Is Emmet that well liked?" I scrubbed my arms, getting rid of the last layer of mountain dirt.

"I don't know how many people like him, but we all owe him, and that's worth even

69

more." Cati knelt by the clothes. "We've got three choices for boots, so we'll see which fits best. All of them are worn, but they're in better shape than the tatters you climbed here in." She rummaged through the pile and pulled out a slightly worn, deep blue skirt. "It'll be a bit short at the ankles on you, but honestly that's for the best up here."

"It doesn't matter to me. If it's clean, I'll take it."

Cati flashed me a quick smile. "Good. I truly don't know how the southern runners manage to get clothes onto all the sorcis they save."

"Sorcis?" I climbed out of the pool, wrapping myself in the cloth she'd laid out for me.

"Sorcerers we save from being trapped by the Guilds." Cati held a shift up to the light of the lae stones. "We don't bring the sorcis here, though. We funnel them south as quick as we can. The farther from Ilara they are, the safer they are."

"Is that what my brother is doing? Bringing children with magic south to keep them away from the Guilds?"

"No." Cati held a bodice up to my torso, tossed it aside and picked up another, which would fit tighter than Lily would have ever allowed. She scowled at it for a moment, then pressed it into my hands. "That'll look nice."

"What is Emmet doing?" I held out my arms for her to drape the shift and skirt across.

"Things that are better not spoken about."

I didn't like the sound of that.

I didn't know Emmet, not as he was. My understanding of my brother was a strange mix of what I remembered of him from when I was little and we still lived together in our parents' home, and the Emmet I'd created in my head over the years of him being gone.

For so long, the Emmet in my mind had been brave and strong, a warrior I could depend on if the Guilds ever came for my blood. When I found out he'd abandoned Nantic and me, I'd decided he was a chivving coward who didn't care for anyone but himself. Now, with Cati holding boots up to the bottom of my foot, I realized I didn't know Emmet at all. I probably never had.

I'd been a little girl when Emmet and I had shared the loft in our parents' home. I'd still thought the fairy stories he'd told me to get me to go to sleep were real.

Then I learned that nothing as beautiful as a happily ever after existed in this world, but he was already gone. Taken far away where I could pretend I still knew my brother.

"This should work for now." Cati left a pair of brown boots by my feet. "Get dressed, and we'll find you something to eat."

She walked out of the cave, leaving me alone.

I tried not to think of who the clothes actually belonged to as I pulled them on. Liam had already saved my life. I didn't like the idea of being beholden to so many people at once. But the feeling of being genuinely clean was enough of a comfort to make me forget how many times I might have to say thank you to strangers.

I picked up my old clothes to take them with me. The dull stink of them sent heat to my cheeks. I'd shared blankets with Liam in these mud-packed clothes.

My face flushed even hotter at the idea of him thinking of me as the filthy little sister of the great Emmet Ryeland. Then I realized he had probably already stopped thinking of me at all, and hurt nibbled at the edges of my stomach.

After days spent with only Liam, it seemed strange to be without him.

But he'd trudged back to his home, a place where he was in charge and had tasks to tend to and decisions to make. I'd left the ruins of my home behind. I had no ink to blend, no chores from Lily to accomplish. I was wearing other girls' clothes in a strange place where the only certainty about my future was how livid my brother would be to find me here.

"Ena?" Cati called in.

"Coming." I stepped out into the late afternoon sun. The wind chilled my neck under my wet hair.

"That's better." Cati gave a nod. "There'll be a comb waiting in your tent. At least there will be if Marta did as I asked."

"Thanks," I said, "for the clothes and all of it."

"Think nothing of it. You just came through the mountains to get here. The fact that you survived the journey makes you worthy of clean clothes and a comb in my book."

"Right." I followed her back toward the cluster of little tents. "Thanks though."

"Sure." She stopped next to the largest tent at the head of the path. A small tent had been set up right beside it. "This'll be for you."

She pulled aside the flap of the small tent and bowed me in. A cot, a stump for a chair, and a taller one for a table had been set up inside. A carved wooden comb lay on top of the thick blankets on the bed.

"It's not much," Cati said, "but this is about all we have to offer here."

"It's all I need." I pushed a little smile onto my face, hoping I looked thankful without having to say it again.

"I'll have someone bring food in a bit." Cati gave a nod, let go of the tent's flap, and I was alone.

For the first time since I'd smelled the smoke in the woods near Harane, there was nothing for me to do. No one for me to try and save, no soldiers to flee from, no mountains to climb.

I stood in the tent for a long while. The chatter of voices cut through the fabric, but the stillness in my little shelter smothered me. I lay down on the bed and shut my eyes, wishing there were something familiar left in the world.

22

Music dragged me from the blackness of my dream. I woke to find myself still surrounded by darkness.

For one terrible moment, I thought the nightmare had learned another new trick, a way to keep me pinned in its grasp by not letting me know if I was awake.

Then I saw the glimmers of light fighting through the fabric of my tent and remembered where I was. I lay on top of my blankets for a few minutes, listening.

Someone plucked at an instrument. A few voices sang along, though not all of them very well. Chatter weaved in and out of the music. Laughter, too. The steady thumping of feet striking the ground kept time with the tune.

Dancing.

Old stories of ghosts reveling in the woods, luring in living men and making them dance until they died, shot a shiver through my shoulders.

"You ran into the mountains with a Black Blood, Ena. You can't afford to become a coward now."

I sat up on my cot and combed my hair. The normality of the motion soothed my nerves. I didn't have a string to tie the end of a braid with, so I let my hair lie loose around my shoulders in a way that would have driven Lily mad.

Remembering her scowling face carved another tiny hole in my chest.

One day, there might be nothing left of me but a vast emptiness.

I pressed my hands to my chest and took a deep breath. My heart beat within my ribs, thumping against my hands. That had to be enough. Breathing and living had to be enough. It was all I could manage.

I ran the comb through my hair one last time and stepped out of my tent.

Lae stones hung along the wide path between the tents, making a trail of blue light to the clearing beyond. Squaring my shoulders, I walked toward the music, determined that, if I was going to walk into the middle of a ghost's revel and be made to dance until I died, I would do it with my head held high and not a hint of cowardice about me.

People filled the clearing—sitting on the halved logs and stumps, clustered around a barrel and small fire on the far side, dancing on the packed earth in the center. Two women stood on one of the benches, playing their instruments, switching between songs with barely a nod or word spoken between them.

Lae stones hung from the trees, casting their light on the whole joyous mess.

I stood at the far edge, watching, searching for the reason for the celebration. I didn't see a pair acting like a new bride and groom, or spot anyone preening like the party was being held in their honor.

But they were all smiling and laughing.

"Ena?" A girl my age with hair so blond it was almost white stepped in front of me.

"Yes." I didn't know what else to say.

The girl smiled, and dimples punctured her rosy cheeks. "I was wondering if you were going to wake up hungry. I tried to bring you some dinner earlier, but you were asleep, and Cati said you'd been through the mountains so I didn't think it would be right to wake you."

I dug my nails into my palms, praying to whatever god could listen so far into the mountains that if this blond girl had seen me sleeping, she at least hadn't found me in the middle of the nightmare.

"Well"—the girl took my hand like we'd been friends since childhood and led me into the clearing—"you're awake now, and you've got to be starving. Bless the stars for Liam, but I'm sure he didn't feed you nearly as well as he should have." The girl gave a bright laugh.

"We managed."

The sounds and movement in the clearing changed as the revelers began to notice me. The whispers started lapping from the far end. One of the women stopped playing, only starting again when the other stomped on her toe.

"Come on." The girl tugged me through the center of the pack.

I kept my face front and my breathing even, refusing to let any hint of pink creep into my cheeks.

"We've got a bit of stew over here," the girl said. "Neil doesn't usually take well to people ferreting for food once he's done feeding the camp for the day, but if you want something more than that, I think he might make an exception for you."

A cluster of men just older than me stopped their whispering as we drew level with them.

"Because I'm Emmet's sister?" I said loud enough for the men to hear.

Three of the four had the good sense to turn their faces from me. One with bright red hair met my gaze and gave me a nod.

"That and you managed to survive being alone with Liam for days." The girl laughed again.

"What's your name?" I asked.

"Oh, sorry." The girl wrinkled her nose as she stopped next to the barrel. "I hardly ever meet new people, so I suppose I forget how it's meant to be done. I'm Marta."

"Nice to meet you," I said, but Marta had stopped listening to me.

"Can I get a stew and ale?" she spoke to the older man who seemed to be in charge of minding the barrel and the fire with the stewpot hanging over it.

The man looked at me with narrowed eyes before nodding.

"We eat pretty well here," Marta said, "at least as far as being in the camp goes. It's not anything compared to what we get in the winter, but I suppose that's the price we pay."

She kept chattering as the older man pressed a wooden bowl of stew into one of my hands and a mug of brown ale into the other. He gave me a nod, and what might have been a smile, as Marta led me away.

"Honestly," Marta said, patting the bench for me to sit next to her, "I think you'll be happy here once you've settled in a bit. Life isn't fancy, but we're safe here, and we're helping, and that makes it all worthwhile. And I am glad to have another girl near my age here. There aren't very many of us, you know, and to have a new person come in, it really is exciting."

"I'm glad." I took a bite of my stew, risking burning my mouth in exchange for a reason not to have to say more.

"I've been telling Emmet he should bring you here for two years now," Marta said. "The look on his face when he finds out you're here will be brilliant. I hope I get to see it. And I hope we get to keep you. Maybe we'll work on convincing him together. Between the two of us, I think we could do quite the job of it."

"Maybe."

Marta kept talking while I ate the thick stew and drank the ale that tasted of pressed flowers. I didn't say much, I just tried to ignore the people pretending not to stare at me, and watched the ones dancing.

There wasn't a hint of fear clouding their joy. People laughed and sang in a way I'd never witnessed in Harane. I hadn't even known enough about what being safe was supposed to mean to realize how much fear had tainted every part of life in the village.

I blinked away images of a dark-stained post, and tamped down the anger even thinking the word *safe* boiled within me.

"If you would only let me do something to help," I said for the fifth time that hour as I followed Marta through the camp.

"You need to rest," Marta said. "Don't worry about helping."

"Marta, if—"

She ignored me and ducked into the open kitchen tent, leaving a sheet of paper under a stone on the table and giving Neil a wave before hurrying on toward the makeshift stables near the western side of the camp.

"I could be useful." I spoke through my teeth as I chased Marta through the trees.

I'm not proud of the three days I spent following Marta through the camp.

The first full day I had with the Black Bloods I mostly just slept. The climb through the mountains had taken more out of me than I cared to admit.

After that, the horrible itching ache to be doing something set in. I didn't care if it was climbing through another mountain range, digging for roots, or mucking up after the horses. The idea of sitting still and waiting for my brother to come back set my every nerve on edge.

Marta paused at the fence of the horse paddock. There were only six horses roaming between the trees. Truth be told, I wasn't exactly sure how they'd gotten the horses up the mountain. They certainly wouldn't have made it on the path Liam and I had climbed.

Even thinking his name set a chill on my neck and a stone in my stomach. I hadn't seen him since he'd left me in Cati's care when we'd arrived. From the little people were willing to tell me, he wasn't even in the camp anymore.

"It'll only leave us with four horses for now." Marta chewed the tip of her thumb. "I don't like it at all, but I suppose we haven't got a choice, have we?"

"Are you actually asking me?" I stepped in front of her. "Because if you'd tell me what the horses were for or where they were going, maybe I could help you work it out."

"It's nothing for you to worry about." Marta gave me a smile just large enough to display her dimples. "We have plenty of supplies here. There's no reason for you to fret."

"I'm not fretting."

"Good." Marta dodged past me and spoke a few whispered words to the woman who minded the horses.

The woman's tan brow furrowed. She pursed her lips, glaring at Marta for a moment before shrugging and going to the tent where the saddles were kept.

"I could help her with the horses, you know," I said as Marta hurried through the trees back up to the main body of the camp.

"She'll have it done in no time," Marta said. "Tirra's quite used to working on her own."

"It's not Tirra I'm fussed about. It's me losing my chivving mind."

"You're not going to lose your mind from a few days' rest." Marta waved a hand in the air as though batting away the foolish notion that the lack of work could be rapidly stripping me of my sanity.

We passed through the clearing where the camp gathered every night—dancing, laughing, talking, perfectly secure in their home far up in the mountains.

I wanted to stand in the middle of the packed dirt and scream. Shout to the entire camp that if they didn't give me something to occupy my time, I might catch fire from the inside out and burn the whole mountain down.

Sleeping brought nightmares. Sitting idle allowed thinking, which brought memories I couldn't bear. I had been reduced to chasing after Marta as she bustled through camp, organizing things in whispers, just so being angry at her would give me something to do.

"If you won't let me help with the horses, food, laundry—"

"There are already people doing all those things," Marta said.

"Then I'll leave camp and gather some plants for healing. You can never have too many supplies if an illness comes."

Marta turned back toward me, chewing on the tip of her chivving thumb again. "I can't let you do that. Liam said you weren't to be allowed out of camp under any circumstances."

A flash of white hot anger burned away the little self-control I'd managed to retain. "Liam says I'm not allowed out of camp? And the chivving slitch didn't see fit to tell me himself?"

"Ena." Marta blushed.

"And why am I not to be allowed out of camp? Am I a prisoner now? Is he afraid there will be soldiers hunting me this high in the mountains?"

"He only wants to keep you safe."

"Don't you even—"

A slow clapping cut me off. I turned to find Cati leaning against a tree in the shadows.

"She's finally cracked." Cati pushed away from the tree, a tiny smile playing on her lips. "I thought it would have happened sooner."

"Cati," Marta warned.

"I bet you were going to explode yesterday." Cati ignored Marta. "Rothford won the bet. I'm out a copper."

"You bet on me losing my mind from sitting still?" I asked.

"That wasn't a very welcoming thing to do," Marta said.

Cati shrugged. "So what's wrong then?"

"I can't just sit around here waiting for precious Emmet to show up," I said. "And I won't be told I'm not allowed to leave camp."

"But Liam—"

"I'm not a child who needs to be kept in the garden." I spoke over Marta. "I'm not useless, and I won't be treated like I am."

"Well, Marta?" Cati crossed her arms, still smiling.

"I suppose," Marta said, looking up to the treetops as though seeking answers from the gods, "there is always a use for more people in the kitchen tent. Neil tells wonderful stories—"

"I don't—"

"Sounds like you don't need Ena's help." Cati stepped between us and looped her arm through mine. "Come with me, Ena. I've got something to keep you busy."

She led me off through the trees, not bothering with a path.

"Wait." Marta chased after us. "Where are you going?"

"To train," Cati said.

"No," Marta said. "Absolutely not. She is not going to train with you. She is to be kept safe until Emmet returns."

"I'm not going to stab her," Cati said.

"She is not a fighter," Marta said.

Cati let go of my arm and rounded on Marta. "I don't care what Liam said. I don't care what Emmet will think. Whatever ends up happening, wherever Ena ends up going, she'll be better off if she knows which end of a knife to shove into someone's eye. Consider her training an investment in her future survival, whether or not she ends up staying with the Black Bloods."

Marta bit her lips together as her face turned bright red.

"Go tally supplies and save Ilbrea." Cati shooed her away.

"If this goes badly, you're taking the blame." Marta gave one final and decisive shake of her head before striding away.

Cati didn't speak again until Marta had disappeared through the trees. "Ready then?"

I wanted to ask what I was supposed to be ready for, but I was too afraid Cati might change her mind and leave me to sit on a stump.

I followed her deep into the trees toward the largest clearing in the camp.

I don't know why they had set the training field so far back from the tents. Maybe it was to keep the clanging swords from making it seem as though the Guilds had come to rip through their canvas homes and kill them all. Maybe it was because there was so little flat space in the mountain refuge, it had to be used where it could be found.

It was a ten minute walk to the open space where the trees had been cut down and the stumps cleared away. The first time I had wandered through the camp, I had wondered at the size of it all. How had so many massive stones been laid to be able to protect a place so large?

But the idea of the mountain shooting talons of stone up around us, as though the rocks themselves held us in their grip, had been frightening enough I'd decided not to worry about how the camp had been formed. If it had that much to do with magic, it was probably best I not know.

The clangs of swords and twangs of bows carried through the trees.

"I meant it, you know," Cati said. "You do need to learn to fight, whatever ends up happening when Emmet gets back. A girl like you needs to know how to protect herself."

"What's that supposed to mean?" I watched as the young man with the flaming red hair hoisted his sword and charged at another man.

"The Guild paun who attacked you—" Cati began.

"Liam told you?"

"Of course, and the sad part is, I wasn't surprised." Cati turned to me, looking at my bodice that showed my curves a bit too well, before staring into my eyes. "You do know you're very beautiful?"

"So men will decide they want to come after me whether I want them to or not?"

"They can try it. But once you know how to fight, you'll be able to slit the throat of the next chivving bastard who tries to touch you." She pulled a knife from her boot and pressed the hilt into my hand. "Sound good?"

I gripped the heavy blade. The weight of it absorbed the hopeless, helpless worry that had been stinging my chest. "All right."

2 4

Every muscle in my body hurt. Bruises had formed on my arms and stomach from Cati's blows. We'd both used wooden knives for practice, thank the gods, otherwise I would have been sliced to ribbons.

I'd never seen someone fight the way Cati did. It was as though someone had taught her a fancy dance that just so happened to involve killing people. When the men on the field watched her, their faces filled with a beautiful mix of admiration and fear.

She showed me no pity as she taught me how to block an attack, and I was grateful for it. Even as I sat in the clearing, too sore to join in the evening's dancing, I was grateful for every blow.

She'd let me keep her knife and had given me a sheath so I could tuck the blade into my boot as she had. Having a weapon pressed against me felt like the most powerful secret I could ever hold. I was not helpless, and someday, I would be dangerous.

When the dancers had begun to slow for the evening, Liam walked into the clearing, his pack on his back and dirt covering his boots.

He gave a wave to the ones still frolicking but didn't slow as he crossed through his people and toward his tent. No one stopped him to speak to him.

His footfalls were heavy and his shoulders rounded. He looked exhausted.

We'd climbed through the mountains for days, and even in the worst of it, he'd never looked like that.

I waited until he'd disappeared up the wide row of tents before following him. I gave a nod to Marta, who'd been avoiding me since I'd gone off with Cati, and blushed a bit as the redheaded boy smiled at me.

The music followed me up the lae stone-lined path. Shadows flickered around me as though the night wanted to take over for the tiring dancers.

The flaps on Liam's tent were still swaying when I reached them. I raised my hand to knock, but the canvas wasn't a door. A foolish, nervous fear pressed on the front of my chest. I shook it away and settled for knocking on the tent post.

"What do you need?" There was an unfamiliar, harsh edge to Liam's words.

"Wanted to make sure you were all right," I said. "But if you're bent on being in a sour mood, I won't offer to bring you a mug of ale."

My heart thumped against my ribs as I waited for him to reply.

He didn't.

"Night then." I turned toward my own tent.

Liam pushed the flap of his open.

He stared at me for a long moment, then held out a small waterskin.

I took it, not even needing to get the skin close to my nose to smell the frie. "So you don't want ale then?" I took a sip, letting the fire of the liquor burn away the bit of me that was embarrassed for following him.

"I find the two don't mix well," Liam said.

"Depends on the person, I think." I took another sip from the skin. "A few of the fellows back in Harane took combining the two to a near masterful level. It was rather impressive."

A smile lifted one corner of Liam's mouth.

"So you're all right then?" I asked.

"Fine," Liam said, "nothing you need to worry about."

"So you're worried?"

"That's not what I said."

"As good as. Did it go badly? Whatever it was you disappeared to do?"

He looked at me for a long moment. It felt like he was judging the weight I could bear. Like I was a bridge he wasn't sure was steady enough to be crossed.

"It didn't go as well as I'd hoped," Liam said.

"Want to tell me about it?" I held the frie out to him.

"There are some things it's better for you not to know." He took a long drink.

"Because when my brother decides where I'm to be placed for safekeeping I might go running to the nearest paun soldier and tell them all about your plans to free Ilbrea of the Guilds?" I took the skin and had another drink.

"You wouldn't betray us." Liam leaned against the pole of his tent. "It wouldn't even matter if you felt any loyalty to the Black Bloods—you hate the Guilds too much to offer them help."

"Well then." I ducked under his arm and into his tent.

A bed, a table with two chairs, and a trunk left most of the space in the tent empty.

"Tell me what's wrong." I took a seat at the table before he could argue with me.

Liam stared at me for a long moment, as though warring with himself as to whether or not to toss me out.

I waved the frie at him and nudged the other chair at the table with my toe. "Come on."

My brashness started a steady thrumming in my chest. I don't know if it was the knife tucked in my boot, the frie in my belly, or the simple fact that I didn't care if he got mad at me as long as I got to speak to him.

Liam sighed and let go of the tent flap, shutting out the rest of the camp. "We need more."

"More what?"

"More fighters, more resources." He sat opposite me with a soul-cracking sigh. "We need more everything."

"And you can't get it?"

"I thought I had a chance," Liam said. "I went to speak to one of the other clans—"

"Other clans?" I leaned in.

"There are five clans in the Black Bloods. Unfortunately, none of the others seem to care as much about Ilbrea as we do. I thought telling them what the Guilds had done to Emmet's home would make them see how bad things have gotten. I thought it had worked." He reached into his pocket and pulled out a bird carved of black stone.

He ran his finger along the bird's spine, and its wings shivered as the stone came to life. The bird hopped around the table, its stone-making the only thing giving away that it wasn't a natural creature. Liam held out his palm, and the bird lifted its chin.

A short, tightly wound scroll grew out of the bird's throat. Liam unrolled the paper and read it aloud.

"Trueborn Duwead. Your bravery is the pride of all Black Bloods, but we can see no path forward to a free Ilbrea that will not bring suffering to all the mountain's people. We will continue to protect the magic you bring us and ferry the power safely away from the Guilds' control. If the chance for freedom comes, we will stand with you. Until then, we must protect our own. Blood Leader Brien."

Liam crumpled the paper. "And he didn't even bother to tell me to my face. It sounded like he'd help us. Then I get this when I'm halfway back here."

"Sounds like he's a chivving coward." I held out my hand and the stone bird hopped toward me. "Would you really want someone like that helping you?" The bird leaned into my fingers as I pet its cold head.

"I don't have anyone else." Liam took another drink, watching as the bird nibbled at my fingers. "We do well enough rescuing the ones who want to hide from the Sorcerers Guild. And I'm not saying it isn't important work."

"Freedom for them and one less trained sorcerer ready to kill any common folk who cross the Guilds."

Liam nodded, rubbing his hand across the scruff on his chin. "But it's not enough. How can the other clans not see it? After what the soldiers did to Harane, after what that bastard tried to do to you." He froze, staring at me.

He thinks I'll shatter.

I took a deep breath, testing myself for cracks. "The Guilds torment us. It's how it's always been."

"That doesn't make it right."

"No, it doesn't. Not even a little. But up here"—I let the bird hop up onto my palm as I tried to fit the words into the right order—"I can understand how the other clans ignore it. Up here, the mountains block out the entire world. They swallow everything beyond. All of Ilbrea could be on fire, and we wouldn't know. We might not even get a hint of smoke on the wind."

"If I hadn't lived it, if I hadn't watched so many people bleed because of the Guilds, I don't know if I'd be willing to leave the mountains to try and fight the most powerful people in the world either."

Liam passed the skin of frie back to me. The bird hopped up onto my shoulder while I drank.

"There are people dying down there every day," Liam said.

"I know."

"What kind of monsters would we be to ignore that?"

"The kind that stay alive."

"Only until the Sorcerers Guild gets strong enough to conquer the mountains." Liam looked up to the canvas above him. "It'll happen. Maybe not for another generation, but Ilbrea won't leave the mountains free forever. If we just hide and let them slaughter and gain power, then how will we be able to say the Black Bloods deserve aid or freedom when the Guilds come for us?"

"Did you explain it to the Blood Leader like that?"

"I tried. But he's so caught up in this year's rations, he can't think of the people starving outside his control."

"Then find another way to get more people," I said.

"If the Brien won't fight with us, none of the other clans will."

"Who says you have to have Black Bloods? You recruited my brother. Haven't you gotten more out of Ilbrea?"

"Some."

"Then you'll find some more." I nudged his chair with my toe. "You've got magical rocks on your side. You'll find a way."

Liam held out his hand. The bird soared over to him, landed on his palm, and became lifeless. He tucked the bird back into his pocket.

"I—" I began, but Liam met my gaze. Fatigue bordering on defeat filled his dark eyes.

"What happened to Emmet and me when we were young, we're not unique. We're not the only children the Guilds stole everything from. What the soldiers did to Harane, how they killed Lily—she expected it. She knew they'd murder her for helping people eventually."

Liam took my hand in his. His callused palm pressed against mine, the warmth of his touch giving me courage.

"And what that man tried to do to me. No one would be shocked at that either."

"It's not right." Liam squeezed my hand. "People shouldn't have to live like that."

"No, they shouldn't." I leaned closer to him. "And you and I, and the rest of the Black Bloods in this camp, aren't the only ones who see that. There are people who will want to help you. You just have to find them."

"I thought you didn't believe we could overthrow the Guilds."

"I don't. But I don't think you're capable of sitting idly by while the world burns either. And if you're going to fight against the flames, there are a lot of other people incapable of doing nothing who will fight with you. And who knows? Perhaps, if you get enough fools together, you can save us all."

"Maybe." His gaze fixed on my hand clasped in his. He moved his thumb toward my wrist, his skin just barely grazing mine.

The edge of my sleeve shifted, falling up my arm. A flock of bruises darkened my skin. I moved to pull my sleeve down, but he'd already taken my arm in both his hands.

"Who did this to you?" His face turned to stone, even harder than the bird's wings.

"No one."

"Did someone in this camp hurt you?" I could hear death in his voice. He'd already slit one throat to protect me—he wouldn't hesitate to do it again.

I didn't say anything.

"Ena, I brought you here to keep you safe, and if one of my own people—"

"It's not like that." I lifted my arm from his grip.

"It's not hurting you to leave you covered in bruises?"

"She did hurt me, but not like you think."

Liam opened his mouth to speak, but I pressed a hand over his lips.

"It's Cati. She's teaching me to fight. Which does involve hitting me quite a bit, but not in a way for you to get fussed over."

Liam lifted my hand away from his mouth. "Why is she teaching you to fight?" He kept my fingers locked with his.

"Because I can't count on there always being someone around to save me. I have to know how to protect myself."

"You shouldn't have to." He held my hand tighter.

"But I do, and learning something is better than sitting around waiting for Emmet. Besides, since the Brien won't help you, shouldn't you be grateful for anyone who's willing to fight on your side?"

He let go of my hand. "I'm glad Cati is teaching you. She's one of our best."

"She is."

"You should get some rest." Liam stood and opened his tent flap. "I'm sure she'll want to leave more bruises on you in the morning."

"Right." I pushed away from the table and stood, refusing to let the chill night air make me shiver. "Rest well, trueborn Duwead."

I lifted the flap from his hand and let it fall shut behind me.

I closed my eyes, warring with myself as to whether to go into my tent, knowing I wouldn't be able to sleep, or to go back to the clearing, knowing someone might notice I wanted nothing more than to tear a tree up by its roots.

A prickle that had nothing to do with the cold touched the back of my neck. I opened my eyes, searching for whatever had set my senses on edge.

A head of bright blond hair glinted in the moonlight. Marta stood in the trees far off the main path, an over-large mug of ale in one hand, a bowl of stew in the other.

Our eyes met for a moment before she spun on her heel and stalked off into the darkness.

I turned the other way and ducked into my tent. I didn't bother lighting the lae stone. I pulled the knife from my boot and set it under the thin thing I pretended was a pillow. I yanked off my shoes and let the cold bite at my skin as I undressed.

I could hear him through the canvas. He couldn't have been more than fifteen feet away from where I stood. From the soft thumping of his feet, he was pacing in the open space of his tent.

I tried not to picture it. Him pacing and drinking frie. Him plotting to find more people to help save Ilbrea. Him worrying about saving villages and stopping the violence of the Guilds. Him thinking of how to get me away from the mountains and the Black Bloods and him as soon as my brother returned.

I crawled under the heavy layers of my blankets and stared into the darkness at where Liam paced, listening to the sound of his footsteps as I faded to sleep.

25

When I was a very little girl, my mother swore I would be the death of her. I loved to run and climb and tear down the road on our horse, even though my legs weren't long enough to reach the stirrups.

When I was six, my mother found me sitting on the roof of our house.

She screamed and screamed. My father bolted out of the barn to find my mother wailing like I'd already fallen to my death and me giggling at the spectacle of it all. Soon, the neighbors came to see what the fuss was all about.

The Ryelands' girl had gotten herself into trouble again. No one was shocked, and everyone but my parents seemed to enjoy the afternoon diversion.

While the villagers offered suggestions of how to get me safely down, no one noticed Emmet climbing up the far side of the house to join me. He hated heights, but he thought I was in danger. So he braved falling to come collect me. He took my hand and led me to the side of the house where the boards had cracked wide enough to create handholds for child-sized fingers, and matched me step for step the whole way down.

The adults had been so busy arguing as to whether it would be safe to have me jump and if my father was strong enough to catch me, they didn't notice I'd disappeared from the roof until Emmet led me over to make me apologize to the crowd for causing a fuss and to my mother for making her worry.

26

"How long did it take you to learn to fight?" I asked, shaking my wrist out, trying to get feeling back into my fingers after Cati's latest blow.

"Does it matter?" Cati tossed her wooden blade from one hand to the other.

"Yes. If you've only been training for a while, then I'm a hopeless slitch who will never get any of this right. If you've been fighting for a long time, then I should resign myself to years of bruises and pain while I try and learn how to not get stabbed."

Cati's laugh rang out over the clanging of the swords next to us.

"And when will I get to use bigger weapons?" I pointed to the blades glinting in the light.

The ginger boy dove under his opponent's sword, leaping back to his feet with a wide grin on his freckled face.

"You won't. I'm teaching you to defend yourself, and keeping a sword tucked under your skirt isn't very practical now is it?" Cati winked at me and mouthed something that looked like *soon.*

She hadn't said anything, but I was fairly certain Liam had laid out what Cati was allowed to teach me in no uncertain terms.

It really was the most practical course—teaching me how to throw a proper punch, kick someone who grabbed me from behind, and the simplest way to gut someone who tried to hurt me. And, though I was improving day by day, it was still far too easy for Cati to disarm me.

But the idea that Liam had forbidden me from learning the weapons that would be used in a real fight grated against every fiber of my being.

"Let's go again." Cati took her place opposite me, her legs set apart, her wooden blade resting in her hand. She didn't even look like she was trying to hold onto the hilt.

I wiped the sweat off my palms and prepared myself for her inevitable attack.

She waited until I was ready, then began shifting her weight ever so slightly from side to side.

I watched her movements, trying to predict where her attack would come from. Just when I was certain she would lunge at me from the left, she leapt straight for my center and knocked my feet out from under me.

I hit the ground hard, coughing all the air from my lungs, but I managed to hold onto my wooden knife. She planted one foot on my chest. I tapped the back of her knee with my blade before she managed to swipe hers across my throat.

"Well done!" She gripped my hand and hoisted me to my feet.

I sucked air into my lungs as casually as I could while pretending the trees weren't swaying from how hard I'd hit my head on the ground.

"We really should get you a pair of pants to practice in." Cati pursed her lips at my skirt. "Liam might not like it, but that will only make it more fun."

"Right." I blinked at the trees, trying to get them to stop drifting around.

"I'll find you something for tomorrow then."

Cati took her place opposite me again, but I still couldn't look away from the trees. The shadows of them had become familiar in the days I'd spent learning from Cati, but a figure that didn't belong lurked under the branches, staring at me.

I took a step toward the trees and felt the world tilt, as though I'd been knocked to the ground again, as Emmet walked out into the open.

He favored his left leg as though he'd been hurt, but that didn't slow his pace as he stormed toward me.

No, not toward me. Toward Cati.

"What do you think you're playing at?" Emmet pointed to the wooden blade in Cati's hand.

"I thought it was better than using the real thing and risking your sister's life." Cati crossed her arms and glared at Emmet.

"She has no business on the training field," Emmet said.

"Don't even start with me, Ryeland." Cati tapped her blade against his chest.

"Your job is to train warriors," Emmet growled. "She will not become one of your minions. She is not going to fight."

The rest of the people on the field had given up on their own training to watch.

I wanted to say something, but everything inside me had gone viciously cold. I couldn't remember how words were meant to work.

"I am training her to defend herself," Cati spat. "Your sister was nearly murdered. I am trying to make sure that doesn't happen again. She should be able to protect herself."

"It's my job to protect her," Emmet said. "It's my job to keep her safe."

"Grand chivving job you've done of it so far," Cati said.

"She is not yours to train." Emmet stepped in front of me like he was shielding me from Cati. Like of all the things in Ilbrea, Cati was the true danger.

Through the chilling numbness I felt my feet move as I walked around to stand in front of Emmet. I felt the blade fall from my hand and my fingers curl into a fist. My weight shifted as I drew my arm back and punched my brother straight in the jaw.

He stumbled, blinking at me like he couldn't quite make sense of why his face suddenly hurt so badly.

"You do not speak for me." The words scratched like stones in my throat.

"Ena, I—"

"You have no right to say what I'm allowed to do."

"You don't understand—"

"What?" I shouted, letting my voice ring over the field. "What don't I understand, dear brother? That you abandoned me? That you left me with a woman who defied the Guilds every day? Let me grow up in the house the soldiers burned to the ground with Lily swinging out front?"

"I didn't know." Emmet's face paled. "I didn't know Lily was a healer."

"How could you have? You weren't there. You never showed up for long enough for me to tell you the sort of danger that hid beneath the floor in Lily's house. You weren't there when the soldiers murdered her."

"I'm sorry." Emmet reached toward me. "I never wanted anything like this to happen. I only wanted you to be safe."

"Safe." I spat the word. "Safe in a village where the soldiers whip people to death? You're right, that's so much better than being here where my dearest chivving brother has been hiding. The gods would hate you for bringing your sister into this dangerous place where there are no people being hanged from trees."

"Ena, you don't understand. The work I'm doing—"

"Has worse consequences than being executed by the Guilds? Than watching the only thing close to family you have swing? Than having a chivving stranger save you from being raped in the streets?"

Emmet just stared at me, pain creasing the corners of his eyes.

"Well, you needn't bother yourself with me ever again. You abandoned me a long time ago. As far as I'm concerned, I don't have a brother."

I turned and strode away into the woods.

I forced myself to breathe. To pull air into my lungs like somehow that might make the shattering in my chest stop. I pressed my palms to my stomach, trying to keep my hands from trembling. But all of me had started shaking like I might crack apart at the seams.

The trees began to sway again as my breath stopped filling my lungs and a sob broke free from my chest. I swiped the tears from my cheeks, but more took their place.

My sobs banged against my ribs, threatening to split me in two, but I couldn't make them stop.

I had lost Lily. She was gone, killed, and I hadn't been there to help her. My home had been burned, the life I'd known ripped away, and there was no hope of ever getting it back.

For the second time in my life, I'd been stripped of everything I was and everyone I'd cared for.

I had run from the flames of Harane, but I couldn't escape what had happened. Emmet pretending he cared had fractured the dark place where I'd hidden the reality of what I'd lost.

I wanted the tears to stop. I tried to shove everything back into the void where it couldn't hurt me. But the pain had broken past its boundary, and I didn't know how to shut it away.

A hand touched my shoulder, the weight of it familiar even through the haze of grief.

"Ena," Liam whispered my name.

A deeper crack cut through my chest. Nine years' worth of grief and fear refused to be tucked away any longer.

Liam wrapped his arms around me. I lay my cheek against his chest.

The harder I cried, the tighter he held me. Like somehow he could hold together the shattered pieces of my soul, keep them safe in his grip and make sure no part of me tumbled away and was lost forever.

I don't remember him lifting me, but somehow he was sitting with me cradled in his lap. His cheek pressed to my hair, his body arching around mine.

Sense started to come back as the tears slowed, and part of me wanted to explain. To offer some excuse for why I had shattered into so many pieces. But he had seen the nightmare torment me, and I didn't know if I was strong enough to start the story from its true beginning.

Liam held me without question until the tears finally stopped.

"I'm sorry," were the first words I managed to say without sobbing.

"For what?" He kept his arms tight around me.

I closed my eyes, trying to memorize the way my body nestled into his. "All of it."

"You've nothing to be sorry for."

I coughed out a laugh that made my ribs ache.

"I mean it, Ena. You've nothing to be sorry for."

"I'm not going." I listened to the wind whisper through the branches while I waited for him to speak.

"What do you mean?"

"I don't care what Emmet wants. He is not in control of my life, and I'm not going to let him choose a place to send me."

Liam leaned away and tipped my chin up so he could look into my eyes. "Then where do you want to go? Pick a place, and I'll do everything I can to see you safely there."

"I'm staying here. I want to help you."

"No. Ena, no. You can't stay here. You can't be a part of this."

"Why not?" I wiped the tears from my cheeks, trying not to think of how swollen my face might be. "You need people, and I can help."

"No, you can't." Liam lifted me off his lap and stood me up.

"I'm useful, and I'm not afraid."

"It doesn't matter." Liam stood.

I didn't back away. "I don't know how to fight, but I can learn. I know enough about healing to be of good use. You should be grateful I want to stay."

"You can't."

"Give me one good reason why not." I laid my hands on his chest. His heartbeat thundered under my palms. "And it better not have anything to do with helping you being too dangerous. Life in Ilbrea is dangerous. If the Guilds are going to kill me, let it be because I was doing something worthwhile. Lily taught me that. It's all I have to hang on to. Do not try to take that from me, Liam."

He looked down at my hands. "This isn't an easy life, Ena."

"I'm not fool enough to think it is."

"If you want to join the Black Bloods, I won't stand in your way."

"Thank you." I took his face in my hands. The rough feel of his stubble beneath my skin sent fire flying up my fingers. "You won't regret this."

He shook his head, and creases wrinkled his brow. "We'll talk to Marta about getting you work to do."

"Good." A tiny shard of something a bit like hope broke through the shattered bits of my chest.

Liam held my gaze for a long moment. "I'll see you back at camp then."

"Right." I watched him walk away, disappearing into the maze of trees.

I sank onto the rock where he'd sat as he cradled me in his arms. One by one, I tucked each of the bits of my life I didn't want to remember back into the shattered void. But the hollow blackness wasn't there to swallow them anymore.

So, I folded the horrors beneath layers of fierce fire. If I was to be a Black Blood, then maybe I didn't need a vast nothing to protect me. Perhaps it was time to use fire to burn the pain away.

27

"I'm happy to help," I said, careful to keep the smile on my face as Neil squinted at me.

The entire camp seemed to have heard about my punching Emmet in the face. Some seemed offended, others impressed. From the whispers floating on the wind, most of the camp had also heard Emmet shouting at Liam when he was told I would be staying.

I wished I had been there to hear Emmet shout and to hear Liam's defense of my joining the Black Bloods. But the whole thing had been over before I'd trusted my face to look normal enough for people not to know I'd been crying.

As far as I knew, Liam hadn't told anyone what had happened in the woods. I was grateful. If this was to be my new home, I didn't want everyone to know I'd won my place with tears on my cheeks.

Neil pursed his wrinkled lips and leaned closer to me. I don't think his eyesight was that bad. It just seemed to be how he always looked at people.

"Go foraging if you like," Neil said. "I've plenty to keep our people fed, but only a fool says no to extra food in their larder."

"Good." I hurried out of the food tent before Neil could change his mind.

I trusted Liam to tell Marta I needed work, but I didn't want to wait. Crying had left me a kind of tired I hated. But climbing around, foraging for useful things, would leave me the kind of tired that might allow me to sleep.

As much as I longed to run, I kept my pace steady as I walked to my tent to get my bag. I didn't want to risk looking like I was misbehaving as soon as my older brother returned to camp.

I had no reason to think myself unworthy of staying, but knowing how everyone spoke of Emmet made me afraid. Like the Black Bloods might decide they didn't want me, even if Liam himself had said I could stay.

I grabbed my bag and headed east of the camp, to the slopes that cut steeply up the mountain. I searched the ground for berries, or places where some might grow later in the season. If the camp would even still be in the same place when the peak of summer came.

I didn't know where the Black Bloods stayed when they weren't in that camp, or how long they would be there for. I didn't know how they traveled from place to place. I didn't know much of anything. I pressed my forehead to the rough bark of a tree.

The deep scent of the sap calmed me.

Liam was in charge of the camp and of his people, and I trusted him.

I remembered the feel of his arms around me. The warmth of his face beneath my fingers.

I shook my head, flinging aside thoughts of Liam's hand touching mine, and climbed farther up the slope.

I found a patch of mushrooms that were safe to eat, and a bit of sour grass to help season food.

I was so busy searching the ground for edibles, I almost strolled past the boulders that surrounded the camp.

The stones were just like the ones Liam and I had passed between when he brought me into the camp, formed of black rock with the bottoms swallowed by the earth and not a bit of moss daring to mar their surface.

Glancing around to be sure no one had followed, I laid my palms on the boulder. I waited, trying to see if I could feel some pulse or spark of the magic the mountains had granted the stones. I leaned my weight against the boulder as though I were trying to merge my body with the rock.

A laugh at my own foolishness bubbled in my throat before a tingle of something tickled my skin. Not like fire or a bee's sting, because it didn't bring pain. I pressed my hands against the boulder as hard as I could.

A pull.

That was the feeling. Like something inside the stone called to the blood in my veins. My blood answered with a hunger and a wanting that crackled and sparked.

I lifted my hands away, severing the pull of the magic.

A longing tugged at my heart as I turned west and foraged my way back to camp.

I kept looping up and down the slope until my body was tired enough to make sleep a possibility, then headed back to the kitchen tent.

The line for dinner stretched out along the path, so I cut through the back way. I caught a glare from the woman stirring the pot, but I gave her a nod and started unloading my bounty onto the table.

"I know it's the same meal as yesterday," Neil shouted down the line of hungry Black Bloods, "but if the hunters keep bringing back deer, then you'll keep eating deer."

"Couldn't you make something other than stew with it?" a voice called.

I bit my lips together and dumped the mushrooms out of my bag.

"If you don't like the food I'm offering, you can feel free to eat some hardtack," Neil said. "And anyone who takes the hardtack won't be needing any ale to wash it down."

Swallowing my laugh, I snagged a bit of seed bread and a bowl of stew from the table before ducking back out the far side of the tent.

The woman stirring the pot tsked after me, but I didn't stop.

I felt like I'd been wrung out. Every bit of my being was exhausted.

By the time I reached my tent, I'd finished my dinner. I set the empty bowl on the stump that served as my table and lay down on top of my cot, boots and all.

I didn't remember falling asleep or the start of the dream. The pounding of the hooves had been dulled since I'd arrived in the camp, and the terror of the unending darkness unable to consume me. I waited through the nightmare, clinging to the hope that morning would come and wake me, but angry whispers carrying through my tent dragged me from sleep long before dawn.

2 8

"We can't." Liam's words drifted through the canvas.

I blinked at the darkness, trying to reassure myself I really was awake.

"It doesn't matter how much it needs to be done," Liam said. "We just can't."

"Why not?" Emmet said in a low, measured tone. Even when we were children, he spoke like that when he was angry. It used to make our mother laugh.

A pain shot through the newly sealed armor of flames in my chest.

"It's too dangerous," Liam said.

"He knew the risks when he agreed to the assignment," Emmet said. "Gabe is willing to sacrifice himself for the cause."

"But it's more than just Gabe we'd be losing."

"You've got to take a chance like this when it comes," Emmet said. "How many people are you prepared to let die?"

There was a thump like a fist pounding a table.

I sat up and ran my hands over my braid, trying to coax the stray strands into submission.

"We aren't going to get many chances like this," Emmet said.

I stepped out of my tent and walked the few feet to the front of Liam's.

"We would be setting ourselves back," Liam said.

Without giving myself time to wonder what the consequences might be, I knocked on the pole of Liam's tent.

Liam and Emmet fell silent.

I had time to look up at the stars in the moonless sky before Liam opened the flap of his tent.

"Ena, are you all right?"

I ducked under his arm and into the tent. "Oh, I'm just fine." I smiled at Emmet, taking a tiny bit of pleasure at the new bruise on his cheek. "I was actually sleeping fairly well until you two started worrying about Gabe's fate. I hope the poor fellow is all right. From the way you talk, he might as well be a sheep lined up for slaughter."

"This has nothing to do with you," Emmet said.

"Then maybe you should be careful talking about poor Gabe ten feet away from my bed." I sat in one of the chairs.

"I'm sorry, Ena," Liam said, not lowering the tent flap, "we should have been quieter."

"It's fine," I said. "What's a little lost sleep compared to the sacrifices Gabe is willing to make?"

Emmet looked from Liam to me as though waiting for Liam to kick me out. When Liam said nothing, Emmet leaned across the table toward me. "Ena, we're discussing important things here. Matters of life and death."

"Sounds like it." I crossed my arms and leaned back in my chair. "Of course, when you're dealing with the Guilds, sneezing at the wrong moment can be a matter of life and death. So, what makes Gabe's impending doom so important to the Black Bloods?"

"It's not your concern," Emmet said.

"Ena"—Liam let go of the tent flap—"I know you want to stay here."

"And you agreed that I can." I swallowed my glee as the veins on the sides of Emmet's neck bulged through his skin.

"But there are some things it's best if fewer people know," Liam said. "The work we're trying to do is dangerous. We may not have the forces to fight on a grand scale, but if we keep the small things we do hidden, the people we have are safer."

"Sound reasoning," I said. "But, as I already know about Gabe's death wish, since you failed to take into account that fabric is easy to hear through, is there anything I can do to help?"

"Yes," Emmet said. "Go back to bed."

"Because you think I'm a useless child or because you just don't like me?" I asked.

"Because you don't belong here," Emmet said. "You're not a Black Blood. You're not a fighter or an assassin. You've no experience killing people. You can't help."

"How many lives have you ended?" I looked to Emmet's hands, foolishly expecting the blood of the people he'd killed to be staining his fingers.

"Enough," Emmet said.

"And what about Gabe?" I hid my shudder at Emmet's cold glare. "Is he an accomplished killer? Does Cati need to go and make the kill for him?"

Emmet glanced to Liam.

"We couldn't risk losing Cati either." Liam pressed his knuckles to his temples.

"Sounds like whoever you want dead isn't worth very much trouble," I said.

"He is." Liam paced the open space in the tent. "That's the problem. We have a chance to rid Ilbrea of a monster."

"But you don't want to sacrifice one of your own?" I asked.

"Ena, you should go," Emmet said.

Liam stopped. He looked at Emmet and me both staring at him.

"I would be losing more than just one good man," Liam said.

Emmet gripped the edge of the table.

"We would be losing a spy we spent a long time putting in place," Liam said.

"Because if the spy kills the monster, he'll have outed himself and most likely be hanged?" I said.

"It has to be done," Emmet said.

"But how many lives will be lost if we don't know what's happening in their ranks?" Liam began pacing again.

I watched him tramp back and forth across the tent, treading the dirt path his boots had worn.

"Gabe can't slay the monster without anyone knowing?" I asked.

"I don't want to shock you, but it's usually pretty easy to tell when someone's been killed," Emmet said.

"I'm aware," I said. "I've seen more than my share of killing and corpses."

Emmet looked up at me.

I turned my back on him, focusing my gaze on Liam. "But does he have to stab the monster in front of a crowd?"

"No," Liam said, "but trying to make a death look like an accident would take more resources and men than we have."

"It doesn't need to look like an accident," I said. "Just poison the monster, and people will think he died of an illness."

"What?" Emmet said.

"It wouldn't even be that hard. A few years ago, Han decided she hated her husband, baked him a pie filled with shadow berry pulp. He died, and no one thought anything of it until Han went mad from the guilt and tore about town half-naked, confessing her crimes. If Lily didn't know Han had poisoned her rat of a husband, no one else would have guessed at it either. Lily had to treat shadow sickness all the time."

"Shadow sickness?" Liam asked.

"In children, mostly." I nodded. "Shadow berries smell sweet, and they grow in the shade of other berry bushes. The little ones eat them without knowing they've done anything wrong. By the time their parents notice they're sick, they're most of the way to dead.

"You can save them if they haven't started coughing blood yet, but that's the first symptom most people show. Got so bad last summer, parents started rushing their children to Lily if they found a trace of berry stains on the little ones' faces."

Liam sat down on his bed.

"You can't be considering this," Emmet said.

"Does it look like a normal illness?" Liam asked.

"Close enough to a fever fit, you can't tell unless you know what they've been eating," I said.

"It could work." Liam looked to Emmet. "Gabe could poison the chivving bastard, and no one would need to know it was him."

"We are freedom fighters," Emmet said, "not murdering mad women."

"If you're trying to kill a monster, does it really matter how you do it?" I asked. "Have the Guilds ever once stopped to think about what the good way to murder us would be?"

Emmet shook his head, but didn't look at me.

"Could you make the poison?" Liam asked.

"No," Emmet said.

"I'm not asking her to deliver it," Liam said, "only to make it. Could you do it, Ena?"

I bit my lips together, trying to sort through the realities of making a tonic not to save, but to kill. "Theoretically, yes, but I've never tried making a poison before. My work with Lily was always on the lifesaving end of herbs."

"Then we'll come up with another plan." Emmet stood.

"If I can get my hands on some shadow berries, it shouldn't too hard to mix them down into something subtler than a deadly pie." I stood up as well, looping around the table to stand closer to Liam. "I'd have to test it to be sure it was strong enough, and we'd have to choose the right way to mask it to be sure poor Gabe isn't caught serving something that tastes like poison."

"Who are you going to try the poison on?" Emmet asked.

"You could volunteer," I said.

"Where can you find shadow berries?" Liam asked.

"They grow all over around Harane, anywhere people haven't found them to rip them up," I said. "I've heard tell of children dying of shadow berries in other places, too, so they've got to be spread out along the mountain road."

"You haven't seen any in the mountains?" Liam looked up to the peak of the tent.

"No." I followed his gaze, though I didn't see anything but plain canvas above us. "The soil isn't right, I suppose."

"She can't go near the mountain road," Emmet whispered. "Liam, please."

Liam met my gaze, a battle warring behind his eyes.

I couldn't tell which side I should be fighting for.

"She'll only have to go far enough out of the mountains to find the berries," Liam said. "After that, you can stay with her in the woods while I take the poison on to Gabe."

"Congratulations, Ena. You've just agreed to kill a man." Emmet stormed out of the tent.

"I should be going with you." Cati shoved stockings into my bag. "I should be going instead of you. What does Liam think he's playing at?"

"I'm happy to help." I passed her the few fresh rolls I'd been granted, along with the packet of hardtack and dried meat Marta had given me for the journey.

Marta hadn't said a word to me as she passed off the food, turned on her heel, and hurried away.

"If he needs a woman, it should be one who hasn't just arrived here," Cati said. "I don't want to hurt your feelings, Ena, but it's not as though you're ready for a fight."

"I know that," I said.

Liam had warned me not to tell anyone of our plans to mix poison. I didn't know why it mattered if Cati knew or not, but I'd only just been allowed to join the Black Bloods and had actually wheedled my way into being given something important to do, so I only shrugged under Cati's glare. "Maybe he thinks they'll need a healer. I don't want to brag, but I've a fine hand for stitching flesh together."

"That is a valuable skill." Cati tied the top of my pack closed. "Just try not to forget everything I've taught you while you travel. And if anyone tries to hurt you—"

"Gut them?" I laughed.

"Be careful." Cati squeezed my hand. "That's all I ask."

I let her lead me out into the bright morning. She gave my hand one final squeeze and headed off toward the training field to torment some other student.

It seemed strange to be leaving camp. I'd never packed to leave a place with the intention of returning.

A few people gave me curious looks as I walked toward the paddock. I held my head high and my shoulders back, ignoring the weight of my pack. I'd salvaged a few small things from the kitchen tent when Neil hadn't been looking. I didn't know if the weight of the items felt heavier because they'd been pilfered or because of what they were meant to help me do.

Marta waited by the side of the paddock, watching as Tirra checked the saddles on four horses.

"Who's the fourth?" I looked to Marta. "Are you coming with us?"

"Me?" Marta gave a low laugh. "Not me. I, unlike some people, remember the promises I've made and intend to keep them."

"What?" I dodged around Marta. Dark circles stained the pale skin under her eyes. "Are you all right?"

"Why wouldn't I be?" She gave a smile that didn't show her dimples.

The tromping of boots came up the path to the paddock.

"Safe journey." Marta turned on her heel and strode away, barely bothering to give a nod to Liam, Emmet, and the red-haired boy.

A stone weighed heavy in my stomach. I wanted to chase after her and ask what I'd done to make her mad. But Liam had reached the rail around the paddock, Emmet was glaring at me, and I was too afraid I might already know why Marta no longer liked me. So I watched Tirra minister to the horses instead.

"Are you a comfortable rider?" Liam asked.

"She loves to ride," Emmet said.

"I can answer for myself," I said. "And if I was a slitch who couldn't ride a horse, wouldn't now be a bit late to be worrying about it?"

The red-haired boy chuckled.

I waited patiently while Tirra glared at each of us before passing over the reins of a horse. I was given a beautiful brown mare who didn't fuss as I strapped my pack of pilfered goods to her back. She wasn't the sort of horse one would dream of riding through fields, but she didn't look like she was going to drop down dead either.

No one spoke as we rode out past the edge of the camp. Liam led, then the ginger boy, then me, with Emmet riding in back as though making sure I didn't run away.

As we passed beyond the boulders that protected the Black Bloods, the pull of the magic within the stones sparked in my veins. I took a breath, letting the scent of the forest dissolve the heat in my blood.

The branches on the trees left patches of shadow scattered across the ground. I kept myself busy, scanning every plant in view, trying to find the treasure we sought. Trying to ignore the growing whispers of Lily's voice creeping into the back of my mind.

You fool of a girl. Leaping right out of the only safety you've ever known.

The day slipped past as Liam led us on a winding trail down the mountains. The slopes on this side were far kinder than the ones we'd climbed farther east. The horses didn't seem to mind them at all. Though, I suppose the paths through the mountains were what they were used to traveling.

We rode until dusk neared.

Liam stopped beside a stream and hopped off his horse. "We should rest here. There won't be another chance for a while."

"You know the path that well?" I climbed down from my horse, gritting my teeth to hide how sore my legs already were from riding.

"He's a trueborn," the ginger said. "Even the Guilds' fancy map makers couldn't know the mountains as well as Liam."

"There are some places in the mountains I'm sure I'll never know," Liam said. "But I have learned this is the best path for the horses to reach the mountain road."

"And the fancy map makers of the Guilds are too coward to do much exploring in the mountains anyway." The ginger began tending to the horses, removing their saddles and tying them close to the stream.

"What's your name?" I knelt by the edge of the bank and splashed chill water on my face.

"Finn," ginger Finn said. "Nice to meet you, Ena."

"You as well." I took a long drink of the water, feeling its cold trickle all the way down past my lungs. "How soon do you think we'll reach the base of the mountains?"

"Tomorrow," Liam said.

"We really did take the long way then," I said.

Liam caught my eye and held my gaze for a moment. "The paths in and out of the mountains aren't the same."

"And there are only a few men can survive?" I dried my hands on my skirt. "I'm thankful I've had such a fine guide."

Liam chose a spot and laid out the black stones around it. Emmet gathered wood for a fire while I pulled the few bits of almost fresh food from our packs.

The dread didn't trickle into my stomach until the sun began to fade from the sky. I had been so excited to be doing something that might hold a bit of meaning, I hadn't really thought through the actual journey.

Finn said cheerful things every few minutes when the silence seemed to become too dull for him, but the rest of us didn't speak much. Once Finn had finished eating, he untied his bedroll from his pack and laid it on the ground.

My heart raced as though the nightmare had already begun. I had to warn Finn that terror would come for me while I slept, but I couldn't warn Finn without Emmet hearing.

No one in the camp had mentioned me screaming in my sleep, but the four of us were packed in together. There was no god I could think of to silently beg for mercy, and whatever thin veil of safety had comforted me in my tent had vanished.

Emmet would know about the nightmare soon enough. As soon as I started screaming, he would know something was wrong. But Emmet hadn't been there on the night the terrible dream had been born. Even he wouldn't understand the darkness that trapped me.

Liam unrolled his blankets, leaving a space between him and Finn large enough to fit my bedding. "You should get some sleep."

"I'm not tired." I met Liam's dark eyes, trusting the fading firelight to hide my fear.

"We'll need you rested when we reach the valley." Liam unrolled my bedding and laid it out beside his. "Don't worry, Ena, I promise to keep you safe."

"We've got magic stones," I said. "Why would I be worried?"

Finn laughed from his bed.

I took a long time untying my boots and retying my pack. The others had all lain down by the time I crawled under my thick blankets.

I lay, staring up at the branches crisscrossing in front of the sky, wondering if I should find a sharp rock to put under my back to make sure I didn't fall asleep.

I was a chivving coward. I would have to sleep eventually, but the idea of Emmet knowing the monsters that still stalked me...

Liam's fingers grazed the back of my wrist. The panic in my chest ebbed. He laced his fingers through mine and squeezed my hand. He didn't let go.

When I woke in the morning, our hands were still locked together.

30

"It's not that I mind berry picking. It's just not what I pictured when we left camp." Finn popped a handful of blackberries into his mouth. "Definitely worse ways to spend an afternoon."

"Thanks, Finn." I weaved between the trees, searching for a briar patch that might hide our quarry. "Just be careful not to eat anything you shouldn't."

Finn's eyes widened.

"Don't worry. You can eat blackberries. I'll tell you when we find the poison kind," I laughed, trying to shake off my fear.

We were searching for berries to murder a monster. As much as I hated the Guilds, as often as vengeance for the horrible things they'd done had flitted through my mind, I'd never actually thought through the process of killing a person.

"They are much sweeter than hardtack," Finn said. "I really doubt hardtack should be eaten."

"Better than starving, I suppose." I moved on to the next patch of trees. A few low plants grew in the shadows, but nothing like what I was searching for.

"Maybe." Finn sounded unconvinced.

Liam and Emmet walked close behind, leading the horses and keeping an eye out for anyone who might want us dead. At least, that's what it felt like with Emmet keeping one hand resting on the hilt of his sword and Liam holding a fistful of rocks.

We'd reached the edge of the forest before midday, and Liam had turned our path north, keeping us within the safety of the trees and out of view of the mountain road.

"Supposing we don't find the death berries," Finn said.

"We will," I said with as much determination as I could after hours of fruitless searching.

"But if we don't," Finn said, "you could find something else that would work, couldn't you?"

I pinched my nose between my hands. "I don't know. There are plenty of plants that could kill a man, but I don't know how we'd drop flower petals into a paun's stew."

"We'll keep looking then," Finn said.

The low rumble of Emmet muttering carried from behind, but I couldn't make out the words.

"What?" I rounded on him.

He stared stone faced at me.

"What were you saying?" I asked.

"We might be too far north," Emmet said. "We're more than fifty miles above Harane. Shadow berries might not grow here."

"We've got horses," Finn said. "We can ride south."

"They should grow up here," I said. "We just have to find them."

"Or maybe we should accept this as a sign from the sky and go back," Emmet said.

I tipped my face to the sky and laughed. "You would rather let a monster torment people than let me help. Well, I am not a coward, and I am not helpless, Emmet Ryeland. I'm not going back up that chivving mountain until we've found the chivving berries."

I turned and stalked toward the edge of the forest.

"Ena," Liam called after me. "Ena, where are you going?"

"I've always seen shadow berries in the open, so I'm going out into the open," I said.

There was a muttering of curses before boots pounded after me.

"Ena, you can't." Liam took my elbow.

The sun peered through the trees just ahead of us, unobstructed by the shade of branches.

"Soldiers could be hunting for you," Liam said. "We're fifty miles north of Harane, but we're only fifty miles. If you had stuck to the mountain road, you could have easily walked this far."

"So you want to give up?" I yanked my arm from his grip.

"I want to keep searching the forest," Liam said.

"Just keep walking north in the trees and hope we get lucky?"

"We need to keep heading north anyway. And this is already the easiest path for us to safely travel. We're only looking along our way."

"Way to where? Is Gabe in the north?" I waited for a moment, but he didn't answer. "Because if he's not, we're wasting our time. I'll dodge out of the trees and do a quick search around. It's not as though soldiers are quiet when they travel. If I hear any trace of a great host of murderers coming my way, I'll run straight back into the forest."

"We need to head north," Liam said. "We have a friend there. We'll need to see her before I can go to Gabe."

I seized that one tiny seed of information he'd been willing to give since we'd left the camp, setting it aside to think about later.

"Will we need the poison for when we meet her?" I asked.

"Yes," Liam said. "There would be no point otherwise."

"Then I suppose when we get to her, you'll finally have to let me out of the woods to search."

"Do these look poisonous to you?" Finn held a bright red berry in the air.

I peered at the low weeds Finn had been digging into. "They won't kill you, but they'll make you wish you were dead."

Finn let his handful of berries tumble to the ground. "Good to know."

"Don't they have bird bushes in the mountains where the Black Bloods live?" I asked.

"Not really." Liam bowed me north. "We've got plants in the mountains near Lygan Hall, but none like this."

"What's Lygan Hall?" I marched north, carefully searching for any sign of shadow berries, though I knew full well I wouldn't find a chivving thing.

"It's our home," Liam said.

"The camp's called Lygan Hall?" I asked. "It's a nice name, but a bit fancy for the tents, don't you think?"

"Can you imagine those tents being Lygan Hall?" Finn tossed a tiny green thing to me. "Can you imagine living in those tents year round?"

I looked at the thing he'd tossed me before scowling and tossing it back. "Can you imagine mistaking a tree tip for a berry?"

"At least I'm trying to help." Finn winked.

"You can eat that if you want," I said. "Might not taste the best unless you're brewing ale."

"Hmm." Finn popped the bright green bud in his mouth and chewed. "I've definitely tasted worse when Neil's in charge of the kitchen."

"Is he not in charge of the kitchen in Lygan Hall?" I asked.

"Things don't work the same way there," Liam said. "People have homes. Most cook for themselves."

A wide patch of fallen trees blocked the path in front of us. The ground beneath them had collapsed, leaving a dark crater under the tangle of trunks.

"If people have homes at Lygan Hall," I said, climbing up onto the trunk of one of the wider downed trees, "why are you living in tents?"

"Camp is closer to the mountain road," Liam said. "It makes it easier to do our work. We can't stay year round—we'd freeze to death come winter—but for the warmer months, it helps to get more done."

"And helps us protect the people we care about at home in the Hall." There was an edge to Emmet's voice.

I walked across the trunk, heading toward the center of the sunken-in earth.

"Careful, Ena," Liam said.

"How does it keep them safe?" I took a long leap onto another tree, picturing Emmet's terrified face as I jumped.

"The mountains protect us," Liam said, "but going back and forth as much as we do, we'd risk someone managing to follow us home."

"There's not a Black Blood in the camp who wouldn't die before giving up the path to Lygan Hall," Emmet said.

"Not that the Guilds would be able to follow the path," Finn said.

I climbed down close to the cracked earth.

"Ena, what are you doing?" Emmet said.

"Looking for berries. Didn't you know?"

There was nothing in the darkness beneath the tangled branches but a dug out lair where some great beast had made its home. From the scratches in the dirt, the animal would have had no trouble tearing out Emmet's intestines.

Or mine, for that matter.

My heart battered against my ribs as I scrambled onto the highest of the downed trees' trunks and ran to safety on the other side. I leapt down onto solid ground, not sure if I should be grateful the animal hadn't been home or terrified it was out in the woods.

"Is Lygan Hall beautiful?" I resisted the urge to glance behind to make sure the others hadn't been eaten alive.

"I think so," Liam said. "Not like the grand halls the Guilds have built with gold and blood. But the Hall is beautiful in its own way."

"I'd like to see it someday," I said.

"You're one of us now, Ena." Liam gave a small smile that actually reached his eyes. "I don't know where else you'd go come winter."

We spent the next ten miles walking and searching. Finn ate everything I knew wouldn't kill him, while I got more eager to go search out in the open as the sun drifted down. Emmet stayed silent and angry through it all.

The forest we trekked through was the same as the one that bordered Harane. The mountains that blocked us to the east were the same range I'd seen my whole life, but somehow it felt as though no one had bothered to tell the trees.

The air in the woods had a different taste than it did near Harane. The ground had a spring to it, too, like there was something alive hidden right beneath our feet. I tried not to wonder what magic might lurk in the forest floor. If the legends of the stones in the mountains holding magic were true, what other wonders had been hiding from the Guilds?

Liam switched with Finn, taking his place at the front of the group. Between searching for berries, I watched Liam's shoulders growing tighter and higher.

We're almost there.

I thought the words a dozen times, but didn't dare say them.

When the light had begun to slant through the trees, Liam stopped, rolling around the stones in his hand before turning to look over my shoulder.

I glanced behind to find Emmet staring back at Liam.

"No." Emmet gripped the hilt of his sword. "Absolutely not."

"Absolutely not what?" I looked back to Liam.

"We can't," Emmet said.

"Can't what?" I asked Emmet.

"I'll go out," Emmet said. "I know what the berries look like. You make camp in the forest, and I'll meet you here tomorrow. I'll bring the shadow berries with me."

"You want to go tromping out of the woods and leave us here?" I asked.

No one bothered to respond.

"It's better this way, and you know it," Emmet said after a long moment.

"No." I rounded on Emmet. "I don't know it, because you're a chivving slitch who doesn't say anything when he speaks. I need to find the shadow berries, not you. I have to make the poison, not you. Because I'm the only one among us who has even the faintest notion of how poisoning a person should work. So once again, me, not you."

Finn let out a low whistle.

"I am going out of these trees to find what I need to make this whole chivving trip worthwhile," I said. "Now, either you can come with me, or you can hide in here and wait for me to come back. But if any of you so much as mentions it being too dangerous for me to be out where the soldiers might spot me, so please the gods I'll poison the lot of you."

"You're a fool," Emmet said.

"Don't." Liam stepped forward. "We'll head into the city and search along the way. If we can't find anything, we can come back out and look again tomorrow."

"You think she'll be pleased to have four of us knocking on her door?" Emmet asked. "And that's if we can get through the city without trouble."

"Why would there be trouble?" I said.

Emmet scowled at me with one eyebrow raised.

"Fine." I stomped over to the horses and pulled my bedroll free. I draped my blanket around my shoulders and shook my hair from its braid, letting it hang limp over my face. I gave a cough that would have made Lily cringe.

"Ena?" Finn said.

"No one is going to get close enough to a sickly girl to see if she might have been around when a soldier got his throat slit." I glared at Emmet. "Besides, of the four of us, aren't I the one who's done the least to anger the Guilds?"

"Shockingly, I think she might be right." Finn shrugged.

"But we've all been careful to keep our faces away from soldiers," Liam said.

"I'm a girl. I'm certain the last thing those soldiers were staring at was my face."

Emmet gripped the hilt of his sword so hard, if it had been wood, I'm sure it would have broken.

"Unless you want to tie me to a tree, I'm walking out of these woods." I looked to Liam. "Would you like to travel together, or should I just be on my way alone?"

Liam stared at me for a long moment before speaking. "We stay together. We'll go straight to Mave's and wait there until tomorrow."

"She won't like it," Emmet said.

"I don't like it." Liam headed to the edge of the woods, still clutching his fistful of stones.

I kept close on his heels, not letting myself look back at Emmet for fear he might come up with some better argument for keeping me hidden.

It only took a few minutes for us to reach the tree line. The sunset glimmered over the valley beyond.

A city built of stone and spires sat nestled in the bend of a roaring river. I'd never before seen a river so wide, with a current so fast, I'd have no hope of swimming across it.

On the far side, a second river flowed between two rocky cliffs, racing toward the city and down behind the silhouettes of the buildings. The mountain road stretched from north to south in front of us, but a smaller road by the big river was where dozens of wagons had gathered.

There were more buildings than I'd ever seen in one place, and no trace of the hint of Harane my heart had been longing for.

As Liam led us toward the city, the weight of how little I knew of the world sank in my gut.

The stench of sweaty men and horse dung tainted the scent of the river and the tang of spices coming from the carts.

Young boys lifted crates larger than themselves off the boats bobbing in the river, hauling them up the dock and into the waiting wagons. The wagon men leaned against the sides of their carts, chatting while the children did the work.

"Are those men Guilded?" I asked, keeping a close eye on the river dock as my horse followed Liam toward the city.

Liam's neck tensed before he looked at the wagons. He studied the people there for a moment before speaking. "No, just laxe."

"What?" I guided my horse to ride beside Liam.

"I thought you were supposed to be ill," Emmet said.

I gave a great cough in his direction. "Better?"

"Do you not call your merchants *laxe* in Harane?" Finn asked. "Or are they not filthy enough to have earned that title?"

"There isn't a merchant class in Harane," Emmet said. "The village isn't big enough."

Finn gave a low whistle.

"Everyone in Harane works to survive," Emmet said.

Doesn't everyone everywhere work to survive?

The question crept toward my lips, but I swallowed it, too afraid they might decide I was ill-prepared to meet the frightening world of a proper city and send me back to hide in the woods with whatever clawed beasts lurked there.

"So the laxe make the children work for them?" I asked.

"They pay whoever needs coin," Liam said. "Sometimes children, sometimes adults, whatever tilk they can find."

"And the Guilds allow it?" I watched as the sun reached the tops of the low mountains to the west, casting the great city into golden shadows.

"The Guilds encourage it," Liam said. "They have to get their fancy robes, wine—"

"Jewels, shoes, houses," Finn added in.

"The Guilds only do their own work," Emmet said, "and they aren't going to go bargaining with the tanner to have a saddle made. The merchants sell to the Guilds. Profit off the Guilds abusing the common folk in Ilbrea. The lot of them are nothing but filthy collaborators."

"Ink for the scribes, blood for the healers, steel for the soldiers, wind for the sailors—land for the makers of maps to behold, and for sorcerers, magic, to defend royals' gold." Finn spoke in a sing song voice. His cheerful verse sent a shiver down my spine. "No bankers, traders, or builders in the Guilds. Those low positions are filled by merchants."

"Traitors," Emmet said.

"I think you've made your opinion clear," I said. "Though I can't say I remember anyone asking you to speak."

Finn chuckled.

"It takes all types to keep Ilbrea running." Liam looked back at Emmet. "We have to remember who the real enemy is."

Emmet's face hardened, but he nodded.

"If we make good time to Mave's, we might even be able to get a decent meal," Liam said. "The streets shouldn't be too crowded tonight."

I tried to picture streets crowded with people. Enough people in my path that it would change my time going from one place to another. I couldn't imagine it.

The walls surrounding the city rose up thirty feet, with turrets sticking up at steady intervals. Tall, thin windows had been built into the stone. I peered into the shadows of each, trying to spot a person staring back at me.

High gates stood open at the end of the road, and a line of wagons, horses, and people waited to be let into the city.

"Twelve soldiers," Emmet said, his fingers twitching as he reached toward the sword he'd tied under his pack.

Men in black uniforms flanked the gates.

My heart leapt into my throat, and I pulled the blanket higher around my head.

"We'll be fine," Liam said, either to Emmet or me—I don't really know.

The scent on the wind changed as we reached the back of the line of people waiting to enter the city. Hints of baking bread, strong frie, and too many people packed together wafted through the gates.

"It shouldn't be taking this long to get through." A woman perched on a fine horse spoke to the young girl tending the horse's reins.

"I'm sorry, ma'am," the young girl said.

The woman glared down as though expecting the girl to have something more than an apology to offer.

I gave a rattling cough that grated my throat.

The woman shifted her glare toward me, horror filling her face as she lifted her sleeve to her nose and turned back to the gates.

My horse fidgeted beneath me as we made our way closer to the soldiers. I watched as a farmer was let in with his giant containers of milk, and a merchant with wooden crates slipped a few coins into a soldier's hand before being allowed through. A young man entered the city, his arms wrapped tightly around the waist of a giggling girl.

We never would have survived in Harane if the Guilds had guarded who went in and out of the village. If they had been able to see who had snuck off with a giggling girl and had the chance of checking any goods that came down the road to us, half the town would have been whipped on a weekly basis.

But we hadn't survived anyway. They hadn't lurked over us every day, only come to kill us when the fancy struck them.

"What is your business here?" A soldier glared between the four of us when our turn came. He wasn't as soft as I would have expected from someone told to guard a gate. His chiseled jaw, narrowed eyes, and firm grip on the sword at his hip made it seem as though he expected an attack rather than a pair of young fools back from rolling around in the forest.

"We're traveling north on the mountain road and seek a warm place to stay for the night," Finn said.

I glanced over to Liam, but he was looking daftly up at the wall as though he'd never seen something so big in his life.

"What's your business in the north?" the soldier asked.

"I've got a friend in Marten who might be willing to marry my sister," Finn said.

The soldier glared at me.

I gave another rattling cough.

"We want to get her rested and well before we get there." Finn gave a hopeful smile. "We've money to pay for a good room."

"Is she catching?" the soldier asked.

"No," Finn said, "her lungs have always been a chivving wreck. But if we get her rested, she'll look well enough he might take her."

Anger rolled in my stomach, and I gripped my reins to keep from punching Finn in the back of his chivving head.

The soldier eyed me for another moment before giving a low laugh. "May the gods help you in getting that one married." He stepped out of our way.

"Thank you, sir." Finn gave a little bow and led us in through the gates.

The wall was thicker than I'd imagined it to be when we were looking at it from the outside. We traveled under twelve feet of stone, which loomed over our heads as though waiting to drop and murder us, before riding out onto the cobblestone streets of the city.

The people didn't spare a glance for the soldiers waiting by the inside gate. Women in fancy silk dresses strode past on the arms of men in finely made coats. Children ran by, giggling as though the soldiers weren't even a threat to be feared.

"This way," Liam said when I'd fallen too far behind our party. "We have to get the horses settled."

Finn stopped in front of a wide stable with a giant white horse painted across the front.

"What is this place?" I stared at the entrance of a pub that had a sparkling silver sign above the door, which read *River of Frie*.

"Frason's Glenn." Liam took my hand, helping me down from my horse. "It's a trading port. Ships stop on the northern coast by Ilara. Some of the goods stay there. Some get loaded onto smaller river boats and brought down here. Then the laxe load them onto wagons and haul them south to be sold."

"So"—I pulled my pack free from my horse, dodging out of the way of a cart selling sweet bread and honey—"this whole town only exists because people earn coins off the goods from the river."

"The whole of Ilbrea only exists because someone is making coin. The only thing that changes from place to place is whose pockets get heavy and whose back gets whipped." Finn took the reins of my horse and tried to hand them to a gangly boy who stared open mouthed at me. "Take the chivving horses." Finn flapped the reins at the boy. "I promise you haven't a chance with the girl."

Finn waited until the blushing boy had gotten all four horses inside before leading us down the street.

I stayed close to Liam, taking his arm as we passed a towering building made of white stone. People in red, blue, white, and purple robes lingered by the glittering metal doors.

I had heard of Guilded folk beyond the normal soldiers, scribes, and healers we dealt with in Harane. I'd seen the black, white, and red robes marking each of their Guilds. I'd even seen a sorcerer in purple robes once. But to see a pack of Guilded paun, chatting on the stone steps that some poor fool had carved swirls and leaves into, sent a cold sweat on the back of my neck.

A lady healer tipped her head back and laughed to the twilit sky. Joy filled her face like there was no duty that called for her time besides standing with her fellow paun enjoying the late spring evening. Like there were no common folk in need of her aid.

Good folk who went hungry to pay their taxes to the Guilds so they could have the right to a Guilded healer's aid. Good people who would die because the lady in the red robes was standing on the steps instead of saving lives.

My stomach twisted so hard I thought I might be sick on the stone street.

Liam took my hand, holding it tight as we passed shops with sparkling glass windows. Dresses, lace, boots, sugar cakes, books—everything I could imagine anyone wanting to spend coin on was displayed in the shops. Lamps burned brightly, inviting customers in, even though the sun had faded from view.

Emmet took the lead, veering off the main street and onto a narrow road lit by lamps that hung from the sides of the stone buildings.

There were fewer people on this street, and most of the businesses had already closed for the day, though the colorful signs describing their trades still hung in the shadows.

There was beauty in the details of the signs, almost as though someone had made up a competition for the most intricate plaque. I didn't know which would win—the cut out of a platter of sweets that had been carved so deep in places, it looked like I might actually be able to pry a slice of cake free, or the woman with long hair, where each strand seemed to have been painted on individually.

My shoulders relaxed as houses took the place of shops, and lamps only hung on the corners of the cross streets. The darkness and quiet might have been frightening if I were alone, but with the others, the isolation seemed safer. Fewer prying eyes and less of a chance someone might spot the girl from Harane who had run from a dead soldier.

Just as I began to wonder how big the city was and how much longer it would take to reach Mave, laughter floated up the dark street. A quick melody of a cheerful tune came a moment later.

Emmet picked up his pace, leading us around the corner and closer to the music.

"Where is that coming from?" I asked.

"Mave's," Liam said.

We reached a set of tall stone buildings that blocked the street we had been traveling down. There were no windows on the first floor of the buildings, but on the second, third, and fourth stories, bright light shone out of the windows. Swirls and flowers of twisted iron surrounded the small balconies that dotted the buildings.

A few of the balconies had been taken by couples enjoying the darkness. Others sat vacant, as though inviting people to come and fill them.

The song ended, and a cheer rose from beyond the buildings.

Emmet shook his head and cut through an alley toward the music.

The dazzling light of a hundred lanterns bathed the square beyond. Five buildings surrounded the open space, all facing each other like old men gathering to gossip. A fiddler, a drummer, and a woman with a tin whistle stood on a high platform at the center of it all.

Around the sides of the stage, young men in matching orange shirts minded great barrels of drink. People stood in line, waiting for their chance at the barrels.

The players began another song, and the crowd hollered their joy.

A man darted out of the barrel line, sweeping a girl into his arms and leading her into a dance. In a few moments, the whole square had filled with couples dancing.

I smiled under the cover of my blanket. I didn't recognize the song, but it was nice to see that even people who lived with soldiers at their gate could find a moment of joy in music.

Emmet led us around the edge of the dancers to one of the buildings on the far side. On the front of the building, the windows started on the ground floor, peering out over a wide porch packed with tables. Men and women filled the seats, some sitting on each other's laps when there were no extra chairs to be had. Plates of food and glasses of chamb had been set out on every surface. Smoke drifted from pipes, laying a haze over the whole scene.

"Fresh ones!" a girl called to no one in particular as she peeled herself off a man's lap and sauntered toward us.

Her blond hair had been pinned up, leaving only a few curls to drip around her long neck. The laces of her bodice had been pulled so tight, she was one quick move away from her breasts falling out and making her having worn anything on top utterly pointless. Her painted red lips curled into a smile as her gaze drifted from Finn to Liam then finally landed on Emmet. "This is turning out to be a lovely night."

"We're here for Mave." Emmet stepped in front of our group.

"Why?" The girl narrowed her kohl-lined eyes.

"Mave and I are old friends," Emmet said.

"Pity." The girl shrugged and headed toward the pale blue painted door. She didn't bother shutting it behind her.

I peered through the doorway to find more tables. Girls dressed to please the men around them, and handsome young men with their shirts unbuttoned prowled through the crowd.

"What is this place?" I whispered to Liam.

"Mave's brothel," Liam said.

"Why are we standing on the steps of a brothel?" I asked.

A pair of red-haired girls led a man inside. One of them had already begun unlacing her bodice.

"Mave's a good friend," Liam said.

A woman stepped into the doorway, blocking out the room beyond. I don't know if it was the mass of dark curls surrounding her face, her perfect features and dark complexion, or the way she held herself that made me forget to breathe. She tipped her head to the side, and a slow smile spread across her face.

"I didn't think I would see you here again," the woman said.

"Hello, Mave," Emmet said. "It's good to see you, too."

"Should I be returning the compliment or kicking you out of my square?" Mave stepped forward. The lantern light caught her dress, glistening off the tiny beads that had been sewn into the maroon fabric.

"You should be pulling down your best bottle of chamb and bringing us in." Emmet stepped forward, reaching for Mave's hand. "Have I ever brought anything you haven't wanted to your door?"

Mave crooked an eyebrow. "More than once. And I don't like having filthy girls dragged to my home. You know my thoughts on men who do such things."

"She's my sister," Emmet said. "The blanket's just to make her feel safe on her first trip into Frason's Glenn."

Mave looked to Liam for a long moment before nodding. "Then welcome, weary travelers. May you find rest and the best of life's comforts within my walls."

3 2

The music from the square carried up to the second floor window, drifting into the parlor where Mave had left us.

A painting of the seven-pointed star of Ilbrea hung over the mantle, though no fire burned in the stone hearth beneath. Blue fabric woven into a flower pattern covered the walls and the furniture that took up the center of the space. Three chairs and one, long fainting couch surrounded a table made of rich, cherry-stained wood.

I sat on the very edge of the seat I'd been given, too afraid of tainting the fabric with my forest filth to get comfortable.

"Not like Harane then?" Finn winked at me.

"Careful." Liam nodded to the open window.

Finn shrugged and leaned back in his chair.

"You can take the blanket off," Liam said.

"Right." I lifted the blanket over my head, folding it up before laying it at my feet. I ran my fingers through my hair, weighing how awful it must look against how much the others would laugh at me for digging in my pack to find my wooden comb. For all the world, it felt like I'd been brought in front of the Queen herself.

"Not everywhere outside Harane is like this," Emmet said. "Most places are closer to the village. But Frason's Glenn has a lot of money—"

"And coin buys fancy things," I cut across him. "I am smart enough to have figured that out for myself."

"Just be kind to Mave and she'll like you," Emmet said.

"Of the two of us, which usually has trouble with being kind?" I asked.

"Enough," Liam said. "We made it into the city without any fuss. Let's not go feeding the shadows ourselves."

A knock on the door kept me from answering.

A man in a bright orange, silk vest stepped into the room without waiting for us to answer. He carried a tray of food with a bottle of chamb sitting right in the middle.

"Compliments of Mave." The man set the feast on the table, took a moment to look at each of the men, and went back out into the hall.

"By the gods, I'm hungry." Finn dove toward the table, grabbing a roll and a slice of meat before the rest of us even stood.

"Are you always hungry?" I examined the bowl of berries, plate of cheese, pile of fresh baked rolls, slices of meat, and bottle of chamb.

"I was born starving, and it hasn't stopped since." Finn spoke as soon as he'd swallowed. "Honestly, when my mother found out I'd chosen to travel outside the Hall, she openly wept. The neighbors all said it was because she loved me so much, but I'm smart enough to know they were tears of joy that she wouldn't have to worry about feeding me any longer."

"Smart woman." Liam smiled. A bright, comfortable smile without any trace of the hardened Black Blood I had followed through the mountains.

The door swung back open.

"Now that I've fed you"—Mave sauntered into the room, closing the door behind her with a sharp click—"tell me why I should let you stay here. Unless, of course, you've come to enjoy an evening of the flesh, in which case eat up and go choose a partner before all the good ones have been claimed. Don't worry"—Mave looked to me—"I can find someone for you as well."

Heat flooded my face.

Liam walked to the window and pulled it closed. The glass dampened the music but didn't block it out. He looked toward the door.

"We're safe." Mave sat on the fainting couch, fluffing the folds of her skirt around her.

"We need a favor, Mave," Liam said.

"I thought as much," Mave said. "Why else would I find a trueborn Black Blood in my home?"

I glanced toward the door, waiting for everyone from the square to come storming in to murder us.

"Do you have any prisoners?" Liam asked.

Mave smiled. "As far as you're concerned, no."

"We need one, Mave," Emmet said.

"Why?" Mave asked. "Who of yours was foolish enough to be caught and important enough to be traded for?"

"No one," Emmet said. "We're not looking for a trade."

"We're looking for a victim," Liam said.

Mave stood, poured herself a glass of chamb, and sat back on the couch. She watched the bubbles rising in her fluted glass for a moment before speaking. "Victim for what?"

"Poison," Emmet said.

Sour rose in my mouth.

"We're planning something," Liam said. "I've got to know everything will work as needed."

"So you want someone to poison?" Mave said. "Should I just haul a victim in here? I'm sure there's plenty of filth in the square who deserve a bit of death."

"We aren't murderers," Emmet said. "But your prisoners are already going to be executed for crimes against the people of Frason's Glenn. They might as well do a bit of good on their way out."

Mave sipped her chamb.

I looked to Liam who gave the slightest shake of his head. I nodded and stayed silent.

"I like you, Emmet Ryeland," Mave said. "I'd go nearly so far as to consider you a friend."

"Thank you, Mave." Emmet knelt in front of her and kissed her outstretched hand.

"But there are some risks I can't take, even for friends," Mave said. "I won't put my family in that kind of danger."

"There is no danger," Emmet said.

"Having Black Bloods in my home is a danger," Mave said. "Bringing you to my dungeon is too much to ask."

"We wouldn't need to go." I waited for Emmet to glare at me for speaking, but he kept his gaze fixed on Mave. "I could give you the poison, and you could just…" I swallowed, wishing I had my own glass of chamb. "Tell me how it worked. How long it took for the symptoms to show, and how quickly your prisoner died."

"We're trying to make a difference," Liam said. "This is how we save lives."

Mave studied my face for a long moment. "Fine. I'll let your brew be the end of one of my prisoners. It's not how things are usually done, but I can make an exception. Though, a debt like this will need to be repaid."

I gripped the edge of my seat, no longer caring about the dirt on my fingers contaminating the fancy fabric.

Emmet looked to Liam.

"Our aim is worth owing a friend a debt," Liam said. "I will see you repaid for the prisoner and for sheltering us while we are in Frason's Glenn."

"The shelter I give freely out of friendship," Mave said. "The prisoner is what comes with a price."

"Thank you, Mave." Emmet kissed her hand again.

"Do you have the poison?" Mave asked. "I have a paun fit for the task."

"Not yet," I said. "But I will soon. Tomorrow night, after I've had time to search outside the city walls."

"I'll search," Emmet said. "We can't risk you being seen."

"Why would that be?" Mave sipped her chamb.

I stood and poured myself a glass. "I was a bit too near a soldier who ended up dead."

I heard the rustle of her skirt before she took my chin in her hand. "You're pretty."

"I know." I met her dark eyes, willing myself not to flinch.

Her gaze swept down to my breasts and back up to my face. She took a bit of my hair and rubbed it between her fingers before tracing the line of my jaw.

"Mave," Emmet said.

"Do you want to hide in a filthy blanket?" Mave asked.

"No," I said.

"Would you like to roam free, not worry about who spots you?"

"Yes."

The right corner of Mave's mouth twisted into a smile. She leaned in and kissed my cheek. "Good girl."

The scent coming off her skin sent my head swimming, like she had somehow bottled sunshine, firelight, and longing and had found a way to bathe in their perfume.

"You boys go get washed up before the stink of you taints my parlor forever. You, girl—"

"Her name is Ena," Liam said.

"Ena, come with me," Mave said. "By morning, I'll have you fit to catch the eye of every soldier at the gates."

"We don't want her to be seen." Finn froze with a slice of cheese halfway to his mouth. "Unless I've missed something."

"No one questions the feathers of a beautiful bird. They only marvel at her beauty and let her fly away. Come." Mave reached for my hand.

I downed the rest of my chamb, letting the bubbles tickle my throat as I took Mave's hand and followed her out of the parlor.

The sound of voices carried up the stairs from the floor below. A man gave a booming laugh. A chorus of female titters answered.

"Mave." The man in the orange vest bowed as we passed.

"You're free to go." Mave gave him a nod.

The man slipped back down the stairs to the first floor.

"This way." She led me down a long hall with doors on either side.

I bit my lips together, trying to focus on the sounds of Mave's rustling skirt instead of the noises coming from the rooms around us.

We stopped at a narrow door at the end of the hall. Mave pulled a key from the folds of her skirt and slipped it into the lock. "Don't go wandering while you're here. I like your brother, but that doesn't mean I'm willing to trust you with a key."

"Yes, ma'am."

A staircase waited for us through the door. There were no fancy fabrics covering the walls here, only bright, unstained paint. Voices drifted down the stairs, but they weren't the same as the raucous crowd below.

"Charge her double and make her buy you a bottle of frie next time," a girl said.

"Double wouldn't cover it," another girl laughed. "She's as sweet as a lamb, but there's only so much a girl can take."

We stepped up into a brightly lit room, and everyone around us froze.

"Mave." A girl in a pink robe was the first to spring to her feet.

The other four were up a moment later, nodding to Mave while keeping their eyes locked on me.

Mave looked at each of the girls in turn, though what she was searching for I had no idea.

"Is everything all right, Mave?" a girl with bright blond hair asked after a long moment.

"I have a project for you, Nora." Mave put a hand on my back, guiding me toward the blond. "This little bird angered the wolves. Give her a new pair of wings."

33

"Of course, Mave." Nora bowed her head, then narrowed her eyes as she studied me. "She'll be beautiful."

"Good girl." Mave swept back toward the stairs. "Now I've got to manage her brother."

I watched Mave disappear down the steps, feeling the stares of the five women prickling the back of my neck.

"Who's your brother?" the girl in the pink robe asked.

"I..." I felt as though I were withering under their gazes. "I'm not sure you'd know him."

The girl in pink raised an eyebrow.

"Emmet Ryeland," I said.

"Emmet's here?" A girl with chestnut curls started toward the stairs. "*The* Emmet?"

"Leave it, Lolli." Nora caught her arm. "I don't think Mave would like you storming in."

"How do you know my brother?" I asked.

A chorus of laughter rang from the girls.

Nora fluttered a hand for the others to stop. "The poor thing is covered in mud. At least show an ounce of compassion." She bit her red painted lips to stop her own giggle. "Now come with me, little bird. Stories of Emmet Ryeland are best told in the daylight."

"What's that supposed to mean?"

Nora didn't answer my question, but I followed her anyway.

This floor hadn't been built on the same pattern as the one beneath. The stairs had brought Mave and me up into the large room where the girls had been sitting. There was space in the room for twenty more to have seats at the table, near the fireplace, or by the bookshelf. I blushed as I tried not to think of where the others who normally sat in the room might be.

Nora led me down a brightly painted, narrow corridor. The rooms lining either side were quiet. Some of the doors had been left open. I slowed my steps enough to peek

116

into one of the rooms. A plain, wooden-framed bed stood next to a rack of beautiful gowns.

"We never leave this floor without our paint on," Nora said. "It's safer that way."

"Safer?" I ran a few steps to catch up.

"Soldiers wear armor to protect themselves. We wear paints, powders, and silk. We step into battle every time we leave the safety of the haven Mave has built for us. I, for one, would never be foolish enough to go into battle unarmed." She stopped in front of an open door.

A set of four brass tubs took up the center of the room, with shelves and mirrors lining the walls. Two of the tubs had women in them.

"Fresh blood?" One of the girls sat up out of her tub.

I averted my gaze from her naked breasts.

"Oh, she won't make it long," the girl said.

"Ha!" the other bathing girl laughed. "When you first came here, you couldn't look at a naked man without vomiting."

"Oy." The first girl splashed the second, sending a wave of water onto the floor.

"Hush, both of you." Nora held up a hand, and the two fell silent. "Either mind your baths or get out."

The first girl ducked sheepishly under the water, while the second picked up a sponge and dabbed at her arms while staring at me.

Nora sighed. "I will never understand these girls. Ah well. Get your clothes off. We've got to get you clean before we start on the real work."

"Right." I reached for the laces on my bodice but couldn't manage to make my fingers work. "A proper bath would be nice."

"By the Guilds." Nora swatted my hands away and untied the knot herself. "We sell pleasure to people at an exorbitant rate. We aren't perverted, and we won't eat you alive."

"Unless you've got the coin to pay for that sort of thing," the sponge girl said.

"I don't think we could convince Mave to agree to host such a horror." Nora wriggled my dirt-covered bodice over my head. "I've seen some strange things in Mave's halls, but there are limits to everything." She unbuttoned my skirt, and it fell to the floor. "Get your shoes off, and I'll find a comb."

I untied my boots, tucking my knife into the bottom where the hilt wouldn't show, and tried to ignore the dark smears of dirt I'd left on the tile floor.

"What sort of new feathers are you hoping for?" Nora pulled a basket down from the shelf.

"I don't know," I said. "I mean, I haven't thought about it."

"You should cut her hair short," the sponge girl said. "A bunch of the Guilded have been asking about short-haired girls. I think it might be a fashion in Ilara."

My stomach rolled at the idea of a Guilded paun touching me. Pain ached in my throat where the soldier had tried to squeeze the air out of me.

"Hush now." Nora petted my cheek. "Breathe, little bird. Just breathe."

"Who hurt you so badly?" the sponge girl said. Or maybe it was the other one. The room had started to go blurry around the edges.

"Out, both of you," Nora ordered. She didn't look away from me or take her hand from my cheek. "No one here is going to hurt you. No one in Mave's home will make you do anything you don't want to do."

The baths sloshed as the girls got up and scampered out of the room.

"We'll get you in a warm bath and give you a fresh set of armor." She took my hand, leading me to the tub on the far right side of the room. "You share Emmet's blood. Whatever wrong the world has done to you, you're strong enough to survive."

"I am." I pulled off my shift, let it fall to the floor, and stepped into the hot bath.

"It's really not frightening here." Nora pressed a brick of soap into my hand and knelt behind me, lifting my hair away from the water. "We're lucky. You're lucky Mave let you up here. Outsiders aren't permitted above the second floor. I don't think she would have allowed it if you weren't Emmet's sister."

"The most amazing luck." I scrubbed at my hands with the sweet-smelling soap. I'd only been away from the camp for two days, but it had already begun to feel as though I might never be properly clean again.

"Are you staying with us?" Nora ran a thick-bristled brush through my hair.

"I'm only here for a day, maybe two, I suppose. Not that there would be anything wrong with staying." The last part tumbled out.

Nora laughed softly. It was the gentlest laugh I'd ever heard. If the wind could laugh as it swept through a summer field, I think it would have made the same sound.

"Our way of life isn't for everyone," Nora said. "There are times I wish I hadn't chosen it."

"Why did you?" I scrubbed at my arms. "If you don't mind my asking."

"My father drank away any money that would have seen me into a decent marriage. Duck down."

I dunked my head below the water, reveling in the silence for a moment before coming back up into the world.

"I had a few men who wanted me anyway." Nora ran her fingers along the teeth of a carved comb. "But I didn't want any of them. To marry a man I didn't love, to spend the rest of my life rolling on my back for him, and then popping out his screaming children, I couldn't stomach it.

"I could have found work as a domestic for a Guilded or a merchant, but then I would have spent the rest of my life toiling in someone else's home only to die old and lonely, owning nothing of my own. With all those years of drab misery laid out in front of me, I couldn't turn down what being a part of Mave's family provides."

"What do you mean?"

Nora started working through the ends of my hair with her comb. "By the time I'm not fit to work the downstairs anymore, I'll have enough coin for ship passage south to the kingless territories with plenty left over to live comfortably for the rest of my life. I'll be done working before I'm thirty."

I tried to imagine that sort of riches, but I couldn't. Cal's family had more income than anyone I'd ever met, but even they couldn't survive if they stopped working.

"It can't be said for the poor souls who whore on the streets." Nora stood and went to the shelves on the right hand wall. "If they aren't beaten to death and manage to stay healthy, they still barely make enough to eat and have a solid roof. The Guilds forget our profession existed long before they took control of Ilbrea, but Mave never forgets. She's built a family, and strength. I wouldn't be surprised if she's the richest woman in Ilbrea outside the Guilds."

"And when you're done, you'll sail away from the Guilds forever?"

"Exactly." Nora held out a thick, black cloth.

I stood and let her wrap me in the soft fabric.

"I'll gladly pay the price for my freedom," Nora said. "I won't ask what brought you to Mave's door, but is what you came here for worth the cost the stars will demand?"

I touched my neck, where the remembered pain had pounded. "Yes."

"Good." Nora kissed my cheek. "In case Mave didn't warn you, beauty is not a pleasant process."

34

I ignored the pain in my neck and shoulders that having my head tugged at strange angles all night had brought, but I couldn't get my fists to unclench as Nora flitted around me, dabbing pink on my cheeks.

"I'll leave your hair down," Nora said. "The color brings a nice contrast to your fair complexion."

I didn't bother trying to answer. After protesting her using the kohl pencil on my eyelids, I learned Nora didn't actually care what I thought of the manner in which she preened me. It had been two hours since she'd finished with my hair and dragged me into her room. She dressed me and painted me like I was nothing more than her doll. A doll she preferred to remain mute at that.

Nora dabbed a bit of tingling cream on my lips. "It really is a pity." She looked at me as though waiting for me to speak.

"What's a pity?" I asked, careful not to let any of the cream get into my mouth.

"That you were born so pretty," Nora said. "It's a waste. Do you know how many girls come crawling to Mave's door who would give their left tit to be half so beautiful as you?"

"No."

"Well, it's a lot." Nora pulled the blanket from around my shoulders. "I'll have to make you a box of treasures when you leave us. It would be wrong to dress you in armor and leave you helpless when it washes off."

"Thank you."

"Come take a look." Nora waved me toward a floor to ceiling mirror in the corner of her room.

Let there be something left of me.

I stepped in front of the glass, examining myself from my toes up.

The boots were the same pair Cati had found for me back at the camp. The long, deep green skirt had more material to it than I was used to. The fabric was finely woven, soft with a hint of texture that pleased my fingers as I trailed them into my pockets.

120

The black bodice cut low in front and left no need for imagining the curves of my body. Nora had pulled the neck of my shift down to meet the bodice, displaying enough of my chest to send heat to my cheeks.

"Don't blush, you'll ruin the look." Nora squeezed my hand.

The deep brown of my hair had been swallowed by black dye.

Like a raven's feathers.

I took a deep breath, straining against the laces of my bodice, and looked up to my face.

I still looked like me, but the girl in the mirror was different. Fierce and powerful in her beauty. A more romantic version of me, one meant for moonlight and love. The Ena Ryeland that would exist if I had been created in a daring story.

Is this how Cal saw me?

"No one will suspect you've ever even passed through Harane. You are a true girl of the city now." Nora furrowed her brow. "Do you hate it? I could go a bit further with your face, but you've said you aren't staying here—and that much paint would be suspicious on the road."

"You've done wonderfully." I managed to make my voice cheerful. "It's just very different. I'm not used to it."

"That's the point." Nora leaned her head on my shoulder. "If you don't feel like you, what chance does the rest of the world have of picking you out in a crowd?"

"None." A blissful sense of freedom tamped down my trepidation.

If the soldiers who had been in Harane saw me on the streets of Frason's Glenn, they'd never guess I was the girl they'd attacked a few short weeks ago. I shifted my weight, letting the sheath of the knife hidden in my boot press into my skin. If the soldiers came after me again, I would not be helpless. I wouldn't allow myself to be.

"We should get you down to your brother." Nora took my hand, drawing me away from the mirror. "I'm excited to see what the great Emmet Ryeland thinks of my work."

"Why do people here know Emmet?" I followed Nora out into the corridor that ran between the sleeping quarters of Mave's girls.

Nora laughed, then whispered, "I'm not sure I'm the best one to tell that tale."

"You said it was best told in daylight, and the sun has risen." I slowed my steps as we reached the big room that led to the stairs.

A girl in a deep blue dress slept in a chair next to the bookshelves. Another girl sat at a table, sipping out of a steaming mug.

"By the Guilds, last night flew," Nora said.

The girl with the mug looked up. "Maybe for you."

"Oh hush." Nora wrinkled her nose at the girl and dragged me toward the stairs.

"Just tell me," I said.

"I wasn't even there," Nora said, "so I couldn't do a proper job."

"But—"

"Ask one of the kitchen folk about the time a naked boy caught the square on fire." Nora pulled a key from her pocket and unlocked the door at the bottom of the stairs. "You'll get a far more accurate and thrilling rendition than I can provide."

We stepped out into the hall, and Nora locked the door behind us.

Women in plain dresses bustled between the rooms on the second floor, hauling buckets, baskets, and rags. They nodded to Nora and me but kept buzzing about their work, moving in a manner that seemed to imply they'd performed these very same tasks a hundred times before.

There was no music pouring in from the square and no laughter drifting up from below. The sound of the floorboards creaking beneath my feet felt like an intrusion on the quiet of the women's morning work.

"Do you know where the others I arrived with are?" I whispered to Nora as we passed a room where the bed had been turned on end. "Liam and Finn?"

"They might be on the fourth floor, sleeping in the men's rooms," Nora said, her voice barely above mine. "If not, they'll be in the kitchens."

"Are the men not fed where they sleep?"

"They are, but Mave eats in the kitchen. If your friends came to see her, that's where they'll be." Nora let her hand glide along the banister as we climbed down to the ground floor.

The great room that had been packed with people the night before sat empty—all the chairs carefully tucked around the tables with not a rogue chamb glass lying around to ruin the perfection. The faint sounds of voices and pots clunking together carried from the far back of the dining room.

The temptation to sit down at one of the tables and revel in the shining solitude grew in my stomach, but a low rumbling voice kept me at Nora's heels.

"I'm not sure it's worth the risk," Mave said as Nora swung open the door to the kitchen, "but if anyone has a manifest, it's him."

I opened my mouth to ask what sort of manifest was worth any sort of risk but lost my question in marveling at the sheer size of the kitchen. The space was bigger than any of the houses in Harane. Larger even than the tavern. Five iron stoves sat along one wall, with a fireplace large enough to burn a bed at one end, and a sink the size of a bath at the other.

"There she is." Mave's words drew my gaze to a long table in the center of the room. She'd changed out of her maroon gown and into a finely made day dress of the same color.

Liam and Emmet sat opposite her.

Liam turned toward me, freezing with his mug halfway to his mouth, while Emmet stood, glowering at me.

"Emmet"—Nora stepped forward, extending her hand—"how lovely to see you with your pants on."

"What have you done to her?" Emmet looked from Nora to me.

"Exactly what I was told to do." Nora planted her hands on her hips. "I created a new and glorious creature and spent the whole night working on it. Some gratitude would be in order."

"Say thank you to Nora, Emmet," Mave said.

Emmet clenched his jaw for a moment before speaking. "Thank you, Nora. No one would suspect this girl is my sister."

"I would." Liam lowered his mug.

Nora turned to me, tapping her lips with one, well-manicured finger. "I could take her back up and change the color of her hair."

"No." I stepped away. "Getting my hair to black was bad enough."

"I don't think the soldiers will know it's her." Liam stood, his chair scraping against the stone floor. "But she looks the same to me."

My heart flipped in my chest so hard I was certain everyone could see its movement through the fabric of my bodice. "Then I'll be going out of the city today?"

"I still don't think—"

"I wasn't speaking to you," I cut across Emmet.

Liam studied me, the line of his jaw set like stone. "We can ride out together. Hopefully, we won't have to go too far."

"I should fetch Finn, then." Emmet started toward the door. "If we're going to go, the sooner the better."

"You and Finn have other things to attend to," Liam said.

"They can wait." Emmet stood in the doorway, glaring at Liam as though he could change his mind through sheer force of loathing me.

Liam didn't flinch. "I'll keep my word, Emmet. I hope I can trust you to keep yours."

Emmet looked at me, his eyes resembling our father's more than I remembered.

"We won't go far," I said.

Emmet looked back to Liam and nodded.

The entire kitchen stayed frozen as Emmet's footsteps thumped away.

"Must be an exciting outing you have planned," Nora said when the only sound left was the girl in the corner scrubbing out a stove.

"Get yourself to bed, Nora," Mave said. "You need your rest."

"Yes, ma'am." Nora bowed her head and floated out of the kitchen.

"Feed the girl." Mave seemed to speak to no one in particular, but a man in an orange coat appeared before I could think to look for him, bearing a tray of pastries the likes of which even Cal's mother could never have dreamt of.

The man bowed and extended the tray toward me. My fingers hovered over the confections as I tried to choose between the shiny one with the chopped nuts on top, the thing filled with jam, and a roll that looked so fluffy I wasn't sure it counted as food.

"We should go," Liam said.

"Let the girl pick something to eat," Mave said. "Beauty is a tiring process, and she's had a hard night."

I picked the nut-covered thing.

The man winked and kept his tray toward me. I grabbed a fluffy roll as Liam waited by the door.

"Thank you," I said. "Thank you, Mave."

"Get out before Liam has a fit." Mave shook her head, her curls bobbing around like a living crown.

I slipped out the kitchen door behind Liam, barely able to believe I'd not only gained two cakes for breakfast, but was also going to be riding out of the city without Emmet.

Bright morning sun bathed the square outside Mave's house. The men sweeping away the debris of the revelry paused as Liam and I passed, holding their brooms steady as though wanting to be sure they didn't kick a stray bit of dirt onto my skirt.

I waited until we were out of view of the workers to bite into my breakfast. The sticky sweetness of the nut-covered pastry made me feel like a little girl who had stolen a bit of pie.

"Are you all right?" Liam glanced sideways at me.

"Fine." I held the roll up to him. "Want some?"

He shook his head. "Mave's already stuffed me full."

Liam weaved a different path through the streets than the one we'd followed Emmet on the night before. He turned down an alley so narrow it looked like people shouldn't be allowed to cross through. Before I could ask where he was taking me, we'd stepped out into a square packed with market stalls.

"How often do you come here?" I asked over a vendor's shout of, "Morning remedies! Take a swig and clear your head."

"It depends." Liam took my arm, guiding me past a man selling vegetables and eggs and a woman offering slabs of meat. "I only make my way to Frason's Glenn when I've no other choice."

A pack of children ran by. The girls had ribbons in their hair. The boys had bright rosy cheeks. This wasn't the Frason's Glenn I'd seen the night before when only the laxe and the night workers had been out. In the fresh morning air, normal people filled the city.

Buying milk, trading gossip, looking for a new packet of needles. Doing normal things like Black Bloods and monsters were no more than myths. I studied the people as I passed, wanting to memorize the beautiful blandness of it all.

The more I watched the people, the more I realized they were watching me as well. I ate the fluffy roll as quickly as I could, just waiting for someone to come charging after us.

We passed out of the square and onto a wide road. No one chased us, but the man with the candle cart and the little girl selling flowers both stared at me.

"Liam," I whispered, "I think people might recognize me."

I felt his arm tense beneath my touch, but he didn't change his pace. "Who?"

I swallowed hard, trying to rid myself of the urge to be sick on the cobblestones. "All of them. They keep looking at me."

Liam scanned the street. I stepped closer to him, holding his arm tight.

He didn't speak until the gate came into view. A line of people had already gathered to exit the city. "They don't recognize you. They just want to look at you."

A prickle sprang up on the back of my neck. The feeling of being watched by a horde drained the warmth of the sunlight from my shoulders.

Liam's tone held no trace of fear as he chatted with the gangly stable boy, asking for our horses.

I steeled my courage and looked at the people around me, searching for the eyes of a monster that sought to destroy me.

Instead, I found a tiny boy with his fist in his mouth as he stared up at me, and an older woman who smiled gently as she looked at me like she was remembering someone else. A boy my age blushed scarlet when I met his gaze.

They all watched me like I was a curiosity. A beautiful bird who had landed in a garden and would soon fly away and be forgotten.

I am wearing my armor, and they don't even see it.

The stable boy brought me my brown mare, and Liam and I rode through the gate, past the soldiers and the river docks, and to the open fields beyond.

35

I know my memory of that day isn't right.

I remember the sun kissing my face and the wind lifting my hair as I rode through the fields beyond the reaches of Frason's Glenn.

I remember laughing with abandon.

And Liam laughing with me, the deep tambour of his joy burning in my soul with a fire I didn't understand.

I remember the sun glinting off my darkened hair in a new way, and somehow not being frightened by the change.

If the perfection in my mind were somehow true, the first blooms of spring had begun to appear, and white flower petals clung to the green fabric of my skirt as I wandered, searching for treasure. The sweet perfume of the blooms tickled my nose, and I tucked a pink flower in my hair.

We rode for miles, searching and knowing the city waited for us, but somehow still wanting to ride a bit farther. To find another meadow to wander through, Liam by my side, a solid pillar of a man that somehow made the sun burn brighter.

The way his eyes burned brighter when we found the shadow berries and piled them into a black pouch. The way he kissed the back of my hand and thanked me for helping him while in the same breath telling me he would find a way to see the rest of our work through without me. I didn't have to do anymore.

But I did.

Walking away from him, from what had begun the moment I'd decided to follow a Black Blood into the mountains, was impossible. So I touched his cheek, the warmth of his skin calling to every bit of my being, and told him I would do the work that needed to be done.

I remember the ride back to Frason's Glenn being too short.

I remember desperately wishing my time by his side would never end.

I remember the smoke hovering over the western edge of the city and drifting out over the river, like morning mist gone mad. Trying not to breathe in the smoke because I didn't want to lose the scent of sunshine and spring the day had left etched in my soul.

But I know not all of the perfect sunshine can be true. Such wonderful days do not exist in a world ruled by the Guilds. Their torment taints even the brightest joy.

I will never know how much of that day was truly how I remember it. I rode out of the city an innocent girl who had never done anything a decent man would judge as wrong.

I returned to the gates a Black Blood with the power to murder hidden in her pocket.

The Guilds had stolen so much from me. My innocence I gave willingly to destroy them.

3 6

There were more people trying to exit the gates than enter when Liam and I joined the end of the line. The sun had begun to sink, and the smoke left an ominous haze over the city.

I wished I had a cloth or something to hold over my face, but the clothes Nora had dressed me in left lifting my skirt to my nose as my only choice. I might have been tempted to try it, but the black pouch of berries burned in my pocket, and I was too afraid of calling attention to myself to do anything more than wrinkle my nose at the stench and wait patiently in line.

Liam kept his horse next to mine as we moved slowly forward.

I glanced around before leaning toward him. "Are they searching people?"

The thought brought me no fear. I doubted the soldiers were smart enough to know the berries in my pocket were deadly. And, even if they did, it would be easy enough to pretend I was a fool bringing bounty home to be made into a tart.

Liam didn't answer right away. He sat up straight, staring at the gate, looking angry at being kept from his supper. "They're searching the people leaving, not entering."

"Leaving?" My brown mare shifted as I stood in my stirrups, trying to see past the gate.

One by one, the people entering crept past a pack of soldiers searching every person exiting the city. The soldiers had pulled down all the crates from a man's cart, leaving the merchant with bolts of fabric lying in the dirt.

Another man had been stripped of his pack and stood pale-faced as a young soldier dug through his possessions.

Why? Why should they care what leaves their protected city?

I opened my mouth to ask, but a different question came out. "Will you promise me they're safe?"

Liam kept his gaze fixed on the gate.

"Liam?" I gripped my horse's reins.

"We should be able to make good time once we get through the gate." Liam gave me a smile that didn't reach his eyes.

All the joy from the day's sunshine drained from my chest.

"Keep moving in." A soldier climbed up onto a stack of crates so he towered over the crowd. "If you don't want us to shut the gates and keep you all out for the night, keep moving in."

"We're trying," an older man in a fine coat shouted up at the soldier. "Don't blame us for your soldiers blocking our path."

I flinched, hunching my shoulders out of instinct. There were people in line behind us, but not so many I couldn't turn my horse and ride away.

A scuffling came from the front of the crowd, inside the gate where I couldn't quite see.

"Stay, Ena," Liam said.

"I am a soldier of the Guilds," the man on the crates spoke above the growing voices by the gate. "Any citizen of Ilbrea who questions my authority will be taken to the prison and dealt the Guilds' justice."

Prison.

I rolled the word around in my head, trying to reason through the Guilds locking up the man who had spoken rudely to the soldier instead of just whipping him on the street.

"I'm sorry," a woman wailed from the front of the crowd. She was inside the gates, hidden from view by five soldiers. "I've done nothing wrong. Please!"

"Stay, Ena," Liam said again, as though he could scent my desire to run.

But as the woman wordlessly screeched, I wasn't sure which way I wanted to run. To the forest, or toward her? I had a knife in my boot and berries in my pocket, but neither would have done much good against so many paun.

The soldiers parted as two of them grabbed the woman. She screamed as they dragged her down the street.

"Help her," I whispered.

Liam looked to me, pain filling his eyes. "I can't."

I reached across the distance between us, needing to feel his skin against mine to assure myself I hadn't fallen into some new nightmare.

The line started moving forward more quickly. The people exiting the city plastered themselves to their side of the road, keeping their heads bowed and staying silent as the soldiers searched them.

Liam moved to ride behind me as we passed under the stone wall and into the city. Ruined skeins of yarn, trampled food, scattered papers, and a shattered doll lay on the ground. Parts of people's lives the soldiers had cast into the dirt without care.

The stable boy stood in front of the white painted horse, his hands behind his back and chin tucked as he watched the soldiers search a fresh batch of tilk.

"Do you still have space?" Liam hopped down from his horse and reached up to help me.

I didn't argue that I could chivving well climb down from a horse without his help. The soldier outside the gate had started shouting again, and Liam's hands on my hips soothed my desire to flee.

"I do." The boy didn't look away from the gate.

"What happened?" I asked.

Liam wrapped an arm around my waist, keeping me close to his side.

"Not sure," the boy said. "Bells rang across the city. There was a bit of a panic about a fire spreading and burning all of Frason's Glenn. Then people said we wouldn't burn, but there were bandits out to steal all our gold. Then the soldiers came.

"Truth be told, I doubt any of what I heard is even true. I can't think of a sane reason any bandit would break into the sailors' offices. There are plenty of places with more gold in them. And if they wanted to break in, why do it during the day?"

"I can't see any sane purpose for it," I said.

The stable boy smiled at me. "I'm glad I've not lost my reason." He stepped forward, taking charge of our horses. He glanced to the gate before leaning in close to Liam and me. "If you want to know what I really think, some Guilded slitch got drunk off their knob and set their office on fire. Now the whole city's stuck paying for the fool's mistake."

Liam gave a laugh that might have sounded real if I hadn't known him. "You just be careful not to down too much frie and light the stable on fire."

"I care for these horses as if they were my own." The boy gave a nod. "Most of them are good as babes, and even the chivving bastards among them deserve a safe stall and fine hay."

"Thank you for taking care of them," I said.

The boy bowed. "I am at your service." He blushed and led our horses away.

Liam gave a laugh that came closer to real. "We should have you fetch the horses when we leave. He might not charge you for their keep."

I aimed an elbow at Liam's stomach. He dodged away, but kept his hand on my back as he guided me through the city. He walked just behind me, as though terrified someone might sneak up and try to steal me away.

We cut back through the square where the common folk had been doing their morning shopping. The vendors were still out finding buyers for their wares, but the cheerful note the scene had held earlier had vanished. Shoppers moved quickly from one stall to the next, taking the goods they wanted and handing over coins with barely a word exchanged. The children had disappeared altogether.

"What did you send them to do?" I asked.

Liam led me into the tight alley without answering.

"What did you ask them to do that's affected a whole city? Liam"—I stepped away from his hand and turned to face him—"what have they done?"

Liam ran his hands over his face. "Nothing that should have caused this. If everything went as I'd asked, there shouldn't be any fuss or fire. Maybe it's not them at all."

"Do you really have any hope of that?"

"I'm not one to give up hope." Liam laid his hand on my shoulder, his fingers touching my bare skin. "But I'd like to get to Mave's and find out what's happened."

"If Emmet's gone and mucked everything up with Mave—"

"Come on." Liam skirted around me and took my hand, leading me out onto the street.

We heard the music coming from Mave's long before the backs of the buildings that surrounded her square came into view.

While the market had gone quiet, Mave's folk seemed to have taken the smoke in the air as a sign from the stars that the revelry needed to be bolder than before. Seven musicians stood on the platform, playing for a packed crowd who whooped and hollered along with the tune.

The girls on Mave's porch swept from man to man, flirting and teasing as easily as butterflies flitting from bloom to bloom.

Nora perched on the edge of a table filled with men who gazed at her like she was a goddess fallen from the sky.

She wore her armor well.

I recognized her face, her hair, the way she smiled in a pitying way at the men who fawned over her. But there was a façade covering the Nora who had spoken gently to me as she dyed my hair and painted my face.

She'd become a knight, going into battle against all mankind.

She is a beautiful warrior.

A man leaned back in his chair to look at me as we crossed the porch. Liam tucked me close to his side, wrapping his arm around me. The man raised an eyebrow and turned back to his drink.

The dining room had filled with patrons as well. The scent of roasted meat and fresh baked cakes wafted from the kitchen. Men in green, chest-baring vests roamed the room as the girls had on the porch. Men in orange carried silver trays heavy with glasses of chamb.

"Can I help you, love?" A girl stepped in front of the stairs, blocking our path, and eyeing Liam.

"I'm Emmet's sister." I tipped my chin up, meeting her gaze.

Her face paled, and she fumbled for the pocket in her skirt. "You should come with me."

"Why?" I followed her up the stairs. "Is he all right? What happened to him?"

The girl spun on the steps and glared at me. "Don't ask such questions in front of the guests."

"Sorry." I stayed close on her heels as we cut through the long corridor of rooms.

Some of the doors were still open. The beds had been made and the lamps lit.

If something were horribly wrong upstairs, life below wouldn't be continuing uninterrupted. But Mave kept her business going while holding prisoners and planning executions. If she could do a thing like that, there was no way to know she wouldn't have my brother's corpse upstairs while her family plied their trade in the long line of rooms.

The girl unlocked the door and stepped aside. "They're on the top floor."

"Thank you." I ran up the steps to the girls' floor.

The big room was empty. I climbed the stairs to the floor above. Another large room, built like the one below but painted a calmer hue, waited at the top of the steps.

Two men stood from their seats at the table.

"Where are they?" Liam asked.

"In the back." One of the men eyed me. "It might be best if she waits out here. It's not a pretty thing."

I ran down the hall without bothering to reply.

"Ena." Liam chased after me. "Ena." He grabbed my arm. "Let me go in. Let me see what's happened."

"Don't be a chivving slitch." I didn't have to ask what door I was looking for. Both Finn's voice and the smear of fresh blood on the handle gave it away.

Gritting my teeth against the feel of blood-covered metal, I opened the door.

The room was small, like Nora's. But instead of beautiful gowns, this room had been taken over by the spilled contents of Finn's pack, a pile of bloody clothes and bandages, and a bowl of red-stained water.

"What under the stars have you done?" I glanced between my brother sitting in a chair, looking pale as a corpse, and Finn kneeling beside him, trying to tie on something they seemed to think was a proper bandage.

"Evening, Ena." Finn gave me a fleeting smile. "Your new hair looks lovely."

"Thank you, Finn." I lifted my skirt over the blood-stained shirt on the floor. "Emmet, what have you done to yourself?"

Emmet glared at me, wincing as Finn tugged on his bandage. "I didn't do anything to myself. Things didn't go as planned, and I had a bit of a run in with a sword."

"If I didn't know better, I'd think you were trying to be funny." I shooed Finn away.

"We got the papers." Finn leaned against the wall.

"What chivving papers?" I knelt beside Emmet.

Liam shut the door and leaned against the frame. "Cargo orders for the river boats."

"That's what you're bleeding for?" I untied Emmet's bandage. "Did you start the fire in the city, too?"

"We didn't have much of a choice." Emmet hissed through his teeth as I began unwrapping the thin cloth they'd used to bind his arm. "We got into the sailor's office saying we had a shipment coming in and needed to know where they'd want it."

"Paun bought it, too," Finn said. "Went searching through the records for where we should deliver our grain. Got him out of the room, got everything we wanted from his desk. Then a soldier walked in from the street, shouting about needing supplies before we could fade into the distance."

"And the soldier carved you up on your way out the door?" I asked.

"More or less," Emmet said.

"How long ago?" I peered at the cut. It was longer than my hand and deep enough to need stitches, though the edges were clean and not too swollen.

"A couple of hours," Emmet said.

"It should have stopped bleeding by now," I said. "Could Mave not find a healer?"

"I won't have trouble brought on Mave's head over my bloody arm," Emmet said.

"You're a fool, Emmet Ryeland." I sat back on my heels. "Your arm needs to be cleaned and stitched if you don't want a nasty infection."

"I'll be fine." Emmet pulled his arm away from me, sending a fresh trickle of blood sliding down his skin.

"How many men have said that only to end up armless or dead?" I looked toward my pack, hoping against hope Lily's basket would appear. "Liam, I need a sturdy needle, thread, strong liquor, clean water, soap, and a bandage these fools haven't made a mess of."

"No," Emmet said, "absolutely not."

"Don't fuss like a baby. It won't take long."

"You're going to stitch him up?" Finn said.

"Of course I am."

"She's not," Emmet said.

"Liam, go fetch the supplies to stitch up this fool." I glared at Emmet as I spoke.

The door clicked closed behind Liam.

"We don't have time for this," Emmet said. "Mave is going to her dungeon tonight. You have to make her the poison."

"Did you even find the mythical berries?" Finn asked.

I pulled the pouch from my pocket and tossed it to him.

"Work on the berries, Ena," Emmet said. "I'll be fine."

"Stop arguing with me and be grateful I'm here." I dug in my pack, pulling out the things I'd pilfered from Neil. A tiny pot and a tight-knit sieve were all I'd brought with me. It didn't seem like enough now that it was actually time to brew something to kill a man.

"Finn, empty the berries into the sieve," I said.

"All right." Finn took the pot and sieve from me.

Footsteps thumped toward the door.

"I've got everything but the soap and water." Liam came back, a bottle of frie in one hand and a needle, thread, and bandages in the other.

"I'm coming," a voice called from down the hall. A boy my age stepped into the room, carrying a bowl of steaming water and a brick of soap. He wore only a thin green wrap around his waist that hid absolutely nothing.

"Get out of here dressed like that," Emmet said.

"You"—I nodded toward the boy—"get me a spoon and two empty vials."

"Yes, ma'am." The boy ran out of the room.

"Press the berries through the sieve." I looked to Finn while I washed my hands in the near burning water.

"With my fingers?" Finn asked.

"Sure," I said. "Just don't lick them afterward."

I took the bottle of frie from Liam, pulling out the stopper with a pop.

"Ena, you're being ridiculous," Emmet said.

I lifted his arm, twisting the gash toward the ceiling. "This is going to hurt." I poured frie into his wound.

Emmet gave another satisfying hiss through his teeth.

"I've got the berries pressed through." Finn held up his deep-violet stained fingers.

"Find a bit of thin cloth." I took the needle and thread from Liam's outstretched hand.

"Can we send the naked boy to get that, too?" Finn asked.

"Just use a bit of the bandage you ruined." I held the needle in the lantern's flame.

"But it's all been bled on," Finn said.

"You only need a bit, and there are some clean patches." I threaded the needle and knelt back down beside Emmet. "Besides, I think the man we're making it for will have bigger things to be fussed over than how cleanly we strained the juice."

Emmet laughed.

I looked up to find a faint glimmer of true mirth playing in the corners of his eyes.

"This is going to hurt, but I honestly don't feel too badly about it." I stuck the needle into my brother's flesh.

3 7

I'd washed the blood and berries off my hands before I'd even left the men's floor. Mave had come to take a vial of the dark liquid. I'd tucked the other vial into my pocket as she led me downstairs to a room at the very end of the row on the third floor.

The bed was made and the lantern lit. I'm sure Mave told someone to make the room up for me, but it didn't seem like it at the time.

With the music still playing and laughter rumbling up from below, it felt as though the house itself were a living creature. And the animal made of stone and wood had created a room for me. A little cave where I could rest huddled in its embrace.

I hadn't slept in more than a day. I should have been able to topple down onto the clean bed and drift instantly away. But I couldn't. I scrubbed my face and hands in the washbasin, and stared out the window at the dark street instead.

Had I been facing the square, I could have watched the dancers and musicians. But my window gave me a view of the sleeping city away from the revelry.

A boy passed beneath my window, moving like he was hurrying somewhere. I wondered if maybe Mave had given him the poison.

No one had told me who would be feeding the man the berries I'd mixed. All I'd been offered was a promise of a full report as to how it had worked once the thing was finished.

If I'd done my job well, a man would be dead by morning. A man whose face I would never see, whose name I would never know. If it was even a man at all.

The air in my room pressed against me, too heavy for me to breathe properly. I unlatched my window, swung the tall panes inside, and stepped onto the small balcony beyond. The chill night air kissed my bare neck, easing my nerves.

"Don't be a fool, Ena," I whispered to the darkness. "You begged to be here. The choice has already been made."

"That doesn't mean you have to be happy about it," Liam said.

I looked up, half-expecting him to be floating in the air, hovering on his stones.

Instead, he leaned over his railing, watching me from the balcony above mine.

"What we're doing is right," Liam said. "It's for the good of all tilk. That doesn't make it any easier."

"No. It doesn't."

Liam looked up toward the sky. The sliver of moon cast shadows on his face.

I wanted to be closer, to gaze into his eyes and see what had truly kept him awake to this horrible hour of the morning. I wiped my palms on my skirt and stepped up onto the metal railing that bordered my balcony.

"What are you doing?" Liam looked down as the rail clanged beneath my boots.

"Climbing." I stood perched on the metal rail for a moment, testing my balance and reveling in the wind blowing around my ankles.

"Ena, get down from—"

I jumped, catching a spiral loop on his balcony in each of my hands. My arms burned as I pulled myself up. I enjoyed the pain of it, the way my muscles remembered how I wanted them to work. I got myself high enough to sneak my toe onto his balcony, and pushed the rest of the way up with my legs. Keeping my back to the open air and my hands on the iron, I looked down at the ground far below.

There was nothing between me and falling but my own strength and calm head. Such a simple path to death with no tricks, plotting, or malice to be found.

"Can you climb over to this side now?" Liam said. "Before the wind gusts and you fall?"

"Wind wouldn't knock me over." I kicked a leg up and over the railing, careful to keep my skirts low enough to not give the sort of show the people downstairs sought. "Maybe if there were a horrible storm, but not a normal wind."

"I'd still rather you stay on this side of falling." Liam leaned against the rail opposite me.

We stood together in silence for a moment. The crowd on the other side of the building cheered as a new song began.

"I suppose it's good thing I didn't have my heart set on sleeping," I laughed.

"You should try anyway," Liam said. "We've a long ride ahead of us tomorrow."

"Even if the berries don't work?" I gripped the rail behind me. The edges of a metal flower cut into my palms.

"They will."

"I hope." I sat on the ground, bending my knees to fit in the small space that was no wider than the window. "It's an awful thing to hope for."

"Maybe." Liam sank down, scooting toward the edge so both of us could fit. "But Ilbrea will be a better place without him."

"Are you sure?" A knot I hadn't noticed before squeezed my stomach tighter.

"I asked Mave who the prisoner was. I thought you might want to know eventually, even if not for a long time. Questions about things like this tend to linger."

I looked up to the stars fighting to shine against the lamps on the streets below.

"Who is he?" The question caught in my throat.

"A Guilded scribe."

I let out a long breath.

"He embezzled tilk taxes," Liam said. "Made it look like some of the farmers north of here hadn't paid."

"Were the farmers killed?" My hands shook.

Liam reached forward, taking my hands in his. "One. Two others were whipped and stripped of their land."

"That scribe is a murderer."

"And the Guilds would never have given him true justice. They'd have kicked him out of the Scribes Guild at worst—sent him to a lesser post more likely."

"Where he could destroy more people's lives for his own selfish greed."

"He'll never harm anyone again." Liam held my hands tighter. "The people he hurt may never know justice was given, but at least they're safe from the monster who placed his desires above common folks' lives."

"Then I'm glad I had a hand in his end. Does that make me awful?"

"Not to me." Liam gave a tired smile. "Not to any of the Black Bloods in the camp. This is the only scale we can fight the Guilds on right now. We do the best we can to stop one monster at a time."

"And tomorrow we ride to Gabe? Help him slay a beast?"

Liam leaned forward, looking straight into my eyes. "We ride to rid Ilbrea of a man who has harmed hundreds of innocents."

"Good."

He let go of my hands and leaned back against the railing. "You should get some sleep. It'll be a long day tomorrow."

"Sleep isn't something I'm very good at." I nudged his leg with my foot. "You've seen it. Better not to disturb the people below my room."

"You shouldn't have to carry such a burden."

I shrugged. I hated myself for not having anything brave to say.

"The nightmare"—Liam pulled something from his pocket and held it up to the sky—"what happens?"

"Does it matter?" I leaned in, examining the thing he held between his fingers. A small black stone, like the ones he'd protected us with in the forest, glinted in the hint of moonlight.

"Perhaps." Liam rolled the stone between his fingers. "Maybe it's only the way the Black Bloods live, but I was always taught you can't fight a monster you can't name."

"There is no monster in the dream." I looked up at the moon, holding on to its faint light so the darkness of the nightmare couldn't surround me. "I honestly don't know if it would make sense."

"Just try."

"Has Emmet told you," I began, fighting to keep my voice steady with every word, "has he told you how our parents died?"

"Fever took them both."

I looked to Liam, searching his face for a lie. But I could see it in his eyes. He honestly believed that was what had happened to them both.

"Emmet's a liar." I laced my fingers together, tucking them under my chin. "Or maybe he doesn't remember. He was so sick when it happened, maybe no one told him."

I waited for Liam to ask a question, or to defend Emmet, but he just sat watching me.

"I was the first to catch the fever. It wasn't that bad for me. I felt chivving awful, but I got better in a few days. Then Emmet and our mother took ill. They didn't get better."

The long-forgotten scent of sweat and sick brought bile to my throat. "Emmet could barely breathe. Mother got so bad she started having seizures. Lily came. She did every-thing she could, but they were beyond her help. We needed a proper healer. But there's never been a Guilded healer assigned to Harane. The nearest is in Nantic, thirty miles north of the village."

"That's too big a territory." Liam clasped the stone between his hands.

"The villagers in Harane have been asking for a healer since before I was born. But the answer is always *just ride to Nantic*. Father had started to get the fever by the time Lily said she couldn't help us any further. I was well enough, and I loved to ride, so he told me to race for Nantic. Set me up on the horse and told me not to stop for anyone. My mother and brother would die if I didn't find the healer before sunrise."

Tears pooled in the corners of my eyes, but I couldn't reach up to brush them away. My body had frozen, trapped in the memory of that terrible ride.

"The sun had set, but I knew the way. There's only one road between Harane and Nantic. All I had to do was follow it. I rode and rode, crying, begging the horse to go faster, but the night stretched on, and there was nothing but darkness and the pounding of the horse's hooves.

"The poor creature collapsed before we'd even reached the city. So I ran. I ran and ran, until there were finally buildings along the road. I didn't know where to find the healer, so I just kept screaming for help. An old woman came out of her house. She was kind. She led me to the healer's door. But there was a note pinned up. A soldier had broken his leg on the crossroad, and he'd gone to tend to the wound.

"The woman begged me to come into her house. Promised me food and a bed, but I had to find the healer. If I didn't, Mother and Emmet would die. I found the crossroad and ran west. There was blood in my shoes, and the road swam in waves as I tried to keep going. I found the camp just after sunrise. I begged the soldiers to help me, to take me to the healer. I told them my family would die.

"They just laughed. Their own healer had gotten too drunk to help anyone, so they had called for the one from Nantic. I told them I'd raced all the way from Harane for help, I sobbed and pleaded. They spit on me, and hit me, and tossed me out of their camp. By the time I could stand again, the sun was already high."

"Ena." Liam took my hands, guiding them away from my chin. "I'm so sorry."

"It took me two days to walk home." The heat of my tears tortured my face. "By the time I got there, Mother was dead. Those soldiers arrived a few hours after me. They'd come to collect spring taxes. Father didn't have the money. He'd sent it to the scribe in Nantic to get the papers so mother could be buried. The soldiers threatened to take our fields. Father argued.

"He stood there, screaming at a silver-haired soldier holding a shining sword. When the soldier got tired of it, he ran Father through. My father bled to death in the cold mud. The soldiers left me weeping next to his corpse. They rode away like nothing had happened."

Liam pressed my hands to his lips. "You survived, Ena. I'm sorry for what those bastards did to your father, but the horrors of the nightmare, you survived those soldiers in the real world. You're strong enough to survive them in the dream, too."

A horrible laugh cut through my throat. "The nightmare never gets that far. I'm trapped on the ride to Nantic, knowing I won't make it. Knowing my parents will die because I failed."

"That's not true." Liam touched my cheek, brushing away my tears. "Your mother died because she was ill, because the Guilds didn't see fit to make sure there was a healer to help her. Your father died—"

"Because the greed of the Guilds murdered him? I know. Lily told me that for years. I can repeat her whole speech if you want me to. None of it changes the nightmare."

Liam leaned away from me and took his hand from my cheek. I thought he'd given up, realized there was nothing to be done to help a girl who'd let her parents die because she couldn't ride fast enough.

But a deep blue light glimmered in his hand, emanating from the stone. He breathed onto his palm and the light grew brighter.

"I wish I could take away what happened to you." He pressed his finger onto the stone, bending the light. "I wish I could change the past so your father never placed that responsibility on your shoulders. I wish I could make the healer be in his home and force a shred of compassion into the soldiers' hearts." He pinched the stone between his fingers. "None of those things are within my power, but at least the nightmare can stop."

The stone faded to a shining black oval with a hole pinched through near the center. He pulled his purse of coins from his pocket, untied the leather cord that held the bag shut, and tucked the loose coins away.

"I wish I could protect you from more, but at least I can let you sleep." He strung the leather through the stone. "May I?"

I leaned forward, holding my breath as he lifted my hair to tie the cord.

"It won't protect you from monsters, but it will keep you safe from your own mind."

His face was so near, only a breath between his lips and mine.

A pull began at the center of my chest where the stone touched my skin. A burning that reached deep into my veins as though my blood itself had discovered longing.

He brushed the rest of my tears from my cheeks with his thumb.

"Liam…"

He pressed his lips to my forehead. "You should rest now."

Our gaze met, and the whole world froze. There was no sound from the square, no wind chasing in the coming storm—nothing had ever existed but Liam and me.

His fingers touched my lips, and I leaned into his warmth.

His lips grazed mine, and I forgot to breathe. A hunger like I'd never known ached inside me.

Before I could memorize his taste, he stood, letting the cold night air reclaim me.

"Mave will be looking for us at sunrise." He pushed his window open. "You should get some sleep."

A wave of laughter carried up from the dining room below.

"Right." I stood, sliding my fingers over the smooth pendant at my neck.

"You can cut through here and take the stairs down."

"I'd rather climb."

"Be careful." Liam stepped inside.

"Emmet and Finn," I said before the window closed, "they were seen by the soldier at the sailor's office. They can't be given new feathers like me. They won't be able to travel with us."

"They didn't leave any witnesses behind." He closed the window, and I was alone in the night.

I climbed down to my bed and lay on top of the covers, waiting for the world to come crashing down on me, or for the Guilds to come burn me alive. But the flames that singed me didn't come from the torches of evil men.

I stared at the ceiling above, wishing I could close the short distance between us. Wanting to taste his lips again if only for a moment, just long enough to be sure I would remember the feel of his hand on my cheek.

But sleep came instead, and there was peace in the darkness.

38

Tap, *tap, tap.*

I opened my eyes, blinking at the early morning light spilling in through my window.

Tap, *tap, tap.*

It took me a moment to remember how I had ended up on a soft bed in a fancy, painted room.

"Yes," I called.

"It's Nora. I've been sent to collect you."

"Come in." I sat up, running my hands over my face. My fingers grazed my lips and heat burned in my chest.

Nora stepped into my room carrying a small leather box. "By the Guilds, your hair."

"What?" I leapt to my feet. "What's happened to it?" I ran to the mirror, afraid it had somehow become orange or purple or some other outlandish color.

The black had stayed in place while I'd slept, but the mass of my hair had tangled in an almost impressive way.

"You can give a mouse peacock feathers, but it takes them more than a day to learn to fly." Nora set the leather box on the windowsill and pulled out a brush. "You're going back through the gate today, and you can't do it looking like a gutter snipe."

"Are the others up?" I wondered if Liam had slept, if he'd had even a moment to remember kissing me.

"They're all locked in Mave's parlor."

"Without me?" I started for the door.

"Come back here."

"There are things they could be talking about that I need to know."

Nora dodged around me and planted herself in front of the door. "The man died. He was a fat, old slitch, and it took an hour for him to go. It wasn't pretty either. Whoever you have in mind for that potion, I hope they deserve a painful death."

"They do."

Nora hugged me tight. "Then I'm glad the Black Bloods have found someone like you." She gave a shaking sigh and stepped away. "Now, let's get you ready to go."

"I didn't know you knew." I let her lead me to the mirror without a fight.

"I've been helping Mave for years." Nora combed roughly through the knots in my hair. "I have private clients around the city. It makes my coming and going at odd hours an easy thing to explain."

"What else is Mave talking to them about?"

"One thing at a time, little bird. You haven't earned Mave's secrets, only Liam's."

Heat rushed to my cheeks at the sound of his name.

Nora looked at me in the mirror, one eyebrow raised. "Guard your heart with that one."

"I don't know what you—"

"Liam loves his cause. I don't how much affection he has left for anything else." She pulled a tin of powder from the leather box. "I hope this will all fit in your pack. I cut it down to the bare minimum of what a girl really needs to survive."

I glanced into the kit of weapons Nora had chosen for me. She'd packed more powders and pigments than Karin could have thought up in her wildest daydreams.

"I've already tucked a few clean clothes into your pack. Eyes shut."

I closed my eyes, careful to keep still as she drew the kohl across my lids.

"Thank you, for all of this," I said, "but you really don't have to."

She bopped me on the nose. "Of course I do. Eyes open. The world may be cold and cruel, but that doesn't mean we shouldn't help where we can."

"Thank you." I hugged Nora again.

"Promise to take care of yourself in your travels, and that will be thanks enough for me." She dug back into the box and pulled out the cream. "Lips."

It only took her a few minutes to primp me back into a well-groomed bird. We walked arm-in-arm down through the empty dining room and into the kitchen. The boys stood around the table with Mave, their coats on and all our packs ready.

"She's fit to travel." Nora presented me to the group.

Emmet tossed a warm roll to me and turned to dig in his pack. Liam didn't look my way at all.

"Thank you, Nora," Mave said.

"It's been my pleasure." Nora tucked the box into my pack.

"Can you even ride in a top that tight?" Finn asked.

I swatted him on the arm. "Faster than you can."

"We should be on our way." Liam hoisted his pack onto his back. "We've a long road ahead, and the sooner we're out of your hair, the better."

"Are you sure you wouldn't rather take my path out of the city?" Mave asked.

"We need our horses." Emmet kissed Mave's hand. "Thank you, Mave, for all you've done."

Mave took Emmet's face in her hands. "Be safe, and come back again someday."

Emmet nodded and headed for the door.

I tucked my roll into my pocket. My stomach had started to squirm too much to consider eating.

"Pleasure meeting you both." Finn gave a nod and followed Emmet.

"Trueborn," Mave said, "don't forget what we're fighting for."

"Never." Liam picked up my pack, balancing it on his shoulder.

"I can take that." I reached for my bag.

"A girl dressed like you wouldn't be carrying a pack in the city." Liam held the door open for me.

"Take this and be well." Mave lifted a bundle of black fabric from the table and pressed it into my arms.

"May we meet again in a land of freedom." Nora kissed my cheek.

"Thank you." I gave them both a brief smile and walked out into the dining room.

Finn and Emmet stood on the porch out front, watching the men cleaning the square.

"Do you think the soldiers will be searching people at the gate?" My voice echoed strangely in the empty room.

"Probably." Liam didn't say anything else as he ushered me out of Mave's house.

I clutched the black fabric tight and touched the pendant at my neck. The smooth stone held the warmth of my body, it had no imperfection in its making, and it was very much real.

What have I done to anger you?

I wanted to ask Liam, but as we weaved through the streets, more pressing questions had to come first.

"Do we have anything we can't let them find?" I asked.

"Not that you need to worry about," Emmet said.

"We're traveling together," I said. "We'll be searched together."

"You and Finn will go through first," Liam said. "He knows which way to ride. We'll catch up to you."

"We should stay together." I clutched the fabric closer as panic crept into my chest.

"You don't trust me, Ena?" Finn clapped a hand to his heart. "You have wounded me beyond healing."

"It's not that."

We entered the market square. The children were back out, running and laughing as though the soldiers weren't a thing to fear.

The noise of the shoppers made speaking softly impossible. The man selling milk joked merrily, and a drunk woman laughed above the rest of the chatter.

We reached the far side and stepped out onto the main road. I slowed my pace to walk beside Liam.

"What if something goes wrong at the gate?" I asked. "How will we know? What if you can't find us? It makes more sense to stay together."

"Ride with Finn, we'll catch up," Liam said. "Emmet."

Emmet stopped, waiting for Liam and me to reach him.

"Let them get their horses before we do," Liam said. "I don't want the soldiers guarding the gate to see us at the stable together."

Finn took my pack from Liam's shoulder. The bulk seemed absurd on his smaller frame. "See you on the road."

I looked at Emmet and Liam but couldn't come up with a thing to say that would let us all stay together.

I tried to think of an argument to make as the stable boy blushed and passed me the reins of my horse. But the poison lay tucked in my pocket, and the papers Liam had wanted badly enough to warrant theft were with him.

Liam's decision made sense.

I mounted my horse and draped the black fabric over the saddle in front of me. A carved wooden clasp caught my eye. A little bird to fasten the neck of the thick black cloak. I smiled, sending a silent thank you to Mave and Nora.

The soldiers gave a quick search through our packs and sent us on our way.

"All we've got to do is ride," Finn said. "They'll find us."

He headed north to the glenn that bordered the city. I followed him, hoping to soon hear hooves pounding behind me.

39

For the first hour, it was easy to make excuses for why Liam and Emmet hadn't caught up to us. I made Finn stop in the trees by the glenn so I could scavenge for a few more supplies. They hadn't come by the time I ran out of reasons to linger.

I looked behind as we took the road that headed west, but they still weren't there.

When the storm came and lightning split the sky, I took comfort in the downpour. With the rain whipping across us, blurring the road and the towering trees surrounding us, they could have been riding just behind and we wouldn't have seen them.

It wasn't until the lights of the town came into view that I gave in to the dread that had threatened for hours.

I was soaked through. Mave's cloak had protected me from the storm for a while, but the protection wasn't meant to last forever.

The rain finally slowed to a manageable pace as Finn led me into the town of Marten.

I clutched my reins with half-frozen hands, studying the stone buildings around me.

The place looked more like Harane than Frason's Glenn. No great wall surrounded the houses that had been built close together like those at the center of Harane. But, if whatever fool had placed the businesses in Harane had also been charged with the planning of Marten, here their gamble paid off.

Shops, a tanner, two taverns, and a proper inn had all been packed together on the main road with more businesses on the two streets that cut through it like a cross. The buildings were taller than the ones in Harane, built three and four stories high to make up for not being able to expand from side to side.

The houses were all made of sturdy stone, and most had their shutters closed tight. I couldn't remember which houses in Harane had even bothered with shutters.

Finn turned down a smaller road and stopped at a tavern that looked a bit sadder than the others we'd passed.

There was no music pouring through the windows. The front door had been solidly shut against the storm, and the paint on the sign out front, which read *The Downy Loft*, had been worn away in places so I had to squint to make out the words.

"They've a stable back here," Finn said. "You stay with the horses, and I'll run in and get us a room. I think..." He scrunched up his face. "I think it would be better if we shared, told them we were together. I don't fancy the idea of leaving you alone in a room here."

I gripped the stone pendant. "Whatever you think is best."

He passed me his horse's reins and dashed inside.

I held my breath, playing out a beautiful scene in my head.

Liam and Emmet would appear behind me. Liam would be cross that Finn had left me alone in the dark. Emmet would say something rude about my needing to be more careful.

We would all go inside and have a hot meal and cup of frie to warm us up. Emmet and Finn would fall dead asleep, and Liam and I would be alone.

I would tell him I'd been worried about him. That I was sorry if I'd somehow tricked him into kissing me, but if he wanted to, I would be happy to kiss him until all the stars fell from the sky.

"They've had a hard ride." Finn came back out of the tavern, leading a sour-looking girl behind him. "If you could give them a bit of extra attention, I'd be very grateful."

"I love gratitude," the girl said. "It does so well when buying food at the market."

"Too right you are." Finn untied my pack from the back of my saddle. "Just see that you care for them as you'd like me to care for you."

I slid off of my saddle, not bothering to hide my wince as my legs protested being asked to straighten.

"I've gotten us a nice room, my love." Finn took my hand, awkwardly shouldering open the door as he balanced both our packs. "I'm told there's already a fire burning in the grate, and the kind lady who owns the place has promised to send up frie and soup."

The murmurs in the dining room, not that a place like that deserved such a fancy name, stopped as everyone turned to look at me.

I resisted the urge to wipe my face in case any of Nora's paint had dripped all the way down my nose. Keeping my chin high, I followed Finn through the crowd of men. Two older women sat in the booths tucked up along the walls. I tried to give them the same sort of smile I'd have given Nora, but both just stared at me.

The wooden stairs had filth lodged in the corners and creaked as we climbed them.

"Second floor, third room down, my love." Finn let go of my hand to fish a key out of his pocket. "We'll get you dry and settled in no time."

"I doubt I'll ever be dry again."

Finn stopped at the third room down and fitted the key in the lock, which gave a heavy thunk as it turned.

The woman who'd rented us the room hadn't lied about the fire in the hearth. The flames crackled mercifully in the grate, the bed had been laid with thick blankets, and before we could close the door, a little boy thumped up behind us with a tray of soup and frie.

"Thank you, sir." Finn set our bags aside and took the tray from the child. "Would you be a fine gentleman and fetch us a pitcher of hot water to wash up with?"

The boy grinned and ran down the hall.

I closed the door behind him.

"It could be worse." Finn set the tray down on the shaky table beside the bed. "It could definitely be better, but it could be worse."

"They'll know to find us here?" I unfastened my cloak and hung the soaked fabric on a nail beside the fireplace.

"It's the choice Liam would make." Finn kicked off his boots. "Can't say I agree with him, but such is life."

I sat in one of the two spindly chairs in front of the fire, letting the flames warm my fingers before I even bothered trying to untie my boots.

"Here." Finn pressed a cup of frie into my hands. "Drink up before you lose a finger."

"I'm not in much danger of that." I sipped the frie, wrinkling my nose as the liquor burned its way down my throat.

"Can't be too careful with those types of things. We can always have the boy bring more up."

"Will Liam and Emmet find us tonight?" I took another sip of frie. "Will they ask what room we're in?"

"Not unless there's a reason for us to run." Finn sniffed his soup before daring to sip from the bowl.

"What if they've already arrived and decided to stay somewhere else?"

"They haven't."

"What if they got lost along the road?"

"They didn't."

"What if they were stopped at the gate and are trapped in Frason's Glenn?"

"Eat your soup." Finn nodded toward the bowl on the table.

"When are we supposed to meet Gabe?" The bowl nearly burned my fingers, but I drank anyway, grateful for the distraction as panic welled in my stomach.

"It's not so much a set time," Finn said. "His regiment is stationed just north of Marten. As far as I know, they aren't set to move anytime soon."

"So we just sit here and wait?"

"No. We wait for the lad to come back with some water to wash up, order some more frie and something other than week old soup to eat, then go to sleep and dream of better food for breakfast."

"You really do think only of food, don't you?" I downed the rest of my soup.

"Food, freedom, and love, sweet Ena. Those three things occupy all the space my mind has to offer."

4 0

I slept on the bed while Finn curled up near the fire. Lying under the heavy blankets, I clutched the stone pendant, trying to promise myself I was brave enough to sleep. As the storm's wrath began again, I finally drifted off.

When I woke in the morning, the storm hadn't changed. So little sun peered through the thickness of the rain, it was nearly impossible to tell day had come at all. The floor creaking as Finn paced was the only thing that dragged me from my dreamless slumber.

"What's happened?" I asked as soon as I managed to remember where I was and what we'd come for.

"Nothing." Finn stopped midstride. "Just lots of rain and a bit of thunder, but now that you're awake, we might as well go and eat."

I rubbed my hand over my face. "Why don't you go down and order us some food while I try and make myself presentable."

"If that's what you want." Finn flipped the lock on the door. "I just didn't want to have you wake up alone." He stepped out into the hall. "See you down there then."

"Squeaked the floor to wake me up and ran for food," I said after the door had closed behind him.

I took my time brushing my hair and painting on my armor, checking the vial I'd hidden in my bag to be sure it was safe, making sure the other plants I'd gathered in the glenn hadn't been ruined by the rain. I dawdled for as long as I could.

There were only two possibilities I could think of. Either Liam and Emmet were downstairs, in which case they would still be there watching Finn eat an extraordinary amount of food even if I lingered in my room.

Or they weren't downstairs. The soldiers had caught them with the papers they'd taken from the sailors. They'd been trapped somewhere awful and needed Finn and me to rescue them. They could already be dead.

I didn't know if I was brave enough to face that possibility.

I tore the brush through my hair one last time and headed downstairs.

The scent coming from the kitchen promised a better meal than the soup we'd had the night before. Voices carried from below, though I didn't recognize any of them.

Holding my breath, I stepped down into the dining room.

The same two women sat in the booths along the wall. Another woman stood behind the bar, polishing metal mugs with a rag browner than my boots. A pack of men waiting for drinks from the woman leaned against the bar, and a few others sat at the tables dotted around the room.

The young boy shuffled from the kitchen, carrying a tray laden with food, heading toward a table near the door where Finn sat, his red hair as bright as a beacon against the dull brown surrounding him.

There was no one else sitting at his table.

My nails bit into my palms as I walked toward him, keeping my face calm so no one would see my panic.

"There you are, my love." Finn stood and pulled out a chair for me. "I'm afraid I've already eaten my breakfast, but I didn't want you to eat alone, so I ordered another round."

I stared down at the roast pig, vegetables, and porridge on the little boy's tray, wanting nothing more than to throw the food against the wall.

"I'm not very hungry." I sank down into the seat opposite Finn.

"Well, eat what you like and I'll finish the rest." Finn set a plate in front of me.

I stared at him.

"Perhaps some tea for my love, young sir." Finn smiled at the boy. "It seems she needs a bit of perking up."

The boy bowed deeply and backed into the kitchen as though Finn and I were the King and Queen of Ilbrea.

"We don't have time to eat." I spoke through clenched teeth as Finn skewered a roasted potato.

"Of course we do."

"They aren't here."

"I figured that out for myself, shockingly enough." Finn popped the potato into his mouth, closing his eyes at the ecstasy of food.

"Finn," I said, gripping the edge of the table to keep myself from tossing the tray aside, "they could have been captured, they could be dead. We have to ride back to Frason's Glenn and find them."

"That's the part where you're wrong." Finn ate another chivving potato. "What we have to do is wait right here and make sure no one notices us lingering. So we eat."

"We can't just—"

"Hush now, my love." Finn held his potato laden fork to my mouth. "You've got to eat, darling. I know you're exhausted from the trip, but I promise we can rest here for a few days."

I bit the potato from his fork as the little boy shoved a tea tray onto our table.

"Thank you, young sir," Finn said.

The boy backed away again, giving an even larger bow, his face split in a wide grin.

"They might not have stuck to the road," Finn said in a much softer voice. "If something went wrong at the gate, then they're probably keeping to the wilds. Which would mean, if we headed toward Frason's Glenn on the road, we'd miss them. They'd arrive here. We'd be nowhere to be found. Liam and your brother would think we'd gotten ourselves killed, and that is a type of wrath I don't care to see."

"We can't just sit here forever." I shoved another chunk of potato into my mouth to keep from screaming.

"Not forever." Finn took my hand. "We wait a few days. Get our gift to our friend on our own if we have to. If they still haven't come, we head home."

"Without them?"

"To find them there." Finn looked up to the spiderweb-strung ceiling. "That's why Liam split us the way he did."

"What do you mean?" I leaned across the table.

"There are paths through the mountains that are open to Liam and me that you and Emmet wouldn't be able to travel alone."

"You're a trueborn?" I whispered.

"No." Finn laughed. "Thank the gods I'm not. I'd never want to carry that sort of responsibility. But the mountain runs through my veins. As loyal as you and Emmet may be, the mountain cares for those born of her child."

I buried my face in my hands, picturing the mountain swallowing Liam and Emmet whole.

"I've seen Liam get out of scrapes that would have killed the best paun," Finn said. "And, to be honest, I've seen Emmet get out of a lot worse. They are fine. We have to focus on getting our own work done, or there will have been no point in leaving camp. Except escaping Neil's cooking for a while. That is quite the welcome change."

I poured myself a cup of tea, letting the steadiness of my own hands give me courage. "So, where do we find our friend?"

"We can look for him tonight." Finn held his cup up for me to pour for him. "If you want no part in it—"

"Tonight will be fine. I have a few more things to do before we meet him anyway."

I spent the day in our room, working on things that would have horrified Lily.

Or maybe she would have been proud. Maybe she would have smiled, glad the skills she had taught me would have a hand in saving lives, even if one man had to die to do it.

I looked up every time a floorboard squeaked in the corridor, hoping it would be Liam and Emmet, terrified it would be a soldier come to hang me. The day passed without either happening.

When night came, I hid three packages in my pocket and polished my armor.

41

The rain had turned to a fine mist by the time I walked out of The Downy Loft, arm-in-arm with Finn. He hadn't said exactly where we were going, only that I should look my best. He had put on a clean shirt and run my brush through his hair.

We wandered up the side street where we'd been staying. I studied each building we passed, better able to see them now than when we'd come into town in the rain. The buildings were a bit sadder than I'd thought, with the mortar between the stones crumbling. The paint on the doors peeled away in places, and the shutters all had heavy hooks on the inside, as though ready to be locked against a terrible storm at a moment's notice.

"Are most towns this sad?" I leaned in close to whisper in Finn's ear.

"Only the ones who have an army camped on their doorstep," Finn said. "If a demon were lurking in the garden waiting to steal your child the moment they showed a lick of magic, you'd stop caring about everything but keeping your doors locked tight, too."

"What?" I tugged on Finn's arm, stopping him midstride.

"Didn't Liam tell you why we were coming to kill Drason?"

"No." A heavy weight pressed down on my chest. "I never even asked for his name."

"The Sorcerers Guild noticed a strange number of sorci children being born in Marten." Finn drew me into his arms and spoke close to my ear. "They sent Drason and his men to investigate. He's been stalking the city for more than a year, trapping the children born with magic, then taking their mothers, too. The children are shipped to the Sorcerers Tower in Ilara. We haven't been able to figure out where the women are taken."

A heavy weight sagged in my stomach as I looked at the hooks on the windows. Locks could keep out a storm but not the Guilds.

"This is why we slay the beast." Finn squeezed my hand and led me onto the main road.

Light and music poured through the taverns' windows. Soldiers in uniforms roamed the streets, but not as though they were patrolling. A fair handful of them seemed to be very drunk for the sun having just gone down, and the rest seemed intent on joining the

149

stumblers soon enough. They strode through the town without a hint of guilt for the pain they'd caused.

Finn stopped in front of a common man carrying a sack on his back. "Sorry, sir." Finn gave a little bow. "I'm looking for a recommendation for a lively tavern."

The man wrinkled his brow. "They're all right behind me."

"Yes, I can see them." Finn gave a smile that would have looked foolish on anyone else. "But I wanted to know which you'd say was best."

"Fiddler's Mark." The man nodded. "Good barkeep, good ale, good music, and I've seen them wash the glasses once or twice before. There are soldiers in there, but…" The man shrugged and shook his head.

"Thank you very much, sir." Finn bowed and stepped around the man as though to lead me to the tavern.

But when the man had turned a corner and was out of sight, Finn veered away from Fiddler's Mark and back out to the center of the street to step in front of a young man with a lady on each arm.

"Excuse me, folks," Finn said. "Which tavern would you recommend?"

"Fiddler's Mark," the girl to the left of the boy said. "We're going. You can come if you like." She gave Finn a wink as the boy led her away.

"What are you doing?" I asked as Finn stopped to stare into the window of a bookshop before looping back out to walk down the street.

"Whenever the soldiers camp close to a town, they always flock to find a drink away from their commanders," Finn said. "Gabe will be at the most popular tavern, not recommended by the soldiers, but the locals. That's how we find him."

Finn asked three more people which tavern would be best. Only one answered anything but Fiddler's Mark.

"I think it's time for a drink." Finn smiled as the elderly woman he'd spoken to toddled away.

"No food?" I asked.

"Of course food," Finn said. "But I was thinking we'd start with a drink and have food to celebrate a job well done after I've finished our work."

"No."

"Fine," Finn sighed. "Food first if you insist."

"I'll be doing the work. Not you."

Finn stopped ten feet in front of the door to Fiddler's Mark. He dragged me away from the cheerful music and into the narrow alley beside the tavern.

"What are you talking about?" Finn whispered.

"I'm giving it to him, not you."

"Don't be a chivving fool, Ena." Finn held out his hand. "Give me the vial and let's be done with it."

"There's more than just the one vial. Liam wanted to be sure Gabe wouldn't be found out."

"Which is why you've brewed the berries," Finn whispered.

"A single death from an illness, taking a commander no less, would still be suspicious."

"So we should just kill the whole regiment? I'm not opposed to it, but I think we should have spoken to Liam about this new idea."

"I'm not talking about killing." I leaned in as though moving to kiss Finn's cheek. "If a group of people take ill and one doesn't recover, they'll blame the food or the gods and not spare a thought for anyone plotting."

"By the stars, Ena."

"I have everything I need in my pocket. I just have to give it to him and be sure he knows how to use it."

Finn leaned against the tavern wall.

"I can do this, Finn. Trust me. I'm sure I'm right."

"Chivving cact of a god's head. Do you not understand, Ena? Liam and Emmet will both kill me if they ever catch wind of me letting you do this."

"They don't need to know." I took Finn's face in my hands. "But I do need to be sure Gabe understands what he's got to do, or the wrong person could die."

"You've literally cornered me." Finn kissed my cheek. "If you get yourself captured or killed, I will never forgive you. I may seem cheerful enough, but I've stone in my blood and fury in my heart."

"I'm terrified of you." I took his hand, leading him back out of the alley.

A chorus of whistles and laughter sprang up as a pack of soldiers spotted us stepping out onto the main street.

"Didn't know they had such beauty available in Marten." One of the soldiers gave a mocking bow.

Heat rushed to my cheeks.

"Oh, Emmet is going to murder me." Finn looped an arm around my waist and ushered me into Fiddler's Mark.

The place was packed with as many men in black uniforms as there were in common clothes. Women dotted the crowd, some huddled together at tables of their own, others mixed in with the men.

I wanted to tell the women to run away, to hide from the soldiers.

But Lily had told me to hide, and my world had been burned in my absence.

A long bar took up one side of the room. Three women poured for the customers, and a panicked-looking man ran food from the kitchen. A woman sang on a stage tucked into the far corner, surrounded by four men playing stringed instruments.

"I hate to say it, but the locals have decent taste." Finn weaved through the tavern, searching for an empty table. "If I could smell anything from the kitchen over the liquor in the air, I might even be excited about dinner."

"How do they do it?" I watched a pair of tilk men laughing as though the soldiers at the table beside them weren't their enemies.

"Allowing your hate for the Guilds to show only gives them reason to suspect you and your family." Finn pressed his lips to my forehead. "Better to drink with a demon than to have him look too closely at your children."

A sick feeling rolled through my stomach.

Finn tipped my chin up and spoke loudly enough for the people around us to hear. "Give me a laugh, girl. If I'm going to pay for our drinks, that's the least you can do."

I hovered on the edge of telling him I owed no man my smile before coming to my senses and giggling as the woman onstage pulled out a pipe to play.

"There we are." Finn darted to the back of the room where a table had yet to be claimed.

We were far from the front door, nestled against the wall, with a flock of drunken soldiers between us and the way out.

"Are you sure we want this table?" I asked. "We could wait for another."

"This is perfect." Finn pulled out a seat for me. "You wait here, and I'll grab us a round of drinks."

He walked away before I could tell him the nerves in my stomach might make drinking anything a disaster.

I unbuttoned the carved bird fastening at the neck of my cloak and let my fingers graze my stone pendant to be sure it was still there. Even after wandering in the chill mist, the stone still held a blissful warmth to it. I draped my cloak over the back of my chair, sat, and began watching the people around me.

Gabe had been placed as a spy among the soldiers, so he would be wearing a black uniform. But beyond that, I couldn't guess what he might look like. Of the Black Bloods I'd met, there didn't seem to be one trait that ran amongst all of them. Between Finn's red hair and Liam's dark eyes, any man in the room could say they had been born a Black Blood and I'd have no way of knowing if they were lying.

"Here we are." Finn set a mug down in front of me. "The woman who owns this place swears by her ale. It may be awful, but honestly I was too afraid to order anything else."

I laughed and took a sip of the bitter brew that tasted like dried flowers.

Finn leaned in to whisper in my ear. "He's here."

"Where?" I started searching the crowd for Liam and Emmet before realizing who Finn was talking about.

"Table on the far side of the bar, facing the door to the street."

"Are you sure?"

"Of course I'm sure, I've met the fellow before." Finn tucked my hair behind my ear. "He's got two others at the table with him. Gabe will stay late. We'll wait and hope his friends leave."

"Do they call him Gabe?" I trailed my finger along Finn's cheek.

"Gabe Louers is his name registered with the Guilds."

A big man in a soldier's uniform came in from outside, giving a booming laugh as though making sure everyone in the room would notice his entrance.

"This"—the man raised his arms toward the sky—"this is an evening to celebrate."

A roar of approval shot up from all the soldiers.

"This, this could be a long night." Finn sighed as the big man lumbered his way to the bar.

Other soldiers followed him, buying drinks for everyone in sight.

I shuddered even thinking of reasons a paun soldier would want to celebrate.

"Maybe we should try again tomorrow night." Finn took a long drink of his ale.

I sipped from my own cup. "No. We should get it done tonight."

"We'll be here till morning."

"What does Gabe look like?" I ran my fingers through my hair, making sure it hadn't been matted by the mist.

"It doesn't matter until the place clears out." Finn took my wrist.

"It does if I want to do a little flirting." I glared at him. "Just tell me what he looks like, and I'll go see if I can spot a way to talk to him."

"You do realize if anything happens to you, I'll be killed. By the Guilds' hand or Emmet's, I will die."

"I'm well aware. Now tell me before I start shouting *Gabe* to see who answers."

Finn froze for a moment as though thinking through his chances of getting me out of the tavern quietly.

"Blond, curly hair, devilishly green eyes, and a scar on his lip that makes him look like a rogue."

"Sounds fascinating." I yanked my arm from Finn's grip and stood. "Try not to panic while I'm gone."

"Thanks."

Pressing my shoulders back, I started through the tables. I didn't know if it was taking off my cloak or not being held close by Finn, but more men eyed me as I worked my way toward the front of the room.

I can be Nora. I have the armor she's given me. I can have her strength as well.

I scanned the tables I passed, offering little smiles to the handsomer men.

"A fine evening." A man in common clothes nodded to me as I passed.

"I don't fancy the mist." I turned away from him.

His friends' laughter followed me as I made my way toward Gabe's table.

I spotted him without trouble. While Finn's description of Gabe's eyes and scar had been accurate, he had understated the color of Gabe's hair. Flaxen ringlets topped the head of the soldier who sat laughing with his friends.

My gut told me to hate him. Laughing with a pack of soldiers, probably telling stories of the tilk lives they had destroyed.

He is one of us.

I fixed a coy smile on my lips and walked up to his table.

The men stopped laughing as they spotted me.

"Good evening." One of the soldiers nodded, his gaze drifting none too subtly to my breasts.

"Not really," I said.

You are brave. You are a warrior.

"The man I came in with is a horrible bore. You"—I pointed to Gabe—"come buy me a drink. I've asked all the locals and they promised this is the best place to find decent ale."

I ignored the simmering disappointment on the other men's faces.

Gabe stood, downing the rest of his frie. "If a man was fool enough to bore you, then please allow me to be the one to regain the dignity of my sex."

"What a kind man." I held out my hand for him, taking his elbow as he stepped away from his table. "Is Fiddler's Mark ale really wonderful?"

"It's not to be missed."

I kept my gaze fixed on Gabe's face as we waited at the bar, carefully ignoring the stares of the other men.

"Two ales please," Gabe called when he caught a barkeep's eye. "It's not usually this hard to get a drink around here. I suppose everyone's come out now that the storm's passed."

"Pity it's so crowded." I leaned closer to him. "I was hoping we might be able to get a table to ourselves."

Gabe unhooked his arm from mine and laid his hand on the back of my waist. "I don't care the size of the crowd. I'm sure I can find us a private table."

"Here you are, Gabe." The barkeep shoved two mugs our way with a smile for Gabe and a glare at me.

"This way." He wrapped his arm around my waist and led me closer to the musicians.

The woman had begun singing.

"As the stars gleam above, so our love shall survive,
As the moon falls from the sky, our children will thrive."

"Fellows," Gabe said, stopping at a table filled with boys who didn't seem old enough to be wearing soldiers black, "do us a favor and find other seats."

Two of the boys leapt to their feet. The third stared at me wide-eyed until his friends hauled him away.

"That wasn't too hard." Gabe pulled out a chair for me.

I sat and he moved to sit across from me.

"Sit here." I patted the chair beside me. "No point in putting a whole table between us."

Gabe smiled and sat.

I took a deep breath, trying to think of how to say who I was.

The players started a new, faster song.

"So where is he?" Gabe asked.

"Who?" I twisted in my chair, leaning close to him.

Gabe trailed a finger from the top of my bodice, up my chest, and to the pendant at my throat. "The one who made this. Where's Liam?"

42

"I don't know." I leaned closer, pressing my lips to his ear. "But I have a gift he's sent for you."

"A gift?" Gabe tipped my chin so my lips brushed against his. He tasted of ale. "What sort of gift would I be sent?"

"Poison to slay a monster."

"That doesn't sound like Liam." He traced his nose across my cheek and nibbled the bottom of my ear.

"It was my idea. A way to keep you in place while getting rid of the beast."

"I've no experience in poison." He kissed the side of my neck.

I tipped my head to the side, offering more skin for him to explore. "That's why I'm here. All you have to do is exactly as I say." I shifted to sit on his lap, draping one arm around his neck.

Gabe's eyes widened.

I whispered in his ear. "There are three things in my pocket." I took his hand, guiding it down my hip to where my treasures hid in the folds of my skirt.

The song ended, and everyone in the tavern cheered.

I tipped my head back, laughing at the racket of the drunken men.

Gabe pulled me closer to him, slipping his hand deep into my pocket.

"Gabe's having a good night," a burly man hollered through the crowd.

I winked at the man as Gabe kissed the skin just below my pendant as though there were no one watching us.

The musicians struck up a fresh tune. Men began stomping in time with the song. The sound of their thumping rattled into my chest, shaking my lungs.

I tipped Gabe's chin up, kissing him, then guiding his lips to the side of my neck.

"The little vial is for the beast. It'll have a taste of berries. Slip it into his drink."

Gabe ran one hand up the side of my ribs, while the other stayed in my pocket.

"Dump the powder into a small food pot, there's enough to make ten men ill. Make sure it's not too diluted, or it won't work."

"What will it do?" He lifted me, shifting my weight so my torso pressed against his.

"Nothing they won't survive." I twined my fingers through his ringlets. "The pouch of berries is for you. Eat them as soon as the others show signs of illness."

"Why?" The ridges of his muscles tensed.

"To be sure you look like one of the fallen." I kissed him as fear flitted through his eyes.

"What will it do to me?" His lips teased mine as he spoke.

"You'll wish the gods would take you for a few hours and be fine by the next day." I rested my forehead against his. "Compared to being hanged, whipped, or burned alive by the paun, your suffering won't be much."

"When should it be done?"

I hadn't thought about the when, hadn't thought about setting a time to end a man's life.

I looked toward the ceiling, wishing the room were quiet and I could have one moment to think through the best time for murder.

Gabe kissed the tops of my breasts, his tongue grazing the skin just above my bodice.

I gripped his ringlets, tipped his head back, and kissed him, trying to tell him I was sorry for giving him such a terrible task and for the pain my plan would cause.

Forgive me. May we meet again in a land of freedom.

I whispered in his ear, "The first chance you get. Let it be done."

I kissed him on the cheek and stood. His hands trailed along my waist until he couldn't reach me anymore.

I walked toward Finn, to our table in the back of the room.

A man took my hand as I passed him. "Did he not have enough to please you? I can promise I do."

I didn't look down to see the man's face. I couldn't see anyone in the tavern but Liam, standing at the back of the room. His jaw set and eyes dark.

43

"That's not what I brought you here for." A hand pinched my arm, dragging me away from Liam.

"What?" I blinked, trying to get my eyes to focus on anything besides Liam's face.

Someone shook my arm. "I pay to bring you here, pay for our drinks, and this is how you thank me?"

My gaze found a head of red hair and a livid face.

Men sniggered as Finn dragged me through the tables toward the front door.

"I have never met such an ungrateful, wretched whore in all my days." A light shone in Finn's eyes, a glint of something between triumph and warning.

I pulled my free hand back and slapped him hard across the face. "If you'd like me to pay attention to you, perhaps you should try being more interested in me than ale."

Finn pulled me to him and kissed me. I wrapped my arms around his neck, and leaned my weight against his body.

He scooped me up and carried me to the door. "This night is for me, and I'll not be sharing you." He kicked the door open and strode out into the misty night, still cradling me in his arms.

A round of hoots and cheers to lift the roof of the tavern followed us toward The Downy Loft.

"Tell me you got him everything he needed," Finn whispered as he turned onto the side street.

"He has everything, and I gave him as clear instructions as I could."

"May the gods bless you, Ena." He kissed my temple. "That was a damn fine performance."

"Did Liam see?"

"Liam and Emmet came in about when I thought Gabe was going to tear your bodice off with his teeth." Finn set me down in front of The Downy Loft. "I'm not sure what your brother thought of Gabe nigh on rolling his sister in the middle of a bar, but I don't think anyone could suspect anything but sex came of that meeting."

He opened the door, and the scent of stale soup greeted us.

Finn wrinkled his nose. "I wish we could've eaten elsewhere, but it seemed best to make a dramatic exit before more fiends came looking for a taste of you."

The little boy ran out of the kitchen, his face bright as he beamed up at Finn.

"Young sir"—Finn bowed—"I'd like any breakfast leftovers you have brought straight up to my room, along with a bit of frie."

The boy bowed so low it looked like he might tip over.

"And a pitcher of hot water for washing up," I said.

I could still taste Gabe and Finn. My neck burned where Gabe had kissed my skin. I wished I was back at Mave's where I could soak in a bath and wash Gabe's scent from my skin.

"Come on, my love." Finn took my hand, dragging me toward the stairs. "The night is young, and we mustn't waste it."

The two women hunched in the booths furrowed their brows at me as we passed.

"A bit of food and a nice night's sleep," Finn whispered as he closed the door to our room behind me. "Liam and Emmet are here, we've done our work, and tomorrow we can turn our attention toward getting home."

"Right." I untied my boots.

"Unless Liam wants to linger until the thing is done." Finn paused halfway through unbuttoning his jacket. "I'd rather be well away, but Liam is the one in charge."

"We'll see what he says."

Tap, tap, bang.

Finn opened the door and ushered in the little boy. I took the pitcher from the tray and went straight to the wash stand in the corner.

"That will be all for the evening, young sir."

I poured water on the cloth and scrubbed at my neck. Liam had seen. Had been standing there watching as Gabe…

I moved the cloth to wipe the kohl lining from my eyes, but I wasn't ready to remove my armor.

"Eat." Finn held out a plate of food. "It's cold but still better than the gray soup."

"Thanks." I sat by the fire and ate cold potatoes, listening for boots in the hall. "Do you think he'll be caught?"

"Gabe's smart. He'll find a way to do as you instructed."

"I hope so."

Boots thumped up the stairs.

I held my breath.

Knock, knock, knock.

Finn was on his feet before I could decide if I thought it was soldiers or Liam and Emmet, and which possibility was more terrifying.

Finn opened the door, and Liam and Emmet stepped through. Neither spoke as Emmet closed the door behind them.

"I'm glad you've made it here safely," Finn said. "Was it trouble at the gate?"

"What under the chivving sky were you thinking?" Emmet tossed my black cloak down at my feet. "What sort of madness has taken your mind?"

"It worked," Finn said. "We've done what we set out to do."

"You put my sister into a pack of men." Emmet stepped toward Finn, seeming to tower over him as anger pulsed from his skin.

"It was my idea." I set my plate down. "And truth be told, I didn't give him much of a choice."

"What?" Emmet rounded on me.

"I needed to speak to Gabe myself, to be sure he understood how to use everything I gave him." I brushed my skirt off and stood. "I made Finn tell me who Gabe was and went after him myself."

Emmet's jaw tightened.

"And if you're looking for an apology, you won't get one from me." I tipped my chin up. "Frankly, I think I did a wonderful job. No one will think anything of Gabe having a bit of fun with a girl, so if you're searching for any words to say to me, you'd best start with *thank you*."

"Thank you for playing the whore to aid our cause," Emmet said. "I'm glad you take such pride in placing yourself in danger."

"Would you say such a thing to your beloved Mave's girls?" I growled.

"I don't like them putting themselves in danger either, but they aren't my chivving sister." Emmet stormed out of the room, slamming the door behind him.

"That went about how I expected." Finn dug his fingers into his hair. "Shall I make sure he doesn't tear apart the town stone by stone, or would someone else like to claim that pleasure?"

I stared at the door. There were things I wanted to scream at Emmet but had nothing to say that would make him any less angry.

"I'll do it then." Finn grabbed the bread from his plate and his coat from by the fire and slipped out the door.

I couldn't bring myself to look at Liam. I didn't want to see the same anger in his face I'd gotten from Emmet.

"What did you give Gabe?" Liam said.

I picked my cloak up off the ground and hung it on the nail by the fire.

"You said *everything*," Liam said. "What did you give him besides the shadow berries?"

"A powdered root to cause a fever for some of the other soldiers, bird berries for Gabe to eat to get a bit sick as well."

"You asked him to poison himself?"

"He'll be fine. He may wish he'd never heard of food, but it'll keep him out of the way while people are worrying about the beast's death."

Liam paced the room.

"Tell me I wasn't right," I said. "Tell me I didn't protect Gabe."

Liam kept pacing.

"It's done." I spread my arms wide. "I got the work done. And if you don't like—"

"You could have been killed." Liam's boots thumped against the floor in a maddening rhythm. "If you had been caught carrying poison, you'd have been hanged."

"Any of us would have been. I knew this was dangerous going into it. Didn't you?"

"You walked into a room packed with foul paun men, teasing them, luring them—"

"That's what Mave's primping made me fit to do."

"I saved you from that soldier in Harane. I didn't do it so you could throw yourself straight back into a den of beasts. Letting Gabe paw you like that, do you have any idea what sort of ideas that puts in evil men's—"

"Stop chivving pacing."

Liam stopped, still staring at the wall in front of him.

"Look at me."

He didn't move.

"I said look at me." I took his face in my hands.

He met my gaze, his eyes dark and unreadable.

"I had Finn," I said. "I was safe enough."

"You think Finn could protect you from a whole tavern of paun soldiers?"

"You sent me away with him. If you trust him with my safety, shouldn't I?"

He hadn't shaved since the balcony. The stubble on his cheeks had lost its coarseness.

"If Finn had been caught, we both would have hanged anyway. The ending was the same if either of us failed."

Liam stepped away from me, rubbing his hands over the place where my fingers had touched his cheeks only a moment before.

"I said that I wanted to be a Black Blood, that I wanted to help."

"By letting Gabe kiss you with a room full of men leering at you?"

"It had to be done."

"Not by you!"

I stepped forward, close enough that I had to tip my chin up to look into Liam's eyes. "What are you mad about? That I got it done, that I let Gabe touch me, or that you ever kissed me in the first place?"

Liam's gaze drifted down to my mouth. I remembered the feel of his lips against mine, and the burning of wanting flared in my chest. I leaned closer, begging the stars for him to take me in his arms and kiss me.

"Ena." He brushed his thumb over my lips and trailed his fingers down the side of my neck.

"Do you want me or not?"

Our eyes met, and then he was kissing me.

He wrapped his arms around my waist, drawing me toward him. He tasted of fire and honey and sweet winds and freedom. I parted my lips, wanting to savor more of him.

He held me closer. His heartbeat thundered in his chest, keeping time with mine.

I laced my fingers through his hair as my hunger for him burned as bright as a star destined to consume worlds. Every bit of my being knew nothing but wanting Liam.

His hand moved up my ribs, his thumb grazing the side of my breast.

I gasped as heat seared through me. I pressed myself to him, feeling every ridge of his body against mine.

"No." He stepped back.

My head spun at the absence of his touch.

"No." He stared past me, through the window to the night beyond.

"Liam." I reached for his hand.

He shook his head, turned, and walked out the door, leaving me frozen in place.

44

I have never believed in true love or happy endings. They are not things that have ever existed in my world.

I have always believed in pain. In agony that cuts so deep, you fear your very soul will pour out of the wound and be lost to you forever.

That torment I know well. It is as familiar to me as the scent of the air after a storm.

But my soul has never poured out of me. Somehow, I have always woken up the next morning.

Mine is not a happy love story. But there is a monster to be slain, a multitude of demons that torment our land. As long as they steal innocent souls, at least I have a beast to battle.

That fight must be enough to keep me breathing.

4 5

Finn had slept on top of the covers next to me. He'd tried to sleep on the floor beside the fire, but given the bruise growing on his cheek, I'd insisted he rest somewhere soft.

I woke before he did in the morning and lay in bed, fingers wrapped around the pendant on my neck.

Part of me cherished it, a bit of Liam that was mine even if I couldn't have him. Part of me wanted to throw it out the window as a first step in shedding all thoughts of how badly I wished he were lying in bed beside me.

But I'd slept through the night, and that was a gift even the horrible mixture of shame, hurt, and longing that buried me couldn't convince me to toss aside.

The sounds of movement on the street below began just after dawn. The rattle of cart wheels fighting through mud and mumble of sleepy voices made the morning seem so peaceful for a town that had a regiment of soldiers camped nearby.

The scent of burned food drifted up the stairs. I forced myself to grin as I imagined the little boy telling Finn there was nothing for breakfast as every edible scrap in the place had been turned to ash.

Finn woke, sniffing the air. "Is that breakfast?"

"You are a mockery of yourself." I tossed my pillow at his back.

"That implies a consistency of character that is difficult to find." Finn sat up. "So, I will take it as a compliment."

He gave me a lopsided grin, wincing as his swollen cheek moved. The bruise on his face took up most of the left side of his jaw. The right side, where I'd slapped him, had only been left a bit pink.

"Emmet should be walloped for hitting you." I crawled over him and out of bed. "What was the slitch thinking?"

"He didn't hit me." Finn gingerly touched his cheek.

"Did you fall and smack your face on something fist-shaped?" I tore my brush through my hair a bit harder than was wise.

"No." Finn grabbed his boots and tugged them on. "He got into a fight with some local boys, and I got punched trying to get the poor slitches out of Emmet's way before he pummeled them into the dirt."

"Why would he do that?"

"I imagine he pictured each of them as the men from the tavern who were quite openly fantasizing about shoving themselves inside his sister."

"Finn!" I tossed my hairbrush at him.

He caught it and began brushing his own hair. "I did manage to ensure no one sustained life-threatening injuries in your brother's rampage. I should be given quite a bit of credit for that feat."

"Credit to you and an earful for Emmet. How has such a chivving fool managed to keep himself alive?" I picked up the box Nora had given me.

"You've never seen him fight, have you?"

My fingers hovered over the tins of powder. Part of me wanted to throw it all away, like somehow I could blame the paint for luring Liam close enough that I thought I could have him. But there were soldiers all around, and I couldn't go back to being the girl from Harane, even if that was what a very large part of me wanted.

"Do you think we'll ride out today?" I brushed pink onto my cheeks.

"I doubt it. Liam and Emmet don't have horses."

"What?" I froze with a brush of pigment halfway to my eye.

"I haven't heard the full story, what with the neck kissing and fighting, but they made their way here on foot."

"No wonder it took them so long." I tamped down the tiny bit of sympathy that rose in my chest at the idea of the two of them traveling through that storm on foot.

"I'm sure it will be a delightful story." Finn inched closer to the door. "Once we get some food in them, and make sure Emmet's gotten past his rage at having a beauty for a sister, we can ask them to tell us the whole thrilling tale."

He stopped with his hand on the doorknob.

"You can go." I trailed the kohl along my eyelid.

"I'll wait." Finn shrugged. "Wouldn't want to leave you alone."

He gazed longingly at the crack in the door as though the scent of burned food were somehow appealing.

"Are you afraid of facing them without me?" I laughed. The feel of it grated against the wound in my chest.

"Not afraid, just wise enough to better my chances with your presence."

I finished drawing on the face of someone who cherished their beauty and let Finn lead me from our room.

"Well, my love," Finn said as we stepped down into the dining room, "a bit of breakfast, and I'm sure we'll both feel better about last night."

A hint of smoke drifted out of the kitchen and lingered on the dining room ceiling, swirling through the spiderwebs. The woman behind the bar had red in her cheeks. I couldn't tell if the hue had been born of anger or tears.

Emmet sat alone at a table, facing the front door.

"We could ask the boy to bring food to our room," I whispered to Finn.

"I hear the kingless territories are beautiful this time of year," Finn said. "We could hop a boat and leave Ilbrea behind forever."

I nudged him in the ribs. "Do not tempt me, Finn, or you'll find yourself on a ship sailing south."

"We all must have dreams." Finn laughed.

Emmet turned toward the sound, glowering as though his glare could burn the world.

"You woke up cheery." I set my face in a pleasant grin, delighting as Emmet balled his hands into fists on the table. Cuts and bruises marked his knuckles. "A good night's sleep can fix the worst of woes. Though those"—I pointed to the fresh wounds—"could use a bit of care. Have you even bothered to wash them properly?"

"I'll order some food." Finn darted toward the bar.

"Of course, in a place like this, who knows how clean the water is?" I said. "We could find some strong liquor to pour on them. I'll have to check your stitches, too. I'm sure not all of them are still in place after you ran around like a chivving fool last night."

I waited for Emmet to say something. I wanted so badly for him to scream and rage so fresh anger could drown out the hurt in my chest.

"Do you want to die of infection?" I sat opposite Emmet, blocking his view of the door. "It's a terrible way to go, but I suppose it's your choice to make."

He inched his chair to the side to see around me.

I stood, leaning in toward him. "Answer me, Emmet."

"I've lived through far worse than this with no one to tend my wounds. I'm not concerned about scrapes and pulled stitches. A few more scars won't damage me. Now sit down and pretend to be a proper girl."

"A proper girl?" I perched on the edge of the table. "What makes a proper girl? Should I find myself a nice man to marry, stay out of the way while the men do the work?"

"I'm not fool enough to expect such a thing of my sister." Emmet laid his hands flat on the table. "But as you played whore and assassin last night and we still need to get back to the mountains alive, a smart girl would sit nicely and eat her chivving breakfast. The best we can hope for is no one taking notice of us."

I slid into the chair to Emmet's right, clearing his view of the door. "Is that what you were doing when you went out to pick a fight last night? Was that you not being noticed?"

"At least I kept my clothes in place."

Finn froze beside our table.

"I wish you hadn't waited so long to tell me shifting my skirts upsets you," I said. "From now on, I'll have to make a point of being naked as often as possible."

"Perhaps I will eat in the room." Finn backed away.

"Of course not." I pushed the chair opposite me out with my toe. "*Proper* people eat breakfast in the dining room, and we must appear *proper*."

"Right." Finn sank down into his chair, his ears turning pink as he glanced between Emmet and me. "I asked about breakfast. It might be a minute as there was an incident, which we can all smell, of course, but I've been promised there will be edible food available soon."

"Good," I said, "we can't have you going hungry after you so bravely helped Emmet last night. As a matter of fact, I think Emmet should thank you for saving him from himself."

"That's not necessary." Finn widened his eyes at me.

"Of course it is," I said. "You got hit in the face for him."

"You're the one who slapped him," Emmet growled.

"Oh, Finn didn't mind that," I laughed. "Matter of fact, I think he liked it. The kissing wasn't bad either."

"Ena!" Finn said at the same moment Emmet leapt to his feet and a bell rang outside.

Everyone in the tavern froze.

The ringing came closer, like whoever held the bell was running along the street.

"What does the bell mean?" I whispered.

Emmet glared at the front door, and Finn shook his head.

I crept toward the bar as the ringing came closer still. "What does the bell mean?" I whispered to the barkeep.

"Someone is searching town for the healer," the woman said. "They ring the bell to call her if she's not at home."

A sense of dread trickled into my stomach. If the healer were being called, then the time had come for the beast to die.

But soldiers traveled with their own healers.

That didn't make a difference nine years ago.

I dug my nails into my palms to keep my hands from shaking as the ringing moved past us.

Nantic's healer had been helping the soldiers when my mother died because their own healer had been drunk. Maybe this healer was drunk as well. Maybe the soldiers' healer had been confounded by the poison and wanted help. Maybe it wasn't a soldier who needed help but a woman gone into labor.

Movement in the dining room resumed as the ringing faded away.

I walked silently back to the table and took my seat. "Where's Liam?"

"Finding new horses," Emmet said.

"Probably best you didn't go with him. Who knows if you punched the stable boy last night?" My joy in needling Emmet had vanished.

We sat at the table, waiting for food, as the bell rang again, traveling back in the opposite direction.

I buried my hands in my pockets to hide their shaking. If the healer had been called to the camp and a tilk was looking for the healer as well, then it would be my fault their call for aid was going unanswered.

I could help. If someone was ill or bleeding, I should help. But offering my skills to strangers could too easily end in my being hanged.

The bell had long since faded away by the time the little boy brought us a tray of food.

"Thank you, kind sir." Finn's bow lacked it usual playful joy.

The boy didn't seem to notice.

We ate half-cooked potatoes and some sort of meat. The three of us kept glancing toward the door, searching for Liam.

"Does he have enough money for two horses?" I asked after a long while.

Emmet nodded.

A sound began in the distance, not the ringing, but a different noise. A steady booming like the beating of a massive drum.

I stood and crept toward the bar again. "What does that mean?"

"I've no idea." The woman furrowed her brow.

There was something in the booming that made me afraid, though I wasn't sure why.

"I'm going to look for Liam." Finn stood as I returned to the table.

"No, you're not," Emmet said.

"We need to leave," Finn said.

"And if he shows up a minute after you walk out?" I took Finn's arm. "You're the one who said we couldn't risk missing each other in the wild."

"Fine." Finn pinched his nose between his hands. "You get our packs, I'll make sure the horses are ready."

I shoved one more cold, crunchy potato into my mouth and headed for the stairs. Emmet's boots thumped against the wooden floor as he followed me.

"You don't think I can get my pack without a man toying with my breasts?" I asked as I hurried up the stairs.

"I have my own bags to gather."

We split ways as he ran two stairs at a time to the floor above. I shoved the few things Finn and I had used back into our packs, hoisted them onto my shoulders, and draped my cloak over my arm. The tightness of my bodice made it hard to breathe while bearing the extra weight.

The door to my room flung open before I could reach it.

"Ena." Liam stood in the doorway, sweat slicking his brow, worry marring his eyes.

"What's wrong?"

He lifted Finn's pack from my shoulder. "We have to go."

"Why?" I followed him down the stairs, lifting my skirt so I could run. "Liam, why?"

A dozen horrible possibilities raced through my mind.

Emmet ran down into the dining room the moment after we'd arrived.

The booming had grown louder in the few minutes we'd been gone.

Boom. Boom.

The women who had been in the booths were gone. The barkeep had disappeared as well.

"Where's Finn?" Liam asked.

"Getting our horses," I said as Liam shoved me out the door.

Two new horses waited for us, tied up outside The Downy Loft.

The booming carried from the main street, and voices sounded over its resonance.

"Emmet, take Ena. Ride to the edge of the woods." Liam yanked my pack from my shoulder, tying it onto the back of his horse.

"You take her," Emmet said. "I'll go with Finn."

"He's in the stable. He's right behind us," I said as Liam grabbed me around the waist, lifting me toward the horse. "We should—"

A familiar clink of metal carried from the north, a sound I had only heard a few times before and would grow to know too well by the end of my life.

I broke free from Liam's grip.

"It's not too late." Emmet met Liam's eyes.

Finn tore around the corner, the reins of our horses in his hands.

The main street fell silent.

"We are not mud!" a voice shouted. "We are not filth to be abused. Our women do not give birth for the pleasure of the Guilds. Our children are not born to be hoarded by the Sorcerers. Our lives are worth more than waiting to die at the hands of the golden demons."

I walked toward the shouted words. I had never heard such things spoken of in the open, let alone shouted for an entire town to hear.

The clinking came faster, surrounding us from the south and the west as well.

"We have spent years convincing ourselves we deserve to be punished, to have our children stolen by the Guilds. If we have suffered for so long, then the stars must have ordained our punishment."

A hand took mine, but didn't try to hold me back as I continued toward the voice.

"But the gods have seen fit to teach us how wrong we have been. Drason is dead. The monster who tormented us has been killed by the gods. They have brought illness among his men. The gods themselves have smiled upon us. They have set us free."

I reached the corner and looked down the main street.

A hundred people surrounded a wagon.

A man stood on top of the wagon, a club in one hand, a wide-stretched drum in the other. He tipped his face up to the sky. "What will you do with that freedom?"

4 6

The world seemed to slow as the man on the wagon looked back toward the crowd. The clinking stopped, and an arm wrapped around my waist, pulling me toward the side of a building.

"You have not been granted permission to gather," a voice shouted.

A sea of black had closed off both ends of the main street and come up behind us to block our path back to The Downy Loft.

"Disperse at once." A soldier stepped in front of his fellows. The golden star stitched onto the chest of his uniform glinted in the light.

"The gods have granted us freedom from you." The man on the wagon raised his arms toward the sky. "The beast Drason is dead. Leave our home."

"This town, all land in Ilbrea, is the property of the Guilds," the soldier said. "You dwell here at their pleasure."

"My family's been on our land for five generations," a woman shouted. "How can that not give us a claim to it?"

"There is no claim but the Guilds'." The soldier took another step forward.

The men behind him matched his movement.

"They claim our land, our blood, our children." The man on the wagon struck his drum with a boom that shook my ears. "The gods have freed us from the monster, and we will not lose that freedom."

"The Guilds will send a new commander," the soldier began. "Commander Drason's death—"

"Is a miracle," a young man shouted. "Chivving bastard got what he deserved."

A roar of approval rose from the tilk.

"Get out of our town!" a woman shouted.

"He deserved to die twenty times for what he stole from us." A girl reached down and picked up a clump of mud.

I watched her gather the dirt in her hand. Watched her throw the filth at the soldiers. I strained against the arm that held me, as though I could somehow outpace the flying mud and catch it before it struck its mark.

The scraping of swords clearing sheaths cut through the shouts of the mob.

"We will not allow you to steal the freedom the gods have granted us!" The man banged his drum. An arrow tipped with black feathers struck his chest before the boom had died.

A moment of calm, quicker than a heartbeat, stilled the street.

With a roar, the tilk charged toward the soldiers, carrying no weapons but their rage.

"No!" I fought against the arm that held me. "Stop them. You have to stop them!"

A clang of metal close by drew my gaze from the bloodshed on the street.

A pack of soldiers surged toward us, their weapons raised. Finn met them head on, parrying the blows of the pauns' weapons with his sword.

Bellowing, Emmet leapt into the fray, unsheathing the daggers at his hips.

"Stay here." Liam let go of me and ran toward the others, both hands raised.

Emmet ducked beneath a slicing sword, driving his blade into the throat of a soldier as Finn slashed through the belly of another.

"Get down!" Liam shouted.

Emmet and Finn dove, rolling away from the soldiers.

Liam opened his hands. A horde of stones hovered above his palms then shot toward the soldiers, striking a dozen of the beasts in the chest. But as the men fell, ten more stepped up behind them.

Emmet and Finn were already on their feet, diving back into the fight. Liam ran forward, drawing his own blade.

"Help me!" a voice shouted from the main street.

The soldiers had surrounded the tilk, cutting them down like they were no more than weeds. A boy broke free of the soldiers, clutching a wound in his side.

I started toward him, desperate to help stop the bleeding. An arrow struck him in the back of the neck. He didn't even scream as he fell toward the ground.

A hand grabbed my arm, whipping me around. A soldier with blood on his face seized my hair, flinging me into the mud as though I were no more than a doll. The fall knocked the air from my lungs, and mud blurred my vision.

He raised his sword, its point aimed at my gut.

"Please don't," I begged, my fingers fumbling as I reached for the blade hidden in my boot. "I'll do anything you want, just don't kill me."

The man smiled.

I closed my fingers around the hilt of my knife and yanked it free. It glinted in the sunlight for a split second before I drove the blade into the soldier's thigh.

He screamed, whether from pain or anger, I didn't know.

I pulled my knife free and aimed higher, stabbing just above his hip as his sword slashed for my neck.

I rolled to the side, wrenching my blade from his gut. Pain sliced through my back as I scrambled to my feet, my skirt heavy with mud.

A roar of rage came from behind me.

I set my teeth, determined not to scream as the soldier killed me. I spun to face him, but he was already dead with Emmet's dagger sticking out of his chest.

"Get up." Finn rode toward me, my horse beside him.

169

"But—"

"Now." Emmet shoved me toward my horse.

I fought against the weight of my mud-laden skirt, trying to get my foot into the stirrup.

Emmet lifted me, setting me stomach-first on the saddle as he had done when I was too little to climb up by myself.

By the time I had gotten astride, Liam and Finn were mounted on their horses beside me, facing the soldiers on the main street.

"We have to help them." The words tore at my throat.

"There's no one to help." Finn kicked his horse and rode away from the Massacre of Marten.

4 7

I wished for a storm during that horrible ride back to the mountains. I wished the sky would open and rain would wash away the blood and dirt that covered me. But the sky seemed as determined as I not to shed a tear.

I didn't speak in the hours it took to reach the forest, or stop to tend to the others' wounds or let them look after mine. Our injuries were not as dangerous as being out in the open.

Dusk had come by the time we reached the canopy of trees. The forest smelled of new life. No one had told the woods of the death that surrounded us.

"It's my fault." My voice crackled as I spoke. "It wasn't the gods who killed the beast, it was me. I started it, and now those people are dead."

A heavy burden beyond grief weighed on my entire being.

"It's not your fault." Emmet guided his horse to ride next to mine. "The soldiers didn't come to town seeking vengeance for a murder. They came to stop a man from spreading hope. Hope is more dangerous to the Guilds than we could ever be."

"It started with me," I said.

Finn passed me a waterskin. "Don't think like that. Unarmed men who run against swords—they're already dead. We saw them choose the end of their torment. They had a moment of freedom, one choice that was theirs alone. Many would be willing to die for that."

"More will before the end of it." Liam didn't look back. He kept riding in front of us, guiding us to safety in the mountains. "But we have to keep fighting. If we stop, there won't be any hope left at all."

48

Hope and freedom. The words pounded in my head for weeks, burning themselves into my memories of the Massacre of Marten. The blood washed away, the wounds healed, but hope and freedom—they carried me into the darkness that lay ahead.

MOUNTAIN AND ASH

BOOK TWO

To the ones who have been afraid.
You will destroy the darkness.

1

"Look at me." I took the child's face in my hands, blocking her view of everything but my eyes. "Look at me, love. Don't look at anything but me."

Her tear-filled gaze found my face.

"Good girl." I smiled.

A banging echoed from the street, but I couldn't tell the distance. The next house over, maybe the one beside that—my heart raced too fast for me to be sure.

"You are the bravest little girl in the world," I said. "Did you know that?"

She took a shuddering breath but didn't answer.

"You are so brave, you can do anything. I promise you can." I picked the child up. She weighed nothing in my arms. "Do you know what we do when we're brave?"

The girl looked over my shoulder toward the corner of the room.

"No, look at me." I balanced her on one hip, using my free hand to block the side of her vision. "When we are very brave, we look into the darkness, and we say, *I am not afraid.*"

A woman screamed in the distance.

The child gripped the front of my bodice in her little hands.

"We do not scream, we do not cry." I moved closer to the window. "We stare into the shadows and whisper, *I am not afraid.* Say it. Say, *I am not afraid.*"

Her lips wobbled as a fresh batch of tears glistened on her cheeks.

"Say, *I am not afraid.*" I slid the window open.

The crash of splintering wood carried from the street.

The child didn't look away from my eyes.

"Say, *I am not afraid.* Come on." I wiped the tears from her cheeks. "*I am not afraid.*"

"I am not afraid." Her voice cracked as she spoke with me. "I am not afraid."

"You are the bravest girl in the whole world," I whispered in her ear. "You will not scream when you're scared. Only whisper, *I am not afraid.*"

"I'm not afraid."

"Good girl." I held her out the window and let go.

She didn't scream as she fell, but a gasp came from the corner of the room.

"What have you done?" The woman cowering deep in the shadows shook with quiet sobs.

"What's best for your daughter," I said.

A bang came from close by, but the floor didn't rattle. The soldiers hadn't reached this house.

"Do you want to join her or not?" I said. "We're out of time. You have to choose."

"I…" The woman stepped toward the window. "I have five children. I have a home and a shop."

"May you find peace with the choice you've made." I lifted my skirt and climbed onto the windowsill.

"Please"—the woman grabbed my arm—"she's my baby."

"Not anymore. You have four children. Your baby does not exist."

"She needs me."

I took the mother's face in my hands as I had done with the child's. "She will never know fear again. She will not know pain or darkness. For the rest of your days, think of her in sunlit fields, running through bright spring flowers. You have given her endless peace, and she will always be thankful."

The woman fell to her knees, coughing through the sobs that wracked her chest.

"Remember her laugh and her smell." I turned toward the starless night. "Remember that it is still your duty to protect her." I stepped from the window ledge and plummeted into the darkness.

The warm wind lifted my hair from my neck as I fell. I exhaled all the breath in my body, bending my knees as I landed in the wide bed of hay.

"Ena?" Finn leapt up onto the front seat of the wagon. "Are you hurt?"

"Go." I scrambled through the hay, fighting my way to the front of the cart. "Is she under?"

"Didn't make a peep." Finn clicked the horse to walk. "I've seen grown men crumble at what that five-year-old faced silently."

"She's strong." I climbed into the seat beside Finn, brushing the hay from my skirt. "She'll make it."

"Of course she will. She's got us looking out for her." Finn steered the cart out of the alley behind the houses and onto the rut-covered thoroughfare of the tiny chivving town called Wilton.

"Halt." A soldier stepped in front of our cart.

"Whoa." Finn reined in the horse. "Happy to stop for you, sir. Is there something I can help you with?"

I clung to Finn, sliding my hand beneath his to coat to grip the hilt of his knife.

"We're searching for a sorcerer hidden in this village," the soldier said.

Four men in black uniforms stepped out of the shadows to surround our wagon.

"Sorcerer?" Finn said.

"Like magic?" I asked. "By the Guilds, you've got to find them. Are we safe? Is the sorcerer going to try to kill us?"

Two of the soldiers climbed into the back of our wagon.

"Do you really need to search our wagon?" Finn asked.

"Who cares about where they're searching?" I swatted Finn on the arm with my free hand. "We've got to get out of here. Unless the sorcerer is on the road. Oh, by the Guilds, do you know which way the sorcerer ran?"

The soldiers dug through the hay in our cart, tossing it out onto the dirt road.

"Hush, my love." Finn wrapped an arm around my waist.

"What if they're waiting in the dark?" Fat tears slid down my cheeks. "What if they're lurking by the road, waiting to attack? I told you I didn't want to leave home. My mother warned me of all the horrors that wait in the world."

"You're fine, my love." Finn wiped the tears from my cheeks. "I promise, I will not let any harm come to you." He brushed his lips against mine.

I pulled myself closer to him, letting my chest press against his as I parted his lips with my tongue.

"Hey." A soldier smacked his hand against our wagon.

"Sorry," Finn said.

"Sorry." I pulled away from him, tucking his blade under my skirt.

"The wagon's empty." A soldier hopped down from the back of the cart.

"Move on then."

The men stepped aside to let us pass.

"Thank you." Finn bowed his head. "Thank you for reminding me there are some things in Ilbrea that are worth protecting." He laid his hand on my thigh.

"You are such a wonderful man." I leaned in to kiss Finn again.

"Get out of here before we have to take you in for indecency." The soldier had a smirk on his face as he waved us on.

"Sorry about that." Finn clicked for the horse to walk. "Have a lovely evening."

I clung tightly to his arm as the wagon rattled forward, smiling at the soldiers and listening for the sniffles of a small child coming from below.

2

It was well into the night by the time we'd gotten far enough away from Wilton to risk sleep.

Finn stopped by a stand of trees, cooing lovingly to our horse as he unhooked her from the cart.

"You are such a good girl." Finn patted the horse. "Such a pretty, kind girl."

"Should I be jealous of the horse, my love?" I hopped down from my seat, taking one last look around before heading to the back of the wagon.

"Never," Finn said. "There is nothing in this world that comes close to my adoration of you."

"Careful, you might make a girl blush." I ran my fingers along the back of the cart, searching for the latch to our hidey hole.

I slipped the metal aside and lifted the three long boards that made up the center of the cart. The compartment below was wide enough to fit two adults if they lay side by side, and just deep enough to leave a few inches of space above a person's nose.

I held my breath as I squinted into the shadows. I'd come up with a hundred different things to say to comfort the child and a dozen apologies for having locked her in the dark.

The child lay in the corner, clinging to a folded up blanket.

"You're all right now," I whispered as I climbed into the compartment. "Let's get you someplace more comfortable to sleep."

The child didn't move.

"You can come out now." I knelt beside her.

She didn't stir.

My heart skittered against my ribs as I laid my fingers on the child's throat. She gave a shuddering sigh and nestled her face into the blanket.

"Oh, thank the gods." I ran my hands over my face.

"She all right?" Finn peered in from the back of the wagon.

178

"Sleeping." I lifted her, cradling her to my chest. "I wonder how long it took her to drift off."

"Hopefully not too long." Finn reached for the child.

Part of me didn't want to hand her over. I'd taken the girl from her mother. I should be the one clutching her in my arms until we could leave her someplace where she wasn't in any danger. But her safe haven was still very far away.

She would be passed from hand to hand a dozen times before she'd truly be free of the Guilds. Finn and I were just one tiny cog in the massive clockwork that would ferry her south to a place where she would never need to be afraid again.

"Come on." Finn held his arms higher. "The sooner we get to sleep, the happier I'll be."

"Try not to wake her."

It didn't take long for us to get the tent up, a circle of stones placed around us, and the bedrolls down. I tucked the child in, and she still didn't fuss. Finn and I slept on either side of her, each with a weapon tucked beneath our heads. I stared at the canvas of the tent for a long while, waiting for sleep to come. I drifted into darkness, clutching the stone pendant around my neck.

3

"Mama."

A voice scratched against the edges of my mind.

"Mama!"

I sat up, tossing my blanket aside and grabbing the hilt of my knife. Finn was already at the flap of the tent before I could look around.

"Where is she?" the little girl asked.

"Who?" I crouched beside her, ready to leap to my feet. "Did you see someone?"

She shook her head. "No, but I want to see mama."

"Oh, darling"—I slid my knife back under my blanket and out of sight—"I know it's hard, but you can't see your mother."

"There's no one outside." Finn ducked back into the tent, curls of early morning mist lapping at his heels.

"Good," I said. "So we're safe. We've got our blankets and our tent, and we're perfectly safe."

"Is mama safe?" The child wiped her tears away with her fists.

"What name do you like to be called?" I held my arms out to her.

"Riesa." She buried her face on my shoulder.

"Well, Riesa, I think your mother is very safe." I lifted her and mouthed *pack up* to Finn.

He ran his fingers through his bright red hair but didn't argue.

"Do you know that you are special?" I asked Riesa as I slid out of the tent.

She shook her head, her face still on my shoulder.

"Well, you are," I said. "You are very special. You are a precious gift. Have you ever heard of someone stealing coins?"

"Yes." Riesa wrapped her arms around my neck.

"Well, you are a massive, shiny gold coin, and there are some who are very greedy and want to steal you from your mother. And in Wilton, she didn't have a way to keep you safe from people who might see how precious you are and try to take you. So she did the best thing she could. She asked us to come and take care of her beloved daughter."

"To take me away?" Riesa asked.

"Yes." I paced by the side of the wagon. "Finn and I are going to take you somewhere you can be very safe. Where there aren't any greedy people who might try to steal you. You will be protected and have every chance to be happy."

"Is mama going to meet me there?"

I took a breath, making sure my voice would sound strong. "No, Riesa, your mother isn't going to meet you. She has to stay in Wilton with the rest of your family. But there are going to be people who will take very good care of you. I promise you will have someone to look after you."

"Are you going to look after me?" Riesa stared up into my face.

"For now I will."

"But you won't stay with me?"

The wrinkles on the child's forehead stole the air from my lungs.

"I can't, darling." I made myself smile. "I have other precious children I need to protect. But you will never be alone. Finn and I will stay with you, and then you'll go on an adventure with someone else. You'll get to see so much of the world, and the place you are going is absolutely beautiful."

"Have you been there?"

"No, I'm not special enough. You are a gold coin." I bopped her nose. "Me, I'm nothing more than bronze."

Riesa gave a teary-eyed grin.

"We're ready." Finn climbed up into the front of the cart.

"I don't want to go in the dark." Riesa clung to me.

"You don't have to." I grabbed the side of the cart, hoisting us both into the front.

Finn gave a longing look to the patch of grass where our tent had been before urging the horse on. The animal seemed as pleased as Finn to be awake.

"Where are we going?" Riesa asked.

"The mountains," I said. "They are a beautiful place, and nothing at all compared to the wonders of where you're going."

"Oh." Riesa played with the end of my braid. "I don't think you're bronze."

"What do you suppose she is then?" Finn barely disguised his laugh.

Riesa shrugged.

"Hmm. If I'm not bronze, am I a fish?" I asked.

Riesa shook her head.

"Am I a tree?"

A giggle trembled in the child's chest.

"Am I a stone?"

I could hear her laugh that time.

"Am I a bird?"

The game lasted until Riesa fell asleep, nestled in my arms.

We let her rest for as long we could.

Wilton was farther west in Ilbrea than I'd ever been, though still far enough from the shores of the Arion Sea not to allow me a hint of salty air. A tiny bit of me, the part that could laugh through playing guessing games with Riesa, wished we had gone a bit farther west—far enough to have reached the beaches covered with powdery sand—and seen the tall sailing ships heading off on great adventures.

The more reasonable part of me, the portion that wished Riesa had chosen to fall asleep in a position that made it easier to reach the knife hidden in my boot, wanted to get back to the safety of the eastern mountains as quickly as we could. Riesa's life had been entrusted to Finn and me. The weight of keeping the child alive was much heavier than the girl herself.

"I don't like being this far west," Finn said as though reading my thoughts. "It feels like I'm naked."

"Naked?" I asked. "I thought you liked being naked."

"I do enjoy not wearing clothes, but without the mountains surrounding me, I feel like a fool who's walked into a bear's den with nothing but his skin on."

"Better than without your skin on."

"Fair enough."

We slipped back into silence as we passed a line of wagons heading west, seven of them in a row, all piled high with goods.

I held Riesa tighter and nodded at the drivers of each of the carts.

One held barrels of frie, another wide crates, but most held goods someone cared enough about they'd covered the loads with waxed canvas to keep the rain off.

Riesa stirred, fidgeting in my arms.

"Shh, darling, it's just some carts," I said.

My fingers itched to reach for my blade. I needed to know what hid beneath the canvas.

Was it weapons paun soldiers would be using against common folk? Was it books being sent to a scribe in some distant territory? Was it people being transported far from home against their will?

"Where are we?" Riesa whispered.

"Still on the road," Finn said. "And half-starved. Ena, can we have a bit of food? Riesa's a growing girl, after all."

I shifted Riesa to sit between Finn and me.

"Just be sure you don't eat all the food we have, Finn," I said. "Riesa, did you know that Finn would eat this whole cart if we let him?"

The road began to curve around a wide stand of trees. A pair of birds shot out of the branches and circled up into the sky.

"Would you mind me eating the whole cart, Riesa?" Finn asked. "Ena always says no, but I think she's being unfair."

Riesa laughed.

She's young. Her life before the Black Bloods will only be a strange dream.

The copse of trees ended, opening up into a wide field covered in tents and wagons. Men in black uniforms moved between the tents. A few wore red healers robes, and five wore map maker green.

I lifted Riesa back onto my lap. "Would you like to hear a story?"

Riesa nodded.

"A long time ago, there was a brave little fish." My heart thundered against my ribs as our wagon drew level with the Guilds' camp. "The fish had always lived in a tiny little pond, but it wanted to know if there was more to the world beyond the tall grasses and bugs."

"Afternoon." Finn nodded to a soldier who stood next to the road, watching us pass with narrowed eyes.

"But a fish can only travel by water, so there was no way for our little fish to hop out of his pond."

We passed the cluster of green-clad map makers.

"So the fish decided to ask a bear for help."

"Stop," a man commanded.

I tightened my grip on Riesa and looked up to find a soldier standing in the middle of the road.

4

"Hello there," Finn said in a cheerful voice. It was one of the beauties of him. He could stare a demon in the eye and greet him with a foolish charm. "Lovely day to be out, though I can't imagine it's ever nice being packed so close together."

The soldier stared at Finn for a long moment. "What is your reason for travel?"

"How do you mean?" Finn said.

"Why are you on the road?" The soldier stepped closer to our horse.

"Well..." Finn said, "we've got the cart, and I thought the road would be better than hoping for good luck in the woods."

"I don't have time for—"

"I'm sorry, sir," I cut across the soldier. "This one gets a tad slow when he's tired, and last night was a bit long for us."

"What business do you have traveling on the Guilds' road?" the soldier said.

"Had to move some things. We're coming from Gint's End," Finn said.

Riesa tightened her grip on my wrist.

"Hush," I whispered in her ear. "You're safe with Finn and me."

"Move some things?" The soldier nodded and walked around to peer into the back of our empty wagon. "What things are you moving?"

Finn's pulse beat quickly in his neck, knocking against his skin like a clock running out of time. "It's a bit of a complicated story."

"Take Riesa." I lifted the child, setting her in Finn's lap.

"Ena, no." Riesa clung to the top of my bodice, pulling it down low enough to catch the soldiers' eyes.

"You are brave, my love." I smoothed Riesa's blond hair, which wasn't close enough to Finn's red or my current black to hope for an easy claim to kinship. "Could I speak to you on the ground, sir?" I looked to the soldier.

"Why?" the soldier said at the same moment Finn said, "I can."

"There are some things best kept away from tender ears." I leaned over the side of the cart toward the soldier, giving him a fine view of the top of my breasts. "Please, sir. I'll only take a moment of your time."

"This had better be good," the soldier said.

"I can speak to him, my love," Finn said.

"Riesa is better waiting with you." I hopped down from the cart. Being on the ground somehow made the reality of being surrounded by a hundred paun soldiers more real. "Do you mind?" I nodded to the shadow cast by one of the map maker's tents.

The soldier's jaw tensed.

"Please, sir." I tried to speak sweetly, like a girl who relied on her pretty face for survival. The kind of girl a soldier would have dreams about—the sort of lurid dreams he'd hold on to until morning when he could brag about them to his fellows.

The soldier's neck eased. "Be quick."

"Of course, sir." I tucked my chin and headed straight toward the shadows. "Thank you for your kindness."

More men dressed in black had noticed me. They peered around the tents to watch me.

"Out with it." The soldier crossed his arms as he studied me. He didn't bother unsheathing his sword or asking one of his fellows to stand with him.

You are surrounded, Ena Ryeland. You will not be a chivving fool.

"We're coming from my sister's, sir," I said. "The child is my niece."

"And you can't say that in front of her?"

"Not really," I said. "She thinks we're just on an adventure. You know, taking her through the country for some summer air. But the crops in Gint's End were river flooded already this summer. There's no hope for a decent harvest."

"I've heard." A crease formed between the soldier's eyebrows.

For a moment, I wondered if he had been one of us. If once, a long time ago, before he donned his black uniform and became one the Guilds' demons, he had been a little boy on a farm where a flood could be as terrifying as an enemy's blade.

"They've no hope of paying their harvest taxes," I said. "My sister will lose everything. She doesn't want her child to be there to see it. She asked me to come get the girl and take her Frason's Glenn where I live. Raise the child on my own until things get better for my sister. *If* they get better for my sister. I just haven't had the heart to tell Riesa yet."

The soldier looked to the wagon.

Riesa had curled herself into a tight ball in Finn's arms.

"That's quite a thing to ask of someone," the soldier said, "even a sister."

"I wanted to say no, but I couldn't," I said. "And she's a good girl. Once she's settled, I think she'll be fine."

"What about the man?" The soldier nodded toward Finn.

Finn whispered something in Riesa's ear.

Riesa huddled closer to him.

"A suitor," I said, "and one with a wagon and the means to leave Frason's Glenn for a few days."

"A lucky man," the soldier said.

"At least until I get the child safely home. I hope you won't mind my being honest with you, but he flips between chattering like a bird and utter silence. Either end drives me mad."

185

"Poor fellow." The soldier's gaze slid from my face to my chest and back up again. "It would be an awful thing to lose a creature like you."

Heat rushed to my cheeks. "You're too kind, and I'm not sure you're right."

"I am." He leaned close to me. His scent of horse, sweat, and mud slammed into my nose. "My company travels through Frason's Glenn quite often. Perhaps you might allow me a moment to convince you?"

"I work in the market square." I held my hand out to him. "Look for the girl selling the best pastries in the city."

He took my fingers and pressed his lips to the back of my hand. "I look forward to seeing you in Frason's Glenn."

"And I look forward to expressing my appreciation of your generosity." I gave him the sort of smile I had learned in my brief time in Frason's Glenn. A hint of a joyful promise mixed with a joke no man could hope to understand.

"Safe travels." He stepped out of my way.

I kept my pace even as I strode back to the wagon. If I had been a sorcerer, I could have torched the camp with a snap of my fingers. If I had been a trueborn Black Blood, I could have shot a hailstorm of stones from my hands and cut the paun down where they stood.

But I was neither. So I smiled nicely as I let the men watch me walk, and gave a wave to the soldier who'd let us pass as Finn urged the horse to trot us away.

He kept Riesa in his lap, one arm wrapped around her as though he were shielding her from an oncoming storm.

I waited to speak until the road had twisted us out of sight. "We're safe, Riesa. You don't have to hide."

"I think she does." Finn loosened his grip just enough to allow me a glimpse of Riesa's hands.

Bright red sparks leapt between the girl's fingers. "I'm sorry."

"Don't be sorry, darling." I covered her hands with mine. Heat peppered my palms. "There is no shame in magic. Where you're going, you won't ever have to worry about how special you are."

Riesa hiccupped. Tears spilled down her cheeks.

"I need you to breathe for me." I scooted close to Finn and transferred Riesa onto my lap. Her sparks stung my arms, and Finn's shirt bore black flecks where he'd been scorched. "We're going to take nice, big breaths and calm down. I told you I would keep you safe, and didn't I keep my promise?"

"Yes." Riesa buried her soggy face on my shoulder.

"And I will keep protecting you." I held her tight. "All I need for you to do is take nice, deep breaths."

It took an hour for the red sparks to die entirely away. We didn't speak to anyone else the rest of that day and all through the next. I told stories until I couldn't remember the proper endings and sang silly songs until I thought I'd go mad. I kept Riesa jabbering and laughing, careful to stop her from noticing how Finn kept scanning the sides of the road for people waiting to attack, and how I kept shuddering, hoping it was a man who sold the best pastries in Frason's Glenn.

5

When I was a little girl in Harane, I believed in magic. In wishing on stars, fairies that danced in the moonlight, and beautiful spells made to save the world.

I learned very young that the sort of magic in stories does not exist.

I didn't know until much later that the sort of magic that does survive in Ilbrea is both more wondrous than fairies and more terrifying than Death's own axe.

Still, there was something about witnessing magic that always took me a little off guard. Like I was a character who had fallen into the wrong story. My tale was that of an orphan from a small village. A girl who was destined to watch everyone around her die until it was her turn for the grave.

Somehow, I had ended up in a saga of bravery, murder, and magic.

I had spent the last four months ferrying sorci children away from the hands of the Guilds. Taking them from Ilbrea to the woods of the eastern mountains, where they would meet the sort of Black Bloods that did not venture into open territory.

Finn and I would hand over the children we'd gathered and never see them again. They would become a part of a different tale, venturing to a faraway, hidden realm where magic reigned above all.

My part in Riesa's story ended before her tale truly began.

I would do as I had with all the other children. Give her a hug, tell her to be brave, and pray to the stars she would find a happier place than Ilbrea.

Repeating my role in the prologue of someone else's story did not make playing the part any easier.

6

"I don't want to be blindfolded." Riesa squirmed away from me.

"Believe me, you do." Finn leaned against a tree.

"I'll make you a deal." I knelt in front Riesa. "We'll tie your blindfold on, and I will hold you tight the whole time you have to wear it. I won't let go of you, so you'll know how safe you are."

Riesa pursed her lips at me and wrinkled her forehead. She'd been in a sour mood since we'd left the horse and cart with a friend of Finn's.

"Riesa," I said, "I know it's been a difficult few days, but I promise it will be worth the hardship when your journey is done. You can be brave, I'm sure of it."

"I can be brave." Riesa nodded.

"Of course you can." Finn pulled a cloth from his pocket.

I lifted Riesa onto my hip.

She gave a giant sigh and scrunched her eyes closed.

Finn tied the cloth around her eyes and leaned back against the tree to take off his boots.

"What happens after this?" Riesa asked.

"You're going to go with some of our friends who will take you farther along on your adventure." I twisted to turn Riesa's closed eyes away from Finn.

"But what happens to you?" Riesa asked.

"We go home and take a hot bath and eat awful food." Finn pulled off his shirt, tossing it onto his boots and socks.

"Where is home?"

"Far away where the Guilds can't find us." I looked up to the canopy of leaves as Finn dropped his pants.

"And I'm not allowed to come with you?" Riesa asked.

"I'm afraid not, darling," I said. "See, where we live, there aren't any other children. If you lived with us, you would get very bored and lonely."

Finn's footsteps crackled across last season's debris on the forest floor. I looked down from the leaves in time to see his bright white, naked bottom disappear through the trees.

"I wouldn't be lonely." Riesa nestled her head onto my shoulder. "I'd be with you."

A tiny pang shook what little was left of my heart. "But I wouldn't be there all the time. There are other people I have to help." I slid the cloth from around Riesa's eyes. "It'll be better for you to stay where the same person will be there to feed you breakfast every morning."

Riesa made no move to scramble down from my arms. "When I'm older, can I come and be with you?"

"Maybe." I held her tight even as I kept my gaze fixed on the woods where Finn had disappeared. "You'll have to see what you want to do with your life by the time you're all grown up. You might have fallen in love with a merman by then and decided to live your whole life at sea."

Riesa giggled. "I am not a fish."

"Too right you're not."

She played with the end of my black braid.

I strained my ears for any sign of Finn.

A small creature rustled through the rotting leaves trapped under a bush. A bird chirped high above.

"Will we have a new horse for traveling?" Riesa asked.

"I don't know. But I'm sure you're going to have a grand time either way."

A branch cracked in front us.

"Hop down, darling." I pried Riesa's arms from around my neck and set her down behind me. I pulled the knife from my boot, savoring the weight of the blade in my hand.

"Ena"—Riesa clung to the back of my skirt—"are soldiers coming?"

"Of course not. We're perfectly safe," I said, though the racing of my heart screamed I was lying. "I have a horrible fear of rabbits, so I like to be ready to defend myself."

"Rabbits?" Riesa stepped in front of me, staring up with a furrowed brow. "What's frightening about rabbits?"

A crackling came from closer by and farther east than the first sound.

"It's the way their noses twitch," I said. "I've never managed to figure out what they're smelling that I can't."

Riesa scrunched up her whole face. "Probably rabbit food."

"I think you're right. You may have just cured my fear of rabbits."

A bright smile lit Riesa face. "That's good! I'm—"

"Another tiny one." A woman stepped out of the trees. She was small, barely breaking five feet, though she might have managed to look larger if the man behind her weren't a good head taller than Finn.

"They keep showing magic younger," the giant man said.

"Honestly, it makes it easier on us." Finn stepped out from behind them, a thin blanket wrapped around his waist. "Easier to ferry someone small."

"Finn, why did you take off your pants?" Riesa asked.

"The seams were too itchy." Finn shrugged. "Needed to give my legs a break."

Riesa giggled for a moment before looking to the tall man. She backed up to lean against my legs.

189

"Come on." I scooted her far enough away to be able to tuck my knife back into my boot. "Let's meet your new friends."

The tall man knelt down. "What's your name?"

"Riesa." She kept her cheek pressed to my leg as we walked toward him.

"Well, Riesa, I'm like you." The man circled his finger along the ground.

Riesa knelt, peering at the dirt.

A sprout of green appeared, poking up through the brown. Before Riesa had managed to crawl all the way to the man's side, a tiny blue flower had blossomed.

"We're going to take you south," the woman said. "We're going to stay in the woods and move very quietly. Do you think you can manage that?"

Riesa nodded.

"Good girl." The woman stroked Riesa's hair. "We should get going, then."

"But..." Riesa turned to me, tears sparkling in her eyes.

"Don't cry, little one." I bent down and kissed the top of Riesa's head. "You are the bravest little girl, and you are heading off on an amazing adventure."

"I am not afraid." Riesa tipped her chin up.

"Don't forget that," Finn said.

"Goodbye, Riesa." I pressed my face into a careful smile. "May you always enjoy your freedom."

She clung to me for a moment before reaching for the woman's hand.

"Up we go." The woman lifted Riesa onto her hip, and the three of them disappeared through the trees.

Finn and I stood quietly for a long while.

"Put your chivving pants back on."

"Really?" Finn nudged me with his elbow. "I thought you liked me better naked."

"Don't be a fool." I couldn't tear my gaze from where Riesa had disappeared. It seemed too awful for a sane person to consider sending a child off with strangers.

Her mother sent her away with you.

"She's going to be all right, isn't she?" I asked.

"Sure." Finn tossed his cloth at my feet. "Henry and Jess are old guard in the Brien Clan. They've been running children south since I was young. They're two of the best."

"Then why haven't I seen them before?"

"Don't know. Lots of work to be done during the warm months. My pants are back on."

"Good." I turned to face him as he raised his arms to pull on his shirt.

The dark outline of a mountain range marked the right side of his ribcage. I wanted to touch the image, not for the sake of being near Finn's skin, just to promise myself the mountains were where I belonged.

"It does get easier." Finn tugged on his boots. "The sorci saving runs aren't my favorite activity, either. I'd rather be sticking a blade between a soldier's ribs than smiling and being nice to one. But we're helping, Ena. We're getting these children beyond the reach of the Sorcerers Guild. We're saving them from a lifetime trapped in the Lady Sorcerer's stone tower."

"It still feels awful to take a child from their home and then abandon them to people I don't know." I untied the end of my braid. Bits of my hair had already fallen loose from

Riesa's fidgeting with it. "I know we're just one part of the beast that saves the sorcis, but doesn't Riesa deserve more than to be tossed from hand to hand?"

Finn wrapped his arm around my waist. "We're doing good work. Let that be enough."

I leaned my forehead against Finn's shoulder. "Right. You're right. We are doing important work, and we are quite excellent at getting the chivving thing done."

"Chivving true." Finn tipped my chin up and kissed my forehead. "Just do me a favor. Next time we have to separate, let me be the one to walk away with the soldier."

"Why?" I picked up my pack. The weight seemed heavier than it had on our walk into the woods.

"If he had suspected anything and decided to murder you—"

"Then I'd have begged for mercy until I got a chance to stab him in the throat." I shooed Finn east.

The mountain sloped up in front us. She would make us climb to find the riches she hid.

"I can see where a proper throat stabbing would come in handy. But what about when word got around camp that you'd shoved a blade into a soldier's windpipe?"

"I suppose I would have to deal with being the toast of the camp." I took a few quick steps to walk by Finn's side. "Just imagine how proud Cati would be of her favorite student."

"And what would I do when Liam and Emmet came to murder me for letting you put yourself in danger?"

An ember of anger flared to life in my stomach. "The two of them aren't allowed to have a chivving opinion about anything I chivving well do."

"Liam is the trueborn in charge of our camp, and Emmet is your brother."

An involuntary growl rumbled in my throat.

Finn held up both hands. "You want nothing to do with them, fine. That wouldn't stop them from coming for my hide if anything happened to you. And quite frankly, either one of them angry is bad enough without having to worry about their anger being rightfully directed at me."

"I'm running sorcis with you." I lifted my skirt to leap over a thin stream that cut through the slope. The sunlight caught the water as it danced downhill, leaving specks of gold shimmering on the surface. "They've got to accept there are risks involved. And if the slitches don't like it, they can very well go marching on a bed of hot coals."

"I appreciate your imaginative punishments."

"I've had time to ponder."

Finn stopped beside a tree bearing little white berries. He sniffed carefully before pulling a berry free.

"Don't even think of eating those."

Finn frowned.

"Trust me," I said. "It's not worth the fever and chills you'll get."

"To distract you from your vengeance on members of my clan? I might chance it."

"I'm not dragging your trembling body through the mountains." I knocked the berry from his hand. "Now get a move on before I decide to tell Neil you couldn't stop talking about how much you missed his root stew while we were traveling."

"You'd condemn the whole camp to eating sludge just to punish me?" Finn clutched his chest.

"Definitely. So don't test me."

"Fine." Finn let his hand fall, all hint of pretense gone. "Just be careful, Ena. Believing in a cause doesn't mean you have to take unnecessary risks for it. You're amazing with the sorcis—their families, too—but I'm better with a blade. If someone is going to have to try and stab a soldier, it should be me."

"No." I started climbing again, grateful for the distraction of the burning in my legs. "If you had died, Riesa and I would have been stuck. I couldn't hand her to the Brien without you. I couldn't take the way home without you. Like it or not, you are more valuable than I am."

"That's a chivving lie, and you know it." Finn took my elbow, steering me north. "This way if you want to get back to camp."

"See." I winked at him. "You, Finn, are irreplaceable."

7

We chatted off and on as we climbed through the mountains, Finn mostly asking if every new plant he spotted could be eaten. He nabbed some sour grass as we passed through a wide clearing, a few mushrooms not too far above a waterfall that tossed enough mist into the air to dampen my clothes, and a handful of leaves, I'd only have chosen if starving, from a twisted tree growing out of a cliff face.

The mountains had bloomed with their full summer bounty. Birds chattered, animals scurried, and it seemed hard to believe there could be anything wrong in the world.

When darkness came, we both pulled our lae stones from our pockets, trusting their blue light to lead us until we found a nice place to rest. I didn't miss the tent we'd left behind with the horse and wagon. Now that we were in the mountains, the rocky overhang we chose suited me perfectly.

Finn carefully surrounded us with dark rocks as I laid down our bedrolls.

"We'll be back to camp by tomorrow afternoon." Finn stretched out under his blanket.

"A bath will be nice." I untied my boots and laid my knife at the top of my bed.

"Are we taking bets on how long we get to stay before they send us back out again?"

"Do you think they'll send us together?" I crawled under my own blanket. "They might give you another partner."

"I don't think so," Finn yawned. "There are so few people willing to put up with me."

"I do tolerate you rather well." I wrapped my fingers around my pendant and closed my eyes.

"You're a gift from the gods, Ena Ryeland."

I don't think I finished laughing at Finn's words before drifting into darkness.

Crack.

The sound yanked me from sleep.

Crack.

It came from right in front of our camp.

I sprang to my feet, my knife gripped in my hand.

"Finn," I whispered his name, hoping it was him I was hearing moving through the dark.

"I hear it." Finn's voice came from right beside me.

I glanced down.

He crouched on top of his blanket, a blade in each hand.

I swallowed my instinct to call out or reach for my lae stone.

A scuffling and a rustling carried from the right.

A growl came a moment later.

My heart slowed a little.

Not a soldier. A soldier wouldn't make a sound like that.

Another crack came, and then another.

"Do you see it?" Finn whispered.

I squinted into the darkness. "No."

A sighing growl sounded like it was coming from just beyond the trees.

I stepped forward, to the very edge of the stone-marked barrier.

A thing moved in the shadows, taller than any person and broader than two men put together.

The beast opened its mouth and gave a snarl that sent my heart racing.

Still gripping his knives, Finn slid an arm in front of me, pushing me away from the stones.

Thump, thump. Thump, thump.

The ground shook as the beast charged forward.

I caught a glimpse of massive claws as the monster swiped for us. It struck our boundary, sending a shimmering blue light blasting out into the night.

The beast roared and swatted again.

I tried to get a clearer view of the monster, but again the light flashed, dazzling my eyes and leaving bright spots in my vision, blocking out the details of the massive beast.

Over and over, the monster battered our protection. I caught a glimpse of it between every flash.

Sharp teeth in a mouth big enough to bite my head clean off. Dark fur matted with something that smelled like old blood. But not on the head. The monster's scalp had barely any fur. Thick scars on black flesh left ridges down its muzzle.

"What is it?" I whispered.

"A monster."

The thing roared, the strength of its rage shaking the leaves above us. It slammed its head into the barrier over and over again, sending flashes of bright blue into the night.

"What do we do?" I asked.

Finn stepped forward so his toes nearly touched the rocks.

The beast growled and gnashed its teeth.

"Hope it's gone by morning," Finn said. "Pray to the gods there aren't any paun in the woods for the light to attract."

"Wonderful."

The beast gave a bellow that sounded almost human.

"Are you sure it's real?" I asked.

"I mean…" Finn tipped his head to the side as the beast attacked our protection. "How do you mean?"

"Not a ghost or figment of our imagination?"

I stood on top of my blankets, feeling like a child woken by a nightmare as Finn slowly stepped side to side, squinting at the monster.

The beast roared.

"Don't know what it is." Finn sat down on his bedroll. "Don't honestly know if it matters."

"You're a Black Blood. You have the mountain running through your veins. Shouldn't you know every creature that roams this range?"

"Yes. I should also know every plant I'm allowed to eat, and we've seen how well I do on that end."

"Shouldn't you have heard of a great beast roaming the woods?" I sat with my back pressed to the rock wall.

"That's the problem with being a Black Blood. There are so many myths and legends, it's hard to keep them all straight."

The beast bellowed and moved to the cliff face on the side of our shell of safety. Stones clattered to the ground as the monster tore at the rock.

"You've got the myths that really are myths"—Finn raised his voice to speak over the scratching and clacking—"and the myths that are real. And the legends that are no better than fairy stories, and the legends that are about my great uncle, which my family swears are true."

I laughed and dared to set my knife down by my side.

"And that's just in the Duwead Clan," Finn said. "There are five Black Blood clans, and I promise you not all of our stories line up. This is probably Narek the Bumbling or some such nonsense."

"What?" I laughed louder this time.

Narek snorted his displeasure.

"Sure"—Finn scooted back to sit beside me—"flitted around on his lover and got turned into a great smelly beast so no one would let him into their bed. Poor Narek here is probably only trying to get in because he finds you so unbelievably attractive."

"Finn!" I swatted his arm.

"You're right," Finn sighed, "it's me the cursed bloke is after. Should I let him down with kind words, or just tell him right off I know better than to mess around with chivving curses?"

We kept laughing and chatting until the beast lost interest and left.

Finn and I drifted in and out of sleep, both leaning against the stone wall, knives by our sides.

I was glad Riesa wasn't with us. I didn't have enough left inside me to bear protecting an innocent against the horrors of the world.

Better to laugh at the monster in the dark than to face how truly terrifying the beast is.

8

I held my hand up to one of the scratch marks in the stone. The gouge cut three inches deep and was longer than my forearm. "Do you think he'll know what it was?"

I couldn't bring myself to say Liam's name, even if he was the person I wished were standing beside me as I ran my fingers through the gouges.

"We can hope." Finn passed me my pack. "I don't want to sound as though I'm a Black Blood who fears the mountains, but I'd rather not have that beast come sneaking up on me in the forest."

"Narek might steal you away," I said in a hushed voice. "Keep you in his cave forever."

"Don't test the gods." Finn started climbing the rock face.

I checked the knife tucked in my boot before following him.

In the daylight, all fears began to seem foolish.

Birds soared overhead, taunting us with how easy it was for them to fly from place to place.

I didn't envy their wings, not really. Not as I once had.

My arms were strong enough to help me scale the side of the cliff, and my balance good enough that I beat Finn to the top. My legs had ample strength to carry me wherever I wanted to go, even if they did burn in protest as the soft forest floor gave way to scree and the ground began shifting beneath our feet with every step.

Wings are delicate things. They can be broken. Then the bliss the birds sing of in their love ballads is gone. Having something as wonderful as wings only gives a person something precious to lose. In a world where the Guilds reign, everything you treasure can be ripped away from you. Everything you love is a weakness the paun will use to shatter you.

Better to have normal, sturdy limbs than beautiful wings. Better not to have anything it would break your heart to lose.

We'd already passed midday by the time we reached the high wall of stone even I wouldn't have had a chance of climbing. Sheer and more than a hundred feet tall, any normal traveler would have seen the cliff and tried to find a way around.

While I waited for Finn to woo the mountain, I amused myself by trying to think through a path up the cliff face. I couldn't do it.

I leaned against a tree fifty feet away as Finn paced back and forth in front of the rock, trailing his fingers along the cracks.

I loosened the cord on the pendant around my neck and retied it so the stone hung below my bodice and out of sight. The wind bit my skin, freezing the place where the pendant had lain. I felt naked without the stone resting above my heart. But I would rather have strolled through camp actually naked than let people see me wearing it.

Finn cursed at the rocks.

"Did you lose your way, Black Blood?" I shaded my eyes to stare at the rock face. "Did we end up at the wrong cliff?"

"No." Finn smacked his hands against the stone. "Though sometimes getting through this entrance is as bad as convincing my grandmother to give me a fourth helping of pie. I know she'll give in eventually, she just likes to make me beg for it."

"I think I'd like your grandmother."

"Stay with us until winter and you'll meet her." Finn stepped back and stared up at the top of the rock wall. "Though I will warn you, I get vicious when asked to share her pie."

"Warning taken."

Finn froze, like he had heard a noise that didn't exist to my ears. He looked to his right and beckoned me forward.

I crept slowly toward him as he slunk to his right. Before I'd made it thirty feet, most of Finn had disappeared. The only part of him I could see was his left arm reaching out through a crack in the stone I would swear to the gods and stars had not existed a moment before.

I took Finn's hand and slipped sideways into the slit in the rock. The world went black.

The birds' singing, the warmth of the sunlight, the smell of the forest, all vanished in an instant.

I took a deep breath, letting the scent of the stone soothe the instinct that shouted I would be crushed by the darkness.

The scent held more than just stone, though. The air was damp. I could smell the moisture on the rock, but it wasn't a stale thing like a puddle in a cave. The air was alive, as the mountain was alive.

I took a second breath. My body stopped panicking at the sudden loss of the outside world, and a strange feeling began. A pull right in the center of my chest. An ache that penetrated the bone above my heart as though the mountain itself had tied a string to me and would drag me through the darkness, whether I liked it or not.

And I wanted to follow the pull.

There was a longing deep inside me that wanted nothing more than to follow wherever that magic led, even if it meant walking into my own destruction.

After a third breath, I managed to shove the longing down. Push it aside with all the other things I was smart enough to know I couldn't bear to feel.

I squeezed Finn's hand.

He pulled his lae stone from his pocket. The walls were close together this time, like the mountain had barely bothered to give us safe passage.

I waited for a nod from Finn before daring to pull out my own light.

Neither Finn nor I spoke as we wound our way through the tunnel. The ground beneath our feet was clear with not a pebble in sight to trip us. The dark stone of the walls was packed close together, leaving scarcely enough room for Finn's shoulders to pass.

I trailed my fingers along the walls as we traveled. Most of the stone was cool, as you'd expect from a rock kept out of the sunlight, but every now and then, there would be a warm patch, like a vein running to the heart of the mountain.

Magic.

I wanted to ask if I was right, but there was only one person I knew who was a true-born Black Blood and really understood the way the magic of the mountain worked. Strong as my curiosity was, it couldn't make me go to him.

The tunnel opened into a wider space. The chamber's walls looked like they'd been cracked by time, and debris lay along the sides of our pristine path.

A gentle, blue light glowed off to one side, barely peeking out from behind a boulder.

I squinted at the shadows, trying to see where the light might be coming from. Something white lay on the dark ground. I took a step toward the glow.

Finn grabbed my arm, keeping me on the path. His red scruff glinted in the light of his lae stone as he shook his head. He kept his hand on my arm as we passed the boulder.

There was white on the far side, too.

Human bones lay on the ground, as though whoever had died while trapped in the mountain's embrace had been intentionally stripped of everything else.

I bit my lips together and stared at the back of Finn's head until we entered a tunnel three times as wide as the first. I walked by Finn's side as the tunnel twisted around itself, as though avoiding some unseen barrier.

A rumble of rushing water joined the sounds of our footsteps.

My heart leapt into my throat. I slid my arm from Finn's grip and held his hand as the sound became louder.

I have come too far to drown in a tunnel.

I gritted my teeth, sending the thought up to the gods and stars or down to the root of the mountain itself. I didn't really care where my plea went, so long as I didn't die buried deep beneath the ground.

Finn held my hand tighter as flecks of moisture filled the air. He stopped short and took a shuddering breath before holding his light close to the ground.

A foot-wide stretch of stone continued uninterrupted in front of us, but on either side, the rock disappeared. A torrent of water rushed beneath our feet with enough strength to wash away an entire village.

Shaking out his shoulders, Finn gave himself a nod before stepping onto the stone bridge.

The ground was slick beneath my feet. I clung to Finn's hand just as much for his safety as for mine. He was born a Black Blood—the strength of the mountains ran through his veins. The mountain itself recognized him as kin and gave him passage through the darkness. But I didn't know if the mercy of the mountain would go so far as to save Finn's neck should he slide into the racing water.

The torrent raged under us for a long time, reaching wider than any river I'd ever seen. Then suddenly, it was over, and the ground was solid rock once more.

Finn looked back at me, giving me a strained smile and a kiss on the cheek before striding quickly through the darkness.

As it always was when traveling beneath the mountains, just when I thought we would never see the outside world again, the tunnel narrowed and twisted, and then we were back out in the forest as though nothing strange had happened.

The sun sinking in the west gave away how long we'd been underground. The terrain was different as well. Tall trees surrounded us. Some even grew from the rock face we'd stepped out of, though I'm not really sure how they survived the vertical stone.

Finn let go of my hand and took a long moment studying the trees before heading north.

"You know," Finn said once the rock face was out of sight, "I'd find being swallowed by the mountain to be a much more pleasant experience if I knew there was decent food waiting on the other side."

"Don't be too harsh with Neil," I said. "You and I are lucky. We get to run off on adventures and save children from terrible fates. Poor Neil waits for us all to come home. Hungry, tired, sore, cranky, and he's got to feed the lot of us. I don't envy Neil."

"I never said I *envied* Neil, or that I thought I could do a better job. I just wish that whatever brave soul had Neil's job would also have some talent when it came to food."

I laughed louder and harder than I had since we'd left the camp more than a week before. A feeling of being home settled into my stomach, easing my fears and lifting a terrible burden from my shoulders.

We both walked more quickly in the last hour before we arrived at the camp.

I tucked my hands behind my back as we passed between two of the giant boulders that made up our boundary, steeling myself against the warmth that filled my chest as we stepped through the magic that protected us.

"Finn?" a man shouted from high up in a tree.

"Indeed it is." Finn bowed to the unseen person. "We have returned from yet another triumphant journey."

I balled my hands into tight fits, pushing away the heat that felt like a terrible hunger had taken over my soul.

"Good to hear." A man dropped from the branches of a tree, keeping an arrow nocked in his bow even as he fell. "Not all who've come back have fared so well."

"What do you mean?" I asked.

"We lost one." The man, Patrick I think was his name, put away his arrow and scratched his beard. "And another party is late in coming back."

"Were they all sorci runs?" Finn asked.

"Don't know." Patrick shook his head. "I try to keep my nose out of who's running what into the open. I have enough to worry about just with the people who are coming back."

"Right," Finn said. "Thanks for keeping watch."

I wanted to ask who had been lost and whose party was late coming home, but there was something in the way Finn strode toward the center of camp that kept me silent.

I'd only been with the Black Bloods since the spring. They'd accepted me as one of their own to a point, but there were rules and funny little ways of doing things I still didn't understand.

If it had been Emmet who'd been hurt, Patrick would have told me. I was new, but the Black Bloods nigh on worshiped my brother, and they all knew we were related.

Cati and Marta hadn't left camp all summer, so it couldn't be either of them.

Liam.

Panic pinched my lungs, making my head swim.

It's not him.

Liam was the trueborn Black Blood who commanded our camp. Patrick would have said if it was Liam. I resisted the urge to pull out the pendant I'd tucked into my bodice.

He's fine, Ena. They are all fine.

I stayed close enough to tread on Finn's heels as we took the path to camp. The scent of food and clatter of pans were the first signs of life.

A wide tent with all the flaps tied open came into view. A few hearty souls had already lined up to be fed. Neil glared at them as he stirred the stewpot, which was large enough for me to sit in.

Finn sidestepped so I could walk next to him. "It doesn't smell too bad. But I suppose I still shouldn't get my hopes up."

There was an unnatural tension beneath his words.

I opened my mouth to say something funny back but couldn't manage it. Not even to see Finn smile.

We entered a wide clearing surrounded by benches and chairs carved out of wood. A few of the seats were filled. A woman stitching in a patch of sunlight, an older man flipping through papers, a younger man staring into the shadows.

The largest chair, with a great bird carved into the back, sat empty.

There were more signs of life on the far side of the clearing, down the path that led to the tents where all of us lived. Voices carried from within the canvases. A man worked his way down the row, placing lae stones in each of the lanterns that hung along the trail.

The largest sleeping tent waited at the end of the path. My small tent sat right beside it. I wished I could go and hide inside my tiny fabric home, but someone had died. Delaying finding out who it was wouldn't keep the people I cared about any safer.

9

"Liam," Finn called out when we reached his tent.

I raised my fist and banged on the tent pole.

"Liam, are you in there?" Finn asked.

"Finn." Liam's voice came from behind us.

The pinching let go of my lungs.

"They told me you were back," Liam said. "How did it go?"

I turned to look at him. His skin shone from sweat. The edges of his hair had curled from it. He'd rolled up the sleeves of his shirt, and the beginnings of a giant bruise marked his arm.

"Well," Finn said. "The tracker was dead right with the location of the girl. Mother gave her to us, but the rest of the family stayed behind."

Liam dragged one hand along his jaw. The other rested on the hilt of the sword attached to his belt.

"It's probably for the best," Liam said. "The fewer we move, the fewer chances of being caught."

"Who was caught?" I asked.

Liam barely glanced at me before shifting his gaze to the palm of his hand. "Roland."

"Roland?" Finn asked. "What was he doing?"

"We needed supplies," Liam said. "His source turned him in. Mary barely made it back."

Roland and Mary, I could put faces to both of their names, but I'd never had a proper conversation with either.

I was grateful for it. My gratitude brought bile to my throat.

"Are we going back out to make sure the slitch never betrays our people again?" Finn asked.

"Emmet's already gone." Liam glanced at me again before looking to Finn. "He left two days ago."

"Good," Finn said. "Some need to be taught the consequences of betrayal."

"What party is late returning?" I asked.

"Sorci run," Liam said. "Kian and Erin—they left before you did. They should have been back two days ago."

Kian and Erin I knew. They liked to sit together at night in the clearing. Kian was fond of ale, and Erin loved to laugh loud enough for the whole camp to hear.

"Maybe they just got held up," I said. "We nearly had to lie low for a bit. They could be hiding in a barn somewhere, waiting the paun out."

"Why would you have to lie low?" Liam turned to me, actually keeping his gaze on me for more than a second.

"The soldiers were searching for the girl," I said. "We got away from them and met a pack of paun on the road."

"Shocking thing is," Finn said, "we didn't have to use our knives once."

"Come in, Finn." Liam stepped around me to his tent. "I want to talk through what you saw."

Finn moved to follow him.

"Have fun, boys," I said. "I'm going to try and figure out how eyes are meant to work. Since I clearly didn't see anything."

"Ena," Finn began.

Liam cut across him. "I just need Finn for now. I'll have things to speak to you about later, Ena."

I gave Liam a low curtsy. "I am honored, trueborn Liam."

Finn's eyes widened at me as Liam went into his tent.

I winked at Finn and ducked into my own tent.

The blankets were still carefully folded just as I had left them days before. A bag with the few extra bits of clothing I owned sat on the foot of the bed, safe from the ground's moisture. My comb lay on the little table made of a cut log, and the shorter log I refused to ever sit on waited beside it.

That was the funny thing about the Black Bloods' encampment—it was all permanently impermanent.

The tent was the closest thing to a home I'd had since Harane. It was my space, but only for now. When the cold came, it would be packed up, and all the people from camp would retreat to Lygan Hall, a place I still had trouble believing existed.

We would be gone, but life in Ilbrea would go on. Sorci children would be caught, and we wouldn't be there to stop it. The army would move, and we wouldn't know.

I didn't blame the Black Bloods, or even Liam, for fleeing from the snow. If we tried to stay in tents in the mountains, we'd all freeze to death well before the spring thaw. But the thought of Riesa being taken by soldiers with swords and shipped off to live in a stone tower because I was keeping warm in some mythical hall, made me so angry I thought I'd be sick on the dirt floor of my tent.

"Don't be a chivving fool, Ena." I dug through my sack of clothes, grabbed my comb, and left my tent.

The low rumble of Finn and Liam talking carried through the canvas as I strode past Liam's tent. Part of me wanted to smack the canvas and tell Liam he could chivving well cut his toes off if he thought I would be running around helping him if he didn't want to speak to me after.

But Liam was right to only want to speak to Finn.

Finn had been making sorci runs for three summers. Finn was a Black Blood. Finn was familiar with the maps. Finn understood things lowly little me wasn't supposed to know about. Finn hadn't kissed Liam and had his bleeding heart handed straight back to him.

I tried to slow my steps as I walked down the narrow path that led to the cave.

Humid air filled my nose before I reached the mountainside. The scent of dried flowers drifted out of the dark.

"Hello," I called into the shadows. I waited a moment before calling out again. "Anyone in there?"

I peered into the cave. Dim blue light left shadows drifting through the space, but there was no one inside.

"Thank the gods."

I dug into the back of one of the stone niches and fished out my soap, setting it beside the bath before sitting to unlace my boots. Dirt from the forest clung to my hands and dusted my bare legs above the ankles of my boots. I set my knife beside my shoes and stood to finish undressing.

The hot water of the bath wasn't enough to melt my anger away, but it did help to smooth out the edges. Scrubbing the filth from under my nails made me want to scratch Liam's eyes out just a little less.

I washed my hair and was just beginning to make a list in my mind of what I'd need to gather to give it another coat of black dye when a voice called from the entrance.

"Hello? Ena, are you in there?"

I ducked my head under the water.

You can't hold your breath forever.

I let my head drift back up above the surface.

"Ena?" A stone clacked under Marta's foot as she peered around the corner. "Ena?"

"Marta." I pushed my hair away from my face. "Come to have a bath?"

"Come to find you, more like." Marta's gaze swept through the corners before she stepped all the way into the cave. The light played across her pale blond hair as she walked to the side of the bath, carefully checking the floor before sitting beside me. "How are you?"

"Fine." I scrubbed my already clean arms. "Had a nice, healthy trek through the mountains and it's almost supper time. What more could a girl ask for?"

"Hmm." Marta pursed her lips, making her dimples disappear. "I could make you a list if you like. It would start with big, soft bed. There would be fine chamb and a proper dinner table included as well."

"And here I thought you liked ruling over our camp." I flicked water at her.

"I rule over nothing." Marta brushed the droplets off her skirt. "I just like to be useful wherever I can. Helping in Liam's work, even if my part is only making sure the lot of you don't fall into chaos and starve, makes me feel needed. I like it."

"You are most definitely needed. I don't know what we'd do without you."

"Good." Marta smiled. "How did it go out there?"

"Didn't you already get a full report from Liam?" I almost kept the edge out of my voice.

"A report from Liam doesn't tell me how you're actually doing. You went out into Ilbrea and had more than one run in with soldiers."

"It's not as though I never had to deal with them before I joined the Black Bloods. Honestly, the lot we met were downright gentlemanly."

"Ena, I'm being serious. When I found out about Roland and Mary, I was worried about you."

"Marta, it's kind of you." I took her hand. "But I promise, I was fine."

"It wasn't just me who was worried."

I climbed out of the tub, not caring as water sloshed toward Marta's skirt, and headed for the pile of folded cloths in the corner. It was probably Marta who made sure there were always some there waiting for us. I don't know who else in camp would have thought through such comforts.

"Emmet was worried sick, Ena." Marta snatched a cloth from the pile and handed it to me.

"Should I thank him for his concern?" I dried my arms so hard, my skin turned pink. "Perhaps a nice, heartfelt letter?"

"When he and Liam found out what had happened, it looked like both of them had seen a ghost." Marta beat me to my comb and handed that to me as well. "Losing Roland was a huge blow, Emmet was angry about that, but the fear was for you."

"And I'm sure he's taking that fear out on whatever cact of a demon spawn—"

"Ena."

"—betrayed Roland and Mary."

"Yes." Marta handed me my clean shift. "If I'm being totally honest, someone is going to die at Emmet's hands before he returns to camp. And whoever the poor fool is won't be leaving this world in an easy manner."

"Do you pity the one who caused Roland's death?" I grabbed my skirt before Marta reached for it.

"No, but I do wish your brother hadn't torn out of this camp as though he were off to slay the world."

"Then Liam should have stopped him."

"Liam sent him."

My hands shook as I threaded the laces on the front of my bodice.

Marta batted my fingers away to do the work herself.

"No one can bring Roland back," Marta said. "No one but the gods can save the fool who betrayed us from Emmet's wrath."

"No one can stop the Guilds from tormenting the tilk or the winter from coming. Don't you think I know that?"

Marta tied off my laces and started combing the tips of my hair. "There is precious little we can control in this world. I can't give the Black Bloods a homeland that will always be safe from the Guilds, but I can make sure our fighters don't have to worry about a warm bed or supplies. You can't bring Roland back, but you could stop resenting the fact that people worry about you. That your brother worries about you."

"Don't." I snatched the comb from her hand. "It's bigger than that. It's so much more than Emmet thinking I'm incapable of keeping myself alive. I'm grateful to have you as a friend, but my problems with him are too large for even you to fix."

"He's your brother, Ena. Doesn't that count for something?"

"It used to."

Marta didn't say anything else while I gathered my things and left the cave.

I wasn't fool enough to think she was done with me.

10

The fire crackled merrily in the corner of the clearing.

Neil stood beside the barrel, doling out ale to anyone brave enough to withstand his withering glare. He hadn't brought a pot of stew or a basket of bread from the cook tent. I suspected that was how you could tell what sort of a mood Neil was in. If he brought food, he was vaguely unhappy. If he didn't bring food, he was miserable and wanted all of us to be miserable with him.

Of course, I had no way of proving I was right, since Neil glowered no matter the occasion.

Two fiddle players had brought their instruments to the clearing. They took turns playing and drinking, so a cheerful tune always filled the air.

Did they play the night they found out Roland had died?

Probably.

I watched the shadows shift as people drifted in and out of conversation. The night was still young, and no one had settled into true frivolity.

"Going to lurk like a lump?" Cati sat beside me. The knife tucked in her boot glinted in the light of the lae stones.

"I just climbed a mountain for two days." I raised my mug to her. "I think I've earned a bit of sitting."

"I don't buy it." Cati took my mug from me, stealing a long drink of the ale I'd braved Neil to claim. "You love scrambling up and down the mountains. Holding you in one place for too long might wear you down, but not climbing."

"Does it matter?" I took my mug back and had a sip. I was grateful they managed to get any ale at all to camp, but I still couldn't help but wrinkle my nose at the perfumed taste of the brew.

"Sure it does," Cati said. "I'm to take you to the training field tomorrow. If you're ill or injured, I might have to go easy on you."

"Never." I laughed. It was a small laugh, but at least it was sincerely felt.

The fiddlers seemed to have decided they were sufficiently lubricated to begin playing in earnest. They set their cups down and began a dancing song. Within the first chorus, four couples had moved to the center of the clearing.

"I'm not Marta, Ena," Cati said. "I don't have the fortitude to sit here all night trying to slowly wheedle out what's wrong with you. If you're not ill and you're not injured, why under the stars are you sitting all alone?"

Finn appeared from the shadows, yanking Case off a bench and weaving him into the dance.

"I shouldn't be here." I ran my hands over my face. "I should be down in Ilbrea, helping. I should be ferrying the sorci children south. I should be doing something."

"Ahh." Cati drank from my mug again. "The first time Liam forbade me to leave camp, I almost murdered him. I had a sword in my hand and everything. I was going to run my blade straight through his gut then stomp down the mountain to kill as many paun soldiers as I could manage."

"Then why is he still alive?"

"Because"—Cati downed the rest of my ale—"I'm not the hero of our fight. No one is going to sing songs about me. I am one tiny piece in the little clockwork that is trying to keep the Guilds from gaining enough power to destroy my people's home while the bastards decimate everything in their wake. And my little cog is most useful teaching the other little cogs how not to die in a fight. Each of us has to do our part if we want any good to come out of all our work, and sadly enough, not all our parts involve getting to kill the chivving bastards."

"But what's my cog meant to do? Because sitting in this clearing doesn't seem to be helping anyone."

"Your part of the clockwork isn't in use at the moment." Cati knocked her shoulder into mine. "So have a bit of fun, forget about the world, get some rest. Then, when it's time to do your bit, you'll be ready. You'll have a recent memory of something in this chivving world that's actually worth fighting for. Now get some more ale and dance hard enough that you'll hate me on the training field tomorrow."

I didn't move.

"Go." Cati pressed my empty mug into my hand. "Be merry, whether you like it or not."

I swallowed my sigh as I stood and headed for the line of brave Black Bloods waiting for ale.

A shout rose from center of the clearing. Finn and Case bounded through the growing number of dancers, lifting and twirling each other with an enthusiasm to make Cati proud.

Join them, Ena. Abandon everything and jump into the dance. Just keep going until you're too tired to remember the outside world exists.

"Back again?" Neil grumbled at me when I reached the front of the line.

"Yes." I held my mug out. "My drink was pilfered, and I wanted to talk to you anyway. I'm going to go foraging tomorrow. If you like, I can keep an eye out for anything special you might be looking for."

In the light of the lae stones and fire, I could almost make out a gleam in Neil's eyes.

"Of course, if there isn't anything you need—"

"I'll think on it." Neil filled my mug to the brim. "Can't say I really do, but I'd be a fool not to spend a moment thinking on it."

"I'll stop by in the morning and see if you've come up with anything." I hid my smile as I turned back toward the clearing.

"What do you want more for, you lout?" Neil railed behind me. "Is your aim to be a no good drunk? Because I won't have any part in it."

I laughed through my sip of ale.

"Maybe I don't need any more," Pierce said as I crossed behind the end of the line. "Is he actually in that bad a mood?"

"That depends," I said.

"All I want is a drink, Neil!" The shout came from the front of the line.

"On what?" Pierce looked at me, his forehead creased in something between concern and amusement.

I considered Pierce for a moment. He was on runs into Ilbrea as often as I was, so I'd only spoken to him a few times. I didn't know him well enough to be sure what he considered a funny joke.

"On whether he likes you or not." I sipped my fragrant ale. "I didn't have a problem."

"You're cut off," Neil shouted. "For the rest of the season. If you want a drink, march to Lygan Hall."

"I don't think I need another ale tonight." Pierce stepped out of line.

"You're drunk on power!"

I peeked around to watch one of the older guards shouting at Neil.

"Probably for the best," I said. "You can have mine if you like. I don't really enjoy it."

"No." Pierce shook his head, his pale blond hair shimmering in the faint blue light. "Doesn't seem worth it now. Would you like to dance instead? Then I don't have to worry about anybody's wrath."

"I…" My mouth had gone suddenly dry. I winced as I took another sip of the ale.

"Can I have that, Ena?" Cati appeared by my side. "I'm thirsty, and I don't think I could speak to Neil without punching him."

"Sure," I said after she snatched my mug away.

The fiddlers struck up a new tune.

Finn whooped his joy.

"You two should dance," Cati said. "It'll keep you out of the way if a brawl comes."

"Shall we?" Pierce offered his hand.

Cati winked at me and sipped my hard won ale.

"Sure."

Pierce took my hand, leading me toward the other dancers. His skin felt foreign against mine. His calluses lined up in places I didn't recognize.

He twirled me under his arm and led me into the circle with the other couples.

Finn and Case had given up on moving with the rest of the pack and danced in the center all by themselves.

I forgot to worry about following Pierce's steps as I watched their pure joy.

Finn tipped his head back, laughing to the sky. Case joined in as they tripped over the dance steps in their mirth.

By the time I realized I should be paying attention to where I was going, my body had already adjusted to Pierce's hold on my waist. He spun me faster, and I leaned back against his hand, letting him take all my weight.

His smile creased the corners of his bright blue eyes. Their color, along with his light hair, made my heart forget to beat for a moment. It was like a ghost from the life I'd left behind had somehow found his way to the mountains.

Pierce spun me under his arm, and the world disappeared in a blur of shadows and glowing blue lights.

I hadn't tied my hair back, so the black sheet of it floated out around me.

Pierce laughed as he spun me back in and lifted me in a circle.

I liked the sound of his laugh. It was easy and low, as though joy somehow came naturally to him.

The song ended, and Pierce held me tight, one arm still around my waist, as I caught my breath.

In the quiet between songs, Marta's voice rose above the rest of the chatter. "Now, Neil, no one is trying to steal ale from anyone. It's for everybody. If you don't want to work the tap, you can just go to bed."

The musicians started back up, playing louder than before as Neil began shouting.

"Again?" Pierce's blond eyebrows rose up his forehead.

"Best not to risk being caught in that mess," I said.

Pierce laughed as he swept me into the new dance.

I glanced toward the center of the clearing, wanting to see if Finn had noticed the sound of Pierce's laugh.

Finn and Case had disappeared.

The new dance had a series of jumps scattered through the pattern. Pierce's hands shifted from my back to my waist as he lifted me so easily I might as well have been flying.

"Just a bunch of ungrateful—"

Neil's shout startled me. I missed a step. Before I could even begin falling, Pierce had clutched me to him, shifting us out of the path of the dancers.

"Are you all right?" Pierce asked.

"I work my fingers to the bone to feed you lot," Neil shouted. "Does that not earn me a bit of respect?"

"I'm fine," I said.

"It's not about respect," the older guard said. "I do my job. Why can't you mange yours?"

"Everyone here is grateful for everyone else's work." Marta held her hands up between the two men, like a dimpled doll trying to hold back two angry hounds.

"Should I do something?" Pierce asked.

"I don't know." I took his hand, drawing him farther away from the dancers, whose weaving pattern had broken down as more of them stopped to watch Marta and the men.

The music broke on a foul note.

I looked to the bench where the fiddlers perched, but they were both staring at the path to the sleeping tents.

Liam stood at the edge of the light, behind his chair with the carved bird.

"Oh no," Pierce breathed as Liam strode across the clearing toward the fight.

I kept Pierce's hand in mine as I backed away from Liam's path.

Liam didn't even glance at me. He kept his dark gaze fixed on Marta.

"We should go." I turned to hop up and over a bench. A bit of me expected Pierce to let go of my hand. He didn't.

He kept our palms pressed together, even as he placed his free hand on the back of my waist, like he was ushering someone important into the woods.

"The last thing I need is one more man trying to fix a problem started by male egos!" Marta shouted.

Pierce and I laughed together as we ran farther into the woods.

11

We didn't stop running until the lights of the clearing had faded and the only sounds were the leaves rustling in the trees. The wind picked up, lifting my hair off my neck.

I sighed and slowed my steps.

"That happy to be away from the clearing?" Pierce matched his pace to mine.

"Yes," I said. "Maybe. It would be nice to watch sweet Marta give every man in this camp what for."

"Do all of us deserve it?" Pierce stopped to look at me.

"Probably." I ran my fingers through my hair, getting the stray strands away from my face.

"Do I?" Pierce lifted my hand away from my hair.

"I don't know. I'm not sure I know you well enough to have a clear view of what you might have done to anger Marta."

"I don't argue over ale." Pierce kissed the back of my hand. "And I was raised to be kind to ladies."

"Ladies?" I tipped my head back to stare up at the sky. Stars shone around the glimmer of the moon. "What about the women who don't really qualify for that title?"

"But you do qualify." Pierce stepped closer, halving the space between us. "You're brave enough to go into Ilbrea to save sorci children. You're beautiful enough to turn every head in camp. You're hard enough to have survived what life has given you, and you're a fine dancer besides."

"You seem to know a lot more about me than I know about you."

"You're fascinating. I'm not." Pierce smiled. The corners of his eyes lifted, and creases appeared. Not lines of anger or worry, just little hints of joy.

My fingers buzzed as I reached up to touch their texture.

He turned my other hand, kissing my palm. "We can head back if you like, cut around the great ale brawl."

I didn't want to head back. I didn't want to see Liam and wonder if he was ever going to truly look at me again.

"No." I closed the gap between us, tipping my chin up.

He let go of my hand and wrapped his arms around my waist.

Slowly, he lowered his mouth, brushing his lips against mine.

A tiny flare of something like hunger bubbled up from my spine as I leaned closer to him, letting my chest graze his.

He kissed me in earnest.

He'd shaved not long ago. There was no stubble on his chin to rake across my skin.

I wrapped my arms around his neck, teasing his lips with my tongue. I couldn't taste him beyond the fragrance the ale had left on both of us.

He held me closer, pinning his hips against mine, as his left hand roamed up my side, his thumb caressing the side of my breast.

I wound my fingers through his hair, kissing him more deeply, letting what my body craved drown out the aching of my heart.

He lifted me, carrying me to a wide tree. The bark cracked as my back pressed against it.

His lips roamed, kissing down my neck and back up to my ear. I took his face in my hands, guiding his mouth back to mine as he undid the tie at the top of my bodice.

He trailed his lips back down my neck, kissing the soft spot beside my collar bone.

The thrumming in my body extinguished all thought beyond wanting to be touched.

He pulled the laces of my bodice loose, lowering the neck of my shift as he kissed the top of my breasts.

I shuddered a gasp as he ran his hand up the side of my thigh, lifting the hem of my skirt.

"Ena," he whispered my name.

"Ena." A voice boomed through the trees.

12

Pierce straightened up, clutching me to his side as though protecting me from the noise.

A shape appeared between the trees, the shadow of the first and last person I wanted to see.

"Who's there?" Pierce pulled his knife from his belt.

My heart froze and shattered as Liam stepped into a beam of moonlight.

"Liam?" Pierce squinted at him. "You nearly gave me a heart attack."

"You shouldn't be out here, Ena." Liam's gaze drifted over me, from my falling off top to my mussed up hair, before locking onto Pierce. "She doesn't know the mountains well enough to be wandering in the dark."

"I won't leave her alone," Pierce said. "I can see her safely back to camp."

"I'll take care of her," Liam said. "We still haven't talked about her last sorci run."

"Right." Pierce eased his hold on my waist. "Can't afford to wait. Lives could be in danger." He kissed my temple. "I'll see you tomorrow, Ena."

The chill of the night air sent a shiver up my spine as Pierce turned and walked back toward camp.

"What do you want to know?" I tucked my hands behind my back, resisting the urge to retie my bodice.

Liam glowered up at the trees.

"Oh," I said, "you didn't want to know anything? You just wanted to follow me to be sure poor, incompetent little Ena didn't get lost in the scary woods?"

"The girl," Liam said, "you should have left her in the compartment below the wagon."

"Left her terrified and alone in that tiny space? No." I stepped closer to him. "I didn't know enough about her magic to risk her panicking out of my sight a moment longer than necessary. Was I supposed to leave her back there and wait for the cart to catch fire or for lightning to strike? Better to keep her where I could see what I was facing.

"That and I'm not a heartless slitch who wants to snatch a little girl from her mother

213

only to leave her locked up and terrified. That's what the Guilds would do, and I am not like them."

"And what if Finn hadn't been able to hide her magic when the soldiers stopped you?" Liam looked down at his hands.

"Then I guess we would have had to fight."

"Against a hundred soldiers?"

"I didn't say we would've survived."

"You can't do that, Ena." He finally looked at me. His dark eyes held none of the warmth I longed for. "You have to be careful."

"Careful?" I crossed my arms over my chest. It made my unfastened bodice look worse.

"Yes." Liam stepped away from me. "I am trying to protect you."

"Like you protect Emmet?" I walked straight up to him, stopping with barely a foot of air between us. "Do you think he's being safe right now? Do you think he's carefully doing everything he can to avoid a fight?"

"That's different."

"Because I'm a sad little girl who might get lost in the woods at night? Do you think I'm incapable of accomplishing the tasks you've given me? Do you think I'm dumb or weak—"

"I'm trying to keep you alive!"

"Why should my chivving life matter more than Emmet's or Roland's?"

Liam scrubbed his hands over his face.

"I am not a child. I am not innocent. I don't need you coming into the woods to make sure I can find my own chivving tent."

"Ena—"

"If I die, it's my life that's ended. Let my death be my own concern. It wouldn't matter to you any more than losing anyone else in this camp. Go find someone else to protect."

I turned and strode off through the trees.

"Ena," Liam called after me, "we're not done here."

"Find me tomorrow."

I didn't look back. I couldn't manage to mask my hurt any longer.

The fire in the clearing had been put out for the night, leaving only the blue glow of the lae stones.

I searched the shadows, hoping Pierce might be waiting for me.

There was no one.

I wanted a mug of ale, but the barrel had been rolled away.

"Just sleep, Ena." I forced myself down the path to my tent. I dragged my fingers through my hair, picking out the bits of bark caught in the strands.

A few people lingered outside their tents, whispering in gleefully hushed voices.

I should have retied my bodice, or at least cared as gossipy Nessa spotted me out of the corner of her eye and her face lit up like the King himself had died.

I ducked into my tent and tied the flaps shut behind me, like a thin bit of fabric could somehow serve as a barricade between the night and me.

My comb waited on the stump table. I sat on my bed and brushed my hair until there wasn't a hint of forest left behind. I placed my knife under my pillow and my boots under my bed, then folded my bodice and skirt so cleanly, no one could have guessed they'd been mussed in the woods.

When I had nothing left to occupy myself, I lay down, clutching the stone pendant, wondering what would have happened if Pierce had kissed low enough to find it.

I lay there for hours, waiting for exhaustion to claim me.

I never heard Liam return to his tent.

13

There are some people you love so deeply they remake your entire soul.

It is not a beautiful process. It is painful and permanent.

I remember the girl I was before. I think like her. My face is the same as hers. But my soul is different.

Where the wind through the trees once called to me, now I long only for him. His scent is what fills me, and I would follow it to the end of the world.

14

"Better." Cati planted the tip of her staff on the ground and reached down to help me up. "But you've got to learn to attack, not just defend."

"Right." I took Cati's hand and jumped to my feet, doing my best to pretend I couldn't feel the stinging pain behind my knees where her staff had pummeled me. "I'll try and attack you and see how much faster I end up in the dirt."

"Survival isn't meant to be easy." Cati handed me my staff. "If learning to fight wasn't hard, the Guilds would have overrun the mountains last century."

"Then I will take the pain, knowing the paun feel it as well."

Before Cati could respond, I twirled my staff over my head, bringing one end down toward her shoulder.

Cati swiped her own staff through the air, knocking my blow toward the ground.

I slackened my grip on my staff and let the momentum of her strike kick the bottom of my weapon toward me. I grabbed the staff with my free hand, spinning it toward Cati's neck.

She ducked just in time.

Before I could tighten my grip on my weapon, a blow caught me right above my shoulder blades, and I was on the ground again.

I pushed myself to my knees and spat the dirt from my mouth.

Clapping carried from across the field. Finn strode toward me, his sword sheathed at his side. "Nicely done!"

"She'd still be dead." Cati held my staff out to me.

"But she'd have gone down in a blaze of glory I could recount around the fire in my old age," Finn said.

"All of my wishes granted." I brushed the filth from my face.

"You've improved so much." Finn clapped me on the shoulder, barely avoiding my growing bruise. "I think it must run in your bloodline. The Ryelands are a deadly crew."

"Am I a deadly Ryeland? Or am I just a child who gets tattled on for doing her job?" I glared at Finn. His mirth melted away. "Is there even a reason for me to learn how to fight if my place is just to sit prettily in the wagon? In fact, I think the Black Bloods and all Ilbrea would be better served if I sat by the fire sewing. I can make dolls that look like women. You can take one on your next sorci run. Prop it up in the front of the wagon to sit beside you. No one will know the difference. Don't worry, if you don't like how the pretty doll handles herself, you can just tell Liam."

Cati let out a low whistle and lifted the staff from my grip.

"Cati"—Finn looked to her—"I think you've hit Ena on the head a bit too hard. She seems to be confusing me with a chivving slitch instead of the partner she's run through Ilbrea with more than once."

"If you didn't tell Liam about my keeping Riesa out of that chivving trap and speaking to the soldiers, who did?" The heat of anger rushed through my chest. I enjoyed the way it filled me.

"Of course I told him what happened." Finn stepped close to me, speaking in a low voice. "He's the commander of the camp. I also told him what a brilliant job you did, and that I would be pleased to keep making sorci runs with you, because I stand a better chance of getting those poor children out with you by my side."

A tiny hole punctured my chest, deflating my anger.

"If Liam's giving you a hard time, it's got nothing to do with me," Finn said. "But sort yourself out quick. We're two pairs of runners down, so it won't be long before they send us out again."

He strode away, back toward the ring where the Black Bloods practiced their sword fighting.

"Damn," I breathed.

"Go," Cati said. "I've bruised you enough for today anyway."

"Thanks." I ran after Finn.

He stopped before I reached him.

"I…" I bit my lips together, wishing Lily had spent more time teaching me the proper way to apologize. "Did you tell Liam about the beast we saw?"

"I did." Finn turned to face me. "He said he'd send a message to Lygan Hall, see if any of the elders or story keepers had heard of such an animal."

"Right." I took Finn's hand and pressed his palm to my cheek. "I'm sorry. I shouldn't have snapped at you. I just—"

"Came home last night with your top untied?" The glimmer of mirth returned to Finn's eyes. "Had your fun interrupted and got to see Liam's better side all at once?"

"More or less."

Finn kissed my forehead. "Like it or not, you Ryelands have the same chivving temper. At least when you're angry, I only have to worry about my feelings getting hurt instead of needing to protect a small village from destruction."

"Give it time." I poked Finn in the ribs. "I'm getting better at fighting. Next warm season, maybe I'll go take out my wrath on Ilara."

"I believe it of you. The destruction of Ilbrea's mighty capital at the hands of a beautiful raven. Just remember who's fighting on your side, little bird."

He wiped a streak of dirt off my chin and headed to the boundary of the sword ring where Case waited with his blade drawn.

Case's face lit up as Finn approached. I wished I could hear the words they exchanged before facing off to fight.

The sun beat down on my shoulders, warming my skin as I listened to the clanging of their blades. They fought with such fury, it seemed as though they were deadly foes.

Do your work, Ena.

The words echoed through my head. The voice sounded like Lily, or at least, the way I remembered Lily speaking.

I didn't remember the sound of my parents' voices. They had been gone too long. Soon enough, time would steal Lily's voice from me, too.

The need to move and climb burned through my legs. I had to get out, away from the clanging weapons and people of the camp.

I ran all the way back to my tent, but the effort didn't lessen my need to flee.

The bag I'd carried with me from Harane waited under my bed. I snatched it up and darted back out of the tent as though the canvas had caught fire.

Nessa stood on the path between the tents, leaning toward Marta, whispering in her ear. Glee filled Nessa's face when she spotted me.

I bolted through the trees, heading south.

"Ena," Marta's call followed me, but I didn't look back.

I ran and ran, not bothering to loop around to see if Neil wanted me to search for anything in the woods. I didn't care about having an excuse to escape the camp. I just needed to get out.

My breath tore at my throat and stung my lungs.

I ran harder, leaping over fallen logs, not pausing as tree branches ripped the skin on my arms.

I didn't stop until I reached the boulders that marked the edge of camp.

Even gasping for breath couldn't mask the longing that filled my chest as I neared the great rocks. No moss or filth marred their surface, as though the stones were meant to be solitary and perfect, untouchable by the realities of mortal life.

I rested my palms on a boulder, letting the ache that pulled at the place just above my heart tear through every other horrible thing I didn't want to feel.

The cool surface of the stone welcomed me. I pressed my forehead to the rock, savoring the knowledge that my touch couldn't warm it.

The mountain had made the boulder. The mountain didn't care about my fate. I was nothing to the magic that lived deep below the ground.

A knot pressed on my throat as the pull in my chest threatened to shatter me.

I let out a long breath and stepped away from the stone and beyond the spell that protected us all.

15

I had fled from camp often enough to know the mountainside well. My feet carried me to the mushrooms Neil always asked me to gather and to the tiny clearing where the roots I wanted to grind into tea grew.

My path had become so familiar to me, I began untying my bodice before I even heard the faint rumble of the waterfall.

The trees changed as I drew near the river's narrow banks. The moisture allowed the trunks to grow thicker and the leaves broader. The scent of damp earth hung heavy in the air, and the ground gave gently under my feet.

The waterfall itself wasn't massive, only twenty feet high. But time had created a deep basin at the bottom. I'd found my secret swimming place a month before when I'd dodged out of camp after Emmet had a fit about my coming back from a sorci run with a bandage on my arm.

I sat on a wide rock to untie my boots. The sun caught the mist off the falls, sending little rainbows dancing in the air. I slipped out of my clothes, using the heft of my knife and bag to protect them from being stolen by the wind.

A breeze played across my naked body, not caring which bits of me were bruised or scarred. The stone pendant hung low around my neck, its warmth a constant comfort against my skin.

A bird swooped through the sky, chirping his joy at the freedom he'd found.

"Fly on, little bird," I whispered to the wind.

I didn't let myself run to the side of the waterfall. I picked my way through the rocks and moss, careful not to let any thorns pierce my bare feet.

A stone cliff reached to the top of the falls. Time had created enough cracks that scaling the twenty feet didn't hold enough difficulty to make my arms ache. I wished the cliff were higher—fifty or a hundred feet, enough to make my head swim and my body burn from the effort.

I pushed myself up onto the ledge and rolled onto my back, shutting my eyes against the bright sunlight.

The rocks beneath me were warm.

"Does the mountain want the boulders it presses magic through to be cold?" I ran my fingers along the rock. "Is it only some stones in the mountains that hold magic, or is it all of them?"

The bird swooped overhead again but didn't offer an answer.

Liam would know. Liam could tell me all about the magic that surrounded me.

I leapt to my feet and ran along the rumbling riverbank.

Not far from the ledge, the path of the water twisted, arcing north. I stopped at the curve, turned, and sprinted back toward the falls.

The thin mist coming up from the cascading water blocked my view of the pool below. The drop could have been a thousand feet, or an infinite plunge into a vast darkness. There was no way for me to be sure the earth hadn't opened up to swallow me whole.

I took a breath as I reached the edge of the cliff and leapt into the open air.

The rush of falling, the way my stomach surged up into my lungs, pummeled every other feeling from my body before I hit the cold water below.

The river surrounded me. The rumbling of the falling water was the only sound left in the world. My limbs were weightless, nothing more than bits of debris to be pushed around at the current's will.

First, the cold stole the soreness of my limbs, numbing the aches and bruises. My feet grazed the rocks at the bottom of the river as the current carried me away from the world.

I didn't fight it.

Then, the calm of the nothing began lifting away other, deeper hurts. Pains I was too terrified to even begin to name. A bit of anger drifted downstream. The jagged edges of a longing that could never be fulfilled were smoothed.

A vice wrapped around my ribs, squeezing all the air from my lungs.

I kicked back, fighting to free myself, but the horrible pressure only increased. I grabbed at my ribs, finding an arm wrapped around me as my head broke through to the open air.

I coughed, gasping for breath.

"You're all right." A gravelly voice spoke in my ear. "I've got you."

I elbowed back, knocking my captor in the stomach.

He grunted from the impact but tightened his grip.

I twisted to the side, ready to bite, but it was Liam who held me.

"Stop fighting me," Liam panted as he shoved me toward the shore.

"What are you doing?"

He tossed me onto the bank, sinking out of sight for a moment before dragging himself up after me.

"Are you hurt?" He swiped his soaking hair away from his eyes.

"Why would I be?"

"What under the stars were you thinking?"

"That this was nice spot to have a swim." I sat up, wringing the water from my hair.

"You could have died." Liam got to his feet. His whole body shook right down to his sopping wet boots.

"I was doing quite well until you tried to drown—"

"Do you have any idea how long you were down there?" Liam shouted. "I thought you were dying."

"Well, I wasn't." I stood and headed back toward the rock wall. "I was having a grand old time, so you can feel free to leave."

"What are you doing?" Liam chased after me, the water in his boots squishing as he ran.

"Climbing." I dug my fingers into the rock and began pulling myself up.

Liam grabbed me around the waist, lifting me off the stone. "No, you're not."

"Why?" I rounded on him. "Is it against some Black Blood rule? Is this a sacred water-fall from some myth that happens to be true?"

"Don't be ridiculous."

"What's ridiculous is you trying to save me." I brushed away the moss that clung to my ribs. "What are you doing out here anyway?"

"Put your clothes on, we're going back to camp." Liam turned away from me.

"Why? Do you need me for a run into Ilbrea? Am I supposed to be leaving now?"

He stalked over to my clothes.

"Are you afraid I won't be able to find the camp by myself?" I leaned back against the stone cliff. "I promise I can. I don't need you to hold my hand and lead me through the scary woods."

He pulled my clothes from under my knife and bag and held them out to his side. "Get dressed."

"Why?" I strolled toward him. "The weather is lovely, and I'm enjoying being naked."

"Just put your chivving clothes on."

"Why do you care if I'm naked or not? It's not like you look at me anyway."

I watched the sides of his neck tense. I stopped right behind him.

His shirt clung to the muscles of his back. My fingers burned with the urge to touch him, just for a moment. Just long enough to memorize the contours of him.

"You don't care anything about me," I said.

"That's not true."

"Of course." I dodged around his outstretched arm to stand in front of him.

He tipped his gaze up to the sky.

"You are the trueborn Black Blood in charge of our camp," I said. "You care for all your people. Even the ones you won't look at."

The line of his jaw hardened as he looked at me. Not a glance or a glare.

For the first time since we'd come home from Marten, he actually saw me.

"It's better if I don't." He spoke just above a whisper.

I froze as his gaze searched my face.

"I have to keep you safe, Ena." He reached out, his fingers barely grazing my cheek.

"Why?" I wanted to lean into his touch but was too afraid I might shatter whatever magic kept him near me as his thumb slid down the side of my neck.

"I have to protect you. Sending you out into Ilbrea is bad enough, but the most dangerous thing I could do is let you anywhere near me." He stepped away, pressing my bundle of clothes toward me.

"That doesn't make sense." I shoved the clothes aside.

"You don't understand."

"Understand what? What have I done to make you believe I am so foolish or weak that I can't understand, that I need to be protected?"

"I'm a trueborn." Liam tossed my clothes back onto the rock. "In camp, that makes me important, in Ilbrea, it's a death sentence, and in Lygan Hall, it puts a target on my back."

"What's that got to do with—"

"The safest place for you is far away from me. I put you in danger by bringing you to the Black Bloods—"

"You saved my life."

"Your place is with us now, but letting you stand by my side is one thing I will not do. I have to protect you, and that means keeping you away from me." He dug his fingers into his hair, pulling at the roots.

I held my breath as I stepped toward him. I took his hands in mine and lowered them between us.

"You don't want me," I whispered. "You kissed me, and you walked away."

He stared down at our hands.

"Tell me you don't want me, Liam." I moved his hands to my waist, then lifted his chin so his eyes met mine. "Just say it."

"I…"

My heart shuddered and stopped.

"I want you safe. I want you protected." Pain filled his dark eyes.

"What about what I want?" I stepped closer to him, my bare chest touching his. My skin burned as his hands tightened around my waist.

"I'm not worth it. You are better off far away from me."

I rose up on my toes so my lips skimmed his. "No, I'm not."

The world froze as I kissed him. His scent flooded through me, and everything else vanished.

He trailed his hand up my side, and fire filled my stomach.

I laced my fingers through his hair and deepened our kiss.

My body hummed as he held me tighter. Wanting pulsed through me as I began to unbutton his shirt.

If the gods had destroyed the world in that moment, my story would have had a happy ending.

Fate is not that kind.

Liam broke free from our kiss and took my hands in his. He met my gaze before pressing his lips to both my palms.

"It isn't about wanting you, Ena." He touched the pendant hanging around my neck. "It can't be."

He let go of my hands and picked up my clothes.

"I followed you because I need to talk to you. I received a message from a trueborn Brien."

"Is Emmet all right?" I took my clothes from him.

"It wasn't about Emmet." Liam looked into my eyes. "The Brien have heard about your poison, the way you took care of Drason."

"How?"

"The death of a monster like Drason was never going to go unnoticed."

"An entire village was slaughtered." I pulled my shift over my head. "Do they want vengeance for the innocent blood on my hands?"

"They want your poison."

"What?" The world froze again. There was no bliss this time.

"There's a problem on the route they use to ferry the sorci children. The Brien need to get rid of the problem."

"And they've never heard of a sword?" I fastened the back of my skirt.

"It needs to happen quietly."

"A knife, then."

"They want the poison."

"No."

Liam took my hand. "They need it, Ena. Just a dose, maybe two."

"Absolutely not." I pulled away from him. "I'm not going to package up a nice vial of death to murder a stranger."

"You never met Drason."

I wiggled into my bodice, yanking at the laces to keep my hands from shaking. "Drason was different."

"How? One paun monster is the same as the next."

"I don't know the Brien. I don't know their definition of a monster. I don't know how careful they'd be to get the poison to the right person."

"Ena—"

"Drason was different because I trust you." The words tore at the back of my throat. "Blame the stars if you want, but I do. I won't have a stranger die by my hand based on the word of a person I've never met."

I sat on the rock to yank my boots on. My nerves finally gave out, and my fingers started shaking as I tied the laces.

"I'm sorry to have to ask you." Liam knelt beside me.

"I can't have another massacre on my head. I can't survive it." I shoved my knife into the ankle of my boot. "You want to protect me from you but think I should help the Brien? By the gods, you're a chivving fool, Liam." I snatched up my bag and headed for the trees.

"Ena, wait."

"If the Brien really want to poison someone, it's not that hard to figure out." I rounded on him. "Line up a batch of volunteers and start feeding them every plant from the forest it looks like they shouldn't eat. When one of the slitches dies, they'll know what to use for murder."

Liam stared at me, his expression a mix of pain and confusion.

I wanted to comfort him, to soothe away every worry.

Before I could move, he nodded and turned toward the waterfall. I swallowed my hurt and walked back to camp.

16

My hair had nearly dried by the time I reached the cook tent.

Neil had a bruise blossoming around his left eye and was busy chopping roots with such fury I didn't even speak to him as I laid the mushrooms on the table and dodged back out into the open air.

I thought of trying to find Marta so she could tell me what had happened the night before, then I remembered Nessa whispering in her ear.

No sooner had the dread at what Nessa might have said dripped into my stomach than Marta appeared on the path in front of me.

"Ena." She gave me a bright smile, setting her dimples on full display. "I've been looking for you."

The dread in my stomach doubled.

"I was out gathering some things." I patted my bag. "I left goodies with Neil, and I'll be able to make some nice tea for the next batch who have too much to drink."

Marta circled around to loop her arm through mine before leading me on toward the sleeping tents.

"Winnie will be so grateful. She's a fine healer, but having you to gather things for her is such a help. Especially when people bother her with silly problems of their own making," Marta said. "It is funny the things that can happen when people get too deep into their cups. Honestly, if I didn't think I'd be killed in my sleep, I'd stop allowing the stuff in camp at all."

"That would be a dangerous decision." My laugh came out close enough to genuine that Marta continued.

"Take last night, for example."

"What happened to Neil's eye?" I stopped to look at Marta.

"Nothing." She waved a hand through the air. "Old men with bad tempers. Those two would like to punch each other stone sober and well fed. There are some people who love being miserable, and there's not a thing you can do about it."

"That's still a nasty black eye."

"There are worse things than black eyes." Marta tugged on my elbow, guiding me off the path to a stand of trees just out of the way of anyone passing by. "And some choices made in the dark can have awful consequences."

"Sure." I nodded before adding, "What are you talking about?"

Marta reached into her pocket and pulled out a little glass bottle. "I don't want to interfere, but I can't let this sit on my conscience."

"I still don't know what you're talking about."

"Pierce isn't a monster or anything, but deciding to run off into the woods with him because Neil's having a tantrum? That's a dangerous thing to do, Ena."

"Yes, Pierce might have left my corpse for the wolves."

"It's not funny." She pressed the bottle into my hand and closed my fingers around the glass. "I'm not overly fond of gossip, but I'm glad I heard about this before it was too late. Consider whose child you'd be willing to carry before running into the dark next time. Or at least be prepared for morning."

I opened my hand to stare down at the glass bottle. "I don't know what you think happened—"

"What I think doesn't matter. Just know there are people who genuinely care for you and want to keep you safe." She kissed my cheek. "Best to drink it when you've got a bit of water on hand. It's nasty stuff."

Marta patted my shoulder and strode away.

I stood for a long moment, staring down at the little bottle. The sun peeked through the leaves above me, glinting off the glass.

A deep anger bubbled in my stomach, seething up into my throat. I let out a yell as I threw the bottle against the tree, smashing the shining glass into shards.

I went into my tent and lay down on my cot, counting the minutes until Finn would come bursting in to tell me it was time to go back out into Ilbrea and far away from the den of chivving Black Bloods.

17

The first day, I stayed in my tent, hiding from whatever rumors Nessa had started.

The second day, I went out to the training field and let Cati beat my rage out of my body.

The third day, I realized I wasn't insane. Pierce had started avoiding me. He wasn't as subtle about it as Liam.

Liam had at least managed to start looking at me again. He even gave me a nod when I nearly ran into him as I stumbled to the breakfast line, my eyes barely open.

Pierce, on the other hand, caught sight of me, turned sheet white, and left without getting any food.

That afternoon, I convinced Finn to start training me in sword combat.

The fourth day, I finished training, bloody and bruised, and walked far enough into the forest that I could scream my rage without anyone hearing.

The fifth day, a little stone bird flew into camp and landed on Liam's shoulder. Word had finally come—Kian and Erin would never be returning to camp. They had been killed by paun soldiers while fighting to protect a sorci child.

Finn didn't dance with Case that night. He sat on a bench with me, holding my hand.

It took six days for Liam to finally speak to me again.

18

"It's not that hard a job." Neil banged his spoon against the side of his massive metal pot with a clang that pounded into my ears.

None of the three of us working in the cook tent were foolish enough to speak.

"Go out into the woods, find an animal, and kill it," Neil railed. "Bring the chivving thing back, and I'll do the real work of preparing the chivving beast to feed the hundred-odd ungrateful chivving mouths I've been charged with."

I tucked my chin and kept my gaze fixed on the dried root I was shredding.

"But when the meat doesn't come"—Neil picked up his knife and began hacking his way through a tuber—"it's not the useless hunters that get blamed. It's me."

A brew for an ill temperament, that's what he needs.

Lily had grown herbs for such things in her garden in Harane. She usually doled them out to soothe women who found dealing with their chivving husbands nigh on impossible. I hadn't seen any such plants in the mountains, but I was sorely tempted to find myself a few seeds the next time Finn and I ventured out into Ilbrea. Start brewing Neil a morning cup of tea.

"Ena." Liam's voice broke through my thoughts.

I looked up to find him standing outside the tent, his face unreadable.

"Liam"—Neil stepped forward, still clutching his knife—"I will not be blamed for the lack of meat. You've got to do something about these hunters."

"I'll send Marta by," Liam said.

"But you're the trueborn," Neil said. "It's you who's in charge of this camp. It's you who can make sure the slitches get what's coming to them."

"Marta will handle it," Liam said. "Ena, I need to speak to you."

I swallowed the fear that balled up in my throat. There was something in his tone, in his stillness, that didn't seem natural.

"People are going to be hungry, but by all means." Neil bowed me toward Liam.

I stood, leaving my half-shredded root on the table, and stepped out of the tent. Being closer to Liam didn't make his manner any less disconcerting.

"This way." He nodded toward the path that led to the sleeping tents.

Neil's angry mutters followed us as I walked beside Liam.

He didn't speak until we were out of hearing distance of the others. "It's not Emmet."

The knot of fear in my throat dissolved a little.

"Then what am I supposed to have done?" I placed my hand over my heart. "I've been keeping my clothes on, I swear it."

Liam winced and shook his head.

"Have rumors of my running wild in the woods become enough of a bother that I'm in trouble?" I asked. "Am I being thrown out and sent back to Ilbrea to take my chances with the Guilds?"

Liam stopped and turned toward me, his shoulders and jaw tense. "That wouldn't happen. I would never let that happen."

"Then what is it?" I reached out to touch him.

He flinched again.

I tucked my hands behind my back. "Whatever you need to tell me, you're just going to make it worse by brooding like this."

"We have to meet with the others first." Liam cut off the path and into the woods.

I swallowed my questions as I followed him, studying the trees we passed instead of letting my mind race through the hundreds of horrible things that could have possibly riled Liam so badly.

We reached a small clearing in the trees with a giant stone sitting right in the center.

If we had been in Ilbrea, I would have said that someone had taken a great deal of time to grind the top of the rock into a perfectly flat surface. But we were in the mountains, and though it sent a shiver through my shoulders, I was quite sure the stone had been smoothed by magic.

"Liam." Cati stepped out of the trees. Her gaze locked on me, but she offered me no greeting.

Finn stepped out of the shadows beside her with the horse minder, Tirra, close behind.

Tirra glanced between Liam and me. "Why's Emmet's sister here?"

Liam laid his palm on the flat top of the stone. He stayed that way for a moment, his eyes shut tight.

I held my breath, waiting for some great magic to happen.

"I received a message from a trueborn Brien." Liam opened his eyes and pulled a tiny stone bird from his pocket. He ran his finger down the bird's spine, and the creature came to life, wiggling its wings and tipping its chin up so a tiny scroll could poke out from the front of its neck.

Liam handed the scroll to Tirra.

"The trueborn wants to meet Ena," Liam said.

"What?" Finn stepped around the stone to stand beside me. He wrapped his arm around my waist, keeping me close to his side. "That's ridiculous. If the slitches think it's going to happen, they're out of their chivving minds."

"Why?" Cati asked.

"The poison," Tirra said. "They want to meet her in person to ask for her help."

Cati gripped the hilt of her sword and looked to Liam. "You told them no, of course."

"With the first request," Liam said. "I don't know if I can deny this message."

"Why should you?" I asked. "If someone wants to meet me, that's fine. Have the true-born come with the next pair to ferry a sorci Finn and I rescue. I'll meet them, tell them to find their own chivving poison—"

"That wouldn't work," Finn said. "The Brien trueborn don't leave their camps."

"So they want me to go to them?" I asked. "Is it far?"

"It's not about far," Cati said. "The Brien are worse than most when it comes to who they allow to enter their camp, and how, and what they consider to be proper hospitality."

"Which is why she's not going," Finn said.

"We don't have a choice." Tirra read aloud from the scroll. *"The risk of ferrying the children grows with each passing day. We are committed to protecting all Black Bloods from the threat of a magically-dominant Ilbrea. But, if we cannot trust the Duwead Clan to stand fully with us, to commit every available asset, we can no longer allow our own clan members to take on the dangers of moving the children south. We will have to find other ways to deal with the sorcerer threat."*

The wind picked up, rustling through the trees.

"What does that mean?" I asked. "Is there another path to take the sorci children on?"

"No," Finn said.

"It means they'll kill them." Cati kneaded her knuckles into her forehead.

"The children?" A horrible, freezing fear settled into my lungs. "That's not true. Cati, it can't be. I've met some of the Brien. They're kind to those children. They promised they would take care of Riesa."

"They will," Finn said. "Riesa will already be far enough south by now."

"But not the others." I leaned on the flat stone. It didn't feel like the boulders that surrounded our camp. There was no pull drawing me to the stone table. The cold, flat surface offered no distraction from the fate of the sorci children.

"How many are left to be taken?" Tirra said.

"There's one I've been sent word of, but there's nothing to be done without Brien runners to take the child south," Liam said. "I don't know how many more might be found before winter sets in."

"So we find a way to take them south ourselves," Finn said.

"We can't cut through the Brien lands," Cati said. "That sort of fight would end badly for all of us."

"We could write to Lygan Hall," Tirra said. "See if the elders would be willing to let us take the children straight there."

"Orla would never allow it," Liam said.

"So then let's go." I pushed away from the table and ran my fingers through my hair, gathering the mass of it over my shoulder.

"Go where?" Finn said.

"To the Brien trueborn." I began weaving my hair into a braid. "If we're going to have to travel to them, it's best to get started. How far away are they?"

"It's not that easy," Cati said.

"Yes, it is," I said. "They want to see me, or they'll slaughter the children we're all living in tents to try and save. It's incredibly simple, actually. I have to go, so let's just do it."

"You can't," Finn said.

"Are you going to put on a wig and pretend to be me?" I asked.

"You're not a Black Blood," Liam said. "Not by Brien standards."

Finn reached into my pocket and pulled out the string I always kept tucked away. "You know how when we give the children to the Brien, I always go prancing into the woods naked?"

"I have noticed," I said.

"The Brien are picky about who they'll appear to." Finn tied the string around the end of my braid. "I go bare to prove I have no weapons."

"I know that."

"I'm marked as a Black Blood so they'll know I'm not just a naked paun," Finn said.

"The mountains on your ribs?" I said. "I thought you just liked them."

"No. Though I mean no offense to the artist." Finn nodded to Liam. "I was given the mark when I swore my allegiance to the Duwead Clan—"

"But you were born into the Duwead Clan," I said.

"And gave my oath to the trueborn Black Blood." Finn bit his lips together. "It's not an easy choice to make. Most people in this camp haven't even taken the oath. It's not something you can ever back away from."

I covered my face with my hands, wishing I could jump back into the river and make the world go quiet, if only for a minute. I took a long breath. As my chest rose and fell, I could feel the weight of the pendant hidden under my shift.

I allowed myself one more breath. "All right. How do I take this oath?"

"Ena—" Liam began.

"Do you need a blood sacrifice or something?" I asked. "Is there a test I have to pass?"

"There is no test, only an oath," Liam said.

"And a bit of pain," Finn said.

"Sounds fascinating." I stepped away from Finn. "When can we start?"

"This isn't something to just dive into," Cati said.

"There are children who need us in Ilbrea," I said. "There are children who will be taken by the Sorcerers Guild if we don't get to them. You're telling me the Brien would rather kill those children than take them south if I don't go meet their trueborn. Is there anything I've misunderstood?"

"No," Tirra said.

"Then how is there any question?" I asked.

"You don't want to help the Brien," Liam said.

"I don't want innocent blood on my hands," I said. "If those children die, it would be on me."

"It wouldn't." Finn took my hand. "You can't blame yourself for the way the Brien do things. It's best not to even try to understand it."

"I don't—"

"Ena," Cati spoke over all of us, "are you prepared to swear allegiance to Liam? Do you offer your life as payment for disobeying our trueborn? Are you willing to die at the command of our trueborn? Will you fight to your last breath for the cause our trueborn has chosen?"

I met Liam's gaze. My heart thundered in my chest. "Yes."

"Then we had better do this before Emmet gets back," Cati said. "We'll be lucky to survive his wrath when he finds out."

"Tonight then?" Tirra said.

Liam nodded. The solemnity of the motion stilled my heart, replacing fear with deadly acceptance.

"I'll have horses ready for you in the morning," Tirra said.

"Two," Liam said.

"Three." Finn took my hand. "She's not going without me."

Liam nodded again.

I wished I could hear whatever thoughts brought such darkness to his eyes.

"You should get some rest," Cati said. "It'll be a long night."

"Sure," I said.

Finn kept a tight hold on my hand as he led me away from the stone table and into the trees.

I glanced behind to watch the others go their separate ways.

"What sort of ceremony is it?" I asked.

"Nothing fancy," Finn said, "but don't let that fool you. You'll be making a vow that can't be broken."

"How does that even work?" I whispered.

"Liam will explain everything." Finn took me by the shoulders and turned me to face him. "You don't have to do this."

"Yes, I do."

"In theory, sure. You would be a chivving awful person not to."

"Then why are you arguing with me?"

"Because you can't save everyone." Finn tucked a stray hair behind my ear. "I know it's a horrible thing to say and an even worse thing to understand, but not everyone gets to live, regardless of how innocent they might be."

"Do you think I don't know that? I understand that good people die. I probably know it better than most Black Bloods."

"Knowing the facts and accepting there are some sacrifices not worth making are two different things."

19

As the shadows of dusk darkened my tent, I began to pace the tiny space. Finn had told me not to leave my tent until Liam came for me. His words had turned my little home into a cage.

Cati brought me dinner and a good-sized mug of frie. I tried asking her about the ceremony, but she wouldn't answer. All she did was urge me to eat before she slipped back out of my tent.

Her words didn't make eating the sour, chopped tubers she'd brought any easier. I wanted to go to the clearing and see if everyone else had been given the same food. See if Neil was still raging about the hunters not bringing in any meat.

But Finn had said to stay, so I'd set my lae stone on my table and perched on my cot, drinking the frie and shifting the tubers around my plate.

The pacing had begun when I'd run out of frie and couldn't stand staring at the tubers any longer. I don't know how many passes I did, pacing the six feet of ground in my cage, before a sharp knocking shook the front pole of my tent.

"Come in." My voice sounded strong. Cati had been smart to bring me the frie.

Liam stepped into my tent. The same darkness I'd seen in the woods still filled his eyes.

"Is it time, then?" I slipped my hands into my pockets to hide their sweating.

"It doesn't have to be," Liam said. "You can still change your mind."

"From what I've been told, this is going to be a long night. As we're meant to ride to meet the Brien in the morning, I'd just as soon skip you trying to convince me not to swear an oath to you and get started. There's no point in wasting time."

Liam stared at me for a moment before nodding.

"So where do we go?" I asked. "Is it back to the fancy flat stone? That seemed like a nice place for a ceremony."

"We can stay here if you like," Liam said. "Or go to my tent if you'd be more comfortable."

I studied him standing in my tent, a little rounding in his back as he hunched to fit his height under the canvas. There was only a few feet of space between us.

Suddenly, it seemed like there wasn't enough air in the tent for me to breathe properly. Like the heat of him, the magic hidden so deep inside him I'd rarely even noticed it, had somehow absorbed everything around him.

I didn't mind the sensation.

"What sort of a ceremony is it?" I asked. "If it's going to involve flinging my blood all over the tent, we can use yours instead."

The tiniest hint of a smile played at the corner of his lips. "Very little blood will be spilt."

"Then here's fine." I looked toward the stump that was meant to be my chair. "Do you need a seat?"

"Not yet." He didn't move.

We stood, staring at each other for a long moment.

The music began in the clearing. Faint notes of the tune drifted all the way down the path to find me.

"By swearing your loyalty to me…" Liam's voice faded away.

I stepped forward, taking Liam's hands. His skin was warm against mine. My fingers longed to twine through his. "There are far worse people I could be swearing my loyalty to."

"By swearing your loyalty to a trueborn Black Blood, you accept their cause as your own. You accept their word as your law. You give your life and death to them." He tightened his hold on my hands. "By giving you my mark, I accept you as one of my own. You are a member of the band of brothers that will fight by my side even as the sky falls. Your victories and shame shall be mine in equal measure.

"The mountain herself gave the magic in my blood that makes such a bond possible, and the stones that shield my people shall be your death if you break your oath."

A chill trickled down the back of my neck.

"Is this a burden you are willing to bear?" Liam asked.

"Yes."

A crease formed on Liam's brow. "I've spent the whole day trying to think of a way out of this."

"Are you afraid I'll shame you?" I tried to give a little laugh.

"No," Liam said, "but being marked isn't a thing to take lightly. I've told you before, being near a trueborn can be dangerous."

I laid my hand on his cheek, reveling in the feel of his stubble beneath my fingers. "I've never been afraid of danger. And some things are worth any price."

Liam pressed my palm to his cheek. "The next part hurts a bit." He let go and reached into his pocket.

"Is this the bit where I bleed?"

"Only a little. I've got to give you your mark." He pulled what looked nearly like a pen from his pocket, but instead of a metal nib, a piece of deep blue stone sat at the tip.

"Oh." I stared at the glistening stone. "That does look a bit painful. Should I just take off my top?" I reached for the laces on my bodice.

"Just pull your shift up so I can get to your ribs." He turned to face the canvas.

"Who in camp is marked?" I loosened my laces and pulled my bodice over my head, trying not to think of how many tents Liam and his stone pen had visited.

"We have four now."

"Only four?" I froze with my shift pulled half out of my skirt. "But they all follow you. They're all here."

"By giving you my mark, I am accepting everything you do amongst the Black Bloods as my responsibility. If the Clans Council should whip you, they'd whip me, too. If they execute you—"

"We both swing together." My mouth went dry. "I'll have to be on my best behavior."

"If I found out you had betrayed me, it would be my duty to execute you."

"Crushed by the stones of the mountain?" I pulled my shift free of my skirt, clutching the length of it in my hands. "I'm ready."

Liam turned to face me. "There's a reason the mark is drawn on the ribs and made with a stone from the heart of the mountains. The pattern leaves a bit of the rock behind, too small to matter to any other trueborn, but my magic will have placed it there. A trueborn can use the tiny pieces and—"

"Ram them through my heart and lungs?" I took a deep breath, feeling my lungs fill without any hint of magic tainting them. "This is what the Brien require? Are all of their people marked? Do they all live knowing their trueborn could kill them without a moment's notice?"

"Everyone who is allowed to leave their stronghold hidden far belowground."

I let out a long breath. "I'm glad it wasn't a Brien who saved me."

He gave another faint smile. "Are you really sure you want to do this?"

"If you're willing to have me." My heart froze for a moment as I waited for him to say he wouldn't give me his mark. That he didn't want to have any sort of a connection to me, let alone one deemed sacred by his people.

"It's best if you lie down."

"Right." I lay on my side on my cot, feeling foolish as I tucked my arm under my head.

Liam took the stump seat and placed it beside me. "I really am sorry for the pain. If I could change it, I would."

"I believe you."

I held my breath as he lifted the edge of my shift, exposing the side of my ribs.

He ran his fingers along my skin.

"I never thought I'd have any sort of a mark," I said. "Let alone mountains."

"It won't be mountains." He placed his palm over the curve of my side. "There are a shocking number of rules as to how marks are given. In the Duwead Clan, no mark can be repeated by the same trueborn."

"That seems like a lot of pressure." I gave a little laugh.

"Try not to move." He lifted the tip of the stone pen and placed it on my flesh.

A strange pain cut into my ribs, as though I could feel the stone magic funneling into my bones where it would lurk, waiting for me to commit an offense worthy of execution.

"You don't see common folk with marks in Ilbrea." I forced my words to stay steady as the pen cut a white hot line down my side. "Only the paun with their Guild marks."

"They use the same sort of magic." Liam moved his left hand up, lifting my shift out of his way, exposing the side of my breast. His fingertips sent fire flying through my skin that made me forget the pain of the pen. "I'd like to believe they stole it from us, but I don't think there's really a way to know where the legend came from, or if the paun's version came first."

"What legend?"

He paused, lifting his hands away. The pain doubled in the absence of his touch.

"I should have told you first," Liam said. "I've never even considered giving a mark to a person who didn't know. I'm sorry."

"Don't be." I touched his knee. "This wasn't your idea in the first place."

"It has to do with the descendants of the mountain's child returning home." Liam started his work again, and heat burned through my side. "The mountain wanted the blood of her child brought home. She called to the descendants, luring them back into her embrace. But the mountain didn't understand the ways of men."

He placed his left hand back on my side.

I fought the urge to lean into his touch.

He didn't seem to notice what skin his thumb grazed as he tipped his head, his brow furrowing as he focused on his work.

"The mountain's child had gotten married and had children. Those children had gotten married and had children. The blood of the mountain spread to each new generation but not to the spouses chosen by the offspring."

I gasped as a new, sharp pain dug all the way into my lung.

"I'm sorry," Liam said.

"What happened to the spouses?" I said. "Did the children leave them behind?"

"Some did. Others tried to bring them into the mountain's embrace. But the mountain wouldn't accept them, and many were killed."

"That's horrible."

"The mountain had spent a long time keeping outsiders away, and her stone couldn't tell the difference between enemies and those loved by the descendants."

"What happened?"

"Some fled, refusing to believe the mountain hadn't turned to evil. Some took their own lives, unable to bear the pain of their loss. But some were still determined to return to their home. There was a girl with stone in her blood who loved a man from Ilbrea with all her heart. She wanted to go to the mountain where she could live her life in peace but would not be parted from her mate.

"They say she begged the mountain for a path that would allow her love to live. Spent weeks kneeling in front of a great cliff, pleading for the mountain's mercy, until the rocks beneath her opened up and swallowed her whole. Her love mourned for her, begging the mountain to return his heart to him. The girl and the mountain both heard the man's pleas. So the mountain made a pact with the girl. If she would claim the man as her own, tie her fate to his by the magic in her blood, the mountain would let the man pass.

"The girl pledged her life in return for her love's safety, giving her vow to claim any pain caused by her mate as done by her own hand. Claiming every step he took as her own. The mountain returned her to the surface, and she grabbed a sharp stone to carve the mark of her devotion into her love's side. The mountain accepted her child's mate, and both were allowed to pass through to the safety of the land beyond Ilbrea's reach."

Liam fell silent.

The fiddlers in the clearing played a happy song with a bounding rhythm that didn't seem to fit the tale of the girl pledging her life for her love's passage.

"What happened to them?" I asked.

"I don't know. I'd like to think they lived long lives and died at peace. But making a vow to take responsibility for another is no easy task. I'm not sure what end they met."

"I suppose that would depend on what sort of people they were before they begged the mountain for mercy. It would be easy to claim a good man's deeds."

"Even good men do awful things when the world pushes them to it."

"I don't think I've ever believed in the existence of enough good men to think any of them turned into the evil slitches who torment the tilk."

"Even the paun aren't born evil." Liam twisted in his seat, leaning closer to me. "It's the Guilds that do it. They're our only real enemy. We fight against the soldiers and try to stop the sorcerers, but at the root of it all lies the Guilds."

"Are we going to stop them? The Guilds, I mean."

"I want to." Liam lifted his pen and pressed his palm to the painful spot on my ribs. Sparks tingled through my flesh. "But the elders in Lygan Hall don't think we can. Without their support, we've no hope of rallying enough fighters to make a real dent. I could spend a decade trying to recruit Ilbreans to stand with me, but I don't think I'd gather enough to make it past the gates of Ilara."

A scene of blood and men falling at soldiers' feet sent sour soaring into my throat.

"You're wrong." I hissed as he lifted his palm and touched the pen to my skin again. "It's not the Black Bloods' fight. Not as it is Emmet's and mine, anyway. It's easy to put off facing an enemy that may never come. It's harder not to fight when they're burning your house down."

"Watching a house burn and doing nothing to help is nearly as bad as setting the fire yourself."

"So," I said, "are *we* going to destroy the Guilds?"

Liam froze.

"I'm one of your band of brothers now, and I don't mind running into the flames if I can drag the paun with me."

20

Liam worked on my side until long after the music in the clearing fell silent. By the time he finished, I'd gone numb to the pain. My ribs had lost their ability to feel the bits of magic drifting into my body.

When he finally stood to leave, dark circles had formed under his eyes, as though the work had cost him more than a sleepless night. He warned me not to touch the raw skin and slipped out of my tent.

I drifted to sleep, though it wasn't the pure blackness I'd become accustomed to.

I stood at the bottom of a cliff, my palms pressed against the cool rock, waiting for something. I didn't know what it was exactly, only that I was willing to wait forever rather than give up hope.

A tapping on my tent pole woke me.

"Ena, its Finn," he whispered.

"Yes." I sat up. A dull throb reminded me of the pain in my side.

"I've brought a bandage." Finn popped his head into the tent. "You'll need to be careful while we ride."

"Right." I rubbed my hands over my face and stood. "How soon are we leaving?"

"As soon as you're ready." Finn held a rolled bandage out to me. "It's a chivving long journey."

"I'll be out soon." I took the bandage, watching the tent flap flutter as Finn disappeared.

I lifted my shift, holding it up with my teeth.

The skin on my side was red and angry, but it wasn't the sting as I touched it that took my breath away.

A raven.

That was the mark Liam had chosen for me. A beautiful bird with its wings spread wide.

I laid my palm on the image as he had done hours before. I tried to feel for any of the magic that was now housed beneath my flesh, ready to kill me should I commit a horrible enough offense.

I couldn't feel it. No hum or heat. Like my body had absorbed the stone and destroyed its magnificence, turning it into something completely ordinary.

Gritting my teeth against the ache, I wrapped the bandage around my ribs, tucked my shift back into my skirt, tied on my bodice a little looser than usual, and pulled on my coat. It only took me a minute to toss the few things I would have carried if I'd been venturing into Ilbrea into a pack. Then I stepped out into the early morning mist.

It seemed strange that no one darted out of their tent to stare at me as I passed down the long row. The camp was filled with people who had been born Black Bloods, and now I was one of only five who bore Liam's mark.

The thought of it brought a bubble of pride into my chest. Then I remembered he hadn't wanted to give his mark to me, had only done it to stop the Brien from murdering sorci children, and the pride gave way to a dull itching in my side.

Liam and Finn waited by the paddock where three horses had been saddled. All three beasts shifted their weight, as though Tirra had told them we were going to see the Brien and none of them were pleased to be making the journey.

"Where's Tirra?" I asked when I reached the others.

"Making sure no one decides to go on an early morning stroll around the camp." Finn lifted my pack from my back.

I gritted my teeth as the strap brushed against my side. "Who do we not want knowing we're leaving?"

Finn kept his gaze firmly away from me as he tied my pack to the back of a sturdy bay horse.

"Liam," I said, "who isn't supposed to know we're leaving?"

Liam shook his head before speaking. "Marta. Cati will tell her once we're well out of camp, but I don't think any of us want to face Marta's wrath this early in the morning."

"Right." I didn't take the hand Finn offered me as I climbed onto the bay. "Why would Marta be so angry?"

Finn's eyes grew wide, but he stayed silent and mounted his own horse.

"Liam, why would Marta be angry?" I asked again.

He rubbed his hand over his face. His skin was pale, like he hadn't even managed to steal a few hours' sleep.

"Am I not allowed to ask?" I said. "Is this part of being sworn to you? I'm just supposed to ride into the forest and not ask questions?"

"No." Liam mounted his horse.

"You should think about adding it in," Finn said.

Liam turned to Finn, a wrinkle forming between his eyebrows.

"Should the occasion for another marking ever arise." Finn shrugged.

Liam kicked his horse and led us south. He didn't say anything until we'd passed through the boulders that protected the camp.

"Marta is not going to be happy when she finds out I've given you a mark," Liam said. "When she finds out I've taken you to meet the Brien—"

"She'll have a chivving fit." Finn spoke from behind me.

"Cati is going to tell her?" I asked.

"Yes," Liam said.

"Don't worry," Finn said. "I'm sure Cati will go into the meeting well-armed."

I tried not to picture Cati and Marta squaring off to murder each other on the training field. Then I tried not to wonder what Marta was going to say to me when we came back from meeting the Brien.

A few solid hours passed with me trying to think as little as possible.

The cheerful green of the leaves overhead offered a bit of distraction. Listening to the different calls of the dozens of types of birds managed to keep me from asking why Marta would care so much about me getting a mark or leaving camp.

I had been going into Ilbrea on sorci runs for months. And if she was peeved about me being marked by Liam...

She and Liam can commiserate.

Counting the number of plants that could be used to kill a person lasted me until the sun was high.

Liam led us east into the rougher part of the mountain range, where solid ground gave way to scree that shifted under the horses' hooves.

The gait of the bay I rode rocked me from side to side so it felt like I might fall down the barren slope. I waited for Liam to hop off his horse and lead her the rest of the way to the rise above us. But he kept riding silently on, his gaze fixed forward.

My horse's hoof struck a stone, sending the rock tumbling down toward Finn.

His mount grumbled its response.

"Should we walk?" I gripped my reins.

"The horses are used to it," Finn said. "Honestly, I think it might offend the poor animals if we hopped off. Might make them doubt their own abilities."

I managed to muster a bit of a laugh.

"That and I don't fancy walking all the way to meet the Brien," Finn said. "Not that I mind a good wander through the woods, but a fellow has his limits."

"You've yet to tell me how far away the Brien actually are." I squeezed my mount with my thighs as she took a few quick steps to the top of the rise.

The expanse of the eastern mountain range stretched out before us.

My breath hitched in my chest as the feeling of being so small I barely existed pressed down on my shoulders. Summits peaked up on the horizon, the shimmering white snow resting on their tops giving the only real hint to their true height.

The vast field of mountains reached so far, it was nigh on impossible to believe anything could exist beyond the eastern edges.

"The Guilds could never conquer this land," I said. "It's too big. They'd never have enough soldiers to patrol it."

"They wouldn't have to patrol to conquer the mountains," Liam said. "They'd only have to kill all the Black Bloods."

21

I never feared the eastern mountains, not as the others in Harane did. I knew the woods on the western slopes, and the trees were my sanctuary.

I joined the Black Bloods, and the mountains became my home. I was never fool enough to believe I could understand the ways of the mountains as a born Black Blood does, but I loved them. I cherished the towering trees. The power deep within the stones grew a storm of longing in my chest.

It wasn't until the third day of riding behind Liam on our way to the Brien that I actually began to understand the depths of the mountains' mystery. What I learned gave me no comfort.

2 2

The rain poured down, creating a thick curtain of water that blocked our shelter from the rest of the world.

Finn paced at the very back of the cave, tucked behind the horses, humming a tune I'd often heard in the clearing at camp.

Liam sat, leaning against the side of the cave, staring out into the rain.

I sat opposite him, trying to convince my fingers they didn't want to trail along the hard lines of his jaw.

"We should just keep going," Finn said.

Liam waited a moment before speaking. "The path is dangerous in the rain."

"Danger lies in front of us no matter the weather," Finn said.

I untied my hair and shook it free of its braid, trying to occupy my fingers with working the sodden strands into a reasonable order.

"The Brien won't like us being late." Finn knelt and dug into his pack.

A minute stretched past before Liam spoke again. "The meeting isn't going to go well. Being late won't make it worse."

"You don't have to fake being cheery on my account," I said.

Liam fixed his dark gaze on me.

I wove my hair back into a braid, trying to ignore the longing in my fingers and the terrible itching on the side of my ribs.

"I don't want to risk it in the rain." Liam looked back toward the solid sheet of water that blocked us in.

I finished braiding my hair and shook it loose again. I needed something to do with my hands to keep from scratching the chivving mark on my side.

Thunder shook the rocks over our heads.

"Could you ask the mountain for a path?" I asked.

Finn stopped mid-step.

"No," Liam said. "The mountain offers us pathways, but only when she chooses and to where she chooses. It wouldn't be wise to ask a favor of the mountain so close to another clan's territory."

"Besides," Finn said, "you'll get plenty of walking through stone before we get back to camp."

Emmet's going to murder them both.

"Now that I've vowed to let Liam kill me if he wants," I said, "will the mountain see me as a real Black Blood?"

"How do you mean?" Liam asked.

Finn stepped around the horses to join us in the front of the cave.

"Will I get to open the secret tunnels?" I began weaving my hair into a more intricate, time-consuming braid.

"That part of the legend is just a story." A smile curved one corner of Liam's mouth.

"Pity," I said. "It would make sorci runs a bit easier."

"Are you trying to get rid of me?" Finn stopped chewing on his scrap of dried meat.

"Never, my love." I winked at him.

The smile left Liam's lips. "I don't think you should go on sorci runs anymore."

"Do you have more important things for me to do?" I asked. "Or do you think the Brien will trap me and never let me go?"

Neither of them laughed.

"We've lost too many," Liam said. "It doesn't feel right."

"No, it doesn't." Finn sank down beside me.

My heart skittered in my chest. There was a weight to their words that seemed too private, like I should find myself some pretty roots to play with and let them speak in peace, but there wasn't anywhere for me to go.

"Three in two weeks," Liam said. "We've had failed runs before, but not like this. Not with the Guilds just waiting to catch us. We stole the sailors' manifest in Frason's Glenn so I'd have a chivving shot at knowing where the soldiers were going to be moving over the summer. I've kept my runners well clear of the soldiers' encampments, but the paun keep finding them."

I stopped fiddling with my hair and slowly lowered my arms, trying not to break whatever spell had tricked them into speaking in front of me.

"They have to know where we're going," Finn said. "Ena and I had two run-ins with soldiers. Even if they were trying to find the same sorci as us, we shouldn't be cutting it that close."

"It doesn't make sense." Liam ran his hands over his face. "Do you think someone in camp has betrayed us?" He looked to me.

"Do I think one of the Black Bloods has been telling the Guilds where you're sending people on sorci runs?" I waited for Liam to look away or ask me to step out into the rain so he and Finn could have a nice chat about important business.

"People are dying under my command," Liam said. "If one of my own people—"

"How could they do it?" I leaned forward. "Every time Finn and I have gone on a sorci run, we've left the morning after you were told where the child was. Is it that way for everyone?"

"Yes," Liam said. "Word comes to me that the children are ready to be moved, and then I send two from camp to collect them."

"Are there any other trueborn hiding in camp?" I asked. "Anyone else who can send a fancy message in the neck of a pretty stone bird?"

"No," Liam said. "The Duwead only have two trueborn, and I'm the only one at the camp."

"Then your problem isn't with any of the people there," I said. "They'd have no chance of getting word to the Guilds before the runners you sent after the sorci were well out of danger."

I reached to scratch my side before stopping myself.

"Smack it," Finn said. "A sharp slap dulls the itch."

"I don't think it's our trackers planted in Ilbrea," Liam said. "The ones watching for signs of magic have been there longer than I've been allowed out of Lygan Hall."

"Could they have gotten tired of the righteous path?" I asked. "Decided gold from the Guilds was worth more than innocent lives?"

Finn's forehead wrinkled as he looked to Liam. "I've never even met any of the trackers. Ena could be right. It could be one of them."

Liam gripped his hands together. If he had been a proper sorcerer, his anger might have exploded in a wave of fire large enough to engulf the cave. "The trackers aren't under my command."

I could hear my own breath as I waited for one of them to speak.

"Then on Orla's head be it," Finn said.

He snaked his arm through mine and took my hand.

"I…" My unsaid words pressed hard against my chest.

Don't be a coward.

"I don't know if a Black Blood has betrayed you," I said. "I don't know who Orla is, or if the trackers can be trusted. But the Sorcerers Guild, they are cruel and powerful. If they want a child with magic, if they know there is quarry hidden in a town, they will find it. I don't know if you should doubt your own people, but do not doubt the Guilds' will to slaughter everyone who stands in their way."

Finn squeezed my hand.

"Talk to Emmet when he gets back," I said. "He knows almost as much as I do when it comes to the wrath of the Guilds. Let him say if it's worth tearing through your own people or if the Guilds are just enjoying murder."

The horses scuffed their hooves as a fresh round of thunder shook the walls.

"Is this the sort of thing you usually chat about without me?" I asked.

"Yes," Finn said.

"You're bound to me now." Liam looked up to the stone above us, as though begging the gods for aid. "It would be wrong of me to keep information from you. If we burn, we burn together."

"The Brien had better be reasonable and willing to accept a polite *no*," I said. "Either that, or I've got the weight of potential betrayal and an awful itch in my side for nothing."

Finn lifted my arms and smacked my ribs, right on the raven mark. "You'll thank me when you stop seeing stars."

"Thanks." I swallowed the bile that rose in my throat.

23

You did not understand. You did not understand.

The thought kept rattling through my mind as my horse carried me along the spine of a mountain.

I had thought I could see the expanse of the eastern mountains from Harane. Then I truly believed I had seen the scope of the range from inside the mountains themselves. But as we traveled farther south, there was no hint as to where the mountains might end.

Finn was the first to stop his horse.

"There we are." Finn soothed his mount.

I looked behind me and watched him jump to the sodden ground before I pulled on the reins of the bay I rode. "Are you all right?"

"We can ride a bit farther." Liam stopped his horse but didn't dismount.

"You can also live through being stabbed," Finn said, "but I don't fancy trying that, either."

Liam kicked his leg over his horse and jumped to the ground.

The silty scent in the air filled my lungs as I waited for him to move or give some sort of an order.

To the east of us, there was nothing but a rocky slope that even our mountain-trained horses couldn't have survived.

To the west, the slope had a gentler feel. If Death had come flying toward me, I would have run that direction, seeking refuge in the woods far below.

Along the ridge in front of us rose a peak the horses would have had no chance of climbing. I wasn't even sure I'd be able to reach the summit.

Liam stared at that peak for a long while.

"We're here, Liam," Finn said. "We can't turn around."

I kicked my leg over my horse's back, willing my stiff limbs to stay steady as I dropped to my feet.

Liam still stared at the peak. I let go of my horse's reins and walked to his side.

"Liam." I touched his shoulder. A foolish tingle ran up my arm.

"I shouldn't have told you," Liam said. "About the letter, about any of it."

"I've known darkness, and I am not afraid."

He laid his hand over mine. "You are stronger than any of us."

I began to say *no*, but I heard the echo of Lily's voice in my mind. "I am as strong as I have had to be to survive."

A crack shook the rocks, sending loose dirt tumbling down the slope to the east.

The horses stamped their fear into the ground.

"I will do everything in my power to protect you." Liam held my hand for one more moment before starting toward the southern peak. "Leave your lae stone hidden. Duwead magic can't be used in Brien territory."

I waited for another crack to sound or for the earth beneath our feet to crumble entirely away.

My bay nudged me with her nose, offering her reins.

I looped the leather around my hand and followed Liam.

I kept waiting for the mountain to devour us as I listened to the dirt crunching beneath our feet. Or for a hundred Brien to leap out of hiding to slaughter us. Anything to explain why my gut had twisted up as though Death himself blew the breeze that tickled the back of my neck.

Liam stopped in front of the rocks. He didn't look back before disappearing into the stone.

I kept my gaze fixed on the swishing tail of his horse as I followed. The stone swallowed the horse, and I held my breath as I stepped into the darkness.

I had expected pitch black, but as the outside world disappeared, the blue gleam of two dozen lae stones surrounded us, leading us toward a dark tunnel.

The sounds of footsteps approaching sent my heart leaping into my throat, and the rasp of a blade clearing its sheath turned my nerves to steel.

"I am Liam Duwead"—he kept walking forward, leading his horse farther down the dark stone passage—"trueborn of the Duwead Clan. I have come at the request of the Trueborn Brien."

Another rasp of a weapon being drawn carried from the shadows.

I peered into the dark patches between the lae stones, trying to find where an attacker might be hiding. I could see nothing but black.

"I have come to request transport to the Brien enclave, for myself and the two who travel with me," Liam said.

The passage narrowed in front of us, leaving barely enough room for the horses to fit.

"Will you grant us passage?" Liam stepped in front of his horse and walked into the tighter tunnel.

I couldn't see him past the bulk of his mount. I wanted to shout for him to stop.

A clack of rocks carried from the darkness ahead.

"Liam." My voice bounced off the tunnel walls.

The lae stone beside me flickered out.

"Keep walking," Finn said in a steadying tone.

A dozen more of the lae stones went dark, leaving only enough light to cast foreboding shadows around us.

I stepped into the narrow tunnel where there was no light at all. Penned between two horses, the animal that had carried me for days now seemed like an instrument of my enemy.

I wished I had a weapon in my hand. Something to give me a chance of taking whatever ghoul lurked in the shadows to the grave with me.

The knife in my boot pressed against my ankle, begging me to free its blade with every step I took down the darkening corridor.

"We ask for passage," Liam said. "We are Black Bloods called to the Brien enclave by your trueborn."

A low grinding of stone came from overhead. I looked up to the ceiling and found only darkness.

These are the people I gave Riesa to.

A dim anger replaced my fear.

May the gods forgive me.

All light vanished.

"I travel with Ena Ryeland," Liam said, "and Finn Duwead. I am a trueborn Black Blood, and I demand passage."

A scraping carried through the pitch black.

The crunch of boots came toward me.

I reached down, pulling my knife from my boot.

The sounds of footfalls surrounded me.

"Do not touch me." I spoke into the darkness. "Your trueborn has asked to see me, and I've come. Let us pass, or let us leave. But if you touch me, I will kill you."

A low laugh sounded by my shoulder.

My horse stomped her displeasure.

The footsteps shifted around me. If there had been any light, I would have thought the people were examining me.

It sounded like three, maybe five people. And there were more moving through the darkness near Finn and Liam.

I gripped the hilt of my blade and kept my breathing steady. I'd no hope of fighting anyone in the dark, but I had been threatened by worse monsters and would not allow these fiends the pleasure of seeing me cower.

All at once, the footsteps stopped.

My heartbeat thundered in my ears.

"You may pass." A whisper surrounded me.

I turned, trying to find where the person had spoken from, but the words had seemed to come from everywhere at once.

A dull crack sounded from my left, and a weak blue glimmer fought through a slit in the wall.

"Thank you." Liam guided his horse toward the light.

Keeping my knife gripped in my hand, I followed.

I could still feel them, the people lurking just out of sight, staring at me. I didn't search for them. I kept my gaze fixed on the blue glow in front of us.

The light didn't come from specific points as the gleam of the lae stones had, but seemed to grow in a vast sheet in front of us.

I squinted at the glow, trying to figure out what trap the people in the dark had laid for us. Then Liam's horse stepped through the gap and out of the way, giving me a full view of the space beyond.

Water.

A glowing lake so vast, I could not see its far bank.

Are we to swim?

The question balanced on my tongue. I didn't dare speak in case my fear should sound in my voice.

I followed Liam away from the gap in the stone and onto the rocky bank surrounding the lake.

Large metal rings had been set into the stone wall, and a boat waited on the water.

The craft was large enough for the three of us to fit, but there was no hope of bringing any of our horses.

Liam tied his reins to one of the metal rings and lifted his pack off his horse's back.

I took a slow breath before speaking. "Are we just going to leave them here? In the dark?"

"They'll be cared for," Liam said. "And waiting when we come back."

I tied my bay to the wall and kissed her nose. "If they try to hurt you, stomp them." I stroked the soft hair on her neck and untied my pack.

The boat gave a soft thump as Liam climbed in. He settled his pack in the bow before reaching for my hand.

He held on to me as I lifted my skirt high enough to step into the boat, which swayed beneath me.

I leaned close to him, pressing my lips to his ear. "Should we trust them?"

"We don't have a choice." He squeezed my hand and helped me over the wide bench in the center of the boat and to the narrow seat up front.

Finn waited until I'd tucked my knife back into my boot before giving the boat a shove and leaping into the back.

The glowing water smacked against the hull as we drifted out onto the lake.

A numb fear pinched my spine as we floated away from land, away from any hope of defending ourselves against the people who lurked in the darkness.

Two oars were attached to the sides of the boat. I waited for Liam or Finn to take charge of them, but both of the men just sat.

The boat slowed and rocked to a stop twenty feet from the shore.

"Should I row?" I asked. "I haven't done it before, but I don't mind."

"The mountain isn't ready for us yet," Liam said.

"Right." I twisted in my seat, scanning the water around us, waiting for darkness to fall again.

Nothing happened.

There were no waves to lap against our boat, no current to carry us—only the faint blue glow coming up from the water.

I tried to listen for any hint of movement. There was nothing beyond the shifting of the horses onshore.

I dug my nails into my palms, trying to be patient instead of letting panic make monsters out of shadows.

"There." Finn pointed into the distance.

A gleam of light streaked toward us, not through the air, but through the water, as though some giant fish were swimming right for Liam.

I gripped the sides of the boat, waiting for a crash to capsize us.

As the light came closer, I still couldn't see what was forming or leading the glow. Then, a sparkling gleam surrounded our boat.

It was beautiful.

Pure, blue light shone all around us, like the fire trapped inside the lae stones had been set free.

I had never seen anything so exquisite.

My breath caught in my chest, and I reached for the water.

Liam grabbed my hand. "Best not to tempt what lies beneath."

His fingers lingered on top of a mine for a moment, as though he too longed to touch the dazzling blue.

"I'll take the first turn at the oars." Liam sat on the wide bench and twisted the oars out over the water.

"I would fight you for it, but I'm sure I'll have plenty of time to get a fine set of blisters." Finn sat in the bottom of the back of the boat, rubbing his palm against the red scruff on his chin.

Liam rowed us along the path left by the light. I waited for the glow to fade into the dull gleam that filled the rest of the water, but the bright shimmering did not cease.

"How long will we be in the boat?" I asked when we were far enough from shore I didn't think anyone would be able to hear us.

"I don't know," Liam said. "It's like the path the mountain gives us to reach camp. It's different every time she offers us safe passage."

"Will they feed the horses?" I asked.

"They'll be brushed, fed, and rested," Finn said. "Strange as it seems, protecting the animals is one point of kindness the Brien have never faltered on."

"Should I take comfort in that, or be worried I'm not a horse?" I leaned out over the water, wondering what creatures lurked below that the Brien might consider worthy of protecting.

24

It took a few hours for Liam to finally allow Finn to row us along the glowing path.

The beauty of the light hadn't faded, but being trapped on the water for so long had begun to wear on my nerves.

Before Finn had started to show signs of fatigue, I made him give up his spot so I could have something to occupy myself with besides waiting for something terrible to happen.

As I rowed, I stared at the trail of light, waiting to catch a glimpse of the shore. It took me a long time to realize I wasn't seeing the end of our watery path, only the end of what was in view.

When my strokes shortened from the fatigue in my arms, Liam took the oars, and I curled up in the back of the boat, trying to lure myself into sleep.

The boat rocked gently beneath me. I wished the motion were soothing.

"I haven't had a massive set of blisters in ages," Finn said. "It'll be refreshing to be in pain every time I move my fingers."

"It's not that bad," Liam said. "Just think of the sympathy you'll get back at camp."

"Treat them properly, and they'll be gone before we get back," I said.

"Do you happen to have any wonders in your bag?" Finn asked.

"Of course." I sat up and leaned against the back of the boat. "Best to wait until you're done rowing, though. No point in putting a salve on just to rub it off on the oars."

"I adore you, Ena Ryeland," Finn said. "You do know that, right?"

"I am aware," I said, "but it is always nice to hear you confess your love."

Finn laughed. The sound seemed strange against the soft slopping of the oars.

"Suppose this lake goes on forever," Finn said. "How long do you think it would take us to starve to death?"

"That depends." I gave a deep sigh. "Are you in charge of our rations, or am I?"

"I'm going to starve to death." Finn leaned against the bow of the boat.

We all slipped into silence for a long while.

The sound of the oars lulled me into a stupor. All I could do was stare at the place where the light disappeared in the distance and wait for the end to come closer.

My eyes drifted shut, and the peace of sleep surrounded me.

"Ena." A warm weight pressed on my shoulder. "Ena."

I opened my eyes to find Liam looking down at me. The blue glow of the water had faded, leaving deep shadows on his face.

"What's happened?" I sat up quickly, setting the boat to rocking.

The shimmering trail we'd been following had faded in front of us. Terror gripped my ribs as the horror of being stranded in the dark shot through me. Then I spotted the dark outline of a rocky shore.

"Thank the gods." I sank back down in the boat. "Are there going to be more people hiding in the dark to taunt us?"

"There shouldn't be." Liam furrowed his brow. "We shouldn't meet anyone else until we near the enclave."

"But?" I checked the knife in my boot under the pretense of tightening my laces.

"The Brien are protective of their territory," Liam said. "If the thought of traitors has plagued me, I can't imagine how far down that dark path the trueborn Brien's mind has journeyed."

"Good thing none of us are traitors, then," Finn said.

Liam gave two powerful strokes with the oars, and the tip of our boat scraped up onto the shore.

Finn hopped out and towed the boat farther onto the rocks.

I listened past the noise of wood grinding against stone, trying to hear any hint of people lurking in the shadows.

Finn grabbed my pack out of the boat before offering me his hand.

As I stepped onto the rocks, the air around me seemed to change. A chill breeze blew across my skin as though the first fall storm were sweeping down upon us.

"I'm not ready for this," I said.

"Ena—"

"I'm not." I gripped Finn's hand. "I don't know about magic, or the clans, or how a lake this large can fit under a mountain."

Finn wrapped his arms around me and pressed his lips to the top of my head. "Knowing won't make it better. Do you trust me?"

"You know I do." I held Finn tight.

"I came on this chivving trip to keep you safe," Finn said. "Everything else is just stone and nonsense."

I laughed and felt Finn's ribs shake as he joined me.

"Right." I stepped away and lifted my pack onto my back. "Into the stone and nonsense, then."

"Into the stone and nonsense." Finn nodded.

Liam stepped in front of us and toward the wall of darkness that bordered the shore.

"Still no lae stones?" I whispered.

"No." Liam's voice bounced off the rocks. "It's against the treaty between clans to use magic while in another's territory."

"Makes sense, I suppose." I put my hands in my pockets, trying to dry the sweat on my palms. My skin stung where rowing had rubbed it raw.

The breeze picked up, setting goose bumps on my arms.

Liam headed left, toward the source of the wind.

A slit cut through the dark stone. The crack reached high up, above the dim light still glowing from the surface of the lake.

Liam ran his hands along the sides of the opening. "It'll be a tight fit."

"Good thing I haven't had a proper dinner," Finn said.

Liam took off his pack and held it to his side as he slid into the crack.

You will not break. Blood has not shattered you, and neither will darkness.

I shrugged back out of my pack and balanced it on my hip as I had done with Riesa. Feeling the rough stone with my free hand, I stepped sideways into the gap.

I could hear Liam moving in front of me, slowly sidestepping as though wanting to be sure he didn't get too far ahead.

Finn stepped into the crack and blocked most of the light from the lake.

I closed my eyes, making my own darkness rather than waiting for the tunnel to steal the light from me.

Did Riesa have to travel through a place like this? Did the Brien trap her in darkness as I did?

I sent a silent plea up to the stars that Riesa might forgive me. Still, I couldn't regret ferrying her from her home.

Even knowing the Brien would be willing to murder children rather than let the Sorcerers Guild have them, I couldn't think of any Black Bloods as more villainous than the Guilds.

I will make them protect you.

A rumbling carried through the tunnel up ahead.

I pressed my palm to the stone, feeling for any sign that the mountain had finally decided to tumble down upon me.

The rumbling grew to a growl.

My leg ran into Liam's bag.

The noise stopped.

I heard Liam take a deep breath before he started moving again.

A trickle of light silhouetted Liam as the tunnel twisted and widened. The light wasn't the blue of a lae stone, but the dull gray of twilight.

A breeze rushed toward us, filling the air with the smell of leaves, and fertile earth, and life.

Liam took another deep breath, as though scenting the magic of the mountains, and stepped out into the open.

25

I'm not sure what exactly I had expected to find on the other side of the mountain, but the woods I stepped into were beyond my ability to imagine.

Trees, whose trunks were as big around as a wagon, dripped with leaves the size of my head. In the dull light of dusk, the rich colors of the flowers surrounding my feet seemed thick and dense, like something out of a painting. A stream ran down the mountainside behind us, filling a pool with water so clear it reflected the gray hue of the sky.

We had stepped into a forest created for a fairy story.

The growl came again.

I spun toward the sound and caught a glimpse of a black tail swishing between the branches of a berry-laden bush.

"He won't attack," Liam said. "The animals know people aren't food."

"What a relief," I said.

The great cat gave another rumble.

Liam turned in a slow circle, examining the canopy of trees before nodding and leading us forward.

I put my pack back on, wincing as the weight bumped against my mark, and trotted after him.

We were high up in the mountains. We had to be. We'd never traveled down. But it didn't seem as though the forest had been told.

As Liam weaved his way deeper into the woods, different sorts of trees began to dot our path.

The bright white bark of birch trees stood out in shockingly pale veins against the deep needles of evergreens. Tree limbs hung heavy with jewel-colored fruit. Tiny animals scampered through the branches, darting from feast to feast. Birds warbled as they settled into their nests for the night.

I've fallen into a fairy story.

I couldn't shake the feeling as a new form of beauty appeared with every twist in our path.

I wished the sun wouldn't set. I wanted to see the true colors of the bushes laden with berries and the deep hue of the moss growing alongside the bubbling stream.

A bright light flickered up ahead. I squinted toward the gleam as Liam slowed his pace.

I held my breath, waiting for something wonderful or terrifying to happen, but it was only a torch planted in the ground.

Liam stopped beside the torch, staring down at its flame.

Finn stepped up next to him. "No point in delaying."

Liam stayed frozen for a long moment before nodding. "I wish it didn't have to be this way."

"Old traditions." Finn took off his pack and shrugged out of his coat. "Centuries of mistrust." He pulled his shirt over his head. "A bunch of men worried about assassination attempts." He kicked off his boots. "And the lot us still too afraid of destroying the treaty to object." He yanked off his socks. "Put all those things together, and you have naked Black Bloods tramping through the woods." He dropped his pants around his ankles.

I looked up to the stars just beginning to show through the darkening sky.

"I've gone first," Finn said. "Now you two strip down so we can get this over with."

I tried to think of something witty to say as I turned away from the others to undress.

I set down my pack and bent to unlace my boots. I held my knife in my hands for a moment before opening the top of my pack and tucking it away.

"You know," I said while I untied my bodice and slipped it over my head, "when you said Emmet was going to be furious with you for bringing me here, I didn't think it would be for this."

"I'm only moderately terrified of Emmet," Finn said. "And I'm a faster runner than he is, so I might survive the coming wrath."

"Perhaps he'll finally give up." I dropped my skirt and pulled my shift over my head.

"How do you mean give up?" Finn asked.

"He could either call me a lost cause and wash his hands of me, or realize I can live my own life without him shouting about it." I folded my clothes and set them next to my boots. "Either way. I'm not picky."

You will not blush.

I took a breath and turned back toward the men.

"Not so bad right?" Finn said. "A good breeze around your nethers to keep you awake."

"Thank the gods it's warm." I kept my gaze locked on Finn's face.

"You've got to leave that, too." Finn pointed to the pendant hanging between my breasts.

"Right." I wrapped my fingers around the smooth black stone. "Forgot it was even there."

I lifted the leather cord over my head and waited for months' worth of nightmares to come flooding into my mind to destroy me.

You have to protect the children. It's just a stone, and you have to protect the children.

I tucked the necklace into my bag. Without the stone touching my skin, it felt as though my flesh had been torn away. I was worse than naked. I was utterly exposed to the world.

"We should go," Liam said. "Regan has never been patient."

"Is that a trait of all trueborn?" I asked.

"Yes," Finn said.

"This way," Liam said.

I waited until I heard him walking to look in his direction.

He'd pulled the torch from the ground and kept his gaze locked on the path in front of him.

He'd seen me naked before, he'd touched my bare flesh. But the fact that Finn now knew I'd been anywhere near Liam without my clothes on brought heat to my cheeks.

Don't be a chivving idiot.

I made myself breathe. I touched the place on my chest where the pedant had rested. The patch of skin felt cold.

The flickering light of the torch sent shadows dancing across Liam's back. The ridges of his muscles left tempting valleys. I wanted to memorize the feel of them. But there was more than the beautiful strength to be seen.

A foot-long scar marked his right shoulder, and another left a raised line on the back of his right thigh. Whatever had made those marks had been brutal. Wounds that large would not have healed on their own.

Someone had tended to him. Someone knew why he had been made to bleed so badly. And that someone was not me.

I looked up to the stars, wrapping layers of fire around the emptiness that dug into my chest.

Creatures moved through the shadows beyond the torchlight, and the woods lost their wonder in the darkness. The forest floor stayed soft beneath my bare feet, but there was no other hint of hospitality to be found as we wandered naked through the woods.

I was only a foot behind Liam when I realized he'd slowed his pace. I tucked my hands behind my back and let him get a few steps in front of me.

He swept the torch from side to side, scanning the shadows. "I've come at the request of the trueborn Brien. I have traveled across the mountains to speak to a fellow child of stone. Grant me safety at your hearth."

With a rustle of branches, a woman jumped down from a tree. Her long, light-gray braid seemed somehow out of place against the dark colors of her clothes. She tipped her head to the side as she walked closer to us, squinting in the torchlight to examine each of us in turn.

I balled my hands into fists as her gaze lingered on my face.

"Is that the one?" the woman asked.

The muscles in Liam's back tensed. "She is."

"Huh," the woman said. "I thought she would be older."

"I'm sorry to disappoint." I dug my nails into my palms. "If I'm not what you're after, I'd be more than happy to go home."

The woman wrinkled her forehead. "That, I expected." She gave a whistle.

The crackling and swishing of people moving through the darkness surrounded us.

"Arms up," the woman said.

Liam raised his arms to be straight out to his sides.

My arms tensed behind my back as the certainty that raising them would somehow place me in greater danger overwhelmed my reason.

Figures appeared in the darkness. The steel of their weapons glinted in the torchlight.

"It's all right," Finn said. "After this, we'll nearly be to the part where they give us a cloth to wrap up in. Raising your arms gets you closer to getting your clothes back."

Gritting my teeth, I lifted my arms.

The woman peered at my side, examining the bird Liam had drawn on my flesh.

"A fresh one," the woman laughed. "I'm sure Regan will be honored." She whistled, and the figures faded back into the trees.

"We weren't given much of a choice," Liam said.

"There's always a choice," the woman said. "Some people are just too blind to see it."

She started walking away, reaching the edge of Liam's light before beckoning us onward.

As we followed her, I kept as close to Liam's heels as I could, searching the trees for any glint of the weapons that had threatened us.

For a while, we weaved between the trees without any pattern I could see. Then she led us onto a path worn smooth by years of travel.

Great trees loomed up on either side of us, planted in long, straight rows with their branches arching over our heads, creating a living tunnel.

I stared up into the branches, marveling at the glimpses of stars I managed to catch through the thick leaves. Except it wasn't stars lighting our path. Tiny lae stones had been suspended from the branches, mimicking the night sky.

I wished I had my clothes. I wished there weren't people hiding in the shadows with weapons.

But I do not live in a fairy story. I do not receive beautiful things without pain.

Voices carried from the distance. Not the rough tones of warriors, but the sounds of everyday life lurking in an enchanted wood.

The lae stones hanging above us grew bigger and brighter as the path in front of us grew wider. Up ahead, where the voices waited, more lights glimmered, sitting on top of posts like torches made of stone magic.

The tone of the voices changed as the people noticed our party.

I waited for Liam's shoulders to tense or his pace to falter, but he walked toward the voices without any hint of fear or modesty. Before we had reached the end of the tree-lined path, two dozen people stood in front of us, watching our approach.

I couldn't press down the heat that flared in my face as the men and women whispered and stared. I looked to the structures behind the pack of gawkers, trying to pretend the people weren't there.

Wooden houses made of thin branches surrounded the clearing. They weren't like any homes I had ever seen. They all seemed too flimsy, too light to survive a proper storm, almost as though nesting birds had advised the Brien's builders.

A rock face rose in front of us, forming the back of the clearing. A small, wooden structure had been built right up against the stone. Swirls of light emanated from the door of the tiny building.

The people parted ways as we reached the end of the path, and the gray-haired woman led us toward the rock face.

"Duwead."

I heard the name whispered.

"She doesn't seem fit for it." The voice spoke louder.

I kept my gaze fixed on the tiny building up against the stone. The walls hadn't been built any more soundly than the houses, but someone had gone to great pains to ensure the structure would stand out amongst the others.

Giant lae stones hung from the front corners of the building, with smaller glowing orbs dripping beneath like water trickling downward. The door had been carved from a single piece of wood, and gleaming symbols had been painted along the edges. The blue that shone from the paint looked almost as though someone had split a lae stone in two and drawn with whatever magic lived inside.

I didn't know what the symbols meant, but I wanted to touch them, to see if they held any heat or were as cool as the stones that lit the camp I called home.

The gray-haired woman stopped in front of the building and just stood there, not knocking or reaching to open the door.

I waited behind Liam, trying to silence the battle in my mind that raged between my desire to reach out and touch the scar on his shoulder and my need to scream at all the people in the clearing to run away before I scratched their eyes out.

The markings on the wood glowed brighter, and the door swung aside. The woman stepped through, and Liam followed her. I didn't like the idea of entering such a small place.

You will not be broken.

I pressed my palms against my bare thighs as I stepped inside. A gasp pulled itself from my throat as I blinked at the space around me.

The little, wooden building was only the entryway to a cave larger than the Guilds' shining, white cathedral in Frason's Glenn.

Lae stones dotted the cavern, arcing high above us on the rock ceiling as though all the stars in the sky had come to peer down upon us.

Ten men with swords at their hips lined the sides of the great room. A gleaming blue stone shone from the hilt of each of their weapons.

The sounds of our bare feet against the smooth stone floor barely carried over the thumping of my heart in my ears as a woman stood up from the throne at the far end of the cavern.

She didn't wear plain brown or black as the people in the clearing had. Her deep violet gown, worthy of a princess, swished around her ankles as she strode toward us. Her long, golden hair flowed down her shoulders as she tipped her head to the side, considering Liam, then Finn, then me. She nodded to the gray-haired woman, who bowed and left us.

The door didn't make a sound as she closed us in.

26

"Trueborn Duwead," the blond smiled as she spoke, "I didn't imagine I'd see you in our enclave again so soon."

"Your letter didn't leave me much choice, Regan." Liam bowed, and Regan's smile grew broader.

"You." Regan pointed to Finn. "You, I've met before."

"Several times, in fact." Finn bowed. "Don't worry, I'm used to not being memorable."

Regan gave a laugh that didn't sound remotely real and turned to me. "You must be the one I've heard whispers about. Rumors of you flit in and out on the wind. A poor little girl who kills great monsters."

I bit the inside of my lips to keep from speaking.

"Quiet? That, I did not expect." Regan examined my face. "Arms up. Best to get this over with so you can get wrapped up."

Finn and I raised our arms, but Liam did not. He turned to face Finn.

Finn's jaw tensed as Liam curled his fingers through the air. The dark lines of the mountain marked on Finn's side shifted, as though a breeze had stirred the image.

A wrinkle formed on Liam's brow as he looked to me.

Breathe. He mouthed the word.

I took a deep breath as he swept his fingers through the air as though stroking the head of my raven mark.

A tingling ran through my ribs and burned my lungs as though thousands of miniature ants had bored their way into my flesh. Before I could decide if I was going to be ill on the floor or rip the skin from my own bones, the terrible sensation vanished.

"Hmm." Regan turned and walked back toward her throne. "I suppose I should be honored."

Finn lowered his arms, and I followed suit.

"Honored?" Liam said. "I don't know what you mean."

"Her mark is still raw." Regan turned back to us. "So much trouble to go through to visit me."

She waved her hand through the air, and a square of rock on the side of the wall slid open, creating a doorway where there had been nothing but solid stone.

"You didn't give me much choice," Liam said. "We have spent years protecting the sorcis together, and now you threaten to abandon them or worse."

"I have my people to think about," Regan said. "I must protect them, as you should yours."

Liam went still as stone.

People entered through the newly-formed door. Three men, all carrying bundles in their arms.

"Is that what we've come to?" Liam stepped toward her. "I ask the Brien for more men to aid me in Ilbrea, and I am told no. My people alone must bear the risk of venturing west of the mountains."

"Taking those children south is no small feat." Regan strode back toward us. Where Liam's face had turned to stone, fire danced in the blond trueborn's eyes.

"It is the risk you agreed to," Liam said. "We have a common cause, Regan."

The three men stopped in front of us, each holding out their bundle.

The man in front of me was thirty, maybe a bit older. He had wrinkles on his tan forehead, as though he had spent too much of his time despising the world. His eyes were gray-blue and his hair mousy brown. There was a tiny white scar on his top lip.

"I think you and I see the end of our journey differently, Liam," Regan said. "My aim is the survival of my people, my clan. That, I prize above all."

The man's gaze swept over my naked body as he unfurled his bundle, presenting a wide, black sheet.

"I have seen the power of the Guilds," Liam said. "I have seen the malice they hold. None of the Black Bloods will survive if we continue to allow their power to grow."

"I agree," Regan said. "We cannot allow them to gain an even stronger foothold in magic."

The man moved toward me, reaching to wrap the sheet around my body.

"And you would be willing to slaughter innocent children to keep them from the Sorcerers Guild?" Liam said.

A smile lifted the corners of the man's eyes as his fingers grazed my breast.

"Don't!" I leapt away from him, covering my chest.

"Ena." Finn ripped the sheet from the man's hands and wrapped it around me.

"Get them out." Liam stepped between the man and me, not bothering to cover himself.

"Go," Regan ordered.

The smile disappeared from around the man's gray-blue eyes. He stared at me for a long moment before following the other two through the door in the stone wall.

"We should get you settled." Regan strode back to her throne. "You've had a long journey. You need rest and food."

"Regan—" Liam said.

"We can discuss our partnership in the defense of all Black Bloods in the morning." Regan kept speaking like she hadn't even heard him.

"Do not make Ena a part of this," Liam said. "She has seen enough horror at the hands of the Guilds. Do not make the Black Bloods another terror she must endure."

"I will see that you all have places to rest comfortably." Regan gave me a smile that did not reach her eyes. "Everything but your weapons will be waiting for you."

"This way."

I looked toward the voice.

The gray-haired woman waited in the open doorway.

"The three of us will stay together," Finn said. "I don't care if we're all huddled on the cold ground."

He wrapped his arm around my waist, keeping me close to him as we followed the woman out of the cave.

My heart thundered in my chest, battering a rhythm I didn't recognize against my ribs. My flesh felt contaminated where the man had touched me, but there was something else. A scent in the air I couldn't name.

Liam stepped forward to flank me with Finn. He walked so close to me, his arm brushed against mine.

I looked to him, wanting his face to bring me comfort, but there was a shade of darkness in his eyes that made my heart scream in terror.

The woman stopped in front of one the wooden houses.

Up close, it was easy to believe the home had been built of twigs. We'd somehow fallen into a strange and magical land, and this was a house a child had built in the garden to lure in a tiny bit of magic.

I stared at the scar on Liam's shoulder as he pushed the door to the house open. Glittering wings did not sprout from his back.

He checked all the corners of the one room the house provided before beckoning Finn and me in.

Finn closed the door behind us, shutting out the fairy lights, and the man with the scar on his lip, and all the things I had thought I understood.

27

"No," Finn said as he slid the wooden bolt into place, locking the door. "No, no, no."

"Are you all right?" Liam took my face in his hands.

The feel of his fingers against my skin brought heat back into my body, cracking through the strange numbness of fear. "I'm fine. You shouldn't worry about me."

"He touched you." Finn paced the length of the room. "That chivving, slitching, cact of a letching—"

"I said I'm fine." I stepped away from Liam. "That was nowhere near the worst I've gotten from foul men."

Finn stopped pacing and sank down onto the only bed in the room. The things Liam had abandoned in the woods lay on top of the blankets.

"I don't know if Regan will be willing to take a *no* from me." I pulled the sheet tighter around my chest. "If she's really so eager to kill the sorci children, I don't know if anything we do will be able to stop her."

"We'll do what we can," Liam said.

I tipped my gaze to the ceiling as he pulled on his pants.

"Do you think you'll be able to convince her?" I asked. "I don't want murder on my hands, but I cannot let those children die because of me."

Knock, knock.

Liam darted to the door before I'd even turned to face it. He slid the lock aside.

Three women waited in the clearing. One held my things. Another, Finn's. The third held a tray of food.

"On the table." Liam stepped out of their way, extending his arm as they passed, as though creating a barricade between the women and me.

He stayed that way until the women left then locked the door behind them.

The scent of roasted meat and fresh baked bread wafted from the table in the center of the room.

Finn didn't run for the food. He just sat, his head in his hands, not even moving to get his clothes from the table.

"Is there anything we can say to her?" I asked. "Any bargain we make?"

Liam pulled his shirt over his head.

I hesitated for a moment before going to my pile of things. I dug into my pack, searching for the pendant. The smooth stone had lost none of its warmth in its time away from my skin. I gripped the pendant, waiting for it to soothe me, to quiet the fear that still thundered in my chest.

The calm did not come. I turned away from Liam as I slipped the leather cord around my neck.

"Can they grant us safe passage to the south?" I asked. "I would rather spend months leading the sorcis through the mountains myself than give Regan poison to use as she pleases."

Pulling my shift over my head did not calm my nerves.

"Or we can send the children to Lygan Hall, or out to sea," I said. "Maybe we could keep them in the mountains near the camp. You could use your magic to hollow out a cave big enough for them to survive the winter."

Neither Liam nor Finn spoke.

"We were only with her for a few minutes." I buttoned my skirt around my waist. "We traveled for days to get here. We can't just give up after a few minutes."

They both stayed silent.

"What?" I yanked my socks and boots back on. "What bit of Black Blood lore am I missing? Is the Brien trueborn's word law? Do women have more of a say in how things are decided than men?"

"He touched you," Liam said.

"I am quite aware." I stepped in front of Liam.

He kept staring over my head at the door.

"It wasn't a pleasant experience, but the lives of children are at stake," I said.

Liam closed his eyes. "There are laws we must uphold."

"What laws?" I asked. "The only ones I've ever known are those the Guilds use to ruin the lives of common folk."

"The Black Bloods have their own laws," Liam said. "Rules written into the treaty."

"What rules?" I looked between Finn and Liam. "Is there some law that says I'm obligated to help Regan?"

"No." Finn stood up. "But there are laws of safe harbor."

"What does that mean?" I asked.

"We came in good faith," Liam said. "We used no magic and hid no weapons. We came with honor to speak to the trueborn of the Brien Clan."

"And?" My heart crashed even harder against my ribs. "Is any of that wrong?"

"We committed no act against the agreement," Liam said. "And that man touched you. He violated your right to safety under the treaty."

I jumped as Finn slammed his fists on the table.

"There's a code to be followed," Liam said, "a way things must be done to maintain the peace between the clans."

My shift and skirt suddenly didn't seem like enough covering to protect me from the world. I snatched my bodice from the table, wishing it were a suit of armor.

"What does that mean?" I kept my voice steady. "What does the code say, and what has it got to do with me?"

Liam's face was still unreadable, set in stone as though the mountain in his blood had taken hold of him.

"Finn." I lifted his fists from the table. "What rules are there to follow?"

Finn wrapped his arms around me, holding me close. "Just breathe for a moment. It could be nothing. It could all come to nothing."

Knock. Knock.

Finn tightened his hold on me as Liam slid the lock aside.

The gray-haired woman had returned. "Three of our men witnessed the violation of the treaty. Justice is yours to be served. He will be waiting to the west." She took the door from Liam's grip and shut us inside.

"What is the Brien's justice?" I could feel my mouth form the words, but somehow they seemed to come from far away.

"Death." Liam didn't turn to face me. "The penalty for violating an envoy's safety is death."

2 8

"Death." The familiar word rattled in my mouth as I tried to discover some new meaning.

"The treaty between clans guarantees our safety." Finn didn't let go of me. "It's a part of the oldest pact. That man violated the agreement, and now he must pay the price."

"Pay the price." My legs lost their strength. I pushed away from Finn to sit at the table. "Death? The letch slides a hand along my breast, and the penalty is death?"

"Safety cannot be violated." Liam slid the bolt back into place, locking the Brien out of our house of twigs.

"Regan really will harm the children, won't she?" The table seemed to sway before me. "If she's so willing to execute one of her own, she won't hesitate to murder the sorcis."

"It's not about Regan," Finn said. "The treaty was created long before any of us were born. She has to follow it."

"So, she just hangs him and has a good night's sleep?" I asked.

"It's not her that's got to do it," Finn said.

My heart stopped. The thundering in my ears disappeared.

"If the one who was harmed is not dead, the treaty requires they carry out the sentence," Liam said.

Sound came crashing back into being.

"Me." My chair fell to the packed dirt floor as I stood. "They want me to execute him?"

"It's our law," Finn said.

"No. No, I won't do it."

Finn reached for me, but I stepped away and began pacing the maddeningly small room.

"Cut off his hand," I said, "that seems like a fair punishment for groping. Or whip him. Just tie him to a post and whip him."

I needed more space. I needed to run, to climb, to disappear from this false fairyland.

"It doesn't work that way," Finn said.

"Then cut off his bits!" I shouted. "Brand him. Lock him up. Shatter the bones in his feet. Or gouge out his eyes, then he'll never leer at any girl again."

"The treaty names death as the penalty for violating an envoy's safety," Finn said.

"I don't care what their rules are. I will not kill a man." My side burned, itching where Liam had drawn his mark. My steps slowed. "Our rules. I don't care what our rules are. I won't kill him."

"You don't have to," Liam said.

I turned to him. His face was still set like stone, and his eyes were still dark with danger.

"You are an envoy," Liam said. "You entered the enclave in good faith. They cannot force you to do anything against your will."

The pressure against my ribs didn't lessen. "So he'll be all right, then? They'll find some other punishment for him and we can speak to Regan tomorrow about the children?"

"Don't think any more of it," Liam said. "It's not what we came here—"

"You can't, Liam," Finn said. "I'm sorry, but you can't."

"Finn." Liam's voice held a note of warning.

"You have to do it, Ena," Finn said. "You have to follow the laws of the treaty."

"Stop—"

"Why?" I cut across Liam.

"If you don't follow the rules of the treaty and you let him live," Finn said, "you become responsible for his actions. If he violates another envoy, his crime would be on your head."

"I would protect her," Liam said. "I would never—"

Finn raised his voice to speak over Liam. "And not just your head. You swore an oath to a trueborn, and he accepted your fate as his."

"I command you to stop," Liam said.

"Then kill me." Finn spread his arms wide. "Use your magic and end my life. If that is my penalty, so be it. But you cannot lie to her. You want to protect her? Fine, but she deserves the honest truth."

"That isn't your decision to make!" Liam shouted.

"If you believe she can't take it, you don't know her half so well as you think." Finn looked to me. "If the letch gropes another woman, you and Liam would both be held accountable. Both of your executions would be ordered by the Clans Council."

I waited for my head to spin or to be sick on the floor. Neither happened.

"So, I kill him, or we wait for him to do something wrong and then they kill us." My voice sounded calm to my own ears.

"Yes," Finn said at the same moment Liam said, "No."

"There are ways around it." Liam stepped between Finn and me. "I can speak to Regan, remove the burden from your hands."

"At what cost?" Finn said.

"The price is mine to pay." Fire flickered in Liam's eyes. "I brought her to the Black Bloods, and I will not allow her place with us to harm her."

I wanted to believe he could make everything right. That Liam could strike a bargain, give a handshake, and we'd be able to walk away as though nothing had happened.

I was not fool enough to believe Regan would be so kind.

"You didn't try to make me a Black Blood," I said. "You saved me, and I asked to stay. You wanted to send me away, find a place for me in Ilbrea, but I said no. It was me who suggested poisoning Drason, not you."

"It doesn't matter," Liam said.

"I won't allow you to be punished because I don't like the Black Bloods' laws." My chest had gone hollow. I couldn't understand where I was getting the air to speak. "I won't sacrifice your life to save a man who touched me. I won't let you make a bargain with Regan to protect me."

"Ena." Liam took my hand. "I don't want you to bear this burden."

"I'm strong enough. I haven't broken yet. If the Guilds haven't managed it, then one man's death won't be enough to shatter my soul."

I remember thinking that my hands should be shaking, or my legs should give out. That I should collapse to the ground or vomit in utter revulsion at the horrible acts survival demanded of me.

But I was calm as I squeezed Liam's hand then went to my bag to dig out my wooden comb.

"How is it to be done?" I asked.

Liam sank silently down onto the bed.

"They'll have him waiting," Finn said. "You'll just have to go and—"

"Kill him." My comb caught on the knots in my hair. "Do they care how it's done?"

"By the blade," Finn said. "It won't be quick."

"I doubt I was the first. He smiled at me before he touched me. I don't think he would have done that if he'd never been so bold before." I pulled my hair over my shoulder and wove the black strands into a braid. "Why would he risk it? If he knows the laws of the Black Bloods, why would he give his life to touch me?"

"He probably thought you'd be too afraid to react," Finn said. "That you'd let him get away with it rather than allow the treaty to be invoked."

"Should I have stayed quiet?" I asked. "Just let him touch me so Liam could convince Regan to help the children?"

"Men like that cannot be allowed to continue to hurt people," Finn said.

"No." I tied my string around the end of my braid. "But death is not the only punishment the world offers."

My knife had not been replaced in my bag. I felt naked without it. I stared at the ankles of my boots for a long time, just waiting for my weapon to appear.

"You don't have to be the one to do it," Liam said. "I can be the one to wield the knife."

"What would the punishment be for that?" I rolled the sleeves of my shift up as high as they could go.

"I don't care," Liam said.

I shut my eyes, willing the world to stop for just a moment.

"If you won't tell me, then it is more than I am willing to pay." I walked toward the door. "Where to the west am I to find him?"

"We can come with you," Finn said. "There is no law against that."

I froze with my fingers on the wooden bolt.

Better to let them watch your guilt, or to have them imagine it?

"We stay together," Liam said. "I don't care what the treaty says, we aren't trusting them with Ena's safety."

I pushed the bolt aside, grateful I hadn't had to choose if Finn and Liam would follow me.

The chill night air greeted me outside the little stick house. The air wasn't as cold as it should have been this far up in the mountains, but the wind swept around us as though trying to lure me into a dance.

All the people who had gawked at me before had disappeared, but the lights in the clearing hadn't faded. They gleamed around us as though, even in that dark moment, I was still supposed to find beauty in magic.

Someone had left a long knife lying on the ground outside our door. The hilt held a lae stone that shone with inordinate brightness. They had not left a sheath. The bare blade sparkled in the light.

I picked the weapon up, weighing its heft in my hand. This blade was larger than the one Cati had given me. The extra weight of it seemed right, like the knife knew it was going to end a life.

"You don't have to do this." Liam stepped in front of me.

I stared at his face, a face I had not bothered to find beautiful the first time we met. But now I would burn the world to protect his dark eyes. I would destroy the Guilds with my bare hands rather than let one more line of worry appear on his brow.

I reached out and trailed my fingers along the sharp angle of his chin.

A new pain appeared in his eyes.

I leaned in and pressed my lips to his cheek. "Where do we find him?"

"This way." Finn pointed to a path between the trees. He'd gone pale, leaving his freckles as the only color on his face.

Liam pressed my hand to his cheek.

"We should go." I slid my hand out from under his. "If the gods are thirsty for blood, we can't let them decide they would rather taste ours than his."

Liam nodded and started down the path.

I followed, and Finn stayed right behind me. We passed between the houses on the opposite side of the clearing and out into the trees.

I didn't let myself look at Liam as we walked. I was too busy searching the shadows, not for men hiding in the darkness seeking to slaughter us, but for any hint of my victim.

A tree crackled overhead as a large black cat prowled through its branches, but the birds had all gone silent. Even the wind stopped rustling through the leaves as we walked along the path with nothing but starlight to guide us.

I heard the man before I saw him. He screamed through the gag in his mouth, shouting words I could not understand.

Liam slowed his step and spread his arms to his sides as though trying to keep me from reaching the man whose life I was to end.

I ducked under his arm and kept walking up the path.

They hadn't hidden the man in a cave or even locked him in a cage. Perhaps the laws of the clans did not allow for such kindness.

The man stood between two trees, his arms tied out to his sides, the ropes so tight, they pulled at his wrists. His ankles had been tied as well, keeping his legs spread wide so the man could not shift his weight without pain.

They'd taken his clothes, leaving him naked and helpless in the darkness. They'd stuffed a black cloth into his mouth to stifle his screams. The cloth did not hide the scar on his top lip.

I stood before him, gripping the knife in my hand.

"What am I supposed to do?" I asked.

"I'll do it." Liam reached for the blade.

"And if they're watching?" I held the hilt tighter. "I wanted to join you. I will not let you suffer because of me."

Liam stepped closer to the man. The man screamed against his gag as tears fell from his gray-blue eyes.

I wanted to ask him why. Why had he been chivving foolish enough to touch me? What under all the gods and stars had stripped him of his senses and doomed us both to be in this dark forest?

"Where do they want me to stab him?" I moved closer to the poor naked beast left to die in the woods. "Am I supposed to strike him more than once?"

"A slice along the gut," Finn said. "Deep enough to cut through to his organs. Then leave him for the animals."

A pressure pinched around my lungs, threatening to suffocate me. "This is the treaty the Black Bloods agreed to?"

"It was forged a long time ago," Liam said. "The treaty has kept the Black Bloods alive."

"Am I only allowed one cut?" I asked. "Do I have to stick to his stomach?"

The man begged through his gag.

I couldn't understand his words, but I knew his desperation.

He was the beast who had broken the law, but I was the monster who had come for his blood.

"Am I allowed to cut him wherever I like?" I shouted over the man's screams.

A rustle of bird's wings carried from high up in the trees.

"Yes," Liam said.

I tightened my grip on the knife and stepped up in front of the man.

I wanted to say something. To beg forgiveness for taking his life or tell him he owed me a debt that could never be repaid. He had begun this horror, not me.

But my mouth had gone numb as my hand had gone numb.

I drew my arm back and stabbed.

The man's scream echoed in my ears.

I forced my knife down. His warm blood flowed over my hand.

I pulled the blade free and fought my instinct to throw the awful weapon aside.

In two quick moves, I cut a deep gash at the top of both of his thighs.

The knife tumbled from my grip, and I stepped away from the blood seeping into the dirt.

Holding my gore-coated hand in front of me, I walked back up the dark path to the clearing surrounded by fairy houses built of sticks.

29

My hands will never be clean again.

I had thought the very same thing many times before and had always been wrong. But somehow, as I scrubbed my hands in the bucket of cold water, it seemed like this time it might be true.

The door closed behind me, and the bolt scraped into place. I didn't turn to see who had come in. If they wanted to slit my throat, I was too tired to fight them.

Two sets of footfalls moved slowly behind me. A chair scratched across the dirt as it was pulled away from the table. Someone stopped beside me.

"I've brought soap." Liam held out a cracked brick of soap that smelled like fat boiled with rosemary.

"Thanks." Pink dripped from my fingers as I took the soap.

"Are…" Liam's voice faded. "Is there anything I can do to help you?"

"To help me wash my hands?" I shook my head. "No. I've washed plenty of blood off my hands before. Getting the red out from under your nails is the tricky bit, but I can manage."

"Ena—"

"Honestly, it was tidier than I expected." I dug my nails into the soap. "I even managed to keep my skirt clean. It's a wonder how much easier it is to avoid getting blood on you when you're the one who's causing the injury."

I rubbed the soap against my hands until my skin stung. "He should be dead by now." I rinsed my hands in the water one last time. "It doesn't seem like it should work that way, but one cut to the wrong part of the leg, and you'll bleed out. It happens much faster than dying of a gut wound, or an animal tearing through your flesh."

My breath caught in my chest. I stood and took the black cloth I'd been wrapped in from the table. If the man with the scar on his lip hadn't been assigned to bring me something to wrap up in, he would still have been alive.

And waiting to touch a girl who's too afraid to say no.

I dried my hands on the cloth, balled it up, and tossed it into the corner.

Then it was done. My hands were clean. The man had been killed. There was nothing more for me to do.

"We should eat." I looked to the table. The scent of the food sent my stomach rolling. "Or make a plan. What are we going to say to Regan? Do you know anywhere we can take the sorci children? Can you send a stone bird to Lygan Hall to ask for help?"

Liam took my hands in his.

"There has to be another place we can keep them safe," I said.

He kissed both of my palms.

"Liam." I should have pulled my hands away from him but couldn't find the strength. "We have to do something."

He gathered me into his arms and held me tight. "I'm sorry. I'm so sorry, Ena."

I laid my ear against his chest, listening to his heartbeat.

It thumped a steady rhythm. His blood stayed safely in his veins. He would not be killed in the woods because of one lecherous man's sin.

I could not regret the blood I had shed if it meant protecting Liam.

He pressed his lips to the top of my head, and I wrapped my arms around him, holding him close.

We stayed like that for a long time, until his scent replaced the stench of blood and foul soap.

"You need rest," Liam said.

"I don't deserve sleep." My own words chipped at the armor in my chest.

"You do." Liam led me to the bed. He moved his pack from on top of the blankets and set it on the floor.

"What are we going to say to Regan?" I didn't fight as he sat me down at the head of the bed and loosened the laces on my boots. "We have to plan. You have to know something about her or the clans that can help us."

Liam slid my boots off and pulled down the covers on the bed. "Sleep, Ena."

True terror welled in my chest as I stared at the pillow.

"I'll keep the nightmares away," Liam said.

I lay down on the bed, wishing the feather mattress would swallow me whole.

He pulled the blanket up over me.

Finn watched from his seat at the table. His face had lost even more color. Like I had killed him instead of the man and he had become one of the ghosts of the eastern mountains.

I rolled to face the wall, choosing to stare at the sticks rather than my friend's face.

"I'll keep you safe."

The bed shifted as Liam lay down behind me. He wrapped his arm around me and held me close, protecting me from every monster he could fight.

"Just sleep." His whispered words carried me into the blissful void of sleep.

30

The sun still hadn't risen when I woke up. I lay very still in bed, listening to Liam's steady breathing. Even through the blankets, his warmth wrapped around me like a cocoon. But I would not emerge from his embrace a beautiful butterfly.

I had killed a man. Not by passing a means of execution on to someone else. I had held the knife, and I had cut into his body, making sure he would die.

I remembered the warmth of his blood on my hand, yet somehow my part in his death didn't seem real. The whole thing was too quick, too absurd. As accustomed as I'd grown to the swift brutality the Guilds called justice, it was hard to make myself believe that I, Ena Ryeland, had ended up in a magical stronghold and been ordered to kill a man.

I nestled closer to Liam. He stirred and tightened his grip on my waist.

I had chosen to join this magic and madness. The Black Bloods had laws, and I had followed them. I would not plead innocence, and I could not regret my choice.

But there were innocent people left in the world. Children who had power running through their veins, magic they could not rid themselves of, that would see them locked up by the Sorcerers Guild if they were caught.

We needed a way to help the children escape that did not involve the Brien.

The gray light of sunrise filtered through the one window in the room.

There had to be a place we could keep the sorci children safe.

I had heard of lands beyond Ilbrea, across the Arion Sea or farther east than even the eastern mountains reached. But I had never seen those places. Even if I found a way to ferry the children to the kingless territories far to the south, I couldn't just pack the little ones up and send them to a place they might not be able to survive.

Wherever the Brien took them was supposed to be safe, Liam had promised me that much. If the Brien had found a safe place to take hundreds of magical children, surely we could as well.

But what if we couldn't? What if the children died because of me?

What if I gave Regan the poison and she caused a horror even worse than the Massacre of Marten?

There were no choices I could see that did not leave more death in my wake.

It all circled around and around in my head until Liam finally stirred behind me. He took a deep breath as he woke then shifted his head on the pillow.

I lay very still, hoping he would think I was sleeping and hold me for just a little while longer.

"Ena," Liam whispered, "did a nightmare wake you?"

"No, I don't have those anymore." I rolled over to face him.

The hard edges of his face had softened while he slept. His eyes held none of the fierce danger of the night before.

"I trust you, Liam," I said. "I have since you told me to run into the woods with you when Harane burned."

He brushed a hair away from my cheek.

"If you tell me to give Regan the poison, I will. But I don't trust her. She had me execute one of her own men."

"It's the law of the Black Bloods—"

I pressed my fingers over Liam's lips. "She smiled when she spoke of hurting the children. If she can do that so easily, will the life of one letch weigh on her conscience? If death is the justice she's used to, who would she be willing to kill with my aid? What if it isn't a monster but someone who simply refuses to do as she says? What if people die, from my poison, just because they're in her way?"

Liam lifted my fingers from his lips. "Then we tell her no. Refuse to give her anything."

"What about the children? We can't leave them out there waiting for the Sorcerers Guild to steal them, and we can't let Regan harm them."

"We'll figure something out."

"Or"—a shiver shook my shoulders. Liam drew me closer to him—"I can stay here. If Regan wants someone poisoned, I'll do it myself."

"No."

"That way, I'll know if the people killed by the brew I mix are guilty of a crime worthy of death."

"Absolutely not." Liam held me tighter still.

I lay my head against his chest, nestling under his chin, trying to memorize the feel of lying so intimately close to him.

"You will not stay here," Liam said. "I don't care what Regan demands. Your place is with the Duwead Clan. You swore an oath to me."

"But if it's stay here or—"

"No." Liam stood up, leaving the bed feeling too big without him lying beside me. "I am your trueborn, and my decision is final."

He pulled on his boots, slid the bolt aside, and stepped out into the dim morning light.

Follow him, a tiny voice called from the very back of my mind.

I wrapped the blankets tightly around my shoulders, trying to convince myself I wouldn't freeze without his warmth.

Finn lay on the floor with his back to me. I watched his side rise and fall.

"Do you agree with him?" I asked.

Finn kept breathing evenly.

"I've been sleeping next to you for months," I said. "I know you're not asleep."

"I don't know which of you is right." Finn rolled onto his back. "The Brien are power-ful. They control the path south, have controlled the route for hundreds of years. You don't gain that kind of strength without being brutal."

"But?"

"I don't know if their kind of brutality would help our cause or make us worse than the monsters we're trying to fight."

I pressed my palm against the pillow. Liam's warmth still clung to the fabric. "If I stay, I can make sure helping them doesn't make things worse."

"You can't stay," Finn said. "It doesn't matter what either of us thinks. Your trueborn has made his decision."

"But if he hadn't, what would you think I should do?"

"It doesn't matter." Finn tossed his blankets aside and sat up.

"It does to me."

Finn stared at the wall for a moment, rubbing his fingers along the ginger scruff on his chin.

"I wouldn't have you stay," he said. "If we're the ones taking the risks in Ilbrea, then we should be the ones setting the rules. If we keep going on as we are now, we'll never move beyond saving sorcis. And as glad as I am to help the children, it's not enough to topple the Guilds."

"So it's better for Ilbrea if I refuse to help Regan at all?"

"I don't know." Finn stood and walked over to the bed. He took my hand in his as he sat down. "But I'm not going to lose you because the chivving Brien can't find a way to take care of their own chivving problems. You and I are partners, Ena. I would no more leave you behind with Regan than I would with the Soldiers Guild."

I kissed the back of Finn's hand. "I adore you. You know that, right?"

"Everyone adores me. It's impossible to resist my charm."

31

I ate the breakfast two women delivered without being ill. It seemed strange that my stomach should so cheerfully accept food when I'd gutted a man the night before.

The women didn't stare at me, didn't curse and call me a killer when they cleared away my empty plate.

I wished they had. It would have been easier to hear the word from someone else's lips than to listen to the constant echo of it in my own mind.

Finn chattered on as we waited in the stick house. Food, Lygan Hall, the people around our camp, the people of the Duwead Clan who hadn't come to the camp. He talked without pause for hours. It was almost as though he too could hear the word echoing in my head and wanted to drown it out.

"We should go look for him," I said for the fifth time when the sun had grown to full brightness outside our window.

"Better to wait here." Finn squeezed my hand. "Liam will come back when he needs us."

"What if he needs us now?"

"Then he would be here now," Finn said.

"Not if someone hurt him." I pushed away from the table to pace the small, open patch of dirt. "What if someone wanted revenge for the letch's death? What if he's tied between two trees, bleeding?"

"He's not." Finn shifted to sit on top of the table. "He's probably out stomping through the forest, trying to convince himself not to level the mountain."

I made a sound somewhere between a whimper and a laugh.

"Either that, or he's decided it's better for him to speak to Regan on his own and they're already meeting inside the cavern."

"He wouldn't." I froze. "He can't."

"Of course he can. He's the trueborn. We are but his marked minions."

"No." I started for the door.

Finn leapt off the table and ran to block me.

"Finn, we have to make sure he isn't trying to meet with her on his own."

"We can't. It's not our place."

"Our place?" I shouted. "I'm the one who started this whole chivving mess. I'm the one who suggested poison. I'm the one who caused the Massacre of Marten. I will not be the one who leaves the sorci children to die!"

"You wouldn't be." Finn spoke in a low tone like I was a dog about to attack. "There are things in this world that are bigger than all of us, Ena. Only fools try to take the credit or blame for acts done by the gods."

"Get out of my way, Finn."

"Going out there will only make things worse."

Knock. Knock. Knock.

Both of us froze at the gentle knocking on the door.

I glanced to my bag before remembering I no longer had my knife.

"Come in." Finn stared into my eyes as the door opened.

Regan stood in the doorway.

"Good morning." She gave each of us a smile before crossing the threshold. "I was waiting to be sure you were awake enough for company. I would find it rude to impose after such a trying evening."

"An evening you—"

"We slept quite well," Finn cut across me. "And breakfast was delicious. I'd never want to make anyone think badly of my own clan, but the food in our camp is nothing like what you have here in the enclave."

Regan laughed. "Call it a personal fault. I cannot feel like there is any safety in the world if I am being ill fed. The haven the mountain has granted us provides great bounty. I insist on that bounty being skillfully used. After all, what's life without a good meal?"

"Does it count as a good meal if there's poison in it?" I asked.

"Ena—"

"It just seems like a betrayal to taint the thing you love with death," I said.

Regan examined me.

I tipped my head to the side, mimicking her motion, and kept my face bland.

"Perhaps," Regan said, "but we marry for power, murder for justice, breed to honor the past. There are a great number of things that go against what we would do in a perfect world. It is the way we must behave to survive."

"Is that what you think?" I laughed. "There are some things you cannot compromise for survival. Better to die than live betraying everything worth living for."

"Do you really think yourself wise enough to educate me?" Regan stepped closer to me. The stiff skirt of her violet dress swished as she moved.

"Not wise," I said, "just experienced. I've lived in Ilbrea. With no enclave to hide in, no clans or magic to protect me. I've lost everyone I ever cared for. Twice. My story is not strange. Suffering, pain, loss—those are the realities of life for every tilk in Ilbrea. And you would abandon the sorcis to the Guilds. You would allow children with magic in their blood to be locked up by the Sorcerers Guild."

"The Brien have spent years working to keep those children from the hands of the Sorcerers Guild. I have spent my life making sure they are ferried safely south."

"And now you would kill those same children?" I stepped toward her. "Is that the sacrifice you are willing to make? Is that what your laws and morals and chivving survival demand?"

"Yes." There was no hint of remorse in her tone.

"You shouldn't fear the Guilds invading the mountains. You are so much like the paun, you could become great friends. Slaughter everyone who displeases you and leave a river of blood in your wake."

Regan smiled.

I waited for men to come storming in to murder me, or for Regan herself to shoot a stone through my body and end my life.

"I see we will not be able to come to an agreement," she said. "Pity. Killing one of my people came so easily to you in the darkness, I had hoped by the brutal light of day you would see our situation as it truly is. I had hoped we would be able to continue saving those poor children."

A desperate fire flared in the center of my chest, blazing even brighter than my anger. "You want poison that badly? It's not even a hard thing to accomplish. Is there no one in your own clan you can order to brew something fatal?"

"Not with the subtlety you managed," Regan said. "I am perfectly capable of having a man killed. Ending his life without losing my allies is another matter."

The fire disappeared, replaced with an ice even more frightening.

"If it's only one," I said. "If you could promise you would keep the children safe. I could go and get the job—"

"I forbid it." Liam stepped into the house. Sweat coated his brow, and darkness filled his eyes.

"Forbid what?" Regan asked. "You, trueborn Duwead, do not hold that power in my enclave."

"I forbid Ena to brew poison for any purposes but my own," Liam said. "She shall not mix it, she shall not give instructions, she shall not work to kill by anyone's orders but my own."

A shiver shook my whole body as though the stone in my bones had recognized the command.

"That power I do hold here, Regan," Liam said.

I held my breath, once again waiting for Regan to rage or for her guards to come racing in to gut us.

"I'm impressed," Regan said. "I thought you were too soft for such a thing, Liam."

"I am not too soft to protect my own," Liam said.

"Then the sorci children must be dealt with." Regan brushed an imaginary speck of something off her perfect skirt. "I suppose it is time we stop risking so much to save children already tainted by Ilbrea."

"You won't be touching the children." Liam walked over to our line of packs by the wall. He picked mine up and thrust it into my hands. "Don't lie to yourself, Regan. Your people don't have the will or the resources to reach to the sorcis in Ilbrea without us. Don't bother sending your people into the woods to meet us. We won't be coming."

I slung my pack onto my back.

"And where will you take them, Duwead?" Regan said.

Liam tossed Finn his bag.

"It's nothing to do with you, trueborn Brien." Liam put on his own pack. "There's not a chivving rule in the treaty about a clan's right to give safe harbor to outsiders, so it's got nothing to do with you."

Liam stormed toward the door.

I kept close on his heels.

"What will Orla say?" Regan followed us out into the clearing. "Will she be generous? Will she accept the Ilbreans into her hall?"

Liam rounded on Regan. "To the Hall, across the Arion Sea, up to the white north itself. Whichever way we send them is none of your concern."

People appeared in the clearing, stepping out of their homes, emerging from the trees, surrounding us on all sides.

"You cannot make this decision for all Black Bloods," Regan said. "You are one tiny pebble born of the mountain. Do not think you are so mighty as to topple the summit."

"If the summit cracks, it will not be my doing," Liam said. "It will be the fault of those who forget the mountain granted shelter to a child."

He stormed up the long path of trees.

Finn took my arm, staying close to me as we followed behind him.

The forest around us held more magic during the daylight. The greens of the trees' leaves shifted from emerald to pine to mint. Birds with feathers of obscenely bright colors cooed as they flew overhead.

With the sunlight beaming down, I could see that we weren't in a valley as I had imagined, but in the hollowed-out summit of a mountain. Perhaps it was the gods themselves who dug out the top of a high peak to create a paradise for Regan to rule. Perhaps the mountains favored children born of the Brien line.

Either way, as I leapt over sparkling streams and dodged around brightly-hued wildflowers, I wanted nothing more than to return to the plainness of the camp. Featherbeds be damned, feed me slop all my days, I wanted to return to the camp as I had never craved a place in my life.

As I chased after Liam, I kept thinking that maybe I just didn't recognize our path through the woods since we were moving in the opposite direction by daylight, but when we reached a crevasse that dug deep enough into the ground to swallow the sunlight, I knew we had traveled a different trail.

I glanced up and down the fissure, searching for a way across, but the split in the earth reached as far as I could see in either direction.

Finn stepped up to the very edge of the crack, gazing down into the darkness below.

I waited for Liam to turn and follow another path, but he just stood beside Finn, staring into the black. Digging my nails into my palms, I stepped up between them.

The blackness below was not complete. It held shadows and textures that marked it as something different than a nightmare.

"It's not too late to go back," Finn said. "Ena could brew the poison and give it to me. I could feed it to the poor slitch Regan wants dead."

"I meant what I said." Liam knelt by the edge of the crevasse. "We've spent too long bowing to the other clans. Every sorci we deliver to Regan makes the Brien stronger. The more power we give them, the worse it will be for all of us if they start pushing down a path the Duweads cannot follow. The Brien will not gain one drop of poison made by Ena's hand."

"Where are we going to keep the children?" I asked.

Liam took my hand. "I swear to you, I will find them a safe place."

A bit of the pain in my chest ebbed away.

"I see them." Finn pointed farther along the crevasse.

I held on to Liam's hand as we followed Finn, not caring if I seemed like a frightened child.

Straining my ears, I listened for the sounds of a coming attack, waiting for an animal to leap out of the trees to devour us, or the Brien to charge out of the woods seeking vengeance for the blood on my hands.

"There." Finn stopped by the side of the rift, squinting into the darkness.

I followed his gaze, trying to find what might have caught his eye.

A thin staircase poked out of the rock wall, each step barely big enough to support a foot. The path led down into the pitch black below the reach of the sunlight.

"I suppose the mountain isn't feeling very generous today," Finn said.

"Any path out of here is a gift." Liam let go of my hand and stepped onto the first stair.

My heart leapt into my throat as sense told me he would plummet into the darkness and disappear forever.

Liam shifted his weight back and forth before moving to the next stair down. "We'll have to go slowly, but if the mountain wills it, we should make it to the bottom alive."

Finn waited until Liam's head had sunk below ground level before bowing me toward the steps.

"You don't want to go first?" I stepped up to the lip of the rift.

"Being marked by Liam won't make the mountain recognize you as one of her own," Finn said. "Better to have a Black Blood behind you so she doesn't decide the path is no longer needed."

"Thanks for that." I adjusted the pack on my back and stepped down.

3 2

I have never been a tiny waif of a creature, but my frame was still much smaller than Finn's or Liam's.

Even so, as we traveled down the rock staircase, it seemed like there wasn't enough width to the steps to keep me from toppling sideways and into the darkness. The shadows cast by the sun distorted the shape of the black rock below my feet. I tried to find the slanting shadows comforting, promising myself there was really more stone to the steps than I could see.

Then I placed my heel too close to the edge.

I swayed, and panic rushed through every nerve in my body.

"Ena!" Finn rammed his arm into my shoulder, slamming me against the solid wall.

"Are you all right?" Liam tried to look back but couldn't turn enough to see me.

"I'm fine." My voice came out too high. I took a deep a breath. "Wishing I had some decent light, that's all."

"We'll be out of here soon," Liam said.

"Good." My voice sounded stronger. "I've always loved to climb, but this is not the sort of challenge I crave."

Liam started down the steps again.

"I don't think any sane person would like these stairs." Finn lifted his arm away from me.

The shadows below seemed to taunt me, like they were waiting for me to slip again and fall into their terrible clutches.

I pressed my palm to the rock wall, wishing I could find even a hint of a handhold.

This is not the way your life ends, Ena Ryeland.

I steadied my nerves, taking slow breaths until my heart calmed. I kept my gaze locked on my feet as I stepped down.

"Is this always the way out of the enclave?" I asked.

"No," Liam said, "there are many paths in and out of the Brien's haven, but this was the only one that called to me today."

His voice soothed me almost as much as if he had been touching me.

I wanted him to keep speaking until I learned how to fill my body with the sound of his words.

"What's it like," I asked, "feeling the stone as you do?"

Liam didn't answer until I'd already opened my mouth to apologize for being too bold in asking.

"I don't really know how to describe it," Liam said.

The stone wall curved, leading us away from the shadows and into pitch black.

"Lovely," Finn said.

I felt for the next stair down with my toe.

"It's like a pull," Liam said. "Or an instinct, I suppose. I don't know if it's a scent, or magic, or the stone in my veins being pulled by the mountain itself. I can feel the stone around me. Some bits are dull and normal. Others call to me. When the mountain offers me a path, it burns bright."

"What about the boulders that protect the camp?" I kept feeling in the darkness for each new step. "Do they burn bright, too?"

"They're a part of me."

I could hear the smile in his voice. I wished there were light so I could see one side of his mouth arc up.

"It's my magic that creates the spell that protects us."

"It is?" I froze in the darkness.

"Why do you think the camp is run by a trueborn?" Finn said. "We've got to have one to work the stone magic to protect us. Liam wasn't chosen for his charm."

"Hmm." I couldn't think of a better thing to say.

"I can feel the boulders, though." Liam's voice sounded farther away.

I stepped as quickly as I dared to catch up.

"Returning to the camp feels like putting myself back together," Liam said. "And when the spell ends as the cold comes, it's like losing a slice of myself. It's not painful, but there are no more bits of me in the great stones. I am reduced to a being a normal man."

"Nonsense," Finn said. "You've scattered your magic in the little stones we use to protect ourselves outside the camp. You aren't normal, only small enough to travel in a pocket."

Liam and Finn both laughed.

I tried to join in, but the bouncing of my ribs jostled the pendant against my skin.

The warmth of the smooth stone sent heat soaring into my cheeks.

"Slow down," Liam warned.

I stopped with one foot in the air. My heart thundered in my ears as I listened for whatever danger lurked in the darkness.

A scratching and dull tapping carried from below.

My ankle itched as I longed for my knife.

The tapping carried out to my side and then behind me.

"We've reached the bottom," Liam said. "There's a tunnel for us to follow."

"Thank the gods," Finn said. "I try to be cheerful no matter how dark things get, but I don't think I could have climbed back up these chivving stairs with a smile on my face."

"Ena," Liam said.

Something brushed the side of my skirt.

"Take my hand. I'll help you the rest of the way."

I reached down and took Liam's hand. I had managed to climb down into the crevasse on my own, but knowing he waited for me in the darkness eased my fear of the black.

"Don't fuss over me," Finn said. "I can make it on my own."

"Last stair." Liam took my elbow as I stepped down onto the blissfully smooth ground. He guided me through the darkness to the side of the stairs.

"If I wasn't so eager to be out of Brien territory, I might suggest we take a bit of a rest," Finn said.

"I just want to reach the open air soon enough to put a fair bit of distance between us and the way out before it gets dark." Liam let go of my arm and placed my hand on a smooth wall of rock. "This way."

I stretched my other hand to the side, touching the opposite wall.

The tunnel was large enough for me to walk easily down, but the stone I trailed my fingers along sent shivers up my arms.

To my right, the rock was smooth, as though a mason had spent years meticulously grinding the surface.

To my left, the rock was cracked and uneven, as though the magic within the mountain had somehow missed this part of her stone.

I wanted to see what the ceiling looked like, to know if there was any design or reason as to why our path had been created this way. I settled for gratitude at being away from the stairs.

A rustling carried through the tunnel. I stopped, trying to hear details in the sound.

"Keep moving," Liam said.

"Of course." I tried to think through anything in my pack that might be used as a weapon. Beyond choking someone with my spare shift or smacking them with my comb, I had nothing but my fists, teeth, and utter will to survive to defend myself with.

The rustling came closer faster than we were moving. Another new sound joined the noise, flapping and squeaking.

"Liam!"

I barely managed to say his name before something heavy knocked me to the ground.

"Just hold still." Liam spoke close to my ear.

The rustling and flapping surrounded us.

Liam shifted to cover my head as a smack sounded right behind us.

"Chivving cact of a paun chivving, slitching—" Finn shouted. "I hate chivving bats."

My nails bit into my palms as the bats continued to surround us.

"Just hold still, and they'll give up," Liam said.

"I have never liked Regan." Finn's voice sounded muffled. "It's not that she never remembers my name. It's her chivving temper tantrums that drive me mad."

"It that what this is?" I spoke into the crook of Liam's shoulder.

"I knew she'd send a goodbye," Liam said. "At least she only chose bats."

The flapping faded away toward the terrible stairs.

"And this isn't against the treaty?" I asked.

"Not in any way that matters." Liam pushed himself off of me and took my hand, helping me to my feet. "There was no one here to witness it and no way to prove she sent her animal minions to scratch at us."

"Petty," Finn said. "That's what she is, plain petty."

"Come on," Liam said. "I'm tired of being down here."

"If either of you got cut, we'll have to clean the wounds," I said.

"Later," Liam said, "when we're free of Regan."

I strained my ears as we kept moving, listening for any more visitors in the darkness. But Regan had only been bold enough to scratch at us, not deliver a mortal wound.

We walked for a long while before a faint blue glimmered in the distance.

"Thank the gods," Finn muttered behind me.

The light grew brighter as we approached.

Soft sounds of movement carried from up ahead, but not the flapping of wings.

Leaning sideways, I peered around Liam.

We hadn't returned to the unground lake. A vast cavern, larger than even Regan's hall, waited for us.

Liam slowed as he reached the end of the tunnel, taking a moment to look around the cavern before letting me step into the open.

Our horses had been tethered to the cavern wall. A pile of our weapons lay nearby.

"Thank the gods." Finn's voice rang around the cavern.

33

The ride north through the mountains didn't hold the same dread as our journey to the Brien, but as the miles passed, a weight still hung over us.

Where will we send the children?

I didn't ask. Neither did Finn, but as Liam rode silently in front of us mile after mile, I knew Finn was wondering the same thing.

We made it all the way to the bit of the mountains we called home before any of us did anything but think.

It was the sharp scent of blood I noticed first, carrying past the earthy fragrance of the woods.

"Liam." I stopped my horse, sniffing the breeze.

The bay fidgeted beneath me, like she too could smell death on the wind.

"What is it?" Liam looked back over his shoulder at me, his face calm.

"There's something wrong." I slid down off my horse. "I think something's been killed."

"It's a forest, Ena," Finn said. "Things are killed in forests all the time. It's how the bigger creatures eat."

"I know that." I walked east, leading my mount behind me. The wind picked up, blowing a sweet and sickening stench of decay.

"Something has died." Finn jumped down from his horse and strode up beside me, covering his nose with his hand. "Do we really need to go near whatever is making that foul stink? Let the animal decay in peace."

I handed him my reins but didn't answer. I was too busy searching the trees for whatever had died.

I'm not sure why I needed to find the creature whose life had ended. Perhaps it was the familiar scent of blood that called to the bit of me that had been trained as a healer. Maybe the mountain was calling to me, begging to tell me her secret.

The mountain sloped down, cutting a gentle path around a place where the ground had collapsed, leaving a stream of boulders scattered between the trees.

Bile rolled into my throat as the wind carried a fresh wave of the stench.

"Ena." Liam thumped up behind me. "What are you looking for?"

"That." I pointed to the side of a moss-covered boulder.

A spray of blood had coated the green, dying it a putrid shade of black. The corpse of a deer lay on the ground, its stomach ripped open but the rest of its body intact, as though the scavengers of the forest had somehow been warned away from this feast. There wasn't even a fly buzzing around the rot.

But it wasn't the death that drew me forward. It was the long lines of claw marks sliced into the boulder, cutting through the moss. The same claw marks gouged the ground around the deer's body.

"It looks like the same beast who came after Finn and me." I picked my way around the corpse to get a better view of the claw marks. "It wasn't a bear that did this, Liam. There's no animal I know whose claws could cut so deep into stone."

"What did Orla tell you of the beast I warned you about?" Finn asked.

"Nothing." Liam turned away from the decay. "Only that she'd have to speak to the story keepers."

"Wonderful." Finn's mouth twisted as though he might be ill. "It's always nice when you have to refer to legends to gather information. Makes knowledge so reliable. And I was worried this summer was getting to be a bit dull." Finn climbed back up the slope, the horses outpacing him to the top.

"Could Regan have sent a beast after the camp?" I asked.

Liam frowned.

"She sent her bats to scratch at us," I said. "Maybe other animals with bigger claws obey her as well."

"I don't think she'd be foolish enough to send a beast into Duwead territory." He scrubbed his hands over his face.

"What are we supposed to do?" I backed away from the corpse, trying to rid myself of the fear that Death himself hid in the trees, watching me.

"We get back to camp," Liam said. "Make sure everyone there is safe, and see if any of the hunters have spotted anything."

I followed him up the slope, trying to convince my stomach I didn't need to be ill.

"Why are you being so calm about this?" I asked. "There's a monster in the woods. I've seen it, Finn's seen it, and it's close to camp."

"You don't run when you hear signs of danger," Liam said. "You don't flinch at the sight of blood."

"Of course not," I said. "I grew up in Harane living with an illegal healer. If got sick at the sight of blood, I wouldn't have made it this far."

"The legends of the mountains are in our blood," Liam said. "The creature you saw was only a bit bigger than a bear. It's killed a deer."

"But Regan—"

"Compared to the monsters that have roamed the eastern mountains, it's no worse than a wound that needs stitching," Liam finished.

I let out a great sigh and took my reins back from Finn. "Will I ever stop feeling like I'm stumbling through the dark?"

"If you can't tell there's sunlight, we have bigger problems than the beast." Finn mounted his horse.

"That's not what I mean," I said. "Every time I feel like perhaps I understand a bit about the Black Bloods, it all slips away in oaths, and marks, and bats, and monsters."

"If it makes you feel any better, I was born in Lygan Hall, and I still don't have a chivving clue what's going on half the time," Finn said. "Think of your confusion as a sign that you're accepting your life as a Black Blood."

"Thanks, Finn." My horse stomped her hoof as I climbed onto my saddle.

"I'll speak to the hunters as soon as we get back," Liam said. "Don't fret about the beast. The boundary will protect the camp."

"I'm sure it will." I urged my horse to follow Liam. "But I don't fancy meeting the monster on our next sorci run."

Liam's neck tensed.

"You said you'd gotten word about one we might need to rescue," I said. "We'll have to leave straight away if we want any chance of keeping them from the Sorcerers Guild. With how long it took us to find out we're truly on our own, we might already be too late."

"They'll have to hold on a bit longer," Liam said. "We have to prepare for them."

"Prepare for them how?" I asked.

"I still don't know," Liam said.

There was a sad resignation in his voice that I hated.

Self-loathing curdled in my gut. Liam could blame the clans and Regan, but it was me who had made the system begin to crumble. If those children were taken by the Sorcerers Guild, it would be because of the choices I'd made.

I placed my hand on my chest, pressing the stone pendant against my skin.

He stopped the nightmare. Liam can save the children, too.

The great stone boulders that surrounded our camp came into view, but the wonderful relief I'd expected didn't come.

The longing filled my chest, and hunger devoured my soul as we passed through the spell Liam had cast to protect the camp. I lingered between the stones for a breath, trying to feel a hint of him within the magic.

The longing threatened to shatter me.

"Liam," a man called from high up in the trees. Rothford dropped from the branches a moment later. "We've been hoping you'd be back soon."

There was something in the set of Rothford's jaw that replaced the longing with fear.

"Emmet's back. He's been pacing in front of your tent for two days now," Rothford said before Liam could speak. "Won't tell any of us what he's so fussed about, and no one fancies telling him he's got to stop."

"I'll go to him," Liam said.

"And a hunting party went out two days ago and hasn't come back. Neil's raving like it's a plot against him, and Marta's barely managed to keep the camp calm. She sent a search party out after the hunters, but we haven't heard back from them yet."

"Case," Finn said. "Where's Case?"

"Far as I know, he went out with the search party," Rothford said. "They didn't pass this way, so I'm not really sure who went."

Finn kicked his mount and raced toward the camp.

"I have to see Marta," Liam said. "We have to go after the rescue party."

He rode off as well.

"Why is he so worried about the rescue party?" Rothford asked. "I'm more concerned about your brother tearing the camp apart."

"Have you seen any animals?" I said. "Monsters prowling beyond the stones?"

"Haven't seen much of anything as far as animals," Rothford said. "Why? What's going on?"

"Just keep a close watch."

Rothford grabbed the reins of my horse. "It's my chivving job to keep a close watch, and I'll continue doing my duty well. What are you going to do about your brother?"

"Liam can…" I shut my eyes, trying to sort through everything that needed to be done to find my place in the madness. "I'll take care of Emmet."

"Thank you." Rothford let go of my reins. "All of camp thanks you."

I kicked my horse and galloped off toward camp.

I'd never ridden through the paths around camp before. I leaned close to my horse's neck, ducking beneath the tree branches and trying to pretend I didn't notice the people staring at me.

Liam's horse was by the cook tent, but neither he nor Marta was anywhere in sight.

The usual people sitting scattered through the clearing started when I came charging through, and others peeked out of their tents as I slowed my horse right in front of my brother.

"Ena." Emmet looked up at me. He hadn't shaved in a while. The dark brown scruff on his face had nearly grown into a proper beard. Dark rings stood out against the pale skin under his eyes, which did not brighten as he looked at me. "Where have you been?"

"Did no one tell you?" I draped my hands over the front of my saddle.

"I was told you'd gone to speak to the trueborn Brien," Emmet said.

"Well then, why are you asking questions?" I tipped my head to the side, keeping a look of innocent ignorance on my face.

"You should not be speaking to the Brien." Emmet stepped closer to my horse.

The bay sighed her displeasure.

"Well, it's done." I stroked the horse's neck. "I'm back now, so there's no use fussing over it."

"The Brien trueborn shouldn't be trusted, let alone—"

"Are you pacing in front of Liam's tent waiting for me?" I cut across him.

Emmet's face darkened.

"If you are," I said, "you can stop now. What's past is past, so go get some rest. You look like a chivving corpse."

"I need to speak to Liam," Emmet said. "So you go get some rest. Quite frankly, you look like the gods have tried to take you as well."

"I can't rest. I have work to do."

"What work?" Emmet took hold of my horse's bridle.

"Do not try to pretend you have any control over me, Emmet." I kept my voice steady. "If you want to speak to Liam about whatever men you killed on your rampage of vengeance in Ilbrea, so be it. But as for my work, my seeing the Brien, anything to do with my life, leave it be."

Emmet kept his grip on the bridle as he stared at me. "Where's Liam?"

"He went to find Marta at the cook tent. I don't know where they went from there. There's a monster roaming the woods. We found a deer it had killed. He's worried about the hunters."

Emmet looked up to the sky.

"What did you need to tell him?" I asked. "If it wasn't about me, why would you spend two days pacing?"

He didn't say anything.

"I was fine with the Brien," I said. "They kept to the word of the treaty."

"You and I were not born Black Bloods, Ena." Emmet reached up and took my hand. A barely-healed wound marked his wrist. "We were born Ryelands. We are children of Ilbrea, not the mountain. We cannot trust their magic to protect us, and no one can trust their treaty."

"What's that supposed to mean?"

"You'll have to ask the one you swore yourself to." Emmet let go of my hand and the horse's bridle. "I don't care if you like me, Ena. But I hope you know I would never betray you."

I shut my eyes, pressing down the old hurts that flared in my chest. "Is there a traitor in the camp?"

"I don't know. I'm not sure who's betrayed us."

"Is the camp in danger?"

"The whole chivving world is about to burn."

34

I have never been one to trust easily. I'm not sure if I was born that way or if the Guilds stole that childlike habit when they stole my parents.

But in Harane, I had always known who I could not trust. Every paun was an enemy. There was no need to question, no need to guess. Anyone in a Guild uniform was out for our blood.

Standing in the clearing, I missed that simplicity.

"We only have a few hours until dark," Liam said. "I want you traveling in groups of three. Everyone is to be fully armed. If you find the beast, protect yourselves first, but if the opportunity comes, kill it. You have to be back inside the camp before dark. Do not add yourself as another person we have to save. It will only make our job in looking for the others more difficult. Go, all of you."

It didn't seem like Liam to dismiss everyone so abruptly, but then I'd never seen him address the whole camp before.

"This is chivving ridiculous." Finn checked the sword on his hip and arrows on his back. "I need a horse. And I can't come back before dark."

I took his face in my hands. "We will find Case. I promise you."

"You aren't going out there." Emmet spoke from behind my shoulder.

"Yes, I am." I rounded on my brother. "And as you are not the trueborn in charge of this camp, you really don't have a say in it."

Emmet glared at me for a long moment.

"We have to go. I can't waste time with the two of you bickering." Finn strode south.

"If you're so fussed, join us," I said. "I'm not letting Finn go out there without me."

"You should stay behind in case someone comes back injured," Emmet said. "Winnie may need help if anyone needs healing."

"I should go out there and find the ones who are too hurt to make it back to camp." I patted the bag at my hip. "I'm not wandering into the woods unprepared. There are people out there who might need my help."

"There's a lot of mountain around us. Do you really think you'll be the one to find them?"

I leaned close to whisper to Emmet. "If you really think someone in this camp may have betrayed the Black Bloods, I'm not sitting here alone waiting while everyone else leaves. And I am not letting Finn go out there without me. He's your friend, too, Emmet. Abandoning him when he's afraid is a betrayal, even if you don't see it."

I took off running, following Finn's bright red hair through the trees. I smiled without even meaning to as Emmet's boots thundered behind me.

"Where did you find the deer?" Emmet asked as soon as we reached Finn.

"About a mile south of the boundary," Finn said.

"There wasn't a sign of the monster, but the kill wasn't that old," I said.

"Ena!" Marta shouted.

We paused as she tore through the trees behind us.

"Ena, are you going out there?" Pink had crept into Marta's cheeks, and sweat beaded on her brow.

"Yes," I said. "This is our party of three."

"We have to go." Finn shot a glare at Marta before continuing his path south.

"The three of you are a group?" Marta glanced to Emmet. "Liam didn't mention you joining the search, Ena. I think he meant for you to stay behind."

"Did he give that order?" I asked.

"Well, no—"

"Is he still in camp?" I cut across her.

"He rode out with Tirra and Kerry," Marta said.

"Then I suppose it's too late for him to tell me to stay behind." I turned and headed south.

"Emmet," Marta said, "I could go as the third."

"Get back to camp," Emmet said. "I don't have time to wrestle my sister into reason."

I ducked under the drooping bows of a pine tree to catch up to Finn. "Case will be all right."

"The search party left at dawn," Finn said. "A beast with claws that large could have torn through all of them in a minute."

"We saw the beast at night," I said. "If it came after us at night, it's probably sleeping right now."

"Maybe," Finn said.

"So, we'll find Case and bring him back before dark." I gripped the hilts of the knives on my hips. It seemed strange, almost foolish, to have three knives on my person. What could I accomplish with three knives that I couldn't manage with two? But Cati had handed them to me, and the weight of them offered a strange comfort.

The boulders of the boundary loomed in front of us.

"We can go as a party of two." Emmet shoved aside a tree branch to walk next to me.

"Liam ordered groups of three," I said.

"I just got back from slipping in and out of an Ilbrean city on my own," Emmet said. "Finn and I will be fine."

"You haven't seen the monster," Finn said.

Dread settled like a stone in my stomach.

"Ena—" Emmet began.

"I thought you'd learned not to argue with me." I pulled one of my knives from its sheath as we stepped through Liam's spell.

Please stay safe. I sent the wish into his magic, hoping he could somehow hear me.

Finn didn't slow his pace as we headed straight for where we'd found the deer.

The stench had somehow worsened in the short time we'd been away from the carcass. The stink led us straight to the awful scene without even needing to think about retracing our steps.

Emmet strode around the body and straight to the gouge marks in the rock. "What under the stars..."

"It left the same scratch marks in the stone when it tried to attack us," I said.

"This thing tried to attack you?" Emmet spun toward me. If the stench bothered him, he showed no sign.

"On the way home from our last sorci run," I said. "We told Liam when we got back."

Finn examined the ground where the beast had left scratch marks in the dirt.

"We should track the monster," Emmet said. "If it's attacked the search party, we'll find them along his trail. If not, we still stand a chance of finding and killing the beast."

I searched the dirt around me for signs of tracks. There was lichen, and mushrooms, a bit of sweet grass. My eyes spotted all the things I'd trained myself to look for but no sign of animal prints.

"Did it leave a trail after it attacked you?" Emmet knelt between two trees.

"Not that I noticed," I said, "but I wasn't exactly looking."

Finn kicked a tree, cracking off a great chunk of bark. "Why? What legend spawned a monster that doesn't leave tracks?"

"We'll keep looking." I circled off through the trees, squinting at the earth, searching for any oddity left in the dirt.

"Ena, do not walk that far from me," Emmet said.

I pressed my palms to the sides of my head. "We need a plan. We need a search pattern or..."

We'd never had to search for anyone in Harane. If something horrible happened to one of the villagers, it was usually at the hands of the Guilds and done in full view so everyone could watch in powerless horror.

"Case!" Finn shouted, heading east down the slope. "Case, can you hear me?"

"Hello." I cupped my hands around my mouth and called into the trees. "Is anyone out there?"

It seemed foolish to make such a racket, like we were calling the ill will of the gods down upon us, but I followed Finn and shouted into the forest anyway.

I had spent enough time wandering through this part of the woods to recognize where we were.

My steps veered away from Finn's path.

"Ena, where are you going?" Emmet caught my arm.

"Toward the falls." I yanked free of his grip. "Animals, people, we all need water. If we're going to wander and shout, shouldn't we go toward something that might draw people in?"

"Finn," Emmet shouted, "come this way."

Finn didn't acknowledge that he'd heard Emmet, but he shifted his path to follow me toward the waterfall.

I gripped my knife tighter as the rushing of the water carried through the trees. At best, we might find the missing Black Bloods huddled by the bank. At worst, my sanctuary would be contaminated by death and blood.

"Case!" Finn shouted. "Can you hear me? Case!"

I held my breath as the falls came into view. There was no hint of blood or terrible scratch marks to be seen.

"Hello!" I called. "Is anyone there?"

"We can head back toward camp," Emmet said. "Cut a wide circle and see if we find anything else."

"Give me a minute." I lifted my bag off my shoulder and tossed it to Emmet.

"What are you doing?" Emmet asked.

"Getting a better view." I tucked my knife back into its sheath and wiped my palms on my skirt.

"I'll head farther south," Finn said.

"We stay together, Finn." I started climbing.

"Ena, don't be foolish," Emmet said.

"You'd rather risk missing something than trust me to complete a task?" I asked.

"Just…" Emmet paused. "Just be careful."

Climbing the rock face naked had been faster and easier, but even with having to move carefully to keep my skirt from wrapping around my ankles, it only took me a few minutes to reach the top.

"Case!" Finn shouted into the woods. "Case, please answer me!"

I dragged myself onto the ledge and rolled over to sit on the rocks. The wind sweeping through the trees held no hint of rot or blood. I squinted into the distance, following the path of the river through the forest. Birds flew from tree to tree, but there was no other movement in sight.

I stood and picked my way across the ledge, peering into every shadow below me.

"I don't see anything," I called. "We could follow the river. There might be something downstream I can't see from up here."

"We haven't got much longer before we have to head back," Emmet said.

"I'm not going back to camp," Finn said. "Not until we've found them."

"I know you want to find Case," Emmet said, "but Liam is right. Wandering through the dark would just leave more people who have to be found."

"Would you leave Ena out here?" Finn asked.

I looked away from them, not wanting to see my brother's face.

"We head back to camp and check in," Emmet said. "Make sure they haven't been found. We'll search a different path on the way back, and if there's still no word, we'll collect what we need to keep searching through the night."

"Thank you," Finn said.

I turned around to kneel at the edge of the rocks and begin my descent. I looked upstream, and my mind stopped.

I could not find a way to process the blood that stained the dirt by the banks, or the bones picked so clean they did not smell of death.

"Emmet." I pushed myself back to my feet. "How many Black Bloods were in the hunting party?"

"Two," Emmet called up, "and there were eight in the search party."

I couldn't feel my feet moving as I walked toward the bones.

They had been shattered and scattered across the bank.

"Ena?" Emmet called up. "Ena, what's going on up there?"

The sounds of him climbing came from behind me, but I couldn't find the words to answer.

I stopped between two crushed skulls. A nauseous grief rolled through me.

"I've found the hunters," I shouted.

"Just the hunters?" Finn called up. "Are they alive?"

Emmet laid a hand on my shoulder. "We need to get back to camp."

"Are they alive?" Finn shouted.

"No," Emmet said.

"What should we do with the bones?" I asked. "I don't know what Black Bloods do with their dead."

"We'll come back for them in the morning," Emmet said. "We don't have a way to carry…"

"All the pieces?" I nodded and headed back to the cliff. "What if an animal scavenges the bones?"

"It won't matter to them," Emmet said. "They're already dead."

3 5

It didn't take us long to get back to camp. We made it well before dark.

The watcher wasn't hiding up in the trees. She stood in the open, her bow drawn as we approached.

"We found the hunters," Emmet said before she could ask. "Tell anyone else who comes in this way."

A gasp caught in her throat, but she nodded just the same.

I wasn't sure who she cared so much for or if she would have grieved that fiercely for anyone from the camp who was lost to the monster in the woods.

I didn't even know who the hunters had been, and now that I'd seen their shattered bones, I didn't want to know.

Neil was in the cook tent as we passed, laboring on his own to provide an evening meal. No one waited in line to eat.

The silence inside the camp prickled against my neck. I'd never noticed all the little sounds the Black Bloods created just in living their lives. Without the voices and footsteps filtering through the trees, the woods felt like a tomb.

Only four people waited in the clearing.

Marta paced a long line down the center of the packed earth, and three others sat together, their shoulders hunched and voices silent.

"Marta," Emmet said.

Her gaze whipped toward us at the sound of his voice. Her eyes brightened for a moment before her face went paler than its usual porcelain.

"What did you find?" Marta's voice didn't waver.

"The hunters are dead," Emmet said. "Ena found them."

"Is the search party back?" Finn asked.

"Not yet," Marta said, "but you're early. There's time before dark, and most will look till the last moment, the search party included."

"Then we should go back out," Finn said. "We should keep trying to help."

"We wait until dark," Emmet said. "Find out where everyone else has searched."

"We can't—"

"Think through it." Emmet took Finn's shoulders. "Actually think through what I'm saying and tell me running through the woods without any information will be better for Case? This isn't about you feeling better because you're doing something. It's about finding him alive."

Finn let out a shuddering breath and nodded.

"You should eat," Marta said. "If you're going to go against Liam and run into the forest, you can't do it hungry. I'll go fetch you some food."

Finn looked like he might argue for a moment before he nodded and sat on a bench.

"I'll help," I said.

"No, you rest." Marta shooed me toward a bench. "If you're going to be running back out there—"

"Ena won't be coming with us," Emmet said. "And I will not to be swayed on it."

"That's not—"

"Food first," Marta cut me off and grabbed my hand. "No point in arguing about anything. The search parties will back soon."

I let her lead me toward the kitchen tent.

3 6

"Do you really think I should let Finn and Emmet run through the woods on their own?" I asked as soon we were out of the clearing.

"Of course not," Marta said. "The two of them are excellent fighters, but it only gives them confidence they shouldn't have. A beast has leapt straight out of a legend and come to terrorize our camp. Neither of them should go back out there tonight."

"Then why are we fetching them food?" I stopped in the middle of the path.

Marta looped back around, took my arm, and dragged me toward the kitchen tent. "Because if I told them they couldn't do it, I would have to spend the next hour standing in the clearing, fighting with two pigheaded fools, neither of whom is capable of seeing reason when they're riled up. Better to feed them and keep them calm while we wait for the others to return."

"But what if they haven't found the search party?"

"Then we make Liam order Finn not to go." Marta furrowed her brow.

"And Emmet?" I asked. "Will Liam order him to stay in camp as well?"

We stopped outside the kitchen tent.

"Emmet has never taken kindly to orders," Marta said, "but we'll do whatever we can to convince him. And if that doesn't work, I'll knock him over the chivving head and tie him up until morning."

She strode into the tent, leaving me staring at her with an open mouth.

"They're all going to complain." Neil slopped stew into bowls. "They'll come back tired and hungry, and all of them will complain."

"And I'll tell them to be grateful for what they have or there will be no more ale this summer." Marta passed me two wooden bowls and tucked two spoons into my pocket. "You're feeding the entire camp on your own tonight. Anyone who isn't thankful is a fool." She patted Neil on the shoulder before taking two more bowls and nodding me out of the tent.

"You're good at that, you know," I said as we followed the path back toward the clearing.

"I do know," Marta said. "My grandmother had five children and twenty-three grand-children. Who knows? There could be even more of us by the time we get back to Lygan Hall this fall. I learned how to handle a pack of rowdy children from her. Minding the camp is honestly the same thing. The only difference being the ones who whine around here are more likely to cheer up if I offer them a mug of ale rather than a sweet."

I laughed without meaning to.

"There you are." Marta shot me a dimpled smile. "A bit of food and you'll be ready to face whatever the gods send us next."

"Thank you, Marta."

Voices carried from the clearing, and more than just the five we'd left behind.

Marta and I picked up our pace, moving as quickly as we could without spilling the stew.

A pack of people had gathered in the center of the clearing.

I headed for the bench where I'd left the boys, but Finn wasn't sitting beside my brother. "Where's Finn?"

Emmet pointed to the middle of the group where Finn held Case tightly in his arms.

Case's dark hair wasn't as carefully-combed as usual. Dirt covered his clothes, but he bore no sign of injury.

"Did the whole search party make it back?" I pressed a bowl of stew into Emmet's hand.

"All eight," Emmet said.

"Did they see anything?" I sat beside Emmet.

"Not the beast you and Finn spoke of, but they did find a wolf den. The whole pack had been slaughtered and left to rot." Emmet began eating his stew.

We sat together, waiting for the rest of the camp to return.

Finn broke the news to the others that the hunters had been killed. I suppose it was right. He was truly one of them. He shared the grief of the people who cried at his words more thoroughly than Emmet or I could.

Since the groups of three returned in stages, the cycle repeated over and over.

Three would return. They would see the original search party, and joy would light their faces. They would see the grief around them, and questions would begin.

I wished the guards would tell the returners. But most of the guards probably didn't know. I pitied the person who would have to circle the boundary of the camp, delivering the horrible news over and over again.

Marta moved quietly around the clearing, taking a tally of who had returned, sending people to get their dinner and warning them to be kind to Neil.

Someone hung the lae stones as true night began to fall. As the blue glow cast shadows across the clearing, the mood shifted again.

I left my empty bowl beside Emmet and crossed calmly to Marta, trying not to spook any of the grieving people. I took her arm and leaned close to her ear, careful to keep my face placid.

"How many still aren't back?" I whispered.

Marta's arm tensed beneath my touch. "Six."

"Where's Liam?"

"I don't know." Her breath shook as she inhaled. "He'll be fine, he's a trueborn. He rode out too far searching, and now he's on his way back."

"We have to find him." I moved to step away, but Marta caught my arm in an iron grip.

"It is dark, and there is a monster out there," Marta whispered. "We cannot have people charging madly through the woods."

"I'm not going to go charging anywhere," I said. "I am going to get a light and Finn's bag of magic stones, and then I will calmly find Liam."

"No, you won't."

"Then knock me over the head and tie me up until morning." I wrenched my arm free. "I will not leave Liam out there."

"Ena," Marta whispered after me as I walked away. "Ena."

I weaved through the crowd to where Finn and Case sat gripping each other's hands.

I knelt in front of Finn. "Liam's not back."

Finn looked around the clearing as though I had somehow missed Liam in the pack of people.

"He's out there, Finn," I said. "I have to do something."

"Do what?" Case asked. "We got back from our search to find that a beast killed Dillon and Pierce—"

"Pierce?" A ringing filled my ears. "Pierce was one of the hunters?"

"Ena." Finn took my hand, lacing his fingers through mine, anchoring me to the world.

"Those bones belonged to Pierce, and I didn't know it?" A burning hot panic rose in my chest. "I should have known. I should have asked who was out there."

"What's wrong?" Emmet knelt beside me.

"She didn't—"

"Liam's still out there." I swallowed the sick in my throat. "We have to find him."

Emmet closed his eyes and curled his fingers into tight fists. The scars on his hands shone in the light of the lae stones.

"He is the trueborn of this camp," Finn said. "Even if he was a chivving slitch, it would still be our duty to protect him."

"Finn," Case said, "think through this, please."

"We should find some others to go with us," Emmet said. "See if we can figure out which direction they rode."

"We can ask if anyone ran into them in the woods," I offered.

"Marta might know," Finn said.

"She doesn't want to cause a panic," I said.

"Everyone will panic," Case said.

A scream cut through the woods, carrying toward the clearing.

"Liam." I sprang to my feet and ran to the bench where I'd left my bag.

"Ena." Emmet chased after me.

"Someone is hurt." I dodged around him, racing toward the sound.

"You don't know that." He sprinted along beside me. "The camp could be under attack."

"It doesn't matter." My heart lurched into my throat as another scream pierced the darkness. "I know that sound, someone is in pain. I didn't get to escape Harane for Nantic when I was a child. I know what agony sounds like, and I will not ignore it."

We passed the cook tent where Neil stood facing the screams, a kitchen knife clutched in each hand.

A lower shout joined the screaming, but I couldn't understand the words.

I raced toward the low voice, running so fast Emmet fell behind.

Liam.

He knelt on the ground. Blood covered his hands, but he was alert and moving.

"We need help." Liam spoke to a gray-haired man. "Go find Winnie. Find Ena."

"I'm here," I panted as I dodged around Tirra and three terrified horses to reach Liam's side.

I started to ask where he'd been hurt, but the woman lying in front of him screamed.

"She's in so much pain," Liam said. "Ena, please help her."

I tore my gaze from Liam's face to look at the woman on the ground. I'd never seen her before. Her clothes looked closer to what was worn in the cities in Ilbrea than the plain colors the Black Bloods in camp favored. Sweat glistened on her pale face, and deep red splotches marked her cheeks and neck.

A gash sliced into her right arm, but there was more blood on her skirt around her thigh.

"Hello," I said, my voice calm even as the woman screamed again, "my name is Ena. I know you're in pain, but I need you to breathe."

She gave a whimpering cry.

"I have to lift your skirt to look at your legs." I took my bag off my shoulder and opened the flap before folding up the woman's skirt. A blood-stained bandage had been wrapped around the woman's leg.

"Did you put this on?" I asked Liam as I pulled a little bottle of liquor and a clean cloth from my bag.

"No," Liam said. "She was already hurt when we found her in the woods. She must have bandaged it herself."

"That was very brave of you." I glanced at the woman's sweat-slicked face. She didn't seem to have heard me. I opened the bottle, and lifted her arm. "I'm sorry about how much this will sting."

She screamed as I poured the liquor onto the cut.

I pressed a cloth over the wound. "Liam, hold this right here, and don't move. It'll need stitches later, but some good pressure will do for now."

The woman whimpered as Liam pressed down on the deep cut.

"I'm going to unwrap your leg." I pulled my knife from its sheath. "I'll get a look at what's happened, and then we'll get you patched up."

She hadn't used a proper bandage to dress her wound. The bloody fabric I sliced through looked to be bits of a shawl she'd torn into strips.

A shiver shook her shoulders as I gently peeled the bandage away.

Her flesh had been torn by sharp teeth. The jaw of whatever had bitten her had been massive, large enough to clamp around her thigh. Lines of indigo blue wound through the broken skin, standing out even through the red of the blood.

"Ena," Liam said.

"Where's Winnie?" I folded the bandage back into place. "Emmet, find Winnie."

My brother tore away through the trees without question.

"What bit you?" I leaned over the woman.

Her glassy eyes didn't find my face.

"Look at me." I patted her uninjured hand. "I just need you to tell me what bit you."

"I think it was the beast you and Finn saw," Liam said. "She mumbled something about the animal's claws, but we couldn't get her to tell us much. She didn't seem to hear all our questions. She kept talking about the children."

"Children?" I looked out to the darkness beyond our boundary. "Are there children out there?"

"She's a tracker from Ilbrea." Liam's voice grew raspy. "She was trying to bring a message about a sorci. She must have been attacked on her way to camp."

"I'm coming!" Winnie's high-pitched voice cut through the trees. She toddled on her bad hip, moving as fast as I'd ever seen her manage.

Emmet kept by her side, both arms extended and ready to catch her.

"I need help." I moved my bag out of the way before Winnie even reached us. "The cut on her arm can be stitched, but she's got a bad bite on her leg. I've never seen anything like it."

Emmet took Winnie's elbow and helped her to the ground. Her hands were steady as she lifted away the bloody fabric.

"By the gods," Emmet breathed.

"I didn't want cleaning it with the liquor to make it worse," I whispered. "I don't know how to treat that kind of infection."

Winnie's hands shook as she covered the wound. "It's not an infection. It's a venom."

"What?" Liam said.

"How do we help her?" I asked.

Winnie picked up the bottle of liquor and handed it to me. "Feed this to her."

"Will it help?" I jumped over the woman and knelt on her other side, carefully lifting her head to drizzle the liquor into her mouth.

"It might dull the pain." Winnie winced as she shifted to sit in the dirt.

"Should we get her back to camp?" I asked.

"We'll wait here with her," Winnie said. "Moving her will only cause pain, and it shouldn't be too long now that she's gone quiet."

I looked down at the woman's face. I hadn't noticed that her screaming had stopped in the rushing of my own fear.

"What kind of animal with teeth like that has venom?" Emmet said.

"No idea." Winnie furrowed her brow, adding extra depth to all the lines on her weathered face.

"It's got to be the beast," Liam said. "At least I hope it is. I pray the gods haven't set two monsters on this mountain at once."

The woman's breathing slowed. The red had swallowed her whole face.

"The hunters," Liam asked, "were they found?"

A sharp pain dug into the center of my chest.

"They were killed," Emmet said.

Liam's face crumpled.

"We found their bones." Emmet placed a hand on Liam's shoulder. "We can gather them in the morning."

"Did everyone else make it back?" Liam asked.

"We were still missing your group and one other set of three when I heard the scream-ing," I said. "Marta was counting everyone."

"I should go to her," Liam said.

"You don't have to hold the wound," Winnie said. "It might be kinder if you didn't."

Liam didn't move.

"What was her message?" I asked. "About the child?"

"It doesn't matter," Liam said.

"Yes, it does," I said. "She climbed through the mountains and faced a monster to deliver it. Her message matters."

"The Sorcerers Guild is circling the sorci she's been watching. She was trying to find out why we hadn't come to rescue the child."

37

I have seen Death too many times.

He is a constant shadow that follows me on whatever path I tread. I see the shape of him lurking in places where there should be only light. I see him mirroring my every movement like a child taunting me.

I have tried to save the people I love from that dark embrace, but I am not that mighty. I have tried to offer myself in place of those Death seeks, yet I am spared.

I will never be stronger than Death, but I have never been reasonable enough to stop fighting against him.

Perhaps Death is not lurking behind me. Perhaps he is pinned to my soul, and all the suffering I have seen has been caused by my own hand.

3 8

The last three returned an hour after darkness had fallen. None of them had met the monster in the woods.

There was no music in the clearing that night, but most of the camp was still there, sitting on the benches and stools, unwilling to leave the comfort of their fellows. Neil built the fire in the corner up to be twice as large as normal. The blaze sent a flickering light dancing through the shadows. It should have been beautiful.

I couldn't find any comfort in the fire. I couldn't manage much of anything but trying not to stare at Liam's empty chair as I wondered what had been done to the tracker's body and if Pierce's bones had been carried away by a scavenger.

"Can I sit?"

I looked up to find Emmet towering over me.

I didn't have the energy to tell him to leave me alone. I patted the empty bench beside me.

"I brought you a drink." Emmet passed me a mug of ale. "I've heard you like the stuff."

His gaze slipped toward the barrel in the corner where Marta stood beside Neil.

"Not really." I took a sip, trying not to wince at the pungent, floral taste.

"You don't have to drink it then." Emmet sipped from his own mug.

"I know, but at least it gives me something to do with my hands."

Emmet nodded.

We sat quietly for a moment. Everyone in the clearing spoke in hushed tones. I wasn't sure if the whispers were born of grief or fear of the monster roaming in the dark.

"Marta told me you and Pierce were friends," Emmet said.

I gripped my mug and waited for him to start raging about my having run into the woods with a man.

"I'm glad you're making friends here," Emmet said, "and I'm sorry you lost one."

"We weren't friends. Not really. But he was a good man."

"I didn't hate him."

I took another drink. The ale tasted like Pierce's lips. I couldn't tell if the pain in my stomach was grief or utter revulsion.

"I didn't know," I said. "When I found the bones, I didn't know he was one of the missing hunters. I know it's absurd…"

The image of his blond hair and bright blue eyes pounded through my mind.

I took a long drink of my ale.

"I feel like I should have recognized him," I said. "There was no way for me to tell, but I knew him. He shouldn't have seemed like a stranger in death."

"It was bones, Ena." Emmet laid a hand over my mug as I moved to take another drink. "His own mother wouldn't have known him. At least you found him. Because of you, we don't have to put any more lives at risk searching the woods. I'll lead a party out to collect the bones in the morning. Pierce will have a proper burial because of you. His family won't have to wonder what became of him because of you. That is a true gift to give a fallen friend."

I lifted his hand off my mug. "Thanks, Emmet."

"Sure." Emmet downed the rest of his ale. "You should get some rest. You look terrible, and the stars have already tormented you enough for one day."

"You don't look much better, you know."

For a moment, I almost believed I caught a hint of a smile on my brother's face. "Some of us deserve more torment than others." He gave me a nod and went back toward the barrel of ale.

I watched him as he was bowed to the front of the line for a drink. Neil didn't argue as he filled Emmet's mug. My brother crossed the clearing to sit on a stump by himself, and all the people he passed nodded to him.

They didn't approach him or try to bend his ear, but they were all aware of Emmet. I didn't know if their attitude came from deference or fear. It didn't matter either way.

I sat alone as I finished the rest of my ale.

Finn and Case were on a bench by themselves, deep in a whispered conversation. Cati sat with the last group that had returned. Those four didn't talk much.

When I finished my drink, I sat for a few more minutes, waiting for something to happen. For the gods to send a miracle or for the world to burn around us. The stars did not send a sign to block my path.

I stood up, returned my mug to Neil, and walked down the path toward the tents.

A blue light glowed through the canvas of Liam's tent.

I knocked on the pole without letting myself hesitate.

"Yes?" Liam's voice still had the same gravelly texture to it as when we'd been kneeling beside the tracker.

"It's Ena." I forced my shoulders to relax. "I need to speak to you."

"Come in."

My fingers froze on the flap of his tent.

Time will not make this easier.

I stepped into Liam's home.

Someone had brought him food and drink. He hadn't touched either. The scent of stale root stew filled the space.

Liam sat at the table, his face drawn and pale. Sheets of pressed paper, a pen, and a tub of black ink waited in front of him.

"What do you need?" Liam said. "Has the beast been sighted by the guards?"

"Not that I've heard of." I started for the other chair at the table and froze.

This could be the end for you.

I shoved the what-ifs, grief, and regret aside and sat at the table. "How are you?"

"Alive," Liam said. "Which doesn't seem fair as I've lost three people under my command in the past two days."

"Did they know it was dangerous?"

"What?" A wrinkle creased the center of Liam's brow.

I wanted so badly to soothe away the worries that plagued him.

"Coming with you to camp, ferrying the sorcis, daring to breathe without the blessing of the Guilds—did they know what they were doing was dangerous?"

Liam looked up to the steep angle at the top of the tent.

"You made it abundantly clear to me when I wanted to join," I said. "I know being here is dangerous. I know helping the sorcis is dangerous. Do you think any of the fallen weren't smart enough to have figured that out?"

"No. They knew. They all knew."

"Then do not give yourself credit for their deaths." I leaned across the table. "They chose to risk their lives for something they believed in. The sacrifice was theirs to make. You do them a disservice by thinking your place in their end was more powerful than their own bravery."

"I should have warned people about the beast," Liam said. "I should have forbidden everyone from leaving camp. Sent out parties to kill the monster—"

"You couldn't kill the monster while keeping everyone trapped in camp."

"I should have found a way." He banged his fist on the table. The cold stew sloshed onto the corner of his papers. He didn't notice.

"How many monsters and legends have you seen in these mountains?" I lifted the papers away from the spill. "Liam, how many?"

"I don't know. Between the ghosts in the Blood Valley, the creatures that lurk below, and the odd things roaming through the mountains, it's enough for a century's worth of stories, but I've never seen anything like it this far west."

I dried the papers on my skirt. "Have any of the other creatures attacked like this?"

"Not here," Liam said. "Not this far from the heart of the mountain. Our camp is settled between the land of myths and the power of Ilbrea. We stay here because it's the thin strip of sanity between two worlds."

"And you've no idea what the beast might be or how easy it would be to kill it?"

"I know absolutely nothing." Liam dug his fingers through his hair. "I sent another stone bird to Orla, but I'm not sure how long it will take her to answer or what she might say. I should have done something sooner."

I set the papers down and leaned across the table, lifting Liam's hands away from his head. "You exist in a world of shadows. When you live in a realm of flickering shades, it's hard to tell which darkness might be a demon. What's done is done, Liam. The important thing is what we do now."

"I'll have to talk to the others." Liam kept his hands locked with mine. "There must be a way to set a trap for the beast. I don't like the idea of luring it close to camp, but I don't want anyone straying away from the boundary, either."

"I'm going into Ilbrea." The words rushed out of my mouth.

"What?" Liam tightened his grip on my hands.

"I'm going after the sorci the tracker was watching. I'm leaving first thing in the morning."

"You can't," Liam said. "You don't even know where the child is."

"I know, but you'll tell me."

"No, I won't." Liam stood and began pacing the worn patch of dirt in his tent. "There is a monster out there, Ena."

"There are worse monsters in Ilbrea. And there is a child who will be snatched up by them if we don't get there first."

"We can't save anyone if we're all dead. We have to protect ourselves. No one can go back out there until we've stopped the monster."

"It'll be too late by then." I laid my hands flat on the table, begging my body not to betray my fear. "We can't afford to wait another day, let alone long enough to stop the beast."

"It's killed three people."

"I've seen all three bodies."

Liam froze.

"I've seen the monster, too, and I am not afraid of it. You promised me we would find a way to save those children, and I'm going to do it."

He covered his face with his hands. "You can't. You can't go out there, I won't let you."

"Will you send someone in my place?" I stood and crossed slowly to him, testing every step for a crack that would shatter and devour us both. "Will you use the magic in my mark to kill me?"

He looked at me. A deep pain filled his dark eyes.

"Just tell me how to find the child and where to take them," I said. "That's all I want from you. The rest is my choice, and the consequences lay on my shoulders."

"There is nowhere to hide the child."

"Then I will put them on my back and swim them across the Arion Sea. I am brave, and I am capable. I am strong, Liam. But sitting in this camp, knowing that an innocent child is going to have their freedom stolen from them…I am not strong enough to survive that."

Liam reached out. His fingers brushed my cheek before he laid his hand on my shoulder.

"If you make me stay here, I will suffocate."

"You'll be safe."

"I will drown." I laid my hands on his chest. "Please, Liam. Let me do this."

We stood in silence for a long moment. Without the normal music coming from the clearing, I could hear his breath shaking in his chest.

"There won't be a horse and cart waiting for you," Liam said.

A spark of the fire in my chest broke free of its shroud. "I don't care. I'll find a way."

"The mountain won't open for you."

"Then I will walk the long way."

"I should go with you." Liam laid his hands over mine, pressing them against his chest. "I have to go with you."

"You have to protect the camp. Your people are in danger, you have to stay here."

"Please don't do this, Ena."

I slipped my hands out from beneath his. I traced the worried creases by the corners of his eyes and took his face in my hands.

"I have to go," I whispered. "I won't be able to survive if I don't."

He pressed his lips to my forehead.

I took a deep breath, reveling in his scent of fresh wind and reckless freedom.

"The child is in the Lir Valley." Liam pulled a blood-stained paper from his pocket. "This is all the information I have."

"Then I will make it be enough." I took the paper and felt the weight of another's soul sink onto my shoulders.

"You can't go alone," Liam said.

"I can't ask anyone to come with me." I tucked the paper into my pocket. "I'll be fine. I can find my way through the mountains on my own. I'll go as soon as the sun's up. You can tell Emmet I snuck out if you like. You shouldn't have to face his wrath because of me."

"I won't lie to him."

"Then at least give me a good head start." I managed a small smile. "However this ends, I am choosing to go. My path is of my own making. I'll find the child and a safe place for them to hide. There are lands outside Ilbrea. There's got to be a place in this world for a sorci child that isn't controlled by the Brien or the Guilds, even if I haven't heard of it yet."

"You would go that far? You would leave everything you know behind?"

"I have to."

"Bring the child here." Liam stared at the lae stone hanging from the top of the tent. "I'll get rid of the monster before you come back."

"But Orla doesn't want—"

"This is your home now, Ena. You've got to promise me you'll come home."

I turned his face to make him look at me and leaned in to kiss his cheek.

He wrapped his arms around me, holding me close to his chest.

"Don't pack up the camp for winter without me," I said. "I don't know how to get all the way to Lygan Hall."

Stepping away from him tore a hole in my lungs. It felt as though I may never be able to breathe properly again.

But I gave him another smile and walked out of his tent, unable to promise myself I would ever see Liam again.

39

I didn't really sleep that night. I had to pack my clothes, then sneak the long way around to steal food from Neil's supplies. When I got back to my tent, I found a little leather bag on my cot. Six black stones waited inside. By the time I'd stuffed the rocks and all my pilfered food into my pack, there were only a few hours left until sunrise.

I lay on my bed, trying to convince myself to sleep. I'd need the rest. Without the mountain providing me a path, it would take days to reach Ilbrea. Then I would have to find the Lir Valley and the child.

I closed my eyes and gripped the pendant around my neck. I trusted Liam. Emmet would tell him about the Black Bloods being betrayed. It was better that the news had been lost in tragedies caused by the monster, and right of me not to mention it. Liam couldn't know until I was gone. I hadn't a prayer of him agreeing to my leaving camp if he thought a traitor might sell me to the Guilds.

Pulling my blankets up to my chin didn't slow the racing of my mind.

The camp would be fine. Emmet and Liam would find the traitor. The monster would be slain. There was nothing I could do in camp to protect the people I cared about.

"The decision's already been made, you fool. Now rest so you can run from the beast."

I squeezed my eyes shut and forced my body to relax, focusing on the weight of the stone pendant against my skin.

"Oy, you."

My eyes sprang open as someone poked my cheek.

"Sun's almost up." Finn leaned over me in the darkness. "If we want to slip out at dawn, we should start moving."

"What?" I pushed my blankets back as I sat up, running my fingers through my hair to get the strands away from my face. "What are you talking about?"

"Have you changed your mind?" Finn handed me my boots. "Are you not going to nab the sorci?"

"How do you know about that?" I tugged my shoes on.

"Does it matter?"

"Yes." I slipped my sheath and knife into my boot.

"You didn't think he'd let you go alone, did you?"

"He had no right to do that." I glared through the darkness toward Liam's bed, swallowing the urge to shout through the canvas at him.

"He has every right." Finn held out my coat. "You swore an oath to him."

"You can't come with me. It's too dangerous."

"And you'd be safer alone?"

"No, but you'd be safer here." I snatched my coat and shrugged on the chill fabric. "Risking my life to go after the child is one thing. I can't ask you to risk yours. I'm going alone."

"Ena"—Finn took my hands and pressed his lips to my palms—"you are my friend. You are choosing to risk your neck to help a child. I'm choosing to risk mine for you. Is my choice any less worthy than yours?"

My anger crumpled at the edges. "No, it's not. But Liam still shouldn't have told you."

"At least he didn't tell Emmet." Finn shrugged.

"I don't like it when you're logical." I swung my pack onto my back. "It makes it more difficult to be angry."

Finn held open the tent flap.

"Do you have a plan for sneaking past the guards?" Finn asked.

"I was going to creep up behind them, then run like the Guilds were at my heels and hope they were too frightened of the monster to follow."

Finn gave a low laugh and waved me down the side path toward the training field.

"I take it you have a better plan?" I glanced back toward the tents. The silhouette of Liam's home stood out against the night.

You've chosen your path, now follow it.

"Where are we going?" I whispered.

"There are blind spots in the guards," Finn said. "The perimeter is too large to have eyes on every inch. If you know where the posts are, it's easy to slip in and out. We don't have to fuss about people getting in since we've got the boundary stones protecting us against anyone Liam doesn't want entering camp. But if you want to slip out unseen, you've got to know where the guards are spread wide enough."

"I've gone outside foraging before. I never thought much of the guards not saying anything as I came and went."

"And this, Ena, is why I am useful." Finn bowed.

It seemed wrong to be laughing as we snuck out of camp, but that was how things were with Finn. Easy, light, like there were people in the world who weren't scarred beyond redemption.

The gray of dawn began as we reached the training field. The strange emptiness of the clearing laid a deep chill across my neck.

I kept waiting for Cati to stride out of the trees and ask where we thought we were going. Or worse, for Marta or Emmet to come storming after us. But we didn't meet anyone on our way to the ring of great black boulders.

We stopped just within the boundary. The sky had yet to turn the golden orange of true daybreak.

Neither of us spoke as we watched the eastern sky, waiting for the sun to touch the horizon.

A faint hint of red kissed the treetops.

I looked to the woods beyond the boulders. There was no trace of living creatures moving through the shadows.

"You should go back," I said.

"So should you."

The orange glow blossomed over the sky.

I took a deep breath and walked out through the barrier.

The longing pulled at my chest. For a moment, I thought the wanting would devour the fire that drove me to risk my life fighting against monsters and vicious men. But the soul-consuming desire nurtured the flames, setting my heart to blazing with an inferno that could devour cities and level mountains.

I will fight to come home.

I sent my silent promise into the stones and turned my path east.

The rasp of Finn's sword clearing its sheath seemed to echo through the trees.

I pulled my own knife from my boot. For the first time, the weight of the blade seemed flimsy and worthless in my hand. I'd seen the monster's claws—what hope did I have battling against the beast with a knife?

Finn and I stayed side by side as we moved through the woods. Neither of us spoke. When Finn wanted to alter our course, he'd give me a wave, and we'd shift our path.

I tried to listen beyond the thumping of my own heart to hear the noises of the forest. The birds had begun to wake for the day. Their chirping held its usual cheer as they swooped between trees. But the forest floor had gone silent. No rustling through the low brush, no chittering of small animals.

What has the monster done to our woods?

An hour passed, then another.

The quiet wore on my nerves, making the sound of every footstep seem as loud as a scream.

Does the beast hunt during the day?

There had been no trace of a camp where I'd found Pierce and Dillon. No hint that they'd been planning on spending the night outside the safety of our stone boundary.

I gripped my knife so hard my hand hurt as I searched the shadows for a flash of deadly claws.

As though the mountain had heard my thoughts, a foul stench drifted on the wind. I turned toward the north where the stink carried from.

Finn tapped my arm and pointed east.

I nodded and kept to our path. What good would seeing another dead animal do anyway?

Crack.

The sound carried through the trees to the north.

Finn doubled his pace, still heading due east.

Crack.

I glanced north but couldn't see anything between the trees.

The ground in front of us dropped away in a steep slope. Finn pushed me in front of him, making me run down the hill first.

I leapt over the deep gouges carved into the earth, slipping on the loose dirt where the mountainside had collapsed.

A crashing carried from behind us.

Rocks had taken over the ground below me. I was too afraid of tripping to look back.

A roar shook my lungs and froze my heart.

I'm sorry, Liam. This was my choice. Please remember.

The ground flattened out near a giant boulder that had a crack straight down the middle.

I dared to glance behind as the pounding of massive paws shook the earth.

The monster stood at the top of the slope, his bare head smeared with dried blood, his massive claws glinting in the sunlight.

I scanned the trees around us, searching for one sturdy enough for me to climb out of reach of the beast's deadly bite.

Debris tumbled down the slope as the monster chased us, his mouth wide and his eyes locked on me.

"Finn, we have to—"

Pain shot through my shoulder as something yanked on my arm.

I raised my knife, ready to slash into the monster. The blade glinted in the early morning light as I brought it down in a wide arc.

"Ena!"

I barely managed to stop my swing from cutting off Finn's hand as he jerked me toward him.

A guttural roar shook the trees, claws swiped at my face, and everything went black.

The roar disappeared. The wind vanished.

If it weren't for Finn's hand squeezing my arm, I would have believed the monster had given me a mercifully swift death.

"Did it touch you?" Finn's voice shook. "Did it bite you?"

"Close, but I'm fine." My words trembled just as much as Finn's. "It didn't get you either?"

"No." Finn pulled a lae stone from his pocket.

Our dark shelter was barely more than a hollow, only a few inches taller than Finn and just wide enough for the two of us to fit.

"My mother always told me the mountain plays favorites." Finn wiped the sweat from his forehead with the sleeve of his coat. "I never quite believed her. All children of the mountain, all loved the same. Except the trueborn, of course, but we can't hold ourselves to their chivving standards. But now"—Finn pressed his palm to the rock above us—"I am willing to believe the mountain may, in fact, love me above her normal child."

The sound of my faint laughter bounced around the tiny space.

"You, Finn, are most definitely favored by the mountain, or gods, or stars." I lay my hands against the cold stone. "Quite frankly, I don't care what force likes you so much. I'm just grateful for the shelter."

"Shall we then?"

"Shall we what?" I looked at the bit of rock Finn had pulled me through. "We're not going back out there. The beast will still be out there."

"You couldn't make me walk straight up to that beast unless I had Liam and Emmet by my side." Finn took off his pack. "Or just Cati. Honestly, I'd go hunting the beast just to see her in her full glory."

Finn knelt down in the back of the hollow where there was a bit of darkness that seemed deeper than the black of the stone.

"What is that?" I peered over Finn's shoulder.

"Our way forward." Finn stretched his arm out into an opening two feet high and barely wide enough for his shoulders. "Shall we allow the mountain to test our gratitude?"

I took off my pack. "I do believe we shall."

40

I have never been afraid of small places, but inching forward through the tunnel tested my nerves. I couldn't see Finn over my pack in front of me. It was only the sounds of him crawling forward that kept me from fearing I was utterly alone.

My body ached from the movement. Bruises covered my arms and legs. My hand cramped from clutching my lae stone as I slithered along. I wanted to stand up and stretch, but even my growing pain did not dull my gratitude for the mountain saving us from the beast.

My pack caught on a rock as I shoved it forward. I wriggled the fabric free and gritted my teeth as the very same rock dug into my ribs as I crawled over it on my forearms.

"Talk to me, Ena," Finn said.

"I'm still here if that's what you're worried about." My knee hit the same chivving rock. "If I find a lovely detour, I'll be sure to let you know."

"I know you're behind me. You keep dropping your pack on my feet."

"Sorry."

"Don't be. I find it comforting."

My laugh jostled the new set of bruises on my ribs.

"Just talk to me," Finn said. "Keep me from going mad."

"What do you want to talk about?" I shifted my pack as far forward as I could, making sure to drop it on Finn's feet.

"Tell me about life in Ilbrea."

"It's hell."

"All of it?" The sounds of Finn's movement stopped. "Is there nothing good out there?"

"You've seen more of Ilbrea than I have. Until I joined the Black Bloods, I'd only ever been to Harane and Nantic."

Finn didn't reply.

"Keep crawling, or we'll never get out."

He began moving forward again. "I've seen most of the cities. But I've never lived out there. Never had a home in Ilbrea."

"I suppose it wasn't all awful." I shifted my bag forward and kept crawling. "There were lots of terrible things. Death and pain and fear taint the corners of everything. But the farmland around Harane was beautiful.

"The men would bicker about whose cows were better and whose sheep kept breaking out of their pastures to harass other animals. But they never hated each other over it. Some of the women hated their husbands, and their husbands would hide at the tavern. Cal would tell me all about the things the husbands said when they were drunk."

"Cal?"

I froze. Rocks dug into my arms.

"A boy I knew. He was very good to me. I don't think I could have survived Harane without him."

"I'm sorry."

"What for?" I shoved my pack forward, trying to blame the ache in my chest on the tunnel.

"That he's not with you now. Do you think…"

"Think what?"

"That you'd still be with him—if the world were a less violent place?"

"I don't know." The truth of it made the ache grow until I could no longer ignore the pain. "He was good and kind, and gods he was handsome."

Finn laughed.

"But his family made their money catering to the Guilds. I couldn't live with that."

"But if the Guilds weren't in power?"

"If there were no Guilds, I would still have parents. My brother would be more to me than some stranger with a terrible chivving temper. My life would have been so different, I can't even begin to suppose who I might have been able to love. It would have been easier if I could have loved Cal, but that is not the life I was given."

"You didn't love him?"

A deeper, harsher pain throbbed through my lungs. "I'm too broken for that."

"I don't think that's true." Finn's voice shifted. "I used to think I was destined to spend my life as a hopeless rogue. Tried to convince myself to fall in love a dozen times, and it never worked. But I figured it out in the end."

"What did you do?"

"I found the right person to fall in love with. Mended my shattered heart."

"Ah, but did it make you any less of a rogue?"

My pack shifted out of my path, and Finn's grinning face appeared.

"No. But I do have a love to come home to, and that's a beautiful thing." Finn winked and held out a hand to me.

I scooted forward, toward the lip of the tunnel.

Finn took my hand, helping me balance as I pulled enough of my body out of the narrow space that I could get a foot on the ground in the chamber beyond.

"I'm going to have bruises from that for weeks." I stretched my arms toward the ceiling.

"Better than being torn to shreds." Finn handed me my pack.

"Much better." I gave Finn a smile.

The chamber the mountain had opened for us offered only one path forward. A tunnel with a mercifully high ceiling cut out of the back of the space and twisted out of sight.

Finn shouldered his own bag and led the way.

I trailed the fingers of my free hand along the stone wall. It wasn't jagged and shattered or perfectly smooth. The rock held a natural roughness to it. The coarse texture soothed me.

I tucked the old hurts away, not allowing myself to examine them before sending them back into the darkness hidden behind the flames.

"What was it like growing up in Lygan Hall?" I asked.

Finn let out a genuine laugh that echoed down the curving tunnel.

"Rowdy," Finn said. "Cold. Wearing. I think the strangest thing was how trapped I always felt when I was little. The Hall is a sanctuary in the middle of the mountains. But the land beyond is wild with untamed magic and legendary beasts. It's like the magic from the heart of the great mountain somehow leaked to the surface and caused chaos."

"Chaos made you feel trapped?"

The tunnel twisted sharply and began sloping down.

"Not being allowed out into the chaos was what trapped me," Finn said. "I could stand on top of the summit above Lygan Hall and stare out into the great wilderness beyond. I could see the epic possibilities for adventure, but I wasn't allowed to get to any of them. I just ended up wreaking havoc in the Hall, causing as much chaos as I could, since they wouldn't let me out. I almost wasn't allowed to venture west with Liam."

"Really?" I tried to picture the camp without Finn. I couldn't do it.

"Orla thought I was too wild to be trusted to Liam's cause. I had to beg and make a hundred promises to be assigned to his camp."

"I'm glad she agreed in the end."

"I'm pretty sure she thought I'd get myself killed right off and then I wouldn't be anyone's problem anymore."

"Finn." I smacked him on the shoulder.

He caught my wrist and kissed the back of my hand.

"I don't blame Orla. I was a terror," Finn said. "But I made myself useful, didn't die, and swore the oath to Liam. So the leader of the Duwead Clan now despises me just a little bit less."

"What does she think of Emmet? Is she grateful for the ruin he leaves in his wake?"

Finn stopped and turned to face me. "We don't tell Orla everything. Only the bits of our work that she really needs to know. Since Emmet saved Liam's life, she thinks he's a bit of a hero, and we choose to allow her belief to continue."

"How did Emmet save Liam's life?"

"You'll have to ask them." Finn started down the tunnel again.

"Why will no one tell me stories about Emmet? If he's done such wonderful things to save people, I'd like to know what they are. It would be nice to have something good to think about him."

The slope of the tunnel pitched even more steeply. The floor didn't have the same rough texture as the walls but was as smooth as polished glass beneath my feet.

I steadied myself with my hand against the wall as my boots slid with each step.

"As much as it shames me to say it"—Finn slipped, tottered, and caught his balance—"I don't actually know how Emmet saved Liam's life." He turned sideways and inched his way forward.

I followed him, sidling my way along.

"All I know," Finn said, "is that Liam went down into Ilbrea, and when he came back, his face was purple, his back had been sliced open, and he'd brought an angry tilk up the mountain with him."

"Hmm."

"Emmet is probably the only one who can give you an accurate account of what he's gotten himself into and how under the stars he's survived. You should ask him."

"No, thank you. I've finally managed to speak to him without wanting to scratch his eyes from his face. Best not to push."

"Fair." Finn stopped moving. "Chivving tunnels."

I leaned away from the wall to peer around him.

The slope of the tunnel became even steeper, beyond our ability to stay on our feet as we traveled.

"I am grateful," Finn shouted to the ceiling. "Dubious of my ability to survive this, but still chivving grateful!"

"What do you suggest we do?" I peered as far into the darkness as I could. All I could see was the slope traveling down at a frightening angle.

"Pray to the gods, and hope they're willing to protect a pair of fools." Finn shook out his shoulders and sat on the ground.

"Are you really just going to slide down there?" I grabbed his shoulder.

"Do you have a better idea?"

I gripped my lae stone in my hand for a moment, savoring the light it provided, and then rolled the stone down the slope. It clacked along as its glow disappeared.

"Shall I fetch?" Finn pushed himself off and began sliding downward.

"It's to light the bottom!" I shouted after Finn. "And give you a warning—"

"It's not that bad!" Finn's voice and light faded away.

Darkness surrounded me.

I sat on the ground and tucked my skirt carefully beneath me.

"This is a terrible idea."

I pushed off as hard as I could and began sliding forward. In the black, I couldn't tell how fast I was going. It didn't seem like an absurd speed, and letting the mountain do the work for me was better than crawling through the tiny tunnel on my stomach.

"Ahh!" A scream carried from far below.

"Finn! Are you all right? Finn!"

I shot my hands out to my sides, trying to grip the wall to stop my descent, but there were no walls for me to touch.

"Finn!"

I leaned farther to the right, trying to find something to catch hold of. The tilt of my body made me spin sideways.

The angle of the tunnel shifted again.

My speed tripled.

I fought to right my body as the tunnel hooked around a bend, banging me into a wall.

Pain shot through my shoulder, but I didn't have time to scream as the tunnel whipped the other way, hurling me into a tight spiral.

I squeezed my hands to my chest, trying to keep my bones from shattering as the tunnel shot me around and around and around.

"Ahh!"

"Finn!" I shouted as loud as I could. "Finn, are you all right?"

I couldn't hear his reply over my own scream as the ground disappeared.

41

Blue light glowed around me, and before I could try to see what sort of place my shattered body would lie in, I hit the ground.

Pain flared through my bottom, my teeth bashed together, and I was still.

"Oh," I groaned.

"I'm glad I managed to roll out of the way in time."

I looked to my right where Finn lay spread eagle on his stomach.

"Still better than the monster," Finn said.

I began laughing, but pain shot through my ribs. "Ow, ow, ow."

"You all right?" Finn pushed himself to his hands and knees.

I made myself sit up. I wiggled my fingers and toes, bent my knees and my elbows. "Maybe a bruised rib, but nothing I won't survive. You?"

"I'll be fine." Finn got to his feet. "As long as no one asks me to sit for the next week."

"Don't make me laugh." I stood up. "Laughing is now a horrible idea."

"Right. No humor from me."

I looked around the space the mountain had chosen to spit us into. Another tunnel continued to our right.

I gritted my teeth as I bent to pick up my lae stone. I checked the crystal-like surface for cracks, but the stone, unlike Finn and I, had been undamaged by the fall.

"Shall we?" Finn grimaced as he bowed me toward the tunnel.

I bowed back and let Finn go first.

"Once we get into Ilbrea," I said, "I'll find us some nice roots and herbs for a balm. Make the journey to the Lir Valley a little less painful."

"Have you ever been to the Lir Valley?"

"No," I said. "I think it's in the northern part of Ilbrea. Closer to Ilara than I've ever traveled."

"I've never been on a sorci run without a map and a plan before."

"Neither have I."

We walked in silence for a long while. I spent the time trying not to think through all the things I wished I knew and how many ways our journey could go terribly wrong. I don't know what busied Finn's mind.

I tried to focus on the child.

In my mind, it was boy. Young with fair hair. He didn't know how to control his magic, and he was terrified. I pictured him hiding, tears coursing down his cheeks, as he wondered why the gods had cursed him with magic.

Then I didn't mind that our work could go terribly wrong. The imaginary child was worth the danger and pain. I would risk my life to keep him from being locked up by a lady wearing purple robes.

"Please." Finn slowed his pace. "Oh, please, please let this be it."

A wall blocked our path.

Finn laid his palms on the wall and pressed his forehead to the stone.

"We are going out into Ilbrea to rescue a child. A little one with magic in their blood. Let us help them find shelter. Please."

I held my breath, half-expecting the mountain to speak.

In a way, I suppose she did.

A rumbling carried from beneath my feet, and Finn stepped back as the wall before us crumbled to dust.

"Thank you," I whispered to the mountain, though I had no hope she would hear one who did not carry stone in her blood.

The full brightness of a summer afternoon waited for us beyond the rock.

I took a breath of the forest air and turned to look back at the tunnel.

The mountain had already healed itself. A flat rock face that seemed as old as the stone around it blocked the path we had traveled.

"It would be wrong to linger, wouldn't it?" Finn said. "We don't know how far we've traveled, and the monster could be on us at any moment."

"Hold still." I dug a packet of dried meat and a waterskin out of Finn's pack. "Eat as you walk. It'll be good for the soreness."

Finn took the food, sighed, and headed down the mountain.

I walked beside him as we tramped through the woods. The fear I'd felt early in the morning didn't return. There was something about this part of the forest, a lightness to it, that the woods around the camp didn't hold. I tried to think back to the spring when I'd first arrived at the Black Bloods' summer home.

It had seemed like such a vibrant and perfect place. A nest of safety hidden away from the world. But when we'd walked away, that air of peace had been gone.

A knot twisted in my gut.

I didn't know when that feeling of sanctuary had disappeared. If it had slipped away so slowly I hadn't noticed the fading, or if it had vanished all at once when death found the Black Bloods.

The mountain had been kind to us. Finn and I made it to the edge of the woods before dark. We climbed back up a bit, away from the mountain road, and found a place to shelter for the night.

Finn set out his six black stones to protect us.

I laid out our bedrolls and climbed beneath my blanket, grateful for the weight of the pendant against my chest.

I drifted into the darkness of sleep, and no monster came to find me in the night.

42

Having kohl drawn around my eyes to walk down the mountain road seemed like a foolish thing to do—the kind of vanity that would have driven Lily absolutely mad, and I myself would have laughed at, before I had a healthy fear of soldiers recognizing me and wanting me hanged.

But the men driving the caravan of wagons heavy with barrels of chamb didn't seem to think the paint and powder I wore was foolish when they offered us a ride north.

I pushed aside the fear that nibbled at my chest and gratefully accepted the ride, careful to keep the men in sight even though Finn sat by my side.

One of the men had a map of Ilbrea and let Finn and me study the roads we'd need to take to reach the Lir Valley.

The path he showed us did not ease my worry.

Liam had given Finn a bag of coins, which allowed us a hot meal to satisfy Finn, and a comfortable bed in a tavern to please me.

The next day, we traveled on foot, leaving the mountain road to head northeast. Finn did not take so kindly to the tavern fare on our second night.

The third day, Finn bought us a ride in a cart carrying a dead body to its funeral. The scent of the corpse did not seem worth saving my feet from the road. But at least the carcass kept the soldiers lurking around the town from asking any questions. We snuck into a barn to sleep that night and slipped out before the sun rose in the morning.

But, somehow, none of it seemed real until we reached a signpost driven into the dirt at a crossroad in the middle of a forest. The sign was not weathered and worn like those I'd seen on my other journeys with Finn. The words on the wood were untainted by the weather and carved in a neat script.

One slat read *Lir Valley*, the other, *Ilara*.

"How long do you think it would take us to reach the capital?" I asked.

"Two more days," Finn said, "maybe three. Why? Do you want to go and burn the place?"

"Do you think we could manage it?"

"Probably not." Finn grinned. "But that doesn't mean I'm not willing to try."

I stared down the road to Ilara. It seemed wrong that a path leading to a city of murderers should look so plain.

"The poor sorci has been living a few days' walk from the Sorcerers Tower. How has the child not died of terror or run far away?"

"Maybe they aren't afraid of the Sorcerers Guild," Finn said. "They could want to join them, you know."

"Then we'd have nearly been killed by a monster for nothing."

"Not nothing." Finn started walking down the road to the Lir Valley. "We'll give the child a choice. An offer of freedom means the world, even if the person you're trying to save would rather stay in their cage."

"I know." I tore my gaze from the path to Ilara and followed Finn. "But I hope none of the children who choose to join the Sorcerers Guild regret it too late."

"I'm sure some of them do." Finn took my hand.

"That's horrible."

"It is, but at least they know there are people in the world who want them to be free."

"Do you think that helps?"

"I hope so."

The road to the Lir Valley wound through the woods, cutting up and down hillsides. We'd started climbing a high hill when the low rumble of water carried through the trees.

I stopped at the crest of the hill, looking down at the long wooden bridge stretching over a rushing river. I barely breathed as we crossed the planks, for fear the whole thing might collapse beneath me.

A small part of me was almost angry it held. I hated the Guilds and didn't want any of their endeavors to succeed, even if their work was only carrying people safely across the water.

On the far side of the bridge, on the western bank of the river, a wide boat was tethered to a large dock that reached out into the water. Three merchant carts waited nearby.

The men around the carts stared at me as we passed. A tall man with ash blond hair whistled at me.

I kept my pace even and my gaze fixed on the road ahead.

"A pretty thing like you shouldn't be walking."

I forced my hands to stay relaxed, not allowing my fingers to betray my rage by balling into fists.

"If the ginger can't provide a proper ride for you, maybe you should set your sights on a real man," the ash blond called.

The men around the merchant carts laughed.

"Too afraid to look?" the man said. "Don't want to know what you're missing?"

"She's not missing anything," Finn said. "She knows plenty of what a real man should be. She doesn't need to spare a glance down your pants to know you don't qualify."

"Why you cacting little chiv"—footfalls thumped up behind us—"of a cow chivving slitch."

"Language, sir," Finn said. "My darling has tender ears."

"Your petal whore should learn the consequences of lingering with a foulmouthed letch."

"Would you like to have a fight with me?" Finn asked. "Honestly, I've been plodding along for days, and I could really use a bit of a diversion."

My heart hitched up into my throat as Finn drew the two knives that lived at his hips.

"Oh, you've brought weapons?" The ash blond's voice didn't lose any of its dripping bravado.

"Yes." Finn smiled. "And I'd be chivving thrilled to use them."

The men around the wagons began shifting toward us.

"I'll tear you to shreds and toss you in the river," the blond said.

"No." I pulled my knife from my boot. "You won't. You'll either climb up onto your carts where you can sit like lazy laxe scum with your pretty cargo boat, or Finn and I will kill you. And we won't bother dumping your bodies into the river. I'll carve your eyes out and drop them on the ground for the ants to eat. Then I'll chop off your tiny, limp pricks and leave them on the road for the carrion eaters."

"You brazen—"

"Now you've worked your way up to being gutted." I pointed my blade at his stomach. "So go back to your carts or pray to the gods that mercy may find you in death."

The men laughed.

"Finn, make the slitch hurt," I said.

Finn threw one of his knives. The blade sank into the blond man's foot.

The man screamed.

His fellows backed away.

"Get them," the blond shouted. "Thrash them!"

"Have a lovely day, fellows." Finn nodded to the men as they climbed up onto their carts.

"You're going to be sorry for this," the blond growled.

"No, he won't," I laughed. "Now give him back his knife."

"What?" Sweat beaded on the man's brow.

"Bring him his knife, or he'll sink one into your other foot," I said.

The man stared at me.

"Careful when you pull the blade out," I said. "It's going to hurt."

"Do it." Finn tossed his second knife from hand to hand.

The man reached down and wrenched the knife from his own foot with a whimper.

"Now bring it nicely over here," I said.

The man limped toward us, the tip of the blade pointing toward Finn.

"Careful there," Finn said, "or I might hit your heart instead of your foot."

The man flipped the knife around and presented Finn with the hilt.

Finn wiped the blood from the blade onto the man's shirt before slipping the knife back into its sheath.

"A word of warning," I said. "Keep that cut clean. Dump some strong liquor on it and bandage the wound well. If it won't stop bleeding, you might need to find a healer. An infection in your foot could steal your life if you aren't careful."

"Enjoy your day." Finn bowed to the men in the carts. "Come along, my love. All this excitement is making me hungry."

"You are a ravenous beast at the best of times." I looped my arm through Finn's, and we strode up the road.

I listened for signs of them following even as Finn and I chatted while we walked out of sight.

"Into the trees then?" Finn said as soon as we'd rounded the bend. He led me south of the road and into the woods, cutting deep enough that the trees nearly blocked the path from view.

"We could have just kept walking." I let go of Finn to lift my skirt over the tangle of branches littering the forest floor.

"Sure," Finn said. "But then they would have gnawed on the next pretty girl to cross their path, and she might not have had anyone to defend her."

I stopped for a moment, listening for any hint of the men following us. "I just hope none of them end up being related to the sorci we're trying to find."

"They're laxe. If they spotted a sorci, they'd sell them to the Guilds straight off."

"A lot of common folk would do the same." The certainty that I was right rolled sickeningly through my stomach. "It's amazing we get any of the children out."

"Cheer up, love." Finn took my hand, dramatically helping me over a narrow log on the ground. "What we do may only be the work of birds pecking at a giant's head, but better that than to wait on the ground pretending we aren't about to be stomped."

"Fair." I pushed away my growing urge to flee.

"And who knows? One of the tiny wounds we make from pecking at the giant's head could get infected."

I laughed, and the rest of my worry shook free.

"I'm not joking." Finn poked me in the arm. "The giant may not have someone as brilliant as you warning him to tend to his wounds. He doesn't pour liquor on the peck marks to clean them, and the tyrant falls down dead with blood poisoning."

"I don't think Emmet told me that story when we were young." I wrinkled my nose.

"That's because we're writing it, dear Ena." Finn stopped and turned to me. "What if future generations sing songs of our heroic deeds and all they know about me is how much I eat? What if instead of being the rogue with the red hair, I just tromp through the ballads eating? Should I stop eating in front of people? Protect my legacy?"

"No, keep eating." I took Finn's chin in my hand. "Eat the most absurd things. When they sing of you, they'll say you ate an entire goat for lunch then defeated the King himself. All the children will love your song best, and tales of your glory will be sung by every scabby-kneed littleling in the land. Ilbrea needs a hero like you, Finn."

"And what of you?" Finn kissed my forehead. "What will your story be?"

"I won't have one. I'm a Ryeland. Apparently, our stories aren't allowed to be told."

Finn laughed, then I laughed, and the woods around us became bright and beautiful. I didn't know what lay ahead, and the mystery of it lured me on through the trees.

We didn't forget the men from the river as we walked arm in arm through the forest. We listened and watched, but there was no hint of any menace in the afternoon shadows.

The reality of the dangers we faced slipped further and further away as we tromped through the woods, until the fact that Finn had stabbed a man's foot seemed like nothing more than a bit of a children's song.

43

We heard the Lir Valley before we saw it.

The mooing and braying of livestock carried into the forest, followed quickly by the scent of their dung. Voices cut through the sounds, and every once in a while a dog would bark, setting the other animals off into a round of calls.

"I didn't think the Lir Valley was farmland," Finn said.

"It's not what it looked like on the paper." I hesitated before reaching into my pocket. My fingers felt cold as they found the bloodstained parchment. I bit the insides of my cheeks as I pulled out the little map and opened it.

A roughly-drawn image took up most of the folded page. One thick line formed a strange shape that seemed to be the outline of the valley. Another thick line, which I assumed to be the road, cut in on one side and ran to the center of the page.

Two circles, one much larger than the other, had been marked in the top left corner. Inside the smaller circle, the tracker had written one word.

Death.

Tiny v's clustered together on the far left side of the page, though I couldn't begin to reason through what exactly they might mean.

At the bottom of the page, a big dot had three little squares leading up to it like stepping-stones.

Near the end of the road, in the center of the page, a set of lines weaved through each other in a pattern I couldn't understand.

"Not the best map I've ever seen," Finn said.

"She must've thought she'd get a chance to explain it."

I tipped the paper into the light, reading the words along the border of the page. The letters had been smeared by her blood in places, but enough was legible that at least the meaning of her writing was clear.

The death is not natural. The people of the valley know something is wrong. The lies began long before. Started in winter. Father must know. Find him for the names.

"Should we start for hunting for the *death* now?" Finn pointed to the word on the page. "Or should we find a place to stay and wait for morning?"

"I say we find a tavern. Can't be caught prowling about at night. We don't want the locals suspicious before we even know what child we're looking for."

"Too true." Finn cut north, toward the road we'd been walking alongside.

I folded the paper back up and tucked it into my pocket.

I won't fail you. I pressed my hand against the map. *I won't let your death be in vain.*

When we reached the last of the trees, we peered up and down the road. There was nothing in sight save some dents in the dirt large enough to wrench a wheel off a cart.

I stepped out onto the road and looked into the Lir Valley.

It was not a sad patch of farmland at all.

The road wound down the slope of the hill, past pastures and fields, then into a proper town at the base of the valley. A web of streets curved as they weaved between stone buildings, with not a straight line among them.

A massive home, grand enough to be a palace, loomed over the hill opposite us.

Large houses, big enough to fit a dozen families, dotted the hill to the south of the fancy estate. In the north, where the circles had been drawn on the map, two little ponds sparkled in the late afternoon sun. To the south, a giant, black hole marred the earth.

"What is it?" I asked Finn.

"Mining." Finn placed my hand on his elbow as he led me down the road and into the valley.

"What are they mining for?" I squinted toward the dark patch but couldn't see enough to guess what lurked below the ground that men might find valuable.

"I've no idea," Finn said. "But I'm sure there will be someone at the tavern complaining about it."

The road down into the valley was longer than seemed possible from the top. We passed herders coming in for the night, travelers on horseback, and a few carts heavy with goods.

My feet ached, and my stomach craved food. But, I smiled pleasantly at everyone who went by, careful to keep my face placid as I studied the fields we passed, searching for both enemies and signs of magic.

By the time we reached the outskirts of the town, twilight had nearly arrived.

The dimming sky gave the dark gray stone of the houses a foreboding feel, even though they all seemed to be well-kept.

"Out of the way," someone shouted. "Everyone get out of the way!"

I leapt off the street, yanking Finn with me as a man in red robes tore around the corner on horseback.

The horse's hooves pounded against the dirt as the healer raced east.

"Huh." Finn stared after the horse.

"What?" I peered around the corner of the stone house, checking for anyone else who might trample us.

"Do you think the healer might be going to look after a foot injury?" Finn whispered.

I turned to look up the road, watching the healer travel toward the river.

"Well," I said, "how clean do you keep your knives?"

"I'm not sure." Finn frowned. "I wipe them."

"I did warn him to tend to the wound. And it may not be the laxe at all."

325

"I don't know," Finn said. "I'm too well acquainted with our luck."

I pulled Finn around the corner and onto the main street of the town.

Someone had taken the time to pack in the ruts in this road, at least on the bit I could see. Beyond the first five houses, the road twisted, blocking the next portion of the street from view.

Little flowerbeds had been planted in front of each of the homes. Pink, blue, purple, and yellow blooms grew from the miniature gardens.

I stepped out of the way of a hay cart and bent to sniff a flower with lavender petals and a scarlet disk in the center. I smiled as the sweet scent filled my lungs.

"Those are pretty," Finn said.

"Lily used to grow them in our garden."

I studied the house the garden belonged to. Built of the same stone as all the others, the house bore no mark of being special. Even the shutters and door were painted a plain, dark green.

"I suppose you don't have to know what a flower can be used for to be able to appreciate its beauty." I breathed in the scent of the bloom again before stepping back out onto the road.

As we wound down the path toward the heart of the town, we passed a young man with a long lamplighter's pole. He carried the flame high, humming a tune I didn't recognize.

We rounded another bend and came upon the first of the shops.

I stopped and looked back up the road behind us.

The boy moved from lamp to lamp, going about his duty with a leisure that seemed to imply a complete lack of fear. The shutters of the homes hadn't been closed against the coming dark. Most houses had their windows thrown wide open, welcoming in the evening chill.

"What are you looking at?" Finn asked.

"They're not scared. We have a map with the word *death* marked on it, and the people in the town aren't afraid."

The color drained from Finn's face. "Are we too late? Did the Sorcerers Guild already claim the child?"

"I don't know." I gripped Finn's hand. "But we'll find out. Until then, we've got to act like someone still needs us."

"Right." Finn nodded. "We'll find out at the tavern. Someone there will know if the sorcerers have been through."

The jingle of a horse's bridle came from the around the bend in the road. Finn and I stepped to the side.

A man with a beautiful black horse to match his shining black cart and slicked back black hair came around the corner.

"Excuse me." I waved to the man. "I'm sorry to bother you, sir."

The man wrinkled his brow as he stopped his cart. He looked from me to Finn and back again. "How can I help you?"

"We're looking for a room for the night," I said. "I'm afraid the winding streets have us a bit confused."

"Ah." The man's face brightened. "Follow this road until you see the dress shop with the red door. Turn right there. Keep going until you reach the open square, then take a left at the far end. You'll pass a public stable, then take another right, and you'll find the tavern."

"Thank you." I gave a careful nod, trying not to shake the directions out of my head.

"You'll probably get lost at least once," the man said. "Don't worry. The people around here are used to confused outsiders. Just keep asking, and you'll find your way eventually."

"Right." I gave the man a smile. "Thank you."

"Best of luck." The man clicked his tongue, and his horse trotted on without pause.

"I'm starting to think I might have judged the tracker's map making skills a bit too harshly." Finn sighed. "I suppose the tavern won't be out of food even if it takes us a while to find."

The man in the fancy cart had been right. It took us nearly an hour and asking three people for help before we found the tavern.

All of the people we spoke to were kind. All of the homes had light peering out through their windows. All of the houses and shops were built of the same stone. The empty square we passed through had a sign marking which days there would be a market, but there was no hint of rubbish or rotting food trampled into the mud.

By the time we stood on the steps of the tavern, a worry had begun tickling the back of my neck. I couldn't name the unease that breathed on my skin, but I knew something lurked in the shadows and feared it might be vile enough to drag me into the darkness.

"In we go, my love." Finn opened the tavern door for me. "After today's journey, I think some food and rest are well in order."

The scents of ale, roasted meat, and fresh baked bread filled the dining room of the tavern. Lanterns hung from the ceiling and along the walls, casting the whole room in a cheery glow.

"Hello there." The man behind the bar waved us toward him. "Can I help you folks?"

I let my gaze slide around the room as we weaved through the two dozen tables. Most of the seats were filled. The people chatted to their fellows, but the place held neither the raucous noise of the places Finn favored, nor the familiar, sad comradery of the tavern in Harane.

"Hopefully," Finn said. "We're looking for a hot meal and a room for the night."

"Oh." The man furrowed his brow and drummed his fingers on top of his balding head. "I'm sorry to have to ask, but are you two married?"

"We are," Finn said. "Though most people don't believe I managed to catch such a pretty wife."

"Good," the man sighed. "Not allowed to let unmarried folks share rooms. The fuss some outsiders make about it."

"No fuss from us." Finn laughed.

The man stepped out from behind his bar, waving for us to follow with his clean white cloth.

"We'll get you a seat over here." The barkeep pulled out a chair for me. "I'll make sure a room is ready for you by the time you're fed."

"Thank you." Finn gave the man a small bow. "After a long journey, your establishment is just what we need."

44

We took our time with our meal and ordered two rounds of ale. The barkeep chatted with the people he served, but there was no one patron who seemed eager to befriend travelers.

"We should get some sleep." I downed the rest of my ale, grateful the hint of honey in the brew made the flavor a little more bearable than the stuff in camp. "We can poke around in the morning."

"I'm not ready to pack it in," Finn said.

"Are you going to waltz up to the bar and ask if he has any interesting stories of death and magic?"

"Probably not the best idea," Finn said, "but I won't be able to sleep if we don't do something."

"I'll go get you another ale then."

"Do you really think you'll be able to flirt answers out of the man who checks to see if his patrons are married?" Finn raised one ginger eyebrow at me.

"I'm more than just a pretty face, Finn." I flicked his ear.

"You also have magnificent breasts, but I really don't want to get kicked out. Or hanged."

"You should have more faith in me." I lifted his mug from his hand.

"I have infinite faith in you." Finn frowned. "It's the men of this sad world I can't bring myself to believe in."

"One more ale and then to bed." I kissed Finn's cheek and headed to the bar.

The patrons in the room had rotated. A fresh batch of people had entered the tavern, but the place hadn't emptied at all. A gray-haired woman had joined the man behind the bar, working the taps and bustling back and forth from the kitchen with trays of food.

I headed toward her and smiled when I caught the woman's eye.

She frowned and went back into the kitchen.

"Right," I murmured. "Not her." I moved down the bar to where the barkeep chatted with a pack of men as he poured glasses of frie.

"It'll be an early winter this year," the barkeep said. "I'm sure of it. You can tell by the way the wert grass grows."

"You'll bring the ice back just by speaking of it," one of the men said. "Keep quiet about your grass."

"The wert grass doesn't lie." The barkeep wagged a finger. "From the mine to the estate, we'll all be covered in ice well before winter should begin."

The men laughed.

"Sorry," I said as soon as the sound began to die.

All the men turned toward me. I gave each of them a smile before looking to the barkeep. "Could I get one more ale for my husband?"

The barkeep rubbed his chin. "Do you think it's a good idea, or will you have a rowdy lout on your hands?"

"Give the girl the ale." One of the men pounded the bar.

"Yes, please," I said. "Truth be told, it's the only thing I've found that keeps him from snoring."

The men laughed again.

"All right, then." The barkeep took both mugs from my hands and led me away from the men to the far set of taps. "One more ale."

"Thanks," I said. "We've had a long day on the road, and a good night's sleep will be welcome."

"We aim to provide a nice place to rest."

"The Lir Valley is much better than I imagined it would be." I leaned closer to the bar. "I don't mean any offense, but from the rumors I'd heard of this place, I wasn't sure I dared to come."

"The Valley is a wonderful place." The barkeep poured the ale. "Anyone who says otherwise is either blind or a fool."

"I wonder where the awful rumors started." I frowned. "The town is so pretty. The valley, too. Why would anyone say that death haunts such a lovely bit of land?"

"I try not to waste my mind on such gossip."

"Isn't it bad for business, though? To have rumors about evil magic scaring travelers away?"

The barkeep's face paled a shade. "It is a bit. I do my best to run a fine establishment. The whole town does everything we can to keep the place clean and respectable. It's hard with the mine lurking at our back door, but we do our best."

"I feel a bit foolish, but what do they mine here?"

"Minerals." He set Finn's mug on the counter. "The Lir family mine digs rocks up from the ground. They built the mine, they built the town, and the estate. Makes it hard to complain about the mine being here, since there wouldn't be anything else in the valley without it."

"But..." I took a moment, trying to find the right words to ask my question. "But why would a mine start stories of evil magic? I was told death had swept through the valley and that a sorcerer came from Ilara, trying to find the one who'd caused it."

The man's face grew paler still. "Bad things happen in all sorts of nice places. The fact that some choose to blame magic instead of accepting tragedy as the gods' will is foolishness that has never made any sense to me. But if you find the one spreading such rumors, tell them we've had plenty of sorcerers come through town and none of them have ever made a fuss about evil magic. This valley is a nice place, and you won't find a soul here who will say otherwise."

"You're right." I picked up the mug. "By the Guilds, it's just not right that fine people like you should suffer because a few fools got bored and decided to make up frightening tales about Death himself taking over a pond."

The barkeep's face shifted to gray.

"Thank you for the ale." I gave him a smile. "My husband will sleep much better now."

45

I woke long before Finn the next morning. I'd slept through the night without any terror chasing behind me, but as soon as I opened my eyes, awful images gnawed at the corners of my mind. I lay by Finn's side, trying to keep still as I battled my own thoughts.

Memories of Harane, of the horror I had abandoned my home to, were better off banished to the deepest corners of the blackness where I tucked the things I was not strong enough to remember. I didn't want the images of Lily hanging from the tree to make my hands tremble, but I could not purge the picture from my mind.

What did people say of Lily? What did travelers whisper to each other of the terror of Harane?

The soldiers had slaughtered our people and burned our homes. Had the villagers tried to erase those horrors? Did they pretend it had never happened and lie to anyone passing through who bothered to ask why charred frames of houses loomed on the sides of the road?

Did Cal's mother flap her bar rag in the face of anyone who dared mention the horrors inflicted on Harane and warn them not to spread dark stories about a lovely place?

"Are you all right?"

I gasped when Finn spoke.

"Ena?"

"Of course I'm not all right. You just scared me, you slitch." I pressed a hand to my chest as though the weight could somehow slow the racing of my heart.

"I meant before I said anything." Finn propped himself up on his elbow.

"I'm fine." I curled closer to his warmth.

"You're not." Finn stroked my hair and tucked a stray strand behind my ear. "I don't think you could be, not after all the world has taken from you."

"I'm strong enough to bear it."

"That's why I adore you, Ena Ryeland. But that doesn't mean you're not allowed to crumple a bit around the edges."

Finn stared at me, waiting for me to say something.

I wanted to tell him to mind his own chivving business and let anger coat everything else I could possibly feel. But Finn kept patiently waiting for me to speak, and I couldn't bring myself to rage at him.

"Ena," Finn whispered, "you're allowed to be afraid."

"It's not that." I gripped the pendant around my neck. "Something horrible happened here. Somewhere in this valley is a child who's got to be scared out of their mind. If they worked enough magic for *death* to be written on the map, they've got to be petrified of themselves and the Guilds and everyone around them.

"I know what it's like to have your whole world collapse around you in a flood of terror and blood and fire. I've lived through it. If Liam had been an hour slower in reaching Harane, I'd..." I let out a slow breath, forcing all the tendrils of fear that crept through my body back behind the rage that burned in my chest. "I'm not a hero, Finn. I'm an inker from Harane who's good at stitching people back together and knows a bit about poison. That poor child deserves someone better coming to their rescue."

"Am I worth nothing?" Finn furrowed his brow.

"You're worth everything. But you should have Cati with you, or Emmet."

"Oh gods, not Emmet." Finn winced. "I'd rather have my mad inker by my side than any of the others. You were the only person bold enough to even suggest leaving camp. And the rest of it, that's just flashy sword work and bravado."

"Is it?" I felt a smile curving my lips against my will.

"Of course." Finn held me tight. "Just act brave, and people think you're a warrior. Swing your sword around a bit, and half of them will run straight off."

"I wish Cati had taught me that trick months ago. It would have saved me a few hundred bruises."

"I'll be sure to tell Cati to update her training methods as soon as we get back to camp." Finn kissed my forehead. "You are exactly what the sorci needs, because we're the only ones who bothered to show up. Now come on, my little mad woman. Let's go be heroes."

I forgot my fear as we dressed for the day and I painted my face to an acceptable hue.

It seemed strange to be leaving our packs behind as we walked out of the tavern, sweet buns in hand, and headed north toward the circle on the map marked *death*.

The people on the streets were cheerful in the fresh morning air. They talked and laughed without any trace of the worry or dragging pain that marked the towns I'd visited with Finn before.

I smiled at the people we passed, trying to look as happy as they did to be out on a fine summer morning. But there was something about their airy nature I couldn't seem to match.

We found the northern edge of the town without too much fuss and from there could easily see the narrow road winding north toward the ponds.

I looped my arm through Finn's and tipped my face up to the sun.

There was an untamed freedom in the way the wind blew about us, as though the land had no idea that anyone had mastered its terrain.

As we moved farther north, the road changed from a wide path, to a narrow trail, to a strip of dirt running through the high grass.

Finn shifted to walk in front of me when the way forward became too narrow for us to move side by side. The grass grabbed at the fabric of my skirt, pulling me back with every step.

"This isn't right." I studied the plants around me, searching for a hint of poison or a predator waiting to pounce.

"It is," Finn said. "The blob of water up ahead is definitely the thing marked *death* on the map."

"I know that." I grabbed Finn's sleeve, stopping his loping stride. "There's a whole town's worth of people back there, and this trail is barely worn. If there had been a pond like this anywhere near Harane, there would have been a pack of children racing to the water on a day this fine. There should be marks in the dirt where carts have been hauling picnics back and forth. What happened in that pond to scare a whole town away?"

The bright sunlight still warmed my face, but fear muted the joy of it. I took a deep breath, trying to catch a hint of decay carrying on the wind.

"Maybe no one's taught the children how to swim." Finn took my hand, pulling me behind him. "Maybe they banned visiting the pond because too many unmarried couples were fraternizing by the water's edge."

"Do you really think either of those things could be true?"

"No. But I'd rather let myself enjoy the morning just a little while longer."

I kept scanning the tall grass as we walked. There were no paths trampled through it by animals come to drink their fill or patches eaten away by hungry livestock.

The ground grew softer under our feet as we neared the water's edge. My boots squished with every step, the sound joining the swishing of the grass against my skirt.

"Finn." I pulled on his hand, but he kept moving forward. "Stop."

He reached for the knife at his waist as he looked around. "What?"

"There are no birds." I froze, listening for any hint of a chitter or caw.

"What under the stars happened here?"

I reached down, freeing my own knife from the sheath tucked into the ankle of my boot. The weight of the blade didn't bring me any more comfort than it had when we'd been chased through the mountains by a monster.

The water came into view, glistening in the morning light. I wished there would be some hint of menace in its beauty, anything to explain the utter dread that curled through my stomach.

A band of barren dirt surrounded the pond. I squinted at the brown, trying to catch sight of any paw prints a thirsty animal might have left behind.

I stepped up to the very edge of the pond, where the water kissed the toes of my boots.

"We could ask in town," Finn said. "Tell the barkeep we fancy a swim, and see what he has to say."

A gentle wind blew around us, and the grass sighed as it swayed. The breeze dipped tiny waves into the surface of the water, giving it a texture that lent depth to the shadows below the surface.

"Finn, look down there." My voice was calm as I spoke. Almost too calm, as though my mind had slowed my words to give my eyes time to understand the submerged shapes.

A man riding a horse, sat at the bottom of the pond. The man wore a dark coat and a white shirt that somehow worsened the pallor of his skin. His head was barely below the surface of the water. He held one hand in front of his face as though trying to protect himself from an attack.

The wind blew again, harder this time.

The water stirred. The very top of the man's head emerged for a moment. His brown hair fluttered in the breeze. Then the wind died down. The water settled, and he was back below the surface. A human statue, carved by a master and dumped into a pond.

"Come on." Finn took my arm, pulling me back down the path.

"It's not right." I kept my gaze fixed on the man, squinting through the sunlight reflecting off the still water.

"Clearly."

"Bodies float. If that's a real man, he should be floating." I paused at the edge of the grass, unwilling to stop staring at the drowned figure.

"If he were killed by natural causes, then I would agree with you. Come on, Ena."

"Come where?" I shut my eyes tight, making white spots dance in front of them.

"Away from the death pond seems like a reasonable start. From there, I would be willing to negotiate."

"We need to see the other pond." I took Finn's hand and started blazing my own trail through the tall grass. The rib-high blades scratched at my bare hands.

"Do we really need to see how many corpses can fit in the big pond?"

"Is he even dead?" My steps faltered. I looked back toward the water, but the grass hid the pond from view. "Is he just frozen, should we help him?"

"I don't have any magic in my blood." Finn stepped in front of me, leading me on a wider path around the water. "I don't claim to be an expert on magic, but I did grow up in Lygan Hall. I have seen my fair share of enchantments and curses, and I can promise you with absolute certainty there is no chance under the stars we could haul that man out of the water and save him.

"I can also say with relative certainty that if we were to try such a chivving foolish thing, we'd probably die. If you want to go see the other pond and check for more death, fine. But we are not touching that chivving water."

"No touching." I nodded, even though Finn wasn't looking at me.

The ground squished beneath my boots, and a shiver shook my spine.

"The people in the town have got to know," I said. "There's no way they could have just always hated that pond and not noticed the man at the bottom."

"I don't think either of us is that lucky."

The second pond came into view. It was larger than the first, at least three times as wide, and surrounded by a similar band of plain dirt.

I held my breath as I stared down into the water, searching for a frozen massacre lurking beneath the surface.

Movement caught the corner of my eye.

"This way." I started around the side of the pond, careful to keep my feet out of the water.

A cluster of reeds grew along the western bank. Flashes of movement darted through the stalks.

"Fish." I leaned over the water.

Finn wrapped an arm around my waist, pulling me back.

"This pond has fish, and the other has a dead man." I stepped away from the water and into the grass, which suddenly felt safer than being in the open. "It doesn't make sense. If there were something wrong with the water, it should be bad in both ponds. They're so close together, a big enough storm would flood it all into one."

"We should go to the squiggles on the map," Finn said. "The tracker was right about the death pond. Maybe whatever she found on the western hill will make a bit more sense."

"We can hope."

I didn't pull the map back out of my pocket as I began leading Finn up the hillside and away from the water. I had a sense of something watching me, following me, and I didn't want it to know about the bloodstained piece of paper in my pocket.

The map was private, sacred. A woman had given her life for the information she'd tried to pass on in those squiggled lines. I would not allow my failure to betray her.

Sweat had begun to bead on my back by the time we made it free of the tall grass. There was no fence, or rocky soil, or any other hint as to why the wild grass that had so determinedly wrapped around my ankles suddenly gave way to low greenery and wildflowers that all seemed to have been recently chewed on by hungry livestock.

A field mouse darted through the grass and down into a hole. The sight of the tiny creature brought me an absurd amount of relief.

"The animals know there's something wrong with that chivving pond." Finn stared at the place where the rodent had disappeared.

"Finn, you know I despise the Guilds." I cut south along the open field. "You know I loathe them with every ounce of my being."

"I do know." Finn tucked his knife back into its sheath.

"I would have sent for them." I knelt, hiding my own weapon away. "If there were a man trapped in a pond and a place even the animals feared, I would have sent for the Sorcerers Guild."

"You wouldn't," Finn said. "You would have thought about it and decided you'd rather be killed by an evil curse."

"At the very least, I wouldn't have hated the one who sent for a sorcerer's aid." I stood up and looked to the pair of ponds below us. From a distance, they seemed innocent. I couldn't see the shape of the man at all. "If the people of the Lir Valley know what's under the water, why have none of them sent for help?"

4 6

A hundred birds perched on the ground. Some of their heads tipped at different angles. A few had spread their wings as though preparing to fly. No two birds were identical, but they were all made of stone.

Is this how Liam's bird was made?

Even as I thought the horrible question, I knew it couldn't be true.

Liam's bird was stone brought to life by his magic.

The birds on the barren hillside were living creatures cursed to become stone.

"What sort of sorcerer could even manage a thing like this?" I knelt beside a bird, studying the prefect outlines of the feathers on its wings.

"I know a few. But none of them are children, and all have spent years training," Finn said.

I balled my hands into fists, resisting the temptation to touch the bird and feel the texture of its stone feathers.

"Either we're here chasing a frighteningly powerful child or an adult who's managed to live in Ilbrea and avoid being taken by the Sorcerers Guild," Finn said. "The trouble is, I don't know which is more terrifying."

I stood and brushed the dirt off my skirt.

The hillside where the birds had met their untimely end was pretty, with a sweeping slope and a wide view of the town below. Farther up, toward the top of the valley, the castle-like estate stared down at everything below.

From this angle, I could just make out a dirt road leading to a giant barn hidden behind the massive stone structure. I tried to think through how many people could live in the castle and how many it would take to maintain it. Even just the people living on the estate could leave us with a dozen possibilities for a child that could be hiding magic.

I dug my fingers into my hair, pulling at the roots. "How do the trackers manage it? How do they find the sorcis for us to save?"

"I'm starting to think they might be using a strange form of sorcery of their own," Finn said. "Either that or a combination of luck and intervention by the gods."

I closed my eyes and tipped my face up to the sky. "How charming are you feeling this morning?"

"Why, my love? Are you considering leaving me for another man?"

"No"—I wrinkled my nose as I looked to Finn—"but I am considering doing something very foolish and may need your charm to save my neck."

"Then point me in the right direction, and I will prove to the world exactly why my mother never chucked me out of the house, no matter how close I came to burning the whole place down."

"Perfect." I turned toward the estate. "Aren't the homes made of stone in Lygan Hall?"

"They are." Finn offered me his arm.

"You almost burnt down a stone home?"

"The stone would have stayed standing." Finn laughed as we strode farther up the hill. "But everything in it—furniture, clothes, my mother's prized collection of books—they would have all gone up in flames."

"Your poor mother."

"Don't be too hard on me." Finn nudged me with his elbow. "It's shocking how flammable bedding can be."

"Poor you."

We chatted all the way up the hill. Finn would take over every time I ran out of cheery things to say. I would respond and laugh, prompt another tale of him angering his mother. But no matter how funny his stories were, I couldn't shake the feeling of something watching me.

I hated that feeling. The powerless knowledge that some unknown thing could see me, but no matter how many times I stopped to take in the view of the valley, carefully searching the open ground around me for a hint of anyone following, I couldn't find whatever it was that had set the chill on the back of my neck.

I stopped one final time as we reached a flowerbed that seemed to mark the beginning of the estate proper. Holding my breath, I searched the valley below for any flicker of movement or wisp of a shadow that could be trailing in my wake.

Nothing.

"Come on." I tugged on Finn's arm, leading him around the flowerbed.

The blooms had been planted in a twisting pattern, with deep black rocks nestled between the rows. The design held a certain beauty, but the plants themselves were the same sort that grew in the little gardens in front of the homes in town.

The castle itself was built of the same stone as the houses and shops far below, though the rocks were where the similarities stopped.

I could only see one entrance cutting through the thick wall of the massive structure, and the lowest set of windows didn't even begin until ten feet off the ground. Even then, all the panes had heavy bars across them, as though whoever had built the place was expecting to be attacked at any moment.

We passed another flowerbed. This one had been planted to bloom into an image of the sun with bright golden rays of light streaking through a field of deep blue.

I don't think anyone in Harane would have dreamt of trying to create such a thing, even if they'd had the time and land to plant so many flowers.

"Ena," Finn whispered, nodding toward the entrance of the castle.

A woman dressed all in black stepped onto the stone slab in front of the shadowed doorway and glared down at us.

"You did say you had a plan when you wanted to come up here?" Finn said.

"Close enough to a plan." I smiled and waved at the woman.

She did not smile back.

A very foolish part of me wanted to shout a hello to the woman just to see if she'd cringe.

But I kept my pace even and my smile bright as we walked toward the stone mouth of the castle. I didn't say anything at all until we were only twenty feet away from the door.

"Good morning." I gave the woman a nod. "It's a beautiful day out."

"The view from the Lir Estate is always lovely," the woman said. "That is why the Lirs have declared this private land."

"A wise decision," I said. "I can't imagine owning a castle only to end up with a town full of people picnicking at my doorstep."

The woman blinked at me for a moment before speaking again. "The Lir family values their privacy, as they always have in the century since this estate was built."

"Of course," I said, "and I wouldn't want to intrude upon the family. I was just hoping someone here might be able to answer a question or two for me."

"You'll have to forgive my wife." Finn stepped around me, bowing to the woman. "She is exceptionally curious. We truly don't want to intrude, but I'll never hear the end of it if she doesn't get to ask."

"It'll only take a moment," I said. "I was just hoping to find out who created the little stone birds."

Finn's neck tensed as the woman's eyes widened.

"Do you know who made them?" I stepped up to Finn's side. "I was hoping you must since they're just down the hill from here."

"The birds are not on the grounds of the Lir family estate," the woman said.

"Right." I furrowed my brow. "I'll ask in town, then. I've never seen anything like them, and I've got to know who's responsible."

"You cannot pester people about the birds." The woman stepped toward me, her tone harsh and low.

"Why not?" I asked. "Do the birds belong to the Guilds? I don't know anyone but them who would have the right to say what I'm allowed to ask about."

"That will be quite enough," a man's voice carried from the shadows of the entryway. The man with the black hair we'd met the night before stepped out into the open. He looked to the woman. "Back to your work."

The woman gave me one final glare before bowing to the man and bustling back into the shadows and out of sight.

"You'll have to forgive her." The man smiled. The expression fit his face, like he had been born to live a life where joy was common. "Birgit means well, but she's overly protective of the grounds."

"I can see why she would be," I said. "The views from up here are lovely. They must be coveted by many people."

"They are by me, at least," the man said. "Though I can't say I have any interest in the stone birds."

"Really?" I said. "So, you don't know who put them there?"

The smile vanished from around the man's eyes, leaving a frightening darkness behind. "If I did, I would make sure the one who defaced my hillside understood the consequences of their actions."

"Can't you just take them down if you don't like them?" Finn asked.

"I will not give the vandal the satisfaction," the man said.

"That's a pity," I said. "I was hoping to find the sculptor. Do you think anyone in town might know?"

"You'll not find a murmur in town regarding the maker of the birds." The man's smile returned. "I'm sorry I can't be of more help."

"Please, don't be," I said. "I'm sorry someone left a flock of birds on your hill. Though I can't imagine anyone from the town would maliciously leave something on your land."

"That's very true," the man said. "Would you like my help in returning to town? I could have my cart ready in a few minutes' time."

"No." I looked out over the valley. "It's a perfect a day for a walk. We'll be off your hill in no time, I promise. Thank you for your help." I took a few steps away from the entrance before stopping. "Is there a child who should be playing around these grounds?" I looked back at the man.

Darkness flashed over his face again. "What do you mean?"

"It's just you prize your privacy so much, and you've had a problem with vandals." I shrugged. "I didn't know if they were supposed to be here."

"What did you see?" He stepped toward me.

Finn shifted his weight, easing his hand up toward the knife hidden at his waist.

"When we were coming up the hill," I said, "I saw a child. They were still for a while then sprinted away. I was never close enough to see much of them. It was a bit peculiar, though. If I see them on our way back to town, should I tell them off or have them come up here?"

"Neither." The man smiled again. This time the expression did not reach his eyes. "I'm sure they are far away by now."

"Ah well." I shrugged. "Have a lovely day."

I held my hand behind me, reaching for Finn, and walked down the hill without looking back. I twined my fingers through Finn's, trying to look like a couple in love as I hurried down the slope.

"Tell me you have a plan," Finn said. "Tell me we didn't just go waltzing up to a chivving castle to shout that we're looking for the maker of some magically frozen birds."

I moved a bit faster, walking as quickly as I could without actually running.

"Ena."

"I don't have a proper plan," I admitted. "But we do have the black-haired Lir very upset."

"Which is a bit of a problem since we're in a valley named after him."

"Oh, calm down." I stopped and turned Finn to face me. "I have to kiss you now."

I leaned in and gave Finn a slow kiss. I wrapped my arms around his neck and pressed my body against his. I pulled my lips from his and whispered in his ear. "Now we're going to run to the tall grass, and you're going to beam and laugh the whole way like you're about to get the best roll of your life."

I took Finn's hand and sprinted down the hill. I tossed my head back and laughed at the sky.

"Is this a part of your non-existent plan or have you finally given in to my charms?" Finn asked through his laughter.

"I have never been immune to your charms."

Sense told me to stop at the edge of the high grass, to stay out in the open and leave whatever the animals were afraid of to the shadows. But I charged into the grass, laughing like a mad woman and dragging Finn behind me.

We ran for a full minute before I glanced behind.

There was no sign of movement in the castle high up on the hill.

I dropped to the ground, yanking Finn down with me.

"Do you actually want me to roll you?" Finn asked. "I take our duty to protect the sorcis seriously, but I don't know if our friendship could survive my crawling up your skirt."

"Oh, hush and be still." I rolled onto my stomach. "We just need to hide here for a bit and watch."

"Watch for what?"

"A man who lives in a perfect castle, on top of a perfect hill, looking out over his perfect town has a batch of mad stone birds glaring up at him. Now he thinks that whoever did it is lurking around his property."

Finn stared at me for a moment. "I still don't understand."

"What does a farmer do when a fox is stalking their hens?" I peered up over the tall grass just in time to see the man with shining black hair ride south on his perfect black horse. "They go fox hunting."

47

The dirt road the Lir man raced down cut along the side of the valley, heading straight south. There were no trees surrounding the lane, or even a long, stone wall to offer a bit of cover.

"This was your plan?" Finn asked as we strode south along the dirt road out in the open for all to see. "You had the brilliant idea to go up to a castle and send a madman charging away on his horse?"

I bit my lips together.

"And now we just saunter along after the angry laxe and hope he doesn't notice?" Finn asked.

"Well, no." I untied the string at the end of my braid and shook my hair free. "Honestly, I was hoping we'd find someone with a loose tongue, eager to complain about the chivving child who'd frozen a flock of birds and murdered a man. But this works as well."

The Lir man rode so far ahead of us, he and his black horse were hardly more than a dark spot on the road.

There weren't many choices for where the man could be going. Along the road, there were only the long buildings and the mine. Still, I couldn't bring myself to stop walking. Not because I was afraid he'd sneak off the road, but out of fear of what he might do to the child. A child I'd sent him after.

I wove my hair into a tight braid as the man stopped his horse beside one of the long buildings.

Finn cringed. "I wish we had a bit of cover. Just a shrub."

The Lir man strode into the second building without glancing in our direction.

"Oh, you made him mad," Finn said. "Very, very mad."

"This way." I tugged Finn off the dirt and into the weeds and wildflowers that surrounded the road.

Vegetable gardens had been planted alongside the buildings, and a few women labored amongst the plants.

I kept my eyes front, locked on the second building as we cut between the garden and the first stone home. At least, it seemed like a home in a sad sort of way.

Built two stories tall and longer than four normal houses stuck side by side, signs of people living packed together spilled through the windows. Washing hung out to dry, the scent of overcooked food filled the air, and murmured words carried on the breeze.

I sensed the women staring at us but didn't look their way. I couldn't, not when the shouting began in the second building.

I couldn't understand the words at first, but I recognized the anger of the shout and the terror in the reply.

Do not let more innocent blood fall on my hands.

"Keep her away," the Lir man shouted. "Keep her inside. Keep her locked up."

"She is," a woman begged. "She never leaves my sight. I swear to you."

"There was a child prowling around my home," Lir growled.

"There are other children," the woman said. "It wasn't her."

"You shouldn't stay here," a voice whispered behind me.

I gasped and spun around, ready to fight for my life, only to find a little girl with black hair and brown eyes staring up at me.

"She is the only one who would be foolish enough to dare," Lir said.

"Come on." The child took my hand. "We can wait below until he's gone. It's best to stay hidden when the master is angry."

"Thank you," I whispered.

"If not her, then who? Which one has been prowling?" Lir shouted. "Someone here has got to know."

"I don't know," the woman said. "I have been in here with Cinnia. I sit with Cinnia. My whole world is watching her. I don't know what anyone else does."

The little girl led me around the side of the building.

I glanced behind to Finn.

He widened his eyes at me but followed all the same.

The girl stopped at the corner of the building. Chewing on her top lip, she glanced up at the windows before running for an open cellar door against the side of the house.

Lir said something, but I was too far away to make out the words.

"Go." The girl pointed at the steps leading down into the darkness below. "Go on."

"It wasn't Cinnia!"

I froze at the woman's shout.

"We have to help her." I looked to Finn.

"Cinnia?" the little girl said. "She doesn't need any help, but we have to hide. You can't let him find out you went to the pond."

The child stood, pointing into the dark as though she hadn't said anything strange.

"Go." Finn nodded me toward the steps.

"Thank you." I hurried down the stairs, blinking against the darkness in the cellar below.

Barrels and baskets lined the walls of the short-ceilinged room. The scent of wet dirt and fresh-dug vegetables made it hard to believe I'd just stepped out of a bright shining morning.

"All the way to the back." The girl darted in front of me and beckoned me to follow.

"Once he knows it wasn't Cinnia, he'll go on a tear. It's better if we keep out of the way when he does that."

She stopped at the back wall and turned around to face us. "You are very big, so it might feel tight to you. Sorry."

Before I could ask her what might feel tight, she'd already leaned against a barrel and begun shoving it to the side.

"Do you need help?" Finn asked.

"I can do it." The child dug her toes into the dirt, pushing with all her might.

The barrel inched sideways, and a tiny slat of light appeared in the back wall.

"Who's out there?" a voice whispered.

"It's Evie." The little girl dropped to her knees. "Scoot over. We've got to make room for guests."

"What?" the voice squeaked.

I knelt down as Evie crawled through the hole in the wall behind the barrel.

"Just make room," Evie said. "The master's on a tear upstairs."

I inched toward the flickering light.

A little boy sat huddled at the back of the dirt cell.

The space was only ten feet deep and not even as wide, but I could tell they'd spent a lot of hours trapped inside. Someone had etched pictures into the dirt walls, and a stack of dirty blankets had been neatly folded in the corner.

"Who are they?" the little boy asked.

I crawled into the chamber. "My name is Ena, and this is my friend Finn."

"You've got to close the door behind you," Evie said.

"Right," Finn said.

I slid out of his way as he wrestled the barrel back into place. It wasn't until he'd blocked us in that the feeling of being trapped settled into my stomach.

"This is a lovely place you have here," Finn said.

"Why are they here?" the boy asked. He looked to be older than Evie, but I wasn't sure if it was only the thinness of his cheeks and fear in his eyes that made me think so.

"I went to the water, to check on the man," Evie began.

"Is he still there?" A wrinkle formed between the boy's black eyebrows.

"He is." Evie nodded. "But they were there, too. And then they walked straight up the hill to the birds."

The boy glared at Finn and me. He balled his hands into tight fists as his shoulders crept toward his ears.

"Then they walked straight up to the estate and spoke to the master," Evie said. "Followed him here, too."

"Why?" the boy said. "Why would they do that?"

"Because we're looking for someone." I sat against the wall opposite the boy, arranged my skirt around me, and laid my hands in my lap.

Neither of the children spoke.

I waited another moment before pressing on. "Finn and I are looking for someone very special. And I think the person we're looking for knows an awful lot about how the man ended up in the pond and how the birds turned to stone."

Evie bit her lips together while the boy glared at her.

"You see," I said, "there are some children who are so special, older people are afraid of them. And when grownups get afraid, sometimes they hurt people. Or send special children away to places they don't want to go."

"No one should be afraid," Evie said.

"Evie." The boy hit her in the arm.

"She never meant to hurt anyone." Evie hit the boy back. "She was only defending herself."

"Quiet," the boy growled. "We don't know them."

"You don't," Finn said, "and you're right to be wary of strangers. But we are here to help."

"You can't help," the boy said.

"I think we can," I said. "I think you know who made the strange things happen by the pond and on the hill. And, if you can be brave enough to trust us, we can help her. There's a place where she wouldn't have to be afraid of her magic. Where she wouldn't have to defend herself."

"Liar," the boy said.

"Breathe, Dorran," Evie said. "You've got to remember to breathe."

"Shut it, you." Dorran took a deep breath.

"Look," Finn said, "where I come from, there's a lot of magic, and it's wonderful. The people born with magic in their blood don't have to hide. They're trained and protected."

"You're from the Sorcerers Guild." Evie's chest sank.

"You shouldn't have brought them here." Dorran rounded on her.

"We're not from the Sorcerers Guild," I said. "We don't even like them. But whoever sank the man and froze the birds, they need help. They are going to be noticed or accidentally hurt someone they don't want to hurt. It's only a matter of time before the Sorcerers Guild comes for them."

"They've tried," Dorran said. "A lady in purple robes went to the estate. The master sent her away."

I looked to Finn. My own fear was reflected in the wrinkles on his brow.

"Can you tell us who it is?" I asked.

"No," Dorran said.

"We'll just talk to them," I said. "If they don't want anything to do with us, we'll go."

"We're not allowed to tell." Dorran glared at Evie as he spoke.

"He's right," Evie said. "We can't tell you. We made a solemn vow."

"Then you shouldn't break it," Finn said. "But maybe you could tell the one with magic that we're here. Let them know we want to help them, and that there's a place where they can be safe that's far away from the Sorcerers Guild and the master. That way, if they want to talk to us, they can, and you won't have broken your vow."

"Maybe," Evie said at the same time Dorran said, "No."

"Either way, it's up to you," Finn said. "Just know that all we want to do is help."

"There is no help." Dorran crossed his arms and pulled his knees up to his chest as though trying to form a cocoon where he might be safe.

"We should go," I said. "Let you two have your hiding place to yourself."

"You can't," Evie said. "He might still be up there."

"We'll be careful," I said.

"And you think you could help." Dorran laughed.

"Why shouldn't we go up there?" I asked.

"It's only the diggers, women, and us children who are supposed to be around the miners' homes," Dorran said. "You're not allowed. It's the rule."

"The master makes rules for everything," Evie said. "He owns everything in the valley. The mine, our houses, the whole town. If you don't follow his rules, he'll boot you out."

"Or worse," Dorran said.

"If you get booted out, there's no way to earn coin," Evie said. "That's when people starve or freeze in the woods. You can't let him catch you where you shouldn't be. You could die."

"Well"—I pushed myself onto my knees—"thank you for being so brave in protecting us. But Lir does not own me or my home. I have no fear of him." I crawled to the barrel and shoved it aside. "We're staying at the tavern in town. If the one with magic wants to speak to us, that's where we'll be."

I crawled out into the cellar, the awful feeling of abandoning those poor children gnawing at my gut.

4 8

Even though I'd told the children I had no reason to fear Lir, I still stood at the bottom of the cellar steps listening for a long while.

There was no hint of angry voices or whimper of distress coming from above.

What if Lir hurt the woman? It would be your fault, Ena. More blood on your hands.

I crept up the steps and peered around the front of the building.

The shining black horse still waited by the road.

"Hasn't the man got anything better to do?" Finn whispered. "Should we crawl back in with the children?"

"We can't let them think we're afraid of him," I said. "Why would they trust us to save the sorci if we're afraid of their master?"

"It's sick."

"I just don't understand it. He can't actually own the whole valley, can he? The Guilds wouldn't let one person own that much."

"I don't know." Finn took my hand, drawing me around to the back of the building. "But I'd rather ponder the matter far away from here."

The women were still working in the garden as we cut back through. I didn't look away from them this time. I studied them instead. Their worn faces, etched with worry lines. The rounding of their shoulders that didn't look as though it could ever go away.

I looked to the mine in the distance. I couldn't see anything inside the great black hole in the ground.

"Liam should be here," I said once we'd stepped back onto the dirt road.

"He's got a monster stalking the camp, remember?"

"This isn't a normal sorci run." I dug my nails into my palms, willing my pulse to slow. "Suppose Evie actually sends the sorci to us. Do we just bolt for the mountains?"

"Yes."

"But what about the people in this valley? Are we just supposed to abandon them to Lir?"

346

"First off, we don't know that he's actually that bad." Finn raised one finger. "Second, short of killing him and hoping a better man takes over as master of these sad people, I don't know what you think we could do." He raised a second finger. "Third, the Guilds are our enemy, not the laxe. As much as I truly do not like this Lir man, he's not the one we're fighting against."

I grabbed Finn's hand before he could raise a third finger. "It seems wrong to ignore people who are being hurt just because their enemy is different from ours. Aren't we all tilk? Does it matter what face the monster wears?"

"Yes, because at the end of the day the Guilds are the root of every evil that destroys lives in Ilbrea. If we spend all our time hacking away at evil leaves, we'll never stop the Guilds for good."

I froze in the center of the road. "You think we can stop the Guilds for good?"

"I bet my life on it every day. Call me a hopeless optimist if you like, but it is freedom for all of us that I fight for, and I can only see one way to make that happen."

Finn looped his arm through mine and dragged me forward.

We cut off the road and through the fields below once we were level with the town. The terrain didn't hold the chilling feel of the tall grass or the crisp neatness of the estate. It looked like normal land leading to a normal town.

Even as we stepped onto the dirt lane that led between the farthest south of the houses, I was still searching for some proof that what the children had told us was true. That Lir genuinely owned everything.

The flowers in front of the houses no longer seemed soothing as we passed by. The blooms were a threat to the owners of the homes. If they did not tend their garden, they would be cast out.

And where would the people go?

I'd left my home and ended up with the Black Bloods. But if I'd been on my own, truly on my own, I don't know what I would have had to do to survive.

Finn chatted with people, getting directions as we weaved through the labyrinth of streets back to the tavern.

The same barkeep greeted us and offered us a table and a hot meal. Finn beamed at the prospect of food, and I tried to smile convincingly along.

The woman who'd glowered at me the night before brought out a tray of meat pies.

"Thank you," Finn said. "We took a nice healthy walk this morning, and I am ready for a good meal."

The woman's face brightened to an expression just above loathing.

"May I ask a question?" I said.

"Didn't you already have all your questions answered this morning, my love?" Finn pushed my plate toward me.

"Nearly." I dug my heel into his toe under the table. "Someone mentioned a tavern in town that's owned by a fellow called Lir. Is this the place?"

"The Lir family owns everything in the valley," the woman said. "We are all fortunate to be allowed to work his land."

She stalked back to the kitchen.

"You are lucky she didn't take the food with her," Finn whispered. "And did you really have to try and break my toe?"

"Yes."

I ate my meat pie without tasting it, trying to look like a pleasant wife instead of someone who wanted nothing more than to run from the valley.

"How long do we wait for the child?" I asked once Finn had finished his fourth helping of food.

"A few days, I'd say. We've got the coin for the room, and we'll still get back to camp before your brother or Liam go completely mad worrying about you."

An odd feeling grew in my gut, one I'd thought I had banished forever.

"I wish Emmet were here." Saying the words felt strange, like someone else had taken control of my mouth.

"Are you feeling ill?" Finn leaned toward me.

"Emmet would storm onto the estate and tell Lir he didn't have the right to control the people of the valley."

"Ahh." Finn leaned back. "I see. You wish a version of Emmet that doesn't exist were here. The real Emmet Ryeland would not go to the odd little castle and tell Lir he's a chivving cact. He'd go pummel Lir and then burn the castle."

"You're exaggerating."

"I'm not."

"What about the mine?" I looked up to the ceiling. There wasn't a cobweb or speck of dust in sight. "Would he sit around wondering what Lir mined that granted him such riches and power? That little girl said Lir sent a sorcerer away. What in this world could give Lir the power to turn a Guilded sorcerer away from their hunt for a sorci?"

"By the gods, I'm glad Emmet's not here." Finn doubled over laughing. "I can see it perfectly in my head. He'd stomp right up to the entrance of the mine looking like a demon fresh from the forge, glowering so badly most would scatter at the sight of him. He'd stride straight to the center of..."

"Keep going." I looked to Finn.

"No." Finn narrowed his eyes at me. "I don't want to give you any foolish ideas."

"It's not foolish at all," I whispered. "There's something wrong with this place."

"Yes." Finn nodded. "It's called a madman owns everyone. All the homes. All the shops. This is what happens when a rich slitch decides who lives and who dies."

"Lir sent a sorcerer away. That's not possible. That's not something the Guilds would ever allow someone to even attempt without the person foolish enough to do the demanding ending up dead."

Finn rubbed a hand over the stubble on his chin.

"There is something going on here, Finn. Something that scared the tracker badly enough to send her racing back to the mountains. Shouldn't we at least try to find out what she knew? Bring the best information we can back to Liam?"

"I love you, Ena Ryeland. I swear to the gods I do, but if we get ourselves killed sneaking around a chivving mine, I will haunt you in the next world."

"Good." I squeezed Finn's hand. "Dead or not, I don't know what I would do without you."

49

I have made many mistakes in my life. Some, I cannot bring myself to regret. Others, I would tear the stars from the sky for the chance to change.

Pain and I have long been acquainted. Grief is a feeling my heart knows well.

I understood the greed of the Guilds. Their love of power and abundance of hate.

I didn't understand the horror one common man's hunger for power can inflict.

I should have known.

I should not have been bold enough to think I could help.

I should have learned from the blood already on my hands.

50

The night wasn't cold enough to warrant wearing my coat, but, as the fabric of it was darker than the sleeves of my shift, I wore it anyway.

Finn and I strolled arm in arm to the edge of town, me doting on him and whispering sweetly in his ear, him nodding and beaming at every person we passed. My nerves didn't begin to shout until we'd reached the southernmost home in town.

There was only a narrow trail leading toward the mine, almost as though the town wasn't meant to acknowledge the hole in the earth near their doorstep.

Once we'd slipped into the shadows behind the last house, we moved more quickly. There were low bushes along the way, but nothing big enough to offer any real hope of hiding. So, we just kept walking, counting on the dark of the night to shield us from prying eyes.

The mine was farther away than it had looked from the top of the valley or even from the miners' homes where we'd met Evie and Dorran.

I looked toward the cluster of buildings. Candles burned in the windows.

I wanted to ask Finn if he thought that was where all the miners lived and if those three buildings would be able to house enough workers to keep a mine running. But the only noises around us were the wind, the soft sound of our footsteps, and the low hoot of an owl. Somehow, it seemed like speaking might break whatever treaty we'd made with the night. I swallowed my questions, foolishly certain I'd have time to ask them later.

I slowed my pace as we neared the mine.

Finn kept beside me, one hand already on the hilt of his knife.

Two lanterns hung by the mouth of the mine. Silhouettes of men moved in the dim light. One pacing. Two standing together, only shifting slightly as though trying to ease the burden on their sore feet.

I took Finn's arm, stopping him behind a low bush. I knelt down, shutting my eyes and trying to reason through how to talk my way past the men.

"Do you want me to knock them out?" Finn whispered. "I can try to do it without hurting them too badly."

I shook my head.

"Unless you can flirt enough to lure all three of them away at once, I can't think of a better plan."

The mine sliced into the hillside, but the slope wasn't at a steep enough angle that I'd have a hope of climbing down from above and slipping in unseen.

"You shouldn't be here," a voice whispered behind me.

I fell to the ground, reaching for the knife in my boot.

"Chivving stars and gods, girl." Finn grabbed my hand, blocking me from my knife.

I looked up to find Evie staring down at me.

"What are you doing here?" I pressed a palm to my racing heart.

"Following you," Evie said. "You said to tell the one who put the man in the pond to find you at the tavern, but you're not at the tavern."

"Evie"—I pushed myself to my knees—"did you put the man in the water?"

She shook her head. "But I told the one that did what you said, and you're not in the tavern."

"We're going to go back to the tavern," Finn said. "We've just got a little chore to finish first."

"In the mine?" Evie cocked her head to the side.

"We need to know what they pull out of the mine," I said. "We're not going to take anything or hurt anyone. We just need to have a look."

Evie bit her lips together. "If you get to look, then you'll go back to the tavern, and then you can take the one who made the man go in the water where she'll be safe?"

"Yes," I said. "I promise. But right now, you need to go where you'll be safe."

"I'm safe here." Evie stepped out from behind the bush. "Come on. She'll get nervous if we make her wait too long."

The child strode straight for the three men.

"Evie," I whispered after her. "Evie!"

She just kept walking.

"The child is chivving mad," Finn said.

"Come on." I stood and chased after Evie. Finn's footsteps thumped quietly behind me.

We'd only been running toward them for a few moments before all three guards saw us coming. They all stopped, turned to face us, and drew their swords.

"Evie, stop." I caught her arm.

A shock, like lightning had struck my skin, shot through my hand.

I gasped, swaying as spots danced in front of my eyes.

"Ena." Finn grabbed me around the waist.

I blinked, trying to get my gaze to focus on Evie.

"Stop," one of the guards ordered. He looked down at Evie. "You? What are you doing here?"

"They need to look inside. I'm sorry." Evie drew her hands back.

A whoosh and a crack sounded as she shoved her hands forward, and all three men fell to the ground.

"Evie?" I ran after her as she strode into the mine. "Evie, stop."

"You said you needed to see," Evie called back. "So hurry up."

I leapt over the men lying on the ground. Their chests were moving, but their eyes were blank as they stared up at the night sky.

"Evie!" I ran after her.

"Ena, wait." Finn thumped behind me. "Oh, by the gods and stars this is a terrible idea."

The lanterns cast an orange glow into the entrance of the mine. The light flickered off the dark gray stone that matched the rock the entire town had been built of.

"Do you have a lantern?" Evie looked at me.

"No." My fingers fumbled as I pulled my lae stone from my pocket.

The blue glow shimmered off the rock, casting strange shadows like the whole world had suddenly been plunged deep underwater.

"That's pretty." Evie wrinkled her forehead, staring at the lae stone. "Is it magic? Are you magic?"

"No." Finn pulled out his own lae stone. "But we have a friend who is, and he made these for us."

I gripped my lae stone tighter. It had never once occurred to me that Liam himself had created the light I carried with me.

"Hmm." Evie turned down the tunnel. "We should keep going. I've only been down here once, and I don't remember much of it."

I followed the child deeper into the darkness. "Why have you been down here, Evie? Lir doesn't make you mine, does he?"

"No." Evie's voice bounced down the tunnel. "She asked me to come down here with her. She was too scared to come alone, and she wanted to see it. Didn't work out so well in the end though."

"Why?" I asked just as Finn said, "Who's she?"

Evie stopped, staring into the dark for a moment before turning toward us. "She never means to hurt anyone, but when she gets scared, she can't always make the magic stop. The men scared her."

"I'm sorry," I said. It didn't feel like enough, but I couldn't think of what else to say.

"Don't be," Evie said. "Just help her."

"We will," Finn said.

"Come on." Evie took off down the tunnel, running through the darkness as though she had no concept of fear.

Finn and I chased after her.

The walls of the tunnel crept closer together the farther down we ran, leaving barely enough room for a cart to pass. The roughly hewn stone had the same dark coloring as the rock by the entrance. As the shadows of the lae stones shifted against the harshly cut angles, it was easy to believe we were swimming down toward some terrible beast.

You will not drown.

"Finn," I said as the tunnel curved and the slope dove deeper still, "does this sort of rock look familiar to you?"

"A bit." A faint trace of fear tainted Finn's voice.

"By the Guilds." Evie stopped short just in front of me.

I wobbled, trying to keep from knocking her over.

"I definitely don't remember this," Evie whispered.

I held my lae stone high, though its dim blue glow barely carried far enough to light the chamber we'd entered.

Tunnels led off in five different directions, not counting the path we'd just run down. The chamber was larger than the clearing the Black Bloods gathered in at night. The size of the space seemed obscene for the three carts that sat in the middle and the one cage of tools tucked behind us.

"Evie," Finn said as he stepped in front of us, heading toward the carts, "how many miners live in the houses with you."

"I'd say..." Evie stared up at the ceiling. "I'd say thirty-four, if you count the three guards out front I knocked out. If you don't count the night guards, thirty-one."

"Such a large space for thirty-one miners," Finn said.

"What do they mine down here?" I asked.

"Rocks," Evie said.

"What sort of rocks?" I bent down to look into Evie's eyes. "Big rocks, like they use for building houses?"

"No," Evie said. "Little rocks. If they find one, the miners are given frie. They all drink and celebrate outside. Then the biddies get angry because the men trod on their gardens."

"Do you know what the little rocks are used for?" I asked. "Are they diamonds?"

"No. They mine rocks, not jewels." Evie ran after Finn.

"Why would they want little rocks?" A heavy fear settled across my shoulders. I looked up the tunnel we had traveled, waiting for one of the guards, or Lir himself, to come charging out of the darkness.

"Do the Guilds buy them?" I asked.

"Chivving cact of a slitching paun's nuts," Finn said.

"Oh dear," Evie giggled.

"What?" I looked to Finn.

"We need to get out of here." He leapt out of one of the carts.

"Why? What did you find?" I ran toward Finn.

He tore past me on his way up the tunnel.

"Finn." I chased after him. "Finn, what did you find?" I grabbed his arm.

He held his hand out. A tiny shard lay in his palm. A simple sliver of black rock that shimmered in the light of my lae stone.

There was something in the tiny shard that seemed familiar and alive all at the same time.

I'd seen mountains of the dark stone without feeling fear—the pendant around my neck that brought me so much comfort had been melded of the same rock—but the tiny, out of place fragment drained the heat from my body.

I pressed my palm to the stone pendant hidden beneath my bodice, needing to feel its warmth against my skin.

"This doesn't belong here," Finn said.

"What doesn't?" Evie ducked under my arm to look into Finn's palm.

"Nothing." Finn tucked his hand into his pocket. "We need to get to the tavern. We need to leave this valley."

"Yes," Evie said. "She'll be waiting for you, and she is not good at waiting."

Evie tore up the tunnel.

I took a deep breath before racing after her.

"Evie," I said, trying to keep my words even while I sprinted up the slope, "if you are the one who put the man in the pond, you can tell us."

"I've said it wasn't me."

"I know that," I said, "but you've got magic. I saw it."

"I know I've got magic," Evie said, "but I'm not the one who put the man in the pond or froze the birds. She's waiting for you."

The child ran faster, moving so quickly, I wondered if her magic were somehow helping her to fly up the tunnel.

Finn's footsteps kept close behind me as we ran, but he said nothing.

The brisk air of the summer night surrounded us as we reached the opening of the tunnel. The men still lay on the ground, their blank eyes turned toward the stars.

Evie ran up the dirt path toward the town without even bothering to check that Finn and I still followed.

I had a hundred questions I wanted to ask of her, of Finn. I even had questions I wanted to shout to the gods, but with the night pressing in around us, there was nothing to do but run.

A stitch pinched my side, and my breath grated my throat as we reached the southern edge of the town.

"Evie," I panted, "we've got to slow down."

I reached forward to catch the child's arm, but she dodged away from me without even bothering to look behind her.

I slowed my steps, forcing myself to walk between the stone houses.

Evie slowed before she rounded the next corner.

"If your friend"—Finn spoke between gasps as he took my arm—"if she's waiting for us at the tavern, we can meet her there."

Evie turned toward us. "She isn't at the tavern. She can't come into town. She's most definitely not allowed in town."

"Right," Finn said. "Of course. But why not?"

"It isn't safe for her," Evie said. "People upset her. She's not allowed to be upset."

"Then where is she?" I asked. "If you tell us, we can get our bags and go meet her. You won't have to stay with us."

"No." Evie turned and kept walking down the street. "I have to stay with you."

Evie led us down the twisting paths of the city without hesitation.

I kept my arm draped through Finn's, though I don't know what innocent defense I could have come up with for following a child through the streets at night.

By the time we neared the center of the town, my breathing had slowed. The scent of flowers and stone filled my nose as we moved from one pool of lamplight to the next. We passed a woman with a heavy basket in her arms, a boy chewing on a hunk of bread, and an elderly woman muttering to the shadows as she shuffled through the night.

Nothing seemed strange or out of place. The town had the same odd uniformity as it had in the daylight. There was nothing to explain the tingling on the back of my neck.

"Are we leaving tonight?" I whispered to Finn as our path became familiar.

"Yes," Finn whispered back.

We followed Evie down a curving alley and onto a wider road.

She stopped dead in the middle of the street, cocking her head to the side like a dog hearing a noise beyond my comprehension.

"Oh quatter wats." Evie shooed us back into the alley.

"What?" I pressed myself against the stone side of a cobbler's shop.

"He's waiting for you in the tavern." Evie chewed on her top lip. "The master's there."

"How do you know?" Finn asked.

"I don't know." Evie wrinkled her forehead. "There's too much noise in the tavern, and I can feel the people being angry and tense. I can smell the master, so I know he's in there, and he's downright furious. I don't know why there would be so many people sitting in a tavern and not drinking if it isn't about you."

"Our packs are in there." I shut my eyes. "Our supplies and our coin. We need our packs."

"I can get them," Evie said.

"No." I grabbed Evie by the back of the dress before she could step out of the alley. "You are not going anywhere near that tavern."

"But you just said you need your bags." Evie twisted out of my grip.

"I'll get them," I said. "Finn, you wait with Evie. I'll pop up, grab our bags, and be right back."

"You'll get caught by the master," Evie said.

"It's not worth it," Finn said. "We'll manage without the bags."

"I'm not stealing from people who are barely surviving." I wiped my hands on my skirt. "It's only one story up. You'll barely notice I'm gone."

I stepped out onto the street before Finn could stop me.

5 1

Low voices carried from inside the tavern, though I didn't see a hint of anyone standing guard around the building.

The large rocks the town had been built of may have been a cheap convenience for the Lir family as they cleared debris out of their mine, but the wide-set stone offered perfect handholds for me to climb.

I loved the burning in my muscles as I scaled the wall to our window. The precision of it, the dependence on every part of my body, made me believe for one beautiful second that I was in control. That my own skill and strength could somehow change the course of things.

I gripped the sill as I pushed the window up. There wasn't even a lock to block my way. I was in the room before I had time to truly think through how I was going to get our bags out.

There was no light in the little room. I squinted through the shadows to the corner where Finn and I had left our packs. I couldn't see anything in the darkness.

As I reached into my pocket to pull out my lae stone, a board creaked in the far corner of the room.

I spun toward the sound.

A man stepped out of the shadows by the fireplace.

I gripped the lae stone in my pocket as I recognized Lir.

His black hair and clothes made him look more demon than man. His pale face twisted into a smile.

"Lir," I said. "What a pleasant surprise."

Lir stepped closer to me. "Is it a surprise? Do you think so little of my people? Did you think none of them would tell me you'd been poking around my valley?"

"I figured they would. When you control people's lives, the line between loyalty and fear becomes so thin there are few brave enough to break away."

"Who sent you?" Lir moved closer still.

I stepped toward him, letting my lips lift into smile. "Who do you think?"

Lir gave a low laugh. "I won't play games with you. This tavern is filled with loyal men. I have more waiting in the shadows to tear you to pieces. Tell me what I want to know, and your end will be considerably less painful."

The crystal edges of the lae stone bit into my palm as I clutched the rock.

Finn will be fine. Finn has gotten out of worse before.

"I was hired by the Sorcerers Guild," I said. "The Lady Sorcerer doesn't like being told she can't take the children she wants."

"I made her a fair offer," Lir said. "If she's unwilling to pay, that's her own trouble."

A rolling hatred bubbled in my gut.

"It's funny how you strut around this valley as though you own the land," I said. "You keep the miners tucked away and the rest of the people living in your stone town too frightened to speak of the man hidden in the pond."

Lir's eyes narrowed.

"You're nothing more than a rich fool in a fancy house." I leaned in so there was barely a foot of space between us. "You don't own anything. Never forget, we all live and die by the will of the Guilds."

"You know—"

I dug my heel into his toe and swung my lae stone for his temple. The impact of the stone against his skull shook my arm, but I held on to the light as Lir collapsed to the ground.

The thump of his fall stopped my heart from beating.

I froze, waiting for a dozen men to charge out of the shadows.

The dull sounds from below, murmurs and movement I hadn't even noticed before, stopped.

You will not fail them.

I held my lae stone toward the corner of the room where our packs had been. The blood on the stone shone purple. Bile rose in my throat.

Our packs were gone. Every hint that Finn and I had ever been in the room had vanished.

Footsteps crept up the creaking stairs.

I glanced around the room one more time.

Not a hint that we had ever existed.

I shoved the bloody stone into my pocket as the footsteps stopped at the door.

The floor creaked under my boots as I leapt over Lir and to the window.

The door burst open behind me.

"She's in here!" the barkeep roared.

I sat on the windowsill and twisted my body over the open air, hanging by my fingers for a split second before dropping to the ground far below.

"Stop!" a voice shouted from the shadows.

I did not stop. I raced toward the place I had left Finn and Evie.

Four people carrying makeshift weapons tore out of an alley. A woman led the pack, brandishing a garden spade.

I do not want to hurt these people. I cannot hurt these people.

I rounded the corner into the shadows where I'd left Finn, but he wasn't there.

Fear coursed through me, but I kept running, desperate to find a way to escape the growing mob that chased me.

I cut out of the alley and onto another winding street.

A faint, blue light glimmered to the north. I headed for the glow, hoping against hope that Finn would be there waiting for me.

A scream carried from the west.

I glanced behind to see flames rising from the roof of the tavern.

A man with a club and a woman carrying a kitchen knife faltered as the fire danced against the night sky.

I ran faster, pushing my legs as hard as they would go. I needed to head to the woods, find Finn in the safety of the trees. I reached the blue glow. The shade and shape were right for a lae stone, but I didn't dare stop to pick it up.

My feet sloshed through a puddle as I rounded the next bend in the road.

"Ena."

I recognized Finn's voice the moment before he grabbed my arm, hauling me out of the way as the puddle I'd just run through caught fire.

The woman with the garden spade screamed as flames leapt onto the hem of her skirt.

"This way." Evie waved us forward. A blue glow shot from behind my shoulder and into Evie's waiting hand. She tossed the lae stone to Finn. "I told you there were people waiting in the tavern."

"Lead on," Finn said.

He kept me in front of him as we raced through the streets.

"Where are we going?" I asked.

"To meet her," Evie said.

Another round of screams carried from behind us.

I risked looking back. The fire had spread to other rooves.

"Evie, did you start the fire?" I asked.

"Only the little one." Evie darted between two buildings as a group of men raced toward us. "It must have been her. I told you she isn't good at waiting."

I kept close behind Evie, resisting the urge to pick her up and carry her as the pounding of boots came closer.

Finn roared behind me.

I pulled my knife from my boot as I turned toward the sound.

The men chasing us had bottlenecked at the mouth of the alley.

Finn sliced through the first man's throat and shoved him back, knocking the others over.

"Stop playing around," Evie called back to us.

"Sorry," Finn said, "hard to resist stopping people from killing us."

We sprinted out onto another street, then through an alley so narrow I was grateful we'd lost our packs.

An open field waited for us beyond the stone buildings.

My moment of gratitude at being able to see in all directions soon vanished as the overwhelming feeling of being watched by a hundred hungry predators made every blade of grass seem like a deadly foe ready to kill me.

"I see them!" a voice shouted behind us.

"Oh dear," Evie said. "Oh dear."

"What is it?" My words rasped in my throat.

"There are too many people coming," Evie said. "She won't like it."

My legs burned as we raced up the hill, scrambling over stone fences, terrifying the animals we tore past.

The woods came into view, their silhouette like jagged teeth devouring the horizon.

"We're coming!" Evie shouted. She gasped in air before shouting again. "We're coming!"

I wanted to shush her, but there was something in her tone that made me quite certain the child was saving our lives.

The ground leveled out as we reached the top of the rise.

I glanced behind just long enough to see the string of torches following us and the massive blaze that had swallowed the center of the town.

"We're coming!" Evie shouted again as she raced into the woods.

I turned my eyes front, squinting into the shadows to try and see where she was running, but unwilling to pull the lae stone from my pocket.

Evie's steps slowed as she veered south.

"We're here," Evie said. "I'm here."

For the first time, there was a hint of hesitation in her voice.

"I've brought them," Evie said. "I did just as I said I would. Come out."

Evie stopped, turning around in a circle as she peered into the darkness.

The crashing of a dozen men carried from the edge of the woods.

"We have to keep going." I reached for Evie's arm.

She shook me away. "It's too late to turn coward. It's run now or stay here and wait for the master's rage."

A girl stepped out of the shadows. Her long black hair shimmered in the starlight. She led another black-haired girl out from behind a tree. Dorran stepped out beside them, worried lines wrinkling his brow.

"Good." Evie turned to look at me. "We're all here. Now, where do we go?"

5 2

I stared at the four children for a moment before remembering how to speak.

"To the river," I said. "We have to move as quickly and quietly as we can."

"Come on, Cinni," the tallest girl said to the one beside her. "We're going to run as fast as we can, all right?"

The girl nodded.

I cut around them, heading east.

I couldn't look back to check on them as we raced through the woods.

I could hear their panting and the steady, heavy thumps of Finn's boots, but there were too many branches and roots to dodge to allow me to watch the children.

We were miles from the river. Finn, Evie, and I had already run for miles. I wanted to stop, to ask the children if they needed to stop, but I didn't know how close behind us the townspeople were.

I pictured the whole forest catching on fire in a blaze of wrathful magic. I didn't know if any of us would be able to escape the flames.

My breath came in exhausted gasps, my feet throbbed, and my legs felt as though they'd been filled with stones. But I kept running.

"Stop," Finn panted behind me.

I swayed, catching a tree branch to keep upright as I turned to face him.

Dorran gripped a stitch in his side, gasping for breath as though he were about to drown.

The two girls held hands as they looked from Finn to me. Evie danced from one foot to the other as though unable to stop moving.

"Hop on my back," Finn spoke to Dorran. "I can carry you."

"We can slow down if you like," Evie said. "They headed too far south. They aren't very close right now."

"Are you sure?" the taller of the other girls asked.

"I can hear them." Evie nodded.

The taller girl looked to the smaller girl, who gave a tiny nod of her head.

"All right," the taller girl said. "We can go slower."

"Good," Finn said. "But we still need to keep moving."

"Right." I turned east again.

I wished I had my waterskin. I wished I had my pack, or the chivving stones Liam had given me so I could protect us from whatever horde Lir had sent after us.

I pressed my stone pendant to my skin, needing to feel that its constant warmth hadn't disappeared.

"We're just going to keep walking."

I turned at the whisper.

The taller girl leaned close to the smaller. "We love walking, don't we? We're going to walk and walk and then we'll find a nice place to rest."

"Sounds lovely," Evie said. "We can all climb in a pile and sleep together, right Dorran?"

"Yes." Dorran's voice wavered as he spoke. "We'll be in a nice, safe place where the four of us can sleep."

"We'll be ready for sleep," the taller girl said. "A nice long walk like this, and we'll be absolutely ready to curl up. That will be wonderful."

The smaller girl gave a tiny nod of her head.

"When we get where we're going," I said, "do all of you want to share a tent? Or do we need one for each of you? We have enough to go around."

"Together," the tallest girl said. "Wouldn't you like that, Cinni? If we all stayed together?"

I glanced back in time to see the smaller girl nod again.

"Do you have cotton to stuff in my ears where we're going?" Evie asked. "I don't want to spend the rest of my life listening to Dorran snoring."

"I do not snore," Dorran said.

"You do," the taller girl said.

They kept on that like as we trekked through the woods. There was a soothing patter to the way they spoke, like it was some sort of game they were all very good at playing.

With my knife in my hand, I searched through the shadows for any sign of attack.

An owl hooted from its nest, and we spooked a family of deer but didn't see any hint of another person before we reached the edge of the river.

"First, I want to sleep late," Evie said, "then I want to eat cake, then I want to lay in the sun all afternoon—"

"And end up with a pink face," Dorran said.

The soft rumble of the river carried through the trees.

"We're going to have to be very quiet," I whispered. "There's a bridge over the river, and I need to make sure we can all get across it."

"I'll go." Finn crept past me.

"Finn," I began.

"You should learn to take turns, Ena," Finn said. "You wandered off without me last time. Now it's my go."

He slunk out of the trees before I could think of a good argument for keeping him with me.

I beckoned the children forward to the very edge of the forest.

The starlight glinted off the water as the river raced south. It was a beautiful thing, and also an obstacle I feared we could not cross. I could swim, but not well enough to carry four, or even two, children with me.

"Look at the river," the taller girl spoke so softly, her voice might have been nothing more than a trick of the wind. "You've never gotten to see the river have you? It's so pretty and fast."

A branch cracked as footsteps sped toward us.

"It's like the water is dancing," the girl said.

Finn raced out of the shadows. "Follow me. Quickly."

We ran after him without question.

I fell behind, letting the four children get between Finn and me.

The two girls still moved hand in hand, while Evie ran in front and Dorran in back. The four of them were like a little unit, like the legs of one giant spider, dodging around tree branches and jumping over roots, while all staying the same distance from each other.

It wasn't until the bridge had come into view that I realized they weren't moving around each other. They were all centered on the smaller girl, as though silent Cinni were the axis their whole world rotated upon.

"There." Finn pointed into the shadows.

A freight boat bobbed next to the river dock.

A feeling of blissful relief flooded through me.

Finn slowed as we neared the boat.

I scooted around the cluster of children to reach his side.

"Did you check inside?" I whispered.

"Not yet," Finn said. "I wanted to get you first."

"We'll go in together then," I whispered.

I stopped at the edge of the dock and looked to Evie. "You all stay here, and Finn and I will be right back."

Cinni flinched.

I bent to look into her dark eyes. "We will be right back, and then we'll all get on the boat and float far away from here. All you've got to do is be brave for a few more minutes."

"Don't worry," Evie said. "I'll take care of us."

"Good girl." I followed Finn out onto the dock.

Even while tiptoeing, the aging wood thunked beneath my feet, but the sound was swallowed by the noise of the boat clunking into the pilings of the dock.

The boat was more than twice as wide as a wagon, and most of the middle was taken up by a cabin.

Finn climbed down onto the boat before pulling out his second knife.

I gripped the hilt of my own blade tighter as I lowered myself onto the deck.

The river racing around us and the knocking of the boat against the dock were the only noises I could hear.

Finn pointed to himself and then to the door of the cabin.

I nodded and pointed around the back side of the deck.

I didn't like turning my back on Finn to circle the cabin. It seemed wrong for us to separate, but we needed to search the boat. I crept quietly along, peering into the shadows between the crates of goods and open water barrels, pressing my back to the cabin wall as I looked around the corner.

I kept waiting for a noise from Finn, listening for any hint of a struggle inside. I paused at the far corner and took a breath before peeking around the back of the boat.

A man sat in a chair, a dark blanket draped over his body, letting him blend in with the stacks of goods around him. His head lolled to one side, and he'd propped his bandaged foot up on a crate.

I'm not sure if I froze for a minute or a heartbeat.

Then I pressed my knife to the man's throat and held my other hand over his mouth.

He jerked awake at my touch.

"Shh," I whispered in his ear.

He made a noise against my hand. I pressed the edge of my blade into his skin.

"If you make a sound, I will kill you. If you try to fight me, I will kill you." I tightened my grip on his mouth. "I don't want to hurt you, but I will. You are going to stand up very slowly. If you move too quickly, I will slit your throat. Now, stand up."

The man lowered his bandaged foot from the crate, wincing as he set it on the ground. Slowly, he stood.

"We are going to walk around to the front of the cabin," I whispered. "You're going to go very quietly."

I dug my shoulder into his back, guiding him toward the far side I'd already checked. We took three steps before he shot his elbow back, hitting me in the ribs, knocking all the air from my lungs.

He spun toward me as I stumbled, drawing his fist back to punch me, but I still had my knife.

The glimmer of the starlight off the metal caught his eye a moment too late.

I drove my knife into his side.

His eyes grew wide. He opened his mouth to scream from the pain.

I wrenched my blade free and kicked him hard in the stomach, knocking him toward the railing.

He coughed at the blow, gagging on the blood that had already begun to fill his lung.

I dodged to the side as he stumbled toward me.

A sound carried from the far side of the cabin.

I swung with my free hand, punching him in the cheek.

He sagged toward the railing.

I drove my knife into the side of his neck. He made a horrible, inhuman sound as I sliced through his throat.

He swayed as I yanked my blade from his flesh.

I dropped my knife and shoved him over the side of the boat and into the river below.

The splash as he hit the water covered the sound of my gasp as I saw the blood on my hands.

The warm stickiness had covered the sleeve of my coat as well.

I stayed stuck for a moment, just staring at my hands.

"Ena." Finn peered around the corner. "Did you find anyone?"

"No." I clenched my hands, hiding the worst of the red. "There's no one here."

"I'll get us untied." Finn disappeared toward the front of the boat.

I tripped over my own knife as I stumbled to the water barrel and plunged both my arms in, using the rough fabric of my coat sleeves to scrub the blood from my hands.

The soft sounds of footsteps came from the dock.

I snatched up my knife and dunked it into the barrel, washing the evidence of death away. I pulled the lae stone from my pocket and scrubbed it clean as whispers drifted from the dock.

I pulled my hands from the barrel and tucked my weapons away. My sleeves dripped onto the blood-stained deck.

I wedged myself between the barrel and the wall of the cabin.

The thump of a rope hitting the deck came from the front of the boat.

I pushed on the top of the barrel as hard as I could. "Please. Just tip."

The barrel crashed down with a splash that soaked my boots and washed away any trace that I had just murdered a man.

53

The children slept during our night on the boat. Finn and I didn't.

I had no idea how to steer a boat, so it became my job to get the children settled inside the cabin, and watch the shadows on either side of the river, searching for anyone coming to kill us.

I stole a spare blanket from the cabin. There were two beds, but all four children had insisted on piling into one.

The tallest tended to the others well enough that it felt wrong for me to hover. Evie waved goodbye, but the others didn't even seem to notice as I crept out of the cabin with my pilfered blanket.

I spent the night pacing the deck, searching for signs of approaching death. By the time the sun started to rise, my clothes had changed from a sopping-wet cold mess, to a damp cold mess. But somehow, pacing the deck in chilly discomfort didn't seem like enough penance for ending a man's life.

I tried to tuck the horror at what I'd done into the darkness where I couldn't feel it, but the look in his eyes when I'd stabbed him wouldn't leave my mind. I tried to burn the guilt away with anger at the Guilds. It was their fault I had to help the children in the first place.

But it wasn't the Guilds who had pressed a knife to the man's throat.

But they're the ones you have to outlive. A voice that sounded horribly like Emmet's rattled through my mind. *The have made a battlefield of our lives.*

"How long will it take us to reach where we're going?"

I gasped and spun toward Evie. The other three children all stood behind her.

"Don't sneak up on people." I pulled my blanket tighter around my shoulders.

"Is it going to be a very long time?" Evie asked.

"I'm not sure," I said. "I've never traveled on this river before. We should ask Finn."

"Finn," Evie called.

"Hush," the tallest girl said.

"I was just told not to sneak." Evie shrugged.

"What's wrong?" Finn peered around the corner from the front of the boat.

"How long until we get where we're going?" Evie asked.

"Ah," Finn said. "We should be off the river by the end of the day. It's actually a nice little shortcut for us. Once the eastern mountain range is in sight, we'll hop up on land, and then it will only be a bit of a climb to your new safe haven."

"How much of a climb?" Dorran asked.

"It'll be a long way," I said. "But Finn and I will be with you, and it will all be worth it in the end."

"A climb will be nice," the tallest girl said. "I think you'll like a climb, Cinni."

Cinni didn't seem to have heard. She stared at the trees we floated past as though trying to memorize all their branches.

"Cinni"—I bent down to be eyelevel with the girl—"is that your name?"

"It's Cinnia, really," Evie said, "but we call her Cinni."

"Cinni, are you the one who put the man in the pond?" I asked.

Cinni's eyes flicked toward me. Her brow wrinkled, and her hands curled into fists.

"She's not mad about it." Evie took Cinni's face in her hands. "Ena and Finn are helping us. They aren't like the pond man."

"It was Cinni," the tall girl said. "She got out on her own. The man saw her using magic. He tried to snatch her."

I gripped my blanket to keep my hands from shaking. "What's your name?"

"Gwen," the tallest girl said. "I should have been watching Cinni. It's my fault the man ended up in the water."

"It's not," Evie said. "It's his for trying to snatch Cinni."

"I'd have done worse if he'd come after me." Dorran laid a defensive hand on Cinni's shoulder. "She was only protecting herself."

"So," I began, speaking slowly, trying to place all the words into an order that wouldn't upset the children, "Evie has magic and Cinni has magic, what about you two?"

Gwen and Dorran exchanged glances.

"Would you send them back if they were normal?" Evie asked. "Because there's no way they could go back to the miners' homes now."

"We wouldn't send them back," I said, "but it will make a difference as to what happens once we get to our home."

"It's all four of us," Dorran said. "We were all born cursed."

"We're Lir's pack of bastards," Evie said. "Well, some of them. We've got more brothers and sisters, but none of them have got magic."

I sank down to sit on a crate. "How many children does Lir have?"

"There are twelve of us," Evie said. "There were fourteen, but two had to be buried."

"They still count," Gwen said. "All of the children born in the miners' houses were Lir's."

"But we're the only magic ones," Evie said. "I told Gwen about you, and she said the four of us should go with you."

"I had to get Cinni out," Gwen said. "She can't travel alone, and I couldn't leave Evie and Dorran there without me."

"Well, you're with us now." I pressed my face into a smile. "And soon we'll be someplace where there are other people like you. People who can teach you and help you."

"Not the sorcerers." Dorran furrowed his brow.

"Where we're going is far away from the grasp of the Sorcerers Guild," I said. "So I need to ask you to be very brave while we're on our journey, but I promise you, it will be worth it."

Cinni nodded.

The children spent the morning on the deck of the boat. Dorran and Evie bickered. Gwen and Cinni sat together, Gwen talking while Cinni studied the trees.

I ransacked the cabin, shoving everything of use I could find into two sacks. I found enough hardtack to make a man sick, and a few packets of spices. I found a coin bag tucked beneath the top of the table with enough in it to feed a small family through a long winter. A crate hid glass flasks of frie. Finn pouted as I dumped the frie and filled the flasks with water from our one remaining barrel.

Finn never asked why I had knocked the other barrel over. I was grateful.

I'd searched the crates and cabin three times before the forest and hills gave way to a beautiful view of the eastern mountains.

I had never imagined I'd be so happy to see the range that had loomed over me my whole life.

"Is that it?" Evie pushed herself up onto the rail that surrounded the boat. "Do we only have to walk as far as the mountains?"

"It's a bit farther than that." I lifted Evie down. "But once we get to the woods, things will be safer."

I didn't allow my mind to wander to the monster that lurked within the trees. Liam had promised to kill the beast. I had to trust him. Without that, I would be lost.

"Everyone up here, please," Finn called from the front of the boat. He stood behind the wheel like he was the captain of a great ship in a daring story about the sea. "I'm going to ram this boat into the shore, and we're all going to hop off very quickly before the river realizes what a foolish idea that is."

"What?" Dorran squeaked.

"Just hop off the front of the boat and scamper away," Finn said. "It'll be easy."

"Come here." Gwen took Cinni's hand and led her to the low part of the rail that had been tied near the docks. "Do you understand what we're supposed to do?"

Cinni didn't move.

"Cinni." Gwen stared straight into her sister's eyes. "I need you to understand that we have to jump."

Cinni nodded.

"Let's keep it quiet for you." Gwen fished in her pocket and pulled out a strip of cloth. Two bundles of fabric had been sewn to the sides. "Hold still." She tied the fabric around Cinni's head, pressing the bundles of cloth over her ears.

I waited for Cinni to rip the fabric away, but instead, the child's forehead relaxed a tiny bit and her eyes stopped darting between the trees.

"Get ready to jump," Finn said.

Gwen held tight to Cinni's hand while Evie shoved Dorran forward.

I grabbed the two sacks I'd stuffed full and carried them to the rail.

"I hope this isn't an awful idea," Finn said.

A horrible scraping came from beneath the hull as rocks and dirt met solid wood. The boat shuddered and lurched against the shore.

Evie was the first over the side, leaping down with a joyful shout.

Cinni and Gwen jumped next.

I heaved both bags over the rail before dropping to the ground five feet below. The damp earth swallowed my boots as I landed.

"Jump!" Finn shouted.

"It's too far," Dorran said.

I yanked my feet free from the dirt.

A scream carried from above me as Dorran flew from the boat and landed face first in the mud.

The boat scraped against the shore with a horrible grating noise as the river dragged it back into its current.

Finn vaulted from the boat, landing on his hands and knees beside me.

The hull of the boat rammed into a rock in the shallows with a great crack.

"Why did you throw me?" Dorran spat dirt from his mouth as he struggled to his feet. His entire front had been coated in a thick layer of mud.

"You weren't jumping." Finn shook the filth from his own hands.

The current pulled the boat away, twisting our vessel downstream.

"I could have died," Dorran growled.

"If you think that was death-defying, you might have a difficult time adjusting to your new life," Finn said.

"Finn." I slogged toward the girls, having to wrench my feet from the mud with each step. "We're all on land. Can we just be happy with that?"

"I'm muddy and wet because he tried to murder me," Dorran said.

"Quiet, Dorran," Gwen said. "You have to stay calm."

"Easy for you to say," Dorran shouted. "I'm going to freeze to death in mud-packed clothes."

Cinni screamed.

At first I wasn't sure where the sound was coming from. Then the pitch of it cut so deep into my ears I could barely think.

By the time I looked to Cinni, Gwen had already wrapped her arms around her sister. I could see Gwen speaking but couldn't hear the words past Cinni's scream.

"Stop it!" Evie's eyes grew wide with horror. "Cinni, you've got to stop. You'll hurt them."

I followed Evie's gaze.

The mud surrounding Finn and Dorran twisted and shifted as though the muck had suddenly come to life.

"Run!" Dorran tried to scramble through the mud, but the dirt around his feet had solidified.

Finn made it farther. He'd nearly reached me before the ground trapped him.

A heartbeat passed where I wasn't sure if I should run toward Finn to try and free him or away from whatever foul magic trapped my friend.

"Cinni, enough!" Gwen shouted.

The screaming stopped.

I looked toward the black-haired sisters.

Gwen held Cinni's face in her hands.

"I'm sorry they shouted, Cinni," Gwen said, "but you're not helping them. I know you want to. I know you're trying to protect us, but you have to let Dorran go. He can't breathe properly, Cinni."

I looked toward Dorran.

The mud on his clothes had solidified, clamping around his torso. He breathed in shallow gasps. The filth on his arms and face had hardened too, turning him into a statue of fear.

All the mud on Finn had hardened as well, but his face hadn't been coated in the muck.

"Cinni," Finn said, "please let us out. I know Dorran was upset about the mud, but we'll get him washed up. We'll light a nice fire and dry him off, too."

"Take a deep breath," Gwen said. "Finn and Ena are helping us. You've got to relax and let them."

Cinni shut her eyes.

"Good girl." Gwen kissed her sister on the forehead.

"Very good," Evie said, "but are you going to let all of us out, or should I?"

I looked down to my feet. The mud around them had turned to stone. I hadn't felt it happen, hadn't even been watching the ground I stood on. I had assumed my capture would come with pain, but it didn't. My feet were simply stuck.

"I'll do it." Gwen stepped away from Cinni.

The ground around the two of them had hardened as well, but a little column had grown beneath them, lifting them above the danger, protecting them from Cinni's spell.

"Uhh." Dorran groaned. "Ah oo, ee."

"What?" Evie said.

"Ee." Dorran tried to speak, though his mouth had been trapped open. "Ee."

"This should be interesting," Evie said.

Dorran's eyes rolled back in his head, like he would have closed them if his frozen face had allowed for it.

A warm breeze, like the first promise of spring, twisted and swirled around me. The wind carried the scent of honeysuckle.

The mud squelched as I began to sink even farther.

Pulling with all my strength, I dragged my left foot free.

Finn cracked through the top layer of dirt surrounding him and ran toward the swaying grass above the riverbank.

I wrenched my right foot up and staggered a few steps before grabbing the two sacks and following him.

I didn't look back at the children until the grass swished around my ankles.

Dorran fell to his knees on the cracked ground, panting and pink-faced.

Gwen held Cinni tight and whispered in her ear.

Evie grunted with each step as she made her way to my side. "Can we go to the forest now?"

"We should rest for a moment," I said. "We'll get Dorran cleaned up and then—"

"We have to go now." Evie widened her eyes at me. "Dorran likes being muddy. It's good for his skin." The little girl mouthed a word to me that looked horribly like *horses*.

"Come on then." My words sounded false to my own ears. "No time to waste. Once we're in the trees, we can all sit for a rest and get washed up."

"But—"

"You heard her," Evie cut across Dorran. "It's time for adventure, so let's get cracking."

Finn took one of the sacks from me. "What are we going to do?" he said in a low voice over the soothing tone of Gwen's coaxing and the grunts of Dorran climbing to the edge of the bank. "What are we going to tell Liam? What are we going to say to Orla?"

I hoisted my sack onto my shoulder. "We tell them at least we got to her before the Guilds."

A frozen terror wrapped around my spine at the mere thought of what the Sorcerers Guild would make of a child like Cinni.

"We tell all the Black Bloods they should be chivving well grateful to us," I whispered.

Bits of hardened earth still clung to the tops of my shoes. I shook my feet, trying to kick the fragments free, but the magic clung to the leather and laces of my boots.

"So just straight to the forest then?" Evie pointed across the sweeping field to the mountains beyond.

"For now," I said, waiting for her to tell me there was some danger only she could hear.

Evie wrinkled her forehead for a moment before nodding and heading off toward the forest.

I let Finn lead the children as we crossed through the weeds and brush. I kept well behind our little pack, searching for horses and men. I wanted to ask Evie why she thought there were horses. If she had only heard the sound of hooves beating the ground, it could just as easily have been deer. But Cinni was still shaking, and I was too terrified of the damage frightening her might cause.

The bright sunlight beat down upon my face. My hands cramped from gripping the neck of the sack I carried over my shoulder. Birds dove and swirled through the sky. Everything was as peaceful and normal as I could have asked for.

We rounded a low slope and cut out onto a wide, flat plain. Without the rise blocking my view, I could see a village perched on top of a hill to the north. Around the edges, farmers had planted their fields and penned in their livestock. It was a pretty scene. Like Harane might have looked from a far enough distance.

A tingle pulled at my feet. The urge to walk up into the village and slip back into an easy life lured me north. But the life that tempted me was a lie. Pretty or not, whether they knew it or not, the people who dwelled in those little homes lived and died at the will of the Guilds. No matter how tired I was, peace was not worth that sacrifice.

Finn paused at the western edge of the mountain road. He took a moment looking up and down the wide dirt path. He raised one hand, beckoning me forward.

I cut around the children and to his side. "What?" I whispered.

The grass rustled as Dorran crept closer to us.

Finn gave a tiny nod toward the pretty village.

I followed his gaze.

Up the mountain road, on the barren dirt between the houses, more than a dozen horses had been tied between buildings. People wearing black stood near their mounts.

I let out a slow breath and looked south down the road.

There was nothing in that direction. We could run south, but even if we'd still had the boat, determined men on horseback could catch us traveling by foot or by water.

"Into the forest then," I said. "On we go."

I hurried the children toward the woods as quickly as I could without risking upsetting Cinni. I glanced north as often as I dared, searching for any sign that someone had decided to follow us. No men or horses emerged from the village to chase us.

The scent of the forest surrounded me as we stepped into the trees, wearing away the edges of the worry clenching my stomach.

"This way." Finn cut southeast. "Once we get in a bit farther, we can stop and get everyone cleaned up and fed."

The children followed Finn without complaint.

Evie dropped behind the cluster the others had formed to walk by my side.

"Have you been in these woods before?" Evie asked.

"Sure," I said. "Not right here, but it's all the same forest, really."

"Oh." Evie bit her lips together. "Are there usually lots of animals in the mountains?"

A cold dread trickled through my veins.

"Why do you ask?" I kept my voice calm.

"I can hear the horses," Evie whispered, "but that's all. I've never been in a forest where there are no little animals before."

5 4

Finn led us on a winding path up the mountains. I kept waiting for the monster to come thundering through the woods ready to kill us all. If I had been able to think of another safe place for the children, I would have led them out of the trees, but I didn't know where else to go and couldn't risk the open with soldiers prowling so close by. Our only refuge was the camp.

I warned Finn of what Evie had said when we stopped by a brook to wash away the worst of the mud. He didn't know what else we could do either. So we kept climbing.

Every step seemed to grant a bit more freedom from the Guilds and give the monster a better chance of killing us with his claws.

But we kept going, climbing higher and higher as the sun sank.

I searched the trees, looking for a place that could offer enough high branches for each of us to perch in safety while we waited through the darkness. My body longed for sleep, but I knew I wouldn't be able to allow myself any rest, not with the chance of a beast seeking our flesh.

The sky had faded to gray when Evie grabbed my arm.

"Are you all right?" I asked. "We'll stop climbing for the night soon."

Evie stared at me, her breath coming more quickly.

"Evie." I took her hand in mine. "Evie, what's wrong?"

"I was wrong. It's not just horses," Evie whispered. "There are smaller creatures, too. That's what all the animals are hiding from."

My worry ebbed for one foolish moment. "Smaller is fine. This is a forest. There should be small animals here. And even small animals hunt other animals."

"But why are they hunting us?" Evie said. "Why are there dogs chasing us?"

"Finn, run." I seized Evie's hand and dragged her up the mountain, outpacing Finn.

"What's happening?" Finn ran beside me.

"Someone's caught our scent."

None of the children cried or questioned as I led them south, hoping against hope I might find something to protect us.

I didn't know who might be in the mountains, let alone coming closer to us with dogs. In the end, it didn't matter what monster chased us. All that mattered was that we couldn't be caught.

A low groaning came from behind me.

"Hush, Cinni," Gwen panted. "You're fine. We're all going to be fine."

The barking of dogs carried through the trees.

I strained my eyes, searching the shadows for any sign of a creek or pond, anything that might shield our scent.

"I can stop them," Evie said. "I can do it. I can stop them."

"No." I held tight to Evie's hand.

Crack.

The sound split through the woods, sending night birds scattering toward the sky.

"Breath, Cinni," Gwen said.

"Up ahead," a voice shouted from far behind us.

Crack.

Trees on either side of us fell to the ground.

"I can do it," Evie said.

I didn't answer as I dragged her around the curve of a slope. A wide patch of boulders waited on the other side.

The dogs howled.

Crack.

The tree above us toppled, twisting away from the boulders as it fell, sliding down the slope toward the dogs.

Evie wrenched her hand free from mine and turned toward the sounds of the approaching men.

"No, Evie." I jumped in front of her.

"It's a sorcerer," a voice shouted from far below. "It's got to be."

Finn grabbed Evie and me, shoving us into the shadows behind a boulder.

"How did they find us?" Finn said. "How could they possibly have found us?"

"Emmet said there's a traitor. Maybe even in our camp." I shut my eyes, forbidding my guilt from overwhelming me. "I thought we left too quickly for anyone to betray us."

"Ena," Finn said.

Dorran whimpered.

The smell of the children's fear cut through the cool scent of the shadowy forest.

"Round them up!" a second voice shouted.

I opened my eyes.

"We fight." Finn met my gaze. His eyes held no fear of death.

"I'll do it," Evie said. "I can stop them. I can kill them."

"No." I tucked her hair behind her ears. "I will not let you carry that burden."

Cinni whimpered as the barking of the dogs came closer.

A tiny fracture cut through the place in my heart where hope had dared to dwell.

I looked to Finn. "Tell him I'm sorry."

I dropped my sack and ran.

Back around the shelter of the boulder and onto the open side of the slope, letting my silhouette cut through the gray of the twilight.

I reached up, smacking a branch with all my might, cracking it off of the tree and breaking the skin on my palm.

The dogs howled.

I didn't try to keep my blood from dripping onto the ground. I pumped my arms as I ran, coating the forest floor with my scent.

The pounding of horse hooves thundered up the hill behind me.

I'm sorry. I'm so sorry.

A cliff blocked my path. I ran at the rock face, leaping up and grabbing hold with both hands. I climbed as fast as I could, digging my toes into the cracks, not caring about anything but surviving for one more minute.

One more minute for Finn and the children.

One more chance for them to find a path to escape.

One more moment before Evie knew what it meant to have blood on her hands.

"Stop!" a voice shouted from below when I was a foot from the top. "By order of the Guilds, I command you to stop!"

"Not a chivving chance." I dragged myself up and over the ledge as the cliff began to collapse around me.

I rolled away from the rocks as a bright orange light flashed toward me. The heat of the spell burned my skin, but I didn't stop, even as I screamed in pain.

I scrambled to my feet and kept running.

Shouted orders came from below, but I couldn't make out the words over the rasp of my own breathing.

The world swayed around me, and fatigue pulled at my limbs.

Just a little farther.

The damage of a long ago avalanche marred the slope in front of me. I raced south, trying to find a path that might lead me up and farther east.

The barking of the dogs came from the north as the animals gained on me.

Another cliff blocked my path. The stone wall jutted out around the edge of the rise, trapping me on the hill of loose debris.

"Up this way!" a voice shouted from below.

I ran to the rock face, searching for any imperfection that would allow me to climb. There was no handhold to be found.

Men in black uniforms appeared at the bottom of the slope, flanking a man in purple robes.

Dogs streaked out of the trees, barking madly as they raced toward their quarry.

I pulled my knife from my boot and pressed my back to the stone.

I hoped Lily would be proud that in the end I had done something worth being murdered for. I hoped Emmet would survive the fire of his rage whole enough to still be of use in this horrible world. I hoped Liam could forgive me, even if he could never have loved me.

The man in purple raised his hands. Green crackled between his fingertips.

Darkness and cold surrounded me.

55

I don't know how long I lay panting in the darkness. It might have been minutes or hours before I realized I was not dead.

I unclenched my hand, and my knife fell with a clatter. The ground beneath me was smooth as I rolled over and pushed myself to my hands and knees.

My palm stung where the tree had ripped open my skin. My fingers trembled as I pulled the lae stone from my pocket.

The blue light gleamed off the black rock surrounding me. A wide tunnel with a high, perfectly-carved arch in the peak of the ceiling stretched out in front of me.

I looked to the rock behind me and pressed my bloody palm to the stone. The mountain did not budge.

5 6

There are legends in this world that will terrify you. There are monsters that no man can slay. There are stories that hold truth and histories rotting with lies.

There are some answers that should never be brought into the light.

I did not have that wisdom as I ventured alone into the darkness.

ICE AND SKY

BOOK THREE

To the ones who fight for change.
Generations will remember you.

1

I am not innocent.

I have killed. I have harmed. I have tried to do good and ended up hurting the people I cherished most.

I cannot argue any punishment the stars torment me with. I deserve to burn.

I have waited for the sky to turn to ash as the gods declare my guilt.

I am waiting still.

2

There are legends of people living deep beneath the stones of the eastern mountains. I had heard the stories long before I knew the Black Bloods were real.

But somehow, even after all the magic and monsters I'd seen, I didn't believe the tales to be true.

I was wrong.

I did not understand how terrible my mistake had been as I journeyed through the darkness. The only sounds in the black stone tunnel were the soft plodding of my feet and the rhythm of my own breathing. There was no sign that any other living person existed.

I don't know how long I walked down the high-arched corridor before the walls began to sway and exhaustion finally won the battle against my own will to escape.

I lay down on the ground, gripping my lae stone in one hand and my knife in the other. I nestled into my coat and pressed my back against the wall as sleep swallowed me.

I don't know how long I slept. When I awoke, nothing had changed. There was no sun to judge time by. As far as I could tell, there was nothing in the world beyond the little pool of blue light cast by my lae stone.

My throat burned from thirst, and my stomach longed for food. But I didn't know if I'd been asleep for hours or for days.

Finn might have made it to the camp before I woke up. Or he might have been taken by the Guilds. There was no way for me to know.

I clutched my lae stone tight, trying to convince myself the answer to that question was worth journeying through the darkness.

My legs trembled as I stood up. My feet ached as I kept walking down the tunnel.

There was no change in the walls, no slope or corner. There was nothing but darkness and moving forward one step at a time.

The pounding in my head began before my hands started to shake.

I had once seen bare bones in a passage created by the mountains. I hadn't thought to ask Finn if he had seen others who had been left to decay far below the ground.

As my fingers began to feel too thick to grip my weapon and light, I wondered if the person who had been trapped had been like me—whisked away from Death's embrace so the mountain might torture them more. I wondered if anyone would find my bones, and what they might think of my fate if they did.

"I'm sorry." My words crackled in my throat. "Whatever I've done to offend you, I'm sorry."

I stopped and leaned back against the wall, resisting the temptation to lie down and sleep. Warmth radiated from the stone. I pressed my palm to the heat.

"Actually, I'm not. Punish me if you like. I am willing to die if that is the price you demand, but I am not sorry for saving those children." My breath caught in my chest. "For trying to save those children."

I thought of the four of them—Evie, Gwen, Dorran, and Cinni—captured by the Sorcerers Guild, trapped in the stone tower in Ilara. I shut my eyes, sending a plea up to the stars that Finn had led them to safety.

My eyes stung, but I didn't have any tears to shed.

I tried to distract myself from the pounding in my head and the pain in my body as I kept walking down the chivving tunnel. I pictured Finn arriving at the camp, all the children safely with him. It was a happy image, a valiant success. Finn and I had not only protected four innocent sorcis. We'd also managed to keep powerful magic out of the hands of the Guilds.

Then I got to the bit of the fantasy where Liam found out Finn had returned without me, and the stinging in my eyes came back.

I banished the images from my mind and kept walking forward.

The blackness that lurked in my chest had always seemed an ally before. A place where I could hide hurts and memories that were too horrible for me to bear.

The blackness I journeyed through taunted me. I was the thing the world did not want to see. I was the pain the mountain could not stand. I had been tucked away and would stay hidden until I died.

I screamed at the high-arched ceiling. My rage tore at my throat and echoed down the corridor. There wasn't even the sound of a scurrying rodent to answer me.

"Keep walking. Even the eastern mountains cannot be endless."

I knew my own words weren't true. But my lie was enough to keep me moving for a while longer.

My throat ached, and my tongue felt as though it might crack with every dry breath I drew. The pain in my legs flared from a dull throb to terrible cramps that left me limping.

I'm not sure how long it took for the pounding in my head to develop a noise my ears could hear. Not long after the sound began, the tunnel started swaying before me. I staggered as I tried to make the walls and floor stay in place.

I wanted to lie down and sleep, but I was afraid if I allowed myself to rest, I wouldn't have the strength to stand back up again.

"If you want me dead, just kill me. If you want to torment me, then bring fire or knives. Do not make me wander down here."

I waited for the mountain to answer.

"Did you save me so you could have the pleasure of watching me die slowly?" I tucked my knife into the sheath in my boot and laid my palm on the smooth stone of the wall. "I am not a child of stone. I'm not a Black Blood. You shouldn't have let me in. Was it a mistake? Can you even make mistakes?"

The mountain stayed silent.

I took my hand from the wall and drew my pendant from the top of my bodice. The stone held a blissful and familiar warmth.

"Please. I just want to get back to camp. I want to help. I want to fight."

I pressed my forehead against the stone wall.

"I just want to get back to him."

I let my eyes drift shut as I waited for rocks to tumble down upon me, granting a bloody end to my captivity.

The pounding in my head amplified.

I pushed away from the wall and kept walking. I wished there were a branch in the tunnel, anything that might offer me the illusion of a choice besides following the mountain's will or lying down and waiting to die.

The pounding in my head developed a new texture. A strange and constant rumbling.

I wondered if it might be a sign that my body was giving out. I'd never seen a person die of thirst before. Through all the misery we'd suffered in Harane, we'd always had water to spare.

As I walked, the sound grew louder. The texture of the noise became familiar.

I moved as quickly as I could, limping as I ran toward the rumble. The ground beneath my feet lost its smooth perfection as the peak of the tunnel dropped to a less impressive height.

"Oh, please."

The end of the tunnel came into view. The walls disappeared, opening up into a vast blackness my lae stone was not large enough to light.

I ignored my fear of what could be lurking in the darkness and followed the sound.

A waist-high wall blocked my path.

I scrambled over the rocks, falling to my knees on the other side. I lost my grip on my lae stone. The light rolled away, stopping under a bench.

Cool moisture greeted my palms as I crawled toward my lae stone. The ground was not hard beneath me. As I lay on my stomach to reach for my light, something soft touched my cheek.

Moss.

The ground was covered in moss.

A plant with pale green leaves twined around the legs of the stone bench.

I wanted to touch the leaves, but the low rumbling called to me. I crawled toward the sound, not trusting my legs to carry my weight.

Another wall blocked my path. My hand slipped as I tried to pull myself onto the ledge.

The rocks were slick with water.

Gritting my teeth, I forced myself to stand.

The blue glow of my lae stone shimmered across the water cascading down from a fountain.

I dipped my hand into the pool and drank.

The coolness raced past my lungs as I drank and drank until I thought I would be sick from the wonder of water.

I was so desperate to quench my thirst, I didn't even have the sense to question how a statue of a woman had ended up in a fountain in the belly of the eastern mountains.

3

I slept beside the fountain once I had drunk my fill. Part of me was terrified I would wake to find the water gone, but I didn't have the strength to stay conscious any longer.

When I did wake up, darkness still surrounded me. I had slept with my lae stone clutched in one hand and my pendant in the other. The chill water of the fountain had soaked through the back of my coat. I didn't mind being soggy and cold as long as I had water.

I sat on the lip on the fountain and drank for a long time. The fullness in my stomach almost disguised my hunger.

The stone lady at the center of the fountain seemed to stare at me as I drank. She'd been carved wearing a beautiful dress with her hair woven into an intricate braid that draped over her shoulder. The fancy hair, long skirt, and drooping sleeves didn't look like they belonged hidden underground.

There was something about her—the severe angle of her chin, the slant of her shoulders—that made me quite certain the sculptor had known the woman, had wanted her in particular to be memorialized.

"Who were you?" I asked the stone. "You must have been very important to someone."

Neither the lady nor the mountain answered.

"How did you end up all the way down here?" I pushed myself to my feet. My body felt weak from lack of food, but the water had made it easier to think. "Why would anyone place a statue and a fountain beneath the mountains?"

I walked toward the rock wall I'd scrambled over before I slept. My lae stone barely shone bright enough for me to see a hint of the rock before I left the safety of the fountain.

Soft moss covered all the ground in view, but it wasn't the sort of moss I'd seen in the forest. The color was wrong, too pale, too silver.

I stopped at the rock wall, trailing my fingers along its surface. The barrier was not made of one solid slab as I'd assumed it would be. Stones had been piled together to form the wall, like a person had put a great amount of effort into creating it by hand.

The bench I'd crawled beneath had been built of three different stones, with no hint of magic in its making.

"Did you trap someone down here for so long they had to build a fancy garden to keep sane?"

I climbed up onto the bench and raised my lae stone above my head.

The angle of my light allowed me to see a bit farther.

There were two more benches on the far side of the fountain. A patch of plants grew clustered together against the wall as though reaching for some impossible light.

"Why?" I shouted to the mountain. "Who lives down here?"

I climbed off the bench and moved closer to the plants. Reason told me I was imagining them, but I'd already seen too many impossible things to be sure what couldn't be real.

Something that looked like sour grass grew in between wide-leafed greens. The coloring of all the plants was wrong. So were the sizes of the stalks and leaves.

I'm not sure if it was desperation or stupidity that made me rip a handful of leaves from the ground and start eating. I spent a long while shifting from the garden to the fountain and back again, eating, drinking, and waiting to see if I'd poisoned myself. I wasn't completely opposed to that end. A plant stealing my life would have been fitting.

But I ate my fill without consequence.

When my limbs stopped their constant trembling, I climbed up onto the lip of the fountain and held my light closer to the stone lady's face. Someone had taken the time to carve tiny worry lines around her eyes.

The longer I studied her face, the more absurd her presence became. She was a work of art, a beauty even the paun would have coveted.

"Does anyone know you're down here? Has the living world forgotten you?"

I turned away from her, toward the vast darkness.

"Is anyone out there?" I shouted. "What is this place?"

The darkness did not reply.

"Show me your secrets," I whispered.

I took another long drink of water and stuffed my pockets with leaves before climbing back up and over the rock wall.

I'm not sure what I expected to find in the belly of the black stone beast. Months later, I still had moments when I couldn't quite believe that everything I had seen was real.

There's a shadow in my mind that still whispers I imagined the entire place.

As I ventured through the darkness, I did not think the path the tunnel had spit me out onto, half-mad and desperate for water, would be a lane leading between houses. Real houses. Built of stone and two stories high. But the dark city was the place I was meant to see.

Decaying wooden shutters hung from the windows of the homes. Doors had been torn off their hinges.

I shoved away my horror as the thought of long forgotten bodies rotting in the homes quickened my pace. I couldn't allow myself to begin to count how many corpses might be hiding in the houses. That was a path I could not come back from.

I passed twenty-seven homes before I reached a crossroad. I couldn't see enough by the light of my lae stone to know what might wait in either direction.

"Do you want me to explore? Is that why you brought me down here? Is there something I'm supposed to find?"

A chill wind blew from my left.

I wanted to run from whatever waited in the darkness, but I had learned enough of magic to know I would not be able to escape, not unless the mountain wanted to set me free.

I walked into the breeze.

More houses stretched down that road, leading to a patch of wide buildings that seemed to have been shops. Pillars supported the roof of a pavilion. Chains dripped down where a sign had once hung. A cracked slat of wood lay on the ground beneath.

I knelt to pick up the slat. The wood crumbled at my touch before I could see if any trace of writing had been left behind.

I brushed my hands off on my skirt and kept walking.

The road I traveled down was longer than the entire village of Harane. Longer even than the streets I'd traveled in Nantic.

The farther I walked, the farther apart the homes were placed.

After a long while, I stopped beside a house where one of the walls had begun to collapse. Loose stones cascaded across the silver moss on the ground, but I didn't see any sign of violence or flames that might have destroyed the home.

I gripped my lae stone so hard, the odd angles of its crystal-like surface cut into my palm.

The road continued in front of me, but there was nothing within reach of my light.

I looked back in the direction I'd come. I didn't know the ways of the mountain. I didn't know if she would block me from retreating to the fountain and food that had saved my life.

You will not die here.

"I will find what you want me to find." I squared my shoulders and stepped beyond the reaches of the stone city.

A feeling of hopeless solitude tore at my chest as I walked through the barren blackness.

The path remained defined in front of me. One line of smooth stone reaching out into the distance. I kept promising myself that there couldn't be a trail leading to nowhere. I tried not to hate myself for my lies.

I walked and walked, munching on the leaves I'd tucked into my pocket like I'd become Finn.

Thinking of him sent a pang through my chest and quickened my step.

I hoped he'd reached the camp unharmed, but I knew that if he had, he wouldn't be grateful for my having led the dogs away. He'd be furious with me.

My brother's rage would be enough to burn through the mountains.

I didn't know if he'd blame me or Finn or the Guilds, but Emmet's wrath would fall on someone's head.

And Liam...

A hole punctured my chest, stealing the air from my lungs. I stopped and pressed a hand to my heart, trying to convince myself I knew how to breathe.

Liam would blame himself for letting me go to the Lir Valley. It had been my choice, but that wouldn't matter to him.

"I'm sorry. I'm so sorry."

I forced my lungs to accept air and continued on my dark path.

I don't know how long I walked before the black stone led me down another tunnel. The ceiling was low and lacked the fancy arch of the one I'd traveled before.

When I grew tired enough, I curled up against the wall again and slept.

I'm not sure how many times I slept under the mountain. I'd been trapped in a world of blackness with nothing to mark time. Without the sunlight, everything began to lose meaning.

I would walk until I was too tired to move. Then I would sleep until I woke up.

When I thought I was too thirsty or hungry to keep going, I would find food and water.

A tiny stream running through the rock, a pool gathered between two great columns of stone. I ate lichen that clung to the walls and mushrooms that grew in cracks in the tunnel. The mountain seemed determined to keep me alive, even if my life consisted only of darkness and walking through her endless realm of stone.

I did not allow myself to wonder if my wandering penance would last forever. I'd not seen much of magic, but the things I had witnessed left me terrified of curses and unwilling to contemplate spending a thousand years trapped in the belly of the mountains.

I did worry that I would go mad. That being alone in the darkness would steal my mind and twist me into a horrible creature that would torment innocents and spread nightmares. I felt my mouth for fangs and searched my hands for growing claws. I did not want to become the beast that had brought so much pain to our camp.

I didn't know if the beast was still alive. I didn't know if the camp still existed. I didn't know if the entire outside world had been a lie I'd created to entertain my own failing mind.

When I was afraid I would lose my sanity, I'd grip my stone pendant, foolishly promising that I would not allow myself to become a monster like the one who'd brought pain to those I cared for.

I'd been gripping the pendant for so long I couldn't move my fingers anymore by the time I reached the walled garden of the manor.

The stone wall had been built up ten feet high, and the metal gate still hung from its hinges.

"Hello?" I let go of my pendant. My fingers barely straightened enough for me to pull the gate open.

The squeak of the hinges sliced through the darkness.

I froze, waiting for monsters to come charging out of the black to devour me.

There was only silence.

"Hello?" I called again as I stepped into the courtyard.

A walkway had been built on top of the high wall, and a garden had been planted in the courtyard, reaching toward the back of the manor. A wide pond took up the center of the garden, and a stone chair sat next to the water, as though someone had once spent hours enjoying their walled-in sanctuary.

If I hadn't been thirsty I would have walked away from the walled garden and continued through the darkness. There was something about the space that felt too intimate to be disturbed.

"Is anyone here? I don't want to intrude. I've been traveling, and I need water and food."

I froze again, waiting for people or ghosts to swoop down upon me.

"Is this where you want me to be?" I looked up to the peak of the cavern far out of reach of my light. "Is this what you wanted me to find?"

I let out a shaky breath and headed for the back door of the house.

The plants in the garden had long since overrun their beds, leaving a knee-high sea of pale leaves and bright white flowers for me to wade through.

The back door of the home hadn't fared as well as the metal gate. The wood had crumbled, leaving a misshapen chunk hanging in the doorway.

"I am not afraid," I whispered so softly not even the mountain could hear as I ducked through the gap and into the house.

4

How did they get so much wood?

I'm not sure why the question seemed so important to me as I moved from room to room in the house.

The kitchen had a wide wooden table, and a set of wooden shelves sat across from the massive fireplace. The dining room had seats for twelve people. There were enough beds and bedrooms for that many as well.

Every time I reached a new doorway, I would take a breath, steeling myself to find some horror in the next room. But as I made my way through the home, there was no trace I could see of anything terrible having happened.

The only damage to the furniture I could find had been done by time. There were no dark stains of long ago bloodshed or bones of a person left unburied.

I stood in the bedroom tucked at the end of the upstairs hall for a long while, just staring at the bed.

It was small, as though built for a child, but there wasn't a toy to be seen. There wasn't anything at all besides the bed.

Months before, I'd spent a terrible night in the Blood Valley, listening to the screams of the long dead. I slowed my heart and tried to hear the pain of those who had once called the grand manor home.

There was nothing. It was as though the family had simply packed up, pushed the chairs in around the dining room table, and left.

"What drove you away?"

I kept silent as I climbed down the stone steps and went back out into the courtyard. I drank from the pond, then scoured the garden for things I could eat. I drank some more and curled up beside the stone chair to sleep.

My head felt muddy when I woke. I drank more and ate. I watched my lae stone gleam off the pond for a long while.

"How did people survive in this unending darkness?"

They were safe from the Guilds, Emmet's voice rattled through my mind. *Why would they have left?*

I dug my nails into my palms, fighting against my wish to have Emmet standing beside me. Not to save me, just to actually hear the voice of another person.

I pulled off my boots and dipped my feet into the pond. The chill water sent goose bumps prickling upon my skin.

A smile curved my lips for the first time in ages as I stripped away my clothing and slipped into the pond. The water wasn't deep, and I sorely missed soap, but scrubbing my skin seemed to tear away a bit of the fear that had seeped deep into my bones in the crushing darkness.

I scrubbed and scrubbed until the cold became too much. Even as my teeth chattered, I basked in the water for a few minutes more. When my feet had gone numb, I climbed out of the pond and got dressed.

Sense told me to stay in the garden a while longer, to rest with the bounty of food and drink, but people had left this home. Some desire or fear had driven them away.

A flicker of certainty sparked in my gut. This was what the mountain wanted me to see. This manor was the reason for my journey even if I had no idea why I needed to witness this deserted place.

I stopped with my hand on the metal gate.

"I am going to get out of here. I am going to find the camp. I'm going home. I…I hope wherever you went, you found a new home. I hope you were happy. I hope it was worth leaving the life you'd built here."

I stepped onto the path, but it only led me back the way I'd come. The mountain offered no new course for me to follow. Holding my lae stone high, I circled the stone wall, searching for any hint of a trail.

There was nothing but the wall and the black stone path I'd already traveled.

I made it all the way back to the metal gate before panic began creeping in around the certainty I'd found.

"I will not be trapped here!"

I strode away from the manor and into the darkness beyond.

"You took a child into your protection, and you let that child go. You saved me"—my steps faltered—"and I am grateful. But I have to tell Liam what I found here. I have to help him. I have to be sure the others are safe."

I tore through the darkness, though I could not name the terror that chased me.

I reached the edge of the vast cavern I'd been traveling for I didn't know how long. A smooth wall blocked my path. I headed right, trailing my fingers along the wall as I ran.

I searched the ground for any hint of a road and scanned the darkness for the shapes of more buildings lurking just beyond my light. My breath had begun to grate my throat before the wall vanished from beneath my fingers.

A gap, barely wide enough to slide into, sliced through the wall. There was no hint that the people who had lived belowground had ever traveled through the crevice. No hint at all that a sane person should try to slip through the crack.

"You've given me worse than this." I held my light in the gap and peered into the shadows. There was nothing in view.

I turned sideways and sidled into the crevice. It was a slow path to travel, and the mountain had left loose stones to tangle my feet.

When I'd left the manor, my hair had been wet enough to leave a chill on my neck. The damp from my hair laying against my coat had dried long before the tunnel finally widened and began to slope up.

The path the mountain laid out for me curved and twisted, dove down deep and forced me to climb back up. But I kept going, charging forward even as my legs burned and reason told me I'd be trapped forever.

Just when a trickle of doubt dripped into my chest, coating the certainty that had kept me climbing, a wall blocked the tunnel.

"No! If you want me dead, so be it, but do not leave me down here alone." My breath hitched in my chest. "Please."

I pressed my forehead against the stone.

"The darkness down here is nothing compared to the outside world. I have to help them. I have to protect him. I need to be with them. Please let me out."

I shut my eyes.

"Please."

The wall trembled beneath my touch.

I opened my eyes to find blinding sunlight surrounding me.

I staggered forward, free of the rock and darkness, and into the wonderfully open forest.

The scent of trees filled my lungs. The wind lifted my hair. A bird soared overhead, twittering its everyday joy.

I sank to my knees as my entire body began to shake.

"Thank you," I whispered into the wind.

I knelt for a long time, watching the leaves twist on the trees.

A rabbit darted in front of me and dove into a patch of low bushes.

I had forgotten to be afraid of the monster that terrorized our camp until I saw the poor animal hide from me.

Pulling my knife from my boot, I forced myself to my feet.

I needed to keep moving. After the uncountable miles I'd wandered underground, I was chivving thrilled to be traveling in the sunlight, but I had no idea where I was or which direction might lead me toward the camp.

The eastern mountain range is massive. Large enough to swallow an entire civilization without leaving enough of a trace for anyone to notice. If I went the wrong way, I could end up roaming the mountains for as long as I'd been underground.

A horrible ache pulled at my chest, and a hunger burned inside me, a longing that tore at my soul until I thought I would crumble. Like a part of me had been ripped away and I was incomplete.

A bit of my soul was missing. I could feel the void the missing part had left behind. The pain of it pulsed through me like a deadly wound.

I shut my eyes and tried to press the ache away, but the longing would not be silenced.

I tucked my lae stone into my pocket and started walking.

There is no explanation I can give as to why I chose the direction I did, but I could not fight it.

Either I could keep following that path, or I could shatter into a thousand irreparable pieces. The stars did not allow any other option.

As the sun began to sink, I knew I was traveling northwest, which by all reason was the absolute wrong way to get to the camp from where I had been when the mountain had swallowed me.

But I couldn't stop. The fire that drove me burned bright. The flames fed the longing.

There was a way to repair the void inside me. I only had to find the bit of my soul I had lost. I could not rest until I had put my soul back together.

The sun set, and I pulled my lae stone from my pocket. I knew I should stop, find a tree, and hope for safety during the night. Even my fear of the monster's claws could not keep me from moving forward.

I cut along a tree-shrouded ridgeline and through a field of boulders that looked as though giants had tossed the great stones in a game. My boots were soaked as I slogged through a stream. The water ran swiftly, as though a storm had let loose in some higher part of the mountains. I searched the sky, but there was no hint of clouds masking the stars.

The moon shone bright across the woods. I scanned the shadows, reveling in the details beyond the reach of my lae stone.

A dark shape, larger than any man, appeared down the slope from me.

I froze, waiting for Death himself to catch me.

The shape did not move.

I crept closer to the hulking mass. A branch cracked beneath my foot.

Still, the shadow did not move.

It wasn't until I was twenty feet away that I recognized the shape of the great, dark boulder.

My breath hitched in my throat as I touched the stone.

The longing that had burned in my chest flared like a sun ready to explode as my fingers touched the cold surface.

Liam.

I stepped into the boundary his magic created, letting whatever spell allowed him to protect us surround me for a moment, before entering the camp.

5

"Ena?" a voice called. "Ena, is that you?"

"Yes." A giddy glee bubbled in my chest at the mere act of speaking to another person.

Patrick jumped out of a tree, an arrow still nocked in his bow. "By the gods, I didn't think I'd ever see you again." He smiled at me, like he was genuinely glad I hadn't died.

A knot pressed on my throat. "Finn. Did he make it back? I left him in the woods. He had—"

"Four demons with him?" Patrick slid his arrow into his quiver. "They're all here."

The trees swayed in front of me.

"Made it back two weeks ago. You've given everyone an awful scare."

"Two weeks?" I blinked, trying to make the trees hold still.

"Your brother charged out of here as soon as he found out you weren't with Finn. Then Finn went back out to search for you. Liam's been going half-mad trying to find out if you were taken to Ilara."

"Liam's gone to Ilara?"

"No, he's here." Patrick furrowed his brow. "Orders came all the way from Lygan Hall—"

I didn't wait to hear about the orders from Lygan Hall.

I cut through the trees and toward the center of camp. I'd come in from the southeast, opposite the clearing and kitchen tent. There wasn't even a hint I was traveling in the right direction until the line of lae stones that lit the paths between the rows of tents came into view.

I'd never appreciated the beauty of their blue glow. Not as I should have. Even if it hadn't been Liam's magic that made the stones, even if their light hadn't been a wonder that cast everything into gentle shadows, the presence of the stones meant people. My people.

The knot pressed on my throat so hard I could barely breathe.

My little tent was still there, sitting next to Liam's. No one had moved it in the weeks I'd been away.

A dim blue light glowed inside Liam's tent. I didn't even think about what I should be doing until I was standing right outside the canvas.

I raised my hand to knock on his tent pole and froze. I wasn't sure if I should wait until morning, or if I should shout that I was home, or maybe that I was sorry for having led Finn into such danger.

In the end, I just needed to see his face.

I knocked on the pole.

"What?" Liam's voice carried through the canvas.

I swallowed the knot in my throat but couldn't find the words to answer him.

"If you do not have news from Ilara, then do not dare to step into this tent." His voice came out gravelly and low, like he hadn't slept properly in weeks.

I brushed the canvas aside and stepped into his tent.

"I don't know anything about Ilara," I said. "But I have had quite the journey. Maybe that could distract you from your worries."

Liam looked up at me. His cheeks had sunken in, and new creases marred his brow. Dark stubble coated his chin. He stared at me but didn't move.

"I can come back in the morning," I said. "Though I'm tired enough I might sleep through—"

"Ena?" Liam still didn't move.

"I didn't mean to be gone for so long. The mountain swallowed me, and I didn't know if I'd ever make it out."

Liam stood and walked toward me.

"I'm sorry that Finn and Emmet went out to find me. I can go after them if you'd..."

He trembled as he took my face in his hands.

"Ena?" A wicked grief flashed through his eyes.

"It's me." I laid my hand over his heart. "I'm here."

"Ena." My name cracked in his throat as he drew me to his chest.

He smelled of fresh wind and reckless freedom. The scent swept through me, brushing away bits of the shadows that clung to my soul.

I buried my face on his shoulder and let his arms wrap around me, circling me like a suit of armor that could not be broken.

He let go of me enough to tip my chin up, as though he needed to look into my eyes. "You're alive?"

"I'm fine, Liam. I got a little lost, but I'm fine."

He kissed my forehead. "I thought they'd captured you. Gods, I thought they'd killed you."

A tear ran down his cheek.

I took his face in my hands and brushed the tear away.

"I took the long way round," I said. "That's all."

He held my gaze. I'd never seen so much grief and fear locked inside one person.

"I thought I'd lost—"

I pressed my fingers over his lips. "I promised I'd come home, didn't I?"

He kissed my fingers. He took my hand in his and kissed my palm.

Heat flooded my veins, racing through my body and destroying every hint of darkness that had festered within me.

I leaned close to him, and he kissed me.

Time stopped. All thoughts of the world disappeared.

His taste was all I knew until his hands trailed up my sides and a new, bright fire burst through my being.

I laced my fingers through his hair, clinging to him as though the world were trying to rip him away from me.

But he didn't back away.

He pulled me closer, like he needed to be near me as much as every fiber of my being longed for him.

I'm not sure when I took off my coat or which of us untied the knot at the top of my bodice. I don't remember our bodies separating until he dragged the fabric over my head. Then there was nothing but my thin shift and his shirt between us.

The heat of him surrounded me.

I deepened our kiss, tasting more of him as he unfastened the buttons of my skirt.

I pulled his shirt off, needing to be closer to him, wanting more of his skin to explore.

His muscles tensed as I trailed my fingers along his bare back. The strength of him sent shocks flying up my arms.

He kissed the side of my neck, and a pulsing fire blazed through me.

I pulled my shift off, letting my bare chest press against him. I needed to feel his skin against mine as I had never needed anything in my life.

I kissed him again, holding him close to me, desperate to feel every ridge of his body against mine before he came to his senses and shied away.

But he didn't back away.

He pressed his hips against mine, and I knew he wanted me as badly as I wanted him.

He lifted me and carried me to his bed.

I tumbled away in a blazing wanting and beautiful peace that I had never dreamt possible.

6

I lay in Liam's arms, our limbs tangled together so I wasn't sure where I ended and he began. Sweat coated the small of my back where he trailed his fingers along my spine.

I nestled my head on his shoulder and let myself drift into the most wonderful kind of exhaustion the gods have ever created.

Liam shifted beneath me, and fear demolished my peace.

"Don't." The word cracked through my chest.

Liam froze. "Did I hurt you?"

"Please don't." I fought the urge to wrap my arm around his chest and cling to him.

"Don't what?"

"Don't say this was a mistake. Don't say you care for me but I'm safer without you. Don't come up with some other chivving reason to kick me out of your bed."

"I thought I'd lost you."

"And now you've realized I'm alive and are going to protect me from you by refusing to look at me." I untangled my limbs from his.

He wrapped his arm around my waist, holding me closer. "I almost lost you. By all rights, you should be dead."

"I'm not."

He tipped my chin up and looked into my eyes. "I was wrong, Ena. From the very beginning, I've been wrong. You burn too bright, you're too vast, too bold for me to protect you by pushing you to the background." He brushed his lips against mine. "If I wanted to keep you perfectly safe, I'd have to lock you away."

"No. I will not be locked away."

"I know." He pulled me closer so my torso fit the curve of his. "You'd never survive captivity. It would break you. The only hope of protecting you I have is to keep you next to me. To stand beside you through whatever storm you choose to challenge. I can't stop you from running into danger. If I want to keep you alive, I'll have to charge after you with my sword raised, ready to fight every beast the shadows have to offer."

I studied his face. There was no hint of anger or jest behind his eyes.

"I'm yours, Ena. For as long as you'll have me, I'll stand by your side."

A pressure dug into my lungs, like something was carving away every broken part of me and replacing it with the undeniable armor of knowing Liam would stand with me.

"Don't say that unless you mean it," I whispered. "You might be stuck with me for the rest of your life."

"Then I will live the best life any Black Blood has ever dreamt of."

He kissed me and I wrapped my arms around him, and every sense of being two different people vanished as our bodies twined together. The terrible longing that had plagued my soul drifted away, and something new filled me and strengthened me.

7

I did not know I was drifting until I found the shore.
  I did not know I was broken until I was whole.
  I did not know what I had to lose until the thieves came.

8

Bright morning light peered in through the canvas of Liam's tent.

I knew I should get out of bed, but the comfort of his arm draped over me was too wonderful to cast away. I lay very still, memorizing the way his weight pressed against my side until he stirred.

For a split second, I worried that everything he had said the night before would be forgotten in the unforgiving sunlight.

He pulled me closer to him and kissed the back of my neck.

"Did you sleep?" he asked.

"Of course. I have a magic pendant to keep the nightmares away."

"Is it enough? You were gone for so long and—"

I rolled over to face him. A thrill shot up my spine as my chest grazed his. "I was fine. I was trapped beneath the mountains in a labyrinth I thought I'd never get out of, but no one hurt me."

"How did you get beneath the mountain?" Liam pushed himself up on his elbow.

"I was swallowed. The soldiers and the sorcerer had me cornered, and then I fell into darkness."

"What?"

"I don't know how it happened, but the mountain took me in and kept me below until yesterday."

"That's not possible." Liam laid his palm on my ribs, on the raven mark he had drawn on my flesh. "The mountain shouldn't have opened for you, and even if she did, how could you have survived for two weeks?"

"There are houses down there, Liam." My heart raced as the memory of the blackness surrounding me shocked through my body. "There was a fountain with a beautiful statue of a woman. There was a garden, and a fancy manor."

"There aren't any people living below the mountain."

"Not anymore, but there used to be. There is a whole abandoned city down there. I don't know who built it or why they left, but I know it's real. I was there. I saw it. I walked through the whole chivving thing for ages. I think the mountain wanted me to see it. I'm not sure why, but I know I didn't imagine it."

"The mountain's magic runs deeper than we want to believe." Liam kissed my forehead, sending a jolt of joy looping through my stomach. "She protected you, kept you safe underground away from monsters—"

"The monster. Is it still in the woods? I didn't see any hint of it on my way here." Reality beyond the warmth of Liam's bed trickled fear back into my veins. "And the traitor. Did Emmet tell you he thought someone had—"

"She's in there." A voice cut through the canvas.

A whispered reply came after.

"No." The voice got louder. "I'm telling you, Ena is in that tent."

"Evie." I dove toward my clothes, which lay scattered across the ground.

"You can't go in there," Gwen said. "Evie, don't you dare."

Liam leapt out of bed and raced for his cast-aside pants.

I swallowed my laugh as he hopped on one leg trying to yank them on.

"Ena will be happy to see me," Evie said.

"I'm sure she will." Gwen overenunciated each word. "But you know how grown folk are before they've had their breakfast."

I pulled on my shift and buttoned my skirt.

"Best to leave Ena alone until she's had something to eat and a chance to wake up!" Gwen shouted the last two words.

I yanked my bodice on as Liam pulled his shirt over his head and ducked out of the tent flap.

"Evie, Gwen," Liam said, "I have the most wonderful news to share. Ena arrived home last night."

"I know that," Evie said. "She's in your tent."

Heat burned in my cheeks.

I jammed my boots back onto my feet and slipped out the back flap of the tent.

"Let's go and see Neil about some breakfast," Gwen said. "I'm sure we'll meet Ena in the clearing."

I looked to the gap between Liam's tent and mine. It wasn't wide. Only two feet. Which was plenty of space for Evie to spot me.

"Let's all go to breakfast together," Liam said. "I'm very hungry this morning."

"I'm sure you are," Gwen said. "You should eat a hearty breakfast so you can feel recovered for the day."

I stayed frozen as their footsteps faded away. I peeked around the side of Liam's tent. There was no one in sight. Feeling like an utter fool, I leapt across the gap between our tents and dove into the back of my own canvas home.

Someone had come in to tidy my things. They'd rolled my blankets to fight off the damp and had laid everything I owned in a neat row on my cot. I couldn't picture Liam doing such a thing, and certainly not Emmet. Finn might have come in and protected my possessions before he left, but it didn't seem like him.

I sat down on the stump that was meant to be my chair.

Was it Marta or Cati?

It seemed strange that there were enough people who might've missed me that I didn't know who could've tidied my tent.

I dragged my fingers through my hair, wishing I had a comb. Digging into the bag that held the few extra bits of clothing I owned, I pulled out clean things to wear. I'd lost my pack in the Lir Valley. My comb, my powders and paints to give me a fitting set of armor to face the foul world of men—all of it was gone.

After I'd changed into my clean clothes, I stood staring at my cot for a long while.

I wanted to go out and greet all the people that filled the camp I called my home, but I wasn't sure what to say to them. I didn't know what they'd say to me.

"Don't be a chivving fool." I tied my hair back with a string and stepped out of my tent.

Nessa lurked on the path leading to the clearing. "You're back! How wonderful." She gave me a smile I couldn't trust as I passed her.

I forced my hands to relax as I strode into the clearing.

I passed Winnie, who gave me a wave from her seat at the side of the wide, open space.

"Nice to have you back." Kerry spoke through his mouthful of food and strode quickly away from me.

Others smiled and waved, but they didn't approach me. They didn't try to ask me questions or block my path.

I'd only ever seen them behave that way with two people. Liam and Emmet.

I stopped at the back of the line of people waiting for breakfast.

Sal offered me his place in line, but wouldn't look me in the eyes.

Do they hate me for sneaking away? Do they think I'm the one who betrayed them?

I shoved my hands into my pockets to hide their shaking.

"Ena!" I heard the shout the moment before Evie rammed into my torso. "I thought you'd died. Everyone thought you'd died. It's been plain awful around here what with everyone grieving for you."

I sucked air back into my lungs as Evie let go of me.

"We've missed you." Evie blinked up at me with her big brown eyes. "I don't blame you for sending us here without you, but it would've been better if you hadn't run away."

"She was protecting us." Gwen stepped up to her sister's side.

The other two Lir children followed close behind.

"That doesn't mean it was nice of her to leave," Evie said.

"At least we made it here alive," Dorran said. He alone seemed the worse for being in the camp.

Gwen and Evie had both gained more color in their cheeks.

Dorran seemed to have lost a bit off his skinny frame, and his brow looked to be stuck in a permanently furrowed position.

Cinni stepped around her siblings and stared up at me.

"Hello, Cinni." I bent down to be level with her eyes. "I'm sorry if you had a rough trip through the mountains, but I'm so glad you're here with my friends."

Cinni reached forward and brushed her finger across the back of my hand.

"I'm happy to be home as well," I said.

Cinni turned and walked straight up to Neil. He passed her a bowl and spoon without question or snipe. Then she sat by a tree to eat.

"Time for breakfast." Gwen shooed Dorran and Evie away.

I felt out of place as I reached the front of the line.

Neil examined me from my boots to the top of my head as he passed me my bowl and spoon.

"Thank you," I said.

"Of course," Neil said. "Of course. Good to have someone back who's slipped through the clutches of the Guilds."

"Right," I said. "Thanks."

I backed away from him and toward the clearing.

A glint of bright blond hair shone in the corner of my vision. I turned in time to see Marta stalk away through the trees.

"Right." I nodded to people, trying not to look like I was searching for Liam as I sat in the clearing. There wasn't a sign of him anywhere. "Right."

I took a bite of what could best be described as gruel. Despite not having eaten anything but scavenged plants in two weeks, the food turned my stomach.

"Not to your taste?"

I looked up to find Case standing over me.

"Not really," I said. "But I'm grateful for food."

"Did they not feed you where you were?" Case asked.

"There were no people," I said. "I ended up wandering on my own after slipping away from the soldiers."

I don't know what made me coat the truth.

Case shrugged and sat beside me. "Finn's been gone for a while now. I hope he has food."

"Have—" I swallowed the sour in my throat. "Is the monster still roaming?"

"Oh no," Case said. "As soon as you and Finn dodged out of camp, Liam went on a tear. The beast was destroyed before Finn got back. Then he, Liam, and Emmet went on a tear about your being missing."

"I'm sorry." I set my gruel aside. "I didn't mean for Finn to go out after me. If you know where he went, I can go and look for him."

"And you'll go one way and he'll go another and you'll end up missing each other in the woods? Best thing you can do is stay here and wait for him to come home."

"I'm sorry," I said again. "I'm sorry you have to wait for him because of me."

"He'll be all right." Case ran a hand through his dark hair, tousling his normally perfect locks. "Cati went with him. She'll make sure he hobbles home."

"But Cati isn't allowed to leave camp. Her job is to stay here and train the fighters."

"That all went out the chivving window when you went missing. All order went soaring into the wind when Finn showed up with four sorcis in tow and announced you'd sacrificed yourself to save him."

"But he made it home, right? That's got to count for something." I wished I had a mug of ale or something to grip in my hands besides a bowl of gruel.

"It counts for a lot that you set your life on the line to protect Finn. I just hope the gods care enough to bring him home safe."

I took Case's hand. "Finn is an impossible, chivving slitch, but if anyone can survive monsters and men, it's him."

"You're right." Case nodded and chewed his lips together. "Want to come and play with swords? My usual sparring partner is absent, and I have a horrible need for exercise."

"As long as you don't mind having to teach me." I shoved a few more bites of gruel into my mouth before following Case to the training field.

9

The rest of the day passed in a haze of flashing steel in the clearing and strained nods and smiles from my fellow Black Bloods. At first, I tried to convince myself they were just glad I was back and too confused about how I'd survived to say hello to me.

Then, I noticed how they whispered when they thought I couldn't see. How Nessa began making her way around the training field, stopping to chat with every person she could catch. How there was a spring in her step as though she were living the best day of her chivving life.

After Case had run me through enough training to leave a fresh set of bruises coating my body, and worn down my need to scream at every person who glanced in my direction, I slipped away for a bath in the cave. As I traveled to my tent, a rustle of whispers followed me like my own personal breeze.

I soaked and scrubbed with fresh-scented soap until my skin was raw. When I got back to my tent, someone had left a new wooden comb and a tiny glass bottle on the stump that served as my table.

I stared at the bottle as I combed my hair. Marta had given me one like it once before. I didn't know if she'd slipped into my tent to leave this one for me.

Maybe Liam had asked her to. Maybe Liam had brought me the comb and glass bottle himself.

When I'd combed my hair so thoroughly there wasn't a hint of stone or tangle left behind, I uncorked the little bottle and drank the foul liquid within.

The vile stuff sent bile into my throat, but I managed to keep it down.

As the sun began to fade, I stepped out of my tent, clean and groomed, and headed toward the clearing.

The whispers still followed me.

I passed by a pack of men.

They fell silent and stared at the ground, as though hoping I wouldn't notice them.

I wanted to shout at them but didn't know what I would say. Screaming that I was sorry didn't seem like it would help, and bellowing that I hadn't betrayed anyone didn't seem like a good way to prove my innocence.

Neil didn't meet my gaze as he passed me my bowl of stew and overly full mug of ale.

I took my dinner and sat on the side of the clearing.

The two fiddlers hopped up onto a bench once true night fell, taking turns drinking and playing as the lae stones became the only real light in the camp.

I wished Finn were in the clearing with me. Or Cati. Or even Emmet.

Marta strode up to the front of the supper line and took her bowl without even glancing my way.

I took a long drink of ale, dousing the bit of me that wanted to walk straight up to her, whether she wanted to greet me or not. Marta was my friend. She'd been a good friend. But I didn't regret journeying to the Lir Valley and couldn't bear the thought of asking her if she believed I'd betrayed the Black Bloods. I didn't want to even think about the other reason she might be angry with me.

Liam trusts you. He chose you. Let that be enough.

Dancers gradually filled the center of the clearing, but there wasn't the pack of them I'd grown used to during the height of the summer. The whole scene just looked wrong without Finn and Case frolicking through the heart of it all.

I tried not to notice the glances thrown my way.

I sipped my ale again. The taste sent me spiraling toward memories I didn't want to dwell upon. My hands shook as I set my mug aside. I ate my meat stew as the players switched from song to song and the few pairs of dancers spun through each other.

I didn't know where the children were. I didn't know where they slept or who had been taking care of them since they'd arrived in the camp. I was sure Marta knew, but I didn't fancy asking her.

The fiddlers began a new song, and a few more brave souls joined the dancers. They laughed and frolicked, but I wasn't tempted to join them.

Nessa appeared from the shadows and flashed a smirk my way before heading toward the men who had fallen silent in my presence earlier.

One of the men tipped his head back and laughed.

Heat soared into my face.

I stood to return my mug and bowl to Neil. But Marta still lingered beside him, and I didn't want to get close enough to look into her eyes and see what she really thought of me. I set my mug and bowl back down, ready to risk Neil's wrath sooner than Marta's judgment, and turned to walk back to my tent.

The dancers parted, and my heart twirled in my chest as I caught sight of Liam sitting in his chair.

I'd never actually seen him sit in the wide wooden chair with the great bird carved into the back. He looked as though he'd been watching the dancers, but a moment after I'd noticed him, he raised a hand, calling me toward him.

My heart hitched up into my throat.

Part of me wanted to flee from him, but he met my gaze and waved a hand toward me again.

A jolt of fear shot through me at the mere thought of walking toward him with everyone around me whispering, but the draw of being close to him was strong enough to lead me across the clearing.

The dancers stopped as I neared them, scattering to make a path for me. I'd have thought the whole world had stopped turning if the fiddlers hadn't kept playing. The walk from my bench to Liam's chair seemed to take hours, but he kept looking at me. And I wanted to be near enough to him to see the dashes of black in his dark eyes.

My heart banged against my ribs as I stopped in front of him. The gaze of every person in the clearing bored into my back. "Is there anything you need, Trueborn Duwead?"

"I'm quite content to sit and listen to the music." Liam's face remained placid.

"Do you enjoy music? I've never seen you sit in the clearing before."

"Honestly, I hate sitting here." He rubbed his hand along the arm of his chair. "This seat feels too much like a throne."

"It looks rather like a throne." I felt a smile curve my lips. "You could be King of the forest birds."

"I'm king of nothing."

"Then why has Your Grandness decided to join us on this fine night?"

Liam looked around the clearing before turning his gaze back to me. "I wanted to be sure you were all right."

"Why wouldn't I be?" My smile slipped into something less genuine. "The flutter of whispers following me is such a delight after spending so long alone."

"I'm sorry for that."

"I just wish I knew what they were all chivving chattering about. What Nessa is whispering to every person in camp about. I didn't mean to disappear for so long. I didn't mean for anyone to go out looking for me. I certainly didn't betray—"

"Ena"—a vague pink drifted up Liam's neck—"all the talk is about us."

My heart stumbled over a beat. "Who did you tell?"

"We live in tents, Ena." He gripped the arms of his chair. "There's never more than a bit of canvas between us and every other person in this camp."

Heat seared my cheeks.

"They all know," Liam said. "I would guess most of them knew before you snuck out of my tent this morning."

The heat turned into an inferno hot enough to melt a mountain.

"What do I do?" I asked. "Oh gods, what are they all saying?"

"I don't know. If they're all whispering that you spent the night in my tent, they're right. There's nothing we can do about that."

"So we should just stand here and wait for my brother to murder you?"

A new wrinkle appeared on Liam's brow. "Emmet is a problem for another day, but tonight we can take care of the rest of the camp."

"How?" The heat of all of them staring at me singed my bravery, threatening to send me running from the clearing like a wounded animal. "Does it involve fleeing across the Arion Sea? I've never sailed before, but I'm willing to learn."

"I can't run away, Ena. I can't stop them from whispering, but we can change what they say."

"Does it involve you making the entire camp swear oaths to you and slaying them all with tiny stones?"

"No." The wrinkles on Liam's brow vanished, and a tiny hint of a smile curved one side of his mouth. "Just sit with me."

"What?"

"Sit with me." Liam shifted in his wide seat, making a place for me by his side. "They want to whisper about you sharing my bed like it's something illicit or wrong, but it's not. I care for you, Ena. I nearly lost my chivving mind when I thought..."

"I'm fine." I wanted to reach out, to touch his cheek, but the stares of the other Black Bloods burning into the back of my neck kept me from moving. "I'm here, and I'm fine."

"I don't ever want to lose you again. I don't think I could survive it. Please, Ena, just sit beside me."

"With everyone staring?"

"Sit with me, and they'll all gape for a moment. But by morning, they'll see we've nothing to hide. I want to be with you, Ena. I don't see the point in pretending otherwise."

I froze, staring at the open place on his throne-like chair.

"Or," Liam said, "you can give me a nod like I've told you something I need you to do for me, and leave. I won't push you toward anything you don't want."

I wanted to sit beside him. I wanted to feel his arm around me. A pull buried deep in my chest screamed for me to close the few feet of space between us.

You are not a coward.

I let out a long breath and sat by Liam's side.

The chair was wide enough for both of us, but his arm still pressed against mine. The warmth of his touch dampened the flames that had plagued me.

I looked out over the clearing. Every single person stared at me. Even the fiddlers had their gazes locked on Liam and me as they played.

"I'm sorry the seat isn't more comfortable," Liam said.

"I hadn't noticed the wood. I'm too busy wilting from the glares I'm getting."

"They aren't glaring." Liam laid his hand palm up on his knee. "They're just a touch disappointed."

"Why's that?" I placed my hand in Liam's, lacing my fingers through his.

"They thought they'd just gotten a wonderful new piece of gossip they could chew on all the way to Lygan Hall." Liam squeezed my hand. "We've deprived them of that."

"So, they are glares then." I nudged my arm against his.

"Maybe," Liam said, "but not for anything worth glaring about."

A flicker of movement at the back of the clearing caught my eye. Marta strode up to the front of the barrel and poured herself a mug of ale.

Marta's movement seemed to have broken the trance that had kept the Black Bloods frozen.

Nessa left the people she'd been whispering to and sat on a bench, still openly glaring at me.

The line for ale shifted as Neil began filling mugs.

Case lured someone up from the benches to dance with him to the fiddlers' new song.

Marta cut across the clearing, looking up at the trees rather than at Liam and me.

"Is she going to hate me now?" I whispered. A sliver dug into my joy.

"It's not you she's angry with." Liam tucked my hair behind my ear.

Marta stormed past us and up the path to the tents.

I froze for a moment, trying to decide if I should run after her. I'd lost too many people I cared for. Most, there was no chance I could ever get back. I didn't want to ruin what I had with Marta if I had a chance of salvaging even an ounce of our friendship.

"I have to go." I brushed my lips against Liam's cheek.

"It's best to let her be," Liam said. "There's nothing you can say to—"

"I've at least got to try."

"Let me go." Liam held tight to my hand.

"Stay here. Be King of the birds. I'll be right back." I stood up and followed Marta, careful not to glance back to the Black Bloods who still stared at me.

10

I didn't allow myself to run after Marta until I'd gotten most of the way down the path to the tents.

Honestly, if her hair hadn't been so pale it seemed to reflect starlight, I wouldn't have been able to find her.

"Marta," I called softly once I was close enough I knew she could hear.

She didn't pause.

"Marta." I ran faster, sprinting to her side. "Could you just stop for a moment?"

She kept striding forward like I didn't exist.

"Marta, I'm sorry." I caught her arm and spun her around. "Please, let me explain."

Marta stepped away and took a drink from her mug.

"I never wanted to hurt you," I said. "You are my friend, and I hope you can forgive me—"

"Forgive you for what? For running out of camp and letting us all think you were dead? Did you even consider the people you were leaving behind when you went stomping off into Ilbrea trying to save the chivving world?"

"I had to help those children." I reached for Marta's hand. She backed farther away. "Have you seen what Cinni can do? What all four of them can do? Can you imagine what the Sorcerers Guild would have made of them?"

"Of course I know what they can do." Marta gave a cold laugh. "I, unlike some people, honor the oaths I have taken."

"I did honor my oath." My side stung as though my mark had come to life just by my thinking of it. "Liam gave me his blessing—"

"Don't you even mention that dishonorable slitch to me." Marta turned away, but I caught her arm again.

"Who are you talking about?"

"We're all here to help him in his chivving cause," Marta shouted. "People have died

408

because they believed in him. People risk their lives for him every day. And he can't keep one chivving vow."

"What vow?" Everything around me went cold.

Marta stared over my shoulder.

I spun around to find Liam standing in the shadows.

"Marta," Liam said, "please don't do this."

"Is that an order, Trueborn?" Marta spat.

Liam didn't say anything.

"Gods, you're worthless." Marta turned and strode farther into the trees.

"Marta," I called after her.

"Ena—"

I didn't wait to listen to Liam. I tore through the darkness after Marta. I wished I had a lae stone. I wished I weren't chasing my friend through the woods. I wished I were still sitting by Liam in his uncomfortable, carved chair.

I slowed my steps as I reached Marta's side.

"Marta." My voice came out wrong, like grief and rage had already taken me. "What vow did he break?"

She didn't answer.

"Please." I dodged in front of her and blocked her path. "We're friends. At least I thought we were."

She stopped moving but didn't look at me.

"I knew..." Self-loathing curdled in my stomach. "I knew you were fond of Liam. But I didn't know you'd made any sort of promise to each other. I would've stayed away from him."

"I've heard enough lies without needing any from you," Marta said.

A pain stabbed at my chest right below where my stone pendant lay. "I'm sorry, I truly am, for whatever part I've had in his breaking whatever vow he gave you."

"The vow wasn't to me." A tear rolled down Marta's cheek. "That doesn't mean I have to forgive him."

She stepped around me and walked off into the shadows.

I couldn't follow her. I wanted to, but a horrible sickness rolled through my entire being, and I wasn't sure if I could breathe without being ill.

"Ena."

I'd felt many things at hearing Liam's voice before. Revulsion had never been one of them.

"I want the truth." I swallowed the sour in my throat. "All of it. Right now."

"Not all of it is mine to tell." Liam stopped right behind my shoulder. I could feel the heat coming off his body.

"All of it." The words tasted foul as I repeated them. "Right now."

"Your brother saved my life."

"I know that."

"I should have died in Nantic. I very nearly did. Emmet killed three men saving me, then hauled me up the mountain. I couldn't have asked that much from a member of my own clan. When I was finally able to do more than babble that we needed to keep climbing, I asked him to join us, and asked what I could offer in exchange for my life."

I dug my nails into my palms, trying to push down the pain that flared in my chest.

"He only wanted one thing in exchange for saving me. He wanted you kept safe. I vowed that I would protect you."

"But you have," I said. "You saved me in Harane."

"And led you through the mountains and brought you to Frason's Glenn and the Brien enclave, and let you go the Lir Valley. And now I've led you into a trueborn's bed. I've told you, you're safer far away from me."

"But it's my life." A tingle of feeling returned to my fingers. "I can make my own choices without my brother's interference. Whose bed I sleep in should definitely have nothing to do with his chivving opinion of where I'm safe."

"I know." Liam took a step closer to me. "And I mean to keep my vow to Emmet. I will protect you. I will keep you safe."

"But that doesn't make sense. If it's just Emmet thinking he knows what's best for me, why is Marta so fussed?" I looked through the trees to where she'd disappeared. "I'm sure he'll rage enough to scare the whole camp when he gets back, but what's that got to do with Marta?"

"She worries when he's gone," Liam said. "And from the way he tore out of camp, I'm not sure how much of Ilbrea he'll burn searching for you."

"Emmet." I said my brother's name like it would somehow make all the pieces of the shadowy mess fit together. "Marta's worried about Emmet. She's not angry because she's in love with you and I hopped into your bed." I clapped my hands over my mouth, muffling my gasp. "No."

Liam said nothing.

"You can't actually mean that Marta's in love with my brother? That sweet woman is in love with my demon of a brother?"

A wrinkle formed on Liam's brow. "Her secrets aren't for me to tell."

"Oh, chivving gods and stars." I took Liam's face in my hands. "They're actually together, aren't they? Is he in love with her? Does everyone in the chivving camp know but me?"

"I have no idea. I stay out of that sort of chatter."

"I thought she was in love with you. I've thought it from the beginning."

He placed his hands on my waist, as though testing to see if I'd want him near me.

I laid my cheek on his chest. "Does she blame you for Emmet going out to find me?"

"She blames me for letting you go to the Lir Valley. She nigh on murdered me when she found out you'd gone. But I am going to keep you safe." Liam pressed his lips to the top of my head. "I would never do anything to harm you, and that includes keeping secrets."

"My brother and Marta is a fairly big secret." I tipped my chin up to look into his eyes.

"It's not my secret."

"You could have told me you'd made some vow to Emmet." A horrible knot wrapped around my stomach. "I always thought you didn't want me. I thought I was a fool for fawning over you."

Liam leaned down and brushed his lips against mine. "You are the bravest, strongest, most incredible woman I've ever met." He kissed me, and his taste filled me. "You are everything I want. I would burn the sky to protect you, Ena Ryeland."

I laced my fingers through his hair and let my body meld against his.

His heartbeat pounded through my chest as I kissed him. Fear and worry drifted away, and there was nothing in the world but Liam and me.

I wished the stars would shine brighter so I could see the ridges of his bare chest. I wished time would stop and I could spend the rest of eternity with my body twined around his.

Embers seared my skin as he kissed every inch of me. Pulsing heat swallowed everything I was, until there could be nothing in existence but Liam. The wanting in my chest burned bright as I wrapped myself around him, and I knew I would crave him for the rest of my life.

We were a beautiful tangle. A mass of limbs and sweat and pleasure so brilliantly sweet I forgot we were in the middle of the forest until it was time to go back to his tent, and I had to spend ten minutes searching for my boot.

He held me close to his side as we crept back to camp, softly laughing as he picked moss and twigs out of my hair.

I slept in his arms again that night, feeling truly safe for the first time since I was a child and had been too naïve to know how cruel the world can be.

When I left his tent in the morning, a little glass bottle waited right outside.

11

I took my time combing my hair in my tent, making sure not a single trace of tree bark or moss had been left behind from the night before. Heat rushed to my cheeks as I remembered him touching me. I could hear him moving in his tent. I wondered how soon I would be able to convince him to sneak back into the woods with me.

When I was certain I looked as respectable as anyone who lived in a tent could, I stepped out into the morning light.

Liam stepped out of his tent a moment later. "Good morning, Ena." A twinkle of a smile lit his eyes. "Are you hoping for some breakfast from Neil?"

"I am, actually. I woke up very hungry this morning."

Liam's smile curved one side of his mouth. His lips were beautiful.

By the gods, I wanted nothing more than to kiss him.

"Shall we?" Liam placed a hand on the back of my waist.

The pressure of his hand against my back shot sparkling joy through my whole being. I tried not to grin like a fool as we joined the line waiting for gruel from Neil. The strange scent coming from the cook pot did not dampen my joy, though it did seem to leave the other breakfast seekers in a foul mood.

"Perhaps I should go foraging today," I whispered. "I might be able to find something to make the food a bit more palatable."

"You can't leave the boundary." Liam spoke so softly, I had to lean closer to him to hear. I didn't mind it. "If you can find something inside, then everyone will thank you for it, but don't go past the boulders."

"Why not?" I turned to face Liam, letting the back of my hand graze against his fingers. A thrill shot up my arm.

"It's not safe."

"The monster is dead," I said. "You killed it."

"That doesn't make us any safer."

The perfect warmth that had surrounded me drifted away.

"The traitor." It felt like the whole camp was staring at me again as I whispered the words. "Emmet told me someone had betrayed us. Did you find out who?"

Liam kissed my forehead. "Not now."

"Do you want food or not?" Neil banged his ladle against the side of the cook pot.

"Food, please." I pried myself away from Liam and gave a smile to Neil. "I was thinking I might prowl through the woods a bit today. See if I can find something interesting to bring to the kitchen tent. I can come and help fix dinner."

"No." Neil shoved a wooden bowl at me. "I'll take whatever you find foraging, but the last thing I need is one more bored Black Blood crowding into my kitchen tent like they think they're going to help me do my job. I've been feeding this camp since before Liam was allowed a sharpened sword, and I know chivving well how to chop a root. I don't need more warriors interfering like slicing vegetables is the same as cutting a man's throat."

"Right." I stepped away and let Liam claim his food. "I'll just drop some things off then."

"Thank you for working so hard to keep us all fed." Liam gave Neil a little bow.

"What's Neil so fussed over?" I asked once we'd retreated with our bowls of slop.

Liam glanced around, giving a few nods to people we passed before answering. "I've banned everyone but the hunting party from leaving camp."

"Why?"

"I don't know how else to keep everyone safe," Liam said. "Someone's betrayed us. I'd like to believe it's not someone in this camp, but I have no way to prove it. The monster's dead, but that doesn't make the forest any less dangerous."

"Why not?" I stopped. "Is the traitor lurking in the woods?"

"Keep walking." Liam led me into the trees, in the same direction we'd traveled the night before.

Heat rose to my cheeks just remembering the taste of his skin.

"You said you wanted the truth from me." Liam stopped once there were no other people in view.

"I do." I leaned against a tree and took a bite of my slop. The goo didn't taste much like food.

"Do you want me to tell you things even if knowing will do nothing but make you worry?" Wrinkles creased Liam's brow.

I set my bowl down and took his face in my hands, tipping his head so I could kiss the wrinkles on his forehead. "You shouldn't worry and stew alone. Besides, I have been known to help once in a while."

Liam stepped away from me and began pacing between two trees.

"The beast was a croilach," Liam said after his third pass.

"I don't have any idea what that is." I picked up my bowl and kept eating my slop, grateful to have something to occupy my hands.

"A stone monster," Liam said.

"It didn't look like stone when it tried to eat me."

"The flesh of the beast was real," Liam said. "Stolen from other animals and molded into one foul being."

"That's disgusting." My stomach rolled, threatening to toss up my breakfast.

"The croilach are animated by a stone heart."

"A what?"

"A stone is filled with magic and then placed in the creature's chest. The croilach then lives to do its master's bidding."

"Someone made that thing and sent it after our camp?" Rage burned through me. "That monster killed three of our people. Who sent it? The Sorcerers Guild? Do they know where our camp is?"

"Creating a croilach requires stone magic." Liam dug his fingers into his hair. "Only a trueborn could create such a creature."

The anger in my stomach turned from a raging fire to a deadly cold beast. The power of that awful hatred filled me.

"A Black Blood sent that monster to slaughter us?" My voice came out calm. "Was it Regan? Are the Brien that determined to stop us from helping the sorcis?"

"I don't know who it was," Liam said. "I sent word to Lygan Hall. Orla is on a war path, but she hasn't offered me any information beyond forbidding me from leaving the boundaries of the camp."

"Why would she do that?" I looked toward the eastern boundary of our sanctuary, waiting for an army of monsters to come charging up to attack.

"If I die, the boundary falls. The camp would be vulnerable."

My hands trembled too badly for me to hold my bowl. I set it back down before the urge to smash it broke through my reason.

"Is the trueborn who made the croilach the same chivving Black Blood who betrayed us?" My voice shook.

"I don't know."

"Could the trueborn send another beast?"

Liam reached into his pocket and pulled out a black stone.

The thing wasn't even as large as his fist. A crack split through the center, but other than that, there was no hint that the rock was anything other than an ordinary bit of the mountains' stone.

"Some parts of stone magic come easily to a trueborn. Others take something out of you, like they're tiring your soul. Creating a stone heart for a croilach is exhausting. I've heard stories of trueborn dying in the attempt. But if whoever made the monster wants to damage the Duweads badly enough to risk an unprovoked attack in our own territory—"

"Then who knows how far they would be willing to go to hurt us?" I reached out and touched the rock. "You'd think I would have noticed the beast had been magically made. It looked like a monster, but I never would have imagined that a person had created it. Even in the daylight—"

"You saw the croilach in the daylight?" Liam moved the stone heart away from me.

"The second time it came after Finn and me. The monster nearly clawed me in half when we left for the Lir Valley."

He slipped the stone back into his pocket and wrapped his arms around me, holding me close to his chest. His breath shook in his lungs.

"I'm fine." I kissed the side of his neck. "The mountain saved our lives. We ended up in a chivving awful tunnel and had to crawl for hours. I gained some nasty bruises, but that's all."

"I should have gone with you." Liam pressed his lips to the top of my head.

"You had a croilach to slay. Didn't Finn mention we'd seen the monster again when he brought the children here?"

"It was all chaos." Liam held me tighter. "He only stayed in camp for an hour. He probably didn't even think of it."

"He's still out there." I stepped away from Liam. "Finn and Emmet and Cati are all out there looking for me. What if a new monster is sent after you and attacks them before they can reach the camp?"

"There are animals roaming near our boundary again. I don't think they'd be here if there was another monster in our woods."

"But you can't be sure." It was my turn to pace between the trees. "We have to find a way to tell them I'm back. We have to bring them home."

"I don't even know where they might be. Finn and Cati were going to retrace his steps to where you'd been lost, but if they'd stopped there, they should have been back by now."

"Then I'll go after them."

"And if they're not sitting in the woods waiting to be found? The mountains are too vast for us to hope to find them." Liam stepped into my path. "Emmet was going to head for Ilara, but there's no way to know where between here and there he might be."

"Then send one of your stone birds. Have the bird bring them a message."

"I can't. It doesn't work that way."

"Why not?"

"I've got to know where the person I'm sending the message to is." Liam looked toward the treetops. "If one of them were a trueborn, I could send a bird without telling the thing where to go. Even Orla's trackers in Ilbrea can send the stone birds she's given them straight to me. The birds can sense my magic wherever I am. But for me to send a bird to a normal person, even sending the bird straight to Ilara wouldn't work. I've got to know a clear destination I want the bird to reach."

I scrubbed my hands over my face. "So we're just supposed to sit here and hope they come back?"

"There's not much else we can do." He laid his hands on my shoulders. "Emmet, Finn, and Cati are some of the best fighters I've ever known. They can make it back."

I let my forehead rest against his chest. "How did you manage to kill the croilach?"

"I ripped the stone heart from the monster's chest."

1 2

I did not want Liam to keep any secrets from me. I was glad I knew an enemy had sent the monster to torment our camp. Being grateful for the knowledge did not diminish the ice-cold rage that filled me.

I wanted to kill the trueborn who had attacked the people I cared for. I wanted to drive a knife into their flesh. I wanted to watch them bleed.

I had killed before, but I had never felt the desire to murder.

After Liam and I spoke in the woods, he had to make his rounds of the camp, checking on all his people, making sure the villain who had tried to destroy us did not seize another from our pack.

I took my bag from my tent and foraged through the confines of camp, choosing the steepest slopes to scramble up and climbing a few trees to try and burn some of the raging energy out of my limbs.

It didn't work.

I dumped my bounty onto Neil's table and went straight to the training ground.

Case was there, fighting with the others. It didn't take much to convince him to give me another lesson.

Working with the sword didn't ease my anger, but it gave me a place to aim the rage, which was better than stomping through the woods trying not to scream my fury to the gods.

"Again." Case prowled around the ring, holding his sword in one hand as though its weight were nothing to him.

I nodded. My arms throbbed in protest as I hoisted my own sword. I tracked Case's movement, waiting for him to come charging at me.

He just kept sauntering around the chivving ring like he hadn't a care in the world.

I tightened my grip on the hilt of my weapon.

"Don't clutch your sword like that," Case said. "You'll wear your hands out before your enemy even gets a blow in."

I forced my hands to relax a bit as he kept circling.

His blade glinted in the morning light. Knowing the edges had been dulled did not diminish the deadly look of his weapon.

Case didn't seem to think there was anything treacherous or dangerous in the world. He barely had a hair out of place after he'd spent the whole morning fighting.

"Are you going to attack me?" I asked. "Or would you rather we go on a nice afternoon stroll?"

"You've got to learn patience." Case twirled his sword through the air.

I tensed at the sudden movement, but he didn't approach. He just kept moving in a slow circle around the ring.

"An anxious warrior will attack too soon," Case said, "go charging against their enemy before the time is right. If you want to win a battle, you've got to learn to wait for the right moment."

"Are you going to wait for me to fall asleep?" I lowered my weapon. "Should I just meet you back here in the morning?"

Case smiled. "You can come back and fight me again tomorrow if you like. Nothing else to do in the camp anyway."

Anger burned through me again. There was nothing for us to do in the camp. Nothing of use at any rate.

Out in Ilbrea, there were sorcis who needed our help. People I loved who could be in danger or even dead, and I couldn't get to them. The world needed us, and we were trapped inside a spell, waiting to see if another monster would come to terrorize us.

The sun flashing off Case's sword was the only warning I had.

I dodged to the side as I swung my sword up, parrying the blow.

Case brought his blade around in a wide arc, aiming for my neck.

I ducked low and sliced my own sword for the back of his legs as I dodged behind him.

The edge of my sword grazed the back of his calf.

"Good job, Ena!"

I glanced toward the high-pitched voice.

A blow to the shoulder sent me staggering forward.

I let the momentum knock me to the ground, using Case's own strength to send me rolling back up to my feet.

A round of cheers came after that.

I spun toward Case in time to parry a blow aimed for my other shoulder, but he used my own trick against me, and let the hit I'd given his blade carry his sword back around to knock me off my feet.

I landed on my back with a grunt.

"It was better before!" the high voice called.

"Thanks." I pushed myself up to my forearms, trying to ignore the throbbing ache in my spine.

Evie ran across the ring toward me. Gwen, Cinni, and Dorran followed close behind.

"I didn't know you could fight with a sword." Evie stood over me.

"I can't," I said.

"You're getting better all the time." Case lifted my sword out of the dirt.

"If that had been a real sword, you would be dead," Dorran said.

"That's why they used dulled swords," Gwen said, "so they can be safe while they practice. Isn't that right, Cinni?"

Cinni had two bundles of fabric tied over her ears, but she nodded at her sister's words just the same.

"I've asked to learn to fight with a sword." Evie took my hand, yanking on my arm for me to stand. "But every time I ask, Marta says no."

"With very good reason." Marta strode up behind the children. "All of you are too young."

"That's not what Neil said." Evie wrinkled her forehead. "Neil said the woman Cati learned to fight when she was even younger than I am now. I'm already behind. I should learn to use a sword."

"Not here, Evie." I brushed the dirt off my skirt.

"Why?" Evie asked.

"Because you are too special to be taught to fight here." I bent down to look straight into her eyes. "You see, Case and I don't have magic like you. You need to learn from someone as special as you are."

"She's trying to say we're frightening enough without teaching us to stab people." Dorran glared at me.

"You think we're frightening?" Evie bit her lips together.

All four of the children stared at me with their matching, dark brown eyes.

"Of course she doesn't," Marta said. "None of us do."

"That's a lie," Dorran said. "You're all afraid."

Cinni flinched.

"You're right," I said. "I am very afraid, but not of you. Not because of anything you've done."

Gwen stepped closer to Cinni.

"What I'm afraid of is failing you." I knelt in front of Dorran. "I don't know how your magic is meant to work, let alone how to help you control it. Finn and I came to fetch you so you could be safe—and you are safe here in camp—but you've got to be patient and wait until we get to Lygan Hall where someone with magic of their own can teach you how to control yours. In the meantime, we'll just have to be grateful that you're all safe and together."

"That is a wonderful thing to be grateful for." Gwen squeezed Cinni's hand. "Aren't you glad we're all together, Cinni?"

I couldn't tell if Cinni had heard.

"We should let them get on with their practicing," Marta said. "We can't distract people from their work."

"It's all right," I said a bit too quickly. "I don't think I can do much more if I want to be able to walk tomorrow."

"Really, we shouldn't—"

"I'll go with you," I cut across Marta. "What are you up to this afternoon?"

Marta's jaw tensed for a moment before she managed to speak. "I was going to take the children to the clearing, let them play for a while before dinner."

"Perfect." I pressed my face into a careful smile. "I'd love to come with you. Hear how the children have been enjoying the camp."

"Well"—Evie took my hand and began leading me toward the clearing—"it was rather awful at first, what with everyone thinking you were dead. And it's still a bit boring since we're not allowed to go past the big stones, which is very sad since there's so much mountain we could explore."

"I would be happy to never see the mountains again," Dorran said.

"But there are some nice things about camp," Evie said. "Neil is very kind and very funny. Sometimes Marta is nice and tells us stories. But the best part is the bath. Have you taken a bath here?"

A much more genuine smile touched my lips. "I have taken a bath here."

"Isn't it the best thing you've ever seen?" Evie bounced as she walked. "In the miners' houses, a bath meant shivering in a tub of chilly water, but here the water is warm and deep enough to swim in."

"The bath is lovely," Gwen said.

"You are all going to be in for a real treat when we get to Lygan Hall," Marta said.

Evie stopped dead in her tracks and rounded on Marta. "That's not for forever. It's still summer, and you said we have to stay here until it snows."

"Well, yes," Marta said, "you are going to have to be patient. But once you get there, you'll see that Lygan Hall is worth all the waiting in the world."

"We can be patient, Evie," Gwen said. "We're very grateful to be here, and we'll be very happy to be there."

"Yes," Evie sighed. "Very, very grateful to be waiting for months."

She let go of my hand and charged through the trees toward the clearing as though the wind were carrying her.

"Evie, do not get so far ahead." Gwen ran after Evie, still firmly clutching Cinni's hand.

"I'm getting so tired of running," Dorran grumbled before taking off after them, leaving Marta and me alone.

We stood silently for a long moment.

"You should go back to the training field," Marta said. "I can manage the children on my own."

"I'm sure you can," I said. "Honestly, Gwen takes such good care of the others, they'd be fine without any of us."

"Gwen is practically a child herself. She shouldn't have the responsibility of raising three young sorcis tossed onto her shoulders."

"I didn't say she should."

I looked to Marta.

She didn't look back at me. Her gaze stayed fixed on the trees where the children had disappeared. I hadn't had the chance to properly look at her in the daylight since I'd been back in the camp.

Her face had lost a bit of its cheerful roundness, and her once porcelain complexion had been tinged with gray. Faint purple marked the skin under her eyes.

"Marta, if you need a break from watching them—"

"I can take care of four children."

"Right." I bit the insides of my cheeks. "Are…" I let out a long breath, trying to reason through what might make things better or worse. "Are you not sleeping with Emmet gone?"

A blaze of anger passed behind Marta's eyes.

"Liam didn't tell me," I said. "But there were only so many explanations for why you'd be so angry about Liam and me."

"He made a promise." Marta's jaw tensed. I missed the dimples I'd become so accustomed to.

"I know." I stepped in front of Marta.

She stared right through me.

"I'm the only relative Emmet has," I said. "It's just him and me in the world. I won't claim to know my brother. You've spent more time with him than I have if you don't count when we were children."

Marta shifted her gaze up to the sky.

"But I do know that no matter how many times I thought I might never see him again, he always came back." I took Marta's hand. "Even when I didn't want him to. Emmet's always come back."

"If you think I'm angry with Liam, it will be nothing compared to Emmet's wrath."

"I'm sure you're right." I squeezed Marta's hand. "But I'm not afraid of my brother, and I do have a right to live my own life."

"I don't think he could survive losing you. Wanting you to be safe is the only thing that's kept him going for so long. He'd be lost without that."

The knot came back, pressing against the front of my throat.

"I can't live in a cage. I won't let him stand between Liam and me. And when he decides to rage over my being a grown woman, I'll remind him that I was born with same blood as him. I am capable of wrath just as terrible as my brother's."

"Gods, the two of you together could burn the world." Marta gave a shaky laugh. "I'm not sure if it would be glorious or terrifying."

"I think that depends on who we Ryelands unleash our wrath upon. Get us riled enough, and maybe we'll march on the King."

"Just promise me you'll stay safe." Marta wrapped her arms around my neck, pulling me into a tight hug. "For Emmet's sake as well as mine. I was so afraid we'd lost you."

I held Marta close. I couldn't bring myself to lie and promise I would hide from danger.

13

Time does not always march along in a logical way. She surges forward, then slows and stops.

Being trapped in the camp was better than being locked under the mountain. Even if I had been all alone, having the sun to tell me the time of day would have been glorious enough to offer me a bit more sanity than the mountain ever granted.

Having Liam beside me was worth more than the sunlight. Sneaking to the far corners of the camp to revel in the wonders of his skin against mine gave me something other than worry and rage to fill my days. Spending my nights wrapped in his arms brought peace to my dreams that was better than pure blackness.

For three weeks, I woke up in Liam's arms every morning. There was a perfect beauty to huddling in the warmth of his bed for a few moments before the world demanded our presence. Even if the only bit of the world we had access to was contained within the boundary of the camp.

The Black Bloods became more restless. My worry and anger grew. But at least I could lose myself in Liam's arms. I should have been more grateful for the rest, for the quiet. For the hours spent hiding away with Liam.

I was not wise enough to understand that the peace was not a punishment.

Perhaps that's why time decided to speed up as though the gods themselves had declared we should be tested again. They pushed the boulder of our fate down the mountain, and none of us were strong enough to stop the fall.

14

I sat by Liam's side in his wooden chair, basking in the light of the midday sun. He'd taken to eating his meals in the clearing where the others could see him. I don't know if he wanted to keep an eye on the Black Bloods to be sure they were staying sane while trapped in the camp, or if he wanted them to see him eating Neil's slop without complaint.

His reasoning didn't matter much to me. At every meal, he'd place his hand on the back of my waist and offer me half of his seat. Taking my place beside him brought me enough joy that I didn't mind the foul food, and getting to be near him soothed the edges of my anxious anger enough to actually allow me to eat.

"I'm going to have to send the hunters out again soon." Liam took another bite of his root stew.

I stared down into my own bowl. I hadn't noticed the lack of meat. I'd been too busy enjoying the warmth of Liam's leg pressed against mine.

"We can survive without meat," I said.

"Marta's worried about our stores." Liam watched the Black Bloods in the food line. "If we go without meat, we'll run through everything else too quickly. Then we'd have to make a run into Ilbrea for supplies or risk having to go back to Lygan Hall early."

"I can spend some more time foraging. People may not like eating what I find, but the camp is large enough, we should be able to get by on the plants within the boundary. At least for a bit."

"It's not something they prepared me for." Liam set his bowl aside. "They trained me in combat. They trained me in stone magic. They taught enough about the evils of the paun to be sure I would fight them with everything I have. None of them ever bothered to tell me how hard leading a camp full of trapped people eating awful food would be."

"That's what you have Marta for." I laid my hand on Liam's leg. A burst of joy shook my chest at being allowed to give such a gesture of affection in full view of everyone.

"We'd be doomed without her." Liam placed his hand on top of mine.

"Liam!" A shout carried through the trees. "Liam!"

He was on his feet before his name had been called the second time.

I followed him as he raced east.

"Liam!"

Dread slithered through my veins.

"Ena!"

As the voice shouted my name, fear locked around my heart. My steps faltered as I looked over my shoulder toward the tents hidden behind the trees. If my name was being shouted, it had to be because someone was hurt.

But Liam was still running forward, and whatever disaster had come, I needed to be by his side to greet it.

"Liam!" Sal raced through the trees. He stopped in front of us, gasping for breath.

"What?" Liam took Sal's shoulders. "What's wrong?"

Sal brushed his sandy blond hair away from his face. "They're back." He gasped for air between phrases. "Looking fit to murder. I'm not dealing with it."

I took off running up the path Sal had traveled down, not slowing my pace as two people stepped into view.

Filthy and worn, there was no mistaking Finn and Cati as they strode through the trees.

A bit of my horrible worry drifted away as Finn smiled through the red beard that had taken over his chin.

"All that, and she's already here," Cati said.

I reached Finn first and dove at him, nearly tackling him to the ground as I hugged him.

"Thank the gods you're safe," I said.

"You were worried I wasn't safe?" Finn held me tight. "You ran off toward a pack of chivving soldiers."

"I had to get them—"

"And then you chivving well disappear!" Finn stepped away as he began shouting. "Do you have any idea the mess you left me in? No? Well, how could you since you went charging away without me?"

"You had to stay with the children. You had to bring them—"

"You don't get to make decisions like that," Finn said. "You don't get to decide to sacrifice your chivving life and leave me standing in the shadows without you. What under the godsforsaken stars did you expect me to do?"

"Get the children here safely, which you—"

"I've spent a month looking for you!" Birds scattered as Finn's voice pounded through the treetops. "We massacred a chivving soldiers' unit trying to find out if you'd been captured. All they would say is that you'd slipped away from them. But did you know there are soldiers along the western edge of the woods now? Whole units scouring the forest. Do you know how far south we had to lead them to make sure they didn't catch wind of our camp?"

"Finn, I'm sorry."

He gathered me back into his arms like he was afraid I might disappear again. "If you ever pull a stunt like that again, I'll chivving well kill you myself."

"That sounds fair." I held Finn tight. "Thank you for looking for me."

"Thanks for saving me, I suppose." Finn kissed my forehead. "But that doesn't mean I forgive you. I'm going to have a chivving chip on my shoulder for quite a while over this."

"I don't blame you," Cati said.

I stepped away from Finn and took both of Cati's hands in mine. "Thank you for searching for me."

"It wasn't all bad, aside from worrying that you were being tortured for information by the Guilds, of course. I finally got to stab some paun soldiers." Cati winked at me. "That made for a nice change."

The sound of running footsteps carried through the trees behind us.

Marta sprinted into view. She stopped for a moment, looking at our little group, before smiling. The expression was not large enough to display her dimples.

"I'm so glad the two of you are back," Marta said. "You were gone so long, we were worried something had happened."

"A flock of soldiers roaming through the woods happened." Cati let go of my hands and looked to Liam. "And not just the usual few prowling the outskirts. They weren't searching for tilk daring enough to brave the mountains for a hope of escaping the Guilds. They're looking for something, and I'm willing to bet, whether they know it or not, we're what they're after."

Liam scrubbed his hands over his face.

"We left a trail for them leading south," Finn said. "Might've led them straight into Brien territory. By accident, of course. It's so hard to tell when it's all just trees and mountains."

"What sort of a trail did you leave?" I asked, foolishly picturing a path of shining black stone.

"That kind that involves lots of dead bodies," Cati said. "Unfortunately, none of the soldiers I had time to chat with knew why they'd gotten orders to search the mountains."

"Best we could get out of any of the sniveling messes was that bandits were roaming the woods," Finn said. "Evil types who kidnap children."

Sour rose in my throat. "Those monsters are the ones who lock children away. We help them. We protect the sorcis from the Sorcerers Guild."

"That's not a very good line to feed soldiers who are terrified of the forest," Finn said. "But saving sweet littlelings from kidnapping bandits—that'll steel a man's nerves."

"How?" Liam said. "How did they find out where we've been taking the children?"

"I don't know," Cati said. "But I've come up with a few new knife tricks I'm eager to show the bastard who's feeding the paun information about us."

"We need to start questioning the people in camp." Marta held up a finger to stop Liam from interrupting. "I hate the idea of doubting our own people as much as you do, but we've got to rule out the possibility of it being one of our own before we start tearing through Orla's trackers or accusing the Brien."

"And how do you suggest we accuse our own people of betrayal and murder?" Cati said. "I'm pretty good at questioning, but I don't think anyone would forgive me afterwards."

"You might have to live with people not liking you," Finn said.

"We send for a sorcerer of our own," Liam said.

Cati, Finn, and Marta all froze.

"Would that be a bad thing?" I asked.

"Asking for Orla's aid is never the best idea," Finn said. "Asking for one of Orla's sorcerers to travel this far west—"

"If the traitor is in this camp, we can't risk them doing more damage than they've already managed," Liam said. "I lost three people because I didn't act decisively when the croilach came. I won't make that mistake again. I don't care what Orla wants in return for her aid."

I took Liam's hand, lacing my fingers through his as though Orla might swoop down from the sky to snatch him away from me.

Cati looked from me to Liam. "At least that got settled while we were gone. I don't think I could have stood you two dancing around each other much longer."

Heat burned from my neck up into my cheeks.

"Can we eat?" Finn said. "I've been half-starved for five weeks."

"Sure." I slipped my hand out of Liam's, still a little convinced my face had actually caught fire. "I won't lie and tell you it'll be decent food, but at least your stomach will be full."

"Good." Finn started down the path. "It's nice to know some things haven't changed while I was gone."

"My adoration of you hasn't changed." I looped my arm through Finn's. "Though I will warn you, Case has been training me with a sword, and I am improving."

"I'll be the judge of that," Cati said.

"He's all right then?" Finn's shoulders relaxed.

"Going a bit mad without you," I said. "But other than that, he's just fine. We're only waiting on Emmet to get back from raiding Ilara, and we'll all be safe and hiding in camp together."

"About Emmet." Finn glanced to Cati.

"What?" Marta said. "Did you see him?"

"No." Cati studied the hilt of the knife tucked into her belt.

"We did hear a rumor of a demon from the mountains who'd set fire to a caravan of soldiers," Finn said. "And another about a scribe's shop catching fire. Seems a beast of a man is working his way north toward Ilara, just sensibly burning his way through every paun he can find."

I was amazed my feet were still carrying me forward when my mind seemed to have shuddered to a stop.

"How far north did the demon get in the rumors?" Liam asked.

"Last I heard," Finn said, "they'd added guards to the gates of Ilara to keep the demon out."

"So he's not late in returning then," Marta said, "just got a bit distracted by vengeance."

"One of the soldiers we caught begged me not to burn him," Finn said. "Emmet is definitely leaving an impression."

"Should I feel guilty?" I asked. "He's on a rampage because of me."

"No." Finn kissed the back of my hand. His beard tickled my fingers. "I only wish I could have caught up with him to join in on the fun."

The kitchen tent came into view.

Neil caught sight of Finn and sighed.

Patrick shouted a greeting, and then it seemed like the entire camp had surged toward us to greet Finn and Cati.

425

Finn didn't let go of me until Case shoved his way through the crowd to reach him. Tears streamed down Case's cheeks as he held Finn in his arms.

I backed out of the pack of people, letting the Black Bloods greet their fellows, wondering if they would ever really consider me to be one of their own.

"We should celebrate tonight." Marta stood at the outskirts of the crowd. A line creased her forehead even as she smiled at the Black Bloods' joy.

"You don't have to pretend you're not worried," I said.

"I'm not worried."

"Liar."

"At least not the way you mean." Marta let out a shaky breath. "I love him, you know. I have for two years now. I know he's got to fight. I know he could never be happy stepping back from the battle while the Guilds are still hurting people."

"But?"

"I worry he'll enjoy fighting so much, he'll forget to come home. But that's just me being silly." Marta flapped a hand through the air. "He'll have to come back here in order to find out if you're safe. He'll come back to make sure you're safe."

"Marta—"

"I think we should pull out the ale early tonight. A bit of fun will do everyone some good." She strode away before I could say anything else.

15

By the time the sun had set, the camp had already spent a few good hours in the clearing. The fiddlers had moved from dancing tunes to tavern songs and back again, while Neil produced a new barrel of ale from wherever he and Marta stashed the stuff. No one seemed to care how foul dinner was as they chatted and laughed and sang.

Even the children got in on the fun. Evie pranced through the couples, making up a dance all her own. Dorran seemed keen to speak to the men who frequented the training ground, though I couldn't imagine the child having much interest in going through the pain required to learn to fight.

Cinni stood on a bench opposite the fiddlers, staring at them as they played. She had the two bundles of fabric tied over her ears, but she looked as close to happy as I'd ever seen her. Gwen sat at Cinni's feet, beaming as she watched her sister enjoying the music.

I stayed close to Liam's side as he made his way through the crowd, chatting with each of his people as I'd never seen him do before. He didn't ask them anything important. Still, I couldn't help but wonder if he was searching for the traitor.

I watched the eyes of the people he spoke to, trying to spot a murderer lurking behind the faces of the people I'd known for months. I didn't want to distrust any of the Black Bloods. Even wondering if someone as dreadful as gossipy Nessa had been the one responsible for all the pain we'd been through made me ill. I hated the girl, but I couldn't think that she'd had a hand in Pierce's death, even if she had whispered to the entire camp about him and me running into the woods together.

"Ena will enjoy it." Winnie's high voice broke through my thoughts.

I looked down to where Winnie sat on a bench, trying to reason through what I could be meant to enjoy.

The healer smiled, deepening the wrinkles on her face.

"I think the healers' garden in Lygan Hall is beautiful," Liam said. "And I've never known what most of the plants are meant to do."

"I'm very excited to see it," I said.

"You could do with some more training," Winnie said. "You've the makings of a fine healer, but you've some things yet to learn."

"Right," I said. "I'm sure I do."

"We should check on Neil," Liam said. "Make sure he's not being stampeded at the barrel."

"Some folks get too eager when they celebrate." Winnie held up her own mug and winked. "We should start taking bets on how many come crawling to me in the morning."

I laughed as Liam led me away.

"She means well." Liam spoke as softly as he could over the music and chatter.

"I know," I said. "But I never asked to be a healer. I've never wanted anyone's life in my hands."

"Then don't let Winnie train you." Liam touched the back of my waist, guiding me toward Neil.

"But what if I don't let her train me and then something horrible happens and I don't know enough to help?"

Liam stepped in front of me and took my face in his hands. "It is not your duty to save everyone in the world."

"That's a bit rich coming from you."

Liam smiled and kissed me. I swear the trees began to spin around us as his thumb grazed the side of my neck.

A flutter of murmurs changed the tone of the chatter as the fiddlers stopped playing.

I blushed and stepped away from Liam, but the people in the clearing weren't staring at us. They were looking to the upper edge of the lae stone light where a black bird glimmered in the blue glow.

The bird made a full circle around the clearing before Liam held his palm up in the air. The bird dove straight toward him, landed on his hand, and froze.

The murmurs didn't stop as Liam tucked the bird into his pocket. He didn't acknowledge all of his people watching him as he walked up to Neil and accepted a mug of ale. He passed by me as he strode toward the tents. He'd made it twenty feet before he stopped and turned back.

I held my breath, waiting for him to say something. I think everyone in the clearing did the same.

Liam reached for me.

I ignored the fluttering in my chest as I walked to him and placed my hand in his.

Whispers surged behind us as we walked out of the clearing.

"You didn't have to bring me with you," I said as we hurried down the path to his tent.

"I want you with me." Liam held the flap of his tent open.

I ducked inside the canvas, wishing we had entered for a chance to enjoy each other's bodies rather than because of a stone bird.

Liam sat at the table before pulling the bird out of his pocket. He stroked the back of the bird's neck and the stone came to life, hopping onto his palm before tipping its chin up. A little scroll of paper came out of the bird's throat.

Liam unrolled the paper. Wrinkles appeared on his brow before he'd even begun to read the note. As his eyes passed down the page, his expression shifted from worried to furious.

"What's happened?" I stepped closer to him, but he didn't reach for me. "Liam?"

He stood and stormed out of the tent without answering. I stepped outside to follow him, but he didn't head back to the clearing where the rest of the camp waited. He strode alone into the shadows of the trees—not toward someone who had caused his rage, but away from me.

I stood in the darkness, staring after him for a moment. The music started back up in the clearing. I took two steps toward the glow of the lae stones and the sounds of the crowd. But the people I'd want to speak to had worries of their own and joys to be celebrated. It would be wrong to bother them with my petty woes.

I went back into Liam's tent and sat at the table. The stone bird did not move.

My fingers trembled as I reached out and stroked the back of the bird's neck.

The bird fluttered its wings as it came back to life. I watched it hop around the table as the noise in the clearing regained it joyous uproar.

I touched the bird's neck again, and it turned back into a statue of itself.

"He'll come back." I rubbed my hands over my face, but the motion didn't soothe me. The minutes ticking past only made me more anxious.

I slipped out the back of Liam's tent and into my own, gathering a fresh set of clothes before walking to the bath.

The music from the clearing didn't penetrate the cave. The trickle of the water streaming out of a crack in the stone wall was the only sound.

The scent of my soap didn't soothe me. Neither did the warmth of the bath.

"Do not be a chivving fool, Ena Ryeland."

I slid beneath the water, but all the silence did was make me think how much better the bath would have been if Liam were with me.

The world does not need another lovesick fool.

I scrubbed myself until my skin was raw, then lingered in the bath like a coward. When I couldn't bear the shame of hiding in a cave any longer, I dried off, got dressed, and headed back toward my tent. I stopped in front of Liam's tent for a moment, listening for any hint of movement inside.

"You're ridiculous." I went into my own tent and lay down on my cot, trying not to worry at what the note in the stone bird might have said, trying not to spin myself in circles wondering what I might have done to make Liam walk away from me.

The music in the clearing had turned entirely to drunken singing before I managed to drift to sleep.

When my eyes snapped open, there was nothing but darkness and silence surrounding me. I lay very still, trying to reason through what had startled me awake and how quickly I could pull my knife from under my pillow.

"It's only me."

I turned toward Liam's voice.

He stood near the flap of my tent, the tiny trace of lae stone light from outside silhouetting his form.

"Are you all right?" I started to sit up.

"Go back to sleep. I didn't mean to wake you, I just wanted to hold you."

I lifted the edge of my blankets. "No boots in the bed."

He gave a quiet laugh.

I turned over as he climbed into my cot.

His clothes were chill against my skin. He kissed the back of my neck and wrapped his arm around my waist, pulling me close to him.

"Your cot is tiny," Liam whispered.

"Not all of us are given big tents and wide beds."

"You could have slept in my bed."

"You weren't there."

He was silent for so long, I thought he'd fallen asleep.

"My bed is yours, Ena. Whether I'm there or not, my home is yours."

I closed my eyes, willing my heart to still. "Where did you go?"

"To beg the stars for mercy."

"Why?" I nestled as close to his body as I could.

"It doesn't matter tonight. Sleep for now. This trouble can wait for morning."

"But—"

"Please, Ena. I just want to hold you."

I lifted his hand and kissed his palm. "Just promise that whatever it is, I won't be separated from you."

"I promise."

I tried to find comfort in his words but couldn't rid myself of the tinge of fear that had flown in with the stone bird.

"Try not to fall off the cot." I laid my arm over his, as though I could somehow bind him to me.

"Wait until we get to Lygan Hall. I have a proper bed there."

I laughed a bit, and we both fell silent. I'm not sure how long it took for either of us to drift into sleep.

1 6

The gray of dawn peering through the side of the tent woke me in the morning. I lay very still, too afraid of waking Liam to take a proper breath.

I wanted to know what news the stone bird had brought, but I didn't want to face another disaster. The weeks I had spent trapped in the camp had left me feeling caged but had also granted me time with Liam. I didn't want to lose that time to whatever new enemy threatened us. I didn't want to mourn another friend, or almost worse, wonder if they'd betrayed us.

"It wasn't about any of our people." Liam's voice came out low and raspy.

"What is it then?" I laced my fingers through his. "Does another sorci need us? Is there a new croilach come to attack?"

Liam held me closer, as though he were afraid I might be stolen from him.

"The Blood Leader of the Healy Clan was murdered," Liam said.

"By a croilach?" I wiggled enough to turn over. I needed to look into Liam's eyes to be sure that another monster hadn't been sent for his blood.

"I don't know." Liam brushed my hair away from my face. "The letter from Orla didn't say."

"Then what did it say?" Cold began at my fingertips and started drifting farther up my hands. "You seemed awfully upset for having gotten news that the blood leader of another clan had been killed."

"She's calling me back to Lygan Hall."

"Tell her no."

"I can't."

"No, you can't leave the boundary." I sat up and scrambled over Liam to pace the tiny space of my tent. The cold of the ground stung my feet. "You've got to stay in here where you're safe. If a blood leader's been murdered, it could have been by the same traitorous bastard who sent a croilach after this camp."

"I don't have a choice. I have to go."

"I'm coming with you. I have to. If there's a monster out there—"

"All of us have to go."

"All of us? She wants all of us to go to Lygan Hall?" I froze, stuck between gratitude and fear. "Can Orla do that?"

"Orla is the Elder of the Duwead Clan. As far as we're concerned, she can do whatever she likes. The whole camp is packing up this morning. I spoke to Marta last night. We're leaving before midday."

"But why? Why would she want you to come back?"

"The letter said nothing but to pack up for the winter and return to Lygan Hall immediately."

I started pacing again. "If there is a beast lurking in the woods waiting to kill us, the worst thing we could do is tramp a hundred people through the mountains. And what about the children? It won't be safe for them."

"We aren't farmers, Ena." Liam stood and took my hands in his. "The people in the camp are prepared to fight. If a croilach comes, we'll kill it."

"We could be marching straight into the traitor's trap. There could be monsters out there, just waiting for us to be vulnerable. This is a chivving terrible idea."

"It doesn't matter. Orla has sent her orders."

"But"—I pulled my hands from Liam to try and pace, but there wasn't any room in the tent to move—"winter hasn't come. There is still work to be done. We cannot leave without my brother."

"Emmet knows the path to Lygan Hall. He can find us."

"What if there are sorcis who need us?"

"We can't help anyone trapped in the camp. In a way, it's good we're leaving. Getting back to Lygan Hall will only help us figure out who's betrayed our clan."

"By going farther from Ilbrea?"

"By getting closer to Orla. By rooting out the traitor before they have time to hurt us again."

"Unless the traitor planned all this to get you out in the open. If they knew Orla would call you back to Lygan Hall, they might have killed the blood leader just to get to you."

"We're going to be all right." Liam kissed my forehead. "I will keep us safe. I will make sure Emmet finds us."

"I believe you." I tried to promise myself I wasn't lying.

"I've got to make sure everything gets packed up properly." He pulled on his boots. "We can't afford to let our hurrying now lose us supplies we'll need for next year."

"Right. I'll pack my bag and find Marta to see how I can help."

Liam gave me a smile that didn't reach his eyes.

"Liam," I said when he'd started to open the flap of my tent, "will I still share your bed in Lygan Hall?"

He stepped back into the tent and kissed me. "I've told you. My bed is yours as long as you will have me."

I tried to remember the feel of his arms around me as I laid out everything I owned on my cot. It wasn't much. I'd lost most of my possessions in the Lir Valley. All I had was two spare sets of clothes, a wooden comb, and the black cloak Mave had given me in Frason's Glenn.

The bag I'd brought with me from Harane still wasn't large enough to fit everything.

When I stepped outside, I expected to be greeted by the usual early morning stupor, but tents along the path to the clearing were already being lowered. Like it was normal, routine even, to pack up our home and leave.

I stuffed my hands into my pockets to hide their shaking as I walked toward the clearing.

Neil stood by his cook pot, but half of the wooden seats were gone.

Case and Tirra carried a bench past me, heading toward the tents.

"Ena," Marta called softly as she hurried toward me.

I kept my gaze fixed on her, not wanting to see if they'd already carried away Liam's wide chair.

"Do you know where Liam is?" Marta whispered.

"He was coming to make sure everyone was packing up."

"Hmm." Marta chewed on her thumb.

"Do you need help?"

"Not with packing. But I want him to send a stone bird. To Frason's Glenn, you know, to Mave. In case Emmet is there."

"Aren't there other places Emmet might go?"

"If he needed help, he'd go to Mave and her girls." Marta gnawed on her thumb. "I just want to be sure he knows that we've gone. That you're here and safe. That he should come back."

"I'll let Liam know when I see him."

"I left a pack for you in front of his tent. Yours should be taken down soon. I hope the children stay asleep until we're done. I don't want to begin to imagine how upsetting this might be for Cinni. I think she was really starting to feel safe here." Marta turned and strode off through the trees toward the bath cave.

I wanted to call after her. I had no idea what I wanted to say, but postponing the walk back to my tent seemed important. I stood with my mouth open, trying to think of some reason to stop the camp from moving, until Marta had disappeared.

"Just pack your bag," I whispered. "That's all you have to do."

I walked back toward the tents. The patches of earth where the benches had sat were darker than the ground around them. The rectangles looked like freshly dug graves. I closed my eyes when I passed the dark swatch where Liam's chair had been.

Most of the tents were down by the time I'd snatched up my new pack and dodged into my tent to shove my belongings into the bag. When I stepped outside, Liam's tent had been taken down. There was a barren patch of dirt where the canvas that had made his home had kept the plants from growing, and four gouges marked the ground where the legs of his cot had dug into the earth.

But that was all.

The place where I had slept in Liam's arms had been shoved away, as though the bed we'd shared meant nothing. I watched the line of Black Bloods walking toward the bath cave. Each of them carried a tent, or cot, or cook pot with them.

I crept beside them until I could peek into the cave. The water had vanished from the bath. The crack in the cave wall had disappeared like a wound that had been healed.

Marta supervised the men laying out the fabric of the tents in the dry basin that had been the bath. One side had been nearly filled with tent poles, while the canvas on the other side had been stacked higher than the lip of the basin.

Neil fussed over the cook pots and stacks of plates and mugs in one corner while Cati stood on the far side of the cave, lovingly packing the practice swords into wooden crates.

I didn't know my feet had carried me into the cave until Marta spoke to me.

"We should be ready to leave within the hour." Marta snatched a bundle of canvas from a gray-faced man. "Could you wake the children? I'd do it myself, but"—she lifted a canvas bundle from Case's hands and shot him a glare—"our Trueborn has charged me with making sure people who are regretting the ale they drank last night don't make us regret losing supplies next year."

Case gave Marta a pained smile. "I regret absolutely nothing."

"You will when the sun comes up all the way and the light pounds through your eyes," Marta said.

"I'll get the children up." I ducked back out of the cave.

I took a deep breath, savoring the scent of the forest. I knew what the high, barren peaks of the mountains smelled like, but I wasn't sure what scents would fill Lygan Hall. I sent a foolish wish up to the stars that Lygan Hall might seem a bit like home.

My tent had been swept away in the few minutes I'd been inside the cave. I knew I should be happy for the efficiency—we needed to leave—but I still clung to the straps of my pack as though someone might steal it as I walked toward the sole remaining tent.

The tent was tucked into the back corner of the rows of canvas that had been standing the previous night. It was the only sleeping tent that had been nearly as large as Liam's. I'd seen the children going in and out of their canvas home, but I'd avoided the place.

I didn't know why. I was too tired and hollow to know if I should feel guilty.

I stood in front of the tent flap, watching two gray-faced women carry a wide bench, trying to decide if knocking or calling out would be less frightening to the children.

"Someone's waiting right outside," a voice whispered from inside the canvas. "Does that mean we're allowed to leave now?"

"Are you awake in there?" My voice stayed steady and calm.

Evie dove out of the tent and lay on the ground at my feet. "I've been awake for hours. Hours and hours."

"That's an exaggeration." Gwen pushed the tent flap aside. "We woke up when the camp started packing."

"I'm sorry about that. We were hoping you'd..." The inside of the tent made my speaking useless.

The children's blankets had been rolled up, and their things had been stuffed into one pack.

"Evie heard people packing," Dorran said. "She woke all of us up."

"We're going to Lygan Hall." Evie lay on the ground, beaming up at me. "We're finally going to learn how to fight with magic."

"We're going someplace nice and safe." Gwen took Cinni's hand and led her sister out of the tent. "We're going somewhere we won't have to fight anyone."

"Absolutely." I made myself smile.

Cinni looked up at me, staring into my eyes with an odd intensity.

"If you're all done in there." Patrick appeared next to the tent. He'd started reaching for the tent pole before I could say the children were ready to be moved.

"Come on then," I said.

Evie bounced by my side as I led the children across the barren patch where the tents had been and cut west, beyond the bath cave, and then up the slope toward the stone boundary.

I didn't really know where the camp was supposed to leave from, but before the ground leveled out, Evie took off in front of me, sprinting through the trees. I followed behind her, not wanting to say I didn't know where to lead the children.

Evie led us straight to Tirra, who waited next to one of the great black boulders.

Tirra watched the five horses she minded as though waiting for one of them to shout that they didn't want to carry the burden they'd been loaded with. The horses huffed and twitched their tails but didn't seem afraid of straying beyond the boundary.

"I suppose this means we'll be walking the whole way." Dorran's shoulders rounded as though he'd already walked a hundred miles that morning.

"Walking is healthy," I said.

"It's only right that you should walk," Tirra said. "The mountains are meant to be traveled by foot."

"Then why do you have horses?" Dorran said.

"Ena."

I turned as Finn called my name.

He'd shaved off his beard and looked positively blissful. "You're ready then?"

"Sure." I made myself smile again. It felt as though my cheeks might crack. "A bit quick, but here we go."

Finn pulled me into a tight hug. "It's for the best. Tromping all the way to Lygan Hall will give Emmet time to cool down."

"Right. I'm sure you're right."

"Everything will be fine now." Finn kissed my cheek before stepping back and tipping his face up to the early morning sun. "You have no idea the wonders that are waiting for us."

"Does it involve a proper house and decent food?" Dorran asked.

"Most definitely." Finn grinned.

"I'll believe it when I see it," Dorran muttered.

"I'm sure we'll be very happy." Gwen stepped on Dorran's toe.

"Will we be leaving soon?" Evie asked.

"Very soon," Finn said.

Evie peppered Finn with questions about our journey and about Lygan Hall.

I wanted to have something useful to say, but I didn't know anything. I just stood next to the boundary, watching as the line of Black Bloods grew longer.

The sun had properly lit the sky by the time Liam strode up the slope to stand beside me.

"Do you have everything?" Liam whispered.

"I've no chivving clue," I whispered back.

Liam touched my cheek and kissed my forehead. "We're going to be fine." He looked out over the people behind us. "Guards, to your posts."

Men and women bearing swords, spears, and bows stepped out on either side of the group.

"We're fine," Gwen murmured to Cinni. "It's good to have people protecting us while we go for a nice walk."

Finn stood on one side of the children, his sword drawn even though he wore a full pack.

Case stepped up to flank our other side. He kept his sword in its sheath, choosing to hold a knife in each hand instead.

A whistle came from the end of the line.

Liam kissed the back of my hand before turning to the black boulder in front of us.

Evie giggled.

"Hush," Dorran whispered, "he's doing magic."

Both children fell silent as Liam laid his hands on the black boulder.

I'd felt the magic that protected our camp a hundred times before. I'd felt the pull of it long before I knew it was Liam who'd created the spell.

Liam closed his eyes and lowered his head.

I wanted to reach for him, but there was something in the way he pressed his palms against the stone that kept me still.

As much as I cherished the magic that surrounded our mountain home, it had always seemed a quiet thing, an invisible cocoon that was not meant to be seen by the world.

I gasped as bright light enveloped the camp.

A brilliantly blue bubble flashed around us, reaching from boulder to boulder and arcing high overhead to surround us completely.

In an instant, the blue shifted, funneling into the boulder in front of Liam. The blue moved faster and faster, ripping out of the sky and racing into the rock.

A light began to glow around Liam, illuminating his face, and making him seem more than human.

The light terrified me, like somehow the magic would swallow the man, and the mountain would claim the one I cared for.

Liam took a deep breath, and the light around him began to fade.

In another breath, the blue glow had vanished.

Liam balled his hands into fists, as though trying to keep them from shaking as he stepped away from the boulder to look out into the forest beyond.

I studied the trees, waiting for a monster to come charging through the woods to slaughter us. There was nothing but quiet.

Liam nodded, pulled his sword from its sheath, and led us east, away from our sanctuary and into the wilds of the mountains where magic roamed free.

17

When I was little, I thought I knew the difference between a lie and a story.

A lie was a thing that had terrible consequences. Whether it was being walloped when the truth came out, or something far worse. Even as a tiny girl, I knew a lie could end a life.

But stories—they were beautiful things. Stories of fairies Emmet would whisper to me when I refused to sleep. Stories of love to give a lonely girl hope. Stories of freedom to make living another wretched day possible.

I knew the stories weren't true. I knew at the heart of the tales there was nothing but lies. Still, I never counted the stories as dangerous.

Never dreamt a story could cost someone their life.

18

My feet throbbed, my shoulders ached from the weight of my pack, and I wanted nothing more than to curl up beside a boulder and sleep. But I kept a smile on my face as we marched through the mountains.

It had been two days of nothing but walking. I wanted to run or climb, but the great caravan of Black Bloods plodded along at a steady pace that drove me mad.

"I never dreamt there could be so many mountains," Gwen said. "Can you believe how many mountains there are, Cinni?"

"My feet can certainly believe it," Dorran said.

"The peaks are so beautiful." Gwen shot Dorran a glare. "I never dreamt I'd see snow on mountains when I wasn't cold."

Cinni didn't seem to care that Gwen had spoken. She was too busy staring at the case lashed across the fiddle player's back. Cinni stared at that stained leather like the case were a magical thing created by the gods. She grinned as she followed the case across ridgelines and alongside riverbeds. I think she would have walked into fire if the fiddle case had led in that direction.

Cinni's perpetual grin didn't stop the rhythm of the chatter between her three siblings. The children kept the pace of their words as the people of the camp kept the pace of their steps.

By the gods, I wanted to sprint in front of everyone and climb something. But Liam had asked me to help mind the children. I wanted to rage at him and shout that I could fight, but Cinni had the ability to wreak havoc on our journey as easily as any monster. If having Marta and me walking beside the children kept Cinni calm, then Liam was right to make me mind the little ones, even if I would rather have been marching on the perimeter of our group, weapon in hand as I scanned the horizon in search of Death himself come to torment us.

"What sort of magic are we going to learn?" Evie bounced on her toes as she walked. "I want to learn all about fire."

"Evie!" Gwen caught her sister by the wrist. "We do not light things on fire."

"Yes, I do," Evie said. "Sometimes by accident, but sometimes on purpose and it saves us."

"Light me on fire," Dorran muttered.

"You'll be able to learn all sorts of magic," Marta said. "There are many people who will be able to help you."

Evie twisted out of Gwen's grip. "What sort of people?"

"There are plenty of people with magic in their blood born into the Duwead Clan," Marta said.

"Then why weren't there any in camp?" Evie asked.

"Why didn't you send a sorcerer to take us away from the Lir Valley?" Dorran said.

I gritted my teeth, swallowing my urge to shout that Finn and I had been the only ones willing to make the journey to the chivving Lir Valley.

"If you were honey, would you go prancing about near a bear's den?" Marta asked.

Cinni glanced away from the fiddle case.

"If I were honey, I wouldn't be walking," Dorran said.

"The Sorcerers Guild searches for people with magic in their blood," Marta said. "They will do whatever it takes to hoard magic. If we brought a pack of sorcerers to the camp and had them run out into Ilbrea to find children like you, the Guilds would catch their scent and steal them away. It's harder for normal people to help sorcis like you, but it's safer for all the Black Bloods if the Guilds don't know what sort of magic we have hidden in the mountains."

A prickle sprang up on the back of my neck.

The Guilds do know. A traitor has risked all our lives.

A whistle sounded from the back of the line. The group stopped.

The sound of weapons being slid from their sheaths surrounded us, followed by the rasp of swords being tucked away a moment later.

I hated that vulnerable noise.

The outermost people came closer to the center of our group as a new batch moved to the edges to replace them. Less than a minute later, a second whistle came from the back, and we started moving forward again.

"How much longer until we reach Lygan Hall?" Dorran said with the air of someone who was quite sure they wouldn't survive the ordeal laid out before them.

"Not too long," Marta said. "But you're lucky we left camp so early this year. The weather is nice and warm."

"It is warm," Gwen said. "We're lucky to have such wonderful weather to travel."

"You don't know how lucky you are." Finn filed into step beside me. "Last time we made this trek, we had snow up to our knees. I'm honestly amazed I made it back to my mother's hearth with all my toes still attached. To be honest, not everyone was so fortunate."

"Who's missing toes?" Evie stared wide-eyed at Finn.

"That is not my secret to tell." Finn winked.

Evie pursed her lips together and began scanning the feet of everyone around her as though searching for signs of missing pieces.

Finn massaged the palm of his right hand.

"I could take your next turn on the edge," I said.

"If he were a sorcerer, he wouldn't need a sword," Dorran said.

"I'm happy to take my turn guarding," Finn said. "What's a sore hand when compared to the honor of protecting one's clan?"

"Well put," Marta said.

"I could be of use protecting the clan," I said.

"You've already been of use," Finn said.

"You're still of use." Marta raised an eyebrow toward Cinni's back.

I took a deep breath. "You know what I'm most excited to see in Lygan Hall? How all the houses are built. I've been told the houses are made of stone, but I wonder how it's done. Are the walls made of lots of rock packed together with masonry, or grown from the ground in one big piece?"

We prattled on and marched along until the sun began to set. As darkness shrouded the mountains, Liam circled the sad pack of Black Bloods, laying small stones all around us while Cati organized the night watch.

Cati took a moment, staring at each of the guards before assigning which watch they were to take. It was as though she were reading a clock set into each of the Black Bloods and judging how much time they had left before the darkness began playing tricks on them.

I was not deemed fit to stand with the other guards, so I dropped my pack onto a spare bit of ground beside a wide rock and pulled my bedroll free.

I wished we had an overhang to offer a hint of protection or even a tent so I could pretend I had a bit of privacy. Neither wish came true and I was stuck unrolling my blankets alongside the children in full view of the rest of Liam's people.

Gwen gave a huge sigh as she dropped her pack to the ground.

"I'm not tired enough to sleep," Evie said.

"I'm tired enough for both of us," Dorran said. "Just sit still and be quiet. I'll manage a double share of sleeping."

"Both of you will sleep." Gwen pulled the blankets out of her pack. "We've got another long day ahead of us, and we all need our rest."

Gwen kept her face calm as she laid out the bottom blanket the children were to share, but there was a tightness in the corners of her eyes I couldn't ignore.

I had made that same face before, when my body and soul were beaten down but my heart was not ready to surrender.

"I think we should find a place for your pack on one of the horses tomorrow." I took extra care smoothing out the edges of my blankets. "A bit more weight shouldn't bother the animals at all, and it will be better for you to move freely, Gwen."

"I'm fine." Gwen sat Cinni down and began unlacing her sister's boots. "I don't mind the pack."

"Gwen is very good at carrying things," Evie said. "She likes it."

"Very true." Finn dropped his pack next to mine. "When you left us in the woods, Gwen carried your sack of goodies all the way back to camp."

"I don't mind being of use." Gwen sat Cinni in front of her and began braiding Cinni's hair.

"There's a difference between being of use and carrying too heavy a burden," Finn said.

Gwen's face went ridged, like she'd somehow become the stone statue hidden beneath the mountain. "There is no such thing as too heavy a burden. There are only people too weak to survive."

I opened my mouth, ready to argue with the child.

But Gwen was only a few years younger than me, and she'd been bearing the weight of caring for her siblings for so long, perhaps I had no right to call her a child.

"I think everyone should have a bite of food," Marta said. "A quick dinner and then off to bed will be best for everyone."

Gwen looked down at the boots she'd already taken off her sister's feet.

"I'll bring food over." Marta gave a quick smile before disappearing into the crowd.

"It's not even real food," Dorran said.

"I've been making that same argument for years," Finn said. "No point in fussing. It doesn't make the stuff taste any better."

I elbowed Finn but couldn't completely hide my smile.

The next hour was lost in everyone trying to claim a spot to sleep and rotating the guards so everyone would greet the night well-fed. Hardtack and dried meat didn't seem like a fitting meal for more than a hundred hungry people, but I was in awe that we had enough of the horrible stuff to feed all of us. I don't know how Marta had managed to prepare for so many people to travel so quickly. Maybe she'd left the supplies for the return journey packed since they'd arrived at the camp in the spring.

When the signal came for the first watch to properly begin, I sat on top of my blankets, trying to convince myself I was actually going to sleep. I'd claimed a decent spot near a wide rock that gave me something to lean on as I watched Gwen shoo her siblings under the blankets.

The fiddler had set up close to us. Cinni lay down, still staring at the fiddle case.

I looked up through the glow of a hundred lae stones, trying to see the sky high above. I could only make out a faint hint of the stars. I knew I would be able to see more soon. The Black Bloods not chosen as the first watch would pocket their lights as they fell asleep, and the growing darkness would welcome more and more stars until the whole sky became a wash of tiny, glowing specks.

Finn clicked his tongue, calling my attention his way.

I glanced over to find him holding out a waterskin. I could smell the frie before I got the skin anywhere near my mouth.

"Not on watch then?" I whispered.

"I'm third shift." Finn sat against the rock beside me.

I took a sip of the frie, letting the strong liquor burn a path down my throat. "How much longer until we reach Lygan Hall?"

"Two days if we make good time." Finn took the skin back and had another sip.

"I don't think I ever really understood the need for the camp, but Lygan Hall really is too far from Ilbrea to be able to do much good during the warm months." I leaned against Finn's shoulder.

"The Black Bloods and the Ilbreans are meant to be two separate people," Finn whispered. "Maybe there's a reason the land tried so hard to keep us apart."

"Wishing you'd never met me?"

Finn shifted away from me.

Hurt flared in my stomach. For a moment, I thought he really did want to be rid of me, but he didn't look angry as he fished in his pocket and pulled out a worn cloth.

"When I was little, I was always taught that Ilbrea was a completely different realm than the mountains, and the people in that distant country were not like us," Finn said. "I was a descendant of the child the mountain had shielded from the gods' storm. I had stone in my blood and a connection to this land no Ilbrean could match. I had a home, an obligation to protect the mountains."

"We do have to protect the mountains from the Guilds," I said. "We can't let those murderers invade the Black Bloods' home."

"It's not just about the Guilds," Finn said. "It's about us and them. The stone in my blood should run deeper than the Guilds' control over Ilbrea."

He looked to the children. They'd all gone still.

"But what if the stone in my blood means nothing?" Finn leaned close to my ear. "What if there is no extraordinary magic in the mountains."

"There is magic in the mountains. It's saved both our lives."

"But what if it's not just in the eastern mountains." Finn unfolded the bit of cloth. A shard of dark stone glinted in the blue light.

It was only a sliver, a fragment of dark rock that should have been nothing but a tiny bit of earth to be crunched under our feet. But I recognized that bit of stone. I remembered the fear on Finn's face when he'd found the shard in the mine beneath the Lir Valley.

"This is mountain stone." Finn held the cloth close enough that I could see the lae stone light glinting off the fragment's dark surface. "This should not have been in the Lir Valley."

I took a deep breath. "Maybe it's not mountain stone. There are other sorts of rock that black. It could be obsidian."

"I can feel it." Finn bundled up the dark stone and tucked it into his pocket. "It holds the same fire as the stone in the mountains."

"But you said you weren't a trueborn."

"I'm not, thank the gods, but that doesn't mean I can't feel the stone that is supposed to course through my veins."

I took Finn's hand, lacing my fingers through his. "The mountain does run in your veins. You were born into the Duwead Clan."

"I know that. I know my family has been in the mountains since anyone bothered to keep track of where people were from."

"But?" I asked, leaning into the question he'd left hovering in the air.

"What if there was no child sheltered by the mountain?" Finn spoke so softly I could barely hear. "What if there is no special magic deep beneath the eastern mountains? What if the stone is just stone?"

"It can't be. The mountains do hold amazing magic. We've both seen it. Liam can use stone magic."

"I know that, I do. But..." Finn looked up to the stars glaring at us through the lae stone light. "What if it's all just chance? What if the magic, or whatever it is that allows the mountain to open to us, has nothing to do with a woman pouring her own magic into the stone? What if the magic was here first, and the Black Bloods just stumbled into something chivving wonderful and made up a story so it would seem like they had a right to claim this land? What if it's magic that Lir is mining in his valley?"

"Is it even possible to mine magic?"

"It's mountain stone Liam uses for the rocks that protect us and to make our lae stones. The clans used to forge the stone for other, darker magic before the treaty. If the Black Bloods could come up with foul uses for the material granted them by the mountain they adore, what horrors could beasts as evil as the Guilds achieve?"

"I…" My mind raced as I tried to come up with an argument to calm Finn. "Have you shown the stone to Liam?"

"No." Finn gripped my hand tighter.

"He's a trueborn. If anyone would be able to tell you if that really is the same stone as in the mountains, it's him. And you can't deny that stone magic doesn't exist in Ilbrea, right?"

"I don't know."

"Then ask Liam."

"I can't." Finn kissed the back of my hand. "There are some questions not worth asking."

"Why?" A hint of dread swooped through my stomach.

"Everything the Black Bloods believe comes from the story of the child beloved by the mountain. Our laws, our clans, our borders. We live and die because a mother poured her magic into the cold, dead stone inside the mountain. If that isn't true, if we're just a pack of wanderers who happened on a magical place and decided to claim it, everything we are has been built on a lie. The clans are barely maintaining peace as it is. We'd be lost. We'd all be lost."

"There's a city under the mountains," I said. "When the mountain swallowed me, I found it. People lived down there once. A whole mess of them. There was a fountain and gardens. It would have taken a long time to build."

"Were there still people down there?"

"It'd been abandoned. A long time ago from the looks of it. I told Liam."

"What did he say?"

"That he was glad the mountain had protected me."

Finn kissed my temple. "Have you told anyone else?"

"No. I almost told Case, but—"

"Don't," Finn said. "Don't tell anyone."

"Why not?"

"Because whether it's the mountain, the gods, or the stars, something has kept me alive this long. And whatever that force might be, it's screaming in my gut that fire and death are lurking in the shadows."

I tried to think of something comforting to stay as the lights kept dimming around us, but the dread in my stomach had turned into a prickle on the back of my neck, as though Death lurked behind me and his own chill breath tickled my skin.

19

Liam's arm weighed heavy on my side when I woke in the morning, assuring me that I was someplace safe and hadn't drifted into a foul and terrible dream.

"You can rest a little longer," Liam whispered in my ear.

"Have you slept at all?" I twisted to face him, finding a new rock to dig into my side.

"Of course." He kissed my forehead.

"You need at least a bit of rest. If you drop from exhaustion, who will keep the stones going to protect us?"

"It's only a bit farther, and we'll be safe in Lygan Hall."

We lay still for a while. I hoped he was drifting to sleep, though from the pace of his breathing, he was still awake.

I didn't want to try to picture Lygan Hall—I knew I could never do the place justice—but a childish part of me couldn't help but imagine grand stone hallways filled with magic.

I drifted back to sleep with images of Liam riding on a stone horse flitting through my mind.

When he woke me for the day, half the bedrolls had been packed up. A string of little cook fires had been lit, and Neil lorded over them, making sure no person or horse disrupted his work.

"What does Neil do in Lygan Hall?" I asked as I rolled up my bedding.

"His family tend sheep in the outskirts of the settlement." A hint of a smile curved one corner of Liam's mouth.

I stopped working on my pack to watch him, not wanting to miss a moment of that beautiful expression.

"Neil's got a flock of children to match his sheep," Liam said. "They tend the animals for him in the warm months."

"But if he's got a family, why is he running off to cook in camp?"

"Almost everyone in the camp has some sort of family in Lygan Hall. They sacrifice their time at home to help protect all Black Bloods against the Guilds. It is a great honor to journey west and work to stop the paun from invading the eastern mountains." Liam leaned close to me. "If you want the honest truth, though, Neil's wife volunteered him to come and cook in the camp."

I bit back my laugh. "I'm not sure if she's brilliant or evil for having dropped him on us."

"We're not starving." Liam tied his blankets to his own pack. "And she's got a bit of peace. Seems like a fair enough trade."

"I wonder what she'll think of him coming home early."

Liam finished tying his pack closed before he answered. "I don't know what any of them will think of us returning so early. We can only have faith in Orla's judgment."

I took Liam's hand and pressed his palm to my cheek. "I'm glad I'll still be with you."

"I don't think I could breathe if you weren't." He kissed my forehead, shouldered his pack, and walked to the eastern-most part of our group.

The morning passed like the others had, with everyone speaking in hushed voices as we all packed up and snagged a bit of slop to eat.

Cati would whistle from the western-most tip of the group, and the first guards would head to the edge of Liam's stones. Once their weapons were drawn, Liam would walk the perimeter of the place we'd slept, collecting the rocks. The children would watch in awe as the stones flew up from the ground and into his leather pouch one by one, stacking in more weight for Liam to carry.

I pressed my pendant to my chest as he tucked the pouch of stones into his pack and started leading us east.

I still wore the pendant hidden beneath my bodice. I didn't have a real reason for not wanting people to see it—all of them knew I'd been sharing his bed—but the stone felt too intimate to be displayed. I'd let the pendant be seen in Ilbrea without worry, but the Black Bloods would know that Liam had made it for me. I didn't know how many might guess why.

I studied the peaks of the mountains around us as the children kept up their patter of words. I'd started to find it soothing, even when I didn't listen to exactly what they were saying. I wondered if Cinni felt the same. If the rhythm of her siblings' speech was nothing more than a gentle rain against the canvas of a tent, hushing the world and lulling her into a steady calm.

The noise stilled my nerves as I squinted against the sun to see the summits around us.

Liam had led us into a valley that cut between two massive mountains, but even the peaks that loomed over us were nothing to the mammoths towering above them. The snow-covered summits stood out against the sky, glittering white in the morning sun.

Even though I wasn't cold, I pulled my coat tighter around me, as though I could somehow stop winter from coming by carefully keeping myself warm.

"Right, Ena?"

I turned toward Evie, scrambling to think what I was supposed to be agreeing to.

"I don't think so," Marta said. "You'll have a nice place to live, but I don't think it will be with Ena."

"Why not?" Evie asked.

Gwen's face turned pink, and she carefully studied her shoes.

"I…" I swallowed, feeling like my throat had suddenly started to close as heat rose up into my cheeks.

"Ena will have to go back to camp to help other sorcis when the weather warms up again," Marta said. "We're going to find you four a nice place to live with someone who will be with you all the time."

"Oh." Evie furrowed her brow. "Can we live with you, then?"

Marta's face paled a shade. "I don't think so."

"Marta's got work to do in camp, too," I said. "She's got the most important job of all."

"What's that?" Evie said.

"Keeping everyone fed and in line," Dorran said. "I can't think of a tougher job."

"Thank you, Dorran," Marta said.

"I would have thought you'd be too smart to say yes to it," Dorran said.

"Then don't go next year." Evie seized Marta's hand. "Stay with us and take care of us. I promise, we'll be just as difficult as caring for the camp."

"I don't think that's how to—"

Cinni's gasp silenced Gwen.

The other three children froze, staring at Cinni.

I tensed, waiting for the ground to writhe to life and trap me.

"You'll be all right." Marta stepped in front of Cinni. "I promise there will be someone to take care of you."

Cinni clapped her hands over her ears and looked to Evie.

Evie wrinkled her brow and tipped her head to the side. "I don't hear anything."

"What is there to hear?" the fiddler turned around to ask.

People looked toward us in a wave as more of the group realized we'd stopped moving.

"There's nothing," Evie said. "Just the thumping of all of us walking."

Cinni's breath came in quick gasps as her gaze darted around as though she were desperately hunting for something.

"You're all right, Cinni." Gwen pressed her own hands on top of Cinni's, adding an extra layer over the child's ears. "We're all together, and we're going someplace wonderful."

Cinni started shaking, like she longed to run or might catch fire and burn us all.

"Just breathe, Cinni," Gwen said. "You've got to breathe."

"Oh no," Evie whispered.

The world seemed to fall silent as I looked toward her.

"Something's coming." Evie met my gaze. "They're so big."

"Liam!" I pulled my knife from my boot. "Which way, Evie?"

"Everywhere." Evie grabbed Gwen's arm. "They're everywhere."

Liam raced toward me, his sword already drawn.

"Something's coming," I shouted. "There's something—"

"To the north!" a man bellowed.

I looked to see what the man had spotted, but a scream from the southern edge of our pack came before I could find what the man had seen.

Liam looked south before he reached my side. He froze, his sword raised. For an instant, it looked as though he were balancing on the edge of the world, trying to reason through which direction led to an endless doom and which to salvation.

Another scream came from the south.

"Stay with the children! Stay at the center." Liam charged south, shouting as he raised his blade.

This time, I did catch sight of the terror that had descended upon us.

The beast had white fur, which had been matted with deep red blood. The creature's claws flashed in the morning light as it slashed through the stomach of one of the Black Bloods. A spray of red flew through the air.

Liam kept running toward the blood.

I wanted to shout his name, wanted to call him back to me, but I was terrified that distracting him might cost him his life.

The fiddler dropped her case and pulled her short sword from its sheath.

A horrible cry came from the eastern edge of our pack.

"Stay right here, children," the fiddler said. "A nice tight group, that's how we do this."

Marta held a knife in her hand. I didn't know where she'd pulled it from.

"Cinni, you've got to breathe." Gwen hadn't looked away from her sister.

A visceral cry of rage and grief came from the south.

Cinni groaned.

"Please, Cinni," Gwen begged. "Breathe. You've got to breathe."

I scanned the chaos around me, searching for an impossible remedy to the bloodshed and fear.

Two beasts attacked us on every side.

Blood and screams swept around me like the raging wind of a storm.

"We can't let them do this. They've all got to stop." Evie charged north, racing toward the monsters.

"Evie, no!" I sprinted after her, gripping my knife.

Evie pulled her hands back before she even reached the edge of our people.

I held my breath as she shoved her palms forward.

A hiss and a crack split the air. The monster did not stagger or sink to the ground.

"Just die!" Evie screamed.

The beast turned its awful pale eyes toward Evie. Its dark fur didn't betray any hint of the blood the monster had spilt as it charged toward us.

Evie lashed her hand through the air as the beast drew near her. I raced to her side, gripping my knife, knowing there was nothing I could do to defend the child against the monster's terrible claws.

But the monster staggered and stopped as flames erupted from its fur. The beast let out a horrible keening snarl and stumbled back.

"Evie, we need to get back to the others," I said.

I don't know whether she heard me or not.

She raced toward the next monster. This one had patchy fur that didn't match in length or color. Its legs were all different sizes, like someone had gotten confused in its creation.

Croilach.

The misshapen beast caught fire as well but didn't slow its attack. The croilach swiped its flaming claws, slashing through Patrick's stomach.

"Stop!" Evie shouted, but a louder cry drowned out her voice as Cati charged the flaming croilach.

My heart leapt up into my throat as Cati plunged her blade into the monster's chest.

"Cut out its heart!" I shouted as I raced toward Cati.

Black coated her sword as she pulled it from the croilach's chest and swung for the beast's neck.

The monster batted Cati's blade aside.

She dove to the ground, rolling beneath the monster's claws, and leapt back up to her feet. The monster lunged toward her, and she drove her blade back into the croilach's chest. The monster growled but showed no signs of dropping.

Cati twisted her blade in the beast's chest with one hand while yanking her knife from her boot with the other.

The monster gnashed its teeth at Cati's neck.

"Stop it!" Evie slammed her fist through the air, and the beast's flaming head jerked to the side as though the child had actually struck the monster.

That moment was all Cati needed. She drove her knife between the monster's ribs and leveraged the blade against her sword, ripping the stone heart from the beast's chest.

20

It seemed like the battle should have stopped. Cati had killed a croilach. But there were seven more monsters attacking our people.

Cati left the bloody stone heart on the ground and charged the other monster Evie had set on fire.

"We need to get back to the others." I reached for Evie, but she dodged away from me, racing toward the fight on the eastern edge.

One of the beasts on that side had been surrounded by a dozen fighters. The other had broken through the ranks of the Black Bloods, leaving its victims screaming on the ground. Both croilach burst into flames as Evie sprinted toward them.

A wail came from the southern edge where Liam had gone to fight.

I spun toward the sound.

A new noise cut over all the clamor of the battle, a scream that pierced my mind and shook the world.

"Cinni." Sour rolled into my mouth as I said her name. I forced my feet to move and ran toward her.

The ground split beneath me, forming cracks that grew with each heartbeat. I leapt over a fissure in the earth, stumbling as I landed on the trembling ground.

Gwen had wrapped her arms around her sister and spoke into Cinni's ear, though what she said I had no hope of hearing over that terrible scream.

The ground shook again. The fiddler's case tipped into a crack in the earth and tumbled into the darkness.

I watched Gwen's mouth move, forming words that looked horribly like *I'm sorry.*

Bright light poured from her skin as she stepped away from Cinni.

"Stop!" I tried to shout the word, but all the air had vanished from my lungs.

Cinni's scream fell silent as the glow around Gwen grew, pulsing and flashing, until a bright burst of radiant light soared from her body, covering the battlefield with its brilliance.

449

The world went quiet for a moment as Gwen swayed and fell.

I leapt forward, catching her before she could slip into one of the cracks in the earth.

Sound came back into being as I clutched Gwen in my arms.

The screaming only carried from one side. The east.

I looked up to see Liam leaping across the shattered ground, racing toward the battle.

Red flew through the air as another Black Blood met a horrible end.

"Gwen." I laid her flat on the ground, but I couldn't tear my gaze from Liam.

He held out his hand, and a storm of stone rose from the earth and plunged into the monster.

The beast reared back, exposing its chest.

A horrible black misted through the air as the croilach's stone heart burst from its chest and soared into Liam's hand.

Then the din of the battle ended, and the sounds of grief and pain took over.

Liam looked back across the battlefield toward me. Gore coated him, but he was on his feet without any sign of life-threatening injury.

"Gwen, I need you to look at me." I tore my gaze from Liam.

Gwen seemed younger as she lay unconscious on the ground, like the child she wasn't allowed to be.

"She won't wake up." Dorran clung to Marta's arm. "There's nothing you can do for her."

"Has this happened before?" I asked.

"Not this bad," Dorran said.

"Then we can't just leave her like this." I pressed my fingers to the side of Gwen's throat. The faint thump of her pulse still carried through her skin. I laid a hand on her chest. Her ribs still rose and fell with each breath.

I couldn't see anything wrong with her that should have left her unconscious.

"I need to find Winnie." I stood to search for her, and the whole world came crashing down.

The cracks in the earth had spread out like a giant spiderweb, leaving chunks of solid ground standing in towers that looked as though they might tip and fall into the darkness from one ill-timed breath. Our safe havens were nothing more than columns reaching to depths reason declared impossible. The little island the children, Marta, and I stood on was the largest patch of solid ground left, with a gap more than six feet wide separating us from the next bits of land.

The rest was all tatters and blood.

Around the edges lay dead and wounded Black Bloods. Cati was already leaping over cracks, trying to reach the ones too wounded to move on their own. Others were trying to help as well, but some of the gaps were too large to cross and some of the people too far gone for help to make any difference.

"Cinni." I knelt in front of her. Tears streamed from her fear-filled eyes. "Cinni, I know you were trying to help. I know you wanted to keep the monsters away, and you did a wonderful job, but I need you to help me again. I need you to put the ground back together."

Cinni looked toward the crack in the earth where the fiddle player's case had tumbled into darkness.

A horrible pained scream came from the east.

"There are people who need my help," I whispered. "There are people who are hurt, and I need to get to them. I need to get to Winnie so she can help Gwen."

"I can try to do it." Dorran let go of Marta and stepped toward me. "But Cinni's magic is bigger than mine. I don't know if I can move that much at once."

"Cinni can do it." Terror clenched my chest as someone called my name from the west. "Cinni, I know you're scared, but that doesn't mean you aren't brave. Being afraid doesn't make you any less strong. I need you to do this for me. I need you to be strong and help me so I can help them."

Cinni reached forward and touched my cheek, running her fingers across my skin as though brushing away tears I was too afraid to cry.

"Please," I whispered.

Cinni balled her hands into white-knuckled fists and screwed up her forehead as though she wanted nothing more than to scream at the top of her lungs.

Crack.

The noise shook the ground, and a fresh wave of cries filled the air.

Crack.

The earth shuddered as rocks flew up from far below, filling the web of gaps with shining black stone that glimmered in the sunlight.

"Thank you." I stood, searching for any hint of Winnie.

The pattern of the black against the mountain dirt should have been beautiful, but as I sprinted across the dark stone, it seemed like a giant spiderweb trying to trap us all, or worse, a dark stain on the land that would become a monument to the horror of the croilach's attack.

"Winnie!" I shouted as I ran west. "Winnie."

"Ena!"

I turned toward the sound of my name.

Nessa knelt on the ground beside a man so covered in blood I couldn't properly see his face.

"Are you hurt?" I sprinted toward Nessa.

The man beside her screamed in pain.

"I'm fine." Nessa's voice trembled. "Shane was bitten by that monster. I don't know what to do."

I knelt next to Shane.

The croilach had bitten his shoulder, shredding both flesh and coat.

I wiped the blood from the wound with my own sleeve. Indigo blue lines trailed through Shane's skin.

"I'm sorry," I said. "There's nothing to be done for him."

"No," Nessa said.

"I have to find Winnie."

"No!" Nessa shouted after me as I sprinted away. "You can't just leave us. You have to help him!"

I passed three more already screaming in pain from the venom in the croilach's bite. Others were luckier.

Patrick lay still on the ground, his blank eyes open to the sky, his stomach torn by terrible claws. His death had at least been quick.

I raced past Tirra, who stood between four horses, trying to calm them.

451

Winnie's dark blue bag was still tied to one of the horse's backs.

I turned around and sprinted back toward the horse.

The bay stomped her foot.

"Don't charge the horses," Tirra snapped.

"I need Winnie's bag."

I don't know if the bay recognized the desperation in my voice or remembered me from the time she'd spent carrying me through the mountains, but she stood still as I untied the dark blue bag.

"Ena!" Liam's voice cut above the rest of the chaos.

I turned to find him racing toward me.

"Are you hurt?" I tried to search him for wounds, but he was too covered in black and red gore for me to be able to see if he had been injured. "Were you bitten?"

"I'm fine." Liam reached for me but stopped before touching me with his bloody hands. "So many people are hurt. I don't know how to help them."

"Where's Winnie?"

"She didn't make it." There was no grief in Liam's voice. He just sounded hollow.

I let myself have one breath—just one moment where panic raced through my veins.

"If the injured can be moved, take them all to the eastern edge," I said. "Put pressure on the wounds of everyone who hasn't been bitten. Try to keep them from losing too much blood."

"What about the ones that can't be moved?"

"Have someone stay with them," I said. "I don't want anyone to die alone."

2 1

Two Black Bloods were missing. I think they fell into the cracks in the ground with one of the horses and three of the monsters.

Twelve Black Bloods were dead before the battle had ended. Dorran used his magic to dig graves for them before the wounded had been gathered.

Six Black Bloods had been bitten. Their screams will haunt me for the rest of my life. I still don't know if it would have been kinder to cut their throats and relieve them of their agony.

Seven Black Bloods were too badly wounded for me to be of any help. I don't think Lily or Winnie would have been able to save any of them either. The croilach's claws had sliced too deep.

Dorran dug that set of graves before I had finished seeing to the people I could help.

Fourteen Black Bloods were wounded in the end. I stitched up the ones I could, stealing the frie from everyone's secret supplies to clean the wounds. I set a broken leg and wrapped cracked ribs with sliced strips of blanket.

By the time I'd patched up everyone well enough for us to start moving again, the ones who'd been bitten had fallen silent.

Dorran dug twenty-five graves before we'd loaded the worst off onto the horses and paired the other wounded with someone strong enough to help them keep moving forward.

I wanted to tell Liam we needed to stop, to set up the little stone boundary and let the wounded rest. But the scent of blood clung to all of us and wafted away from us on the wind like a siren's call luring in other beasts who wanted to slay us.

The whistle came from the back. Cati hadn't been hurt, not badly at least. She'd only needed a bandage and some salve on her burned arm.

None of the people I cared for most had been terribly wounded. I was lucky. My relief made me ill.

I stayed close to Liam at the front of the pack, with the children just behind me.

Neil carried Gwen in his arms.

She looked like a sleeping doll. I still hadn't thought of anything that might help wake her.

Marta had taken Gwen's place, holding tight to Cinni's hand and whispering comforting words.

Case walked with one arm around Finn's waist. Finn had gotten a slice on the arm that cut through to the muscle. Case kept glancing to Finn as we walked, terror creasing the corners of his eyes as though Finn might drop at any moment.

I didn't blame Case for his fear. Finn had lost enough blood that his pale face looked like a death mask.

"This shouldn't have happened." Case's voice was hoarse. I don't know if it was from screaming or from horror at what the monsters had stolen from us. "This should never have happened."

"This is what happens when there's vermin hiding in your home." Finn's voice came out worse than Case's had.

"Don't," I said. "Save your strength to keep moving."

Finn looked at me and opened his mouth to speak.

"We can talk once you've rested." I shot a glance to the children. "For now, we need to keep moving."

"We're not stopping until we reach the gates of Lygan Hall," Liam said. "We march through the night."

I took two quick steps forward so I could see his face.

Blood had smeared and spattered across his skin and clothes. The sword he carried in one hand still had a streak of black on the hilt. In his other hand, he held a fistful of stones, which, in a trueborn's grasp, were more deadly than any blade.

I had seen many sides of Liam before. Protector, friend, confidant, leader, lover. I had never seen the warrior. Not really. I'd seen him fight, but I'd never seen him hungry for blood.

"You're going to love the gates of Lygan Hall," Marta said. "The inside is beautiful, and then you'll get to have a nice meal and sleep in a warm bed. Won't you like that, Cinni? Then all four of you will get to learn from the sorcerers. I can't wait to see what wonderful things they teach you."

Neither Evie nor Dorran added to the patter.

I took a deep breath and forced my rage behind the shroud of fire that crackled in my chest. "I think you're going to learn lots of nice things. And I hear there's a lovely garden packed with all sorts of herbs and flowers. We'll have a long walk, then a nice sleep, and then you'll get to learn and see the garden. Won't that be a wonder, Cinni?"

My throat went raw as the hours passed, but I was too afraid to ask Marta for silence. One of the wounded died. Dorran had a grave dug before anyone asked for his aid. Then the horse was free to carry Gwen.

She lay draped across the animal's back. Still breathing, but with no other sign of life.

Neil stayed close to her even after the horse had taken over the task of carrying her weight.

Cati gave the whistle to rotate the guard, and even though different people took the edge of our group, not a single Black Blood sheathed their weapon.

When the sun began to sink in the sky, no one pulled out their lae stone. We traveled in darkness with only the stars to light our path until we reached the lip of a rise.

Liam stopped and looked down the slope in front of us. Even in the darkness, I could tell the path ahead was too narrow for us to continue in our wide formation.

"We could stop here for the night," Marta whispered. "Lay out the stones and wait for sunrise."

"We aren't stopping," Liam said. "We are not sitting down and waiting for the next disaster to strike."

He pulled his lae stone from his pocket. The magic in the sphere glowed more brightly than normal, as though it recognized the magic in Liam's blood. Or maybe the light fed off his rage.

He stepped onto the winding path that led down the slope.

It was the first proper path I'd seen while traveling in the eastern mountains. I didn't like taking such an obvious route, but as I followed Finn and Case, I understood why enough people had walked this trail to wear down the ground.

The dirt on the trail was loose and shifted with each step, but if I'd strayed from the path, the ground would've given way, leaving me to tumble down the side of the slope.

To the north and south of the trail, rocky cliffs overtook the terrain. I might have been able to make that climb in the daylight but not in the dark. And most of the Black Bloods couldn't have scaled those rock walls, even if a pack of monsters hadn't decided to attack us.

Liam pocketed his lae stone and slowed his pace as he reached the bottom of the rise, giving the rest of the group time to catch up. But he didn't stop. He kept pushing forward through the wide valley that seemed to have been scooped out by a giant's hand. I wanted to ask if there was some sort of legend as to how the valley had been formed, but I didn't want to hear another story. Wondering how much truth hid in legends was more than my mind could bear.

I tried to distract myself by examining the plants in the valley instead. Everyone had put away their lights, so I couldn't see much more than shadows. There were scrub bushes and a few hardy-looking wildflowers, but nothing that gave me any hope of a large group of people being able to forage and survive.

I tried studying the stars above me as I kept up the endless chatter for the children.

None of it could drown out the word banging in my head.

Traitor. Traitor. Traitor.

I wanted to scream the word into the night. Keep screaming it over and over until whoever had brought this hell down upon us confessed their crimes. I would see them cower in fear and then watch them die.

I didn't know the face of the person I hated so badly, but I knew what their fate would be and looked forward to their terrible end.

My legs and feet moved beyond sore to throbbing and then went numb as the cold of the night surrounded us.

Still, Liam led us onward.

When Finn's steps started to falter, I gently looped his injured arm over my shoulder, bearing some of his weight as he sagged closer to the ground.

How much farther?

I wanted to ask but wasn't sure the children could survive the answer.

A great string of mountains rose up in front of us, soaring so high I wasn't sure I had the strength left to climb them.

Liam quickened his pace, and everyone else in the line followed without complaint.

As we traveled through the shadows, the summits never seemed to grow any nearer.

We will be trapped in the dark forever.

I would have thought I'd be more grateful for the stars.

The base of the mountains rose up in front of us.

I gritted my teeth, determined not to be the one who endangered our group by slowing my pace.

"A warm bed and good food, that's what's waiting for you," Marta said. "I need you to be ready for lots of people and bright lights first, but after that, I promise I'll find you a nice, warm place to rest."

Liam stopped. So did Case and Finn. My knees almost buckled as I tried to remember how to stand still.

"I am Liam, Trueborn Duwead, returning to his home in Lygan Hall on the orders of Orla, Elder of the Duwead Clan. We have been attacked on our journey. Many were killed, and we have wounded desperately in need of care. We ask for safe passage and need your help."

I strained my eyes, trying to see who lurked in the darkness. There was nothing but stone.

"Open the gates for your Trueborn." Liam's voice rang through the night.

I leaned down, trying to reach the knife tucked in my boot without letting go of Finn.

My breath caught in my throat, and my body tensed, preparing for an attack, as a bright slice of light cut through the night.

22

I shielded my eyes and blinked against the growing glow.

A crack had appeared in the side of the mountain. The light that shone out of the stone wasn't the blue I'd become accustomed to, but instead glowed a warm, dazzling orange, as though a thousand torches lit whatever wonders waited beyond.

Liam led us forward but didn't sheath his sword or toss aside his handful of stones.

The light of the cavern streamed out into the night, casting him in a striking silhouette, like something out of a story. A warrior venturing into a world of magic.

I wanted to run after him to be sure no magic could separate us, but I couldn't let go of Finn.

"We're nearly there," Case said. "Just a bit farther and you won't have to walk anymore."

"I'll keep walking if you promise a proper chivving meal," Finn murmured.

More silhouettes joined Liam's as we neared the gate of Lygan Hall. Men and women all bearing swords, all flocking toward Liam while keeping their weapons raised to fight off whatever beast waited in the shadows.

"I need to go to Orla," Liam said as soon as he stepped into the mouth of the cavern.

"I'll let her know to expect you." A young man with dark skin and no hair at all on his head ran down the long tunnel.

But it wasn't a tunnel. Not really. That word can't describe the outer chamber.

The space was wide enough to fit three houses. The opening to the outside spanned the entire width, as did the line of armed guards. The ceiling was twenty feet high and set with dazzling orange orbs that cast their shimmering glow on everything in sight.

Real torches burned along the walls, reaching to the back of the wide space where the room narrowed into a tunnel blocked by metal gates.

"Wes," Liam said, "we need healers, everyone you've got available. Now."

A man with black hair sprinted away.

I helped Finn past the line of guards and into the center of the chamber.

A woman with gray streaks in her hair stepped in front of us. "Let's get him down." She took my place under Finn's arm. "Your mother is going to have a chivving fit, Finn, coming home a bloody mess like this."

"She'll be glad of it." Finn smiled as he sank to the ground. "You know how she likes to fuss."

"Ailis," Liam called. "Ailis!"

"I'm here, Liam." A girl with flaming red, curly hair ran toward him.

"Take her to the crag." Liam pointed to me. "See her cared for, and keep her guarded."

"Good to have you back." Ailis started toward me.

"Ailis," Liam said, "do not leave her."

"I won't." She reached for my arm.

"Liam, I should stay with you." I backed away from the girl.

"Go with her." Liam didn't look at me. "Get the outer gate closed!"

Men ran toward the far corner.

I wanted to stay and see what people could possibly do to make the mountain move, but Ailis gripped my arm, dragging me forward.

"I should stay here," I said. "I can help with the others. There are children who need to get settled."

"Someone else will do that," Ailis said.

"How do you know?"

"Because Liam told me to take you to the crag." She strode down the chamber so quickly, my numb feet could barely keep up.

"I can help here," I said.

She squeezed my arm tighter. "I've been told to take you to the crag, and you're going." Ailis stopped at the metal gate.

A man peered through the bars before swinging it open. A second metal gate waited just beyond.

"If you have a problem with Liam's orders, take it up with him." Ailis led me through the second gate.

I wanted to argue, but my mind had gotten stuck on the racks of weapons lining the sides of the room. There were hundreds of swords, bows, spears, and knives all along the walls, as though an entire army hid behind the stone, ready to march at a moment's notice.

A line of people tore past us, heading back toward the outer chamber. Each of them had a heavy pack on their back. I hoped they were the healers.

We reached another gate that another man had to peer through before letting us pass.

On the far side, the tunnel split in five directions. One path led straight forward, two branched up to the right and left, and two sloped downward just beside them. Ailis steered me toward the upper left corridor.

"Stop." I wrenched my arm away from her.

"We should keep moving." Ailis reached toward me.

"No." I held up my hand. The orange light cast a horrible glow on the blood staining my skin. "I don't know you. I don't know where you're leading me. I don't trust you, and I have to know how to find Liam."

Ailis pursed her lips for a moment before speaking. "I'm taking you to the crag."

"How do I know that?"

"Because Liam told me to."

"That doesn't mean anything. You could be leading me anywhere, and I wouldn't know the difference."

"Look." Ailis gave a false smile. "I don't know who under the chivving stars you are. I don't know why you're here. But Liam, my Trueborn, has given me orders to take you to the crag, see that you're cared for, and guard you. I can drag you up this tunnel by your hair, or you can walk nicely. Either way is fine with me, but you are going to the crag."

"Unless you decide to slit my throat." Pain pressed against my chest. "I need to go back there. I have to make sure they're safe. We lost so many today. I can't—We can't lose any more."

A crack appeared in Ailis's armor. "Who did you lose?"

"Winnie, Patrick. Twenty-eight today."

Ailis's neck tightened. I wasn't sure if she wanted to scream or cry. "Do you trust Liam?"

"Absolutely." I pressed my blood-covered hand to my chest, needing to feel the shape of the stone pendant against my skin.

"He ordered me to take care of you. Would he have done that if he didn't trust me?"

"Never."

"All right then, let's go." She started toward the tunnel.

"What about the others?" I took a step back, toward the outer chamber. "I can't abandon them."

"Chivving just—" Ailis laid her tongue over her teeth. "You can't trust a trueborn and think they can't care for their own people. So move. Now."

My breath rattled in my chest.

You have nothing if you can't trust him.

I nodded and tucked my hands into my pockets, as though hiding the awful stains could somehow separate me from the horrors of the day.

"What happened to all of you anyway?" Ailis led me into the tunnel.

The gentle slope of it curved and wound up in a spiral.

"We were attacked," I said.

"By who?" Ailis tightened her grip on her sword.

"Does it matter?"

"If I'm supposed to protect you, then yes."

"Why you?"

"I thought you said you trusted our Trueborn." Ailis looked at me, raising one red eyebrow.

"Good people can still be wrong about evil men."

Corridors branched off the still-spiraling tunnel, but Ailis kept leading me up.

"I've known Liam since before either of us could talk." Ailis cut right, down a wide corridor that led to a staircase.

Two guards waited at the bottom of the stairs. Both nodded and let her pass without asking why the girl with her was covered in blood.

"Liam and I are about as close as two people can get," Ailis said. "I have no idea why he wants you in the crag, but I trust him. So I'll fight and risk my chivving life to protect you."

Six guards with swords drawn waited in front of the intricately carved metal door that blocked the path ahead of us. The guards stepped aside and opened the door before Ailis and I had to slow our steps. A wide hall with walls polished to gleaming black perfection greeted us beyond the fancy door.

"Is Liam safe here?" I asked. "Will there be guards to protect him?"

Ailis glanced over her shoulder, looking at me with a puckered brow. "We are the Duwead Clan. We would do anything to protect Liam."

She stopped at a wooden door. She didn't knock or anything before shoving it open.

"Wash up in the back. I'll see that you have something clean to wear."

I stepped through the door, and Ailis closed me into the darkness.

23

I'd often been grateful for the light of my lae stone, but the gleam of it meant more to me as I stood in that dark room.

A wardrobe sat against one wall, while a vanity and chair sat along the other. A bed, wide enough to fit three people, took up the entire middle of the room. White blankets lay on top of the bed. They looked sickly in the light of my lae stone, like they'd been contaminated by a croilach's venom.

Sour rose in my throat, and my stomach trembled.

A door stood open at the back of the room.

I ran toward it, trying to convince my stomach to be as strong as my heart.

A metal cylinder waited in the corner. I dropped to my knees and emptied the sparse contents of my stomach. My hands trembled as I leaned against the cold stone of the wall.

I wanted to be angry at the world and the traitor. I wanted to rage and fight. I wanted to bolt past Ailis and find Liam.

"He knows her." I gripped my light in my hand and forced myself to stand. My legs wobbled as I walked to the stone tub and turned on the silver taps. "He would not have sent you with her if he didn't trust her." I set my light on the ground and let my pack fall from my shoulders. "Liam would not place you in danger."

My fingers protested being asked to work enough to undress myself.

Steam rose from the tub by the time I'd finally managed to shed my blood-caked clothes.

"He would not have sent you away if he were in danger." I could not stomach my own lie. I raced to empty my belly again.

The hot water of the bath could not convince me he was safe. The soft cloth I dried myself on did not mean he hadn't been killed. The fine feathers of the bed did not mean I would ever be able to sleep in his arms again. But exhaustion still stole the world from me, and I drifted into blackness, unsure of what I would find should I ever wake up.

2 4

Bright light beamed into my eyes, making me quite sure I was back outside the gates of Lygan Hall, left in the open with a herd of monsters eager to kill me.

I reached for the knife under my pillow before I'd even opened my eyes.

But the bright strip of light streaming into my room wasn't from the outer chamber, and I wasn't outside.

I wrapped a white sheet around me as I crawled off the feather mattress, searching the corners of the room for any hint of a person waiting to attack. I crept toward the bathroom, still gripping my knife, but there was no one in there either.

I didn't move toward the strip of light until I was sure I was alone.

Shame weighed on my shoulders as I realized I hadn't noticed the shutters in the stone wall the night before. With the light streaming between them, it seemed a horrible danger to have missed.

The shutters were only made of wood, nothing that could be considered battle worthy, and the window was nearly as big as a door, more than large enough for a person, or monster, to slip through.

I tightened the sheet around my chest before pushing the shutters open.

A vast valley stretched out before me. The bright morning light bathed the houses, fields, and patches of dense trees in a beautiful glow.

Snowcapped mountains surrounded the valley like soldiers standing guard, protecting Lygan Hall.

A cliff face stretched out on either side of me, with other windows scattered in all directions. High above, a balcony poked out of the rock, and far below, a raised garden had stairs that reached down to the valley floor.

People already roamed through the paths of the garden. None of them moved like a monster might come for their blood.

A dark bird soared across the bright blue sky, looping and swirling in blissful freedom.

"How do they convince anyone to leave?"

I had pictured Lygan Hall as a sturdy place made of stone with surviving the mountain winters the only concern in its building. I had never pictured a valley paradise.

A click sounded from the other side of the room.

I spun around, gripping my knife as the door swung open.

Ailis stepped into the room. Her gaze slid from the knife in my hand to the sheet wrapped around my body.

"At least you're clean," Ailis said. "I assume you're hungry as well."

"Where's Liam?" I didn't lower my knife.

"I've no idea." Ailis beckoned in two women. One carried a tray of food, the other pushed in a long, rolling trunk. "Last I heard, he went to see Orla."

"I have to find him," I said.

"If Liam wanted to see you, he would be here," Ailis said. "Since he's not here, you're going to eat and put on a decent set of clothes."

"I'm not hungry."

"I didn't ask if you were hungry," Ailis said. "I told you you were going to eat."

The woman with the tray set the food on the vanity table and left. The woman with the rolling trunk hovered awkwardly for a moment.

"Yes?" Ailis turned to the woman.

"I don't know what size boots?" the woman said. "Liam said to be sure she was cared for—"

"You've seen Liam?" I started toward the woman.

Ailis stepped into my path.

"I will walk through this place naked," I said. "Do not test me."

"Take her boots and work from there," Ailis said.

"Where did you see Liam?" I asked as the woman scampered to my pile of blood-crusted clothes.

"I was called to Orla's council room." The woman gingerly lifted my boots.

"When? Is he still there?" I asked.

"Out," Ailis said. "Now."

The woman curtsied and hurried through the door.

"Where is the council room?" I headed toward my pack.

"It doesn't matter, because you're not going."

"I have to find Liam." I rounded on Ailis. "We were attacked. People were killed. I don't know if he's safe."

"He's in Lygan Hall."

"That doesn't mean anything!" My voice bounced off the stone walls of the room. "If Liam trusts you enough to protect me, I would have thought you'd be smart enough to know that."

Ailis looked up to the ceiling, as though searching for guidance from the gods. "I can't take you to the council room. I can't let you leave this room. If I have to set a pack of guards on you, I will, but it would be safer for everyone if you'd just agree to stay put. If Liam wanted you brought to the crag and protected by me, then it's clear he's worried about your safety.

"So, instead of running around trying to see if you can get into trouble, can't you just stay here and trust that Liam's doing what's best? Or at the very least stay safely in here so he doesn't get hurt running around trying to save you?"

"I thought you said Liam was safe." I looked to the window. "What would he have to save me from?"

"Whatever had him so fussed he ordered your protection and comfort before he bothered to close the chivving outer gate." Ailis sighed. "Please just eat some food. Then we'll get you into some proper clothes. If Liam still hasn't come by then, I'll send a runner to the council room to tell him you're looking for him."

I eyed the door to the hall.

"You won't make it out of this corridor without a flock of guards stopping you," Ailis said.

"Fine." I sat at the vanity, staring at the tray of food.

I'd been brought fruit, cheese, and rolls that still radiated heat. After days of trudging through the mountains, I should have been grateful for the bounty.

"Who are you anyway?" Ailis stepped up beside me and snagged a bit of cheese from the plate.

I opened my mouth to speak but couldn't find the right words.

The one Liam promised to share a bed with sounded absurd even in my head. Petal whore would have been the most common description. Lover might have worked if I'd been able to say the word aloud without feeling like a chivving fool.

"I'm Emmet's sister."

"Emmet?" Ailis said. "I didn't see him last night. He wasn't killed in the attack was he?"

"No." I took a bite of a roll. The gentle sweetness soothed the awful feeling in my stomach. "He's still in Ilbrea. On Liam's orders."

"Good." Ailis stole another piece of cheese. "I've always liked Emmet. He's such a nice man."

I coughed, choking on my roll. I took a sip of berry-sweetened water from a finely etched glass. "You're thinking of the wrong Emmet. No one has ever called my brother nice."

"Emmet Ryeland," Ailis said. "You look so much alike, I might've guessed you're related last night. Of course you were fairly caked in blood."

"How well do you know my brother?"

"Well enough." Ailis perched on the edge of the vanity. "We've trained together the last two winters. Been in some of the same hunting parties as well."

"Don't tell me"—I leaned back in my chair—"you have a wonderful story about Emmet doing something daring, but you can't tell me."

She laughed.

I liked the sound. It was easy, confident, like she wasn't afraid of the stars knowing she was happy.

"I don't have a daring story about Emmet. I was, however, there when he got tossed off the back of his dog sled and left behind."

"What?" I coughed on my berry water.

"Dog sleds are the fastest way to travel once the snow hits. Emmet does well enough hunting, but he learned to hold on tight to the sled the hard way. The dogs just kept racing on without him."

I started laughing along with her.

"He was just stuck standing in rib-high snow, watching his sled race away from him." Ailis spoke through her laughter.

"What happened?"

"I caught up to his dogs and turned them back. The lead dog hadn't even noticed they'd left him behind."

"I would love to have seen that."

"I can try to have him tossed off another sled this winter." She ate one of the berries. "I'd honestly love to see it again."

"He'll be here," I said. "Emmet will join us soon."

"I'm sure he will." Ailis's laughter faded from her eyes. "If you're not going to do more than pick at your food, we should get you dressed. The biddies downstairs banded together when they got word that Liam himself had said to look after you."

"I'll have to thank them." I stared at the trunk but couldn't convince myself to stand.

Ailis walked over and tossed the top open. Three different stacks of clothes waited inside. One of only shifts, one of skirts, and one of bodices.

At least the clothes you recognize.

"I can sort through them on my own," I said.

"Nonsense." Ailis pulled the stack of shifts from the trunk and began laying them out on the bed. "I was told to take proper care of you. You can't be in the crag looking like a little forest rabbit."

"Should I be dressed as a wolf instead?"

"You should be dressed to fit the station of someone in the crag."

"What does that even mean? What is the crag?"

"Right." Ailis stopped fussing with the shifts and pursed her lips as she studied me. "I'd have thought Liam would have told you more. Emmet knew all about Lygan Hall before he arrived. Seemed like he'd memorized a map of the Hall. Did you only just join up with Liam?"

I watched as she laid out a second full line of shifts.

"I've been in the camp since the spring." I picked up another roll just to have something to busy my hands.

"Huh." She moved on to laying out bodices. "Liam's busy during the summer months. It's not surprising he didn't have time to tell you about the Hall."

I stood and walked over to the bed.

I don't know what made me do it. Maybe it was jealousy, or pride. Maybe I wanted to stake my claim, and maybe I was just sick of sitting around wrapped in bedding.

I stopped beside Ailis and dropped the sheet, letting the white fabric fall to the floor. I reached for a lavender-dyed shift, giving a full display of the raven mark Liam had drawn on my side. I turned to Ailis holding the shift low enough that she could not miss the black stone pendant lying against my pale skin.

"This is a pretty color." I ran my fingers over the soft fabric. "I suppose, now that I'm in Lygan Hall, I won't have to worry so much about blood stains on my clothes."

"No," Ailis said, "you won't."

I held her gaze as I unfolded the shift. "I hope not. But standing beside Liam comes with its dangers. I suppose that's the price I have to pay."

Ailis didn't say anything as I slipped the shift over my head. The luxurious texture of the fabric caressed my skin, offering a foreign kind of comfort.

I chose a deep blue bodice and a dark gray skirt with black stitching forming a design of mountains along the bottom. They were the finest clothes I'd ever worn.

I hated them.

I wished I had the skirt I'd worn when I fled from Harane. None of my clothes had been fancy, but I'd been able to run and climb in them.

The weight of the gray skirt would only have been an obstacle if I'd had to escape.

I looked at myself in the mirror once I was fully dressed. I'd hidden my pendant beneath my bodice, covering any hint that Liam and I were connected. Still, I couldn't look at my reflection and claim I was the girl who'd followed Liam away from the flames of Harane.

My face had lost its last traces of childish roundness. My eyes didn't hold fear anymore, only vicious courage. I was not one to wait for the Guilds to slaughter her. I was a demon who would chase the monsters into the flames.

"Where is Cati?" I asked. "Where are Finn and Marta? And the children, where are they?"

"Below, I suppose."

"Where is below?" I turned to Ailis.

"Where the healers live. The children were either taken there or, from what I hear, straight to the sorcerers' compound."

"I should go see them."

"No." She stepped in front of the door.

"I can't just wait here. You say I can't go to Liam, fine. At least let me check on the people who may need my help."

"There is one of me," Ailis said. "Liam put your safety under my care. Defending you in the open is far different than keeping you safe in the crag. Believe it or not, I can't watch all directions at once."

"Then I'm not safe here at all."

25

We'd sorted through all the clothes to find what actually fit me before the midday meal came. Then I sat on the bed and stared out the window for a while. Three more birds had joined the dark shape soaring through the sky.

I hated being powerless. Hated sitting in a fancy room, waiting for Liam to come for me.

Do not be a fool, Ena.

There was no way I could make it past six armed guards. Even if I did, I'd never find Liam or the others.

Knowing I was powerless only made the waiting worse.

Ailis stayed with me, though we didn't speak much. I wondered what she thought of the mark on my side. If she thought Liam was a fool for allowing someone who knew so little of Lygan Hall to swear an oath to him. I wondered what she thought of my pendant. If she thought me weak for needing his protection.

I could bear her thinking me useless as long she knew I was not a stranger to Liam.

Knock. Knock. Knock.

The sound carried through my room. I gripped the white blankets beneath me, trying to decide if I should be ready to fight.

"Ena?"

"Liam." I leapt to my feet and raced to the door before Ailis had time to sheath her sword.

He stood in the hall, alive and whole.

Seeing his face brought me more comfort than I knew a person could feel.

He trailed his fingers along my cheek and down my neck. He kissed my forehead, as though wanting to be sure I was actually real.

His scent filled my lungs and wiped away the hours of worry.

"You're all right?" I whispered.

He kissed me. Heat surged through every fiber of my being. Then he held me tight in his arms, and the stone room no longer felt like a prison.

"I'm sorry." He pressed his lips to the top of my head. "I'm sorry it took so long. I had to be sure Lygan Hall could be defended against croilach."

"Against what?" Ailis asked.

"The beasts that attacked us." Liam stepped away from me and pulled her into a tight hug. "Nine croilach have been sent after us."

"What?" Ailis broke free of Liam and gripped the hilt of her sword.

"Orla is sending messages out to each of the clans," Liam said. "All the perimeters have been warned."

"Will it matter?" I laid a hand on Liam's chest, needing to feel his heartbeat beneath my palm.

"She called us back to protect me from assassins," Liam said. "Orla will not allow an attack on Lygan Hall."

"What about the others?" I asked. "Cati and Finn. Are they safe? Did the healers help them?"

Liam wrapped his arm around my waist, holding me close to his side. "They're up in the keep. The healers have tended to them."

"And the children?" I asked. "Is Gwen awake?"

"Marta is with them," Liam said. "She would have sent word if anything bad had happened."

"I need to go to them," I said. "You need to rest. We have to find out who sent the beasts after you."

"We will," Liam said. "We can see Cati and Finn now. We'll go to the children once the sorcerers send word that we're welcome."

"What?"

"We can't just walk into the sorcerers' compound," Liam said. "But Wyman will send word when it's time."

I closed my eyes, pressing down all the questions rattling through my mind.

"Let's go to Cati and Finn," I said.

I think Liam must have sensed my urge to flee, my absolute hatred of being told I wasn't allowed to see the children I'd taken from their home.

He laced his fingers through mine and kissed my cheek. "Trust me," he whispered so softly I would have thought I'd imagined the words if I hadn't felt his breath caress my neck.

"Shall I escort you?" Ailis asked.

"To the keep, if you will," Liam said. "Then you should sleep."

"Have you slept?" Ailis asked.

"No," Liam said. "But that doesn't give you an excuse not to."

"I'll set a new guard around the base of the keep and then rest." Ailis led us out the door. "The Healy Blood Leader has been murdered, and there've been two attacks on the Duwead Trueborn. I won't trust a gnat as safe until we find whatever vermin is responsible for all this."

Is it the same rat who's killed so many?

I hadn't considered it before. For some reason, I'd thought the beast that had tormented the camp had been created solely to harm the Duwead Clan. In my mind, the beast had been made to hurt Liam and stop our work in Ilbrea. It had never occurred to me that the terror we'd suffered at the camp hadn't been aimed solely at the people I cared for.

The idea that the attack hadn't been so specific, that there was some vile person sitting in a cave, sending death and horror after people they didn't even know, who'd never done anything to offend, just for the joy of spreading bloodshed like so much sheep shit, brought a familiar helpless hatred to my gut.

The Guilds killed without care. That was their world, their unforgivable flaw. I could not believe I had escaped one hell to walk willingly into another.

I kept Liam's hand tightly in mine as the guards bowed us past the carved metal door. We walked down one hallway and up another, passing through a gate and another door before entering a wide hall.

Even though the sun shone outside, orange spheres and torches glowed brightly in the corridor. A fountain shaped like a mountain peak spat water in the middle of it all. Women in well made skirts sat around the fountain like Death himself hadn't chased us to their gates only hours before. Men in perfectly clean clothes chatted in groups like none of their fellows could possibly be plotting murder.

Liam led me through a wide entryway where more guards waited, then up a sweeping set of spiral stairs that seemed as though they'd go on forever.

I wanted to stop Liam and ask him what under the chivving stars was happening and how a place like this had been built in the side of a mountain. But I didn't know Ailis well enough to speak with her walking behind us.

As we climbed higher, windows began appearing along the stairs. The shutters had been left open, and every window we passed offered a vaster view of the valley below.

When I thought my legs would give out in protest at being asked to work so hard after the distance we'd traveled the day before, the stairs opened into another wide chamber.

More guards stood along the edges of the room, and more corridors branched off in different directions.

A person could spend a lifetime lost in this labyrinth.

Two guards nodded to Liam and followed behind us as we walked down a side hall. One of the walls was made almost entirely of windows, with places to step through onto a narrow balcony beyond. I wondered when we had climbed past the wide balcony I'd seen from below.

Liam stopped in front of a wooden door and knocked.

He let go of my hand and slipped his arm around my waist while we waited.

The door opened, and a woman with gray-streaked, red hair peeked into the hall.

"Liam." The woman smiled for a moment before a scowl took over her face. "Finn needs rest. He's been tramping through the wilderness and attacked. I mean no disrespect, but he is not ready to be running about."

"Let it be, Mother," Finn called from inside. "If they want me to march into battle, I'm going to go, so there's no use in fussing."

"I'm your mother." The woman rounded on Finn. "It is my job to fuss. And you will not be fighting anyone or running anywhere until your arm is healed up. I absolutely refuse to let my sweet little boy lose an arm because he's too foolish to realize flesh needs time to heal."

"Mother"—Finn appeared behind her shoulder, wearing a long, purple dressing gown—"can you just go steal a bit of pie from Granny's and let me be?"

"The moment I leave, you'll be running off and ripping your stitches." Finn's mother jammed a finger into his chest.

"I'm stuck here till spring," Finn sighed. "Can't you fuss over me when there aren't people watching?"

His mother's lips turned into one thin line as she looked from Liam, to me, to Ailis, and finally to Finn.

"If I hear one whisper of you doing something foolish, gods help you I'll break your legs and tie you to my hearth."

"Yes, yes." Finn shooed her out the door. "I love you too, Mother. Don't forget about the pie."

Finn's mother kept shaking her head until she turned out of the corridor and disappeared from view.

"We really should find a way to stay closer to Ilbrea year-round," Finn said. "I don't know if I can survive a whole winter of her fussing."

"I thought you said she cried tears of joy when you decided to travel outside Lygan Hall." I stepped closer to Finn.

"Ah, but I live in the keep now," Finn said. "She's not the one to feed me."

"Are you all right?" I asked.

Finn wrapped his good arm around me and pulled me into a tight hug. "We live to fight another day. That's what matters."

"What about the people who didn't make it?" A horrible pain swiped at my throat.

"We find comfort in vengeance." Finn bowed us into his room. It looked much like the place I'd slept—there was a fancy bed and a wardrobe—only Finn had a desk in place of a vanity, and hints of permanent occupation lay scattered across the room.

A worn bow and quiver of arrows had been tucked into one corner. A small painting of a red-haired man sat on the desk. A stack of books waited beside a stuffed chair.

"I'll send new guards," Ailis said before she closed the door behind us.

26

Finn's face drooped into exhaustion as he sank down onto his bed.

"Tell me we know something." He rubbed his good hand over his face.

"I wish I could," Liam said. "I spent the night going through everything that's happened with Orla. She sent messages out and posted more guards, but I've no chivving clue who attacked us."

"It has to be a trueborn." I wished I had my knife in my boot, or even had any chivving shoes at all, so I'd be ready to run from whatever horror lurked in the shadows.

"It wasn't a Duwead trueborn who made the croilach." Liam paced beside Finn's bed.

"I think we can all be sure of that."

"How?" I asked.

"Orla is the only other trueborn the Duweads have," Liam said. "If she wanted me dead, she wouldn't bother exhausting herself making monsters."

"Regan then." I sat on the stuffed chair. The comfort of the seat set my nerves on edge, like the blue fabric were some sort of deadly trap. I stood back up.

"Maybe," Finn said.

"Not alone," Liam said. "To make nine croilach, to know when we were leaving the camp... If it was Regan, she had help."

"Is there any way she could have done it without the help of someone from the camp?" I dug my fingers through my hair, trying to pull through the tangles of this awful mess.

"I can't see how," Liam said. "I wanted it to be one of Orla's people in Ilbrea who'd helped a trueborn send the monster to camp and let the soldiers know where we'd been ferrying the children."

"But someone in Ilbrea wouldn't have known the camp was packing up." I froze for a moment, then started weaving my hair into a tight braid. "It was someone from the camp then."

"Who would bring eight croilach down on their own head?" Finn said.

"I don't know." Liam dug his knuckles into his temples. "I told Orla about the attacks and the soldiers on the western edge of the forest. She agrees that someone has betrayed the Black Bloods."

"But she doesn't have a chivving clue as to who?" Finn said.

"She's allowed me to ask for the sorcerers' aid," Liam said. "I don't think we have any other choice."

A deep cold rattled my spine.

"What do we do now?" I asked. "Sit by and wait for magic to fix the problem?"

"We can ride for the Brien safe haven," Finn said. "Visit their elder and demand answers."

"You're not riding anywhere until your arm is healed," I said.

"None of us can leave," Liam said. "Orla's banned all travel outside the valley. She takes the attack on our caravan as an attempt on my life and an act of war."

"Chivving gods and stars, Liam." Finn shook his head. "We can't leap into a clan war right now. We can't just walk away from the good we've finally managed to do in Ilbrea."

"I know," Liam said. "But we've got to make sure everyone here is safe, convince Orla that what we've accomplished in Ilbrea matters, and avoid destroying the peace that's kept the Black Bloods alive for more than a century."

I wrapped my arms around Liam and laid my cheek against his chest.

"We'll do it." My voice sounded strong, like someone who was capable of challenging a war. "We'll sort all this out."

Liam held me close and kissed the top of my head. I held him tighter. The world could have burned us and I still would have been grateful to be wrapped in his arms.

"Where do we start?" I asked.

"We root out the traitor," Finn said. "Find them, find who they've been feeding information to, kill that whole lot. Then we worry about the clan war. We don't even know who the enemy is right now. We've got to do that before anything else."

"I'll speak to Wyman," Liam said. "Give him a list of everyone from the camp."

"You'll lose a lot of followers if the sorcerers offend loyal people," Finn said.

"I lost twenty-eight yesterday," Liam said. "I'd rather have my people hate me than put any more of them underground."

"Can you send a bird to Mave?" I asked. "In case Emmet turns up in Frason's Glenn. Warn him that there could be more croilach in the mountains."

"I pray to the gods there aren't more of those beasts lurking on our land," Finn said.

"I can't send word to Frason's Glenn." Liam stepped away from me but kept both his hands tightly around my waist.

"Is there news? Is Emmet hurt? Was he captured by the Guilds?"

"Orla thinks Emmet is the one who betrayed us."

The room swayed, and he gripped my waist tighter.

"That is utterly ridiculous." Finn stood and placed his hand on my back.

"Emmet would never betray you," I said. "And he couldn't have known we were leaving the camp. He's out in Ilbrea right now burning his way through the paun."

"I know that," Liam said.

"You told me Orla liked him." I broke away from both men. "You said he'd saved your life so she liked him."

"She does," Liam said.

"Then how could she accuse him of causing the deaths of so many people?" My words

472

echoed around the room. I was sure they'd carried into the hall. "Emmet wouldn't betray you. He'd never risk monsters like the croilach coming anywhere near me. And what about Marta? Does he treat her so casually he'd risk her life?"

"I believe you," Liam said. "I believe in him."

"Did you tell Orla that?" I asked.

"Of course I did," Liam said. "But it's easier for her to believe that Emmet is a traitor than to consider that one of the people who grew up in her halls betrayed their clan."

"This is chivving ridiculous," I said. "My brother isn't even here to defend himself."

"So we'll do it for him," Finn said. "We'll use the sorcerers to find the traitor and clear Emmet's name well before he gets back to Lygan Hall."

"I'll go now," Liam said. "We'll start sorting through people from camp before the end of the day."

"Good." Finn reached for me. "Ena and I will stay here and try to work out how we can slog through this chivving mess faster."

Liam kissed the back of my hand. "I will make sure we find the scum who started this. I promise we'll be safe again."

I nodded. I couldn't think of anything bracing to say.

Liam left. The door clicked shut behind him, and I was alone with Finn.

"We'll need to rally the people from camp," Finn said. "As soon as they're cleared by the sorcerers, we'll need to make sure they spread the word of all the work we're doing in Ilbrea to the rest of Lygan Hall."

"How will the sorcerers know who betrayed us?" I dragged my fingers through my hair again and began weaving the strands into an even tighter braid.

"They have their ways," Finn said. "I can't say I understand the magic they use, and the process isn't pleasant. But if they question the murdering slitch, they'll know."

"Does it count as murder if the traitor never even held a blade against any of our people?" My hands shook as I finished my braid.

"Yes. They worked to kill our people. That makes them a murderer in my book."

"That means I murdered Drason, you know. If that's how you count it."

"It does." Finn went to his wardrobe and fished around the bottom for a moment. "But Drason was a monster who stole women and children from their homes. He was responsible for a lot of death and horror. There's a difference between slaying a beast and murdering people you counted as friends."

"Whoever betrayed us drank with us in the clearing." Sour rolled into my throat. "They grieved with us when Pierce and Dillon were killed."

"And they'll pay for all of it."

"What will Orla do to them when they're found?"

"The treaty lays out the method of their punishment." Finn handed me a short leather cord. "Honestly, if I was the cacting slitch, I hop off the high summit and plunge to a much quicker death than the end Orla will offer."

"What if she won't believe it wasn't Emmet?" I tied the cord around the end of my braid.

"She will."

"But what if she won't?"

Finn rubbed his hand over the red scruff on his chin. "We'll ask the gods for aid and hope they bring an answer that won't make us traitors to the clan."

Knock. Knock. Knock.

My shoulders tensed at the sound, like somehow my body knew it wasn't Liam outside the door.

"Who's there?" Finn called.

Knock. Knock. Knock.

The sound came again.

Finn slipped a dagger with a carved wooden handle out from under his pillow. He held the weapon behind his back, wincing as he opened the door with his wounded arm.

"Hello there," Finn said.

I inched to the side to peer around him.

Four men in blue jackets waited in the hall.

"Can I help you gentlemen?" Finn asked after another moment.

"We're here for the girl," the man in front said.

"I'm sorry," Finn said, "I had an awful day yesterday, so my mind is running a bit slow. You're here for who?"

"Ena Ryeland." The man looked straight into my eyes.

"Ah." Finn nodded. "I see. Unfortunately, Liam told her to stay here with me. Perhaps you might be able to come back for her later, once Liam is here to give—"

"We are to collect the girl by order of Orla," the man said. "Move out of the way before we make you."

The sides of Finn's neck tensed as he gripped the weapon behind his back.

"It's all right, Finn." I laid my hand on his shoulder. "No point in making a fuss over going to see someone, right?"

"Of course not," Finn said.

"You need to rest anyway. Get some sleep, and we'll talk later."

"Right." Finn tucked the dagger into the back of his purple robe's sash. "A bit of sleep is exactly what I need."

I gave him a smile before slipping past him into the hall.

The four men in blue coats surrounded me. They didn't reach for me or brandish any weapons, but the feel of them, the way my heart thundered in my chest like it was shouting a terrible warning, felt like I'd been penned in by Guilded soldiers.

They all started walking without asking me to move along with them. I had no choice but to follow or try and fight.

For one foolish moment, I wished I'd taken Finn's dagger. Then the swords on the guards' hips caught my eye. I'd been training to fight, but I was not Cati. I could not battle four swords and hope to come out alive.

I moved down the corridor with them, keeping step within my cage of men.

I wanted to ask questions, if only to bother the guards, but a whisper in my mind told me to stay quiet. To wear my armor well even if I was barefoot and the only shield I had was silence.

We went into the wide corridor. There were more people in the space than when I'd passed through with Liam. The fancily dressed men and women stared as the guards escorted me past.

We cut down one hall, along another, and out into the grandest chivving place I'd ever seen.

The black stone of the walls had all been polished to perfection and carved into an

474

intricate pattern of swirls that somehow formed a picture of a mountain range. White, gray, red, and blue stone had been set into the black, making the whole room look like we'd stepped into an artisan's masterpiece.

Wide windows granted light to a sweeping staircase that spanned the whole width of the room. The steps cut down and twisted out of sight. A polished set of massive metal doors stood opposite the stairs, but the door the guards had led me through was a normal size, like we'd cut into the grand space through a side passage.

There were more men in blue jackets lining the walls of this hall. Each of them held a sword. Each of them looked ready to kill me.

Maybe all the world is actually the same. Maybe the colors of the uniforms are the only difference from one place to another.

I lifted my hand to press my stone pendant to my skin.

The rasp of swords being drawn from their sheaths stopped my movement.

"Are you really this afraid?" I said, not asking anyone in particular. "You're in a place guarded by the magic of the mountain. You've got dozens of passages between here and the entrance to Lygan Hall. You have sorcerers of your own. What could have made you this afraid? What leader is this terrified of her own people?"

None of the guards bothered to answer.

We stopped in front of the giant metal door. I studied the images carved onto the surface.

At first, it seemed like a simple design of mountains, but the longer I looked at the picture, the more defined the scene became.

Streaks of lightning cut along the top, reaching toward the highest of the peaks. A woman stood on the summit of the mountain, her shawl blowing from her shoulders as she clutched a baby in her arms. At the very bottom of the door, an orb hid beneath the mountains.

I wondered if the person who'd carved the picture had meant the circle to look as though an evil lurked beneath the woman's feet, waiting to devour her.

We stood silently for a long while.

I wanted to ask the guards if they were going to knock, but I kept staring at the orb, wondering what malice would spring up from below to swallow the mother and child.

Without a word or a sound, the doors swung open, allowing us into Orla's council chamber.

27

She sat on her throne at the end of the dark stone room. Tiny orange glowing orbs hung from the ceiling like a king's chandelier. The light should have been enough to give the place a cheerful glow, but the magic within the orbs was not strong enough to banish the darkness.

There was no design in the walls of the black stone room. Nothing at all to suggest the space might offer peace or contentment. A round table and set of chairs took up one half of the room. They had been carved of richly hued wood, but the effect brought no cheer.

Orla's throne was made of black rock molded into swirls and curves that should have been beautiful. But the stone only looked like the tendrils of a great shadow beast ready to taste my blood.

Even the woman herself offered no hint of light.

Her dark hair and eyes were accented by the deep sapphire of her dress. She might have been beautiful if her face weren't filled with quiet loathing.

Orla studied me, starting with my face, moving down to my feet, and coming back up again, as though wanting to be sure she had thoroughly observed the horror of me.

"I should have known you'd be pretty," Orla said.

A bit of rage sliced through my reason.

"Thank you." I met her gaze as I curtsied. "I'd like to know who pays me such a compliment."

I waited for her to rage or laugh, but she only stared.

"Orla, Elder of the Duwead Clan." Her voice stayed calm as she spoke. "And you are Ena Ryeland, sister of Emmet Ryeland."

"Yes ma'am. I'm sorry my brother isn't here to greet you. Last I heard, he was out torching paun as he searched for me. Knowing Emmet, it might be a while before he lets his anger at the Guilds go long enough to realize I'm not being held captive in Ilara."

"Right to it then," Orla said. "How refreshing not to dodge around the conversation."

"Sorry to disappoint you"—I gave another curtsy, not bothering to try and hide my bare feet—"but I've no idea what conversation we're meant to be having."

"Your brother betrayed the Duwead Clan." Orla laid her hands on her lap. "He has been feeding information to one of our enemies. His betrayal has resulted in the deaths of more than thirty of my people."

"Ah." I nodded. "I see. Your people are dead, and you want to blame my brother. Emmet's not perfect, I'll be the first to admit that, but he would never betray Liam. My brother would do anything to destroy the Guilds."

"Perhaps Emmet believes that sending the clans into a war would somehow make them strike out against the Guilds."

"What?" I pushed out a laugh. "I don't know how you think that would work. The clans fighting amongst themselves wouldn't do anything to help the common folk in Ilbrea. It would only leave more dead scattered in the mountains."

"A man who sets off in a blaze of fury to conquer one enemy can easily be turned to believe others are his foe."

"Emmet did not betray Liam." I laid my palms flat against the sides of my legs, refusing to let them display any hint of my anger. "He couldn't be responsible for the croilach attacks. He was in Ilbrea on Liam's orders the first time—"

"How convenient."

"—and he's been in Ilbrea searching for me for the last month," I pressed on. "He's been terrorizing paun soldiers, which you should chivving well thank him for."

"Are you always so foul-mouthed when faced with authority?"

"Only when the authority warrants it." I stepped closer to her dark throne, ignoring the rasps of swords clearing their sheaths all around me. "Three times, croilach came close to killing me. My brother would never, ever place me in such danger. He'd never place anyone from the camp in that kind of danger."

"I'm not naïve enough to believe he genuinely cares for anyone in the camp."

"They really don't tell you much, do they?" I smiled, relishing the deepening of the wrinkles around Orla's eyes. "Emmet would die before allowing a monster anywhere near me. He'd die before he let a beast threaten the camp. I'm sorry one of your own people has betrayed you, but your problem has nothing to do with my brother. He wasn't even in camp when Liam got the orders for us to pack up. He couldn't have sent word that we'd be vulnerable. It's just not possible."

"Then perhaps the two of you are working together," Orla said. "Perhaps you sent word that Liam would be in the open."

"Me?"

"You were in camp when Liam received my orders." Orla stood. "You were missing for weeks. You had plenty of time to run to the fiend who created the croilach."

"I had nothing to do with any of this." I pressed my hands against my legs, trying to squeeze away my urge to run. "I've only met two trueborn—Liam and Regan. Liam was with me when I met Regan, so I certainly couldn't have tossed together some plan to help her. If you don't believe me, ask him."

"Oh, I'm sure Liam would tell me you couldn't possibly have done this terrible thing." A tiny smile curved one side of Orla's mouth.

"He trusts me."

"I'm sure he does. Men with hungry snakes have lost their senses for much less pretty

477

faces. My son may be an excellent leader, but that doesn't make him immune to a beautiful liar."

Her words rang through the room. I searched each syllable, trying to find where my mind had lost its reason.

"He really doesn't tell you anything." I spoke softly, barely loud enough for Orla to hear.

"I know everything I need to." Orla's skirt swished as she walked closer to me.

I hated that starched sound. She might as well have been a growling beast.

"There are two outsiders in Liam's camp." She stopped three feet in front of me. "There were no problems in the camp until the Ryelands inserted themselves into Liam's cause."

"I didn't insert myself into anything." My laugh grated my throat. "Liam came to me as my home burned. He saved me. He brought me through the mountains to the camp. So unless you think I have the chivving power to stage an attack by Guilded soldiers on my own village, then you've lost your mind and are just searching for anyone to blame."

"How dare—"

"I'm sorry you're grieving."

The guards stepped closer to me.

I ignored them and pressed on. "I'm sorry you're hurt and scared, but it's got nothing to do with me. If you want something to blame me for, I'd be happy to give you a list of all the ways I have failed. But I would never hurt Liam."

"You will regret the day you met my son," Orla said.

"Never. Nothing could ever make me regret meeting Liam."

Sounds of shouting carried through the metal door.

"Wanting someone to blame doesn't make me guilty," I said. "It only gives the murderer more time to plot against you."

The shouting grew louder.

I waited for a monster to burst through the door and slash me to shreds with its claws, or for Orla to begin executing me in some horrible and painful manner, but she didn't move. Neither of us did. We just stood glaring at each other until the metal doors banged open.

"Ena."

I turned at the sound of Liam's voice.

Sweat glistened on his brow, and he gripped the hilt of the blade on his hip.

"What is she doing in here?" Liam looked to his mother.

"Being accused of treachery and murder," I said.

Liam stopped beside me, his stance wide as though ready to defend me from an army of beasts.

"Ena had nothing to do with this," Liam said. "She is completely innocent."

"It is so easy to believe the beautiful are innocent," Orla said. "That doesn't make it true. She and her brother betrayed the Duwead Clan. She will pay the price, and I will hunt for Emmet. Justice will be done."

"Then kill me." Liam let go of his sword and spread his arms wide. "If you think Ena is guilty of murder, then run me through right now."

"This is not the time," Orla said.

"Of course it is," Liam said. "There is no punishing her without hurting me. Ena took the oath. Her deeds are bound to my fate. If she is guilty, then I die, too."

Orla froze.

"Even if she hadn't given me her vow, I would not let you harm her." Liam took my hand in his. "She is mine as I am hers. Find someone else to accuse, Mother."

He began leading me away, but I couldn't tear my gaze from Orla's face. There were hints of Liam in the cut of her cheeks. I'd seen the quiet anger that raged behind her eyes in Liam's as well.

"You're a fool," Orla said. "You trust Ilbreans as though the Guilds have not contaminated them all."

"And you trust your people as though one of them has not tried to murder your only child." Liam kept walking.

I looked away from Orla as we neared the door.

"I will find the one who betrayed our clan," Liam said. "Either help me or stay out of my way."

I waited for the guards to leap in front of the door and bar our path, but they did not move as Liam led me out into the grand room with the fancy stone walls. We passed by more and more guards wearing blue, enough to fend off a proper attack.

Who does Orla fear so deeply?

My heart raced too fast for me to form the words.

Liam didn't lead me back the way I'd come. We walked down the wide, stone stairs.

Statues flanked the hall that waited at the bottom—life-sized monuments to men and women who all seemed to look a bit like Liam. Guards waited between the statues, but still, no one stopped us.

We reached another metal door, and two men sprang forward to wrench it open before Liam could touch the handle.

A hall with six doors, all on the same wall, waited within.

Liam led me through the second door on the left, then slammed the door shut behind us and slid the metal bolt into place.

28

The room was beautiful, by far the fanciest quarters I'd ever set foot in.

A massive bed sat on a low stone pedestal. Curtains of gauzy, pale blue fabric surrounded the bed, though I had no idea what purpose such delicate material might serve.

A set of windows covered the front wall, displaying the view of the valley like a work of art. A stone fireplace, carved to look like the profile of a massive bird, took up one side wall. To the other side, an open door led into a room with a table, chairs, and two massive wardrobes.

Liam let go of my hand as he stormed through the door into that room and bolted the entrance from the hall.

I walked toward the bed. A rug woven of blue, red, and silver surrounded the bed's pedestal. The dense softness beneath my feet didn't bring any comfort.

I stepped back onto the stone floor.

Where I belong.

Liam came back from the second room and paced in front of the door.

I watched him go back and forth. Back and forth.

"Did she hurt you?" He didn't stop his pacing as he spoke.

"No." I took a deep breath. The room smelled of fresh flowers, though I didn't see any blooms. "She sent her guards to collect me. Told me Emmet was a traitor, said I was a traitor, then you came in."

"She will not hurt you." Liam shook his head. "I will see to it that she leaves you out of this."

"How could she accuse me again? I've given my oath to her son."

Liam stopped. He stared at the bird carved around the fireplace for a moment before looking at me.

"You could've told me," I said. "You could have mentioned once that Orla was your mother."

"I didn't think you'd be meeting her the day you stepped into Lygan Hall." Liam ran his hands over his hair. "I thought I'd have time—"

"Time to what? Warn me that the man I'm rolling around with is the son of the woman who leads the Duwead Clan? I should have been told before I stripped my clothes off for you."

"Would it have changed your mind?"

There was hurt in his eyes. Actual worry and fear.

I took his face in my hands and pressed my forehead to his. "You could be the son of the King and I would still want you."

He wrapped his arms around me.

"But in all the times I heard her name, in all the plans for Marten, and helping the sorcis, how did no one ever mention that Orla is your mother?"

"It's not important."

"Chivving gods and stars, Liam, yes it is." I stepped away from him and swept a hand around the room. "Clearly it is. I thought Lygan Hall was a cozy cave, not a chivving palace."

"I never said the Hall was a cave."

"You never mentioned the few hundred guards or the giant chivving valley, either."

"I forget what other people don't know."

"You told Emmet." It was my turn to pace. I hated the stone floor beneath my bare feet. I felt too vulnerable without my shoes. "You told him about the Hall and the layout of the whole place. Ailis told me. Ailis was very confused as to why I didn't know a chivving thing about your home."

"Emmet needed to hear," Liam said. "He needed to know there was something in the mountains besides a camp full of people willing to fight. Do you think he would have gone so far away from you if he didn't know he was fighting alongside people with more than five horses and some tents?"

"How many horses do you have here?" I went to the window. A wide balcony waited beyond. I stepped outside and looked down to the valley below. "There must be thousands of people in Lygan Hall. You have sorcerers here. Why can't the Duweads march on the Guilds?"

"We have twelve hundred guards." Liam stepped out beside me. "We have tanners, cobblers, farmers, healers, and sorcerers. There are even Duweads outside the valley. Brave folks who homestead beyond the protection of Lygan Hall. But there are about as many people in Frason's Glenn as in the whole Duwead Clan. We could launch an attack on Ilara, but even if every man and woman in the valley fought, we'd never win. We might make it through a day, but we'd never break the walls or hold the city."

"And Orla knows it, doesn't she?"

"She does." Liam laid a hand on my shoulder.

I leaned into his touch. "Yet she sends her only child to the woods to work against the Guilds."

"I have to go. There has to be a trueborn to protect the camp. The last trueborn to lead the camp died six years ago. Now it's only Orla and me. She can't go, so it became my duty."

I stepped closer to him, resting my head against his shoulder.

"I knew it was coming," Liam said. "I'd been trained to assume the responsibilities of a trueborn since I was too young to understand what that meant. Orla hoped someone in the valley would give birth to another trueborn baby, but there hasn't been one since me."

"She's your mother. All those stone birds have been coming from your mother."

"Orla's never been much of a mother." Liam laid his cheek against the top of my head. "She gave birth to an heir. That's more important to her than a son. To me, she's always been the Elder of the clan. *Mother* is just a title I use when I want to annoy her."

"I'm sorry."

"Don't be. An excellent woman raised me. She's just not the one who carried me in her womb."

I twisted to look into Liam's eyes, searching for some hidden wound I'd never managed to see.

"I will not let Orla hurt you. She can't risk hurting me. I'm the only one who can take her place." Liam gave a tired smile.

"You need to sleep."

"I can't."

"If you don't rest now, it won't be Orla's wrath that ends you."

"There's a traitor. There is work—"

I kissed Liam, cutting off his list of everything that had to be done to protect us all.

"How do I get to the sorcerers?" I asked.

"I'll go."

"No." I stepped around him, making sure he didn't try to head for the door.

"You can't. It's too dangerous to send you out into the open while Orla's angry."

"Fine. You're Orla's son, heir of the Duwead Clan. Send a message and make the sorcerers come to you. Then you sleep."

He stayed silent for a moment before nodding. He stepped in and kissed me.

He tasted the same as he had when we'd been living in tents in the woods. He had the same scent of fresh wind and reckless freedom. His body felt the same as I leaned against him. I tried to find comfort in all those familiar things.

Liam tipped my chin up and looked into my eyes.

"Even if you hadn't sworn an oath to me, I would not have let Orla take you. I need you to believe that. I would fight the entire world to protect you."

I did not know how soon that battle would begin.

29

I stayed on the stone balcony as Liam spoke to the sorcerer in the sitting room beside his bedroom. I sat gazing out over the valley, trying not to be grateful that I couldn't hear what they were saying.

The two spoke for a long time. I watched the clouds race across the sky and looked at the tiny people far below. I tried to picture Liam living in this room, the Liam I cared so much for growing up in a fancy hall, surrounded by guards and catered to by servants.

The door to the side room opened, and a woman stepped through. She watched me sitting on the balcony with an air of modest interest on her angled face.

The woman didn't look magical. She wore her plain brown hair in a simple bun. Her dress was pretty enough but didn't seem to have a special color or any other marking of being a uniform. But there was something about her that screamed she was dangerous and powerful.

She walked closer to the balcony.

I pressed my hands against the stone beneath me, preparing to spring to my feet to fight.

"I'll be sure the groundskeepers know to let her in," the woman said.

"Thank you." Liam stepped out of the sitting room door to stand behind the woman.

She bowed to Liam and started toward his bedroom door.

"Deirdre," Liam said.

She stopped with her hand on the lock.

"Ask Wyman to be gentle," Liam said. "There is a traitor among us, but there are far more innocent people who don't deserve to be in pain."

"He will only be as intrusive as he must." Deirdre nodded, slid the bolt aside, and stepped out into the hall. The door closed behind her, and the bolt slid back into place without Liam reaching for it.

"Makes locks seem a bit pointless." I stood up, trying to convince myself I had no enemy to flee from.

"Locks only work on people who are willing to be kept out." Liam climbed the stone step and sat on the bed. "Gwen still isn't awake."

"Why?" Panic clenched around my heart. "Can the healers help her if the sorcerers can't?"

"She's not ill." Liam rested his head in his hands. "She burned out."

"What does that mean?" I stepped up onto the stone platform and sat beside Liam.

"She pushed more magic through her body than she should have. Her body didn't know what to do, so it shut down. She'll sleep until she's recovered."

"But she will recover?"

"She will. It may take hours or weeks, but she'll wake up when she's ready."

"And the other children?" I did not want to think of the children without Gwen to guide them. I didn't know if Cinni would be able to survive without her older sister.

"Deirdre didn't seem happy about having Ilbrean children in the compound, but she'll learn to enjoy their presence. Marta is still with them. She'll make sure they behave."

"Then that's all you can do for now." I rested my hand on Liam's leg.

"I should go stand guard at the outer gate or send more messages. I should find a way to do more good."

"You will, when you wake up." I took Liam's hand and dragged him to his feet. He didn't argue as I pulled back the blankets, whose thickness and soft texture didn't seem to match.

"Promise you'll stay with me."

"Sleep." I pointed toward the row of pillows along the top of the bed.

"Only if you'll stay with me." He took my hand and kissed the inside of my wrist. "I've lost too many people since the last time I slept. I need to feel you beside me if I'm going to slip into darkness."

I brushed my lips against his. "I will stay right here. My place is with you."

30

I had only had new boots once in my life before Lygan Hall.

When I was little, Lily had bartered for used boots other children of Harane had outgrown.

When I was finally old enough to keep a pair of shoes for a bit, Lily bought me brand new boots. They were plain brown and belonged only to me. I'd destroyed those boots on my way to the camp in the mountains.

When Liam finally woke up the day after we arrived in Lygan Hall, a woman was waiting outside his door. She had a pair of boots with her. They were made of fine black leather and had been built just for me. The cobbler had torn apart the secondhand boots I'd worn since I'd joined Liam and made a brand new pair from the marks my feet had left in the tatters of my old shoes.

The new boots were soft on my ankles and made with a hardy sole. They fit me perfectly.

Those chivving boots were nicer than any shoes anyone in Harane had ever owned.

The woman curtsied to me as she left Liam's rooms.

31

"What exactly do you propose we do about it?" Cati stormed back and forth across Liam's sitting room. "I'm not going to be able to entertain them with blunted swords for long."

"I don't want you to," Liam said.

"Then come up with another plan." Cati smacked her hands against the table. "Yesterday, I had a sorcerer show up at my room. They want me to go to the compound. Fine. Wyman himself wants to be sure I'm not the traitor who got our people killed. Fine. I let him use his magic on me. Why?"

"To set an example for the rest," Liam said.

"Exactly." Cati pointed at Liam's chest. "I let that man question me so the others couldn't be angry. I hop onto the training field to get rid of my will to slaughter everything that moves, and you know what? So does the next one Wyman messes with, and the next. Now I've got a field of raging mad people."

"And I am grateful to you for taking care of them." Liam pushed his chair away from the table and stood.

I didn't move. I stayed in my seat, staring at the remains of my lunch.

"What would really help them is having something to do," Cati said. "Get Orla to open the gates."

"She won't do it."

"Make her," Cati said.

"She's forbidden everyone from leaving Lygan Hall," Liam said.

"All I can see in my mind are those monsters tearing apart my friends." Cati's voice caught in her throat. "There are more of them out there. If not croilach, then whatever the chivving bastard plans to have attack us next. Let me find them. Let me kill them."

"You can't," Liam said. "I'm sorry, but you have to stay here. Work on training the fighters. Bruise them all if you have to, but I need you here and alive. You're the best teacher I've got."

486

"That is going to stop being good enough," Cati said. "I am not a house cat, Liam. I cannot pace in the kitchen, purring. There are monsters out there, and I will slay them."

"I know," Liam said, "but right now, our worst enemy is already in the Hall. I need you here, keeping the men moving, watching for any hint of the traitor. I need you to be ready to help me kill the chivving bastard when we find them."

Cati looked up at the stone ceiling. A series of orange orbs had been set into the rock, leaving a glowing trail of light overhead.

"I have fewer than a dozen people I can truly trust within these walls. I am your Trueborn, and I need you here," Liam said. "Please, Cati."

Cati nodded.

"Thank you." Liam walked over to the window, looking down at the valley below.

I wondered if he knew who lived in all the houses and which trees produced what fruit. I wondered if he was remembering his childhood or plotting the best place to attack the traitor.

"How many has Wyman questioned so far?" Liam asked.

"Based on the ones who've shown up to the training ground," Cati said, "about half of us. The only one who's put up a fuss is Marta."

"Marta?" I gripped the arms of my chair. "Marta would never hurt anyone. There's not—"

Cati held up a hand to silence me. "She's refusing to leave the children. Gwen still isn't awake, and she doesn't trust the sorcerers to take proper care of Cinni without her watching over them."

"Does she need to be questioned?" I asked.

"If she wants people to trust her word on Emmet's innocence, then she should," Cati said. "Anyone who's fought by Emmet's side knows he couldn't have done this. The more people proven innocent who can shout it to the cowardly slitches who hide in Lygan Hall, the better off we'll be."

"I can go to the children," I said. "Cinni knows me. I can mind them while Marta's away."

Cati looked to Liam.

A crease formed on his brow.

"You can't keep her locked in here all winter," Cati said. "There are already rumors of the Trueborn's new beloved flying around the Hall. People are obsessed with whispering about the traitor. People want to gossip about Ena. We can't allow the two sets of rumors to get jumbled together. The more they see Ena, the less they'll envision her as a dark enchantress who's poisoned your mind."

"Is that what they're saying about me?" I looked toward the windows, as though I might be able to see the people peering through, trying to catch a glimpse of my wickedness.

"It's started a bit," Cati said. "On my way to breakfast, I was asked if it was true you'd appeared in camp in the wake of a terrible storm. Before I'd finished eating, I was asked if you were already carrying a trueborn child."

Heat rushed to my face. "Where are they getting any of this? Is it Nessa?"

"She's barely spoken since Shane died," Cati said. "The problem is everyone knows you're here, and that's all. They need something to say about you, and none of them know a hint of the truth."

"So what am I supposed to do?" I asked.

"Nothing," Liam said. "I don't want you involved in clan politics."

"Then you should've kept your pants on or left the romance in the woods like every other sensible tryst." Cati crossed her arms and stared Liam down. "Normally, I'd be a touch less forward, but I've been having a chivving awful week."

"It's not safe for her to go wandering around where people can see her." Liam paced by the window. He looked like a caged animal. "We can't leave Ena exposed while Orla's out for blood."

"I'll go with her," Cati said. "Between Ailis and me, we can take care of the Trueborn's mysterious lover. Then, if someone dares to attack, I'll get to stab them, and you know how much that cheers me up."

"It's too dangerous," Liam said.

"Hiding her now will only make things more dangerous down the line." Cati stepped into Liam's path, stopping his pacing. "Finding the traitor will not make the Hall safe for Ena if the people still believe she's a threat. Let them see that she's only a girl and not some evil magic given human form. I'll take her to the sorcerers' compound to visit the children. The sooner your people accept Ena as the one their Trueborn has chosen, the safer she will be."

Liam rubbed his hands over his face.

"Ailis agrees with me," Cati said. "We are your friends, Liam. We are sworn to you. Let us do our job."

"I want to go," I said. "I don't want to be lied about, and I need to visit the children. I've walked into a tavern full of soldiers and come out alive. I don't want to hide from the people I've joined."

"Fine," Liam said, "but I want a full complement of guards. Ailis can choose who."

"How long will that take?" I asked.

"A few hours," Cati said.

"Good. I will not meet the people who whisper about me without armor."

3 2

I thought when I asked to see the people who'd brought me clothes, I might be laughed at or given a plain *no*. But the women had bustled in with a new rolling trunk and laid out items far finer than what they'd offered when I was only Liam's guest.

When I asked for paints and powders, I was certain they'd say no such thing existed in Lygan Hall. Instead, a man appeared in less than ten minutes, bearing a tray laid out with more pigments and brushes than I'd ever seen in one place.

Cati sat on the balcony as I traced the kohl around my eyes and painted my lips a deeper hue.

I chose a black bodice and skirt from the stores the women delivered to go with a shift of deep blue, just a shade darker than the color the guards wore. The women tucked the rest of the clothes into one of the wardrobes in Liam's sitting room. I don't know if he'd told them to or if they'd heard rumors of me carrying his child and decided I deserved half his space.

Either way, the women smiled as they ducked back out into the hall.

"Are you quite ready?" Cati came back in from the balcony. "I'm starting to regret choosing to accompany you over staying on the training grounds."

"I thought you needed to protect me from the horrible whispers." I dug into the pack I'd carried from the camp. A servant had shoved it into the corner, as though the shadows might hide the blood stains.

"I count you as a friend, but if I lose my chivving mind, I'll be of no use to anyone."

I pulled my knife from my bag. The weight of the blade calmed my nerves. I tucked the weapon into the ankle of my boot.

"You won't lose your mind." I dug deeper into the pack, feeling for thick fabric.

"You don't know that."

"I do." I pulled the heavy black material out. "You trained a camp filled with men, put up with Liam and my brother, stalked soldiers through the mountains, and that's just the bits I've been around for. The awful pictures in your mind are just one more enemy to be defeated. You're a warrior, Cati. You will survive."

"I hate to admit that you've made me feel a bit better."

I stepped in front of the long mirror in the sitting room and fastened the black cloak around my neck. The silver bird clasp glinted in the orange light. I studied the girl in the mirror.

She wasn't the girl from Harane or the girl from the camp. She wasn't even the girl from Frason's Glenn.

The dark hair and clothes gave me the look of one who'd become accustomed to death and was not afraid to face the shadows. I'd painted my face to perfection, as though I'd used my lips to lure Liam in.

If they wanted to think I was dark and mysterious, I would not fight them. Let them point to me and say my beauty bewitched him. I was magnificent and perfect, a mirage the people could not see through. I had claimed their Trueborn, and they would have to accept that he was mine.

The girl in the mirror was powerful and fierce.

I hated her. I did not want to depend on her for my survival, but I was wise enough not to reject any weapon.

Let them stare.

"Are we ready then?" I turned toward the door to the hall.

"Sure." Cati pulled the bolt aside. "Let's go flounce you about and see what new whispers we hear."

"As long as they don't whisper that I am helpless."

Cati pulled the door open, and Ailis stepped into view.

"Huh," Ailis said. "Not what I was expecting for a stroll across the valley."

"What were you expecting?" I asked.

"Clean clothes and combed hair," Ailis said.

"None of that for our Ena." Cati bowed me down the hall. Ten guards in deep blue coats stepped forward to follow us. "A quiet peace is not in her blood."

"Of course not." I spoke loudly enough for all the guards to hear. "I was born in Harane. My parents died in Harane. The Guilds murdered the woman who raised me. They burned my home. I lost my taste for peace when I learned it was a lie."

A guard darted forward and pushed open the door that led out of the hall.

Aside from the blue-clad guards, the statue corridor had only four people in it—three strangers and Finn.

"Ena." Finn looked at me, a knowing smile growing across his face. "Liam told me you were heading down to see the children, and I'd been planning to check in on them today. I didn't feel quite safe making the long walk with my arm all bungled. But if I could go with you, I know my dear mother would feel much better about my leaving the keep."

I bit my cheeks to hide my smile.

"Have you been questioned by Wyman?" Ailis said.

Finn's jaw tensed.

"He went before I did," Cati said. "Liam had Wyman go through all the marked first."

But not me.

"Fine," Ailis said. "Just know that if we're attacked, we've been assigned to protect Ena, not you."

"Fair enough." Finn stepped next to me and offered me his good arm. "I would gladly meet a horrid death to protect my beloved Ena."

"Hush, you," I whispered. "I'm trying to look like I'm brave and in control of my own chivving destiny."

"No offense, my darling," Finn muttered as we cut down a side passage and to a flight of spiral stairs, "but one look at you, and the men will dream of your tits while the women loath you for your beauty. Some of that may be a bit flipped, but you get the general idea."

"It's a little late to change now." I glanced down to make sure my breasts were relatively covered.

"You absolutely should not change. Just know that the whispers will be gales of speech by nightfall." Finn winked.

"Good."

It took a full ten minutes to work our way down the spiral stairs, past guards, through corridors, down more stairs, past a metal gate, and out into the open.

I took a deep breath of the crisp fall air. For some reason, the scent of the wind smelled sweeter and fuller from the valley floor.

Trees with bright white bark rose up on either side of our dark stone path. The edges of their leaves had been kissed with oranges and golds, giving everyone winter's warning.

Along the sides of the path, bright red flowers bloomed at the top of long stalks, like the ground had decided to make living torches.

I tried to look calm as Ailis and Cati led me down the stone path that cut out into the valley proper. The walkway wound through flowerbeds and looped around fountains grander than anything I'd seen in Ilbrea.

"I think the thing I'm most excited for this winter is the solstice feast." Finn gripped my arm hard, as though he sensed my urge to linger beside a fountain made of pure white stone—the figure at the center looked eerily like Liam. "I already feel much better after a few proper meals, but there is something about the feasting season that warms my heart."

"I'm excited to see it," I said. "I don't think I've ever been to a feast before."

"If you're unsure, then you haven't," Finn said.

We cut off the path before we reached the proper town at the heart of the valley. The houses were all made of dark stone, like the rock had been discarded as they dug the tunnels of the crag and keep.

My breath hitched in my chest, and I squeezed Finn's arm.

He kissed the back of my hand. "I know you're not one to revel in fine food, as I am wont to do."

"Really? I'd never noticed."

"But there is plenty of music and dancing as well." Finn fell silent for a moment, not speaking again until we reached a group of men who stood beside the path in a tight clump. "And, since Liam knows how much you love a rollicking dance, I'm sure there will be better music than ever. I don't know if he tripped over himself and fell head over heels for you because you laugh like a fool when you dance or because you killed a Guilded commander. Either way, I don't suppose it matters."

The men all stared at me as we passed. I met each of their gazes, not allowing myself to flinch.

"The important thing is that after months in tents eating sludge, longing for a decent bed, and trying not to be torn apart by croilach," Finn pressed on, "we're safe in Lygan Hall. If anyone has earned a bit of peace, it's you."

We moved beyond the hearing of the men and onto a path lined with white flowers.

"Did you need to lay it on so thick?" I whispered.

"No." Finn shrugged. "But I did enjoy it."

I kept my hand in his as we moved from one path to another.

Just when I'd begun to wonder if the valley reached so far we'd need to camp overnight to cross it, trees surrounded our path.

"A quick word of warning," Finn said. "I never try to be my charming self with the sorcerers. It's best to go with a strict *yes ma'am, no ma'am*, and hope they don't take offense at your breathing."

"This is who we've left the children with?" I squeezed Finn's hand as the shadows of the trees overtook our path.

"They aren't as bad as you think," Finn said. "Only, their magic seems to make them too stern to enjoy a good laugh."

The path lost its stone surface as we ventured farther into the trees.

I took a deep breath, trying to catch the scent of the forest, but another feeling filled my chest. It wasn't the longing I'd felt every time I'd been near the boulders that surrounded the camp. The sensation was more like the prickly feel of knowing a predator is waiting to pounce.

The pressure of my knife hiding in my boot offered me comfort as I searched the shadows, looking for any hint of what had licked cold against the tops of my ears.

I heard the voices before I even spotted the stone wall surrounding the compound. The unseen people spoke in low and even tones.

Maybe this will be a good place for Cinni.

Tree branches laden with bright green leaves dripped over the stone wall. A silver gate blocked our way as we reached the end of the path.

I didn't let myself lean forward to peer through the bars of the gate. I wanted to. The urge to catch a glimpse of what might wait for me made my fingers twitch.

"We've come to see the sorcerers." Cati called out as she stepped in front of me. "I've brought Ena Ryeland to visit the children she rescued from the Lir Valley."

The gate swung open without a sound or hint as to how the metal had moved.

I kept my hand in Finn's as we followed Cati into the compound.

33

The stone of the walls surrounding the sorcerers' compound was thicker than I'd thought it would be. Nearly five feet of solid rock separated them from the rest of the valley.

Are the sorcerers trying to keep something out, or are the normal people trying to lock something in?

The question sent fear prickling on the back of my neck.

The garden that greeted us inside the walls did not quiet my fears. There were no people in the garden, despite the voices I'd heard from the outside.

Flowers of deep hues surrounded the paths that branched off in every direction. Their color was richer than any blooms I'd seen in Ilbrea, almost as though an artist had thickened the pigment as they painted this world.

The trees that grew up against the wall had broad, straight trunks without any hint of deformity. Shorter trees, with fruit dripping from their branches, grew in front of the giants I'd seen from outside the walls. Paths led to the fruit trees, as though inviting me to come and taste their bounty.

I didn't want to consider what the penalty for stealing food from the sorcerers might be.

"Beautiful, isn't it?" Finn said.

"It looks like the Brien enclave." I tried to relax my grip on Finn's hand. I couldn't manage it. "Is that how Regan created her perfect home? Magic?"

"The Brien allow their sorcerers to travel outside their safe haven," Finn said. "Regan keeps a complement of sorcerers with her at all times."

"The enclave isn't the Brien's true home?" I whispered. "They have a larger, grander place than that?"

"Not grander," Ailis said. "Just better protected."

"I suppose that's the price of amassing power," Finn said. "You start to fear everyone is trying to steal it from you."

"With the state we're in, do you blame them?" Cati asked.

493

Three women stepped through the trees on the far edge of the garden.

The first acknowledged us with a nod and led the others in our direction. Before they'd made it ten feet, a squeal of joy shot from behind them as Evie tore out of the trees and raced toward me.

"Ena!" She plowed into my side. "I was starting to think we'd been abandoned here forever."

"You haven't been abandoned." I gave Evie a hug before tipping her chin up so I could look into her dark eyes. "I just needed to wait until you'd settled in before I could visit."

"You look fancy." Evie wrinkled her brow. "Why do you look so fancy?"

So they will not see how lost I am.

"Because we are in Lygan Hall," Finn said. "I will eat, Ena will primp, and we'll all give in to a little bit of folly and enjoy our time here."

"I haven't had any folly," Evie said.

"You'll have to forgive the child," the first woman said. She wore her gray hair twisted into a large bun and had eyes of a brilliant emerald shade I'd only seen once before. "It can be so difficult for children to settle into new routines. We don't normally accost guests when they enter the garden."

"But I could hear them coming," Evie said.

"What has that got to do with running through the compound without permission?" the emerald-eyed woman asked.

Evie pursed her lips.

"It's been a lot of new things for you lately." I took Evie's hands. "But now you're finally somewhere you can get settled."

Evie bit her lips together as though trying swallow her own face.

"I'm here to sit with the children for a bit." I looked to the emerald-eyed woman. "Liam sent me so Marta could pay a visit to Wyman."

Evie's eyes widened.

"Evie would be pleased to take you to her siblings." The woman smiled. "The guards will wait here."

"We'll be staying with Ena," Ailis said. "Sorry, Iona. Liam has his ways."

Iona stared at Ailis for a moment, as though wondering if it would be worth the trouble of using magic to get the intruders out of her garden.

"As the Trueborn wills it," Iona finally said.

"I'm so glad you're going to sit with us for a while." Evie bounced on her toes as she led us back toward where she'd appeared. "Cinni and Dorran will be happy to see you. Gwen still isn't awake, so I don't think she'll care so much."

"Has there been any word on—" I looked back to where the three ladies had been. They'd all disappeared.

"I like Marta." Evie dragged me through the trees. "She tells us stories and tucks us under our blankets. She did it at camp, too. Every night." Evie looked up at me. "All the time."

"It's nice to have someone taking care of you," I said. "You'll finally…"

We stepped out on the other side of the trees, and I forgot what I was going to say.

Somehow, we'd moved from the garden to the inside of a stone hall, but there had never been any sort of door. I looked behind to find a solid wall I had apparently walked through not a breath before. Only Finn, Cati, and I had entered the room, but as Evie dragged me forward, the rest of the guards stepped through the solid stone, too.

If any of them were amazed at the feat, their faces didn't betray them.

"It would be nice to live someplace that isn't in the compound." Evie led me between two long tables where young men and women sat, reading by the light of the lae stones hanging from the ceiling.

There were no windows to offer any sunlight to the room. The only breaks in the walls I could see were two corridors that cut out from the back.

"Wyman said we're all going to have to study very hard and learn to use our magic," Evie said.

"I know," I said. "You've been so excited to learn."

"I thought it would be the fun sort of learning." Evie sighed. "Like the kind Cati taught in camp. I want to learn how to fight, but Wyman said I won't be using any real magic for months. *Months.*"

Finn gave a low laugh.

Evie stopped and spun to face him. "You wouldn't like it if they made you sit still and read for months."

"I'll give you that." Finn shrugged.

"And I'm not sure what they're going to do about Cinni." Evie furrowed her brow. "She's smart, maybe smarter than all of us, but I don't think she can spend months reading. If she sits too long, she gets antsy. That's when bad things happen. She'd been kept inside for six weeks before she snuck out to the pond for a breath of fresh air. That's when she sank the man who tried to grab her."

The echo of the horrible crack as the ground split beneath our feet rang through my mind. I didn't want to even begin to imagine what Cinni might do to the valley if they kept her tucked away for too long.

"I'll talk to Liam," I said, "make sure we get all four of you out for some nice fresh air so you don't feel cooped up. Maybe we can get someone to play a bit of music for Cinni, too. I think she'd like that."

The creases in Evie's brow smoothed out. "I think she'd like the music a lot." Evie tugged on my hand, dragging me into a long stone corridor with wooden doors along either wall. "When Gwen wakes up, can you take us to see more of Lygan Hall? I want to see where you're living."

"It's not all that interesting in the keep," Finn said. "If you want to see the good bits of Lygan Hall, it's me you ought to speak to. I grew up here as a scabby-kneed troublemaker. I learned all the best places to snag a sweet and the cracks and corners children aren't supposed to know about."

"I'm glad you've grown into such a fine influence for children," Ailis said.

"Children need a bit of fun." Finn winked at her. "Helps keep the grownups on their toes."

Ailis raised one ginger eyebrow at Finn.

I'd never realized how alike they looked. I wanted to ask if they were related but didn't want to seem even more ignorant than the guards trailing behind me probably believed me to be.

Evie paused in front of a set of wooden double doors. "I think you'll like this part." She shoved against the wood with all her might.

The doors swung open, and Evie staggered forward into a courtyard made for a fairy story.

Unlike the garden just inside the wall, this place was blatant in its magic.

The same sorts of deeply-hued flowers we'd passed in the front garden grew in ground-level beds surrounding the benches and fountain at the center of the space.

Potted plants sat on stone slabs that hovered in the air, as though they'd been suspended by invisible strings. The tiers of flowers rose all the way up to the second balcony that surrounded the square. Crystal spheres as clear as drops of water dotted the open air. The sun shone down from above, bathing the space in warm light.

I could picture the courtyard in the dark, with all the crystals glowing like lae stones, making the whole place look like the stars had come down to watch the sorcerers work. I wished I could see that sort of beautiful magic.

The hum of chatter stopped as the people in the courtyard caught sight of us. I kept my chin high and my face calm but couldn't drag my gaze from the fountain in the middle of the garden long enough to actually look at the people staring at me.

A statue of a woman stood at the center of the fountain. The angle of her chin and creases around her eyes were too familiar for me to ignore.

"Who's the woman in the fountain?" I asked.

"A lady who funneled all her magic into the mountain." Evie yanked on my hand, tugging me forward. "They've told me the story three times, and I read it in a book, too. I still don't understand it, though. If a lady putting her magic into the rocks is why the sorcerers in Lygan Hall have magic, then who put magic somewhere for the sorcerers in Ilbrea to get? Don't try asking for yourself, though. All you'll get is scowls and told the same story over again."

I sensed the stares of the people tracking us through the courtyard and to an open door on the far side.

"I've brought Ena, Finn, Cati and a bunch of strangers," Evie called into the room.

"Why have strangers come to visit us?" Dorran stepped into the doorway, his arms crossed over his chest.

"If you're rude to strangers, you'll never make new friends." Marta stepped out beside Dorran. She smiled at me. Both her dimples appeared on her cheeks, but the expression didn't quite reach her eyes. "It's good to see you all."

"You too," Ailis said. "You've been missed."

"Thanks." Marta nodded, and her smile disappeared. "Come on in, Ena. Cinni will be happy to have you for a visit."

I took a breath, steeling myself for some horror waiting within the room.

It was a pleasant place, with three big beds, a table and chairs, and a big couch facing an empty fireplace. A stack of books and the remains of lunch sat on the table.

"The food is better here," Dorran said. "Not that it would take much after the slop from camp."

"We should—"

"Be grateful we never went hungry?" Dorran cut across Marta. "I know." He sat down at the table and pulled a leather-bound book toward himself.

"Gwen." Evie ran to the farthest away bed where Gwen lay peacefully, as though she'd been tucked in for the night. "If you wanted to see Ena, now would be a good time to wake up."

Two hands appeared from the far side of the bed as Cinni pulled herself up to look at her oldest sister. Cinni stared into Gwen's face for a moment before sinking back down onto the floor.

"Cinni's taken to hiding behind the bed," Marta said. "If that's where she feels safe, she can stay there for now, but she'll have to start on her studies soon."

There was no hint of a response from the far side of the bed.

"She won't come out until Gwen wakes up," Dorran said. "Keep trying if you like, but you're wasting your time."

"She should get out and walk around," Evie said. "We could have fun, Cinni. Finn said he'd take us to places we shouldn't be."

Marta shot Finn a glare, but there was still no sound of movement from Cinni.

"I was going to ask Liam to send a musician to play for you, Cinni." I walked slowly toward her, listening for any hint of her getting upset. "Would you like a bit of music? Maybe we can get a fiddler to come by."

I sensed her anxiety rather than heard it, almost like a subtle thrum of panic flying through the air. "Or not." I backed away. "Perhaps after all the excitement, a nice bit of quiet would be best. You can let me know when you're ready to hear a few tunes played."

"I should go for my visit to Wyman," Marta said. "The sooner I leave, the sooner I'll be back. I don't want to miss dinner with the children."

"I don't think you should go at all." Evie raced across the room and stood in the doorway, blocking Marta's path.

"Ena will be with you," Marta said, "and I'll only be gone for a while."

"I don't care," Evie said. "You shouldn't go to that man. You should stay with us. It's better for you to stay with us."

I stood very still, waiting to hear whatever sound had upset Evie.

"Evie"—Marta knelt to be eyelevel with the child—"sometimes, we are asked to do unpleasant things."

"It's a bit more than unpleasant," Evie said.

"And even if we don't want to, we have to be brave and face the task," Marta said. "If not for ourselves, then for the people we care about. I will be back very soon. So be good for Ena, and look after Gwen."

Evie bit down on her lips.

"Please, Evie." Marta stood and looked to me. "See you in a bit."

Evie didn't fight as Marta shifted her out of the doorway and stepped into the courtyard. She just stared after Marta, still biting her lips.

"It's not going to be so bad," I said. "I'm here. Finn and Cati are here."

Evie wrinkled her brow.

"Marta will be back soon," I said. "I promise you're going to be just fine."

"It's not me I'm worried about," Evie said. "I can hear them. The people Wyman questions. Their voices carry through the stone in the compound. I can hear all of them scream."

34

There was a certain strange peace to being locked inside Lygan Hall. The size of the valley made it easy to forget that none of us were allowed to leave. And the strength of the stone offered a false sense of safety that I was tired enough to accept.

For thirteen days, I visited the children every morning, letting the people watch me as I walked to and from the compound, always with a pack of guards marching around me. I went to the training ground every afternoon. Cati finally gave in to my request for her to teach me proper sword combat.

I hadn't ventured into the village. Liam was against my going. Cati and Ailis agreed. The village had too many corners, too many shadows where evil could hide.

Every night, Liam would tell me it would soon be over. They would find the traitor, and I would be allowed to walk freely among the people.

Still, the traitor had not been found, and my paths led me only to the training ground and to the compound.

Wyman had questioned everyone from the camp but me. I offered to be questioned, but Liam refused.

So the murderer walked free, and the rumors about Emmet and me kept growing.

We were sent by the Guilds. The King himself had trained me as an assassin. I'd killed Emmet and left him to rot on the western border of the woods. I'd bewitched Liam and forced him to make the croilach.

Finn was the only one who'd actually tell me what the whispers were. Everyone else held their lips tight and their weapons close.

Nights spent in Liam's arms were the only thing that kept me from raging at the gale of accusations.

He wanted to touch me. He wanted to hold me. He didn't think I was a murderer or an enchantress who had stolen his affection.

I would fall asleep tangled in his arms and wake to his skin pressed against mine in the morning. I wanted to spend my life waking up surrounded by his warmth.

I could have lived with the rumors if it meant being by his side, but there are some accusations that cannot be ignored.

35

"They're going to have to try something else." Finn set down his fork and leaned back in his chair. "It's been two weeks. Gwen should've woken up by now."

"I've already spoken to Wyman." Liam kept his gaze fixed on his plate. He'd barely touched his meal. "They can't help her. If they'd seen her use magic before, they might know enough about which bit of her burnt out, but if they just start guessing, they could do more harm than good."

"Cinni won't make it much longer," I said. "I managed to get her to listen to the fiddle player a few days ago, but now she's back to hiding behind the bed."

"We can try and get her out of the compound," Finn said. "Maybe some fresh air will do her good."

"Wyman won't allow it," Liam said. "And I can't say I blame him. We've all seen what Cinni is capable of. If something sets her off, people could die."

"Losing her mind from being trapped in that room, huddled by her unconscious sister could get people killed as well." I stood, went to the window, and looked down over the valley.

The angle of the morning light lent deep and mysterious shadows to the now familiar scene. The thick cluster of trees that shrouded the compound didn't look like anything more than an innocent little forest, but I knew all too well what danger lurked within the stone walls.

"We could send my grandmother to them," Finn said. "Have her bring a pie around, let her dote on the children. That woman's got a comforting presence that would bring a bear to heel."

"I'll see if Wyman will allow it." Liam set his fork aside and dug his knuckles into his temples. "I should be able to do more. I should be doing something to help the children or protect the Hall."

"Don't be too hard on yourself," Finn said. "Orla's banned us from leaving to hunt for monsters. Colm is the Blood Leader, so setting up guards and watches is his territory.

Wyman rules the sorcerers' compound with a magic-laden fist. And as best we can tell, the gods themselves aided the trueborn who made the croilach. As far as I'm aware, you can't use clan laws to punish gods, so there's chiv all we can do."

"I should spend some time on the training field today," Liam said. "Make sure the people from camp are keeping up. Orla will have to open the gates eventually, and we'll need to be ready when she does."

A faint thumping carried from the far side of the door.

"What a happy day that will be," Finn said. "I've always hated the winter hunts. Absolutely loathed getting snow packed into my boots."

The thumping got louder.

I walked toward the door to the hall, grateful for the knife pressed against my ankle.

"But," Finn sighed, "I would trek through snow with a song in my heart if it meant getting closer to the trueborn who started all this."

"There are people in the hall," I said.

A moment later, the sound of voices came through the wood.

"Get to the bedroom." Liam leapt to his feet and grabbed the sword that leaned against his wardrobe.

I opened my mouth to protest.

"Go." Finn drew his own sword.

My heart battered against my ribs as I stepped into the bedroom, the place that had become my sanctuary.

Bang, bang, bang.

A fist slammed against Liam's sitting room door.

Please do not take this peace from me.

"Who's there?" Liam called.

"Your Elder." Orla's voice cut through the door.

Neither Liam nor Finn relaxed.

"Get back." Finn shooed me into the shadows of Liam's bedroom. He didn't tell me to close the door. There would have been no point since there wasn't a lock.

I pulled the knife from my boot and pressed my back to the stone wall.

Liam stepped toward the hall door. The rasp of the bolt of being slid aside sent a shiver up my spine.

"Mother," Liam said. "What an unexpected surprise."

"Don't bother," Orla said. "No amount of sentiment or foolery will help you, Liam."

Footsteps moved closer to the door.

"Where's the girl?" Orla said.

"What do you want with her?" Liam asked.

"The only wish I have for that girl is for her to never have existed," Orla said. "I am not that lucky."

"No, you're not," Liam said. "If you've nothing more to do here than insult the woman I've chosen to share my bed, get out."

"Neither of us is lucky in that regard," Orla said.

Thumps came from the hall as though an army of men were approaching.

"Word has come from the Healy Clan," Orla said. "The blood leader they lost was murdered."

"We knew that," Finn said.

"Poisoned," Orla said. "His death looked like a blood fever until the very end. A handful of others took ill with the same symptoms though some of them survived. What a clever ruse, mimicking an illness to cover murder."

I gripped the hilt of my knife, but my hands would not stop shaking.

"The Healys have been searching for a culprit," Orla pressed on. "It took a while for the rumors on the wind to fly all the way to their fortress. Another military leader had been killed in much the same fashion. A Guilded commander, in fact. Two such similar assassinations cannot be a coincidence."

"Ena had nothing to do with this." There was a hint of fear lying beneath Liam's words.

I wanted to take his hand and promise that everything would be all right. I could not have stomached such a lie.

"The Healys have sent their grievance to the Clans Council," Orla said. "A trial has been called."

"This is ridiculous," Liam said. "Ena has never even met anyone from the Healy Clan. She'd never know how to find them."

"Ena has been summoned to stand trial before the clans," Orla said. "I hope you are happy with the woman you've chosen, Liam. She could very well cost you your life."

"If that's the price of being with Ena, then I will pay it."

"No." I stepped out of the shadows and into the doorway. "No, you can't. They want to accuse me, fine. But they can't drag you into this."

Orla looked at me. Her eyes were cold. I couldn't tell if the ice was born of hatred or terror.

"You will both be taken immediately," Orla said. "The escort leaves in an hour."

"I'll go," I said. "Liam can stay here. He can't—"

"You gave him your oath," Orla cut across my words. "You are bound to him. He accepted responsibility for your steps within the mountains. Your punishment will be his. Take them."

"Will you let your anger go this far?" Liam said.

Orla stepped out of the way.

A pack of blue-clad guards took her place.

"What will you do without an heir, Mother?" Liam asked. "If you let them push you this far, the Duweads will be nothing but filth beneath the boots of the other clans."

"If I do not obey the summons, it will be seen as an act of war," Orla said.

The guards entered the room, but none of them tried to grab us.

"You want to lead this clan with an Ilbrean in your bed, then prove her worth and her innocence," Orla said. "You have made your choices. Live or die by them."

36

The sound of Orla's starched skirt rustled down the hall, but none of the guards followed her.

"I hate to do this, Liam," one of the guards said. "Can you just come with us?"

Liam stayed silent.

"There's a full complement of guards outside this corridor," the man said. "You'll never make it past them. All you'd do is kill a mess of your own people."

"And the path?" Liam said.

The guard shook his head. "I'm sorry, Liam."

Liam handed the guard his sword. "Do not forget that I am your Trueborn."

"Your knife, Miss." The guard nearest me held his hand out for my blade.

Liam gave a tiny nod.

I flipped my knife and laid the hilt in the guard's hand, then reached down and pulled the sheath from my boot. "I would appreciate it if you kept them together. Cati gave me the sheath and blade as a set."

"I..." The guard looked to Liam and then back to me. "Yes, Miss."

"She and I will travel together," Liam said. "If you separate us, I will fight back."

"If Orla orders us—"

"We will not be separated," Liam said. "Am I understood?"

"Yes, Trueborn." The guard nearest Liam bowed.

"I'll just pack you a few things, shall I?" Finn replaced his own sword in its sheath on his hip. "It'll be quite a journey, and you know how the clan elders like to blather."

"You can't," the guard said.

"Why would that be?" Finn's fingers twitched as though he longed to pull his sword right back out of its sheath.

"You've been called upon to be a guard of the escort," the man said. "They looked for you in your rooms. Better toss a uniform on before Colm has a fit."

"Go," Liam said. "We'll meet you below."

Finn stepped between the guards and to my side. "I'll see you soon." He kissed my forehead and weaved back through the men and out of sight.

"Fetch someone to pack for Ena and me," Liam said. "I am the Trueborn of the Duwead Clan. I will not step in front of the council looking as though I have been abandoned by my people."

"Of course not." The man bowed. "I'll send word down and have someone take care of it."

Liam reached for me. I wanted to feel his hand in mine so badly, but still, it took me a moment to convince my feet to move.

I stepped between the two nearest guards and held my breath, waiting for one of them to run me through. I took another step, and still the blue-coated guards only watched me.

Liam took a step toward me, closing the distance between us.

"It's going to be a long journey." Liam took my hand in his. "We should start as soon as possible. The longer there are guards escorting us to the Broinn, the longer Lygan Hall will be vulnerable to attack."

I let Liam lead me into the corridor. Two-dozen guards filled the narrow space.

"Whoever you believe is responsible for the croilach attacks, understand there could be more out there," Liam said. "Any trueborn strong enough and desperate enough to create nine of the beasts would have no reason to stop there. Nothing but death can stop a murderer so filled with fury. Make sure all the guards who are staying in the Hall know how much danger this valley is in. Watch every shadow a monster might hide in.

"I don't know who unleashed this terror on the Duwead Clan, but it is up to the guards of Lygan Hall to protect its people. Do not let this be the end of our clan. Fight to the last man to protect the innocent lives here. And be prepared for battle when we find out which trueborn is responsible for the deaths of thirty of our people. They may think they are defeating us. They are only forging a fiercer enemy."

His words rang through the hall.

The posture of the guards changed. Their shoulders went back as they tightened their grips on their weapons.

"We will protect the Hall," a female guard with short hair said. "They will be taught the consequences of attacking the Duweads."

A ripple of nods went up and down the corridor.

I held tight to Liam's hand as he walked through the guards and into the room of statues beyond.

Another pack of guards waited for us. They added on to the flock trailing in our wake.

Liam didn't stop to speak to those guards as he led me down corridors and through rooms I'd never even seen before.

I may never see this place again.

I forced down the rising panic in my chest and swallowed the dozens of things I needed to say to Liam. I wished I could promise myself there would be time to speak to him later, but I didn't know if that was true.

"The children," I said just loud enough for Liam to hear. "Promise me they'll be safe."

"Marta is still with them," Liam said. "She'll look after them."

A knot pressed on my throat, making it impossible to speak. I nodded instead.

We stopped at a spiral staircase where ten more guards waited for us.

Liam nodded them down the stairs. We followed the blue coats, twisting around and around.

Orange lights had been set into the ceiling, but they didn't offer a cheerful glow. The hue seemed menacing, as though the flames of a battle were lapping at our flesh.

We followed the guards around and around until I was sure we'd gone far below the ground.

There hadn't been any windows to prove we'd gotten closer to the earth, or any doorways where others waited to join our path. Just a twisting descent that offered no clue as to when it might end.

The sounds of voices below were the first hint of there being anything to our journey besides plunging into the earth.

"I'll not have either of them traveling on foot." I recognized Tirra's voice. "You would do well to remember who your Trueborn is and the courtesy you owe him."

Gratitude replaced a tiny bit of my dread.

The stairs ended, and we stepped out into a tunnel forty feet wide and so long I couldn't see anything but darkness in either direction.

Tirra stood to one side. She held the reins of two horses while more of the animals pawed at the ground behind her.

"Liam." Tirra turned to him. "I have horses for you and Ena."

"Thank you, Tirra." Liam gave a tiny smile.

"I won't be accompanying you apparently." Tirra sucked in her cheeks as though swallowing words she longed to shout. "That doesn't mean the two of you shouldn't be riding as your station demands." She shot a glare at a white-haired guard. "This mount should do well for Ena."

A horse with a pure black coat stepped forward as Tirra handed me her reins.

"Only fitting, I think." Tirra gave me a nod and passed the reins of a matching black horse to Liam. "See that you bring them back to me well cared for. These ladies are more than pretty. They're two of the fastest I've got."

"They'll be looked after," Liam said.

Tirra nodded and turned to the swarm of guards in the tunnel. "Who is going to be caring for the horses on this chivving mess of an expedition?"

"Me," a hesitant voice called over the sounds of the masses.

Tirra stormed toward whatever poor sap had been placed in charge of caring for her darling horses.

Liam led me down the corridor.

We passed a man with bright white hair and dark skin. He stood in the center of the guards, lording over their scrambling chaos. From the way the men nodded to him as they passed, it was easy enough to guess he was Colm, Blood Leader of the Duwead Clan.

But there was something different in the way the guards acknowledged Colm and Liam.

Liam nodded at the guards we passed and moved without waiting for anyone to give permission, even though we were both prisoners.

The guards nodded back to Liam. Some even stopped what they were doing long enough to bow. Even as they went about their tasks, everyone seemed aware of the presence of their Trueborn.

I had never walked anywhere in Lygan Hall with Liam, not since the first day when he'd saved me from Orla's wrath. I hadn't seen the way the people reacted to him. Not really.

As we walked to the very front edge of the pack of guards, it was as though, in a strange way, Liam was still in control. Even as we were being forced to attend a trial where both of us could be killed, Liam was still the one they looked to for protection and permission.

I don't think he understood the power he emitted, just walking through his own people. Maybe that's what it's like for those raised to rule. They become numb to the respect and deference offered them.

Liam stopped when there was only a line of twelve guards in front of us.

The guards bowed to him.

He gave them a nod, then offered me a hand to help me onto my horse.

I wouldn't have taken it, but I could feel the stares of the hundreds of guards behind us.

Trust him. Let him show them the Liam they need to see.

I took his hand and climbed onto my horse.

She shifted her weight beneath me, as though longing to run.

Liam kissed the back of my hand before climbing into his saddle.

"Excuse me, Miss."

I looked down to find the young guard with the bald head and dark skin.

"I was told to give you this"—he held up my black cloak—"to keep you warm on the journey."

"Thank you." I threw the cloak around my shoulders and fastened the bird clasp. The metal of the closure was chill against my skin. The dark fabric matched my mount's coat.

I looked behind to the rows of guards, searching their ranks for any familiar faces from the camp. Finn's red hair was easy to spot, and Case stood right beside him.

I could not find anyone else I knew in the mass of blue.

All of them stared at me as though caught in some terrible trance.

I was not an orphan from Harane to them.

I was no longer chased by Death. I had become the fiend.

I would accept their fear if it meant saving Liam's life.

3 7

The mountain did not know that a stone heart can grieve, nor did she understand how deeply a human heart can be damaged by greed.

Long ago, after the mother trusted the mountain to save her child and funneled all her magic into the stone, the mountain learned those horrible lessons.

The mountain called the offspring of the child she raised deep within her stone back to the safety of her lands. The offspring came, bringing their spouses and the children they had born.

The mountain feared the spouses who did not hold her stone in their blood—they were intruders who would ruin her lands and steal from her beloved children—but love convinced her to save them all.

The mountain watched her people thriving in her embrace and learned what wonders the love between a human and her mate can create. The stone at the heart of the mountain felt hope for the first time.

Love and children. Generations of children who would prosper in her embrace. The mountain would never be lonely again.

The offspring gathered in the Broinn, living together and enjoying the bounty the mountain provided. There was a time of great peace and prosperity when the Black Bloods first came to their true home.

But wherever there is anything of worth, jealousy grows.

Fights over food, territory, and rank brought violence to the Broinn.

The mountain wept as the blood of her beloved children seeped into her stones. Her walls trembled and the ground cracked, but the children would not heed her warning and refused to cease their battle.

Magic surged through the mountain as she prepared to end her children's lives rather than watch them become murderers and monsters.

Most fled in fear.

Five mothers were brave enough to kneel before the mountain and beg forgiveness.

They had lived too close, too packed together. The women swore that if they had the space, they could keep their children from fighting each other.

The mountain heard the mothers' plea and gave in to their wishes.

She carved five tunnels leading away from the Broinn, giving each mother a path to follow with her children, granting each of them a home where they could be safe and let generations expand within the embrace of the mountains.

Each woman swore an oath of peace to the mountain and followed the path to the territory where they would build their clan.

The mountain was happy, for her children had found peace.

The mountain did not know how easily humans lie.

3 8

I'm not sure how long we rode the first day in the tunnel. There wasn't even a way to be sure when the sun had set far above us. It was as though the mountain had trapped me underground again, swallowed me whole and left me with no choice but to continue forward. Only this time, there were hundreds of people with me. I had felt safer alone in the darkness.

I knew Orla rode behind us, in the very center of the group beside Blood Leader Colm. Even glancing at the man's dark skin and bright white hair made me uneasy to have him riding out of my view. I could feel the prickle of stares on the back of my neck and wondered if one of those sets of eyes belonged to Orla or Colm. I did not turn around to check. I would not give Orla the pleasure of knowing that I wanted nothing more than to run from the demons marching behind me.

But Liam rode calmly at my side, and I could not leave him behind. I would not even attempt escape without him.

So I kept riding forward.

In the dim blue light of the lae stones, there was no warning of anything in front of us until the wall of the outpost came into view.

Six men in black coats stood on top of the wall, their arrows nocked and aimed at our escort.

My heart leapt into my throat as I waited for the soldiers to attack, but they did not loose their arrows.

"We've come to the outpost for shelter as we journey to the Broinn," a guard at the front of our pack called up. "We travel with Orla, Elder of the Duwead Clan, Liam, True-born Duwead, and Colm, Blood Leader of the Duwead Clan."

With a clinking of chains and creak of hinges, a door in the center of the wall swung down.

A great pool of orange light glowed on the other side.

I tightened my grip on my reins, still waiting for an attack. But the guards at the front of our group walked quickly forward, as though excited to pass through the doorway.

"We only got word you were coming a few hours ago," a man in a black uniform said as soon as the first of the blue-clad guards stepped under the wall. "We've the main rooms prepared, but the guards might have to find a spot and toss a blanket down."

"We can't blame you," one of the blue guards said. "We usually offer more than a breath of warning before coming to you in this number."

The blue guard sounded cheerful, despite the three feet of stone wall we'd ridden beneath to reach the inside of the orange-lit space.

If I hadn't been terrified, I might have been impressed enough to understand his relief.

The orange glow came from hundreds of orbs hanging from the dark stone, just as it had in Orla's council chamber. But this space was not as barren.

To one side, a stable had been carved into the stone wall. To the other, three layers of balconies reached up toward the stone ceiling. Across from the gate, far enough away that all the guards, both black and blue-clad, could have had a fine time dancing and never worried about bashing elbows, another high stone wall and wide door blocked our way forward.

A blue-clad guard stepped in front of me and reached for my reins.

"Kely, that is not how you treat a lady," Liam said. "You will respect her, or you will stay away from her."

"I'm sorry, Trueborn." The guard Kely bowed.

Liam climbed off his horse and offered Kely his reins before reaching up and lifting me down. He passed the reins of my horse to Kely. "Don't be sorry. Just spread the word to the other guards. Ena will be treated with the same respect given to me. You will make sure the guards at the Broinn understand this as well. Am I clear?"

"Yes, Trueborn." Kely bowed to Liam and then to me. "It is an honor to serve the Trueborn."

Liam didn't speak again until Kely had disappeared into the swarm of blue coats. "We should get to our quarters. Tomorrow will be another long ride."

"Of course." I kept my hand in Liam's, refusing to show a hint of the stiffness in my legs as I followed him toward the side of the outpost where balconies rose up the wall.

Four men in black uniforms stood at the bottom of a set of stairs that reached straight up to the third story. All four bowed and stepped out of Liam's path.

"The room at the end if you would, Trueborn." One of the guards gave Liam an extra bow.

Liam gave a stiff nod and stepped past the guards. He led me onto the stairs and nodded to me before beginning to climb.

I let my gaze slip out over the scene below as I followed Liam.

The horses were already being brought into the stable. Colm stood at the center of it all, watching as the gates shut us off from the tunnel back to Lygan Hall. Orla herself was nowhere to be seen.

At the top of the stairs, Liam led me all the way down the long balcony to the very last room.

I'd expected bars on the window and a giant lock on the door, but there was no sign at all that the room we'd been given was meant to be a prison.

Liam placed a hand on the back of my waist, ushering me quickly through the door and shutting it behind us. There was no bolt for him to slide into place.

We both stood staring at the room for a long while.

The bed had been laid out with blankets and pillows. A bottle of chamb and a tray of rolls, honey, and cured meat waited on the table. A circle of orange orbs had been set into the ceiling.

"What is this place?" I asked.

"The outpost. The halfway point between Lygan Hall and the Broinn."

"How far apart are they?"

"A bit over sixty-two miles."

"We did travel a long way today, didn't we?"

"Ena, I'm so sorry." Liam turned to me. Pain I could not bear to witness filled his eyes.

"Don't." I took off my cloak and laid it on the bed. "Why do the men here wear black?"

"They're members of the shadow guard. They take an oath to stay underground protecting the clan. The color is a sign of respect for their sacrifice. There are some below Lygan Hall, too, just nowhere you would've been."

"That is quite the sacrifice to make."

I tried to picture it. Willingly forsaking the sun to protect my home. I would have taken that vow if I could have spared Harane, but we were a village, not a mighty clan with hundreds of men and tunnels the Guilds would have to fight to breach.

"We should eat." I sat at the table and stared at the food, wondering if it had been poisoned. It would have been a poetic end. "Do you think it's safe?"

"Our own people prepared it." Liam sat beside me and poured himself a glass of chamb.

"The Healy Blood Leader probably thought the same thing."

Liam took a sip before passing the glass to me.

"If it were poison I'd brewed, you wouldn't be able to taste it." I sipped from the glass. The bubbles tickled my throat but offered no flavor of malice.

"Then I suppose it's a good thing I'm sure you didn't do this." Liam poured a glass for himself.

"There has to be a way out." My breath hitched in my chest.

"If Orla doesn't deliver us to the trial, it will be considered an act of war against the clans," Liam said. "A clan war would kill thousands of Black Bloods. We could lose all the work we've done in Ilbrea."

"Better to be executed than to live knowing you've caused that much pain." I took another sip of chamb to wash the sour from my mouth.

"They will not hurt you." Liam set his glass down and tipped my chin so I had to look into his dark eyes. "I swear to you, Ena, I will protect you."

"I don't know if you can." I forced my voice to stay calm. "But you have to find a way to save yourself."

"Ena—"

"There is no camp without you." I pressed my fingers over his lips. "The sorcis will be left to suffer. They will be taken by the Guilds. You can't let that happen."

Liam kissed my fingers and lifted them away from his mouth. "Our fates are tied. They cannot judge you as guilty without placing the same judgment on me."

"Then pull the stone back out of my ribs. You drew the mark on my side, take the magic out. Tell them it was only a rumor that I gave you my oath. Then you'll be—"

"It can't be done. There is no way to erase a mark, and removing the stone would mean killing you."

"Regan wasn't punished when that man touched me in the enclave." I pushed away from Liam and stood. "If that man had to die and she was left unharmed, there has to be a way to protect you, too."

"Violating you was a low offense."

"I had to kill that man." As soon as I had spoken, I wished I could swallow my words. I pressed a hand to my chest, feeling my pendant against my skin as I waited for Orla to come bursting in, gleeful of my confession.

A minute passed before I found the courage to speak again. "How can groping me be considered a low offense if he had to be executed?"

"His actions were not horrible enough to be considered offensive to the mountain. If Regan had defended him"—Liam stood and walked slowly toward me, as though afraid I might actually try and run from him—"if she'd hidden what the bastard had done, or tried to keep him from the clans' justice, then she would have been tied up in the woods and gutted with him.

"To murder a clan member in their own territory is one of the highest offenses in the Clan Treaty and goes against our covenant with the mountain. I could tie you up and hand you to the council, and it would not release me from the bond we both agreed to."

"There has to be a way." I made myself speak past the horrible knot of fear in my throat. "There's got to be something we can do. I will not let them hurt you."

"There's only one way out of this for either of us. We have to prove to the council that you're innocent."

"How? You've spent weeks searching for the one who betrayed us. How are we going to be able to do anything different in the Broinn than you've already done in Lygan Hall?"

Liam went still for a moment. I could see him tucking his own fear away so I wouldn't feel it.

"I swear to you I will find a way." Liam pressed his lips to my forehead.

"And if you can't?"

"Then I will shatter the stones above us, and we will flee."

"Across the Arion Sea?" I touched the creases by the corners of his eyes. "Or to the kingless territories?"

"Your path is mine, Ena. And we will walk side by side to whatever end."

I kissed him, trying to sink his taste so deep into my bones that not even fire could burn the memory away.

His hands roamed up my sides, as though he wanted to be sure I was still breathing.

I pressed myself against him, needing to feel every ridge of his body against mine. Needing to know that even as darkness surrounded us, he craved me as much as I did him.

His longing pulsed through me.

He lifted me, and I wrapped my legs around him, unwilling to be parted from him for a single moment.

I forgot about the guards outside as he pressed my back against the stone wall. He trailed his lips along my neck, and the violence of the world meant nothing.

His flesh found mine, and not even the will of the gods could have torn me from him.

39

I don't know who in Lygan Hall packed my things to travel. It could have been Nora, it seemed so much like the way she'd prepared me to leave Frason's Glenn. A small trunk had been stuffed to bursting with fancy clothes to match my black cloak and plenty of powders and paints to ensure I had armor strong enough to take on the Guilds.

A man in a black coat delivered our breakfast tray. A little glass bottle sat beside the rolls and cheese. The shadow guard stared at me as he placed the tray on the table.

I took the little bottle and drank its bitter contents while staring right back into his eyes.

A flush of red overtook the guard's face, and he fixed his gaze on his boots as he bowed back out of the room.

Men who will gladly fight demons will run from the truth of womanhood. I am grateful for the lesson I learned from that cowardly guard.

I rode by Liam's side through the darkness for another long day.

The blackness of the tunnel pressed in around me. The only sounds were the pounding of the guards' feet and clopping of the horses' hooves.

I wasn't sure if time was racing as I neared my doom, or if it had stopped as the mountain tried to rob me of my sanity. Either way, the constant plodding developed a steady rhythm in my mind, and the rhythm developed a voice of its own.

He is mine.

He is mine.

He is mine.

If they touch him, they will burn.

He is mine.

He is mine.

The words offered a violent comfort.

When I had almost become convinced that the words were not born of my own thoughts, another wall came into view.

This wall did not leave a gap for men to stand on the top. The barrier reached from floor to ceiling with only thin slats for windows where archers could aim their bows.

Arrowheads glistened in the blue light as we stopped in front of the gate.

"We've come at the request of the Clans Council," a guard at the front of our pack called up. "We travel with Orla, Elder of the Duwead Clan, Liam, Trueborn Duwead, Colm, Blood Leader of the Duwead Clan, and Ena Ryeland, who will face the accusation of murder."

The metal gate in the wall began lowering to the ground. There was no orange glow to beam into the tunnel. But the sounds of voices and movement carried from the darkness beyond.

Even after the gate lay flat against the ground, the guard at the front of our escort remained still for a moment.

I took a breath, waiting for something horrible or magical to happen. But the guard only gave himself a nod before stepping up onto the back of the gate and leading us through the fifteen-foot long corridor under the wall.

We passed beneath the stone arch, and my whole body tensed as though the gods themselves were staring down at me, already declaring their judgment.

We reached the end of the passage, and a new feeling replaced the fear in my chest. A pull that started at the point right in front of my heart, right beneath my stone pendant.

Have they poisoned me?

The horrible thought raced through my mind before I recognized the sensation.

The longing, the need to follow wherever that pull in my chest led.

I looked to Liam. He rode by my side, his face made of stern stone like he wasn't feeling anything unusual.

We rode past orange orbs set into the wall, passing another set of balconies like in the outpost, before following a twist in the path that led to a wide-open space.

I searched the cavern, trying to find what the pull in my chest might be leading me toward.

There were tiers of seats carved into each of the five stone walls, all facing the center of the room where a pentagon-shaped table had been surrounded by five chairs.

Five tunnels led into the space, cutting in at the corners of each of the walls. A door had been carved into the base of each of the seating sections. All the doors had heavy metal bars crisscrossing their wood.

I studied each of the entryways, trying to find where the pull might be leading me.

Liam climbed off his horse and reached up to me.

I laid my hand on his chest as he lifted me down. His heartbeat thumped against my palm. The lure of him still made me want to drown in him, but the pull was there behind my longing for Liam, drawing me toward something I could not see.

"Don't be afraid," Liam whispered the moment before a ringing cut through the air.

He pressed my hand against the steady thumping of his heart as the bell tolled again and again.

The noise vibrated my ribs, shaking away the armor I had wrapped around my fear.

Sounds of movement came in the slim silences between the awful tolling. Soon, shadows appeared down the other four corridors. Hundreds of people entered the cavern.

Each set of tiers filled with armed guards dressed in a different color. Green, gray, purple, and burnt orange marked each of the other clans. When the guards had reached their places, three from each group would step toward the center of the room. One would sit while two stood behind them.

The bell did not stop tolling until all four sides had gone still, leaving only the Duwead Clan outside the chamber.

A shuffling of footsteps came from behind us, followed by the rustling of a starched skirt.

Orla stepped in front of Liam and me, then gestured the guards forward onto the bottom tiers of the empty section.

"She will not stand with you," Orla spoke under the sound of the guards' feet. "Play whatever games you like in the Hall, but if they see you treat her as though the customs of the clans do not apply to your petal whore, you will set the council against her before we begin."

Liam took my hand. For a moment, it seemed as though he might bolt up the tunnel, leading me to freedom.

There is no way out.

"Follow the last of the guards," Liam said. "Stand on the bottom tier, and wait to be called."

He squeezed my hand as the last of the Duwead guards passed.

I pulled free of his comfort to take my place on the bottom tier. The longing in my chest doubled in the absence of his touch.

He followed Orla to her seat at the center of the room, then stood behind her chair with Colm.

A woman with pale blond hair nodded to Liam from across the table. It wasn't until she smiled that I recognized Regan.

A wave of fury washed over my fear.

"Just hold still," a familiar voice whispered in my ear. "They'll blather for a bit, but the best thing you can do is let them argue."

I glanced over my shoulder.

Finn stood behind me, his gaze fixed on the people at the table even as he spoke.

"Don't react. They'll see it and hold it against you."

I exhaled, forcing my face to be calm.

A man in a gray jacket stood from his seat at the table. "As Elder of the Healy Clan, I call this council to order."

Fear dug into my spine.

"We have come here today to discuss the murder of the Blood Leader of my clan. Warner was a good man and a fine fighter who led the guards of the Healy Clan with honor for many years. He was denied the privilege of dying in battle by a coward who resorted to poison for a traitorous end. The Clan Treaty was broken. The one responsible will face the consequences, or the Healy Clan will seek justice of their own."

The gray-clad guards of the Healy Clan began stomping all together. The rhythm of their pounding quickened as though they were speeding their charge for my blood.

I kept my gaze locked on the table.

"Enough!" The woman sitting in front of Regan waved a hand through the air.

The Healy guards fell silent.

"We all received word of your accusation against a girl of the Duwead Clan," the Brien Elder said. "What evidence do you have of her guilt?"

None!

I wanted to scream the word, but Liam stayed silent. I pressed my hands against my thighs, willing my rage not to betray me.

"I believe we all know what the girl has done," the Healy Elder said. "Word traveled to all of us that Ena Ryeland, sister of Emmet Ryeland, had joined the Duwead Clan. But she was not ferried out of Ilbrea as a sorci running from the Sorcerers Guild. Ena Ryeland is but a normal girl. A normal girl who happens to have a strange skill for murder."

The word rang around the room. There was no stomping this time.

"Ena Ryeland joined the Duweads and less than a month later assassinated a Guilded Commander with a heartless poisoning plot. We all heard about it, didn't we?" The Healy Elder looked to each of the sections of tiers. "Every trader moving between clans carried with them the story of the Duweads' great victory, granted to them by an Ilbrean girl who just so happened to be an assassin. The tales did not warn us of how dark her deeds truly were." The Elder stared straight at me.

I did not flinch as I met his gaze.

"She did not just poison the commander," the Elder pressed on. "She gave people around him a vicious brew to make the commander's death look like an illness. Putting other lives at risk to kill her mark.

"We lost a great man when we lost Warner. I had every healer and sorcerer in my fortress try to save him. In the end, the best of them came to one conclusion. Poison. The symptoms looked like a blood fever, but there was no illness in his body. It was not a disease but an attack that killed my Blood Leader and claimed three innocent lives as the murderer sought her mark."

A rustle of tiny movements carried around the crowd.

"Eight of Warner's men fell ill at the same time he was stricken. Three died." The Elder pointed to me. "This assassin came from Ilbrea and is trying to commit the same atrocities she executed on Guild soil. We will not allow her reign of terror to continue here."

"I'm so sorry." Orla shook her head.

"It is a time of great grief," the Healy Elder said.

"No," Orla said, "not that. I'm sorry that I must be misunderstanding you. Or, rather, I believe you have misspoken."

"What?" The Healy Elder narrowed his eyes.

"You seem to have implied that there was some horror or monstrosity involved in the execution of Commander Drason," Orla said. "Perhaps you aren't familiar with his name, but I am. The man that girl killed was guilty of kidnapping magic born children and handing them over to the Sorcerers Guild. He was also guilty of taking the mothers of those children. We don't know where he took them or exactly what he did with them, but I believe any thinking person with knowledge of the Guilds will agree that his aim must have involved breeding."

There was a long silence as Orla sat and stared at the Healy Elder.

"I'm sorry again, Edric." Orla nodded to the Healy Elder. "Perhaps a woman needs to be completely blunt when speaking to a man. Commander Drason stole magically gifted children from their mothers. He then kidnapped the mothers and raped them to breed new children for him to steal. If you would like to argue that this man did not deserve death, then I suppose we will have to sit through it. If you do not have an argument to make on Drason's behalf, then let us not refer to his death as murder. It was an execution for crimes against innocents, organized and completed by the Duwead Clan. Would you like to accuse me of murdering an Ilbrean commander, Edric?"

"We are here to discuss the murder of my Blood Leader." Furious red crept up Edric's cheeks.

"Then please keep to the topic at hand. I hate being underground and would like to return to Lygan Hall as quickly as possible."

Edric worked his lips together for a moment before speaking. "There is only one person this council is aware of who is known to have brewed the sort of poison that killed Blood Leader Warner. This girl wheedled her way into the Duwead Clan under suspicious circumstances. It is my belief that Ena Ryeland poisoned Warner in an effort to begin a clan war."

"Why?" the Brien Elder asked. "Why would an Ilbrean born care about a clan war?"

"It is my belief that Ena Ryeland and her brother Emmet Ryeland are working on behalf of the Guilds," Edric said. "It is my belief that they desire to start a clan war so the Guilds can steal the land rightfully granted to the children of the mountain."

The rumble of whispers that flooded the hall sounded like an army of ghosts come to haunt me.

My mind stumbled back, sorting through everything I'd done in my life, trying to find one action that might appear as though I were trying to aid the Guilds.

"This is all very interesting," an elder with long gray curls said. "But do you have an ounce of proof, or just whispers?"

"I don't need proof, Elan," Edric said. "Ena Ryeland herself will prove me right."

I squeezed my hands against my thighs so hard I could feel bruises forming on my legs.

"Under the Clans Treaty, I have the right to question Ena," Edric said. "I have the right to question her in front of the full council. The treaty made no mention of an elder not being allowed to question an accused just because that elder was born a sorcerer."

4 0

The torrent of words that flew through the chamber was loud enough to drown out the questions in my mind.

I didn't understand why I wouldn't want to be questioned. I knew I was innocent. Answering questions in front of everyone seemed like a chivving wonderful way to clear my name.

But Finn stepped in front of me, his hand on the hilt of his sword, as Liam left Orla's side to join in protecting me.

"There is no rule in the treaty that forbids my questioning the one who murdered my Blood Leader," Edric shouted over the roar of the crowd.

"We cannot allow such a thing to happen." The Brien Elder stood. "You are using the gifts of your birth to grab at a power never meant to be offered in the treaty."

"Such nonsense coming from the woman who hoards all the magic she can steal from Ilbrea." An elder with a long black braid slammed his hand against the table.

"This is what comes of allowing a clan to have an elder that is not a trueborn," Elan said.

"There is nothing in the treaty that demands an elder be a trueborn," Edric said.

"The mountain created the order the clans should live by," Elan said.

"How has your clan fared with a sorcerer leading, Edric?" the black-haired Elder asked. "Has the death of your crops been enough for the mountain to demonstrate her displeasure? Will she have to collapse the stone over your heads before you finally learn?"

"Do not concern yourself with the covenant my people hold with the mountain, Ronin," Edric said.

"Silence, all of you," the Brien Elder held a hand in the air. "I did not come here to listen to two men preening and bickering."

"Then let us proceed with the questioning," Edric said. "The sooner I prove Ena Ryeland's guilt, the sooner justice will be served."

"The question you have raised is much larger than the murder of one blood leader,"

Orla said. "If you do this, if you use magic to influence the workings of this council, you will be endangering everything the treaty was created to protect."

The room fell silent as Orla spoke.

"If we allow this to happen, what will we become?" She looked to each of the tiers in turn. "What precedent will we set? If the Healy Elder wants to dive into your mind, all he will have to do is accuse you of a crime. He will be given the power to torment based on accusations with no witnesses, no evidence beyond rumors. Is this the choice you would make? If you are all this weak, I fear we have reached the beginning of the end."

"We should conference and vote," the Brien Elder said. "This choice goes beyond the matter of Ena Ryeland."

"There is no choice involved." Edric pointed a quivering finger at me. "That girl murdered my Blood Leader."

Liam stepped to the side, standing between me and Edric.

"The treaty gives me the right to question the accused," Edric said. "I will not allow council politics to steal the Healy's justice for Warner's death."

"We will conference," the Brien Elder said. "Those in favor?"

Orla, the Brien Elder, the black-braided elder Ronin, and Elan all raised their hands.

"I suppose the story keepers who blather warnings in my ear know their history after all," Edric said. "Not all treaties are made to last."

"And not all men are wise enough to rule," Orla said.

The Brien Elder swept her hand through the air before the uproar could begin. "The girl should be locked away."

"Of course." Orla nodded to the guards around me. "I have no qualm with justice being done, only with the ravings of a mad man."

A wave of sound exploded from the tiers of gray-clad Healy guards.

"This way, Miss." Kely stepped up beside Liam. "If I may, Trueborn?"

"I'll stay with her," Liam said.

"Don't," Finn said. "Not with all of them watching."

Anger flashed through Liam's eyes.

"She can survive anything, Liam," Finn said. "Trust me, I know." He took my hand and guided me away from Liam.

The other people in the stands were all funneling back into their tunnels, but that wasn't where Finn led me. He took me to the door at the base of the Duwead tiers instead.

Kely stepped around Finn and unlocked the door. The metal lock turned with a terrible thunk.

"It won't be long," Finn said.

"Take care of Liam." I stepped into the cell. "Do not let his anger make him foolish."

"I'll watch him."

The door swung shut, and for the first time in days, I was alone.

41

The cell was short. A person as tall as Liam wouldn't have been able to stand upright.

A wooden pallet lay along the back wall, as though it were meant to offer a prisoner a place to sleep. I could not bring myself to even sit on that surface.

The stench of the room was an awful mix of terror and human decay.

"He will not abandon you in here, Ena Ryeland." My voice bounced around the tiny room. "You have been trapped in fouler places than this, and you have crawled your way out of every one of them."

I paced in front of the door for a while, trying to calm my nerves with the rhythm of the movement. All I managed to do was make my cage seem smaller.

Pulling my cloak tightly around my shoulders, I stared at the door, willing Liam to come bursting through to tell me he'd found the murderer.

I stood there until my hands grew numb from gripping my cloak. I wanted to sit down, but sitting seemed too much like resigning myself to being trapped for a very long time.

They do not know what we are made of. A voice that sounded like Emmet's echoed through my thoughts. *They are made of stone, but we were born in fire.*

The rumble of Emmet's voice pressed against my ears, but I could not understand the words.

"You will not let them break your mind, Ena Ryeland," I whispered to myself.

The rumbling grew louder, until words carried through the door, and I recognized the unmistakable anger in my brother's voice.

"I've come to stand trial before the council," Emmet shouted, as though he knew I was trapped behind the door and desperate to hear his voice.

There was a moment of muffled speech before Emmet spoke again.

"Guilty men run from accusations. Innocent men clear their names."

I pressed my ear to the door.

"Where is my sister?"

An angry voice replied.

"Then lock me away with her, or question me now," Emmet said. "I have nothing to hide from any of you, and after what I've seen in Ilbrea, there is more important work to be done than sitting around in a cave, accusing people of crimes they couldn't possibly have committed."

A voice that sounded like Orla's spoke. "Will you and Ena willingly agree to be questioned by Edric, Elder of the Healy Clan, knowing that he is a sorcerer?"

I leaned closer to the door.

"Is that what you're all bickering about?" Emmet asked.

"I have the right to interrogate—"

Orla spoke over Edric, "But a precedent cannot be set if the questioning is entered into willingly."

There was a long silence.

I waited for Emmet to speak.

"My sister and I willingly submit to the Healy sorcerer's questioning." It sounded as though Emmet stood right outside my door. "That's what all you Black Bloods forget—children of stone may rule in the mountains, but Ena and I were forged in the ashes. Children of ash cannot be broken."

I held my breath, waiting for my cell door to open. But the tolling of the bell came instead. The rock around me did not dull the sound, but rather amplified it, as though the mountain herself wanted to see if she could shake me into pieces.

A thunder of footsteps pounded over my head as the ringing stopped.

When the footsteps went quiet, a voice spoke. It sounded like the Elder of the Brien Clan.

"Emmet and Ena Ryeland have freely volunteered to be questioned by Edric, sorcerer and Elder of the Healy Clan. This questioning takes place without the treaty being invoked. The findings of this questioning will be held as true before the council, and the fate of the accused will be determined from the truth held within their own minds."

"That isn't what—" Edric shouted.

"Do not press, Edric," the Brien Elder said. "It makes you appear too eager to quarrel. Some might even suggest you are trying to break the treaty between the clans."

There was a long silence before Edric spoke again. "I will examine them thoroughly. What I find shall be sufficient to determine the truth."

More voices spoke, but they were all too quiet to hear.

A rumble like a giant boulder being rolled across the floor grated against my ears.

I willed my heart to beat softly as I waited for Edric to ask his first question.

"Answer loudly, Emmet," I whispered. "I need to be able to hear."

Pressing my palms against the door, I shut my eyes, listening for any hint of speech.

A horrible scream came instead.

The cry held such agony that I could barely recognize my own brother's voice.

"Emmet!" I banged on the door, hopelessly trying to reach him. "Emmet!"

His screams changed pitch, as though shifting from pained to terrified.

"Stop it!" I slammed my fists against the door.

The pitch of his screams changed again. His anguish went beyond fear or pain. It had become the cry of one who had been robbed of everything they loved and wanted nothing more than to leave this world.

I kept beating against the door as my breath hitched in my chest.

"Emmet!"

I slammed my fists against the wood over and over, not caring that warm blood dripped down my arms.

When I thought my brother might choke on his own blood from screaming so loudly, the sound stopped.

The silence was almost worse than his screaming. At least then I had been sure he was alive.

"Emmet!" I pounded on the door. "Where is my brother? Emmet!"

Low voices spoke outside.

"Emmet!"

The lock on my cell turned with a heavy thunk.

A pale-faced guard opened the door.

"Where is my brother?"

"Ena Ryeland." Orla spoke too loudly for me to ignore. "We have been assured by your brother that you will submit to questioning without need of invoking the treaty."

I stepped out of my prison and into the vast room.

Liam stood behind his mother's chair. Pain and fear filled his eyes.

"Where is my brother?" I asked.

Orla did not answer, but Liam glanced over his shoulder toward the place I had stood before.

I followed his gaze.

Emmet had taken my place on the bottom tier. Finn stood right behind him.

A new patch of burns marked the side of Emmet's neck. His face was pale and sweaty, as though he'd been violently ill. He met my eyes and nodded.

Locked in my cell, I was afraid my brother had been broken. But the torment they'd unleashed on him was nothing to a child who had survived the Guilds.

"I am innocent." I spoke loudly, letting my voice ring around the cavern. "I have nothing to hide from the council and will be grateful for a chance to swiftly clear my name."

I glanced back to Liam.

He had his gaze fixed front, away from me.

"What a relief to make quick work of this," the Brien Elder said. "Come, Ena Ryeland. Whether you're guilty or not, I am anxious to start for home."

I kept my head high as I walked toward the table. I could feel the gaze of the hundreds of people around me, but I did not shy away from them.

The blood dripping from my hands was nothing more than another layer of armor, another illusion to keep them from seeing the real Ena Ryeland.

No one told me to stop as I stepped right up to the edge of the table. A cart carrying a giant stone basin of water rested beside Edric.

"On the table, if you will." The Brien Elder pointed to the center of the pentagon.

A blue-clad guard offered me his hand.

I ignored him and stepped straight up onto the table without aid.

"Remove your cloak," Ronin said.

I looked to him.

"It's best to not have any constriction around the throat." Ronin bowed his head.

I unfastened the bird clasp and let the cloak fall behind me.

The stares of the people surrounding me grew in their hunger.

Without the cloak, the curves of my body were exposed. I watched the people on the tiers. Lust, longing, jealousy—they all felt something as they stared at me.

"I submit this questioning for the consideration of the council." Edric stood and locked his gaze on me.

I stayed still, blood dripping from my hands, as I waited for his first question.

But a glimmer of light emerging from the stone basin drew my attention from Edric's face.

A sheet of gleaming water rose up and stayed floating in the air even as lights danced across its surface.

Fear.

The word echoed through my mind, but the voice was not one I recognized.

Show me your fear.

I looked to Edric.

A smile lit his face.

4 2

I thought for a moment that I had already lost my mind. Somewhere in the blood and chaos, all reason and sanity had vanished.

Then darkness surrounded me. Pitch black with the endless thumping of hooves driving into my mind.

I was trapped on the mountain road, and there was no escape. I would be stuck riding on that horse until I died, knowing it had been my failure that had killed my parents.

Bright sunlight flashed before me.

A soldier with silver hair stood behind our house. He smiled as he ran his sword through my father's gut.

Ester with blood leaking from her womb and a baby that would not breathe.

Jesep lying on the ground, surrounded by blood. Too much blood for one person to lose.

The clanking of chains filled my ears as darkness surrounded me again. The slats of a wagon covered me. I was locked beneath. Stored like goods to be sold.

Nantic. A sorcerer with emerald green eyes. But my fear of her didn't steal the world from me. There was a glimmer beyond her form. A sheet of light that showed the images of my horror as though my life were no more than a pantomime performed to terrify the masses.

A smith's forge. Emmet gone, missing.

I kept my gaze locked on the images of my fear as new shapes swirled into being.

Smoke in Harane. A hand at my throat. My body pressed against the side of a shop.

Lily.

Lily hanging in front of our home.

Lily gone.

Stinging in my eyes blurred the images. I lost sight of the water's pantomime as the scene surrounded me again.

A little girl screaming, but I could not save her.

Soldiers attacking unarmed innocents. Blood on my hands I could never wash away.

The man in the woods. His blood blossoming over my fingers. The warmth of his life staining my skin red.

Pierce. Nothing more than bones.

The croilach chasing me.

Torches chasing me.

Dogs chasing me.

Darkness swallowing me. Leaving me in a city long forgotten by the world. Doubt draining my courage as the darkness continued. Houses and fountains. The darkness would never let me go.

An entire city the world had forgotten, as I had been left in the dark, forgotten and abandoned.

Marta shouting. Doubt scarring my joy.

Croilach everywhere. Blood, so much blood.

Red to paint the entire world with Death's own brush.

Screaming and blood.

Cinni and screaming and blood.

Screaming. Horrible screaming.

My breath hitched in my throat.

Screaming and graves. A child making graves.

Liam. Liam afraid.

The darkness swallowed Liam's face, and the pounding of hooves shook all reason from my mind.

Show me your guilt.

A voice joined the darkness, but the black did not falter. The hooves did not stop. They pounded and pounded against the ground, shouting to the world how badly I had failed.

I'd created my own fate when I'd been too slow to save my parents.

Everything else, every other wound, had started there.

"Enough." A voice echoed through the darkness, but the black did not shift. "If there is anything else you want to see, do it. Otherwise, stop this spectacle."

Show me the lives you have taken.

My mother and my father sitting together at our table.

Ester's baby, still and pale.

Jesep laughing as he tried to dance. He'd loved to dance.

Lily, her hair blowing in the breeze as the rope twisted around her neck.

Marten. So many faces in Marten. Hundreds of eyes I did not get to look into before I caused them to close forever.

The man with the gray-blue eyes and the scar on his lip.

The man on the boat who looked afraid as I plunged my knife into his flesh.

The images rotated back to my mother. Red spots dotted her neck. Emmet lay by her side.

"Stop," a voice said. "Unless your aim is to prove how desperate you are, just stop."

The images faded, and the bright lights of the cavern bored into my eyes. I swayed, trying to keep my feet beneath me as fatigue washed through my body.

"I think we can all agree you found nothing to substantiate an accusation, Edric," the Brien Elder said. "Would you like to vote or humiliate yourself further?"

I looked to Edric.

He gripped the edge of the table. Sweat slicked his brow and stained the collar of his shirt.

"The houses, the darkness, what was that?" Edric said.

"Your question does not concern the death of your blood leader," Orla said. "You questioned her on the matter of murder. That vote must take place before other matters distract this council."

"Distract?" Elan had gone horribly pale.

I wondered if my failures had been so terrible they'd actually scared her.

"I am ready for a vote," Edric said.

"All who agree Ena Ryeland is innocent." The Brien Elder raised her hand.

Three more hands followed hers.

"My Blood Leader is still dead," Edric said.

"And you have no idea who killed him." Orla stood up. "Search your own clan before you draw all of us to the Broinn next time."

"You only want her to be innocent to protect your son," Edric said. "You're only concerned with the girl's fate so you can save your heir from execution."

Orla leaned across the table. "Are you going to criticize how I run my clan while your people go hungry? Look to your own troubles before coming after mine."

"Are you really both foolish enough to waste time bickering after the images Edric pulled from this girl's mind?" Elan said. "No petty grudge can be as important as the city below the mountains this Ilbrean saw."

43

"That was a part of Lygan Hall," Ronin said. "It's not surprising. I'm sure all of us have halls we've abandoned with time."

"Are there empty portions of Lygan Hall that vast?" Elan looked to Orla.

Orla stared stone-faced back at her.

"It wasn't Lygan Hall." My voice came out strong, undamaged by screaming. I wondered if I had screamed, or if it had only been terrible memories that echoed in my ears. My cheeks were damp, like tears had betrayed me. I wanted to touch my face, see if I really had cried in front of all those people, but I was too afraid my hands might shake if I moved them. "I was running from a Guilded sorcerer. He had soldiers and dogs with him. The mountain swallowed me, and I ended up in the city."

Silence filled the cavern.

"I'm not sure who exactly built the place I found," I said, "but it wasn't anything like Lygan Hall."

I waited for horrible images to flood my mind again, but the elders just stared at me.

"The girl is mistaken," Ronin said.

"Whatever you like so long as you believe I didn't murder a Black Blood or betray the Duwead Clan." I waited for someone to bow me off the table, but no one moved. "I was trapped in those tunnels for two weeks. That's where I was before the blood leader was murdered, stuck in the darkness below the mountains, so there's no chance I could have had anything to do with a plot against the Healy Clan. I wandered around the underground city and found a compound beneath the mountains. My innocence is proven. Surely I am done here."

The Brien Elder waved a hand through the air. "The Ryelands deserve rest after the ordeal they've been through. Take them to their quarters."

"We have just heard heresy from someone standing on our table," Elan said.

"I agree, Bryana, the Ryelands do deserve rest." Orla nodded to the Brien elder. "The two taken in by my clan have been cleared of the false accusation of assassination. Stew on your own upset before you deliver your troubles to my door."

"How did you get inside the mountain?" Ronin leaned closer to the table.

I turned to Orla. My legs felt as though they might collapse beneath me. I met Orla's gaze and gave her a nod. "Shall I answer, or would you prefer I be taken to rest?"

"This matter cannot be ignored, Orla," Ronin said.

I kept my gaze fixed on Orla's face.

"There are so many matters that cannot be ignored," Orla said. "A trueborn has sent nine croilach to murder my heir. A blood leader has been killed, and we still don't know who is to blame. The mountain sheltered an Ilbrean born girl and showed her an impossible city. Which matter would you like to conquer first, Ronin?"

I waited for Ronin to respond, but it was Bryana, the Brien Elder, who spoke first.

"Nine croilach were sent after Liam?" Bryana asked.

"Yes." Orla looked toward Regan. "Would you like me to accuse your Trueborn? She is the only one I can think of who would hold such a grudge against my heir."

"Don't be ridiculous," Bryana said. "Regan has been working with Liam to aid the sorcis for years."

"Until she demanded that Ena supply her poison," Orla said. "Liam refused to allow that folly."

A shadow passed behind the Brien Elder's eyes.

"The cooperation between the Duweads and the Brien is no more," Orla said. "Didn't you know?"

"Do you mean to tell me the Brien Trueborn sought poison and no one thought to inform me?" Edric smacked his hand against the table.

"You were so busy accusing the Ryelands, I didn't think factual information would matter to you," Orla said.

"I wasn't seeking the poison for anyone in the clans," Regan said.

If I hadn't heard her voice before I might not have noticed the hint of fear.

"There was a problem on the southern path," Regan said. "I wanted to deal with it quietly and requested the Duwead Trueborn's aid."

"And I forbade Ena to brew poison for you," Liam said. "She is sworn to me and had to obey. Whatever trouble you find yourself in, Regan, do not try to draw me into it with you."

"Then it's the Brien who came for my Blood Leader." Edric pointed a quivering finger at Bryana.

"Do not begin to imagine I will allow you to question my Trueborn, sorcerer," Bryana said. "I'd rather meet you on a battlefield than allow you to violate my daughter's mind."

Regan stepped closer to the back of her mother's chair.

"There is a murderer sweeping through the clans," Edric said. "They have killed my Blood Leader and attacked the Duwead Trueborn."

"Are we now on the same side, Edric?" Orla asked.

"How can you bicker about petty sides when the mountain has acted so strangely?" Ronin said. "The matter of men killing men is nothing compared to the mountain sheltering an Ilbrean girl."

"Ena Ryeland, when did you take to the Duwead Trueborn's bed?" Bryana asked.

"What?" The word caught in my throat as I faced the Brien Elder.

"When did you crawl into Liam's bed?" Bryana stared brazenly at me like she hadn't done anything wrong.

Heat rose up my neck. "That is none of your chivving—"

"Is there a chance you were pregnant with the Trueborn's child when the mountain sheltered you?" Bryana cut across my protest.

"No." I wanted to tear her eyes from her chivving head and grind them beneath my fancy new boots.

"Are you sure?" Bryana tipped her head to the side.

"There is no chance of it," Liam said. "Now, leave her alone."

"Hmm." Bryana narrowed her eyes at me. "What about another Black Blood? Could you be carrying a different Duwead's child?"

"Does it bother you that much?" I asked. "Is it that horrible to you that the mountain might have saved my life just because she could?"

"A simple yes or no will do," Bryana said.

"No," I spat the word at her. "I'm done here."

I jumped off the table, snatched up my cloak, and strode toward the Duwead entrance to the cavern.

"You are not done here," Elan said. "Guards, stop her."

A flock of green-clad guards charged down from the tiers to the right of the Duwead Clan.

Without a word from Liam, the blue-coated Duwead guards ran to stand between me and Elan's men.

"What?" I rounded on the table. "What more could you possibly want from me? I have proven my innocence, let you dive into my mind, let you question whose bed I've chosen to share. What else do you want?"

"What you are saying of the mountain is untrue," Elan said. "She would not shelter an Ilbrean, would not lead an Ilbrean to hidden secrets."

"It's a mountain!" I spread my arms wide, shouting to the ceiling high above us. "I think a mountain can do whatever it chivving wants."

"What you think does not matter," Elan said. "What you are saying is blasphemous."

"I am only telling you what happened," I said. "I wouldn't have mentioned it at all if you hadn't gone poking about in my mind."

"We were wrong to vote so quickly," Elan said. "This girl has treacherously fooled the mountain who has protected and nurtured us all. She was clearly taught some vile magic by the Sorcerers Guild that allowed her to fool Edric."

"This is preposterous," Orla said. "Edric, is there any chance of an ungifted girl fooling a sorcerer."

"I…" Edric dried the sweat on his brow with his sleeve.

"Could she have fooled you?" Orla stood, staring Edric down.

"It is possible to fool a sorcerer if they gently examine a mind," Edric said. "I dug deep enough into the Ryelands' minds I would have found any lies."

"I call upon this council to hear charges against Ena Ryeland for treachery against the clans and the mountain herself," Elan said.

"What?" A hand gripped my arm before I could move toward the table.

"I've just told you the girl isn't lying," Edric said. "Everything I showed you is true."

"Then the Ryelands have placed us all in more danger than I feared." Elan took her

Blood Leader's hand and climbed up onto the table. "Are none of you capable of seeing the damage this girl has done? This Ilbrean has employed some dark trickery to make the mountain grant her shelter."

"I didn't make the mountain do anything!" An arm wrapped around my waist, holding me back.

"If the mountain was fooled into sheltering an Ilbrean, will she next offer our sacred pathways to the Guilds' army?" Elan shouted over me. "This girl has done horrible damage to the bond between Black Blood and mountain. There are already Guilded soldiers prowling through the western outskirts of our woods. If they are given a pathway, they could march straight into our homes."

The room fell silent. Elan took a long moment looking at each group around the room.

"The death of a blood leader and an attempt on a trueborn's life are nothing compared to the horror of having Guilded soldiers diving deeper into the mountains." Elan spoke softly, forcing everyone to stay quiet if they wanted to hear her words. "We must find out why the mountain accepted her. We must find out what foul deception this girl is guilty of. We are Black Bloods, and we will protect our home!"

A cheer shot around the crowd, starting with Elan's own people before flying through every group but the Duweads.

"We need to go," a voice spoke under the shouts.

I glanced over my shoulder as Emmet began dragging me back behind the crowd.

"Do not let that girl leave." Elan's command carried over the cheers, changing the pitch of the sound from approval to a battle cry.

"Form a line and defend!" Liam raced toward me, but he didn't have a sword. They'd taken his weapon from him.

I fought against Emmet's grip as he pulled me farther away.

A streak of red and blue dove into the horde of men racing toward us.

"Finn!" I shouted his name, but he'd already disappeared into the throng.

A clang of metal on metal came from the right.

"Stop, all of you!" Finn leapt onto the table and shouted over the masses. "For the sake of the mountain herself, stop."

A crack shook the cavern. Dust fell from the ceiling high above.

"Hold your attack!" Finn bellowed.

I don't know if it was the mountain cracking or Finn's plea that made the two groups pull apart.

"We all know the story of how the mountain sheltered a child," Finn said. "We've always believed that we are special, beloved by the mountain. But we've been wrong."

Finn looked to me and held my gaze. There was no fear in his eyes, only a blazing determination that drained the warmth from my body.

"I found mountain stone in Ilbrea," Finn said. "In the Lir Valley, far from where our legends say the stone should be. The stone that we have worshiped does not belong solely to us. Whatever magic our people have been granted was not born of a pact with the mountain. It exists in Ilbrea as well.

"You say that we are in danger of the Guilds infiltrating our mountains. They already have. I have seen them. I have fought them. Would you rather waste your time fighting over a legend or work together to find a real answer to our problems? The Guilds are coming. They will try to take our land and our lives. Will you stand against the paun, or will you hide belowground, bickering while the world burns?"

"Do you dare—"

"I've faced the Guilds, Elder Elan." Finn jumped off the table. "Yes, I chivving well dare."

44

"We're going." Emmet pinned me to his side and lifted me off my feet, carrying me away from the cavern.

Finn strode after us, holding his sword aloft but not looking at the guards he passed.

"Guards, to our corridor," Liam ordered.

A sea of blue followed Emmet back toward the gate.

"Put me down." I pushed against Emmet's arm. "Put me down. I can walk."

Emmet let my feet touch the floor but kept a firm grip on my arm, dragging me forward.

I clutched my cloak to my chest, taking comfort in its unchanging weight even as the world went mad.

"We can't leave." Orla caught up to us.

Six guards with swords drawn surrounded her as she moved quickly enough she had to lift the hem of her starched skirt.

"My sister has been cleared of murder," Emmet said. "We're leaving."

"I won't leave without Liam," I said.

Emmet didn't reply. The wall blocking the path to Lygan Hall came into view. The horses had been stabled on one side, but there was no hint of anyone in the warren of rooms on the other.

"No one is leaving," Orla said. "The gate opens at my pleasure."

"I came in without your permission," Emmet said. "Will you really make us prisoners?"

"Your sister just triggered an avalanche, and I am not sure any man is strong enough to stop the fall," Orla said. "I offer you shelter. If you've ever held any allegiance to the Duwead Clan, you would willingly stay."

"If the Duwead Elder appreciated the people who put their lives on the line for her clan, then none of us would be here," Emmet said.

"I didn't have a choice." Orla veered toward the wall of balconies.

"There's always a choice," Emmet said. "Some are just too cowardly to see the true path forward."

I expected Emmet to drag me toward the closed gate, but he followed Orla instead.

The room Emmet hauled me into looked more like a fancy dining room than a place that belonged deep underground. A long, wooden table reached down the center of the room as though Orla were expecting twenty people for dinner. A bookcase took up most of the back wall. The bindings on the books were old, as though they'd been underground far longer than I'd been alive.

Orla sat at the head of the table, facing us.

I could hear the sounds of men rushing about outside, but it didn't sound like fighting.

"Are you all right?" Emmet eased his grip on my arm.

"Fine. You?" I looked up at him. The burns on his neck looked worse than they had from a distance. "Has anyone even looked at those?"

I reached to shift his collar away from the wound. Blood still dripped from my hands.

"Hopefully there are some proper healing supplies here." A knot pressed against the front of my throat.

"We'll sort it out."

I just nodded. I couldn't think of anything to say.

Emmet lifted the cloak from my grip and kissed the top of my head.

I leaned my cheek against his chest, and he wrapped his arms around me. I'd forgotten how comforting and solid my brother was.

The agony and fear of everything Edric had shown all those people dug at my chest, like a tiny, vicious monster was picking parts of me away. My breath hitched as pain pierced my lungs.

"You're going to be fine." Emmet held me tighter. "You are strong enough to survive armies and fire. Those chivving bastards are nothing to people like us. You'll be all right."

I wrapped my arms around Emmet, not caring that I was dripping blood on him. "Thank you for looking for me."

"I was getting ready to sneak into Ilara." Emmet laid his cheek against the top of my head. "But I went to Mave's first. I needed help finding supplies. She told me you'd left for Lygan Hall."

"When you tell Marta where you were, be sure to emphasize needing supplies before mentioning Mave."

Emmet took a step away from me.

"She was worried sick about you," I said.

"I'll fetch a healer." Emmet didn't meet my gaze before going out the door and leaving me with Orla.

"This underground city," Orla said, "what did you see?"

I stood at the opposite end of the table from her, watching her for a moment.

"Was Edric wrong?" Orla said. "Did you fool him? Does the place not exist?"

"I didn't see everything that's down there. At least, I don't think so. When the mountain swallowed me, I followed a long path. Then I was so thirsty, I could barely keep going, and I found a fountain and plants. Edible plants growing that far underground. There was a beautiful statue in the fountain, like the one in the sorcerers' compound. And houses, I don't know how many. I kept to the path, just trying to find a way out.

"Sometimes, I would walk for days and see nothing, like there were bits of the countryside no one had chosen for their homes.

"I found a manor with a walled garden. It looked like the people had packed up and moved on, but there was no sign of trouble. Then, when I thought I'd go mad from being alone for so long, the mountain let me out, and I was back in the forest."

"And the stone Finn spoke of?" Orla asked.

"He found the shard in the mine below the Lir Valley," I said. "I don't know if that's what Lir is mining or if they just found it by accident."

The door swung open behind me.

Finn walked in, followed by a livid Liam.

"Just in time," Orla said.

"And you never once mentioned it to me?" Liam shut the door behind him. He looked at me, and for an instant it seemed like he was going to reach for me. But then his face grew hard and he went back to glaring at Finn.

The pain in my chest dug deeper.

"What should I have said?" Finn asked. "I found a bit of stone and I'm afraid we've been lied to all our chivving lives?"

"It would have been better to hear it from you before you leapt up onto the council's table," Liam said. "You could be charged with heresy. Gods and stars, Finn, what were you thinking?"

"That they were going to keep trying to pin every sort of misery on Ena!" Finn shouted. "That we were one against four with those guards charging at us, and I didn't like the odds of the people I care about staying alive. And the stars can blame me if they like, but people have a right to know that what we've been taught is a chivving lie."

"Finn," Orla said.

"I'm sorry, Orla," Finn said, "but I can't reconcile the existence of the Black Bloods with there being mountain stone so far away from the eastern mountains. Not if everything I've been taught is true.

"If the magic that protects us was created by the mother funneling her magic into the heart of the mountain, then this stone"—he reached into his pocket and pulled out a folded cloth—"shouldn't be anywhere near the Lir Valley. If we really are standing right beneath the summit, in the womb the mountain formed to raise the child, then there shouldn't be a random mine of magical chivving stone far west near Ilara."

"Let me see it." Liam held out his hand.

"I'm right, Liam. I'm certain of it." Finn unfolded the cloth and placed the shard of stone on Liam's palm.

The tiny bit of black rock lay against Liam's skin.

For one blissful moment, I thought Finn had been wrong.

But Liam gasped, and the tiny shard glowed a brilliant, pale blue.

Orla stood and hurried to her son's side.

"Give it to me." She held her hand next to Liam's.

Liam stayed staring at his palm, as though seeing something I could not.

"Now, Liam."

Liam picked up the sliver of light and placed it on Orla's palm.

"How could this be?" Orla tipped her hand, examining the bit of impossible magic.

"I don't know," Finn said. "But I found it in Lir's mine. The man owns an entire valley and is powerful enough to ward the Guilds off his land. The two can't be a coincidence."

"Why didn't you come to me immediately?" Orla looked away from the light in her palm to study Finn's face.

"With the Ryelands being accused of treachery, it didn't seem like a good time to cause a fuss," Finn said.

"And the middle of a council meeting did?" Liam asked.

"It stopped the fight." Finn shrugged. "Besides, people deserve to know."

"What will happen now that they do?" I asked.

Liam turned to me.

He looked at my face and the blood on my hands. There was distance in his eyes I'd never seen before. "I'm so sorry. I'm sorry this happened to you." He reached for me.

I lifted my hands away from him, holding them close to my chest. "Don't be." I forced myself to give him a quick smile. "I've been through far worse before."

The door swung open, and an old man burst in with Emmet close behind him.

The man bowed to Orla before looking to me. "I hear you've hurt your hands."

"I'm fine," I said. "Emmet's got burns—"

"You're bleeding, Ena," Emmet said. "My burns are old. A bit longer without care won't make a difference."

"At the table, if you will." The healer pulled out a chair for me.

"Emmet." Liam stepped toward him. "I'm glad you're back."

"I never should have gone anywhere," Emmet said. "I never should have left Nantic. I should have stayed in Ilbrea where I could look after my sister."

"Emmet." I stepped between him and Liam.

"I asked you for one thing, and this is where you've landed her," Emmet said.

"I love her." Liam placed his hand on the back of my waist.

For the first time, his touch did not bring comfort.

"I am doing everything I can to keep her safe," Liam said. "Her being called here was not because of me."

"You should have taken her and run," Emmet said.

"You shouldn't have volunteered her to be questioned by a sorcerer," Liam said.

"If you were truly a man of your word, you would be across the Arion Sea by now." Emmet's voice was low and dangerous. "Then I wouldn't have had to take the only way out she had left."

"Emmet, stop it." I sat and laid my bloody hands out on the table. "I am chivving well capable of making my own choices, and we've got bigger problems right now than both of you thinking you know what's best for me."

"We'll get this bandaged up for you," the healer said. "Won't take long at all."

"I can do it myself if you'd like to tend to my brother."

"There's a healer here," Emmet said. "Just let him do his work."

"We all have our own work to do," Orla said, "and I fear our tasks have just become monumentally difficult."

"What do you mean?" Emmet said.

"The council is in uproar," Orla said. "We are as close to fracturing the treaty as I have seen in the last twenty years."

"What should we do?" Finn said. "You can't deny that Ena and I both spoke the truth."

"First, we send Ena and Emmet back to Lygan Hall," Liam said. "They can take the two horses they rode here."

"I'm not leaving you." I pulled my hand from the healer's grasp.

"If you could hold still, Miss," the healer gripped my wrist.

"The Hall is no safer than the Broinn," Orla said. "Not when we still have a murderer lurking among us. And it would be wrong to remove the one person who's seen the city belowground when people will have so many questions."

"You would have Ena placed back on trial?" Emmet said.

"You cannot be placed on trial for telling the truth, despite what Elan thinks," Orla said.

"Do you think any of them will stay here after the way the council meeting crumbled?" Finn asked.

The healer spread a stinging salve onto my fingers. I'd cracked through the skin on my knuckles and torn the sides of my hands.

"Ronin might leave," Orla said. "The whole Davin Clan has always been prone to dramatics. Bryana will stay for fear of missing information. Edric is still worried about his dead blood leader. Elan will be terrified of this information being accepted and ruining her idea of what the Black Bloods are meant to be. She won't risk the truth getting out without putting up a fight. The bells will be rung again in the morning. Until then, we all stay in this corridor. Colm will see to the guards."

"We should plan," Liam said. "Look at what the best path to peace might be."

"We've thrown a knife at a monster's hide," Orla said. "All we can do now is wait to see how badly we've angered the beast."

4 5

Someone had laid out a clean shift for me. I stood next to the bed, staring at it for a long while.

I wanted to know if they had laid it out while the worst horrors of my life were being displayed for all to watch, or after. Had they waited to see if I'd be found guilty before bothering to find me something to wear that hadn't been stained with my own blood? Had they only done such a kind thing because they'd seen the horrors in my mind and felt sorry for me?

Everyone in Lygan Hall will know my secrets. I can't hide from them any longer.

"Do you need help?" Liam asked.

"What?" I spun toward him and backed away from him all at the same time.

"Your clothes," Liam said. "With the bandages you've got on, I thought you might need help getting changed."

"I can manage." I turned away from him to untie my bodice. Pain throbbed through my fingers, and I could feel the newly scabbed wounds cracking. But I made quick work of the knot and loosening the laces.

"Are you hungry?" Liam asked.

"No." I shimmied the bodice over my head and knelt to untie my boots.

"I'm sorry there's not a better place for you to wash up."

"I don't mind. I'm too tired anyway."

"A cup of tea then, to help you sleep."

"I've just said I'm tired." I kicked off my boots and unfastened my skirt. The heavy material pooled around my feet as it fell.

"Right. I'm sorry."

I yanked off my dark blue shift and pulled on the clean, cream-colored one.

"If there's anything I can do to make you more comfortable, please just—"

"Which one is it?" I cut across Liam.

"What?"

"Which horrible memory of mine bothered you so badly that you don't want to touch me?" I untied the string from the bottom of my braid, grateful for the stinging of my hands as I shook my hair free. "You already knew about the ride to Nantic, so it can't be that. Was it actually seeing the faces of the people I failed? Seeing my parents? Or was it the man I stabbed on that boat? I never told anyone about murdering him."

"You wouldn't have done it if you'd had any other choice."

"I could have screamed." I dug into my trunk for my comb. The bandages shifted as I searched through the fabric, leaving my wounds exposed. "I could have hit him on the head or shouted for Finn. But I killed him instead. Just like I killed the man in the Brien enclave."

"You didn't have a choice."

"There is always a choice!"

"No one can blame you for any of that." Liam laid a hand on my shoulder.

I pulled away from him. "Was it being captured to be sold to the highest bidder? I'd have ended up a whore in a far worse place than Mave's. Did that make you realize how little I'm worth?"

"You're worth everything." Liam held my comb out to me. "I love you, Ena Ryeland."

"Don't." I stood and backed away from him. I couldn't even make myself accept the comb.

"I do. I love you. And no horror, no nightmare, nothing from your past could ever make me stop loving you."

"You deserve someone better." Pain sliced through my throat. "Someone whole and untainted. Orla's right to hate me."

"I've told you before. You are the bravest, strongest woman I've ever met."

"I don't want you to care for me out of some twisted sense of sympathy." Heat stung my eyes.

"I'm sorry for all the terrible things that have happened to you. If I could erase them, I would, but I cannot pity the woman who's survived so much. You are not weak. You are not tainted. You are fierce, Ena. You are a survivor. You are an inferno that will blaze through the evils of this world. I only hope I will be lucky enough to stand by your side to see the flames."

"I'm not brave." A tear raced down my cheek. I raised my hand to wipe it away, but my bandages had shifted, and blood covered my skin. "I'm afraid. I'm always chivving afraid. And people die, and it's my fault."

"No, it's not." Liam reached forward slowly, as though waiting for me to back away. "You may feel fear, but it doesn't control you. You are brave. You are courageous and powerful. You've saved lives, Ena. That is more than most people ever manage."

He wiped my tears away.

"I'm sorry for what Edric did to you." Liam stepped closer. His scent surrounded me. "I'm sorry I let Bryana question you like that. But you are not diminished by their evil. There is no force in this world strong enough to do that."

More tears spilled down my cheeks as Liam fixed my bandages.

He led me to the bed and pulled back the blankets.

I curled up on my side, feeling like a little girl, lying in Lily's loft, too terrified to sleep.

Liam pulled the blankets up to my shoulders.

"Don't go." I caught his hand before he could move away. "Please don't go."

His boots thumped against the floor as he kicked them off.

He kept his hand in mine as he climbed under the blankets, his body cradling mine as though giving a fresh promise to keep the nightmares at bay.

46

I sat between Emmet and Finn at the long wooden table. We'd finished eating our breakfast an hour before, but the bell still hadn't rung. Orla and Liam had left as soon as
someone came to take our plates away, but Finn, Emmet, and I had been abandoned to sit.

I stared at my bandaged hands on the table. The healer had come and re-dressed them.
The wounds felt better than I'd thought they would. I wanted to know what the healer
had used on my skin.

Emmet wore a bandage on his neck that gave off an earthy scent I didn't recognize. I
wanted to know what ointment held such an odor, as well.

"Do you think they all left?" Finn said. "Maybe they've all cleared out, and we can just
pack up and go home."

"We're not that lucky," Emmet said.

We sat silently for a few more minutes.

When I couldn't stand sitting anymore, I went to the bookcase in the back of the
room.

"I think things will be better now," Finn said. "If we can get Black Bloods to believe
there's mountain stone in Ilbrea, maybe they'll see that what goes on out there really
does have something to do with them. It could rally enough people that we can finally
fight."

"Maybe." I ran my fingers along the spines of the books. None of them were titles I'd
encountered in Harane.

"I…"

I looked back to Finn.

He ran his hands over his face before speaking again. "I don't think the legends are
true. I don't think all Black Bloods are descendants of a child raised by stone, but I am
certain there's something special about the mountain."

"There has to be," I said. "Normal mountains don't save people."

"Then there's got to be a reason for it," Finn said. "The mountain wanted us to find the stone and you to see the city. This is how it's meant to be. Everything is happening according to the mountain's plan."

I opened my mouth to argue, but there was something in the certainty in Finn's eyes that I didn't want to test. I had only believed in one person the way Finn trusted the mountain. Losing that faith had nearly broken me.

"Whatever the stars have planned, we'll keep fighting." Emmet clapped Finn on the back.

"I'm glad we're good at it." Finn smiled.

A ringing echoed down the tunnel.

"They didn't all leave then." I could barely hear Finn's words over the tolling of the bell.

"Right." I stared at the door. I'm not sure if I was waiting for someone to come in or deciding if I really was brave enough to go out and face the council again.

"Come on." Emmet stood up and held out his hand.

"Right." I nodded. "Better to get it done."

I took Emmet's arm, careful not to crack the scabs on my hand.

As soon as we stepped outside, the sound of the bells began vibrating in my lungs, and I could feel the pull again. The longing hitched onto the front of my chest, drawing me toward the cavern.

"Miss." Kely, who'd taken my horse, stepped in front of me and held out my cloak. "They cleaned it as best they could," he shouted over the bells. "I thought you might want it."

"Thank you." I gave Kely the best smile I could and took the cloak.

He bowed before running to join the line of guards gathering at the end of the corridor.

I let go of Emmet to fasten the cloak around my neck.

"Ena," Liam called in the silence between the tolls.

He'd reached my side before I could turn toward him. They'd given him a sword to wear at his hip. I wished someone had thought to give me a knife—any sort of weapon.

"To the cavern," Colm called from the front of the pack, his words barely discernable over the throbbing in my ears.

"I'll protect her," Emmet shouted over the din.

"Finn and I will both stay with the two of you," Liam shouted back.

He met Emmet's gaze, and something passed between them. Some understanding I did not share.

Emmet nodded.

Liam stepped in front of me while Finn and Emmet stood on either side.

"Where's Case?" I leaned close to Finn's ear.

Finn pointed toward the front of the group where the guards had pulled their swords from their sheaths. "Colm's orders."

What does the Blood Leader think will happen?

The front of our group started forward. The movement rippled across the pack of guards until the whole Duwead flock began moving toward the cavern.

They were not this ready to defend when my life was at stake.

I scanned the crowd, searching for Orla. She traveled at the back, surrounded by black-clad guards.

I squeezed Emmet's arm and glanced back toward Orla.

He followed my gaze.

"Will there be anyone left at the gate?" I leaned close to his ear.

Worry mixed with anger creased the corners of Emmet's eyes, but he didn't answer.

By the time I could see into the cavern, three of the five sides were mostly filled.

Ronin's section was completely empty.

The first line of Duwead guards stood in front of the tiers, their weapons still drawn. The rest of the guards filed up onto the steps behind them.

I waited for Liam to walk toward the pentagon table at the center of the cavern, but he led me to the corner of the tier where I'd stood the morning before, placing me behind him with Emmet and Finn still standing on either side.

Orla and the shadow guard didn't enter until the rest of us were still.

The three elders already seated said nothing as Orla, Colm, and ten black-clad guards approached the table.

The bell stopped tolling as she reached her seat. My ears pounded in the silence, but still, I could hear the rustle of Orla's chivving skirt.

"Has your Trueborn decided not to join us?" Bryana asked, staring pointedly at Liam standing in front of me.

"My clan was attacked yesterday in this very chamber," Orla said. "And let us not forget the attempts on my Trueborn's life."

"Should we all call guards to stand behind our seats?" Edric said. "Will we resort to petty threats soon?"

"You have no space to judge after your actions yesterday, Edric," Orla said.

"The traditions we have in place hold a purpose," Elan said. "Bringing armed men with you to our table? You are trying to destroy everything the Black Bloods should cherish."

"I am only seeking my own safety as I offer you all the truth," Orla said.

"Have you decided to admit to killing my Blood Leader?" Edric leaned forward, as though ready to pounce.

"I offer physical proof that what Finn told you about the stone under the Lir Valley is true."

"That is blas—"

"And presents a larger threat than I had hoped to face in my lifetime." Orla ignored Elan and reached into her pocket. Finn's worn cloth had been replaced by a square of black silk. Orla unfolded the fabric and placed the tiny shard in her hand.

The extraordinary blue light flared to life, glowing brighter than it had the night before.

"What is this trickery?" Edric stood and leaned over the table, peering into the light.

"You would not be able to see it," Bryana said. "You're a sorcerer, not a trueborn."

"What does that—"

"The stone calls to trueborn," Bryana said. "You see a shining light. We see the blazing potential of magic. We feel its pull in our blood, see its vibrancy in a way you can't begin to imagine. This is mountain stone. This is the essence that runs through our veins."

"This stone was found in a mine far outside our mountain range," Orla said. "In an Ilbrean mine. The enemy we have all feared for years has access to this precious resource."

Bryana pressed her fingers to her mouth, looking afraid for the first time. Regan reached forward and placed her hand on her mother's shoulder.

"The stones that we use for protection," Orla said, "that we alter to create light, that had been used to create the terrifying weapons our own treaty banned—the Guilds have access to this stone."

"Lies," Elan said. "Is this how desperate you've become to interfere with Ilbrea? The Black Bloods' place is in the mountains. The Guilds have nothing to do with us."

"Do you suggest I created this stone?" Orla stood and held the blazing light high.

"You could have gotten that anywhere," Elan said.

"Why would I do such a thing?" Orla asked.

"Desperate people are prone to disgusting acts." Elan stood up. "I did not think I would ever see an elder treat the covenant we hold with this mountain with such disregard."

"I value the bond we Black Bloods have with the mountain above all," Orla said. "But we cannot turn away from the truth, not when we are even more vulnerable to an attack from Ilbrea than we feared."

"You say the stone was found in Ilbrea," Edric said, "prove it. Let us all see where the stone was discovered."

My chest seized as the horror of being asked to let that man display images from my mind stripped away my senses and left me with nothing but a will to flee.

Emmet took my arm, as though preparing to grab me and run.

"I'd be happy to let you prance through my memories." Finn waved. "You'll see a lot of dark tunnel, but I'd like to think my attention to detail will give you all a decent show."

Orla did not look surprised or angry as she turned to Finn. She gave him a formal nod before speaking. "Do you freely volunteer?"

"Absolutely." Finn squeezed my hand before stepping down and through the line of sword-bearing guards.

"I will not stay to watch this masquerade of lies." Elan strode away toward the Hayes corridor. "May you someday remember the duty that comes with the stone in your blood."

"Black Bloods deserve to know the truth." Finn looked to each of the four groups on the tiers as he walked toward the table. "I am grateful for the duty I owe the mountain."

Elan disappeared, unwilling to watch what the rest of us had to witness.

"Can you get someone to fetch the giant bowl?" Finn leapt up onto the table. "I'd prefer to—"

I didn't hear the buzz cutting through the air. I should have heard it, but I didn't. I didn't notice anything at all until blood sprayed from Finn's back, coating Orla and the shadow guard.

4 7

A hand gripped my arm, but I wrenched free, diving through the line of guards to reach Finn's side.

"Protect your Elder!" Colm's voice cut above the screaming.

The shadow guard surrounded Orla, rushing her away.

A bellow carried from the far side of the cavern as the green-clad Hayes guards charged the Duweads.

Still, I ran forward. I had to reach Finn.

Nothing in the world mattered but reaching Finn.

Only one person ran faster.

One streak of blue sprinted toward the wall of green.

I slipped in Finn's blood as I reached the table.

Finn lay on his back, gasping for breath, his eyes wide and his gaze fixed on the crack in the ceiling high above us.

"You're going to be all right." I climbed up onto the table and knelt beside him. The warmth of his blood soaked through my skirt. "Look at me, Finn. You're going to be fine. I just need you to keep breathing."

Finn turned his gaze to my face as I tore the sleeve from my shift and pressed it to the wound.

He gasped in pain.

"I need the healer!" I shouted as loudly as I could. "Someone get the healer."

There was no one to hear me.

Liam had charged straight for the attacking Hayes and fought on the far side of the table, trying to keep them from reaching Finn and me.

But a pack of Hayes had gotten past him, all the way to where the tiers met the Duwead corridor.

Emmet fought at the bottom of the steps, slashing through men as he tried to reach me.

"It's fine," I said. "We can hold on. We can wait."

I kept pressing on the wound with one hand while I unfastened my cloak and draped the thick fabric over Finn.

Boom.

A wave of light flew from Edric's side of the table, knocking both Duweads and Hayes aside, leaving Edric and his men a clear path to flee. But the Brien had joined the fight, pushing the bulk of the Hayes guards back toward their tunnel.

"Case." Finn's hand trembled as he pointed.

"Don't move." I took Finn's hand. "You've got to hold still. Just keep breathing. That's all you have to do."

"Case." Finn gasped.

"Case!" I shouted. "Case!"

I looked away from Finn to see if Case had heard me. It only took me a moment to find him, standing in the middle of the Hayes guards, fighting alongside the bastards as they tried to flee.

"Emmet!" I screamed his name.

"Ena."

I looked toward Emmet's voice in time to see him slash through the throat of a Hayes guard.

"Stop Case." I pointed toward the crowd.

Darkness devoured my brother as he spotted the traitor. He wasn't the boy I had worshiped or the man I had hated. Emmet Ryeland was a demon born of Death himself.

He did not give them the warning of a battle cry as he raced into the crowd of green-clad men. He sprinted silently toward them, blood already dripping from his blade.

"Emmet's fetching him." I looked down at Finn.

His eyes had gone blank. There was no fear on his face, or pain. He'd laid his hand on top of mine as I'd pressed on his wound. I hadn't even felt his touch.

"Finn."

I pressed my fingers to his neck, searching for a hint of life.

"Finn."

The world went silent around me as a sob banged against my ribs.

"Please, Finn."

No amount of love can bring a person back from death. There is not a soul in this world who is that strong.

My tears dripped onto Finn, marring his face.

I wanted to see him smile one more time. To hear him laugh just once so I could try to memorize the sound.

My hand trembled as I let go of the wound.

I took Finn's hand in mine and pressed my lips to his forehead. "I will make them understand. I will burn Ilara. I promise."

I laid his hand back on his chest and pulled his sword from its sheath.

4 8

The battle still raged around me. Guards in blue, green, black, and purple all lay dead on the ground, but the ones left standing seemed determined to fight.

Liam faced a line of green-clad men with purple Brien guards fighting by his side.

Emmet had pierced the pack of Elan's men, leaving the others fighting on our side struggling to follow in his wake. But none of Elan's cowards seemed eager to get near my brother.

A green-clad guard dared to slash his sword for Emmet's side.

Emmet dodged with the slightest lean as he swung his own blade, severing the guard's head from his body. The guard's body fell, toppling into the men behind him.

I leapt off the table and ran toward Emmet.

A green-clad guard had a Duwead pinned to the ground.

My ears rediscovered sound as I drove Finn's blade into the Hayes' back. My arm felt the effort it took to stab the man, but my heart felt nothing as I yanked my blade free and kept running toward Emmet.

A glisten of red-coated metal caught the corner of my eye.

I brought my blade up before I saw who was attacking.

The Hayes guard glared at me with hatred in his eyes.

"Blasphemer." He spat the title like it was worse than *murderer*.

I let my blade sink under his blow.

He raised his sword to swipe for my chest.

I kept my own blade low and sliced through the side of his knee.

The man cried out as his leg collapsed beneath him.

I slashed my sword through his gut and kept running toward Emmet.

The other Duwead guards had finally managed to catch up to him, and the Brien had blocked off the Hayes corridor, preventing the bastards from retreating.

There was no talk of surrender as Emmet's blade pierced the chest of another Hayes.

I reached the back of the pack of Duweads. There was no one there for me to fight. I wanted to get to the front of the crowd, to find someone else to sink Finn's sword into, but the Duwead line was thick, and they would not let me through.

"Keep Case alive!" I shouted. "Keep the chivving traitor alive!"

"Miss." Kely appeared by my side. Blood coated his right arm, and he held his sword awkwardly in his left. "The path to our corridor is clear. You should join Orla."

"I'm not going anywhere until they've captured the traitor," I shouted over the chorus of rage and agony.

"The Trueborn wants you safe," Kely said. "I'm trying to help you."

"If you want to help me, go fetch the healer. The longer he stays hidden, the more good people will die." My own words punctured my bloodlust.

"I can't leave the fight."

"Liam said to treat me as you would him. I am ordering you to fetch the healer. Drag him here if you have to."

Kely nodded and ran toward the tunnel, still awkwardly gripping his sword.

I looked at the cavern.

Finn lay on the table beneath my black cloak. Blood had been smeared across the dark stone of the floor. All around, guards lay on the ground, wounded or dead.

This is not the last fight.

I ran toward the nearest blue-clad guard who was still conscious. He'd been stabbed through the shoulder.

A hand reached out and grabbed my ankle. The man wore a green coat. I thrust my blade down through his throat.

"I need you to sit up if you can." I knelt beside the blue-clad guard.

"I can't feel my arm," the guard said.

"That's all right." I laid my sword by my side and ripped the other sleeve from my shift. "If we get you upright, you'll lose less blood. Can you manage it?"

The guard bit back his scream as I helped him to sit. I used Finn's sword to slice away the bottom of my skirt and made two bundles to tie against the wound.

I grabbed my sword and ran to the next guard. He had a horrible slice through his calf. I tied another strip of my skirt around his leg. I hoped he wouldn't blame me when he lost the limb.

The chaos on the far side of the cavern had quieted.

The next guard was a Brien. Pink frothed at the corners of his mouth.

Panic has never helped anyone, Ena Ryeland. Lily's voice echoed through my mind.

Tears blurred my vision as I lifted the guard just enough to fasten his own thick leather belt around the wound in his chest.

Footsteps carried up the Duwead corridor. I hadn't realized it was quiet enough for me to hear something so small. Two women charged out of the tunnel, each carrying a heavy pack. The old man who had wrapped my hands trotted after them a moment later.

"No!" The scream came from the Hayes side of the cavern.

The fighting had stopped. There was no more clanging of weapons, just the one terrible cry.

"Let me go! I'm one of you. Let me go!"

Emmet broke free of the crowd, dragging Case by his bound wrists. Case flailed along the ground, but Emmet either didn't notice or didn't care.

"Open the cell," Emmet ordered.

Kely limped as he ran past Emmet, pulling a heavy set of keys from his pocket. He opened the door, and Emmet threw Case into the cell.

I heard the smack as Case hit the ground.

"Lock him in and leave him for Orla's justice," Emmet said.

He looked my direction and met my gaze.

We were the same, my brother and I. We'd both been born into a world of flames and come out of the ashes with a blazing fire devouring our souls that not even vengeance could calm.

Emmet gave me a nod and strode toward the Hayes corridor. "Who wants to make sure there are no rats left in the warren?"

A roar rose up from the men.

Both Brien and Duwead followed my brother into the darkness.

I stood and moved on to the next wounded man. He'd been sliced through the gut and was beyond my aid.

"Ena," Liam said.

I couldn't make myself look at him. I was too afraid of turning around to find him wounded and on the edge of death.

"Ena, are you hurt?" Liam knelt in front of me. A small bit of blood stained his side, and a larger wound still bled on his leg. "Are you bleeding?"

"We need to wrap that." I sliced another strip of my skirt away with Finn's sword.

Liam took my hands in his, stopping me from reaching the wound on his thigh.

Blood covered my hands and arms. The red stained the pale skin above my bodice and soaked through my skirt.

"Were you wounded?" Liam tipped my chin up and made me look into his eyes.

"Please let me help you." My words cracked against the knot in my throat. "I can't lose you, too."

Liam sat back and let me wrap the tatters of my finely made skirt around his thigh.

"How?" My hands shook as I tied off the bandage. "How could this have happened?"

"I don't know. But we will find out."

I laid my hand against Liam's chest, needing to feel his heart beating.

"Finn loved him," I said.

"I know." Liam pressed my hand to his chest. "Finn loved you, too."

Everything inside me shattered. There was no joy left to bind the fragments of my soul together.

Liam held me close as I wept for the friend I had loved with reckless abandon.

49

By the time Emmet led the guards out of the Hayes corridor, all the wounded had been tended to and the dead separated by clan.

Finn still lay on the table. They had tried to move him, but I'd shouted like a madwoman until they'd backed away.

I couldn't bear to look at him, but I didn't want him clustered with the others. I didn't want them taking him away where I couldn't find him.

When Orla finally appeared, she wore a fitting air of grief and disgust. She'd changed her clothes and washed Finn's blood off her skin. It seemed wrong that she could undo the damage the battle had inflicted on her so easily while Finn would never come back.

I pressed the terrible pain into the dark void and tucked the blackness behind layers of rage and vengeful fire. It was the only way I could stay standing.

Regan and Bryana returned not long after Orla. They too bore no mark from the fight.

They all clustered with their blood leaders in front of the door to Case's cell, staring at the wood.

Liam kept my hand in his as he went to join them. I think I would have started screaming again if they had tried to separate me from him.

"This is an act of war against the clans," Bryana said. "There is no coming back from this."

"I hope you do not count the Duweads amongst your enemies," Orla said.

"Is the traitor sworn to you or Liam?" Bryana asked.

"No," Liam said.

"Then our enemies are the Hayes and this traitor," Bryana said. "We should tell Edric and Ronin. Make sure they know what demons have swept through our lands."

"I'll send runners down both passages as soon as the execution is finished," Orla said.

"We need more information from him," Liam said. "How did he keep in contact with the Hayes? Who was he feeding information to in Ilbrea?"

"Is there another traitor, or was he working alone?" I gripped Liam's hand as a thick silence swooped through our cluster.

"Case knows the fate that awaits him," Orla said. "Do you think you'll be able to pull information from him?"

"Could a sorcerer do it?" I asked.

"He's already fooled one sorcerer," Liam said.

"Then I'll do it," I said.

"Have the Guilds trained you in assassination and torture?" Regan asked.

"No, only desperation. Leave him in there until I get back."

I turned away from the door to search the cavern.

A healer knelt beside a man with a slice through his side. The man bit down on a strip of leather as the healer cleaned the wound.

Liam stayed with me as I crossed the stained floor.

"Can I borrow something from your bag?" I asked.

The healer glanced up at me. "What?"

"Yarrow tincture if you have it," I said.

"Bottom pocket." The healer furrowed her brow at me. "Why?"

"Liam needs stitches in his leg, and you should clean the wound on his side as well." I let go of Liam's hand and pulled the little glass bottle from the bag.

"What are you doing?" Liam asked.

"Who here might have a bit of frie on them?" I said.

"Colm." Liam furrowed his brow. "Why?"

"A desperate person in a cage can only want one thing," I said. "So, I'll give it to him."

"You can't," Liam said.

"Finn is dead."

"Things are already bad enough."

"And I want to know who is responsible," I said. "Do you trust me to do this or not?"

Liam shut his eyes for a moment. "Promise me you won't untie him."

"I promise." I gripped the bottle in my hand and pressed my lips to Liam's cheek. "Don't let them interrupt me."

I strode back toward Colm. He'd made someone bring him a clean coat to cover the true horror of the day.

Blood still coated my skin. Finn's, our guards', their guards'.

Their blood offered a new form of armor. I was not a grieving girl. I was a warrior. An avenging demon.

Case had started this horror. If he hadn't betrayed us, Finn and I would have been in Lygan Hall eating pie and laughing while looking up at the bright blue sky. There were others to share the blame, but Case would be the first to die.

"I need your frie." I held my hand out to Colm.

"What?" Colm had the nerve to look insulted.

"Just give me the frie, and let me get the answers you can't."

"Do it," Orla ordered.

Fixing me with an angry glare, Colm pulled a little waterskin made of fine leather from his pocket. He winced as I pulled the stopper out with my teeth.

I dumped the full bottle of yarrow tincture into the frie, pushed the stopper back in, and shook the mixture up.

"Now let me in," I said.

"This is ridiculous," Colm said. "The Hayes are to blame. We'll find out who else aided them when we storm the Hayes citadel."

"Citadel?" I said. "Sounds like that cacting slitch really does trust in the mountain to protect her. Now open the door. I am not patient enough to wait for armies to move before I have answers."

"Let her try," Regan said. "Torment and evisceration wait for him either way."

"Open the door," Orla said.

Kely stepped forward and opened the lock with a heavy thunk.

I paused in front of the door. "Don't let them take Finn away. I don't want him discarded in the darkness."

Orla laid a hand on my bloody arm. "I promise you each of my people will receive a hero's funeral. Finn will be cared for."

I nodded, pushing the tendrils of pain back into the void. "Thank you."

I wrenched open the heavy door and stepped into the darkness.

50

Someone pushed the door closed behind me.

Thunk.

I didn't look back as they locked me in. My gaze was already fixed on Case.

He sat on the wooden pallet at the back of the room, his hands still tied in front of him. The orange light of the cell almost hid the moment when the hatred in his eyes shifted to worry.

"Where's Finn?" Case asked. "Have the healers seen him?"

"Finn's dead. It was quick though. He didn't suffer much."

Case shut his eyes, and his shoulders curled in toward his chest.

"Did you actually care about him?" I asked.

"I loved him, and those bastards—"

"Don't bother lying." I stepped closer to him. "There's no way you're making it through this day alive. You betrayed your clan and the man who loved you. You deserve to die."

"If you believe that, then why are you in here?"

"You tricked a sorcerer. How? How did you fool Wyman?"

"I didn't trick anyone. I'm innocent."

"What's the punishment for being a traitor?" I asked.

Case stared silently at me.

"No really, what is it? I don't know."

"Burning with coals, breaking with hammers, and evisceration." He swallowed like he might be ill on the floor.

"Seems fitting." I shrugged. "You got my friend killed and ripped my heart out—they rip your guts out."

Case turned to the side and vomited on the floor.

I waited for the retching to stop before speaking again.

"Finn loved you. And I think you loved him, too, at least a little."

"He was a wonderful man. He never should have been involved in any of this. He should have stayed in Lygan Hall."

"I want to hurt the one who shot a stone through his chest, and I want you to help me find them."

"I don't know anything."

"Lying won't save you from a horrible end. Nothing can save your life, but I can smooth out your final moments." I held up the skin.

"You hope to buy me with frie?"

"Widows brew." I pulled the stopper with my teeth and held the skin close enough to Case that he could smell its scent over the pungent odor of his own sick. "It's a fast end. You'll get a bit dizzy, maybe a little warm, then fall asleep, and you won't wake up."

"You're lying."

"Poison is my specialty. I'm offering you a kind end in exchange for information. Would you like to tell me how you fooled Wyman, or would you like your guts ripped out?"

Case stared at the waterskin. "Wyman was looking for fear and trying to be gentle. He poked around to see what I'd felt when the croilach attacked. All he found was terror. I didn't know Elan was going to send any beasts after us and certainly not a herd of them. I didn't want the monsters to rip through my clansmen. I never wanted them anywhere near Finn. He saw how genuine my terror was and let me go."

I swallowed my rage, forcing air into my leaden lungs before speaking again. "How were you communicating with Elan?"

"Stone birds, like the ones Liam uses. She sent me a batch of them before I left for the camp. I just had to write notes and tell the birds to fly."

"Did she send messages back to you?"

Case nodded. "There's a landslide about six miles north of camp. I'd go whenever I could sneak away and find birds there, waiting for me."

"And you told her everything? Where the sorcis we were trying to save were hiding? Where we were fetching supplies in Ilbrea?"

"I didn't know where everyone was going." Case stared down at his hands. "But when I did, I'd send a bird. Finn always told me where he was headed. He told me about the poison he helped you mix and the things you gave Gabe for the other soldiers. I told Elan about that, too."

I shut my eyes, pressing my self-loathing away.

If I'd never offered poison, so many lives would have been spared.

"Why did they mimic my poison?"

"I don't know. Elan never sent me information, only instructions."

"Why did you tell her what I'd done?"

"Why didn't you give Drason the widow's brew?" Case nodded toward the waterskin.

"It tastes awful. You'd never get someone to drink it without them knowing."

"I don't mind a bad taste." Case reached for the skin.

"Not yet." I moved the skin behind my back. "Who was the Hayes contact in Ilbrea?"

"I have no idea." Case pushed himself to his feet. "I only had a way to send messages to Elan."

"That's it?"

"She always pressed for information about things near Frason's Glenn. I think her contact must have been there if she was so eager for news. Maybe Elan had a dozen people in Ilbrea, I really don't know. Now please, give me the poison before they decide to come in."

"Why did she kill the Healy Blood Leader?"

"I don't know anything about that. All I did was send messages."

"Did you love him?" I shouldn't have asked, but I couldn't help myself.

"Yes, I did." Case looked to the ground.

"Then how could you do this?"

He looked up at me with determination in his eyes. "My love for one man cannot be greater than the love I have for the Black Bloods. Our place is here, honoring the covenant we hold with the mountain. Interfering in Ilbrea will do nothing but bring destruction to our land. I had to stop it."

I nodded and handed him the skin.

He pulled out the stopper with his teeth and drank greedily.

I knocked on the door. My blood still stained the wood from the day before.

"How did Elan find you?" I asked. "How did she know that a Duwead would be willing to betray their clan?"

"It's not hard to find like-minded people if you know where to look." Case sat on the pallet. "I'm not alone in my beliefs. The old ways will return, and the mountain will watch over those who have sacrificed to protect the people descended from the stone-raised babe. No amount of torture could make me turn in the others who are willing to risk everything to protect the Black Bloods."

"We'll see," I said as the door opened. "I'm willing to bet Regan is good with a knife."

"What?" Case stood.

I stepped out of the cell.

The guard caught hold of Case as he tried to attack me.

"May your death be everything you deserve."

51

Fire cannot shatter a mountain's stone, but ice can.

Innocent drops of water sneak into the cracks during the fine rains of summer. No one notices such a meaningless little intrusion. The mountain is too great to fear water as it should.

Winter comes, and the water turns to ice, growing and forging tiny new fissures in the stone.

It may take a hundred winters, but the stone will be defeated. The mountain will crumble.

Fire cannot tear down a mountain.

It's the cracks in the mountain's own stone that will be its undoing.

5 2

The journey back to Lygan Hall took longer as the living carefully carried the dead.

Three hundred men and women waited below Lygan Hall at the end of the long corridor to help us carry the fallen Duweads into their home.

Orla opened a massive stone door, and we walked up a long ramp and into the pale light of dusk.

Mountains of snow covered the ground. By some magic, a path of perfect green had been left for the mourners to tread.

The rest of the people of Lygan Hall waited by the edge of the woods, surrounding a field of emerald green grass.

Emmet squeezed my hand before leaving my side.

A tiny prick of joy managed to reach my heart as he walked across the field to Marta. Tears coursed down her cheeks as Emmet gave her a nod and took his place next to her.

Evie stared up at him before looking across the field to me, poking Dorran in the ribs, and whispering something in his ear. Cinni and Gwen stood hand in hand beside their siblings. Gwen offered me a tired smile.

I watched as the guards laid the shrouded dead on the ground. I knew which one was Finn—Liam had been helping to carry our friend home.

He knelt beside Finn, caressing his head and saying something no else was meant to hear before standing and making his way through the field of bodies to stand beside me.

It was fully dark by the time the last of the families had bade farewell to their dead.

As an elderly woman escorted Finn's mother away, a faint gleam shimmered in the sky.

"We should begin." Orla took her place by Liam's other side.

A man with dark gray hair stepped forward and held his hands flat over the ground. He spoke no words, and the ground made no sound as the earth shifted, and the mountain reclaimed her beloved children.

Liam took my face in his hands and looked into my eyes. I could see his love for me right there. Behind the courage, behind the anger that drove him to face the horrors ahead, his love for me floated beneath it all, keeping the soul of a wonderful man from collapsing.

His kissed my forehead before stepping out onto the empty field.

"People of my clan." Liam's voice rang through the darkness. "The treaty that had long protected us has been broken by the Hayes Clan. Our enemies in Ilbrea are stronger than we knew and diving deeper into the mountains than they have ever dared before."

I looked up to the sky. The shimmer had become a dancing band of green light that swayed without care for the troubles of the men far below.

"We have two choices," Liam said. "We can barricade ourselves in Lygan Hall and hide while the world crumbles. Or we can fight to protect our clan, our families, and these mountains!"

A roar shook the ground as the people of Lygan Hall chose to launch themselves into a deadly battle.

Liam met my gaze and I nodded. I would follow him.

His path was mine, and we would walk side by side to whatever end.

FEATHER AND FLAME

BOOK FOUR

To the ones who are lost and alone.
They should not have tried to break you.
You are the spark that begins their fall.

1

I wish I could give you a different ending to my tale. I wish the words I had to offer brought comfort and joy.

I am not powerful enough to change the path I have tread, and I will not lie.

I will not allow myself to commit that awful offense that ripped my heart from my chest and left me less than human.

I am only an orphan from Harane.

I am broken beyond repair.

There is no other truth for me to tell.

2

The scent of charcoal filled the little room, and a low rumble carried through the door.

I listened carefully as I ground the black lumps into fine powder. The sound from the corridor stayed steady.

Deirdre had brought flowers from the sorcerers' garden. I would need to use a fresh mortar and pestle to grind the petals once I'd finished with the coal.

The rumble grew louder.

If I made good time, I'd be able to finish a fresh set of inks in the next few days.

"That answer is no longer acceptable." The rumble of voices grew into actual words.

The reply was not loud enough for me to hear.

I set the mortar and pestle aside and went to the washstand in the corner. Someone had left sweet-smelling soap and fine, white cloths for me to dry my hands on.

"It's been months!" The angry shout rattled through my door. "If Colm can't manage it, then send someone who can."

I dried my hands on a cloth, leaving pale gray streaks across the pristine white. I didn't feel guilty for leaving a mess. I'd find fresh white cloths in my workroom in the morning no matter how badly I damaged the fabric.

"I don't care about the clans' rules. This war is a chivving waste of time, and you know it."

I fastened my cloak around my neck. The heavy fabric held a chill from being hung against the stone wall.

"Are we just supposed to wait for more people to die?"

I squared my shoulders before opening the door.

Emmet stood in the corridor, glowering at Ailis.

"What exactly do you want me to do about it?" Ailis asked, not bothering to glance my way.

Emmet didn't look in my direction either.

"Take me up to see Orla," Emmet said. "Let me at least try to convince her to allow us to join the fight."

"She wouldn't—"

"You can't tell me you're content to stay locked in Lygan Hall." Emmet spoke over Ailis. "There is a war going on. We should be at the front, making sure Colm does more than drink frie and let the siege continue."

Ailis pursed her lips and gripped the hilt of the sword at her hip. "Orla has chosen to sequester herself while the clan is at war. She is our Elder. There's nothing—"

"We're running out of time," Emmet said. "Spring will be here soon. We have to be ready to go out into Ilbrea. We can't let Colm drag out the fight with the Hayes."

"What a pleasant afternoon, Emmet." I stepped out of my workshop and into the hall.

The guards lining the corridor bowed to me.

I dug my nails into my palms, fighting to hide my hatred of their deference.

"Are you ready for our walk?" I asked.

Emmet stayed glaring at Ailis.

She ran her tongue over her teeth before speaking. "I'm getting really sick of having this fight with you."

"Then let me see Orla," Emmet said.

"Are you going to wade through the whole argument again?" I looped my hand through Emmet's arm and tried to steer him down the hall.

He wouldn't budge.

"Orla won't come out of her chambers," I said. "You're not allowed into her chambers. Even if you were, you and I still wouldn't be allowed to join Colm in fighting against the Hayes Clan."

"You shouldn't—"

"I should stay safely in Lygan Hall, I know." I yanked on Emmet's arm. He finally started walking down the corridor. "The Hayes want me dead, and my going into their territory would only be offering myself up for the slaughter. Besides, my place isn't fighting in the clan war anyway. I am very aware of your opinion, brother."

He didn't respond. The only sound the hall offered was our footsteps against the stone floor.

"Now it's Ailis's turn to speak," I said. "She'll tell you there is no argument she could make to convince Orla that Liam's people should join the war, even if she could get into the chamber to see our Elder."

"It's true." Ailis followed behind us with the rest of the guards. "Liam's duty is to protect us from the paun. The clan war is not his battle, and our place is at our Trueborn's side."

The guards' footsteps echoed through the hall as well, ruining my chance of hearing anyone approach.

"Then Emmet will say something about there being evil in the world and how only cowards hide while innocents suffer," I pressed on. "Ailis will say again that we can't chase after Colm. Our place is with the Trueborn, and his duty lies in Ilbrea."

"We are useless here," Emmet said.

"I'll tell you that, no matter how many paun were creeping into the mountains when you came to Lygan Hall, there's too much snow between us and Ilbrea to attack the Guilds, and you'll sink into a silent rage that will terrify everyone we pass."

A guard who looked barely older than fifteen scurried forward to open the door for me.

I nodded to him before stepping into the wide corridor beyond.

Benches lined the walls, and flames leapt cheerfully in a massive fireplace. Cold swept in through the wide windows overlooking the valley, but it was my presence that froze the people who'd been passing by.

I let them stare at me for a moment, but I couldn't bring myself to acknowledge them.

"Come on," Emmet said softly.

I fixed my gaze on him as we cut through the gawking Black Bloods. "Have I missed a part of the daily argument? Is there anything you'd like to add?"

The long scar on my brother's left cheek twitched.

"Well?" I bumped my shoulder against him.

"You're annoying when you do that," Emmet said.

"I'm your sister," I said. "It's my duty to annoy you. And we all must do our duty."

Neither of us spoke again as we wound the familiar path through the maze of corridors, down three sets of spiral stairs, and to the raised garden just outside the crag.

A sparkling layer of snow covered the ground, laying a blanket of white over the paths. But the fierce winter storms hadn't harmed the blooms of the garden. The Duwead sorcerers had seen to that.

Brightly hued flowers grew up from the snow, as though the summer sun still beamed down upon them every day. The garden was a beautiful thing to behold, but strolling through the blooms brought me no joy.

People stopped and nodded as I passed, always granting Emmet and me the path.

I fought to keep my face pleasant as we walked. Not angry, not joyful, just a blank canvas that would not feed any of their rumors.

We circled the garden twice before Emmet steered me to a bench under the drooping branches of a weeping tree.

Without a word, the guards fanned out around the tree, each with a hand on their sword, none of them seeming to mind the freezing air that whipped through the valley.

I bundled my cloak around me as I sat on the bench. The material was thick enough to block the worst of the wind. But the frozen ground still chilled my feet, and the air raised goose bumps on my neck.

"How was the training ground this morning?" Emmet asked.

"Much as you'll find it this afternoon," I said.

I stared up through the branches to the bright blue sky. I didn't want to talk about how empty the training ground was with most of the Duwead guards off fighting the Hayes. I didn't want to say that Cati looked like she might go mad at any moment either.

"We're not exposed enough," I said in a voice barely loud enough for Emmet to hear.

"I know," Emmet whispered, "but I needed to talk to you first."

"Why?" I twisted in my seat, leaning over to examine the rosebush beside the bench.

"There are too many places to hide around the path you want to take," Emmet said. "If they come for you—"

"Then I'll have eleven people protecting me. I am not naïve, and I am not helpless."

"We should go back inside. Think through another plan."

"We've tried all our other plans, and none of them have worked. We take the path we've chosen, and that's final."

"Do not push me, Ena. I am not some Black Blood who will fall at your feet."

"No." I turned to Emmet, locking my gaze onto his eyes rather than letting it drift to the burn scars on his neck. "You are my brother, which means you know me well enough to understand that I will keep going with or without your help."

"I could tell him what you're up to."

I stood and brushed the dusting of snow off my cloak. "If you want to rat me out to Liam, so be it, but you'd have to speak to him to do it."

"There is nothing I wouldn't do to protect you," Emmet said.

"I am protecting myself." I pressed my hand to the knife hidden at my hip without meaning to. "Pretending danger doesn't exist will not make me safer. Locking me up won't get rid of the people who want me dead. I will do this with or without your help."

Emmet stared up through the leaves as I had.

I doubted he was studying the hue of the sky.

"If I tell you we're turning back, I don't want to hear a chivving word of argument," Emmet said.

"Of course." I took Emmet's arm. "But it's such a fine winter's day, a nice long walk seems like a lovely idea."

I led Emmet back onto the path.

Ailis stepped up to my side, eyeing the people between us and the entrance to the crag.

"I'd like to walk a while longer," I said. "Since there's no snow coming down, it would be a shame to waste the sunlight."

"We can circle the garden." Ailis gave me a nod.

"I'm going into the village." I longed to run but kept my pace even as I headed toward the stairs that led from the garden to the valley below.

"Is there something you need?" Conn stepped up to flank Emmet.

I looked to the guard.

Conn had such a bland face, I couldn't tell if he was trying to be helpful or was furious at my suggesting we venture into the village.

"Nothing that you can help me find, Conn." I offered him a smile.

"If you need one of the ladies from the Hall to fetch you something—"

"There are things I need to see for myself," I cut across Conn. I didn't want to watch the corners of his eyes scrunch up and not know if he was in pain or only squinting in the sunlight.

I didn't pause at the top of the sweeping staircase.

A group of women stepped out of my way, pressing their backs to the carved stone rails to give me the path.

I wanted to curl up inside my cloak and hide as the women reverently lowered their eyes.

Emmet placed his hand over mine as we passed the women.

They bowed to him.

"When did the Ryelands become objects of awe?" I whispered.

"When you found a city under a mountain and defied everything they thought they knew," Emmet said.

"Do not leave yourself out of this mess," I muttered, nodding as an older man bowed to us at the bottom of the stairs.

"All I've done is torment paun," Emmet said. "I'd be bowed to in half the taverns in Ilbrea if folks were brave enough and there were no Guilded soldiers nearby."

I swallowed my laugh as we reached the valley floor.

My shoulders tensed as we walked between the banks of snow along the dark stone path, though I didn't catch sight of anything dangerous.

"If you'd like to take a walk, maybe the sorcerers' compound would be a better destination," Ailis said as the path weaved between snow-covered flowerbeds. "I'm sure the Lir children would be happy to see you."

"I'll visit them later." I veered onto another path, one I had not been allowed to tread before.

Barren trees flanked the narrow lane, and mounds poked through the snow where bushes would bloom come spring.

I knew what was hiding beneath the blanket of white, but the mounds still seemed foreboding, as though monsters might leap out to devour me.

Emmet lifted his arm from my grip and let his hand hang by his side, closer to the hilt of his sword.

I strained my ears, listening for whatever might have set him on edge.

The blanket of snow muffled the sounds of the valley.

I am here. All you have to do is attack.

I sent my silent call out onto the wind.

We passed more Black Bloods on our way to the village. All their reactions to my brother and me were the same.

I hated it.

Their reverence seemed like a part of a terrible lie that I was somehow guilty of telling. But I had spoken only truth in the Broinn.

I had found an abandoned city below the mountain. I had been protected by the mountain, even though I was not a Black Blood.

I had spoken only truth, and still, my friend had died.

My breath hitched in my chest.

"Are you all right?" Emmet glanced down at me.

"Fine," I whispered.

"We should go back," Emmet said.

"I won't sit in my room, waiting to be murdered. If someone wants to attack me, they can chivving well do it in the open."

We reached the edge of the village. Despite my own words, I hesitated just before the first of the black stone houses.

"If you really want to go into the village, we should wait for more guards," Ailis said. "I'll double the lot assigned for tomorrow. We can come back then."

"Are the ten of you not enough?" I squared my shoulders and took my first steps into the village of Lygan Hall.

3

Signs of life poured out of the houses along the main thoroughfare. Smoke drifted up from the chimneys, and the scent of food and animals blended in a way only found where people live packed close together.

A child raced across our path. He stopped at the edge of an alley, nearly tipping over as he spun around to face me.

The boy's eyes went wide before he dropped into a low bow.

I bit my lips together, resisting the temptation to run from the child.

The boy stared up at me, his eyes filled with awe.

"What's your name?" I stepped closer to the boy.

He blinked at me as he straightened up.

"My name is Ena." I waited for the boy to speak.

He silently blinked a bit more.

"It was very nice to meet you," I said. "Be sure to keep warm."

The boy nodded and tugged the neck of his coat higher before turning and bolting down the alley.

"Mother, I've just met Solcha!" The boy's voice bounced between the stone houses.

"We should go back." Ailis laid a hand on my shoulder.

"No." I kept my breathing even as I walked farther down the dirt road between the houses.

The soothing sounds of people living normal lives carried through the windows.

The shutters and doors of the homes were painted cheerful colors that seemed odd against the dark stone of their walls. Reds, purples, yellows, every manner of color had been chosen, but each house had a stripe of Duwead blue right above their door.

I did not want to imagine what sort of legend might have created such a tradition.

Before I'd reached the next crossroad, the dull sounds around me had changed.

"Quinn!" a woman shouted. "Get back here!"

Other voices added to the buzz.

"What exactly were you coming into the village to find?" Conn stepped up to my side. "I can lead you wherever it is you're trying to go."

I'm looking for the ones who are hunting me.

"Solcha."

The sound of the name rattled my spine.

I looked toward the nearest alley.

A woman stood in the shadows.

"We should keep moving." Emmet took my elbow, leading me onward.

"Solcha, you're here." The woman stepped out of the shadows, moving closer to me.

The knot of guards tightened around me.

"I knew you'd come into the village." The woman moved closer still.

Emmet shifted to stand in front of me.

"My husband and son," the woman said, "they've both gone with Colm to fight the Hayes and protect Lygan Hall."

I opened my mouth to speak but had forgotten how to form words.

"We are all grateful for those who have gone to fight," Emmet said. "I pray the stars will watch over them."

"You could watch over them." The woman reached for me.

Ailis gripped the hilt of the sword at her hip. "We should keep moving. Ena has places to be."

"Solcha, the mountain chose to protect you." The woman smiled as tears spilled from her eyes. "She showed you secrets she did not trust to any of her own children."

Footsteps thundered toward us from every direction.

"Move. Now." Ailis grabbed my arm, dragging me away.

"Please!" the woman screamed. "You can help our people, Solcha. You can protect them. Show them how to break into the Hayes citadel. We need—"

The rest of the woman's plea was lost under the roar of the crowd that surged toward me.

Emmet gripped my other arm, using his body to push through the still growing horde of Black Bloods.

"Solcha!"

"Solcha!"

Solcha.

That was the only word I could make out in the clamor of the people.

I hated the name the people had laid upon me, like it was some kind of gift or honor. I couldn't find the word in any books. For all I knew, it could have been invented by whispering drunks in the back of a tavern. But the name had grown alongside the rumors of what I had seen when the mountain swallowed me.

They believed the mountain had shown me wonders so I could light the path the Black Bloods must follow. They believed the mountain had chosen me to help them. They believed I deserved to be called *Solcha*. They did not know that I was only an orphan from Harane. I had no hope to offer them.

I searched the rooftops, looking for a path to freedom or any hint of an attack. But the only blades in sight were the ones raised by Liam's guards.

"Don't hurt them." I remembered how to speak as I screamed the words. "You will not hurt them!"

I broke free of Emmet's and Ailis's grips, but the guards behind me still blocked me in.

"Keep moving," Conn ordered.

I turned to face him. "You will not hurt these people."

"It's not their lives I'm concerned with," Conn said.

"Solcha, tell us what the mountain showed you," a voice cut above the din.

I didn't resist as Emmet wrapped an arm around me and hauled me forward.

If I had been braver, I might have climbed up onto a rooftop and shouted to them all that the mountain sheltering me had not saved me. My life had been spared, but the cost had been too high. I was not worth a clan war. I was not worth losing Finn.

Even as they called after me, I was not brave enough to shout that I was not Solcha. I was not a savior chosen by the mountain. I was only Ena Ryeland. I could not save anyone.

Emmet did not loosen his grip on me until we'd left the village and were safely back on the path to the crag.

The clamor of the people still trailed in my wake.

"Two of you stay behind, and do not let them follow," Ailis ordered.

I didn't look back to see which two had stayed. I kept my gaze front, already forming new plots and plans in my mind.

"Do not attempt to follow her," a voice shouted.

Ailis seized my arm and quickened her pace, dragging me behind her.

"Do you really think they'll chase us all the way to the garden?" My voice didn't shake. My heart hadn't even sped up in fear as the people had surrounded us.

"Only fools try to reason through what desperate people will do," Ailis said.

"Let's just get to the crag," Emmet said.

"And once we get there, you're staying where you can be protected," Ailis said.

"I am not a prisoner," I said. "You have no right to lock me away."

"What I have is a son who needs his mother."

I looked to Ailis. Her face was rigid. She might as well have been formed of stone.

"I am willing to risk my life to protect you," Ailis said. "It is my duty to protect Liam. But the next time you want to go strolling through a pack of people, consider whose life you're putting on the line. If things go badly, you won't be the first to die."

"I'm sorry." My words tasted foul. "You never told me you had a son."

"It is possible to be more than one person, Solcha," Ailis said. "You only have to learn what parts of yourself to offer."

We stepped off the tree-lined path and back onto the black stone walkway that led up to the garden.

Prickles sprang up on the back of my neck, giving me the jolt of fear I hadn't felt when the crowd had pressed in around me in the village.

Four blue-clad guards hurried down the stone steps from the garden. All of them had their gaze locked on me as they trotted down the path.

"Is there anything I should know?" Emmet whispered.

My mind raced back through the morning, searching for what could have made the guards look so serious as they charged toward me.

Liam.

I took off at a run, outpacing my guards as I sprinted up the path.

"Ena," Emmet shouted, "where are you—"

"Where's Liam?" I shouted over Emmet, calling to the approaching guards. "Is Liam hurt?"

The first of the guards gave a merciful shake of his head, though none of them spoke until we met in the center of the snow-bordered path.

"We've been sent to collect you," the oldest of the guards said.

"Do not run ahead of us, Ena," Ailis said.

"Learn to run faster." I cut between the guards, continuing toward the stairs leading up to the garden. "Who sent for me?"

"Liam," the older guard said.

"Why?" I started running again.

The pounding of feet chased after me.

"Where is he?" I asked.

"In his quarters," the guard said. "We're to—"

I sprinted up the stairs and away from the pack of people in blue.

I heard their footfalls chasing after me but ignored their warnings that I should slow down.

By the time I reached the entrance to the cliff face, only one set of footfalls stayed near me.

The people in the corridor shifted out of my way as I tore past, pressing themselves against the walls, as though trying to dodge out of Death's path.

You are right to fear me.

The thought dug painfully into my lungs. I ran faster, drowning out the fear that seized me, fighting for air as I sprinted up the stairs.

The one set of footsteps still followed behind me.

No one even bothered trying to stop me as I raced past fountains and statues. Doors with fancy metal carvings were wrenched open before I had to slow my pace.

The first blocked entrance I came to was the door that led to the corridor where Liam and I lived.

Ten men with swords at their hips stood outside that door.

Kely stepped forward, tightening his grip on the hilt of his blade. "Are you being attacked?"

"Liam sent for me." My breath grated my throat as I spoke.

Kely furrowed his brow but bowed just the same.

"That doesn't mean you should run from the people who are guarding you." Emmet stepped up beside me.

"I knew you could keep up," I said.

A thunder of footsteps pounded into the hall behind me as Kely opened the door.

"Ena," Ailis gasped, "you can't chivving well run away from your guards after you were mobbed in the center of the chivving village."

"There was a mob in the village?" Kely's hand flew back to the hilt of his sword.

"No, just a bit of a crowd."

"That was not a crowd," Ailis said. "Do you know how quickly that could have gotten out of hand? Do you have any idea how fast adoration can turn into madness and murder?"

Kely's eyes were wide as he bowed me into the corridor.

"Ena, will you chivving listen to me?" Ailis darted in front of me before I could reach the door to Liam's room. "I do not want to treat you like some naughty child, but you have got to start taking your safety more seriously. If I cannot trust you to act with your own safety in mind, I will have to speak to Liam."

"Do as you please." I stepped around Ailis. "I am no one's prisoner."

"Ena," Emmet said.

I looked back toward my brother and met his gaze.

He didn't need to say he wouldn't be coming into Liam's room with me because he couldn't stand the sight of the man who had once been his friend. He didn't need to say I'd be given an earful for my failed plan to draw out whatever shadows longed to taste my blood. He didn't even have to say that he expected a full report on whatever had been important enough for Liam to send guards to collect me.

My brother just gave me a nod and faded away to wherever it was he liked to hide.

4

I loved looking at the silhouette of Liam's face. I wanted to devour the beautiful strength of the warrior who had chosen me to share his bed. I wanted to hold his bravery close to my heart, locked away where no one could ever steal it from me.

When I stepped into his sitting room, he wasn't standing over the table he'd covered with maps or meeting with grim-faced guards discussing the latest news of Colm's siege of the Hayes citadel. He stood by the windows that looked out over the valley. The sun kissed his face and glinted off his dark hair.

For one slim moment, I forgot my rage and fear. There was no room for anything in my mind but Liam.

"Ena." He turned to me, and I caught a flash of a smile at the corners of his eyes before the joy vanished and the Duwead Trueborn took Liam's place. "I didn't think they'd find you so quickly."

"We were already heading back." I looked to the closed door behind me, fighting the urge to slide the bolt into place and lock Ailis out. "What's happening? Has there been word from Colm?"

"He sent a message, but it wasn't anything new." Liam rubbed his hands over his face. "The Brien are blocking one end of the citadel, and the Duweads the other. All the Hayes are trapped, and Colm seems content to let things stay that way."

I joined Liam at the window. The snow-blanketed valley below was vast—miles across and reaching even farther into the distance. Towering mountains surrounded Lygan Hall, blocking out any hint of the outside world.

I'd been told the Hayes' citadel wasn't like the Duweads' valley. I'd seen sketches of the stone fortress built between two mountain peaks. Somehow, I still couldn't wrap my mind around Colm and more than three thousand other Duweads just sitting in the snow, waiting for the Hayes to offer a crack in their great stone armor.

"How many good men will freeze while Colm bides his time?" I asked.

Liam wrapped his arm around my waist, and I laid my cheek against his chest. His familiar scent tempered the wrathful fire that flared to life every time I so much as thought of Colm's siege.

"No more than would die if they tried to breach the walls without a solid plan." Liam's chest rumbled beneath my cheek as he spoke.

"And when will Colm finally form a plan? When will Orla stop hiding and decide something more needs to be done?"

"When the mountain forces their hand."

When they realize their fear is more deadly than the Hayes.

"I received another message." He kissed the top of my head before stepping away. He held out his hand, and a black stone bird soared down from the top of his wardrobe and landed on his palm.

"From who?" I laid my hand on my chest, pressing my stone pendant against my skin, as though Liam's magic could somehow protect me from whatever horrible news the stone bird had flown into Lygan Hall.

"The Brien Elder." Liam stroked the stone bird's neck.

The bird raised its chin, and a little scroll pushed out through the front of its throat.

"Why would Bryana send a message to you?" My hand moved from my pendant to the knife hidden at my hip. "Are the Brien abandoning the Duweads to fight the Hayes on their own?"

"Far from it." Liam handed the little scroll to me.

Trueborn Duwead,

In these dark times, we must set aside all quarrels and push toward a future where the Black Bloods retain control of the mountains that are, without any doubt, our rightful territory.

The war with the Hayes will not be won in a single winter. The terrors of the outside world will not stop in our absence.

It is in the best interest of all Black Bloods that the work in Ilbrea, undertaken by the Brien and the Duweads, continue, regardless of the clan war.

My envoy will arrive at Lygan Hall within the week to lay out plans that will ensure the protection of all the mountain's children.

Our enemy to the west is more powerful than we feared. We cannot ignore that threat, even as our own brethren betray us.

~Bryana, Elder of the Brien Clan

I read the letter twice before looking back up to Liam's face.

The note sparked something in my chest that I hadn't felt for months. It wasn't anything as naïve as hope, but I couldn't quite name the feeling. Something between the urge to fight and the need to run through the trees.

"What does this mean?" I asked.

"That despite Orla's indifference, our cause in Ilbrea has not been forgotten." Liam looked back out the window.

"This is a good thing." I took his face in my hands, making him meet my gaze. "You've spent years fighting against the paun and keeping sorcis out of the hands of the Sorcerers Guild. This means the clan war won't make you abandon all the innocent people in Ilbrea you've been trying to help."

"I know. We need to go west. We need to keep the paun out of the mountains and make sure the Guilds don't become an enemy the Black Bloods can't defeat." The worried lines around Liam's eyes did not ease. "But in all the years the Brien and the Duweads have been working together to help the sorcis, they've never sent an envoy to Lygan Hall."

"Oh." A cold dread prickled the back of my neck.

Liam lifted my hands from his cheeks and kissed both my palms. "I have no idea what Bryana is after, but she wouldn't bother sending her people all the way here if it were nothing more than working out a new agreement on where to send the sorcis."

"You mean the sorci children Regan threatened to kill if I didn't give her poison?" I pulled my hands from Liam's grip as the memory of warm blood spilling over my skin sent bile to my throat. "Will Regan demand my help again?"

"She might try, but the answer will remain the same."

"Then why would Bryana send someone here?" The need to flee raced through my veins, but there was nowhere for me to run. "Have you told Orla?"

I left the sitting room and strode into the bedroom I shared with Liam. Flames crackled in the fireplace. The orange glow danced across the carved profile of the massive bird that surrounded the hearth.

"I wanted to tell you first." Liam followed behind me. "I didn't want you to hear any rumors sweeping through the Hall."

I stopped as close to the flames as my skin could bear, letting the heat dissolve the last bits of winter chill that had sunk into my bones.

"I'm so tired of rumors." I didn't fight as Liam undid the bird clasp on the front of my cloak.

I'd made them use the fastening from the cloak I'd been given in Frason's Glenn when the seamstresses in Lygan Hall had fashioned me a new garment, one fit for the girl who shared their Trueborn's bed. Fine black wool, and a deep blue, silk lining. I knew I should be grateful. Never in my life had I been given such beautiful things, but I wanted to be back in the woods where a plain coat and sturdy boots were all I needed.

"I'm sorry." Liam tipped my chin up and brushed his lips against mine. "I'm sorry I dragged you into—"

I pressed my fingers to his lips. "You saved my life, and I chose to join you. You hold no blame for any of this."

He kissed my fingers and slid my hand to his cheek. "You are extraordinary, Ena. You are everything—"

I kissed Liam, cutting off his praise.

I didn't want to hear more comforting words. I didn't want to wonder what demands the Brien would bring to Lygan Hall.

The great void inside me had grown too full of grief and rage. There was not room to tuck any more pain away. Every bit of adoration from the people was only a reminder of how badly I had failed, and how much those failings had cost me.

Liam wrapped his arms around me as I deepened our kiss, and a new simmering heat filled me.

I threaded my fingers through his hair and pressed myself against him.

I did not recognize my own sigh as he trailed his lips along the side of my neck.

Wanting pulsed through me as he untied the strings of my bodice and I pulled free the bottom of his shirt.

With each ridge of his body I explored, the troubles of the world became a little more distant. As my skirt fell to the floor, the weight of the name the people had laid upon me tumbled away. As he tasted my skin, the worries of the war vanished. As I locked myself around him, the entire world faded like a wretched dream.

Nothing existed but Liam and me.

5

"It's not that I mind the studying. It's that it's not actually fun." Evie bounced on her toes as she spoke, as though the force of her magic were burning the bottoms of her feet.

"Not everything that is necessary is fun," Gwen said.

"But not everything that's not fun is actually necessary either." Evie wrinkled her forehead.

I bit the inside of my lips together as I swallowed my laugh.

"Enough, both of you." Marta shooed the sisters apart without even looking up from the tea she was brewing.

Evie huffed and moved off to one side of the wide, stone practice room while Gwen rejoined Cinni on the other.

Dorran sat against the back wall, book in hand, completely ignoring his siblings.

"How are you?" Marta pressed a mug into my hands and came to join me on the one wooden bench the barren space offered.

"Well enough." The floral taste of the tea wasn't something I really enjoyed, but I'd grown accustomed enough to the flavor the sorcerers favored that I didn't wince when I sipped the hot brew.

"Sounds dreadful," Marta said. "What's wrong?"

"Nothing."

Marta narrowed her eyes at me.

"Look. Look!" Evie shouted from her side of the room.

I glanced over to find her balancing a tiny ball of flames in her hand.

"Is that really worth shouting about?" Dorran said.

"Be careful," Marta warned.

Cinni left Gwen and walked slowly toward Evie, narrowing her eyes as she watched the dancing ball of flames.

"Look what I made." Evie held the flames out to her sister.

Cinni reached toward the fire.

"Don't touch it." Gwen ran forward, waving a hand through the air.

Evie's flames disappeared in a gust of chill wind.

"That wasn't nice," Evie said.

"Do not lure her in with fire." Gwen took Cinni's hand and led her younger sister back to the far side of the room.

"So, it's still going well?" I allowed myself a little smile.

"Wyman seems happy with the children's progress," Marta said. "None of them have needed any healing in the past few days, so I suppose things are going as well as I could hope for."

"Huh." Dorran gave a low laugh.

"Wyman is especially pleased with how Dorran has taken to his book studies." Marta gave a wry smile that displayed her dimples. "It seems I have quite the little scholar on my hands."

"Until you leave us." Evie balanced tiny blue flames on each of her fingers. "Then we'll be dumped on someone else."

Marta's smile faded for a moment so brief, I barely caught sight of her dimples flickering away.

"Let's not fuss about something that hasn't happened," she said.

"Of course," Dorran said. "I'm sure they'll find someone else to toss us on. No point in fussing. We're only children. We won't have a choice in who cares for us anyway."

I wanted to say something comforting but couldn't find any soothing words for the children I'd taken from their home.

"We'll all be together," Gwen said. "We'll all be training with the sorcerers. I think that's plenty to be grateful for."

"Well said." Marta gave Gwen a nod.

We sat and watched the children for a few minutes.

"How are things going at the keep?" Marta asked in a pleasant voice.

"Well enough," I said. "We're to have visitors coming in soon."

Marta's shoulders tensed, but her face stayed calm. "That'll be an exciting change."

"Before the end of the week," I said. "They'll be coming up from the south to plan for the warm season."

"I'm sure they'll enjoy seeing the wonders of Lygan Hall." Marta looked to Cinni. "It's a pity they won't be able to visit the sorcerers' compound. Wyman guards his treasures closely."

Cinni knelt on the ground, trailing her fingers along the stone to create some invisible pattern.

"It's best not to display precious things in front of thieves and hoarders," Marta said.

I gripped my mug with both hands, willing my heart not to race and betray my fear.

In all the blood and fighting, it had never once occurred to me how easily we might have passed the Lir children on to the Brien and how horrible the consequences might have been if Marta had not been with the children to protect them.

"I heard there was a bit of excitement in the village today." Marta sipped her tea.

I took a sip from my own mug to keep from cursing about my chivving brother. "It was nothing, just got a little crowded."

"That's not what Ailis said."

"Ailis?" I slopped a bit of tea onto my fancy blue skirt.

"It's been quite the day for visits," Marta said. "Ailis came to see me as soon as she left you. Wanted to know if you'd always been one for such little adventures."

"And what did you tell her?"

"That if you were determined to see the village, perhaps she should take you on a tour late at night, when you wouldn't run the risk of crowds. If you want to do something, you're going to do it. The best she can hope for is to offer you a chance to do it in the way she likes best."

"Did you learn that from dealing with me, or my brother?" A true smile curved my lips.

Marta's smile didn't look as genuine. "A bit of both."

"Are you—"

A tap on the back of my hand cut me off.

I looked over to find Cinni staring at me with her dark eyes.

"Hello, Cinni. How are you this afternoon?"

Cinni pressed one finger to my mug, guiding it out to the side and away from my lap.

"Would you like some tea, Cinni?" Marta asked.

Cinni paid no attention to Marta. Instead, she stared down at the dark spot the tea had left on my lap.

"It's all right," Marta said. "It's only tea. The skirt can be cleaned."

Cinni pressed her palm to the damp spot and stared into my eyes.

"It really is fine," I said.

The child just stared at me for a moment, as though wishing she could tell me something.

"What's wrong, littleling?" I asked.

Cinni lifted her hand from my skirt. The spot had vanished as though I'd never spilled at all.

"That's wonderful, Cinni." Marta beamed. "Such gentle magic is very difficult. I'm proud of you."

"Not proud enough to stay with us," Evie said.

"Hush, you." Dorran didn't look up from his book.

Cinni reached out to Marta, touched both of her dimples, and smiled. Before I could wonder what Cinni might mean, she'd turned and walked back to where she'd been kneeling in the corner.

Marta raised an eyebrow at me, but her smile stayed in place. It was an expression filled with such quiet, placid joy, I couldn't shove away the envy that flared in my chest.

"I should go," I said. "I don't want to make the guards wait for me in the dark."

"We'll see you tomorrow, then?" Marta said.

"Sure. Will you tell Emmet about our friends from the south coming to visit?" I set my mug down and lifted my heavy cloak from the bench beside me.

"If I see him."

"Good." I draped the black around my shoulders and fastened the clasp. "Better for you to deal with his storming than me."

"It could be a good thing," Marta said. "At the bottom of it all, the Duweads and the Brien are on the same side."

"Of course." I waved to the children and slipped out the door into the winter's night.

I took a deep breath of the freezing air, letting the chill of it race to my lungs and wash away the panic that had nibbled at my nerves.

I didn't know how I could envy their peace and find it so suffocating at the same time.

"Leaving already?" Conn stepped forward.

"It's been a long day," I said.

"We'll get you back to the keep then." Conn nodded, and the rest of the guards stepped out of the shadows to surround me.

I took another deep breath before setting off toward the exit of the compound.

In all the months I'd been coming to visit the children, I'd never learned any more about the place than the path to their room and, once they'd started training in earnest, the way to the barren chamber where the children practiced.

I'd never met the sorcerers who worked with the children during the day. I'd never seen the library Evie hated spending time in.

Part of me wanted to dive into all the secrets of magic the compound had to offer. But most of me, the parts that were battered and scarred by everything I'd seen and done, knew I had shadows enough of my own to conquer. Diving into the dark world of magic would do nothing to protect me or the people I cared about.

I could not allow myself the luxury of curiosity, not when I still had so much to lose.

I kept to the same path I always followed—along the outdoor passage, past the wide double doors that led to some hidden secret, and into the inner courtyard where tiny lights hung in the air, as though the stars had come down from the sky to watch the sorcerers work.

Stone tiers bearing blooming flowers hovered in the air, casting strange shadows across the flowers that grew in beds along the ground. All the blooms in the courtyard had been enchanted with the same magic that protected the blossoms in the raised garden outside the crag, keeping the flowers as vibrant as they'd been in midsummer.

But it was the fountain at the center of the square that I could not ignore.

The water flowed freely, despite the ice that shrouded the lip of the basin. The statue of a woman at the center of the fountain had not been marred by a single snowflake.

I stopped to study the lines of the woman's face, from the sharp angle of her chin to the wrinkles that had been meticulously carved at the corners of her eyes. The lights that hovered in the courtyard seemed to have been placed to give perfect depth to the shadows of the fountain, as though even the sorcerers recognized the statue as a work of art beyond even magic.

They worship her.

What do they say of you?

Sour shot into my throat.

"Are you all right, miss?" Conn stepped forward.

"Fine." I pressed my face back into a placid expression.

"The mother watches over us all."

I spun toward the voice.

A woman with pale blue eyes stepped out of the shadows. "She is the magic in our blood and the stone in our walls. The magic of the mother fills the mountains."

"Of course." I gave a quick nod.

"Did the magic of the mother fill the place the mountain showed you, Solcha?" The woman stepped closer to me.

579

The guards tightened their pack around me, though not one of them reached for their blade.

"I don't know," I said. "I'm not a sorcerer or a Black Blood. I know nothing of magic."

The woman tipped her head as she examined me.

I tried not to shrink under the gaze of her pale eyes.

"Perhaps you really do believe that," the woman said. "Pity they don't teach Ilbreans to understand the difference between what they see and what they feel."

I slid my hand closer to the hilt of my knife.

"Rest well, Solcha." The woman bowed. "May the mountain continue to guide you on your path."

She turned, strode away, and vanished into the darkness.

A prickle sprang up on my skin, as though a hundred enemies lurked in the shadows, waiting to attack. Or each of the shimmering stars floating in the air were somehow waiting to kill me.

"We should go," Conn said.

"Right." I nodded and turned my feet toward the path that would lead me home, trying to ignore the fear tingling my flesh as the pull in my chest shouted that I needed to be near Liam.

6

I have never liked waiting for anything. Not supper, not pain, and certainly not for the Brien to arrive.

Not knowing exactly when the envoy would come only made things worse.

Every morning, I would train with Cati and wonder if the next time I drew my blade it would be to defend myself against the Brien. Every time I left my workshop, I would wonder if the petals I'd left to stew would spoil if the Brien kept me from coming back. Every walk with Emmet was a time to plan for whatever tricks the Brien might use to harm us. Every visit to the children brought fear of their being discovered. Every night spent in Liam's arms felt like the last time I would find such blissful escape.

But waiting cannot last forever, no matter how long time might seem to drag.

The Brien arrived, and I wished I could go back to waiting.

7

The pounding of boots in the hall no longer set my nerves on edge. As the sounds carried from the corridor outside Liam's sitting room, I stayed in my seat, eating my dinner.

Ailis's voice rumbled through the door.

A voice I didn't recognize responded. "I don't know anything more than that."

Ailis said something else I couldn't understand as Liam stood and fastened his sword back onto his belt.

I took a sip of my chamb, touched the hilt of the knife hidden at my hip, and twisted my foot enough to be sure my other knife was tucked safely in the ankle of my boot.

"I'm not doing anything but following orders, Ailis," the unknown man said.

Liam squared his shoulders and opened the door.

An older guard with gray hair stood in the corridor, sweat glistening on his brow.

"Trueborn." The guard bowed to Liam. "I've been sent by Orla. The Brien envoy has arrived."

"Am I to meet them in Orla's council chamber?" Liam asked.

The guard glanced to Ailis before bowing to Liam again. "No, Trueborn. Orla will not have visitors in her council chamber."

I took another sip of my chamb and pushed away from the table.

"Where will Orla be greeting the envoy?" Liam said.

"She doesn't want to see them at all," the guard said. "She's sent orders for you to handle the visitors."

"And where has she ordered me to meet them?" Liam asked.

"They're to be kept in the crag." The guard tucked his chin, like a child frightened of being scolded.

"When did Orla make this decision?" Liam asked.

"My guess would be as soon as she heard they were coming," Ailis said.

Liam rubbed a hand across his chin.

"They'll be waiting for you." The guard bowed.

"We should go," I said. "I've never heard rumor of a patient Brien."

"You stay here." Liam turned to me. "There's no need—"

"I'm coming with you," I cut across him. "I don't care about any sort of tradition, and I chivving well don't care if the Brien are fighting with us against the Hayes."

Liam held my gaze for a moment before nodding.

"They'll be waiting in the lower terrace." The guard bowed one last time before fleeing down the hall.

Ailis stood, silently blocking Liam's path until the door at the end of the corridor closed.

"Conn," she said, "I want two dozen more guards at the lower terrace before we arrive. And I want them from our people."

Conn bolted down the hall.

"Why do we need more guards?" I stepped up to Liam's side, needing to be sure that no danger had come chasing after his blood. "Do you think the Brien have come to hurt Liam?"

"No," Ailis said, "but Orla's decided she wants nothing to do with this meeting, which can't be a good thing for us."

"Could she know something we don't?" I asked.

"No," Liam said. "She's just spent a lifetime dealing with Bryana and the Brien."

Liam placed his hand on the back of my waist, and I let him guide me out into the hall.

The sound of the guards marching behind us was the same as it had been for months. Everywhere I went, the dull thump of their boots chased after me.

But there was something about walking down the corridor that night that felt closer to stepping up to the edge of a cliff and waiting for the ground to collapse beneath me.

A few more guards joined our pack as we passed through the hall of statues.

I wanted to ask Ailis to send someone to the sorcerers' compound to warn Marta to keep the children quiet and out of sight. But even thinking of their existence felt too dangerous to be allowed, as though I were inviting the shadows to drag the children into some horrible game.

The pressure of Liam's hand on the back of my waist kept me calm as we cut through corridors and wound down spiral steps into a vast, open space I had never seen before.

Hundreds of orange lights hung from the ceiling, and hundreds more had been set into the walls. A swath of white-leafed trees grew up against the wide windows, which let in enough freezing air to raise goose bumps on my arms. Outside, the moon shone brightly across the valley, bathing everything in a silver glow.

More than thirty guards in blue uniforms stood in a long line, forming a barricade across the center of the room, separating us from the far end where more mirrors than I had ever seen in one place had been set into the wall.

As Liam led me closer to the guards, I stared at the wall of mirrors, trying to reason through which Black blood had wanted such a thing in Lygan Hall and what the mountain might think of so much glass covering her stone.

The guards parted.

A group of twenty Black Bloods dressed in Brien purple waited on the other side.

Liam didn't stop to acknowledge the Brien. He strode straight past them and to a raised stone platform just in front of the wall of mirrors.

I watched our reflections as we neared the glass. We looked like something out of a fairy story—a handsome warrior with a beautiful maiden by his side.

I smiled at the absurdity of the thought.

Three chairs waited on the platform. Ailis and her guards filed up and stood along the back wall, each with a hand on the hilt of their sword.

Liam led me to the right-hand chair and waited for me to sit before taking his place on the throne-like seat at the center.

I laid the folds of my skirt perfectly across my lap as I waited for Liam to speak. But he stayed silent as he examined the group of Brien.

A full minute passed before the guards in purple shifted, and a girl with pale blond hair stepped out to the front of the group.

I pressed my hands to my lap to stop them from shaking as Regan smiled at Liam.

"It's good to see you, Trueborn Duwead." Regan strode toward the throne as though there weren't more than thirty Duwead guards, who would be perfectly happy to kill her, standing just behind Liam. "I never knew Lygan Hall held such wonders." She swept a hand toward the glowing orange orbs overhead. "I've heard stories of lae stones that did not glow blue, but I never thought I would see so many in one place."

"The Duweads that built Lygan Hall held great magic," Liam said. "Is it any wonder their light still shines bright today?"

"Hmm." Regan's smile grew. "I suppose the Duwead Clan is not one I usually associate with great magic. I must reconsider what I know of the Brien's closest ally."

"Ally," Liam said. "Is that what we should consider ourselves?"

"We fight on the same side," Regan said. "Our enemies are the same, and the threats to our people grow all the time. Come, Liam, would you rather sit on your mother's throne talking around the lives that are at stake, or shall we have an actual conversation away from the horde of ears?"

I will cut your throat before I let you hurt him.

My fingers tingled as I longed to reach for my knife.

"Do you expect me to trust you?" Liam asked. "You abandoned the cause we shared for years because I wouldn't allow you to make Ena your assassin."

"The southern route has been compromised," Regan said.

"You had a temper tantrum because you didn't get your way," Liam said.

"How dare—"

"What will you demand of the Duweads this time?" Liam said.

"There are things that are best not spoken of in crowds," Regan said.

"Is it your own people you don't trust, or mine?" Liam asked.

"Hers," I said. "The Brien Trueborn can't trust the ones who are sworn to her. Isn't that right, Regan? Or do you not remember the man you made me kill?"

All hints of humor vanished from Regan's face. "The clan treaty demanded Jareth's death, not me."

A slicing pain bit through my stomach. "You allowed such a man to come near me. Did you really not know what would happen?"

"You think me capable of such treachery?" Regan stepped closer to the platform.

Boots thumped against the ground as the Duwead guards stepped closer to my chair.

"You asked me for the means to murder a stranger," I said. "You wanted to murder the sorci children we found, or worse, leave innocent children to be tormented by the Guilds. Yes, Regan, I think you capable of any amount of evil."

"You're an Ilbrean fool," Regan said. "You know nothing of the clans. You know nothing of the sacrifices the Brien have made to protect the sorcis."

"To hoard their power?" I said.

"There are Guilded soldiers creeping into Brien territory." Regan looked to Liam. "The paun are pushing their way into the mountains. How long until they start bringing sorcerers into our woods? How long until they attack us?"

"Leaving the sorcis in Ilbrea only makes the Sorcerers Guild stronger," Liam said. "And murdering children is not an option I am willing to consider."

"Send the guards away," Regan said. "We have things to discuss, Liam. Matters that belong between trueborn."

"Do you not trust your own people, Regan?" Liam asked.

"Are you foolish enough to trust so many of yours?" Regan said.

I waited for Liam to shout that he trusted each of the sword-bearing Duweads in the terrace, but he only sat, staring at Regan.

"Our people are dangling off the edge of catastrophe," Regan said. "Pride, quarrels, tawdry love affairs mean nothing. Liam Duwead, I am asking you to do what is best for our people. Will you not even listen to what I have to say?"

I dug my nails into my palms, biting my cheeks as I swallowed my urge to scream.

"Ailis, Conn, and Ena will stay," Liam said. "You can send all of your people away."

"You will keep two guards, and I will have none?" Regan asked.

"We are facing catastrophe," Liam said. "Are you not willing to trust me for the good of the clans?"

Regan turned to her purple-clad guards. "Go, all of you."

One guard dared to step out of line. "Trueborn, we—"

"Obey my order, or I will rip the stone from your side," Regan said.

The guard's face didn't pale. He didn't even wince at Regan's threat before stepping back into line with the others.

"Take them to their quarters," Liam said. "See them fed and cared for."

"This way." One of the Duwead guards led the Brien out in the opposite direction of where Liam and I had entered.

"Wait outside." Liam looked to his own guards. "Do not allow us to be interrupted."

Without question or complaint, the Duwead guards left the way we'd come. I wondered what they would whisper to each other as they all blocked the path back up to the keep.

The door shut behind the guards with a soft thud, and the cavernous room went quiet.

"What do you want, Regan?" Liam stood and stepped off the platform.

Ailis and Conn moved forward to stand behind him.

"I want to keep the sorcis away from the Guilds," Regan said. "I want to protect our mountains from the paun."

"And you came all the way here to tell me that?" Liam said. "You had your mother send me a message. She could have written all that down and had a bird fly your request here."

Regan sucked in her cheeks as she looked from Ailis to Conn and finally to me.

"There are troubles that must be dealt with before we can even begin working to protect the sorcis," Regan said.

585

"Still looking for poison?" I stood, brushed off my skirt, and walked slowly to Liam's side. "You'll get no help from me."

"If I need to stab the slitch who interfered with the southern route myself, so be it," Regan said. "I'd like it done quietly, but I am not afraid to end a life for the protection of my people."

"Then why are you here?" Liam asked.

"The paun have mountain stone," Regan said. "They could have a whole stash of it, and who knows what their sorcerers have made of stone magic? If the Guilds bring the sort of weapons that nearly destroyed the Black Bloods before the treaty onto Brien land, I will not be able to protect my people. The enclave will fall. Would you be able to protect your camp from mountain stone-made weapons, Liam? Would you be able to stop the Guilds from taking everything you love?"

8

I lay in bed for a long time, twisting all the things that had happened since I'd left my home in Harane around and around, trying to find the point where everything had tipped off the side of the cliff and left us to fall into the darkness.

The fall was always going to happen. Finn's voice rattled in my head. *Everything will go according to the mountain's plan.*

I gritted my teeth so hard I thought they'd shatter as I fought my need to scream at the top of my lungs.

Liam slept soundly beside me, his chest rising and falling in a rhythm that usually soothed my rage.

But there were some wounds too large for even Liam to mend.

I tried to focus my mind on the weight of his arm draped over my side. But he was not enough to anchor me.

The longer I lay still, the faster my heart thundered in my chest.

I waited for the old nightmare to take hold of me. But the blackness didn't surround me, and the thundering of hooves did not drive into my ears.

Moving as carefully as I could, I slid out from under Liam's arm and slipped out of bed.

The rug that surrounded the bed's platform held a chill. The stone of the floor beyond sent painful cold into the bottoms of my feet.

The women who tutted over the things I wore had made sure I had fur-lined slippers when the first snow came. They were the same women who had insisted I have a new cloak with a silk lining and more clothing than any reasonable person needed to own.

On normal days, the riches they tossed upon me were enough to sour my stomach, but as I crept through the dark, I was grateful for the fur in the slippers and for the weight of my cloak as I lifted it from the hook by the door.

I listened for a moment, trying to hear any sounds from the guards who had been set to watch the door while Liam and I slept. I didn't even know the names of the people who cared for us when we were most vulnerable.

I should have known. I should have asked their names and if they had any children. I should have been sure I had looked into the eyes of each of the Duweads who were willing to die to protect Liam.

The weight of the cloak around my shoulders did not ease my guilt, but still, I crept toward the balcony instead of slipping into the hall to thank the guards.

Frigid mountain air stung my skin as I stepped through the window and out into the night. The wind swirled snowflakes around the corners of the balcony, as though each speck of white were a dancer frolicking to a tune I could not hear.

I shut the wide window, leaving Liam inside to sleep in peace and warmth.

A horrible pressure pushed on the front of my throat as I fought the urge to scream my rage and fear into the night.

I blinked against the heat that stung the corners of my eyes.

"You should be here," I whispered into the wind. "We should be facing these demons together. I do not want to travel into the darkness alone."

I pulled my cloak tighter around my shoulders, wishing I were foolish enough to believe that a miracle might happen and Finn would appear by my side.

He'd say something witty to make me smile, then make me feel brave enough and clever enough to face the demons that waited in the shadows.

But the night wind did not have any comfort to offer, and Finn was dead. Even the sound of his voice in my mind was not enough to steady me.

I walked to the railing of the balcony, picking my way across the patches of ice.

The moonlight bathed the valley below in a soft silver glow.

The angles of the rooftops in the village stood out against the snow, giving definition to all the homes beneath. Smoke drifted up from their chimneys as the Duweads tried to fend off the wrath of the mountains' winter.

A dark patch of trees shrouded the compound where the children lived. I was grateful for the shelter the forest provided.

"I hope it will be enough to keep you safe." My hands trembled as I pulled my cloak even tighter around me. "I am not strong enough to protect anyone."

A gust of wind swirled around me, sending a chill right down to my bones.

As I turned to go back inside, a flicker of a glow caught the corner of my eye.

High up in the sky, a faint band of green shimmered into being.

At first, it didn't look like anything more than a thin cloud drifting across the sky. But the cloud twisted and grew, its glow becoming brighter every second, until waves of dazzling green danced across the sky.

Hints of red and deep purple caressed the bottom of the green light. I tried to memorize the hues, wanting to make inks of those perfect shades that seemed to embody the prettiest kind of magic imaginable.

In a single breath, the light grew to swallow the entire sky, as though the gods themselves had chosen to outshine the stars.

I stood, watching as my hands and feet went numb.

I probably would have stood on that balcony until I froze to death.

But the light dwindled and vanished as quickly as it had overtaken the sky.

So, I went back inside, hung up my cloak, and took off my fur-lined slippers.
I was not strong enough to protect the people I cared for.
I was not weak enough to give up the ones I loved without a fight.

9

"Knowing what we want to accomplish really doesn't help anything." Regan sat back in her chair with a placid look on her face, as though we weren't discussing the fate of all Black Bloods. "We need a plan. A real, workable plan."

"There is nothing that can be done until the spring," Liam said. "I hate it as much as you do, but there's too much snow. Even if we could get our people to the western edge of the mountains, the snow would make it too easy to track us. We have to wait for spring."

A low laugh came from the corner where Emmet leaned against the wall.

I'd insisted he be invited to the meeting. I'd badgered him into coming. But sitting at the table with Liam seemed one step too far for my brother, even if we were discussing fighting against the Guilds.

Ailis, Liam, Regan, and I all stared at Emmet.

He stared silently back.

"Do you have something to contribute?" Regan asked.

"Not really," Emmet said. "Just thinking about how much use the Guilds could be making of their time while we hole up here and wait for spring."

"We don't have any other choice," Liam said.

"I don't know anything about making magical weapons out of mountain stone." Emmet didn't acknowledge that Liam had spoken. "But if it's anything like smithing a normal blade, a month could make a massive difference in how many weapons the paun have forged."

"We're not even sure they are making weapons," Ailis said. "We don't know if they have more than a sliver of mountain stone. We don't know if they want to attack us or if they even know we exist."

"They are searching Brien territory," Regan said.

"But have they found anything?" Ailis said. "You can hunt for something as much as you like. The work doesn't mean anything until you've actually found your quarry."

"We don't know what the Hayes traitor might have passed on to the Guilds," I said.

"Case knew chivving well where our camp was. The Hayes know how to find the Brien. It would be safer to assume the Guilds know exactly where the camp and the enclave are."

"All the more reason to wait until spring," Ailis said.

"Sure," Emmet said, "as long as you only care about protecting Black Bloods. I, for one, don't like the idea of the Guilds slaughtering any innocents, even if the tilk don't have any stone in their blood. There are children in the world who were not born Black Bloods, Ailis."

Ailis laid her tongue over her teeth, as though trying to decide if she should rail at my brother or agree with him.

"We need an army of our own," Regan said. "We need to stop the Guilds before they get any closer to our homes."

"Our armies are already fighting the Hayes," Liam said. "Unless you have guards to spare, we don't have the people to fight the Guilds."

"It would be better to keep the numbers small," I said. "Finn and I found the mountain stone on our own. We slipped in and out of the mine. We managed to kill Drason because we moved without being seen. If we try to face the Guilds head on, we won't win. You've said it yourself, Liam."

"We don't have the numbers." Liam dragged his hands over his face.

"Then forget about an outright attack on the Guilds," I said. "Work as you always have. Keep to the shadows and fight without them knowing you're there."

"She's right," Emmet said. "I can make it into Ilara. Try and find out what they're forging from the mountain stone."

"We need to find out who in Frason's Glenn betrayed us first," Liam said. "Until we know what they've told the Guilds, everything else we do is at risk."

"Then I'll head to Frason's Glenn," Emmet said. "Find the traitor and move on from there."

"I can come with you," Ailis said. "You'll have to run a dog sled to make it through the mountains."

"No, Ailis," Liam said. "Your place is here."

"I have sworn to aid you in your cause, Liam." Ailis gripped the hilt of her sword. "If you are going to risk Black Bloods sneaking into Ilara, then it is my duty to go. You can't ask me to sit in Lygan Hall while you take on this fight."

"You have a son." Liam looked to Ailis. "I won't take you away from him."

"It is my choice," Ailis said.

"It is," Liam said. "But I'm asking you to stay with Beli. As a friend, Ailis. I don't want him going without a mother because of me."

Liam and Ailis stared at each other.

I don't know what understanding passed between them, but when Ailis looked away, she no longer seemed ready to tear Liam apart for telling her to stay.

"One of your other guards can run Emmet in," Regan said. "Surely you have someone else from your camp who can handle a pack of dogs."

"This is too big for two people," Liam said.

"Ena's right," Emmet said. "The party should be kept small."

"Not so small that there's no hope for help if we need it," Liam said. "We need to plan and prepare, not let you burn through Ilbrea."

"Do the paun not deserve to burn?" Emmet asked.

591

"Are we back to waiting for spring?" Regan said. "If this is the best answer you have, perhaps I should not have bothered with the wretched journey to Lygan Hall."

"Riding through tunnels is such a terrible burden," Emmet said.

"I am grateful for the paths the mountain granted the Black Bloods." Regan stood. "That doesn't make this any less of a waste of my time."

"Solcha."

I tensed at the word before even realizing it had been Ailis who spoke.

"What?" Regan asked.

I pressed my hands to the tabletop as Ailis looked to me.

"That's not my name." I kept my voice level.

"The mountain showed you a hidden path," Ailis said. "The mountain showed you where the paun were digging her stone."

"Don't tell me you've started listening to the murmurs on the street." Emmet stepped out of the corner.

"What murmurs?" Regan said.

"Those whispers are what keep my sister in danger," Emmet said.

"The fact that people are whispering doesn't change the truth," Ailis said. "The mountain offered Ena a path. If there were one to the western edge of the mountains, we wouldn't have to wait for spring. If she could lead us to the compound beneath the mountain, we could work from there and be safe from the Guilds as we fight them."

"Even if the mountain chose to open a pathway, my sister would not be coming with us," Emmet said.

"I'd have to," I said. "If you wanted to travel a path the mountain chose for me, I'd have to follow it with you."

"No, we—"

"There's no point in arguing because I can't help you anyway." I laced my fingers together, wishing I had something to occupy my chivving hands. "Whatever names people have tossed upon me, I have no control over the mountain. I am not a trueborn. I'm not even a Black Blood. I don't know why the mountain rescued me, and I certainly don't have any chivving clue how to make her do it again. So, unless you want to try to murder me and see if a tunnel opens, we're going to have to face the snow to reach Ilbrea."

"Then we're back to waiting," Regan said.

"Not if I go now," Emmet said. "I can work on my own until the spring."

"Are you so desperate to flee Lygan Hall?" I asked.

For a slender moment, it looked as though my brother had flinched.

"We're not giving up," Liam said. "There is a way to get enough of us to Ilbrea to make a difference. There is a way to drive the Guilds out of the mountains. We just have to find it."

"I'm going to be stuck here for months, aren't I?" Regan glowered at the window, as though the valley beyond were filled with torment and misery.

"I'll have you escorted back to your room to wait," Liam said.

"Will your guards be keeping me in the crag?" Regan asked.

"All the Brien will be kept to the crag," Liam said. "Ailis will escort you."

"I had hoped for more hospitality from our allies." Regan strode toward the door, her starched skirt rustling as she walked.

"Pouting isn't attractive on any woman," Ailis said. "Although, neither is abandoning allies when they won't murder for you."

A bubble almost like a laugh flitted in and out of existence in my chest.

"Until tomorrow, Trueborn." Liam gave Regan a nod.

Regan opened the door and strode out of the room, Ailis keeping right behind her.

None of us spoke until the sound of Regan's footsteps faded away.

"I can't make the mountain open for me," I said. "If those are the whispers on the wind, the Duweads will be very disappointed in what I'm actually capable of."

"What the people think doesn't matter," Liam said.

"It chivving well does when people want my sister dead." Emmet retreated to his place in the corner by the door.

"Will you not sit with us?" Liam asked.

"I've learned to not to give lying slitches an easy angle of attack," Emmet said.

"Enough." I stood and allowed myself the luxury of pacing beside the table.

"We've all seen the evil the paun are capable of. While I was trying to find Ena, I saw worse from the Guilds than even I expected," Emmet said. "They were tearing through towns, searching for sorcis, killing anyone they thought might have a connection to the bandits who'd been ferrying children into the woods. There were paun combing through the forest, trying to find us.

"If there's even a chance they could be planning to use mountain stone-made weapons on anyone, we have to stop them. That's more important than any clan war or protecting any sorcis. They could wipe out whole villages."

"They already do that," I said.

"But how much more damage could a soldier do with a weapon forged of magic?" Emmet said. "The tilk would never stand a chance."

"If you think it's best to go through the snow, I won't stop you," Liam said. "You aren't sworn to me. I won't lock you in Lygan Hall."

"He can't go," I said.

The creases on my brother's brow deepened.

"There are still people in Lygan Hall who want me dead," I said. "Would my brother really run away and leave me here?"

"You have the guards." Liam stood and crossed into my path, stopping my restless pacing. "Ailis and her men will keep you safe."

"Safety is a lie," I said.

I tried to ignore the flicker of hurt in Liam's eyes.

"Case told me there were others in Lygan Hall who believed the same things he did." I rested my hand on Liam's cheek. "That slitching traitor helped the Hayes because he believed the work you were doing in Ilbrea went against what the Black Bloods should be. The Hayes betrayed us to the Guilds to stop us from protecting the sorcis. Finn was killed because he told the truth about the mountain stone we found in the Lir Valley. We know there are more traitors in Lygan Hall. All I have done, all we are planning to do, will only make them hate me more."

"The people worshiping you doesn't help," Emmet said. "*Solcha* may mean something wonderful to the people who adore you, but it's another reason to murder you for the ones who hate everything you stand for."

Liam's face paled. "We need to keep you inside."

"I will not live locked away while my enemies plot to murder me," I said. "I will not leave Lygan Hall until the murderers have been found. If we allow their treachery to fester, we'll be endangering the people we leave behind. We have to find a way to draw them out. Then we slaughter the traitors.

"Once they are dead, I will beg the mountain for safe passage to the west with every breath I have. But we cannot leave those traitors here with the children and trust the sorcerers to protect them. Evie went into that mine with Finn and me. I will not let her become a target."

"I'll speak to Orla," Liam said. "We'll tear through the village if we have to. I will make sure you are safe."

"I am not safe in Lygan Hall. I am not safe in Ilbrea. There is no such thing as safety. All we can do is choose which danger to face."

1 0

My breath fogged before me as I prowled the outer edge of the sparring ring. The cold of the stone floor bit through the soles of my boots, and the chill in the air raised goose bumps on my arms, despite the hour I'd spent practicing with my sword.

Clangs and shouts echoed through the cavernous space, but the sounds did not make me look away from Cati's blade.

I tightened my grip on the hilt of my sword as she shifted her weight to her left.

"Are you going to attack?" Cati asked. "It's a bit cold to be standing still for so long."

I made myself smile for her. "I'm waiting for the right moment."

"Sure." Cati shrugged. "Just know that I'll be chivving angry if I lose a toe to frostbite while waiting for you to actually make a move."

Cati was right to fear the cold.

They'd closed the proper training field when the snow had gone past two feet deep. The cavern at the base of the cliffs that housed the crag and the keep offered shelter from the snow and the worst of the wind. But the place was still plenty cold enough to risk frostbite if you were fool enough to stand still for too long.

I hoisted my sword, dodged to the right, then veered left, swiping my dulled blade for Cati's middle.

Cati knocked my blow aside without even shifting her weight.

"You should at least try to properly attack me," Cati said.

"I thought I'd give you something to take your mind off being cold." I brought my sword around and swiped for Cati's feet.

She leapt over the blade as she spoke. "I'm not surprised you're distracted. Not with all the excitement."

"Excitement?" I backed out of Cati's reach.

"Sure." Cati darted forward and brought her sword down as though trying to cleave through the top of my head.

I raised my own blade to block the blow. The force of the hit vibrated my bones, and before I could begin my own attack, Cati had slammed her blade into my shoulder.

I staggered forward but stayed on my feet.

"Usually, we have nice quiet winters here in Lygan Hall," Cati said. "We come back from the camp, spend time with our families, and enjoy proper food and real beds. I train up the fighters for the next season and choose what new blood might join our little band. Liam plays with his maps and plots what we'll do once the weather stops trying to kill us. It's a nice little ritual."

"And have you found many new members for Liam's band?" I gripped my sword in my left hand, trying to shake feeling back into the right.

"It seems we won't be needing new members," Cati said. "The whispers on the wind say he'll only be taking a handful of people west and that he might leave long before the snow melts."

"And where did you hear these rumors?" I leveled my blade and charged as though trying to stab Cati in the stomach.

She leapt out of the way, and I twisted my sword, grazing her hip.

"You're getting better." Cati swung for my sword, knocking my weapon out of my hands. My blade hit the ground with a clatter loud enough to draw the attention of the two-dozen fighters training in the cavern. "But don't get cocky."

"Where did you hear that Liam might be leaving soon?" I kept my gaze fixed on my blade as I went to retrieve my sword, trying to keep the flush of embarrassment from creeping into my cheeks.

"It's all over the Hall," Cati said. "From what I can tell, Regan's been speaking about it loudly enough that all the guards set to watch the Brien party have heard. I don't know which of our guards has been whispering to the others, but the rumors have spread far enough, I'd bet most of Lygan Hall knows."

"And you've decided to believe the rumors?" I gripped the hilt of my sword.

Months ago, my arms would have protested hoisting the weapon after an hour spent training. Now, gripping the sword felt right, the weight of the blade balanced perfectly with the strength I'd developed.

The sword was no longer a foreign hindrance, but a tool necessary for my survival.

The weapon feeling right in my hand did nothing to ease the worry that gnawed at my stomach as I watched Cati pace across the center of our ring. The weight of knowing that I should be able to defend the people I cared for only worsened my fears.

"What I believe really doesn't matter," Cati said. "When Liam decides to travel has little to do with me, as long as our Trueborn understands that I will not be left behind."

"Liam hasn't decided anything," I said. "There's the endless snow between us and Ilbrea to begin with—"

"I don't care." Cati held up a hand to keep me silent. "I don't care how many lies the chivving Brien are spreading. I don't care if Liam really has lost his chivving mind and decided he wants to slog through twenty-odd feet of snow and see if he makes it to the edge of the mountains alive. But you, Ena, are going to make it chivving clear to your darling Liam that if he tries to leave Lygan Hall without me, I will chase after him like a demon risen up from the shadows beneath the heart of the mountains.

"I was left behind when you went to the Broinn. I did as I was told and stayed here to keep training the men. I lost more than one friend when the Hayes turned on the

Duweads. I am not going to sit here and let the people I care about fight without me again. Do you understand?"

"I do." I nodded. "But I can't make Liam do anything. He's the Trueborn."

"And you're the one he's rolling," Cati said. "I don't care if you have to ban him from touching your tits until he agrees, but you make sure that when he goes, I am not left behind."

I held Cati's gaze, trying to reason through an argument for leaving her behind.

She has as much of a right to fight the paun as Liam does.

"Fine. I'll make sure you come with us," I said. "But keep quiet about it until we know what's actually going on."

"Sure." Cati winked. "I'm perfectly happy to keep quiet as long as I have a decent chance of getting to slice through some paun."

"You already sliced through plenty of paun in the mountains. Do you not remember the trail you and—" I paused, making myself breathe as a pain sliced deep into my chest. "The trail of Guilded corpses you left leading into Brien territory might very well be why Regan bothered to come here."

"Good." Cati went back to her place at the center of the sparring ring. "If even half of the rumors I've heard are true, the sooner we go out and fight the paun, the better off all Black Bloods will be."

"Only if we manage to do some good." I watched Cati watching me, searching for some sort of hint as to when or how she might attack. "If we just run west and hope for the best, we won't be helping anyone."

I knew the words were true, but still, I hated myself for saying them. Talking in circles with Liam did nothing to keep the Guilds from making terrible weapons to use against the tilk. Just the same as how plotting with Emmet to try and draw out the traitors in the Duwead Clan had accomplished nothing.

I'd spent months spinning in circles, trying to find my enemies and protect my friends. Accomplishing nothing but driving myself a bit madder with each passing day.

Cati's sword flashed through the air as she swung for my arm.

I ducked low and swiped for her legs.

She spun as she dodged out of my reach.

With a shout, I charged forward, bringing my blade up in a wide arc as I attacked her left side.

She blocked my blow, and I let the momentum born of her own strength carry my blade up to strike her on the shoulder.

"Not bad." Cati stepped away from me, shaking her hand as though trying to get feeling back into her fingers.

"I'm done waiting," I said. "It's time to force the fight."

"That's what I was hoping you'd say." A glimmer of joy danced in Cati's eyes.

1 1

If I had been as brave as I pretended, I'd have strode straight back to Liam's room and told him my plan. But I knew Liam. I knew he would do anything to protect me. Even if protection was not what I wanted.

Emmet would do anything to keep me safe as well, but he at least understood that survival was not the only thing that mattered.

I went to my brother's room in the crag as soon as I'd left my training with Cati, but Emmet was not there. I went to my room to wash and get ready for my afternoon walk, but Emmet did not come to meet me.

We'd been planning to walk through the winding paths along the base of the cliff face to see if we could catch the attention of any assassins, but even with Ailis and her guards watching me, it didn't feel right to follow the path I'd chosen with Emmet without him beside me.

I walked through the inside of the keep and crag instead, wandering down corridors I'd never entered before, finding new warrens where Black Bloods lived and labored. Even after months living in Lygan Hall, I still hadn't seen most of the place. Knowing how much of my home was hidden to me only grew my desperate need to do something.

Whispers followed me. People bowed as I passed. But there was no mob demanding Solcha's aid. No villain trying to take my life.

When I'd grown tired of wandering, I ventured out into the snow and across the valley to the sorcerers' compound. I didn't think anything of going to see Marta and the children earlier than I normally would.

I let the winter sun kiss my cheeks as the guards and I wound our way through the snow-lined paths. The cold air flowed through my lungs and surged more determination into my body.

I knew there were traitors lurking around me, shadows that wanted me dead for the crime of telling the truth about what the mountain had shown me. I had hunted for the shadows. I had used myself as bait to try and lure them out.

The time had come to set a trap for the shadows, and I would not wait for anyone's approval.

The gate to the compound opened before Ailis even announced that I had come to visit the children. I walked through the garden where the fruit trees still bloomed, stepped through the solid stone wall, passed the young men and women studying, and got all the way to the door of the children's room before realizing I should not have altered my daily routine, even if my chivving brother had given up on keeping his word to the people he cared for.

I stood outside the children's door for a moment, waiting for Evie to come bounding out to greet me.

Leaning close to the door, I listened for any hint of trouble inside before raising my hand to knock.

Knock. Knock. Knock.

The sound of my own knuckles against the wood seemed strange. Never, in all the months I'd been visiting the children, had I needed to announce my presence. Evie had always heard me coming well before I reached the Lir siblings.

"Yes?" Marta called through the door.

"It's Ena. I've come for a visit."

"Come in."

I opened the door to find Marta bustling toward me with a smile on her face that didn't quite reach her eyes.

"You're early," Marta said. "I'm afraid the children are still in their lessons."

"That's all right." I nodded to Ailis before stepping into the children's room and shutting the guards outside. "I'm just as happy to see you."

"Would you like some tea?" Marta turned from me and headed toward the fireplace where a pot hung from a metal hook.

"I'm fine," I said. "How are you?"

"Never better." Marta poured two mugs of tea and set them both on the table. "How is Regan then? Have you figured out what the Brien want?"

"Not any more than we knew after our first meeting." I sat and accepted the mug of floral brew Marta pushed toward me.

"Which would be?" Marta asked. "You've never told me what Regan said. The children are always around, and I can't imagine the Brien traveled here for any purpose Cinni wouldn't find upsetting."

"I don't think I know anything different than what Emmet's told you."

"I haven't seen him for a few days." Marta flitted a hand through the air, as though the movement might keep me from noticing the pain around her eyes. "Did Regan bring news about the siege?"

"She wants us to go back out into Ilbrea before spring." I gripped my mug, ignoring the pain in my hands from the heat. "If we can sort out a way to manage it, we could all be leaving in a few weeks."

"Oh." Marta blinked at her mug for a moment. "That is much sooner than I expected."

"The children will be fine here. You were going to have to leave them to go back to the camp eventually. Finding someone to care for them now won't be any different."

Marta stood and went back to the fireplace to fuss with the kettle.

"I can help you look for someone to care for the children," I said. "If not a sorcerer, then—"

"That's not necessary."

"I don't mind helping. I took the children from their home. I should make sure they're cared for."

"I won't be going back to the camp," Marta said. "I'm staying in Lygan Hall."

"What?" A gaping hole took up the place where my lungs had been only a moment before. "Even if you don't join the group heading for the western edge of the mountains now, you've got to come when Liam brings people back to the camp. He needs you. We all need you."

"I can't go."

"If it's a matter of finding someone to look after Cinni, then I understand your wanting to take care of the children." I stood up. "But you've got to think of all the sorcis still out in Ilbrea."

"I'm pregnant," Marta said. "I can't leave Lygan Hall. I'm pregnant."

My whole body went numb as I sat back down.

"There's not a chance of my convincing Liam to let me go with him. He'll say traveling the mountains is too dangerous, and I can't think of a good argument against it. I have to stay here."

"Emmet," I said. "Have you told Emmet?"

"Of course." Marta lifted the kettle off the hook. The whole thing trembled as she set it on the floor beside the fireplace.

"He's going to be a father, and he didn't tell me?"

"I don't think he will be a father."

"What?" Shock shot feeling back into my hands. "The baby's not his?"

"Of course it is." Tears sparkled in the corners of her eyes. "But that doesn't mean he wants anything to do with me or the child."

"What did he do?" I gripped my mug to keep myself from shouting.

"I told him I was pregnant." Marta looked up to the stone ceiling as tears streamed down her cheeks. "He said he was sorry and left. I haven't seen him since."

"No." I shook my head, as though I could somehow change reality through sheer force of will. "No, he would not abandon you like that."

"He has. I will be staying in Lygan Hall with the children. Staying here with my child." Marta swiped the tears from her cheeks and pressed a smile onto her face. "It will be good for Cinni for me to stay here. Good for all of them, really. They've been doing well with…" Her voice broke as fresh tears trickled down her cheeks. She took a deep breath as she wiped her tears away again. "They've all been progressing very quickly."

I stood up, walked to Marta, and pulled her into a tight hug.

"I'm fine," Marta said even as her whole body trembled. "I'm just…fine."

"No, you're not." I took her face in my hands and kissed her forehead. "But you are strong enough to carry the entire world. Do not ever forget that, Marta."

I headed for the door.

"Where are you going?" Marta said. "You haven't finished your tea or told me what plans Regan wants to make."

"I'm going to find my chivving brother."

"Ena, no." Marta dodged in front of me, blocking me from the door. "Emmet wants nothing to do with our baby. I can find a way to live with that. Please do not make me the talk of the entire Hall. I don't want to listen to whispers of how he abandoned me."

"There will be no whispers." I took Marta's hands, guiding her out of my path. "But do not tell a Ryeland to shut away their wrath."

"Ena," Marta called after me as I tossed open the door and strode outside. "Ena, please."

I didn't listen to her. My own fury pounded too hard in my ears for me to care about her words.

"Such a short visit?" Ailis asked.

"Send runners ahead to the crag," I said. "I want them to find my brother."

"What happened?" Ailis asked. "Is Emmet in danger?"

"Only from me," I said.

Ailis sent two guards sprinting ahead of our pack.

I kept forming perfect sentences in my mind. Words to shout at my brother that would make him understand that he had finally fallen so low there was no path back to redemption.

He'd left me behind in Harane when he'd gone to be a blacksmith's apprentice in Nantic. He'd abandoned me when he left Nantic to join the Black Bloods. But I had never imagined that my brother could stoop so horribly low.

The storm of my rage carried me across the valley and to the raised garden.

"Where are the runners you sent?" I asked.

"Lygan Hall isn't a small place," Ailis said. "Finding Emmet might take a while. Why don't you go up to your rooms? I'll bring you word when we've found your brother."

"If you can't find him, then I'll do it myself." I entered the corridor inside the cliff.

The people plastered themselves against the walls and lowered their eyes as I passed. But there was something in the way they backed away from me that seemed to say my rage had become a living thing the people could see. The Black Bloods feared the demon my wrath had created.

I did not blame them.

I went from Emmet's room, to the hall where the people in the crag ate, then all the way to the cavern where Cati ran a fresh set of Black Bloods through fighting drills without finding a hint of my brother.

"I am more than happy to have a search party sent out to find him," Ailis said. "But with all the time it took us to get here, he could be back in his room by now. There is no use in us stomping through the halls. I'll set some guards by his room and have Emmet brought to you as soon as he turns up."

I shut my eyes, trying to find reason beneath my anger.

"Ena," Ailis said, "he's here somewhere. I promise he'll turn up."

"Where are the weapons stored?" I asked.

"Most of them are in the halls before the outer gate," Ailis said.

"No, closer than that." I turned back toward the cavern where the fighters trained. "Where are the weapons stored for daily practice?"

"There's a storage room and a small forge nearby," one of the guards said. "The smiths don't use the space very often. I can't think of any sort of reason a person would be there."

"That's exactly where my brother will be."

"It's this way." The guard led me into the cavern where the chill air whipped around my ankles.

The few people not engaged in combat bowed as I passed.

"Why do you think Emmet would be lurking in a storage room?" Ailis asked.

"Blood and violence bring comfort to my dear brother," I said. "If he wants to stay out of sight, he'll find sanctuary among the tools of his trade."

A narrow corridor cut out the backside of the training area.

The tunnel wound down, passing other halls and locked doors. The farther down the tunnel we traveled, the fewer people we passed.

The guard stopped twenty feet away from a wooden door. A faint thump carried from inside the room.

"Wait here." I stepped in front of my guide.

"Not a chivving chance," Ailis said. "I don't care how well you think you know your brother, I don't know who's in there. I'm not letting you walk into a room packed with weapons on your own."

I dug my nails into my palms as I swallowed everything I wanted to shout at Ailis.

"Fine," I said. "Come and see that I am right, then leave my brother and me alone."

Ailis pursed her lips and glared at me for a moment before nodding.

"Wait here," Ailis ordered the other guards.

She walked quietly, as though sneaking up on my brother might offer her some protection from the Ryelands' wrath. There was a keyhole set into the wood, but the latch moved easily as she shoved the door open.

"What do you want?" Emmet's voice carried from inside the room.

"Huh." Ailis let go of the hilt of her sword. "I suppose you do know your dear brother after all."

12

The weapons room did seem like a fitting place for my brother to hide.

A wide stone furnace had been built into one of the walls. A table laid out with hammers, files, and tongs sat near an anvil. Along all the other walls, racks of polished weapons waited to be used.

Emmet stood in the middle of the room, knife in hand, facing a wooden target that had been mounted on the wall.

"Take the guards farther up the tunnel." I stepped in front of Ailis. "You can wait for me there."

"What are you doing here?" Emmet asked. "Run out places to take a nice peaceful walk?"

"Go, Ailis," I said.

"Are you sure?" Ailis said. "I'm not sure I should leave the two of you alone together."

"Do you think my brother would attack me?" I asked.

"From the tone in your voice, it's not you I'm worried about." Ailis closed the door, leaving Emmet and me alone.

"I'm sorry I missed our walk," Emmet said. "Did you take the path along the cliff face?"

"No." I stepped farther into the room. The heat of the fire cut through the chill of my cloak. "I promised I wouldn't go looking for the people who want me dead without you."

"We'll go tomorrow." Emmet threw the knife in his hand, sinking the blade into the center of the target.

"Will we?" I asked. "I keep my promises. I only wish the same could be said of you."

Emmet walked up to the wood and yanked his knife free.

"Did you ever love her?" I asked.

My brother studied the knife in his grip as he walked back to his place and threw the blade again. The knife struck the center of the circle with a thunk.

"Did you ever care for Marta at all?"

"Does it matter?" He walked back to the target and yanked his blade free again.

"Yes, it matters. She is carrying your child."

"I'm surprised she told you." He walked back to the center of the room.

"The whole Hall will know soon. How long do you think she'll be able to hide her belly? I suppose it only matters to you that she keep it quiet until you manage to leave Lygan Hall. No wonder you've seemed so anxious to run back to Ilbrea." I ran over and stood in front of the target, keeping him from throwing his chivving knife again. "How could you do this to her? To the kindest, most caring—"

"This isn't Ilbrea. There are no Guilds here. She'll not be shipped off to Ian Ayres to give birth in a place fit for demons."

"So it doesn't matter that you're abandoning her?"

"She'll be cared for!" Emmet shouted. "She'll have food and shelter. She's not going to be thrown to the wolves or starve."

"She'll just be left to raise your child on her own."

"She's better off."

"What?"

"The clan will make sure she has everything she needs. There is nothing more for me to do."

"I thought I knew you." I swallowed the sour in my throat. "I thought I understood your faults, but you are nothing more than a disgusting coward."

"I'm not a coward. I'm a killer, Ena." Emmet threw his knife at the table, sinking the tip into the wooden top. "That's all I'm good for. I can fight, and I can kill. How is that of any use to Marta?"

"You're more than just a fighter. You have a proper trade. You were apprenticed to a blacksmith."

"I learned a lot from him." Emmet gave a mirthless laugh. "Wouldn't know how to chivving well defend myself if it wasn't for that slitch. The chivving bastard taught me how to hit hard enough to knock someone off their feet."

"The blacksmith? I met him when I went looking for you." I took a step closer to my brother. "He was nice to me."

"He was fine when he was sober. But a bit too much frie, and he'd beat you till you couldn't move. Had to learn to fight back, or he would have murdered me."

Emmet ripped the knife from the table and threw it at the target. A breeze passed my face with the blade.

"I'm sorry," I said. "I didn't know he hurt you. I'm sorry you got dropped some place awful when our parents died, but—"

"It wasn't much better for me when our parents were alive." Emmet strode to the racks and grabbed two more knives. "Mother was a good woman, but our father was a demon with human skin."

"That's not true."

Emmet finally met my gaze. "You don't remember, do you?"

"There is nothing to remember."

"I did everything I could to shield you from him. I didn't think it had actually worked."

"Our father was a good man. He worked hard to feed our family. The soldiers murdered him—"

"Just because the paun killed him doesn't mean he wasn't a violent bastard."

I wanted to shout that Emmet was wrong, but there was something in his steady tone that kept me quiet.

"Our father had a horrible temper. One wrong word, and he'd hit hard enough to make the world go black. I made sure he blamed everything on me. I made sure he didn't touch you. Kept you out of the way when he went after our mother. I taught you to climb so you could chivving well get away from him if you had to. His temper brought terror to every moment I lived in that house. And I am filled with the same demons that made him.

"I learned how to take a hit from our father. I learned how to fight back from the smith. I learned how to kill because there is nothing else for me in this world. I wish I had something else to offer, but I am what they made me. There is enough blood on my hands to drown a village, Ena. I am a killer filled with violence and anger. There is no place for this much blood and death in a child's life. Marta and the baby are better off with me far away from Lygan Hall."

He threw the first knife into the target. And then the second.

I tried to think back through the things I remembered of my parents. I had no memory of my father hurting me. No memory of him shouting at me, not until he'd placed me on the horse and told me to ride for Nantic. Then he'd railed at the soldiers who came for the taxes, his temper blazing even when facing a line of men bearing swords.

A terrible ache pressed against my chest.

"I don't remember you teaching me to climb," I said.

"You were only three." He stepped around me to retrieve his blades.

All three clustered together in a tight group at the very heart of the target.

"I don't remember our father being angry," I said.

Emmet stared at the knives in his hands. "I don't need you to believe me. I remember enough of the truth for the both of us."

"Go to Marta." I stepped into Emmet's path, trapping him by the wall. "Go to the compound, and beg her forgiveness."

"I am not fit to be a father."

"I don't remember our father being evil—"

"I've told—"

"—because you made sure I wouldn't. You protected me. You've always protected me, even when I chivving well didn't want you to. You have fought and killed to protect the people you care for—"

"I fight because it's all I know how to do." For the first time, Emmet looked afraid, diminished. "I have nothing in me but anger. I can't be what Marta needs."

"You don't have a choice. You are the one she chose. You are the father of her child. And you are going to march to that compound and beg her to marry you. If a fighter is all you can be, then your child will have a warrior for a father. If you defend Marta and that baby half so well as you've protected me, then you'll have done more than most men ever manage."

Grief filled Emmet's eyes as he shook his head.

"We were born in fire. We are made of ashes." I took Emmet's face in my hands, making him meet my gaze. "Maybe the Guilds burned away bits of our souls and we'll never be whole, but you can't let the paun win. You can't let them steal your chance at a family. Do not make the woman who loves you suffer because the Guilds left you afraid."

"I walked away from her." Emmet shut his eyes. "She won't accept me. She'll want nothing to do with me."

"Beg until you change her mind."

"How can I do that when I know she'd be better off without me?"

"Because if you don't, I will never forgive you. I will never speak to you again. I will never look at you again. Make this right, or I am done with you forever, Emmet Ryeland." I rose up on my toes and kissed my brother's forehead. "You deserve a shot at happiness, and your baby will need a father to protect her. This world isn't safe, Emmet. You have to protect Marta and your baby. If you won't beg for your own good, do it for them."

Emmet nodded.

"Now go, and do not dare return to the crag until you've won her back."

He stepped around me and laid his knives on the table before going out the door. He didn't offer any thanks or parting words before leaving me alone.

I didn't allow my hands to shake until his footsteps had faded away. Then my whole body began to tremble, as though I might somehow shake away the shadows that crept in around me and launch myself back into the bliss of not knowing.

I'd spent so long being angry that Emmet hadn't taken me to Nantic with him. In Lily's house, there had been danger from the soldiers, but Lily cared for me in her own way. She certainly never raised a hand to me.

Emmet had killed three men saving Liam's life. I knew that much. But I'd thought it had just been a fight gone wrong and he'd run from Nantic to protect himself. The violence in my brother's life reached farther back than I'd known.

I leaned against the table, staring into the fire for a long while.

"Ena?" Ailis's voice cut through the thoughts dancing circles in my head.

"Yes." I pressed my face into a careful smile before turning toward the door.

"Are you all right, then?" Ailis studied me, as though looking for hints of a brawl. "I hear the Ryelands shouting at each other, then your brother leaves, and you stay awfully quiet in here."

"I'm fine." I straightened my cloak around my shoulders and walked toward the door. "There were just some decisions that needed to be made."

"Ahh." Ailis pursed her lips. "And you've done your deciding?"

"I have. Now I just have to convince Liam I'm right."

13

There are moments in time when it seems like everything should stop. All the world should take a breath and revel in the beauty that creeps in through the unending pain of our lives.

Those moments of true happiness are so rare and so brief, it's hard to catch them as they happen. It's only once they've passed that you realize you should have screamed for the world to stop and behold the beauty you've discovered.

By then, the moment has passed, and you are twisting back into a world of darkness and danger, where even the most blissful pleasures are tainted with the knowledge that the demons are still scenting your blood as they hunt from the shadows.

14

Marta wore her hair loose when she married my brother in the common hall inside the crag. Its bright blond seemed to glow in the lae stone light as she beamed at Emmet.

I caught him smiling at her as well.

If my memories were true, his scars vanished for a few glorious moments, and Emmet Ryeland was just a handsome young man, marrying the woman who had stolen his heart.

Marta blushed when the crowd cheered after Liam finished performing the ceremony. But my brother did not hesitate to kiss her in front of everyone.

Tears streamed down Marta's cheeks as she greeted all the people who had come together to wish them well.

I could not remember the last time I had seen someone so blissfully happy.

Neil rolled out barrels of ale and frie, though thankfully he'd had nothing to do with preparing the feast's worth of food.

Evie danced through the crowd as soon as the fiddler struck up the first tune, while Cinni stood on top of a table, beaming as she watched the musicians play.

Through all the joy and laughter, I couldn't stop myself from missing the one face that would have completed the scene.

I was so busy watching the dancers, I almost didn't notice gossipy Nessa strolling past as she prowled for a partner.

"Nessa," I called out, giving a little wave once she looked my way.

She hitched a false smile onto her lips. "Ena, it's lovely to see you. It seems life in Lygan Hall suits you well."

"The Hall is beautiful," I said, "though I can't help but miss life in the camp."

Nessa's smile shifted from false brightness to genuine joy. "I have heard rumor of Liam heading back into the wild sooner than spring. I suppose you'd be happy to join him as he tramps through the snow, then."

"Of course." I lifted a cup of frie from a passing tray. "I'd be happy to stand by his side no matter where he is. Though, I'm afraid I'd have to go with him whether I wanted to or not."

"Oh?" Nessa leaned a little closer.

The fiddlers finished their tune, and the crowd cheered. I waited until the new song began to speak again.

"There are secrets under the mountain Liam would have no hope of finding without me," I said. "We're leaving in three days to head west. I'm glad I was able to see my brother married before venturing back into the labyrinth of stone."

"Right," Nessa said. "You wouldn't want to miss Emmet's wedding."

"There are so many changes coming for all the Black Bloods." I raised my cup to Nessa. "It's nice to begin with a celebration of family."

I walked away, weaving across the room to Liam's seat at the head table. When I glanced behind, Nessa was already leaning in to whisper in another girl's ear.

Liam smiled when I caught his eye, and for a moment, all of my scheming seemed like a terrible mistake. All I wanted was to be with Liam. To sit by his side and revel in being near him.

Enemies do not care if you have found joy.

"It's quite the wedding." Liam stood and pulled out the chair beside his.

"Marta looks happy," I said.

"So does Emmet."

It took me a moment to catch sight of them on the far side of the room.

Marta chatted with the people who had come to congratulate her.

Emmet did not speak to anyone in the crowd. He just stood silently behind Marta, watching her as though he'd been given the sacred duty of guarding her.

"We should leave him behind," I said. "We can go west without him."

"I don't think so," Liam said.

"You're making Ailis stay behind. If she has to stay to care for her child—"

"I'm not disagreeing with you. I hate to ask any parent to leave their child. That is a weight I do not want to carry." Liam kissed my hand. "But I don't think we'd be able to convince Emmet to stay in Lygan Hall. Even if you stayed behind, he wouldn't give up the fight in Ilbrea. I don't think he can."

The song stopped, and Evie cheered so loudly the grownups around her laughed as they joined in.

"If we stopped the Guilds," I said, "if the sorcis were safe and the paun couldn't hurt anyone, do you think Emmet could be happy staying in Lygan Hall?"

"I hope so," Liam said. "That's what some people don't understand—you spend so long fighting, just trying to get from one day to the next, trying to make sure you don't lose any more good people, peace becomes a foreign thing. The quiet of Lygan Hall can seem smothering after a season out fighting the Guilds. It should be restful, but it only makes my skin crawl as I wonder what's happening out in Ilbrea."

"So we'll go," I said. "We'll take a small crew and head west on dogsleds."

"What about the traitors hiding in the Hall?" Liam laced his fingers through mine. "A wise woman assured me the longer we let that fester, the more danger there will be. And not just for you."

I watched Evie prance through the dancers. She held such perfect joy. After all she'd suffered growing up in fear of her own magic, she radiated happiness. I couldn't bear the thought of anyone stealing that sweet innocence from her.

"I've figured out how to trap them," I said. "They'll come for me soon."

Liam stiffened and eased his hand away from mine and toward the sword at his hip. "Ena, what have you done?"

"Nothing." I leaned in and kissed his cheek. "They want me dead, and now they'll know I'm leaving. They're running out of time."

"Let's go." Liam took my arm, drawing me to my feet.

"We're at a wedding," I said. "We can't leave."

"Of course we can." Liam wrapped an arm around my waist, half-dragging me toward the door. "You've just told me you've set a target on your back. We are not staying here."

"Liam—"

"Do you want your blood to be spilled at Marta's wedding?"

I let him guide me toward the door, keeping a careful smile on my face as the Black Bloods bowed us past.

"Trueborn." Conn bowed as we reached the door.

"We're going back to my quarters," Liam said. "Now."

Conn and another guard started leading the way.

"They are going to come for me, Liam." I tried to step away from him, but he tightened his grip on my waist. "I am done hiding."

"Have you been hiding?" Liam said. "Has your traipsing along every path in the valley been you hiding? Has your going into the village and allowing yourself to be surrounded by people been you hiding?"

"Who told you?"

Liam didn't answer as we wound our way up the spiral staircase to his room.

The guards at the end of the statue corridor bowed to us as they opened the door to the hall where we lived.

"Double the guards in the corridor and at the bottom of the steps," Liam ordered Conn. "No one enters this portion of the keep unless you personally can vouch for them."

"Yes, Trueborn." Conn bowed.

Liam didn't let go of my waist until he'd slid the bolt on the bedroom door into place. Then he strode straight into his sitting room to lock that door as well.

"It was Ailis, wasn't it?" I asked. "Has she been telling you everywhere I go?"

"Of course."

"She's been spying on me?"

"I trust Ailis with my life. I trusted her to protect you." Liam checked through the corners of the rooms, even looking out onto the balcony before bothering to face me. "Protecting you often means keeping you safe from yourself, Ena."

"What?" I shouted.

I pictured the guards outside flinching at my rage.

"What is that suppose to mean?" I kept my voice too low to be heard through the door.

"Finn died."

"I know. I was there."

"They killed him to keep him from spreading word of what he'd seen," Liam said, "which wasn't half so much as what the mountain showed you. There are people who want you dead. From what Case told you, there are people in Lygan Hall who would kill you to keep you quiet."

"I chivving well know that!"

"Then why would you give the bastards every opportunity to murder you?"

"Do you think I should silence myself by hiding? Just lock myself away and let the traitors decide when they'd like to attack?" I strode to the vanity the women had set up for me in the corner of Liam's room. As though I was his equal. As though I actually deserved a say in the space I inhabited.

"I want you safe."

I shook out my fancy braid and tore my fancy brush through my hair.

"Have you had any luck finding the traitors hiding in your own Hall?" I asked.

"No," Liam said. "There's no chatter in the taverns. No hiding places in the shadows. Even in the darkest tunnels below Lygan Hall, there are no traces of traitors lurking."

"You've been searching below the Hall?"

"Of course I have!" Liam tore his hands through his hair. "I've spent months searching every chivving corner of this place, trying to find the bastards who betrayed my clan before they hurt the woman I love. Only the gods know what the sorcerers will demand in exchange for all the help I've asked for. And you go tromping about, trying to get attacked everyday!"

"Better to have them attack me in the open than wait for them to kill me in my sleep." I sat in the chair and stared at my reflection in the vanity mirror.

"I promised I would never lock you away," Liam said. "I understand you want to fight. I know losing Finn was a horrible blow for both of us, and I know you want vengeance on the bastards who helped Case do this horrible thing."

"Don't say his name."

"But I can't lose you, too." Liam knelt beside me. "Finn's death was not your fault. And you knew him. You know how much he loved you. The last thing he'd want is for you to put yourself in harm's way."

"He'd do the same for me."

There were no tears on the perfect face I'd painted to attend my brother's wedding. My cheeks were a cheerful hue. My lips looked ready to seduce a king. I'd covered my pain in beautiful armor, but there was not enough paint in the world to fool Liam.

"You want vengeance. I do, too. The whole clan is at war because of what the Hayes did to us. But you don't have to sacrifice yourself to find justice. I will never stop hunting for the vermin who betrayed us. I promise you." He gently touched my cheek, as though waiting to see if I would scream at him again. "Please, Ena. I cannot survive losing you."

"They'll come for me before we leave." I leaned into his touch. "They'll all know I'm going. I've made sure of it."

"Then you can stay in here until it's time to go west. I'll keep the guards packed into the hall so no one can reach you."

"And I won't say goodbye to the children before we leave? Will I be allowed to come back if you can't find the murderers lurking in the shadows?"

"I will find them."

"The Guilds stole one home from me." I kissed Liam's palm. "Do not ask me to let murderers steal another."

He brushed my hair away from my face. "I'm afraid your grief will steal your life."

"Please, Liam. I can't keep waiting for them to come for me. I will go mad if I keep waiting for the shadows to attack. I have to stop them."

"I love you." He kissed my forehead. "More than anything in this world, I love you."

I leaned in and kissed him.

Maybe I should have been brave enough to tell him that he was the only thing that made living in this awful world worth the unending pain. I know I should have told him I didn't mind him wanting to protect me, that having someone who cared for me so deeply made it easier to see why I had to keep fighting each time it felt like the world was squeezing the air out of my lungs.

But I kissed him instead.

His lips tasted of fire and sweet honey. And his heart raced in his chest as I pulled him to his feet.

He kissed the side of my neck as I unfastened the belt that held his sword.

I did not try to stifle the moan that escaped my lips as he sought more skin to explore.

I wanted him. That was one desire I was not too cowardly to express.

Our bed was a haven where our limbs could tangle, and sweat and pleasure mixed in a perfect delight that offered blissful freedom.

We were safe in our sanctuary as he tasted my skin.

I forgot the outside world existed as I found bliss in Liam's arms.

The shadows outside did not forget about me.

15

The morning sun slanting in through the frostbitten windows woke me in the morning.

Liam's warmth had filled the blankets with blissful heat, batting away any temptation that might have lured me out of bed.

I tucked my head onto his shoulder, listening to the soft rhythm of his heart beating in his chest.

I knew he'd woken up when his breathing changed, but I stayed silent until he tightened his arms around me, drawing my naked body closer to the heat of his skin.

"I'll miss this bed." I pressed my chest to his side and kissed the sweet spot nestled right beneath his ear.

"Should I have a better bed hauled to camp when the others join us come summer?"

"No. It would be rude to make the horses carry such a heavy load just for my comfort."

A hint of a laugh rumbled in Liam's chest.

"I don't mind the cot as long as you share it with me."

Liam tipped my chin up and kissed me. "For as long as you'll have me."

"I have an idea."

Liam pulled away from me and sat up, ruining the perfect warmth that had surrounded me.

"You don't want me wandering." I knelt beside him, pulling the blanket around me to keep the chill off my bare skin.

"I don't want you wandering through the valley trying to get people to attack you," Liam said. "I don't want you placing a target on your own back."

"So then I won't wander. Let's bring the traitors to me instead."

"What?"

"Let's throw a party." I pressed my hands to Liam's shoulders, and he shifted as though wanting to bolt away from me. "A nice little farewell before we head west. Make sure the rumor travels through the whole valley that it's the only time I'll be leaving our room before we go. Tell them I'm preparing to ask the mountain's favor in granting us a path if you have to. Just make it clear that it's the only time I'll be in public."

"Then march you into a crowd and see who kills you?" Liam pulled away from me to pace beside the bed.

"No crowds," I said. "Just a small group of people. If there really are traitors who want me dead lurking in the shadows, they'll find a way to be invited."

"Luring clever killers in. That's somehow a better idea?"

"You'll freeze your feet pacing barefoot." I reached for Liam.

He met my gaze and stepped onto the rug that surrounded the bed's pedestal.

"We wait for everyone to arrive—" I began.

"And see if they manage to kill you?"

"We lock the doors," I said. "Keep everyone in and see who tries to attack."

"And if they figure out they're trapped and don't tip their hand?"

"Then we have Wyman search them."

"Would you have Cati question innocent people next?" Liam asked.

"Would you leave Lygan Hall and simply hope no one finds out that Evie was with Finn and me in the mine?"

Liam rubbed his hands over his face and sat on the edge of the bed.

"We can ask sorcerers to come," I said. "We can stack the guards so there will be plenty of protection."

"There is no protection from a stone through the heart."

"If they had that ability, don't you think they'd have used it months ago? You have searched for the shadows. I have tried to lure them out. We have to go west to stop the paun from doing even more damage, and we can't leave here if there are still traitors lurking in Lygan Hall. You know I'm right."

"Fine." Liam took my hand, drawing me to the edge of the bed. "But you don't come to the party. You stay here."

"But—"

"That's the line I will not cross, Ena." Liam held my gaze.

I stared into his dark eyes and saw no chance of compromise.

"Fine. But Marta and the children are kept away as well."

"I'll arrange it." Liam kissed my temple. "We'll have to have a new dress made for you."

"But I'm not going."

"We'll want people to believe you are." Liam lifted me onto his lap. "We'll take Emmet and head west on sleds. Get to Frason's Glenn and work from there."

"Cati's coming, too. She won't be left behind."

I leaned my head against Liam's chest and breathed in his scent, letting it simmer all the way into my bones, where no amount of pain or fear could steal the memory from me.

"We'll take Cati," Liam said. "We'll have to allow Regan to travel with us as well."

Loathing shook my shoulders, and Liam held me tighter.

"Better to have her with us in Ilbrea than here where we can't watch her," Liam said. "Maybe she'll finally learn why we fight so hard to keep the sorcis safe."

"Are there enough sleds for all of us?"

"There will have to be."

A soft knock came from the door.

Liam lifted me up and lay me on the bed. He kissed the skin right beneath my stone pendant before snatching up his pants and heading for the door.

I burrowed into the covers as Liam opened the door and gave a nod to the woman bearing our breakfast tray.

I shut my eyes as he accepted the food.

I don't know why, but even after months of sleeping in Liam's bed, even knowing that everyone in Lygan Hall, including his mother, knew chivving well that Liam and I rolled about all the chivving time, I'd still turn bright red when the serving women actually caught me naked.

I waited until Liam had closed the door to open my eyes again.

He set the tray on the bed and tucked my hair behind my ear.

"It's safe to come out now." A smile curved one side of his lips.

"Would you prefer me to flounce around naked?" I reached for the little glass bottle on the tray.

"Personally? Always."

I laughed as I uncorked the bottle and winced as I downed its foul contents.

Liam passed me a mug of tea. "You don't have to drink that, you know."

"Really?" I sipped the tea, which did little to improve the awful coating in my mouth. "Do you understand what it's for?"

"Would it actually be so terrible?" Liam looked down at his hand resting on my blanket-covered leg. "For us to have a family?"

"Aside from your mother hiding from me, people wanting me dead, a sensible clan war—"

"I mean it, Ena."

"You've grown that tired of having me beside you?" I shifted my leg away from him and pushed myself to my knees. "You'd rather I stay here while you run off and fight?"

"No. I just...I want to build a proper life with you."

I froze for a moment, trying to think through a future I'd never considered.

"Never mind." Liam kissed the back of my hand. "Pay no attention to the lovesick fool."

"You're not a fool." I gripped his hand tighter. "But I will not be parted from you. If you have to go west every year until the Black Bloods are safe from the Guilds, then I'm going with you. If carrying your child means staying in Lygan Hall, I won't do it, not until you can stay with me."

"Destroying the Guilds may not be possible."

"It is. I will burn Ilara. The Black Bloods will be safe. And then I will give you a dozen children, Liam Duwead. My path is yours, and we will travel it together. And when the path leads us home, we will build a family that will terrify your mother. And Lygan Hall will never have a moment of peace again."

16

The dress the women below had stitched together was a work of pure beauty. I could not begin to imagine how they'd achieved it in two days.

The skirt had been dyed in streaks of blue that seemed to imply the wind twirling through the fabric even as the dress lay on the bed. The bodice had been sewn with little glass beads that caught the glimmer of the lae stone light in a way that hinted at magic in their making.

The dress was more stunning than anything I'd seen even at Mave's home in Frason's Glenn, and no one was going to see me wearing it.

I sat at the vanity, painting my face as though I were actually donning my armor to battle with a room filled with Black Bloods. I fiddled with the top of the jar of ground charcoal I'd used to line my eyes. I missed the paints Nora had given me, but being an inker did have its advantages when it came to mixing the hues I wanted.

"I invited my mother to the party." Liam stepped up behind me.

The women had dressed Liam in a billowing blue shirt that cut in at his waist and made him look like a chivving god.

I stared at his reflection in the mirror, reveling in his absolute perfection.

"She's not coming," Liam said.

"I'm not surprised."

"She did promise to send the finest chamb as my farewell."

"I'm sorry." I turned to face Liam.

"Don't be." Liam smiled at me.

I wanted to stare at him and kiss him all at the same time.

"I've said before she's not much of a mother." Liam touched my cheek, and I leaned into the warmth of his hand. "Her heir is going out into Ilbrea to protect the Black Bloods from the Guilds. She didn't attend a going away party for Colm. Why would she care any more about my departure?"

"Because you're her heir." I stood up.

616

Liam looked at me in my plain, white shift, and wanting filled his eyes as though I were actually wearing the perfect blue dress. He trailed his finger along my neck.

"I should stay here with you," Liam said. "Cati and Emmet are already in the hall. I can send Ailis down, have her lock the doors and—"

"Go." I pressed my hand to Liam's chest. "Make a fuss about how I'll be down late. Let them announce my arrival and see who tries to strike. If they don't believe I'm coming, the shadows might not show themselves."

"Swear to me you'll stay safely in here?"

I lifted Liam's hand and pressed his palm to my heart. "I promise. As long as you swear you'll come back to me."

Liam kissed my forehead. "Time to see if we can catch a shadow." He squared his shoulders and strode toward the door. "As long as you're sure you'll be down soon." He spoke loudly enough for his words to carry into the corridor. "I don't think anyone will forgive me if I throw a party and Solcha herself doesn't come."

I cringed at his use of the name.

Liam gave me a smile before opening the door.

Instinct told me to hide so the guards wouldn't catch me in my shift, but I followed behind Liam, letting them all see the curves of my body and my perfectly painted face.

"I'll be down in a bit." I kissed Liam's cheek. "The dress is so beautiful, I want to make sure I show off the ladies' work as well as I can."

Liam gave me a nod and closed the door behind him.

I leaned against the wood, fighting the urge to slide the bolt into place.

I hated the pretense. I didn't believe any of the guards would try to hurt me, but I knew they'd whisper about my joining Liam later as soon as they got downstairs.

I stood by the door for a moment, wondering what exactly I should do.

Liam and Emmet were downstairs trying to stop the traitors, but my role was to hide.

I hated hiding.

If I could have snuck out to slip into the woods, that would have been one thing, but sitting in the room, wondering if lives were ending far below, was enough to drive me near madness within the first two minutes of Liam's leaving.

I pulled on a robe and paced in front of the fire, trying to keep my heart quiet, as though I might hear the screams of the traitors through the thick layers of stone.

When I couldn't stand pacing anymore, I turned to the tray of food the women had delivered along with my dress. They'd given me bread, cheese, and a berry tart, as though expecting I would be too delicate to eat at the party.

I laughed to myself as I poured a glass of frie and bit into the sweet pastry. I was a child of mud and blood, not a lady who belonged in a fine gown. I pictured Lily scowling at the idea of my turning away food because I was wearing a fancy dress. Her furrowed brow and flattened mouth made me laugh again.

I sat in front of the fire with my tart and frie, staring into the flames and wondering what Lily would say if she were in Lygan Hall with me.

She'd be horrified I'd been sharing Liam's bed to start. Absolutely furious that I'd been rolling around with a man and let everyone know about it.

She'd have liked the healers, how skilled they were and how they never asked for more than a family could pay.

She'd have liked Liam. Once she got over the fact that he had an unmarried girl in his bed.

A pain started in my stomach. I set my frie aside and tried to shake thoughts of Lily from my mind.

I wanted to be able to remember her without sickening grief rolling through me, but I could not make the pain stop.

I had never appreciated how lucky I was that she had plucked me out of the mud when my father was killed. If Lily hadn't claimed me, I could have ended up with someone who liked to hit children as Emmet had. I'd probably have ended up in a brothel if Lily hadn't taken it upon herself to teach me an honest trade.

She had taught me a less honest trade as well.

My head spun from the heat of the fire. I pushed myself to my feet and backed away from the flames, but the room kept swaying in front of me.

The sharp pain dug into my stomach again.

I missed Lily.

I needed Lily.

Pain shot through my wrists as the room tipped and I fell to the ground.

"Miss?" a voice called through the door. "Ena?"

I tried to answer, but my lungs had gotten heavy.

The door burst open, and Conn ran in.

I didn't know how bad I was until I saw the fear in his eyes.

"She needs help!" Conn shouted toward the hall. "Just lie down."

I crawled away as he knelt beside me.

"I'll help you to the bed."

I retched on the floor.

"Has someone gone for the healer?" Conn's voice pounded in my head as I stuck my fingers down my throat and made myself ill again.

There were more voices in the hall, and freezing cold hands tried to grab hold of me.

I broke free of the ice and made myself stand.

"I will not fail you." The room swayed as I stumbled toward my vanity.

My skin had gone a pale gray, leaving my painted armor as the only color on my face.

"You need to lie down."

An arm wrapped around my waist as I tipped into the vanity.

Paints and powders tumbled everywhere, but I managed to grab the jar I needed before it smashed on the ground.

Bits of the world faded to gray as I was lifted by someone who did not smell like Liam.

I didn't fight against them. I didn't have the strength to do anything more than unscrew the top of the jar and dump the powdered charcoal into my mouth.

"Stop!" Fingers pinched my cheeks, like I was a child who had eaten something bad.

I swallowed the powder before they could stick their fingers into my mouth.

I smiled as they laid me down on the bed.

Lily's face flitted before me as blackness stole my vision.

She was smiling, too.

618

17

I had never had such a headache in all my life.

Before I even knew I was awake, I could feel the pain boring deep into the back of my skull.

As I realized there was a world beyond the pain, I was not tempted to move. There was something comforting about my surroundings. I did not need to be afraid. I was protected. Guarded.

I lay in blackness, waiting for the pain to retreat.

It took me a long while to realize why I did not need to be afraid.

I took a deep breath, and the scent of fresh wind and reckless freedom filled my aching lungs.

"Ena?" Liam's voice cut through the darkness.

I tried to open my eyes, but even that slim effort proved too much.

A hand lifted mine from under the blankets.

Lips pressed against my forehead.

The darkness swallowed all of my thoughts.

1 8

A grating thirst woke me the second time.

The pain in my head had retreated to a bearable throb, and my eyes slid open when I asked them to.

The dull gray of twilight filled Liam's room.

"Ena?" Liam sprang up from his seat near the side of the bed.

I tried to speak, but my throat burned too badly.

"Water," Liam said. "They've said you're allowed water."

He grabbed a glass from a table someone had left beside the bed.

"Is she awake?" Emmet thumped in from the other room.

Liam looped an arm behind my shoulders and helped me to sit up. He trickled the sweet coolness of the water into my mouth.

Swallowing hurt, breathing hurt, but I could tell from the look of relief on my brother's face I should have been much worse off.

"What happened?" My words came out as an awful croak.

"You were poisoned," Emmet said. "While we were waiting for an assassin at the party."

Liam tightened his grip on my shoulders.

"They used my own trick against me." I took another sip of the water.

"It almost worked," Emmet said.

"It should have," I said. "But I'm too familiar with death."

"We should get the healers back in," Liam said.

"I'm fine," I said.

Emmet went to the door anyway. He didn't even leave. He just popped his head into the corridor and snapped orders at the people outside.

"Did you find them?" My arms shook as I tried to push myself up straighter.

Liam lifted me to lean against his torso.

I let myself sink into his warmth.

"We know who brewed the poison." Emmet bolted the door to the corridor. "But they've gone missing."

"They're in Lygan Hall," Liam said. "There's no way they've gotten out, but we don't know where in the valley they're hiding."

"Who was it?" I took another sip of water.

"One of the kitchen biddies," Emmet said. "Her husband's been arrested and questioned."

"By Wyman?"

"The man shares his wife's beliefs," Liam said. "He thinks the Black Bloods should honor their covenant with the mountain and stay well out of Ilbrea, but he didn't know his wife had gone so far as to join with people who plot murder."

"Then it's all for nothing." I raised my hand and brushed my hair away from my face. My skin felt rubbery beneath my own touch.

"I'll find her," Emmet said. "And when I do, I'll make sure she tells me where the rest of the demons are hiding."

"You'll torture an old woman?" I asked.

"I'll torture the fiend who tried to murder my sister."

A smile curved my lips, and a cough grated against my lungs as I gave a feeble laugh.

"Take another drink." Liam held the glass to my lips.

"Was anyone else hurt?" I asked once I'd managed to draw more air into my lungs.

"No," Liam said.

"It was a fine party until the guards came charging in to tell us you were half-dead," Emmet said.

"We have to find the old woman before we can head west," I said. "And we've got to do it quickly. We can't keep wasting time hiding in Lygan Hall."

"You need to heal," Liam said. "You can't go through the snow like this."

"But the Guilds could be forging weapons. They could be mining more mountain stone every day," I said. "They've already crept too far into the mountains. We can't wait here because of me. We need to find the woman and go."

"I've work to do organizing the party we're to take west," Liam said. "There are supplies to be managed and routes to plot."

"But we were already set to leave," I said.

"Until someone tried to murder you," Emmet said. "Since you've been out, the number of people insisting on joining the expedition has grown."

"What?" I asked.

Liam kissed the side of my head.

Emmet didn't flinch.

"We're a party of twenty heading west now," Liam said. "It was easy for people to think we could wait until spring when the danger from the Guilds seemed far away. We've got a clan war to worry about, and we always spend the cold months in Lygan Hall."

"But then someone tried to murder one of our own in the safety of her home," Emmet said. "Suddenly, finding the traitor the Hayes placed in Ilbrea seems a lot more pressing."

"But they killed Finn. Was his death not enough?" I leaned forward as the urge to tear through the stone of the Hall burned in my veins. Pain shot through my sides.

"Careful." Liam wrapped both arms around me, pinning me in place and offering comfort. "It'll take at least a few days to get the supplies ready. We'll see how you're feeling by then."

"I'm tired of waiting," I said. "I'm sick to death of spinning in circles, waiting for the next disaster to strike."

"By the gods, you're a fool." Emmet narrowed his eyes at me. "You are the next disaster, Ena. You very nearly died. You got your wish—they finally tried to murder you."

"That's not—"

"Stop complaining that your body needs rest because you actually survived. We'll leave as soon as we can. In the meantime, I'm going hunting for the cact of a chivving slitch who tried to kill you." Emmet strode toward the door.

"Don't let your wife hear you talking like that," I said.

Emmet froze then turned slowly to face me. "My wife will be more forgiving of my language than I'll be of you trying to move too quickly and doing yourself more harm. Do not try to use Marta's good nature against me."

I didn't bother hiding my smile as Emmet stormed out the door.

"He actually called her his wife." I nestled against Liam's shoulder. "Marta getting pregnant is the best thing that's ever happened to my brother."

Liam said nothing.

I looked up to see his face. "What's wrong?"

"I agree with Emmet," Liam said. "We need to wait for you to heal. It was wrong to try and go west so quickly."

"We're going as soon as we can. I was only a little poisoned. There's no use in fussing about me."

"I almost lost you, Ena. I've spent the past two days praying to every god who might listen that you'd stay alive."

"Two days?" I searched my memory, trying to reason through having lost so much time.

"You will rest until the healers say you are well enough to travel."

"And Ilbrea will spiral further into chaos while we wait?"

"I will not leave here without you." Liam held me tighter. "Emmet won't go until we've found the woman who poisoned you."

"At this point, we might be here until the snow is gone."

"So be it," Liam said. "I was foolish to think I could outrun the threat to your life. I won't make that mistake again."

19

I cannot recommend healing from poison as a pleasant way to spend time, but the waiting was worse.

The healers poked at me. Marta brought the children to visit me. Liam hovered over me. Cati prepared our party to head west. Emmet and the guards scoured the valley for the would-be assassin. And I stayed in our room, growing more restless with every breath.

"You look healthy enough to me." Evie squinted at me. "Definitely a lot better than you were."

"Everyone looks better than someone on the edge of death," Dorran said. "At least they should hope they do."

"Be nice," Gwen said.

"Yes, be nice," Evie mimicked her older sister. "Some people can't help the wretched way they look."

"All of you be nice," Marta warned from her seat at the other end of the table.

It felt strange, having the children in Liam's sitting room, only a closed door away from where I shared his bed. But the healers hadn't allowed me to stray from the keep, and even as the time before we could leave Lygan Hall dragged out in a maddening way, I didn't want to miss any chance to spend time with the children before we left.

"You know, Ena," Evie said, "your brother isn't nearly as cheerful as you are. And I don't think he likes living in the sorcerers' compound."

"Who would?" Dorran said.

"But?" I prodded, trying not to laugh at Gwen's reproachful glare.

"There is no but," Evie said. "I just wanted to make sure you knew."

"I think Ena is well aware of Emmet's cheerful demeanor." Marta's smile set both dimples on full display.

"He's not cheerful," Evie said. "That's the point."

Cinni abandoned her seat at the table and wandered to the corner where Liam's and my packs waited for us to be ready to leave Lygan Hall.

She knelt by the packs, just staring at the knots.

I wondered if she was examining the faint bloodstains I hadn't been able to scrub out.

"They aren't leaving yet," Marta said. "They're only packed so they'll be ready when it's time."

Cinni looked to Marta with a furrowed brow.

"We have a bit of work to finish here," I said. "Once that's done, we're going to head west into Ilbrea. That way, we can help more children like you."

Cinni sat on her heels and went back to staring at the bags.

"It's all right, Cinni." Gwen left the table to kneel by her sister's side. "Remember Emmet told us about the dog sleds? They're going to take a pack of dogs and head off on a lovely adventure."

Cinni wrinkled her forehead as her breath quickened.

"Don't worry, Cinni." My body ached as I pushed away from the table and went to join the children on the floor. "I'm not afraid of a little snow. We'll go west and do our job protecting children like you. Then we'll come right back here. You'll hardly notice we're gone."

Cinni reached out and laid her hand on my chest, pressing my stone pendant against my skin.

I had grown used to the constant warmth of the stone, but the heat of the pendant grew, as though it were a living thing nestled against my body.

Cinni met my gaze before lifting her hand away and going back to her seat at the table.

"By the time you get back," Evie said, "I will be a proper sorcerer, Dorran will know he's not better than me, and Marta will have a baby."

"Evie!" Gwen warned.

"Marta's staying with us for good now." Evie grinned. "I think the baby is the best thing to happen to us."

Marta's cheeks blushed bright red, but she still smiled, her dimples on full display. "Well, I'm glad you're happy. Now we should go, leave Ena to get some rest."

"I'm really fine," I said.

"You need sleep." Marta shooed the children out of their seats and to the door.

Gwen tucked Cinni into her coat while Evie smacked Dorran with her scarf behind Marta's back.

"We'll see you tomorrow, then." Marta gave me a quick hug. "Out, all of you."

The children piled through the door, and I was alone again.

I read for a bit from an old book of Black Blood legends.

I wondered if a copy of the text had ever made it out into Ilbrea and if that was where the legends of the Black Bloods began.

I ate the soup that Conn brought to me as my dinner. It wasn't very good, but Liam had set clear rules on who was allowed to cook for me.

I paced beside the windows while staring out over the valley.

I tried to a picture a peaceful life in Lygan Hall. Where Liam and I spent our days together instead of him and my brother going out, hunting shadows.

I tried to reason through accepting the adoration of the people and living with being called Solcha for the rest of my days.

I tried to imagine the children Liam and I would share. I wondered if they would be trueborn and what that power would do to their lives.

I wondered what Orla would do if all her grandchildren were born completely normal. If she would hire her own assassin so Liam would have to choose another woman to bear his children.

I despised having so much time to think.

I wasn't allowed to train with Cati.

I could have gone down to work in my ink room, but I didn't want to start any new batches if we were to leave as soon as the shadows were found.

I read some more. And paced for a while.

Finally, a familiar, low rumble came from the hall.

A bubble of joy tickled my chest as Liam stepped into our room. He looked exhausted, but still he smiled for me.

"Did you find anything?" I asked.

"A few more tunnels even the shadow guard didn't know existed, but no sign of people," Liam said.

"Any word from Colm?" I crossed the room to stand in front of him.

"The siege continues."

"The journey west?"

"Cati has everything in place. We could leave with an hour's notice. We're only waiting to find the traitors." Liam ran his hands over his face. "I'm doing everything I can. I swear to you."

I lifted his hands away from his face and placed them on my waist.

"No pressing danger?" I leaned closer to him. The chill of his coat cut through my clothes.

"I'm sorry. I—"

I cut him off with a kiss and kept kissing him as I pulled away his coat and dropped it on the floor.

I lured him all the way to the bed and did not stop kissing him until I had driven every bit of wondering completely from my mind.

20

I woke before knowing I had heard any strange sounds.

My heart thumped in my chest as I reached for the knife beneath my pillow.

A voice carried through the door. The sharp tone brought me no comfort.

"Liam." I shook him awake before scrambling out of bed and snatching my shift off the floor.

"You shouldn't be here." The words carried in from the corridor.

I yanked my shift over my head and bit my knife between my teeth as I buttoned on my skirt.

"Look"—it was Conn who spoke that time—"let's just get you back where you belong. I don't think Marta will be pleased to find you've wandered off."

"Marta?" I ran to the door, ignoring the cold stone stinging my feet.

"Ena, let me." Liam leapt in front of me and slid the bolt aside.

"Just back away then," Conn said.

Liam opened the door, and I peered around him.

All the guards in the hall had drawn their swords except Conn.

He stood in front of the others, both hands raised as he faced someone I could not see.

"No one here wants to hurt you," Conn said, "but we've got to get you back to the compound. The sorcerers will be looking for you."

I slipped around Liam and out into the hall.

"What's going…" My words faded away as Cinni peered around the guards.

"Cinni, love, what are you doing here?" I stepped closer to her, but the guards shifted, blocking my path.

"Stay back, miss," a guard warned.

"She won't hurt me." I tucked my knife into the back of my waistband and pushed the guard's sword down. "Just back away, and let her come here."

"Do as she says," Liam said.

The guards all shifted to one side of the hall, giving me a clear path to Cinni.

The child wrinkled her forehead for a moment before walking straight up to me and taking my hand.

"What are you doing here, Cinni?" I bent down to be eye level with the child. "Marta will be sick with worry when she finds out you've snuck away."

Cinni stared back at me.

"How did she get in here?" Liam asked.

"No chivving clue," Conn said.

"Go check the other guards," Liam said.

"Come on, love"—I led Cinni into Liam's room—"I'll get my boots on, and I'll walk you back to the compound."

"The guards can escort her," Liam said. "It too dangerous for—"

"Nonsense." I kept my tone smooth and cheerful. "There's no danger at all. Cinni got a little lost and found me. I'll walk her back home, and there is absolutely no need for anyone to get upset."

"I'm coming with you." Liam pulled his coat from the wall as I laced up my boots.

"That's just fine." I tucked my knife into the ankle of my boot and wrapped my cloak around my shoulders. "We're going to have a lovely little walk, aren't we Cinni? It'll be nice to have Liam on our walk. The three of us and a few of my friends. We'll walk straight back to the compound and get you tucked back into bed."

Cinni's breathing quickened, and her gaze darted around the room.

I knelt in front of Cinni and took her shoulders. "Is everything all right at the compound?"

Cinni's breathing didn't change.

"Send guards to the sorcerers' compound," Liam spoke softly to the guards. "Make sure the Lir children are safe."

Cinni took my hand, leading me to the door.

"We'll go as quickly as we can," I said. "We'll get you back to the others."

She tightened her grip on my hand as she led me down the hall and out into the statue corridor.

My breath caught in my throat at the state of the room beyond.

A dozen guards lay unconscious on the ground, as though they'd been struck by some unseen foe.

"They're all alive," Conn said. "But I don't know what happened."

"Send for the healers." I kept my voice calm as I glanced at each guard to be sure they were breathing.

Cinni did not seem to like that I had slowed my pace. She yanked on my hand, dragging me down a side corridor.

"Did you send the guards to sleep, Cinni?" I asked.

Cinni quickened her steps.

"I'm not mad if you did," I said. "But why did you need to see me so badly?"

She looked up at me with her dark eyes as though trying to tell me something, all the while still leading me down the hall.

She cut down another side corridor and to a winding staircase.

"This isn't the fastest way to the sorcerers' compound," Liam said. "Would you like me to lead, Cinni?"

Cinni pressed onward.

"I think she knows exactly where she's going," I said.

We passed a pack of guards at the bottom of the stairs.

As soon as they saw Liam, they backed out of our way, as though being led about by a little girl in the middle of the night were a perfectly normal thing.

Cinni never paused or seemed to question her path as she led us deep into the tunnels of Lygan Hall. We passed the common hall where the people of the crag ate, cut down a narrow corridor and into the kitchen. Even though it was the middle of the night, there were women working in front of the wide hearths and at the massive wooden table, preparing breakfast for their fellow clansmen.

A wooden door blocked our path. It swung open before we reached it.

I started to bend to retrieve my knife from my boot before realizing that Cinni had opened the door for us.

My shoulders trembled as we stepped out into the cold night, but it wasn't the icy air that made me shiver.

Once we were outside, it wasn't too hard to see where Cinni was leading us. From the plain, ground level door, there was only one path cutting through the snow.

The trail of frozen mud led straight toward the village.

"We need more guards," Liam said. "Run back and send as many as you can to meet us. Now."

I didn't turn to see which guard had sprinted back into the cliff face.

I wished I had my lae stone with me or had even brought a proper weapon instead of only my knife.

She's a child. What could lead a child to wander at night?

The same thing that made her sink a man in a pond.

"Cinni," I said, "I want to make you a deal, all right? You show me whatever it is you want me to see, and then you and I go back to Marta. Does that sound like a good idea?"

Cinni did not respond.

My heart quickened as we neared the edge of the village.

"Trueborn," a voice spoke softly behind me, "we can't let her enter the village. She could murder our people."

"Cinni wouldn't hurt anyone on purpose," I said. "And she can chivving well hear you."

"We keep following," Liam said. "Let her go where she likes."

Cinni paused at the edge of the village.

I held my breath, hoping she would change her mind and head away from the thousands of sleeping people.

But with a tug on my hand, she led me onward and into the dark village.

21

Even with the moon shining above, I could barely make out the cheerful colors I knew coated the doors of the homes. I squinted in the darkness, trying to take comfort in the stripe of blue above every entryway.

This was a Duwead Clan village. Even if there were people who wanted me dead—even if I had no idea where Cinni was leading me—I was surrounded by Black Bloods, not paun.

Shame sank in my stomach as I realized I felt safer among the Duweads than I did among the tilk in Ilbrea. My own people had been tormented by the Guilds for centuries. I don't believe any thinking person could be shocked that it had turned some of the tilk toward vile acts.

Cinni had been leading me for so long I had started to believe we would keep walking until dawn.

When she stopped in front of a house, I nearly knocked her over before realizing she wasn't moving anymore.

I stared at the door of the house for a moment, waiting for people to come pouring out with weapons raised.

But the night stayed quiet as Cinni stared at the upper windows of the two-story home.

"Is there something here you want?" I spoke softly. "Do you know who lives here?"

Cinni dragged me toward the narrow alley between the houses.

"Wait." Liam cut in front of Cinni. "I need to go first."

Cinni pressed her hand slowly through the air.

Liam tripped and toppled sideways as though he'd been shoved by a giant.

"Liam." I started toward him, but Cinni clutched my hand harder, dragging me into the alley.

"I'm fine," Liam said. "Just stay with her."

"Cinni," I said, "I know you want to show me something, but you can't just push people. Do you understand? We have to be gentle."

Cinni didn't seem to care what I had to say as she led me out the far side of the alley and to the door of a root cellar behind the house. She stood still, her eyes locked on the cellar door, as the guards piled out of the alley behind us.

Once all of them had stopped moving, she looked up at me and smiled.

"Do you want me to go down there?" I asked. "Is that why you brought me here?"

Cinni wrinkled her forehead and reached her free hand toward the door. Without taking her eyes off me, she yanked her hand back.

The wooden doors of the root cellar shattered and exploded out into the night.

I flinched and covered my face with my arm, but none of the wood reached me.

Screams carried up from the cellar.

Cinni pointed down the steps and smiled.

"Who's out there?" a voice shouted from below.

A moment later, a man bearing a battered sword charged up the stairs.

"Stop in the name of your Trueborn!" One of the guards leapt in front of me, blocking the stranger.

But the man did not halt his attack. He swung for the guard's neck.

"Cinni!" I scooped the child into my arms and backed away as the guard drove his sword into the man's stomach.

Cinni sat happily in my arms, grinning at me.

"I am Liam Duwead, Trueborn of the Duwead Clan." Liam drew his own sword as he stepped around the slain man. "Come out now, or we will be forced to believe you mean us harm."

Liam waited a moment before nodding to the guards and climbing down the stairs.

A guttural cry came a moment later.

I wanted to chase after Liam, but I had Cinni in my arms. And I couldn't abandon her.

"Let's get you back to the compound," I said, trying to keep my voice calm even as a woman gave a blood-curdling scream. "Marta will be waiting for you."

Cinni twisted in my arms.

I tried to hold on to her, but heat like white-hot coals flew from her skin. I gasped and let go.

"Keep her alive!" Liam shouted from the basement.

Cinni took my hand. Her skin felt cool to the touch.

She tugged on my arm, trying to lead me back the way we'd come.

Lights began to glow in the houses around us as the commotion woke the villagers.

"If you won't go back to the compound, then I have to stay here," I said. "I have to make sure Liam is safe."

Cinni turned to face the cellar and stood with her hand in mine as the sounds of the fighting below changed.

"Ena." Liam ran up the steps. He'd ripped his coat but looked fine otherwise.

"What was down there?" I asked.

Cinni tugged on my hand, dragging me away.

"Watch the cellar," Liam said. "Keep the traitor alive. I want her questioned by Wyman before sunrise."

"Liam," I said as Cinni nearly yanked me off my feet.

"You two"—he pointed to two of the guards whose faces I recognized but names I did not know—"with me."

I let Cinni drag me along, even though shouting still came from the cellar.

"Who was down there?" I asked.

A man bearing a hammer peeked out the front door of his house. He caught sight of Liam and bowed. "Trueborn, are we being attacked?"

"We've found the beasts who betrayed our clan," Liam said. "Lock your door, and keep your family inside until morning."

The man slammed the door behind us.

I tried to cover Cinni's ears, but, though she flinched, she kept dragging me forward.

More doors opened as we traveled down the dirt road. Liam repeated the same orders over and over.

I wanted to go back to the cellar and see what monsters had been lurking in the village, but Cinni kept dragging me onward. And something in my chest screamed that I needed to see whatever it was she wanted to show me.

We left the village on a different path, cutting farther north toward the entrance of the sparring cave.

A flock of guards ran to join us as we crossed the open field of snow.

"Liam," Cati said as she reached us, "they sounded the bells in the crag. What under the stars is happening?"

"Cinni's helping," I said. "She's a smart girl. Smarter than all of us, I'd bet."

"She led us to the traitors," Liam said. "They were lurking in plain sight. We'd never have found them without ransacking every home in the village."

"Where is she taking you now?" Cati asked.

"No idea," I said. "Just keep up."

Cinni gave my hand a squeeze.

Cati pulled a lae stone from her pocket as Cinni led us into the cavern where the fighters trained.

Even though wind gusted freely through the space, the air inside had a heavier feel, like the stone had somehow absorbed the fears of the ones who had come to train.

"Do you want a light, Cinni?" Cati offer her lae stone to the child as Cinni led us down the narrow corridor at the back.

My heart leapt into my throat as the idea that something terrible had happened to Emmet made me forget to breathe. But even beneath my panic, a pull deep in my chest told me I needed to follow Cinni.

She turned down a corridor that led away from where I'd found Emmet in the weapons room, and I gratefully gulped down cold air.

An old door blocked our path. It opened with a wave of Cinni's hand.

"We're just going to let her keep going?" Cati asked.

"It's got to be something important," I said. "I don't think Cinni would have snuck away from Gwen if it weren't."

I tried to banish the memory of the man in the pond from my mind as the pull in my chest grew stronger still.

The tunnel we entered was not as well used as the rest of Lygan Hall. The air held a scent of mineral rather than people, and dust crunched beneath my boots with every step.

"Where are we?" I asked.

"The old tunnels," Liam said. "There are a few below Lygan Hall, but they haven't seen regular use in my lifetime."

We kept walking and walking until Cinni led us to the end of a corridor and stopped. She kept her gaze fixed on the stone wall in front of us as Cati crept forward with her light.

"Is this what you wanted to show me?" I asked.

Cinni grabbed both my hands and pulled me down so I could look into her eyes.

"I can't see what you're seeing, littleling," I said. "I want to, but I can't."

Cinni ran her finger across my cheek, as though drying my tears, then pressed her hand to the stone pendant hidden beneath my shift.

"I'm sorry, love," I said. "I just don't understand."

Cinni pointed to the solid wall.

With a crack that shook my lungs, a gap appeared in the stone.

Cati held her light into the void.

There was nothing but darkness beyond.

I looked down at Cinni.

The child stared into the black, a triumphant smile filling her face.

22

There are some goodbyes you do not recognize until it is far too late.

You did not try to hang on to the memories of those you left. You were sure you would see them again.

Their smile. The tone of their voice. Their strange habits that you should have cherished are all shunted aside as the stars drag you on to the next adventure or tragedy.

It is not death that has separated you from those you thought you would see again. It is the very act of living.

I have lost many people I cared for to Death.

I have lost more without realizing they were gone.

23

I didn't leave the entrance Cinni had found, not until our party was ready to travel.

Liam sent runners to gather the others and to fetch us clothes and our packs.

I could hear Cati shouting orders as people filtered down into the halls, all of them baffled as to why they'd been called to leave in the middle of the night.

But we didn't know how Cinni had found the opening, where it led, or how long it would stay open. So, she and I stood in the place where Lygan Hall met the vast darkness, hoping the mountain would not see fit to crush us if she decided we weren't moving quickly enough.

Cinni smiled up at me the whole time.

Before I had truly begun to understand that we were leaving Lygan Hall, the rest of our party had arrived.

Cinni pressed my pendant to my chest and wandered away.

The corridor behind us was so narrow, the Black Bloods had to plaster themselves against the walls to let her by. She ran her fingers along the horses' flanks as she turned up the corridor and slipped out of sight.

Liam squeezed my hand, and I took a deep breath and stepped into the darkness.

There was no rumble or crack or anything to mark the greatness of our journey, only thick blackness all around us as we plodded forward hour after hour.

We slept, and we woke. And we slept again. And still, there was nothing but darkness.

The clopping of the horses' hooves followed behind me, as did the low voices of the others in the party.

The endless blackness of the tunnels beneath the mountain pressed down upon me, but I kept moving forward at a steady pace, refusing to acknowledge the helplessness that crept in around the edges of my mind.

I had been chosen to lead our party of twenty through the mountain. Though, truth be told, there wasn't much leading to be done. We'd spent the past three days walking through a twisting tunnel that gave us no choice but to continue ever onward through the black.

Liam walked beside me, Emmet right behind. Their presence offered comfort but did not make me feel any more worthy to lead.

I was not Solcha. I took comfort in the knowledge that the name would not follow me into Ilbrea. Whatever hopes the people of Lygan Hall wanted to toss upon me with that title were untrue. I held no gift capable of saving the Duwead Clan.

But I had been in the tunnels hidden beneath the mountains before. And, as far as most of our party knew, the mountain had chosen to open a passage for me.

The lie coiled through my nerves, making it seem like an enemy waited in the shadows that surrounded me.

But the truth could not be told. There was not a chivving chance I was going to let Regan know that the child who'd slipped by her in the hall held the power to seek out the mountain's secrets or that she was hiding in the sorcerers' compound in Lygan Hall. And I would not let the people of the Duwead Clan lay the expectations they had of me onto a child. Cinni deserved better than that.

For her, I would bear the weight of the lie. For Cinni's sake, I would look confident as I walked through the unending darkness.

The path the mountain laid out for us was tall enough for the five horses to pass through and flat enough for the way forward to seem like it might never end.

Liam brushed his fingers against the back of my hand.

A foolish thrill shot up my arm.

I don't know why—I'd been rolling around with him for months—but that simple gesture of affection dissolved enough of my hopelessness to make me quicken my step.

"We're going to have to eat eventually." The rough grumble came from behind.

I bit my lips to keep from laughing.

"Unless the lot of you have decided eating isn't something you fancy doing," Neil said. "I wouldn't complain about having my job be easier."

"We'll get a bit farther before we stop for the night," Liam said. "We have no idea how long it will take us to find the end of the mountain's path. We should cover as much ground as we can."

Neil did not reply.

I had not expected him to join the expedition into Ilbrea, but he had insisted on coming. Cati and Kely had come along as two of the guards. Tirra had demanded to come so she could mind her beloved horses. Regan had come with three of her own people.

But it was not the Brien that made me fear the shadows. I had already faced Regan's cruelty, and our people outnumbered hers.

It was Allana, the Duwead sorcerer with the pale blue eyes, who I did not like walking behind me.

I had not questioned why Orla had chosen to allow a sorcerer to travel so far west. There was something about Allana's presence that made me sure I did not want to know her purpose in venturing into the darkness.

I could feel the sorcerer's gaze boring into the back of my neck as she watched me, waiting for something terrible to happen. I hated that constant reminder of her power.

The path before me narrowed, leaving barely enough room for Liam and me to walk side by side. I held my lae stone in front of me, squinting into the darkness.

"If the path gets too small, we'll have to send the horses back," I whispered.

"They never should have been brought along in the first place," Emmet said.

The tunnel twisted in front of us.

Let there be an opening ahead.

I sent my plea out into the stone.

"We'll be grateful for the horses when we make it to Ilbrea," Liam said.

"If that is where the mountain is leading us." Allana spoke loudly enough for the entire party to hear.

I gritted my teeth, trying to shake away the feeling of having been spied on.

"The mountain's ways are mysterious," Allana said. "She could be leading us to great wonders that have nothing to do with the Guilds' country."

"Then this whole thing will have been a chivving waste of time," Emmet said.

"Do you think you know better than the mountain?" Allana asked.

"I think saving innocent lives may not be what matters most to magic shrouded in stone," Emmet said. "I'm going into Ilbrea to try and stop the Guilds from murdering people. That is where my journey will lead me."

"If the magic within the mountain wills it," Allana said.

The tunnel twisted back in the other direction.

"If the mountain truly cares for the descendants of the child, she will lead us to Ilbrea," Regan said. "Surely I am not the only one who fears the day the Guilds attack the clans."

"I did not know the Brien held so little reverence for the mountain that shelters us," Allana said.

"Protecting my people is the only thing that matters," Regan said. "I adore the mountain. I am a trueborn. I can feel the magic of her stone all around me. But I am wise enough to know I am too small to understand what lies at the heart of the mountain's magic. Have you imagined yourself to be so great, Duwead sorcerer?"

"The mountain withholds the secrets she does not wish to share," Allana said.

"Then I shall have to rely on human means to protect my people," Regan said. "And that requires reaching Ilbrea and stopping the Guilds from attacking our mountains. Whatever the cost. Whatever path the mountain tries to make us follow. I will protect the Brien. I would hope the Duweads feel the same about their own clan."

I slowed my steps as the tunnel straightened out and widened in front of us.

"We're all under the mountains right now because we want to protect the clans," Liam said. "Arguing amongst ourselves will do nothing but feed the shadows."

"Stop." I froze in place as the path before me disappeared.

The tunnel opened up into a vast darkness. The black offered no hint of what might lie in any direction. Pale moss covered the ground, but there were no wear marks from footsteps.

"Stay here." I stepped out in front of Liam, holding my light high.

The soft crunch of moss beneath boots followed me into the darkness.

"I told you to stay," I said.

"I'm not obligated to obey," Emmet said.

I glanced over my shoulder.

There was no fear on my brother's face as he scanned the shadows.

I kept glancing behind as I walked farther into the darkness, not stopping until Liam's lae stone was only a dim glow in the black.

"Is this familiar to you at all?" Emmet asked.

"No." I cut a wide arc to the left of the tunnel where the others waited. "I might have been near here, but I never traveled that tunnel."

"I suppose the mountain is just taking us where she chooses," Emmet said.

I stopped and looked back to where Liam's lae stone glimmered in the distance. "Do you think the mountain chooses? Really chooses, thinking through how she wants things to go, planning our course forward?"

"I don't know. I don't know if the mountain is alive with magic trapped in her stone, if there's a god hidden in the eastern mountains, or if the whole chivving thing is just a strange mix of sorcerery and luck."

"Thank you for the comfort," I said.

"You don't need comfort. We need a path forward. That's been given to us. So now it's your job to lead us."

"Shouldn't that weight be placed on one of the trueborn?"

Emmet looked back toward Liam's light. "Twice now, paths have been opened for you in ways they shouldn't. Magic aside, I don't know why such a thing would happen if the paths weren't meant for you to travel."

I wanted to argue that this path had opened for Cinni, not for me. But I would not say her name with the Brien anywhere near us. And Cinni had found the path for me.

She had trusted me to take her from her home. I owed the child my trust in following the path she'd given me.

"This way then." I led Emmet in a wide arc to the right of the tunnel where the others waited.

There was nothing but darkness and moss waiting in that direction either.

The weight of the party's expectations sat heavily on my shoulders as I led Emmet back to the tunnel.

"Did you find anything?" Regan asked.

"Moss," I said then looked to Liam. "I think we should camp here for the night. Choose which direction to travel in the morning."

Liam held my gaze for a moment before nodding. "We sleep here tonight." He walked thirty feet into the cavern and took off his pack.

There wasn't much chatter from anyone as we all laid out our bedrolls.

Tirra murmured to the horses, and Neil fussed about organizing dinner. Regan and her three guards made camp off to one side, while the sorcerer sat against the wall, staring at me as I combed and rebraided my hair.

The gratitude I'd felt when I'd first heard of the people who wanted to risk venturing west before spring because I'd nearly been killed had been tempered by the reality of traveling through the dark with such a crowd.

I couldn't speak plainly with the sorcerer lurking. Couldn't mention the children or what had really happened in the Lir Valley with the Brien around.

I missed Finn. I wished it were just him, Liam, Emmet, and me going into Ilbrea. I knew it was a strange thing to long for.

Our enemy was too large. There were too many things to be done to protect the Black Bloods. We needed help to succeed.

As I lay down next to Liam, I wondered if our pack of twenty would be enough to face the giant.

24

I sat alone in the darkness, staring out into the black as though it might suddenly offer some new clue as to which direction would lead us the right way.

We'd all finished eating our morning meal. The horses had been tended to and the bedrolls tucked away.

I still didn't know which way to lead us.

Liam didn't press. He occupied the others with maps of Ilbrea, tracing lines across the hardy scrolls, negotiating plans for how we might break up the tasks ahead. There were daring things to be done, like finding the one the Hayes had been feeding information, and dull tasks as well, like plotting the land the soldiers had scoured in the eastern mountains and finding supplies to last our people until the snow melted.

They'd talked through the whole chivving thing before, and there was no new information that might change our plans.

He's buying me time.

I hated myself for needing it.

"You can't be a coward," I whispered. "Sitting in the dark will help no one."

Choose a path and follow it. Finn's voice echoed through my mind.

My chest ached at the mere act of remembering him. *I don't know which way to go.*

That's a chivving lie, and you know it.

There's too much at stake. I don't want to watch more people die.

Then keep moving. Don't fight against yourself, my love. There are too many other people out there who want you dead.

I took a shuddering breath, trying not to let my chest explode with the pain of missing Finn.

I sat for another moment, waiting for him to speak again.

He stayed silent.

Digging my fingers into the moss did nothing to quiet my grief. I wanted to set the whole chivving cavern on fire just to spite the mountain.

I pictured Finn, rubbing the red scruff on his chin, trying to decide if he should indulge my insanity or tie me up until I'd regained my senses. The fantasy made me smile, and a familiar feeling pushed through the grief in my chest.

A pull right above my heart, like someone had slipped a hook through me and would use it to draw me forward.

I glanced behind to where Liam knelt beside a map with the others.

"This is chivving insane," I whispered into the darkness.

The pull did not stop.

"We should go this way." I spoke loudly enough for the others to hear and pointed in the direction the pull seemed to lead.

Allana walked toward me, peering out into the black. "The mountain has revealed the path."

"Sure." I stood up and brushed the moss off my skirt. "Believe whatever you like so long as we can start moving."

Emmet carried my pack over to me. His face stayed calm, though there was a question in his eyes I knew I would have to answer eventually.

"Ena will lead us on." Liam tucked away his maps and joined me at the head of our group. "Keep tight together. I don't want to risk anyone getting lost in the cavern."

We're all lost in the cavern.

I let the back of my hand brush against Liam's as I set off into the darkness.

The thrill of touching him shot up my arm. I longed to hold him until the ache in my chest disappeared. But the pull led me into the darkness.

I followed it, spending hours walking across the pale moss.

If the others questioned my ability to lead them safely through the blackness, they didn't show it as we trudged forward.

I waited for the pull in my chest to ebb, for me to realize the sensation had been no more real than Finn's voice in my mind.

Before we'd stopped for our midday meal, the blackness in front of me changed.

Texture gave depth to the shadows, transforming the black into a living thing.

I slowed my pace, holding my arm to the side to keep Liam from getting in front of me.

My heart raced as I crept forward, but the pull dragged me on.

The rasp of swords clearing their sheaths came from behind me as something moved in the darkness.

A chill breeze touched my skin as shapes began to emerge.

A copse of black weeping willows blocked our path. The drooping branches swayed in the wind.

"By the gods," Emmet breathed.

"I told you there were strange things down here," I said. "But I never traveled this way."

"What wonders the mountain has created," Allana said.

I glanced over my shoulder to find her right behind me, her face a mixture of awe and ecstasy.

"Stone magic couldn't create something like this," Regan said.

"Not as you know it, no," Allana said. "But there are old stories, from when the children first returned to the mountains."

"There were Black Bloods with this sort of power?" Emmet asked.

"Yes," Allana said.

"It's a possibility. The legends aren't clear enough for anyone to know for sure," Liam said.

"You're all fools," Regan said. "If it was Black Bloods who lived below the mountains, then the legends are wrong. The children weren't led out of Ilbrea and to the Broinn. They lived in the mountains already."

Regan's words hung heavy in the air. I waited for someone to shout that she was speaking heresy or for a stone to fly through her chest.

"The legends we pass down are what the people who came long before us chose to remember," Allana said. "They do not describe the mountain's whole truth. The magic in the mountain is larger than any Black Blood. Let the mountain tell her own story."

"Right," I said. "Feel free to wait here for words to rain down from above. I'm going to keep moving."

I pushed the drooping, black branches aside and studied the ground for any hint of a path.

"Lead on, Solcha," Allana said. "The mountain pulls you along your path."

A cold dread twisted around me. "My name is not Solcha."

I shoved between the trees, letting the branches pull at my coat. I wanted to turn around and scream that I had not been chosen by the mountain. I had been tormented.

I was not a reminder of the love the mountain held for her children. I was a grieving girl with blood on her hands and enough hatred in her heart to burn the world.

But the pull in my chest led me onward.

I veered from the direction my chest wanted me to follow. A hollow ache filled my lungs as though the grief for all I had lost had come surging out of the darkness to end me.

My breath came in shuddering gasps.

"Ena." Liam grabbed my arm.

I pressed my hand to my chest, digging my stone pendant into my skin.

"Are you ill?" Liam asked.

"No." I turned my feet back toward the path the mountain had planned for me. "Just startled myself is all."

Liam took my hand, lacing his fingers through mine, as though he knew I'd lied and wanted to protect me from whatever truth I did not dare to tell.

The dripping, black leaves of the willows glinted in the light of our lae stones, giving a grim beauty to the whole scene. The shadows wanted to lure us in. Wanted us to find enough beauty below the mountain that we'd forget to return to the world above.

The patch of black willows reached all the way to the shore of a lake. The water stretched beyond the limits of my light.

"I wonder how far it goes." Kely stepped up to the edge of the lake.

"We should be able to cut around it." I knelt beside the water and held my lae stone out in front of me.

A bright white something flickered through my light.

I reached out farther. The blue glow barely caught the tail of a white fish as it swam away.

"I could cook that," Neil said. "If anyone cared to catch it."

"We shouldn't," Liam said. "I'd rather not muck around with things that have learned to survive down here."

"Then I don't want to hear any complaints about the quality of the food on this journey," Neil said.

I searched myself for a smile or even a laugh at the exchange. I couldn't bring myself to feel anything but the need to keep moving.

"Come on." I led our pack around the bank of the lake.

The willow trees became sparser and faded away until there was nothing before us but pale moss. Still, we walked for a long while before the water was swallowed by the darkness. I did not take the time to turn around and explore what hid on the far end of the lake. It was not where the pull led me.

Traveling through the great blackness surrounded by nothing but moss muffled the thin bit of certainty I'd gained. But I kept following the pull, too afraid of what I might feel if I chose another path.

When I'd started to think we'd have to camp in the cavern for the night, the blackness in front of us changed again, thickening into a solid wall of rock.

I have doomed us all.

I swallowed my fear and walked straight toward the wall.

The black right in front of me was thinner than the rest.

Relief surged through me as the shadows revealed a tunnel tall enough and wide enough for even the horses to travel. I stepped into the tunnel and pressed my hand to the stone of the wall, grateful beyond reason that I hadn't led us in the wrong direction.

"The mountain has led Solcha well," Allana said.

My fingers twitched as I longed to reach for my knife. "Think what you like."

"Perhaps the people are right about you," Regan said. "Perhaps you are more than just an Ilbrean."

"Just an Ilbrean?" Emmet said. "Don't underestimate the Guilds or the people who have survived them. It'll get you killed."

"Come on." I started down the tunnel. The pull in my chest had not finished with me.

"Are you the pinnacle of an Ilbrean specimen?" Regan asked. "Sneaking around, setting fires, slaughtering soldiers. Is that what Ilbrean men have to offer?"

"Don't flirt with him," I said. "My brother is a married man."

A low laugh carried from farther down the line. "That wife of his may seem sweet, but she's got a temper hidden beneath her dimples," Neil said.

"Why do you think I fell in love with her?" Emmet said.

My heart tumbled in my chest a little. I wanted to turn around and look into my brother's eyes, see if he'd been traded out for an imposter or if my beast of a brother had actually managed to express an emotion beyond rage.

Are you that much better?

I shook away the sound of Finn's voice and trudged on through the darkness.

2 5

It was not the ten-foot-high stone wall that took my breath away, or the whispers of the people behind me. It was the blissful sense of peace that washed over me as we reached the manor.

"By the gods," Emmet's low voice carried over the rest.

"I've been here." I cut around the stone wall toward the gate I knew would lead into the garden. "This is where I spent my last night below the mountain. The manor house is still whole, like the people who lived here just packed up and left."

My excitement faded as the gate actually came into view and I realized the pull in my chest had vanished.

The sense of something a thousand times larger than me—looming over me, watching my steps—made me want to scream at the sky.

But shouting at the stone that I did not want to be dragged through the darkness would not help me find a path to Ilbrea. And letting the others know I was terrified of whatever it was that had led me through the black was too foolish a thing to consider.

I could not let them know my fears. Weakness was a luxury I could not afford.

I touched the gate, waiting for some magic to course through me and end my life.

The gate only squeaked as I pushed it open.

The garden inside the walls was exactly as I had found it months ago.

A stone walkway ran along the top of the high wall, allowing whoever had built the house to see what intruders lurked in the darkness. A stone chair sat beside the pond, as though someone had spent long hours enjoying their garden. White-blossomed flowers overgrew their beds, leaving a pale sea to wade through to reach the back door of the house. The back door had crumbled away with only one chunk of wood still hanging from the hinges.

"Who built this place?" Liam asked.

"I have no idea," I said. "But if you want to follow the path I took to get here, we'll cut through a whole city on our way to Ilbrea."

Liam nodded.

"Safe to say we're camping here for the night?" Neil frowned at the overgrown garden as though offended by the lack of open space to light a fire.

"We should," Liam said. "We've been traveling long enough, and this is as good a place to rest as any."

I swallowed my urge to shout that this wasn't a place that should be disturbed by the living.

"There's a hearth inside," I said. "I don't know if it's usable, but you can check."

"We should set up a watch," Cati said.

"You think there are people down here?" Regan passed her pack to one of her guards and brushed off the shoulders of her deep purple coat. She tenderly touched the fancy material, as though wanting to be sure the task of walking hadn't damaged her garments.

"I think we've found a manor under a mountain, and I don't fancy taking any chances," Cati said. "Don't worry, I wasn't going to put any of your people on watch duty."

I left them to glare at each other and headed toward the stone chair and the piece of ground where I had curled up to sleep what felt like a lifetime ago.

The flowers showed no sign of damage from where I'd lain between them.

"Have there been others who traveled this way?" I whispered.

"I believed you."

I turned toward the sound of Liam's voice.

He waded through the flowers to reach me, examining the stone wall and the high walkway that looped the whole compound.

"When you told me about this place the night you returned to the camp," Liam said. "I knew you were telling the truth, but somehow it didn't seem real."

"Like I'd slipped into a story and popped back out?" I reached for Liam.

He took my hand and drew me into his arms.

"I wasn't sure I would be able to find this place again."

"We could set up a base here," Liam said.

"It's still a long walk to Ilbrea." I leaned my cheek against his chest. "Took me almost two weeks to get this far."

"Closer to the exit, then," Liam said. "If we could set up a camp beneath the mountains, we'd be able to work against the Guilds year-round."

"You'd have plenty of room to hide sorcis."

"We'll find a place. There's got to be somewhere in the underground city we could build a home for the children."

"We could sleep inside tonight," Regan called from near the back door. "I don't want to imply that I'm not happy to sleep on the ground surrounded by a pack of travel-weary Black Bloods, but there is something wonderful about having a door."

"If you can close it without the wood crumbling to dust." I stepped away from Liam's warmth.

Regan shrugged and walked into the manor.

Her three guards trailed behind her.

"I wish they weren't traveling with us," I said.

"We need allies," Liam said.

"We can't afford a knife in the back. Orla allowed a sorcerer to travel with us. If she let Allana leave Lygan Hall, you might be able to convince her to send others as well. We could use Duwead magic in Ilbrea. If we're not planning on fighting the Guilds outright, then we'd only need a few of Wyman's people."

"We need the Brien." Liam took my hand. "We need them to fight the clan war, and we can't refuse anyone who's willing to help us fight against the Guilds."

"I don't fancy being poisoned again." I stared at the broken back door, watching as Allana slipped into the house. "And I don't trust these people."

"I know." Liam laced his fingers through mine and kissed the top of my head. "But the traitors in Lygan Hall were found. Wyman will question them, Conn will round up any shadows we might have missed, and they will all be dealt justice by Orla's hand. Lygan Hall will be safe for us when we return."

I could not find comfort in his words.

"We can't distrust our allies because some monsters betrayed us," Liam said.

"And you can't trust monsters just because they claim to be allies."

"I know." Liam squeezed my hand. "But we can use their aid and watch each other's backs. I'm not blind, Ena. I will keep you safe."

I leaned up and brushed my lips against his. "If they try to hurt you, I will kill them."

I let him lead me toward the manor.

He paused before we climbed the steps and kissed me properly.

A longing burned deep in my chest. I wanted to pull him closer to me, to hold him until all reason slipped away.

He kissed my cheek and whispered in my ear. "Regan's decided she wants to fight in Ilbrea. I'd rather keep her where I can see her. Better to know where her blade will land."

He kissed the back of my hand and led me into the grand house.

Neil was already at work in the kitchen, crouched inside the hearth, peering up as though checking the flue. Footsteps carried from overhead where Regan and her people prowled.

A chill trailed across my skin as I led Liam to the stone stairs and up to the bedrooms.

I did not like trespassing in that place. I liked being there with a horde of people even less. It felt almost as though the noise of our pack might catch the notice of the ghosts and bring their wrath upon us.

But there was no hint of any terrible slaughter that might have created ghosts.

Liam and I stopped at the nearest bedroom.

The bed had been stripped of its sheets, as though the owner had decided to bring the blankets with them to their new home. A chest of drawers sat in one corner and a chair in another. None of the furniture had been knocked over or even looked crooked or out of place.

"They just packed up and left." Liam laid his hand on the bedframe.

"I wish I knew what had driven them away." I leaned my pack against the wall.

"Perhaps they weren't driven." Allana stood in the doorway, blocking our path out of the room. "Perhaps they were led."

"I don't think we'll ever know," Liam said.

"Maybe." Allana tipped her head to the side. "Maybe not. It depends on how badly our Trueborn wants the information."

"Curiosity is one thing," Liam said. "Disturbing the long dead is another."

"Solcha was led here, Trueborn," Allana said. "Twice, the mountain called her to this place. Do you really believe that to be a coincidence?"

"If this place was built by our ancestors, they deserve to be left in peace," Liam said.

"You place peace for the dead before peace for the living?" Allana asked. "Trueborn, you are on a journey to protect our clan. Solcha was brought here. Will you reject the wisdom the mountain is offering?"

"The mountain offered us a path," I said. "Isn't that enough for you?"

"Not if there are deeper truths to be found," Allana said.

Liam closed his eyes for a moment. "Can it even be done?"

"Regan brought three sorcerers with her," Allana said. "Of course it can be done."

The sorcerer smiled, and true fear wrapped around my heart.

26

Knowing I was sitting with four sorcerers I did not trust made the evening meal taste worse than normal, as though Neil's slop had somehow been contaminated by their presence.

Allana had done something to the wood of the furniture, allowing us to sit on the chairs around the large kitchen table without them crumbling to dust.

I hated sitting on something I knew had been made solid by magic.

I did not know any of the sorcerers. I did not trust them not to shatter the wood beneath me if I displeased them.

Regan trailed her spoon through her bowl of slop.

For a moment, I thought of warning her the food wasn't going to get any better so she should just learn to eat it.

Let her starve.

I took a bite of my own slop, swallowing quickly before the stuff could stick to my tongue.

"We should work our magic soon. I don't think the shadows would look kindly on our delaying," one of the Brien sorcerers said.

I laid my hands flat on the table, not allowing myself the comfort of balling them into fists.

"Funny how you so easily admit to being sorcerers now when you didn't mention it before you joined our expedition," Cati said.

"Orla sent one of her own precious sorcerers." Regan stood, leaving her uneaten food on the table. "Do you truly think she didn't know my guards were capable of magic?"

"If you want to know what happened in this place," another of the Brien sorcerers said, "then don't complain about having sorcerers with you. One alone wouldn't be able to control this type of magic."

I studied the sorcerer's face, trying to decide if it was her magic or her allegiance that made me dislike her.

She was the only woman Regan had brought along. She couldn't have been much older than I was, but she watched the world around her like she'd already lived a hundred years and experienced all the most interesting things life had to offer. Being in a long forgotten manor brought her no fear or curiosity.

A gangly-limbed boy and a man with graying hair were Regan's two other sorcerer-guards. Neither of the men seemed quite so bored with our journey.

"We'll center the spell in here," Allana said. "The kitchen is the heart of a house after all."

"I'll have no magic in my kitchen until everyone is done eating," Neil said. "It's my job to keep you lot fed. I won't have sorcerers interfering with my duty."

"Which you accomplish so well," Regan said.

"You should work whatever magic you have outside," I said, cutting Regan off before she could slide into insulting Neil. "In the garden by the gate."

"Why do you say that?" The Brien sorcerer narrowed her eyes at me.

"Because that's where it feels the worst," I said.

A weight pressed on my shoulders. I looked up to find everyone at the table watching me.

"I've seen a lot of horrible things," I said. "I know what it feels like when death lingers."

"Thank you for your wisdom, Solcha." Allana nodded to me. "We are grateful for whatever path the mountain leads you on."

I pushed my bowl away as my stomach threatened to reject my food.

Liam laid his hand on top of my leg.

I wondered if he truly could sense my urge to run into the darkness and flee from these people.

We didn't speak much more as everyone finished what they could of their slop.

Neil scowled at everyone as he accepted the remnants of their dinner.

"Should have brought a pig with us," Neil muttered. "At least the animal would have been wise enough not to waste food."

Allana led the other sorcerers out into the garden. Regan, Cati, and the other Duwead guards followed close behind.

Liam wrapped an arm around my waist, keeping me beside him while all the others left.

"You don't have to go out there," Liam said. "Whatever the sorcerers dig into the shadows to find, you don't have to see it."

"I do. I am not Solcha. I cannot fit their idea of this person chosen by the mountain for some special path. I should not be bowed to, and I have no idea if I'm actually capable of helping to protect the Duwead Clan. But…"

I dug into the blackness in my chest, pulling out the truth I had been too frightened to accept. "I knew the first time I came to this manor that the mountain had led me here for a purpose. This house might be the whole reason the mountain chose to protect me from the Guilded sorcerer and his soldiers.

"This place is the reason Finn was murdered. If there is something to be found here, I need to know what it is. Nothing could be worth losing Finn, but I promised him I would make the Black Bloods believe him. I can't just walk away from that vow because there could be monsters in the shadows."

"I know you hate the people's adoration." Liam held me close, laying his cheek on top of my head. "But they are right. Whether the gods or the mountain or just plain luck led you through this dark place, you have lit the path the Duweads must follow."

"Liam, I—"

"It doesn't need to be fate or destiny. You are a girl from Harane. You are the woman I love. You are the fierce warrior who has done so much to help a people she's only just joined." He brushed a stray hair from my face. "All magic and mountains aside, you are still Solcha. You have still lit the path we all must follow."

A knot pressed on the front of my throat. "And if I lead us all to our doom?"

"You did not lead the Guilds into the mountains. The Hayes had betrayed us before you joined the camp. The clans were already on a road that held nothing but bloodshed. You've offered us hope, Ena. That's why the people love you."

"I don't think I'm strong enough to carry that weight." I pressed my hands to his chest. Even the steady rhythm of his heartbeat could not keep me from trembling.

"You are strong enough to burn the world."

Liam looked at me with such love, such faith, I wanted to believe him. I wanted to think I was brave enough and strong enough that, all magic aside, I could be who the Duweads wanted me to be. What I'd have to be if I wanted to stand by Liam's side as we faced the terrors ahead.

"I am willing to fight," I said. "I'm not afraid to face the Guilds. I don't know what more I have to give."

Liam kissed me.

My heart swooped in my chest as longing filled me with the undeniable knowledge that I would do anything to stay with Liam. I would let them bow to me, and bear the name Solcha, and let them primp me into an image I did not deserve. And find a way to slay every enemy that threatened the Black Bloods.

"I will make that be enough." I took both his hands in mine and made a vow to the gods and whatever had drawn me to the manor that if it meant protecting Liam and the people I cared for, I would do whatever they asked of me.

And I will burn the world if you take them from me.

I led Liam out into the garden.

The four sorcerers stood by the pond, all facing each other like a bunch of old men ready to trade gossip. The rest of the party stood in front of the gate, silently watching the sorcerers.

The crunch of footsteps came from the top of the wall as Emmet and Kely continued to pace and keep watch.

"I should lay out stones," Liam said.

"Will we need them?" My hand drifted to the hilt of the knife at my hip.

"I don't know." Liam let go of me and dug into the pouch that hung from his belt. "But I'd rather keep us protected."

"Both of you down here." Cati waved Emmet and Kely down from the wall.

"We should keep watch," Emmet said.

"You should do as you're told," Cati said.

Regan gave a low laugh and smiled. "I never thought I'd actually like a Duwead."

"I still don't think I like any Brien," Cati said.

Regan's smile only grew.

I stood with the others as Liam laid black stones in a circle around us.

Emmet glowered as he took his place beside me.

I laid a hand on his arm, offering what silent soothing I could.

"We're ready," Allana said.

For some reason, I had expected there to be markings drawn on the ground, or for each of the sorcerers to have a talisman in their hands like something from a scary story.

But the four just stood together, looking a bit travel worn and very focused.

Liam trailed his fingers through the air, as though he were testing the strength of the boundary he'd set around us. No flash of light came from the stones, but still, Liam nodded.

"Do it."

Allana turned away from the other sorcerers, gently raising her hands in front of her.

A moment later, the others mimicked her motion.

Allana's lips moved, though I could not hear any words.

I didn't know if she was whispering some secret spell or sending a plea to the gods and stars that whatever happened in this place would not be a nightmare that would trap us forever.

I forced my heart to slow as the seconds ticked past and nothing happened. There was no rustle in the dark, no scream of terror.

It's not going to work.

Relief and disappointment mingled in my chest.

But then something changed. A breeze wafted around me, carrying with it a foreign scent, as though the magic had had a palpable effect on the air.

I looked up to Emmet to see if he had felt it as well.

His gaze was fixed on Allana's hands.

Pale, white tendrils of light drifted down from her palms toward the blossoms below. The light grew in substance until it seemed like a mist floating out over the sea of flowers.

The other sorcerers had light dripping down from their hands in pale wisps as well.

I held my breath as the mist drifted toward me, but the thin blanket of white stopped outside the barrier Liam had created, leaving a blank circle where our pack stood.

The sorcerers all stayed still, their eyes closed, as more and more of the mist filtered out of their bodies.

Soon, the white coated the ground, hiding the flowers, covering everything outside the safety of Liam's stone magic.

The white thickened into a fog and began to move.

First, it climbed up the walls to hover on the walkway where Emmet and Kely had been keeping watch.

Next, it grew to fill the gap left open by the broken door of the house.

Then, all at once, eight patches of mist began to swirl and grow into pale towers.

The white spirals morphed and twisted, growing hands, adding definition that became faces.

I let go of Emmet's arm and gripped the hilt of my knife as the towers developed pale shades of color, and the eight people made of mist came to life.

27

Laughter.

That was not the first sound I expected to hear.

But the smallest of the six figures in the garden tipped her head back and let out a joyous laugh.

"There's not a chance." The young girl made of mist gripped her stomach and laughed again.

"I don't think that's very kind," a man with pale brown hair said. The mist that formed his face swirled as he frowned at the girl.

"Kind?" the girl coughed. "I'm much kinder than Hoshna will be if this lout tries to declare his love."

"And what do you know about love?" A young man crossed his arms and glared at the girl.

"Enough to know that you don't stand a chance." The girl crossed her arms as well, mocking the young man's stance. "I can picture you riding to the city now. You knock on Hoshna's door, fall to your knees"—the girl knelt in the mist, sending waves of white rippling away from her—"and cry *My beloved Hoshna. I have traveled far to win your heart. Now run away with me, and live in exile with the other spell weavers.*"

The two men made of mist who kept watch on top of the wall paused their pacing to look down into the garden.

"We aren't in exile," the young man said.

"Have you looked around?" the girl asked. "Living where no one else wants to be *is* exile."

"I could move to the city." The young man stepped closer to the girl.

"And who would train you there?" the girl asked.

"Enough, both of you," the brown-haired man said.

The guards started pacing again, gliding back and forth as they watched the blackness beyond the wall.

"Would you give up your training?" the girl pressed on, ignoring the man. "Live your life mucking out stables instead? You're here to learn to be a proper spell weaver. There's no place for Hoshna in that."

"Enough." The misty form of a woman spoke. "If you do not already possess the discipline to be kind to each other, you'll learn it through hard labor."

"Sorry, madam." The girl tucked her chin.

"I'm sorry," the young man said, though he did not seem nearly as contrite.

"Into the house, all of you," the woman said. Her glare did not spare the two child-like forms who had yet to speak. "I will have no more talk of running off to the city. We are in this place to serve a precious purpose. Those who cannot remember why they have been sent here to learn do not deserve the privilege."

"Yes, madam." The girl turned and drifted into the house.

The two silent mist figures followed in her wake.

Only the lovesick boy, the man, and the woman remained in the garden.

"I *will* go to the city," the young man said. "I know I have a duty to understand the power that runs in my veins. I know I need to learn to protect our people as the Lady decreed. But I love Hoshna, and I will tell her." He followed the others into the house without waiting for the woman's reply.

"I worry about him," the man said. "He needs to learn. If he stops his training, he won't be prepared to meet our enemies in battle."

"Don't worry," the woman said. "Hoshna will reject him. If he runs off to declare his love, he'll be back before the end of the week. Let him have his tantrum. He'll throw himself into his work once his heart has been broken."

The man and woman drifted into the house.

Bitter anger filled my mouth. I wanted to rage at the woman for using the boy's heartache to twist him into a better warrior.

Emmet stirred beside me. The pale light of the mist lent deeper shadows to the scars on his neck and face.

Maybe the broken do make better warriors.

I dug my nails into my palms, trying to swallow my own dark thoughts.

We waited in silence for a long while.

The mist in the garden swirled in little eddies, but no more figures grew up from the white.

The two ghostly men on top of the wall were still there, pacing as Emmet and Kely had not very long before.

I watched them prowl back and forth, over and over.

Common sense told me the spell should end. We knew who had lived in the manor. That should have been enough.

But there was a bit of nervous dread scratching at my gut. The kind of worry that always comes from knowing something bad is about to happen and you are not strong enough to stop it.

I think the rest of our group felt that worry as well.

None of the Black Bloods fidgeted or complained. There was no suggestion of giving the whole thing up and going to sleep.

A sudden flicker of movement on the high walkway caught my eye.

One of the men who'd been pacing raced to the other side of his wall. The mists he'd been made of swirled as he ran, leaving a trail of white in his wake.

"Shona!" the man called. His voice sounded younger than I'd thought it would, like the form he'd been given did not show his true age. "Shona, come quick!" He leaned over the wall, peering into the darkness.

I turned toward the gate, wanting to know what the man had seen.

A dim glow in the distance broke through the solid black.

I gripped the hilt of my knife, though I didn't know what hope I might have of defending myself against mist and light.

The glow came quickly closer, moving faster than a person could walk.

The mist from inside the garden expanded beyond the gate, floating into the darkness and reaching toward the light.

"What it is?" The woman reappeared in the courtyard, her face cross as she looked up at the guard.

"There are people coming, Shona," the man said. "A whole swarm of them."

I looked back out the gate.

The light had traveled farther down the black stone path I had walked months ago.

For one brilliant moment, I thought the light and the mist would not join. One would conquer the other, and the manor's story would be done.

But the mist lapped at the light, growing and expanding into the body of a horse. The horse ran toward the gate as the rider on its back swirled into being.

The riding woman held her hand high as though carrying a lantern. Only it wasn't a normal lantern she was holding. She gripped a short chain that had been fixed to an orange, glowing lae stone. The sphere of light swung with the horse's gait.

I studied her lae stone as she rode closer. The hue of it was almost like the lights of Lygan Hall, only this sphere glowed a shade brighter, like it had yet to be tarnished by time.

My breath hitched in my chest, and I moved closer to Liam.

Behind the woman, more figures on horseback emerged. A whole line of them, like the lady was leading a company of soldiers toward battle.

"It's Lady Tiona." Fear filled the man's young voice.

"What?" Shona said.

I turned in time to watch Shona bustle toward our group.

But Liam had set up our barrier right in front of the gate.

I waited for the bright blue light to flash as our protection pushed the woman away.

She strode up to Liam's black stones and vanished. Without any swirling of mist, or sound of pain.

A gasp from the other side of our group made me look back out beyond the gate.

Shona appeared on the far side of our barrier as though we had only lost sight of her for a moment.

"May the stars protect us," Shona murmured as the woman on horseback stopped right in front of her.

I looked up at the mounted woman, and the world began dipping and swimming all around me.

"Lady Tiona." Shona bowed. "We are honored by your visit."

Lady Tiona stared down at Shona.

The hard angle of her jaw, her long braid, the slant of her shoulders, and drooping sleeves of her dress.

I'd seen her before, memorized the stone replica of her face.

The woman from the fountain lowered her light before opening her mouth to speak.

2 8

"Are you honored?" Lady Tiona said. There was no anger in her voice, but there was something in her tone that seemed to promise there would be a penalty if someone were foolish enough not to listen.

"Absolutely." Shona bowed again. "The students have been hard at work, training for you."

Five mist figures stepped out in front of our shield as more of the manor house folk joined Shona.

Lady Tiona considered each of them in turn, not seeming to care that the other riders had caught up to her.

More than twenty mounted figures formed a long line, stretching out across the width of the walled compound. Each specter held an orange lae stone in their hand.

"How close are you to completing their training?" Lady Tiona asked. "If the western barbarians broke into our stronghold this minute, would your students be prepared to defend us?"

The young girl stepped in front of the manor house group.

"I would be, Lady Tiona." The girl bowed. "I am ready to defend our people."

"One girl?" Lady Tiona said.

"I'm strong," the girl said.

A hint of a smile lifted one corner of Lady Tiona's lips. "One strong girl can topple a kingdom."

The girl swallowed hard and bowed again.

"But I did not ask for one girl," Lady Tiona said. "I asked for an army of spell weavers."

"We are training them," Shona said. "Whatever threat you need us to face right now, I will go out there and fight the beasts myself. But we need more time. More children with the gift."

"I can give you neither of those things," Lady Tiona said. "The barbarians are working their way closer to the mountains. I will not sit by and wait for them to find us. We are leaving the Dark Hall."

"What?" the brown-haired man from the manor said.

"There are lands to the east," Lady Tiona said. "We will settle there."

"We can't." The man stepped in front of the girl. "Lady Tiona, there are monsters to the east. Shadows that come up from below, birds that will steal children. Our ancestors escaped those demons. How can we give up our home to go back?"

"Because that is my command." Lady Tiona raised a hand. Sparks crackled between her fingers, like tiny bits of lightning. She curled her fingers through the air, as though molding the light.

The shining image of a great bird unfurled and hovered over her palm.

"Monsters." She twisted her fingers, and the tentacles of a beast wound up her arm. "Shadows. These are the things you fear. You forget that men are far worse demons than anything the eastern mountains have to offer. We will venture east. We will fight whatever monsters the mountains bring us. We will claim our new home."

"It will be an honor to travel with you." The girl darted around the man to bow to the Lady again.

"Lady Tiona"—Shona bowed—"there could be people to the east as well. Here, we are protected."

"Until the barbarians find their way into the Dark Hall," Lady Tiona said. "That day will come. They will not find us here when it does."

"How do you know there is anything but death and monsters in the mountains?" the man asked.

"I can feel it." Lady Tiona lowered her hand, and the light she had created disappeared. "There is wild magic to the east. Pure magic untainted by human hands. Raw magic living in the stones and the beasts since before man ever sullied this continent. Uncaged power that has not felt the demeaning nature of what our spell weavers mold magic into." She lifted her hand again and pressed her fingers to the spot right above her heart. "I can feel it pulling me. Calling to me. The magic bids me to follow, and I will."

"We will follow you," Shona said. "We'll finish our work here and join you in the east."

"We leave now." Lady Tiona lowered her hand to her horse's reins. "Our caravan will continue east. Our people will stay together. Stragglers will not survive the journey."

"We need time," the man said. "We have to pack up the students. Close up the house—"

"Do not argue against me," Lady Tiona said. "I cannot tolerate it. Dissent endangers my people."

"I mean no offense, my Lady," the man said, "but we've built a life here. You can't just expect us to leave without any notice."

Lady Tiona looked down at the man. Tiny wrinkles formed around her eyes, as though his defiance had somehow aged her soul.

She raised her hand again. A low buzz filled the air.

"No!" I shouted.

The people made of mist didn't hear my cry.

A shard of black flew from the Lady's hand and crashed into the man's chest.

The manor people screamed.

The Lady watched as the man crumpled to ground. She waved a hand through the air, and the mist around the man twisted, pulling him down even as he desperately gasped for breath.

"Please don't!" Shona shouted.

As though the rock below followed Lady Tiona's commands, the ground shifted, devouring the man.

Silence hung heavy in the air. The mist smoothed out as though nothing had happened.

"You will join the end of the caravan," Lady Tiona said. "My men will see to it."

She kicked her horse and rode away. The mist that had formed her dissolved before she moved out of view.

"We need to pack." The girl's voice was low and too steady.

I recognized that tone. She had tucked her pain away. I hoped her grief would not destroy her.

The manor people walked back toward the house, disappearing as they crossed through Liam's barrier.

The mist was still not done.

The men on horseback followed Lady Tiona, dissolving as she had as they exited the awful scene.

But more figures emerged in the distance. Some with horses, some with wagons, some on foot carrying heavy packs. A long line of them followed Lady Tiona on her journey east, toward Lygan Hall and the rest of the Black Bloods' territory.

Liam placed his hand on my back, as though needing to be sure I would not be stolen from him as the thousands of people passed by.

I don't know if it was the mist or the sorcerers, but before the line of travelers ended, the fog faded away. And we were left alone in the darkness.

29

The mountain loved her children.

They had vowed to live peacefully in her embrace, separated into five clans so there would never again be a battle over land or leaders.

For a time, great joy filled the mountain's heart, but the eastern mountains are not separated from the rest of the world. Other people lived and thrived in the lands surrounding the mountain's haven, growing in strength to rival the children of the mountain.

The men from the south came first, slaughtering and terrorizing the descendants of the mountain's beloved child. The mountain opened a great chasm and swallowed the invaders, but she was too late. The blood of her beloved children had already slicked the valley floor.

The men from the east came next. They burned the forest, and the children of the mountain starved. The mountain grieved as she watched her children waste away.

The men from the west came. They stole the women, carrying them away from the mountain and beyond her protection.

The mountain mourned and raged, for her magic was no match for the violent ways of men.

One man shared the full weight of her grief.

His beloved mate had been carried away. He begged the mountain for the strength to go west and save his love.

He knelt on the edge of a cliff, screaming into the wind, shouting that he would pay any price if only he could rescue the woman who had stolen his heart.

The mountain heard the grief that echoed her own.

She felt the stone racing through the man's blood and knew he was a descendant of the child she had loved and the mother who had given all her magic to the mountain in exchange for her babe's life.

The mountain knew the power of that magic, knew the good it could do.

She gave the man a black stone from center of her heart where all her power dwelled. She bade him eat it and let the mountain's stone fill him with magic.

The man did as the mountain asked and swallowed the stone. The pain of the magic he should not have possessed coursed through his body. He cursed the sky and begged the mountain to end his suffering.

But the mountain knew that transformation cannot come without pain. Every great triumph comes with great cost. She listened to the man's cries and let him suffer as he was remade into one truly born of the mountain's stone.

When he rose to his feet, the ground trembled beneath him. When he bade the stone lay out a path to lead him to his mate, the stone obeyed. When he willed the stone to kill for him, his battle was won.

The mountain rejoiced, for her children were mighty enough to defend themselves.

She granted her gift to more of the offspring, forging an army that would protect her lands with the strength of her stone.

The mountain did not understand that time ticks on, and even the greatest of armies crumbles.

30

There once was a woman with the power of a sorcerer and the stone magic of a trueborn. Two gifts that should never live in one person.

She ruled a city deep beneath the mountains. Her people built homes, fell in love, carved statues of her.

The woman feared her enemies to the west and did not want to face them in battle.

She felt a pull in her chest just above her heart, drawing her toward a power too large for any person to truly understand.

She followed the pull toward untamed magic and brought her people with her.

Someone lived long enough to carve another statue of her and leave it in Lygan Hall.

Those are the truths I can offer you.

The rest is all legend. Stories that people have fought and died for, but I cannot say how much history is hidden in the words.

I am finally wise enough to accept that I will never understand.

Mountains. Magic. It is for the gods to comprehend.

The rest of us must simply try to endure.

3 1

The days spent in darkness dragged at my soul. The horrible feeling that the world could be on fire and I would not know plagued my every waking hour. Sleep didn't come easily. Liam's magic protected me from nightmares, but letting myself slip into that total blackness tested my courage.

I would lie by Liam's side, staring into the darkness while the others slept. The pull in my chest had begun again, dragging me onward. But the path the mountain laid out was different than the one I had traveled before.

Part of me itched with impatience. There was something else the mountain wanted me to see. If it was something that could aid Liam's cause, I needed to find it.

Part of me hated the pull. If the constant tug in my chest really was leading me toward wild, untamed magic, then the best thing for an orphan from Harane to do would be to run in the opposite direction.

The pull was not merciful enough to lessen when I tried to sleep.

I had been lying still for what seemed like hours, listening to Kely's soft footfalls as he kept watch.

Liam slept soundly beside me.

I wanted to curl up in his warmth and pretend the safety I felt in his arms could somehow protect me from all the dangers of the world.

I rolled over and laid my hand on his chest. His heart beat steadily. I could feel no hint of magic racing through him.

As I lay beside him, a longing filled me. I wanted more of Liam. I wanted a lifetime spent reveling in the wonders of that magnificent man.

I had felt that longing, that pull, before Liam was mine. I had thought the ache that drew me toward him came from my own foolish heart.

But if there was some malformed part of me that was drawn to magic, it might not have been his bravery or rare, crooked smile that had lured me in.

The mountain did not make you want him. Magic did not make you want him.

Pressure pushed on my throat as I swallowed my urge to scream and rage into the blackness.

If untamed magic was what led me through the darkness, like I was nothing better than a dog scenting meat—if that unnatural sense was what had drawn me to Liam...

Liam sighed in his sleep and drew me closer to him, nestling my body against his where I fit so perfectly.

I closed my eyes and breathed in his scent.

I did not care what led me to him.

He was mine as I was his.

I would not let anything take Liam from me.

32

The scent in the air changed before we heard the rumble of the water.

I held my light close to the ground, searching for any gaps in the rock I might slip through and tumble into the rushing current.

But the ground stayed solid, and the source of the noise stayed out of sight.

"It would be nice if we could actually find the water," Cati said. "I wouldn't mind filling the waterskins."

I didn't tell her the mountain had never let me die of thirst when I'd been trapped before. I didn't want to make promises on the mountain's behalf and have the mountain kill us just to prove me wrong.

If the mountain even chivving cared about people. Or was capable of caring at all.

The tunnel twisted, leading us farther down, but the roar of the water stayed steady.

My boots slipped against the stone floor as the tunnel spiraled around itself.

"Watch your footing," I called to the people behind me.

"The horses are never going to trust coming into the darkness again after this journey," Tirra said.

The moisture in the air dampened my coat, and the roar of the water grew louder as our path straightened out. The shadows before me changed as the end of the tunnel came into view.

The walls had been carved with straight, hard edges, as though either mountain or maker had wanted this space to be tidy.

It wasn't until I reached the end of the corridor that I understood why.

A shattered door lay on the ground. The metal bracing across the rotted wood had rusted through but, ages ago, would have been capable of blocking an attack.

The great chains that had once hoisted the door lay broken on the ground, as though they'd been snapped by a giant.

I picked my way through the mess, looking for any other sign of the place having been attacked. There were no bones or weapons to hint at a battle.

A chill dripped into my veins, but it wasn't from the mist that dampened my face.

To one side, balconies had been carved into the walls, leading to rooms whose doors had long since rotted away. To the other side, large niches had been dug into the stone, forming a stable.

"It's just like the outpost," I whispered.

"Look there." Liam pointed to the wall.

Indentations, like half-spheres, marked the dark rock, as though lae stones had once been set into the walls.

I wondered who had pried the lights away.

"I don't think I'll ever know which places my ancestors truly built, and which they only claimed ownership of," Liam said.

"I'm sorry." I reached for him.

He took my hand and kissed my palm. "Never be sorry for the truth."

I touched his cheek. His stubble had softened in the time we'd been traveling.

"Whatever your ancestors were, you are a great man who has helped save so many people. Things that happened hundreds of years ago can't change that." I trailed my fingers along the angle of his jaw.

Gods, I wanted to sneak into one of the dark stone rooms and strip him naked. Wrap myself around him and forget all about magic and evil men.

He kissed me, and a bright flash of temptation made me quite willing to strip him down with everyone watching if that was the only way I could have him.

"We might have a bit of a problem." Kely's voice barely stopped me from threading my fingers through Liam's hair and seeing just how far he'd be willing to let propriety slip.

"Might?" Cati stood beside Kely at the very edge of my lae stone's glow. "They really haven't let you out of Lygan Hall before, have they?"

I laced my fingers through Liam's as we walked toward Cati and Kely.

They stood together, staring down at the place where solid ground disappeared and a roaring river blocked our path.

The remnants of a bridge still clung to our side of the stone bank, as though the structure had once been built to lower over the water to let friends pass and be tipped up to keep enemies from crossing.

Were they that frightened of the western barbarians finding a way into the Dark Hall?

To one side of the tunnel, a waterfall raced down the wall, sending great plumes of droplets into the air. To the other side, the river swept away into the darkness, cutting through a gap in the wall that offered no handholds or any other chance of climbing across.

"None of us will make it to the other side swimming." Emmet knelt by the water's edge, dipping his hand into the river. "Current's running too swiftly. We wouldn't reach the far shore before getting dragged into the tunnel."

"I could form something solid enough for all of us to cross," Allana said. "I might need help to hold the weight of the horses."

"No." Liam let go of my hand and knelt beside Emmet. "This place was built using stone magic. Casting a sorcerer's spell might insult the shadows. I'll get us across."

Emmet stood and backed away, then reached forward, grabbed my shoulder, and pulled me back to stand beside him.

"Are you sure you're up for it, Trueborn Duwead?" Regan said.

There was a smile in her voice.

I forced myself to take a deep breath rather than throw her into the chivving river.

If her tone bothered Liam, he didn't show it.

He looked calm as he laid his hands against the stone floor and shut his eyes.

A gentle blue glow began under his palms, as though he were drawing lae stone light from the ground.

The glow expanded, surrounding him and stretching out toward the rest of our group. Before I could wonder if I should run from the glow, it had spread across the whole space.

The blue light cast everything in the cavern in bold shadows, giving more depth and light to the space than would have been possible with a thousand lae stones.

The balconies hadn't been roughly carved by a careless hand. Their maker had kept the lines perfect and smooth, with a faint pattern of leaves running along the bottom edges.

Above each of the stables, someone had carved beautiful horses. One running, one jumping. Each of them different. Each filled with such life, I wondered if the right spell could make them sprint around the room.

Liam gasped.

I looked back toward him, ready to dart forward and save him from tipping into the rushing water.

A smile curved one side of his lips as the blue from the floor began to expand out over the river, reaching forward like spilled water.

Whenever the light seemed to hesitate, a fresh, bright wave would reach forward, stretching closer to the far bank.

The light touched the other side and spilled out, racing all the way to the solid wall beyond.

Fear surged through my chest first. Then hope.

I had followed where the pull led me. I had to believe it meant something, even if I would never truly understand why I felt it. The mountain would not have led us this far only to leave us trapped.

Liam let out a long breath, and the blue light around him began to fade. The arch that reached over the water dimmed and turned into a solid, black bridge.

When the only light left in the space came from the lae stones our party carried, Liam lifted his hands from the ground. His shoulders rounded, and he stayed still for a moment, as though searching for the strength to stand.

"Liam." I stepped forward, pulling free from Emmet's grip on my shoulder.

He looked up at me and gave a tired smile.

I didn't know if I should be afraid. I'd shared Liam's bed, felt his power in the boundary that had protected the camp, but I had never seen him do magic like that.

His hand felt the same in mine as I helped him to his feet. His lips tasted the same as I kissed him.

"Come on." I stepped out onto the bridge Liam's magic had created.

The stone held fast beneath my feet.

Liam must have been sure it would. He didn't try to stop me as I led him to the far bank.

I wrapped my arms around his neck and kissed him again.

He tasted of honey and freedom. I wanted more of him, needing to be sure that magic hadn't somehow altered him.

"Enough," Emmet said. "There's only so far you can push a man before he snaps."

Liam pulled away from me but kept his arm around my waist, holding me close to his side.

"Has kissing been banned now?" I asked.

"There are other people here." Emmet thumped across the bridge.

If self-righteousness had weight, the stone would have collapsed beneath him.

"There were plenty of people at your wedding," I said. "That didn't keep you from kissing your bride."

A touch of pink crept into my brother's cheeks. "Until it's your wedding, keep it where I can't see it."

Emmet stomped to the solid wall that blocked our path.

I pressed my hand over my mouth, trying to quiet my laugh.

"Please don't tell me you're plotting a way to throw Emmet into the river," Liam said.

"And waste your beautiful bridge?" I leaned my head against Liam's shoulder. "I just think it's funny that that's probably the closest to my brother's approval we'll ever get."

Liam's low laugh was lost under the clatter of the horses' hooves and Tirra's steady urging as she lured the animals across the bridge one at a time.

"Don't get it in your head that you should marry me just to anger your brother. I'm brave enough to kiss you whenever you like, despite Emmet's wrath."

"But driving Orla and Emmet mad at the same time? That would be worth becoming a bride."

"If that's what you want, I will marry you whenever you like, Ena Ryeland." Liam kissed my forehead. "I love you. I am yours. The rest is just tradition and fancy words."

Blissful contentment flooded through me. "Maybe in the fall then, when we're back at Lygan Hall. I wouldn't want Cinni to miss the wedding music."

I brushed my lips against Liam's and walked away from him before my reason had time to flee from me entirely.

Cati stood beside Emmet, both her hands pressed against the wall as she searched the shadows.

"Find anything?" My voice sounded too chivving cheerful for someone stuck below a mountain.

"Rock," Cati said. "Lots of solid rock. If this does open up anywhere near Ilbrea, we might just have the chance of the chivving century."

I looked back at the dark outlines of the balcony, picturing Liam and me happily sharing one of the rooms.

"Let's see where the mountain spits us out," I said.

"If the mountain decides to let us out at all." Neil glowered at the rock.

I laid my cheek against the stone, trying to feel the pull in my chest beyond my utter need to slip back into Liam's arms.

The pull stayed quiet.

The horses huffed, but none of the people spoke as we all waited for something to happen.

"I'm trying to make it count," I whispered so softly no one could hear over the rumble of the river. "I'm trying to keep my promise. I don't understand how all this works, and I know I never will. But I was led here. All I'm asking is for you to show me why." The sharp stabbing of grief dug through my joy. "I will not let Finn down."

The pain of my grief twisted and expanded as the pull in my chest sharpened like it might tear me in two.

My eyes shot open as a loud crack echoed through the cave and the wall in front of us crumbled to nothing.

33

Snow coated everything beyond the entrance to the tunnel. White glistened on the tree branches and made sparkling banks across the mountainside. The wind whipped around us, as though testing our resolve to actually enter the cold.

I pulled my coat tighter around my neck.

"I never thought I'd say it, but I hope we're near Ilbrea." Neil pulled his gloves on. "I don't fancy trudging through three feet of snow for a hundred-odd miles."

"You forget, Neil"—Regan gave him a sweet smile I didn't chivving well trust—"there are Brien sorcerers on this expedition. And I hate being cold and wet."

"Which way?" the female Brien sorcerer asked.

"We can't leave a trail," Liam said. "We don't know how close we might be to the mountain road or a pack of paun soldiers."

"Don't worry, Liam," Regan said as she flipped up her gold-embroidered hood to cover her pale blond hair, "the Brien may prefer comfort, but it is our skill that has afforded us such luxury."

Liam stepped out into the snow. His face had an exhausted pallor from building our bridge, but his eyes were sharp as he looked up at the sky and squinted at the trees around us before pointing along the side of the rise. "That way."

The female Brien gave Liam a nod and stepped around him.

She held her hands in front of her, as though she would push the three feet of snow out of our path. But instead, the snow melted, leaving a trail cutting through the white.

"After me then." The sorcerer kept her hands in front of her, walking barely slower than a normal pace as she magically cleared our path.

"I don't like it," Emmet said softly.

"Me neither," I said. "But at least we've got enough light to be able to spot paun coming for our blood."

"Until the sun sets," Emmet said.

We made quick work of cutting down the slope. Every time we reached a new rise, or a dip in the snow that looked like we should not attempt to cross it, the sorcerer would turn to Liam. He would choose our path, and we'd continue on.

At the very end of our party, the young, gangly Brien sorcerer worked his own magic. Forming the melted snow back into perfect ice crystals and then smoothing a bit of the snow from either side of our path over the top.

The female stopped at the crest of a new rise and waited for Liam to decide our course.

I looked back. The sun shone down through the winter bare branches of the trees, casting a dazzling light on the snow.

Even knowing where we'd come from, I couldn't find a trace of our path.

Liam steered the sorcerer to the left of the rise, and we continued on.

The sun had sunk far enough in the sky to make me wonder how we were to keep warm as we slept in the open, before the depth of the snow began to lessen, and the trees in front of us became taller and sturdier.

"We're nearing the bottom," I said. "These trees grow like the ones near Harane."

"And we'll just be a group of twenty heading into a village for the night," Emmet said. "The paun won't find that suspicious at all."

"You're assuming we'll be lucky enough to find a town," I said. "Even if we pop right out onto the mountain road, it's thirty miles between most villages."

"I'm more concerned with being spotted by soldiers than finding a village," Emmet said.

"Would you like me to stop making a path?" the female sorcerer asked. "It's rather exhausting work, and I don't need to keep plowing ahead for my own enjoyment."

"Please keep going," Liam said.

I chewed the inside of my lips as the sun sank lower still and the slope leveled out.

There was barely a foot of snow covering the ground by the time we reached the edge of the trees.

A wide swatch of frozen, muddy road cut through the glistening white. The gash seemed obscene in the moonlight, like a wound no one had tried to heal.

Dots of light glimmered to the south, though from such a distance, there was no way to know what town we might have found.

"If we can find that opening again," Cati said, "if the mountain will allow it…"

We won't need the chivving Brien's help to fight the Guilds.

34

I won't deny the convenience of the magic the Brien used to clear a patch of ground for us to camp. I won't pretend the heat they laid upon us didn't keep me from shivering too badly to sleep.

I will say that sleeping surrounded by snow is not a pleasant experience, and I would never recommend it to anyone I liked even a bit.

By the time Liam led us out of the woods in the morning, I had little thought for anything but a hot bath and some warm frie.

Liam, Emmet, Regan, and I had been given horses by Tirra. We were to ride to the town we'd seen the night before, find out where exactly we were, and poke about to see what news we might hear of any soldiers in the area.

Cati looked ready to murder us all when Regan was chosen for the party instead of her. Regan looked like she might summon a colony of bats to scratch us to death when Liam forbade her sorcerers from trailing behind her.

But somehow, the fact that neither side was actually happy seemed to mean it was the best plan, so we rode off toward the village, leaving everyone else behind.

There was something oddly comforting in riding beside Liam along the mountain road. I didn't consider Ilbrea my home. I hated the chivving mountain road. But I knew where it led. I had grown up in Harane, a village that only existed so travelers might have a place to rest along their way to somewhere else. The mountain road was a constant in Ilbrea, a path I didn't need a pull in my chest to find.

I knew as soon as the first houses came into view that I had never visited this town before.

The homes were built of a familiar mix of wood and stone. The ones on the outskirts all looked to be in need of repairs that only moneyed tilk would have the time or coin to manage.

The pastures leading up to the houses smelled of animal dung, and the scent in the air didn't improve much once we'd entered the town proper.

669

Regan gave a little cough as the wind swept the stench around us. "Do all places in Ilbrea smell this foul?"

I looked back in time to see her raise a gloved hand to her nose.

"It depends on the time of year," I said, "the direction of the wind—"

"How much time the farmers spend cleaning up sheep shit," Emmet added.

I laughed as Regan's shoulders shook in revulsion.

"Don't worry," I said, "as long as you stick to the road, your boots will probably only be covered in mud."

Emmet and Liam both gave low laughs that time.

We rode past homes where the windows had been patched with stretched leather, and others that looked like they might be owned by what passed as laxe merchants in a town of that size.

I tried not to despise the laxe. I knew it was the Guilds who were the true demons in Ilbrea. But I couldn't quiet my loathing for the merchants who made their gold off of tilk sweat and labor. Not when there were good people with hungry bellies living just outside the rich laxe's doors.

A little boy wearing a man's coat ran past. He gripped the bottom of the coat in his bare hands, keeping the tattered wool from dragging across the frozen mud.

A woman bustled toward the center of the town. She wore a knitted shawl and clutched an empty basket as though she were hurrying to the market. I hoped she would have the coin to buy the food she needed.

I looked down at my boots. They'd been made just for me in Lygan Hall and were nicer than anything that would be found outside of a fancy city in Ilbrea. The rest of my clothes were plain enough I wouldn't catch anyone's eye, but the boots sank guilt into my stomach. I could feed a family for a winter off what I'd get for selling them.

If I stripped Regan, I'd be able to feed a few families.

She'd been smart enough not to wear starched skirts when we left Lygan Hall, but the make of everything she wore screamed of coin to burn. The fabrics were finely woven, and intricate patterns were stitched into every piece. The sort of time it would take to do such a thing either meant enough leisure to do it yourself or enough coin to pay to have the work done.

Both were luxuries most common folk in Ilbrea never had.

The road narrowed as we got closer to the center of town and businesses took the place of houses—smiths, tanners, a dressmaker, a cobbler.

A bit of gold glinted in the light.

My hand drifted toward the knife at my hip as we neared a Guilded scribes' shop.

I glanced back to my brother, who rode at the tail of our party.

His face was dark as he stared at the golden, seven-pointed star that hung outside the shop.

Part of me expected the white building to catch fire just from the sheer force of his wrathful glower. But we rode past, and no flames emerged.

The road widened back out to form a town square. There were even proper cobble-stones set into the ground so the people braving the cold to shop at the merchants' carts didn't have to slog through muck. Behind the carts selling baubles, sweetmeats, and ale, proper businesses surrounded the square.

Two cheerful-looking taverns, with competing music pouring through their doors, stretched along either side of the town square. A stable and a busy bakery took up the two ends.

But it wasn't any of the businesses that drove cold into my veins.

In the middle of the bustling square, three tall posts stood in a row. All of them had dark stains and grooves from years of wear near the bottoms.

People skirted around the whipping posts, eager to do business, not caring that tilk had been beaten and murdered right in the center of their own town square. I couldn't find any sympathy in my heart for the people who ignored such pain.

My lungs ached as I pressed down my need to scream.

I rode behind Liam as we left the square. If I hadn't been following him, I don't know if I would have been able to make myself keep moving.

He stopped in front of a tavern that looked run down and sad compared to the buildings around it.

"A bit of good food and some ale." He climbed off his horse and reached up for me. There was an unnatural ease to his smile as he lifted me down. It was a beautiful expression, but it didn't fit my Liam.

I made myself match his ease as I brushed my skirt out. "Too long on the road, and all I want is food and drink. If they have a spot by the fire, I'll be thrilled enough to dance a jig on the bar."

Liam laughed and squeezed my hand as a girl peered around the side of the tavern.

"Stabling?" She pointed to our horses.

"Only for a bit," Liam said. "But see them fed and watered."

There was something in the way he spoke to the girl that tensed my spine and brought sour into my throat. The tone was familiar. The easy way he handed the reins to the girl like he hadn't a care in the world besides a decent meal.

"In we get." Liam bowed all of us toward the tavern door, like a dashing host ready to charm everyone in sight.

Finn. The sour in my throat turned to pain. *He's playing Finn's role.*

It had always been Finn to speak to the locals and charm out information. Finn who played the handsome fool when we needed to buy time. But Finn was gone, and Liam had slipped into his role as easily as someone shrugging on a new coat.

Emmet pushed open the tavern door, and the sound of enthusiastic fiddling carried out onto the street.

"A nice seat by the fire, I think." Liam placed his hand on the back of my waist and ushered me inside.

A girl with a fiddle stood in the corner, grinning as she played, even though her bow squeaked horribly every few notes.

I gave her a smile and tried not to cringe as the sound dug into my ears.

A man with tufty gray hair hurried out from behind the bar. His clothes weren't terribly clean, and as far as I could tell, any mugs we were given wouldn't be much better. But the man beamed at our party.

"Please, come in." The barkeep bowed. "We've got plenty of food, the best frie in town, and a nice fire for the ladies to warm themselves by."

The patrons in the bar had turned toward us as well. The men scattered around the tables all seemed the sort you'd expect to find in a tavern before midday. A few travelers savoring their time out of the cold, and several men hiding from their wives.

The barkeep shooed away the lone person at the table nearest the fire and dusted the seat off before offering it to me.

"Thank you." I sat down, sighing as the warmth of the fire touched my skin. "I'll be happy to warm up."

The barkeep pulled out a chair for Regan as well. She stared at the seat as though it were covered in dung.

"Come on." Emmet sank into his own chair. "You grumble about being cold, you whine about being on a horse—both your troubles are solved."

"How very thoughtful." Regan gave Emmet a smile that didn't reach her eyes.

I watched the people in the room as Liam ordered food and drinks for all of us and the barkeep hurried away.

"I don't think there are many soldiers near here." I leaned across the table to the others, speaking low enough that no one else could hear over the screeching of the fiddle. "At least not right now."

"Why do you say that?" Regan asked.

I gave her a conspiratorial grin, like she and I were friends in on some joke the men wouldn't understand.

"There's no fear in the locals," I said. "They don't flinch when the door opens. Their shoulders are relaxed. Tilk wouldn't look like that if there were a mess of armed paun prowling the streets, searching for a reason to tie them to the whipping post."

"Is that better or worse for us?" Regan's gaze slid around the room.

"It'll make our work a bit tougher but keep the rest of our party safer," Liam said.

"Do you want to find out where the soldiers are, or shall I?" I asked.

"I'll do it," Emmet said.

"You've got a scar on your cheek and burns on your neck," I said. "You're too easy to recognize and horrible with people besides."

"You try first," Liam said, "but stay where we can see you."

"Of course." I took off my coat, laid it on the back of my chair, and gave a little tug on the front of my bodice to be sure I was showing enough skin to be distracting.

"Do you have to do that?" Emmet said.

"No, but it does make things easier." I winked at my brother and stood. "I'll be right back."

35

I let a smile touch my lips as I strolled between the tables.

The bodice and shift I wore weren't the grandest, but I'd tied the laces tight enough to allow the men a good look at the curves of my body. I hadn't painted on my full armor, but the bit of pink on my cheeks and red on my lips still had all the men in the room staring at me by the time I reached the bar.

The barkeep smiled at me, trying to hide the fact that his gaze had flicked down to the bare tops of my breasts.

"Is there something else I can get for you?" the barkeep said. "I'll have your frie over in just a moment."

"Actually"—I glanced over at the table where the others sat before leaning across the bar—"I was hoping you might be able to help me. I met a soldier a while back, and he said his company is often posted near the town. Do you know where I might be able to find them?"

"If I tell you, is it going to cause a brawl in my tavern?" The barkeep wrinkled his forehead.

"Oh no." I gave a little laugh. "The angry one is my brother."

"That doesn't mean safety for my furniture."

The fiddler finished her song. The men offered some half-hearted applause before she struck up a fresh tune.

"I give you my word." I laid my hand on top of the barkeep's. "I won't bring any trouble to your tavern."

The barkeep stared at me for a moment before giving a heavy sigh. "There are soldiers who come through town about twice a month. They head north and back, then south and back. They don't stay in Lenton for more than a night or two when they travel in either direction."

"Hmm." I let my lips form a little pout. "How long ago did they leave?"

"Ten or so days. Headed south this time."

I glanced over at the table. "If I wanted to leave a letter for a soldier, where would I go?"

"Scribes' shop would be your safest bet. It'll cost you a few coins, but unless it's a soldier I already know, I couldn't make a promise to get anything to him."

"I'll try the scribes then." I shoved down my hatred and forced myself to smile. "It's such a pity they're making those poor men spend the winter tramping up and down the mountain road. It would be kinder to let them stay in Lenton for the cold months."

"It would." The barkeep picked up his rag, twisting it in his hands in an absent-minded manner. "But the soldiers sign on for a life serving Ilbrea, and I can't say I don't sleep better knowing they're out on patrol keeping the shadows well away from us."

"Why? I'd always heard Lenton was a nice town."

"There's not a thing wrong with Lenton." He pulled a mug from under the bar and began polishing the tarnished metal. "It's the woods you've got to look out for."

I leaned farther across the bar. "Is there something out there I should be scared of?" I asked in a low whisper, though no one would have been able to hear me over the screeching of the chivving fiddle.

He worked his lips together but didn't answer.

"Well, I suppose I have got two men with me," I said. "They'll keep me safe enough."

"Don't count on them to protect you. Two men wouldn't be enough." The barkeep set the mug down and pulled out a bottle of frie. He poured himself a nip and downed it before setting four cups on a tray. "There are frightening folk who take to the woods. I'm sure you've heard the stories about ghosts and bandits."

"Of course." I didn't mention that I had joined the rumored ghosts and had three of them sitting by the fire.

"Men'll take advantage of people's fears." The barkeep poured our four drinks. "They've been stealing children and carting them into the woods where the bastards think we'll all be too afraid to follow."

"That's terrible." I pressed my hands to the top of the bar to keep them from shaking and betraying my rage.

"We don't even know what they do to the poor children. But it's the monster that leads the band of bastards the soldiers are after."

"What do you mean?" I twisted my foot, needing the security of being able to feel the knife hidden in the ankle of my boot.

"The Demon's Torch. That's what the soldiers call him. They say he's a great beast of a man, but that might only be people's fear talking. The evil slitch terrorizes soldiers and scribes alike. Lighting them on fire if they dare try to stop him." The barkeep shook his head. "I feel bad using such language in front of a young girl. But I hope the soldiers give that chivving bastard what's coming to him when they find him. And they won't stop hunting for the monster until they do."

"I'm so grateful there are good men in Ilbrea." My heart raced so hard I could barely keep my voice from shaking. I picked up the tray of frie. "I'll carry these. Just don't tell my brother what I asked about." I gave him a smile and a wink before strolling back to the table. I gave the least disgusting of the male patrons a wink as well for good measure.

"There you are." Liam pulled my chair out for me as I reached the table. "I was starting to think he'd run out of frie."

"Not at all." I passed the cups around before raising mine to Emmet. "To the Demon's Torch." I spoke only loudly enough for our group to hear. "May the Guilds never find my sweet brother."

36

I only half listened as Liam, Emmet, and Regan quietly argued over what should be done next. I was too busy trying to hear beyond the terrible music to the noises on the street, though I had no real hope of hearing soldiers coming to murder my brother unless they wanted us to know they were attacking.

Besides, it didn't matter if I listened to the details of the others' bickering. There was only one way for us to move forward.

Still, the old arguments spun around as I ate my meal.

Emmet refused to hide while the rest of us worked. Regan wanted all her sorcerers taken on the next part of our journey. Liam thought Regan would be better off heading far to the south, checking on the places where the Brien's territory bordered Ilbrea, and leaving us well alone. Emmet insisted she should head farther north, where he'd found the most soldiers during the fall.

I allowed them to continue until I'd finished my sweet pastry.

"Are we ready to go then?" I asked.

"Have you not been listening?" Regan said.

"Honestly, no," I said. "I didn't feel the need to listen to you all dicker around in circles."

"Ena," Emmet warned.

"We are going to Frason's Glenn," I said. "A party of twenty will draw too much attention, so we whittle our group down to five. The rest go to the safe house and wait for us there. It wouldn't be wise to spread out our people until we know how much the traitor told the Guilds."

"I see." Regan smiled. "And which five go to Frason's Glenn?"

"Whoever my brother chooses," I said.

"And why does a Ryeland have that much of a say?" Regan leaned forward like she was getting ready to scratch my eyes from my head. "Liam and I are the trueborn here."

"We're not in the mountains. We're in Ilbrea. The fact that you're a trueborn doesn't chivving matter. It's Emmet's contact in Frason's Glenn," I said. "He'll choose who he trusts. And then we'll go to the Lir Valley."

"And let me guess," Regan said, "Emmet will choose who goes on that escapade as well."

"No. That'll be Liam and me," I said. "Because he's in charge of this mess, and I'm the only one who's been to the Lir Valley."

"She must be outstanding between the sheets if you let her speak to you like that, Liam," Regan said.

"Don't you chivving dare—" Emmet began.

"We can't all go to Frason's Glenn, and it has to be people Emmet can trust," Liam said.

"You definitely don't qualify as trustworthy," I said.

"None of us will be swayed." Liam leaned back in his chair. "Do we need to sit here and argue about it any longer?"

"I will not be left behind," Regan said. "The Brien are a part of this battle. Our people are in danger from the paun."

"And you don't think we can get it done?" I laughed. "You don't even know what animal dung smells like. You're of no use out here."

"I will be there to see the traitor dealt justice," Regan said.

"I don't fancy your kind of justice," I said.

"How dare—"

"And I don't trust you anywhere near my contacts," Emmet said. "The last thing I need is for you to decide they're creating too much trouble for you."

"This is absolutely ludicrous," Regan said.

"They're right," Liam said. "Everyone else can hunker down and get organized. Work on finding the supplies we'll need if we do have to go up against stone-made weapons."

"And you couldn't have told me about this absurd plan before we left Lygan Hall?" Regan said. "Or even before we left the woods?"

"While you had sorcerers standing behind you?" Liam said. "I thought it best to wait until we could have a more private conversation."

"In the middle of a tavern?" Regan said.

"This is how things are run out here," Liam said. "You can feel free to flee east whenever you like. But out here, sorcerers are a liability, and traveling in a large party puts a target on your back. Are you willing to accept how things are done, or is it time for our groups to part ways?"

I couldn't read anything beyond loathing in Regan's expression as she stared silently at Liam.

"We need to head back soon," I said. "It'll be best to pass through town before dark, and we'll have to split into groups to do it."

"Fine," Regan said. "You take a small group to Frason's Glenn, but I will be a part of it. I'm coming with you."

"Not a chivving chance," Emmet said. "I take care of the people who have given me their trust. And you aren't going anywhere near them."

37

The mountain was good to us. Or maybe Cinni had known what it was we needed and asked the mountain to lead us to a path near Lenton. The town wasn't of much importance in Ilbrea, but it was thirty-four miles north of Frason's Glenn and only a bit farther of a walk for the group headed to the safety of the little farm where Finn and I had borrowed a cart more than once.

Liam, Emmet, Kely, Cati, and I took the five horses Tirra had brought along, leaving the others to carry their supplies. I didn't like separating from the rest of the group. I wasn't worried about us—I'd been to Frason's Glenn without Cati to defend me. I just didn't fancy abandoning the others in Ilbrea. I liked leaving them with Regan and her sorcerers even less.

Worry nibbled at my gut as we separated from the others. It didn't stop until we neared a road cutting west.

A sick feeling of grief rolled through my stomach as we passed the crossroad that led to Marten, and guilt pushed every other thought aside. My pulse pounded in my ears, and my hands shook as I gripped my horse's reins. Voices of people I had never met echoed through my mind as they screamed their loathing of me. I had caused their deaths. The Massacre of Marten was my fault.

I will not let them forget what they did to you. I will burn Ilara.

The sun was just beginning to set when we reached the great walled city of Frason's Glenn.

Nestled in the bend of a roaring river, the city of stone and spires left a glorious silhouette against the gray of the sky. On the far side the city, two cliffs surrounded a second river that ran behind Frason's Glenn before joining with the first.

The city walls soared thirty feet high. The only breaks in the stone were tall, thin windows that allowed archers an advantage when trying to murder anyone who dared threaten the city.

Turrets stuck up at intervals. Men in black uniforms stood on top, their bows visible even in the dim twilight.

The Guilds are wise not to trust the tilk.

"By the stars," Kely murmured.

I looked back to where he and Cati rode.

"You all right?" I asked.

"I just didn't think it would be so big," Kely said. "Or well defended."

Cati stared up at the top of the wall.

I wondered if she too was in awe of the size of the city, or only wondering the best way to kill the soldiers.

"You should see Ilara," Emmet said.

"Are the walls higher?" I asked.

"No," Emmet said. "But the place is massive, and right next to the sea."

"If it's next to the sea, that should offer some easy ways in," I said.

"Sure," Emmet said. "If you don't mind the hundreds of soldiers on patrol or thousands barracked in the city."

"Don't make it sound like so much fun," I said.

The city gate came into view.

A line of people waited outside, hoping to be given permission to enter the city for the night.

I watched them file through the gate one at a time.

The soldiers would question each group. Some would be allowed to pass with hardly more than a word exchanged. Others would have their belongings tossed from their wagons as the soldiers searched them.

It was the people who shook hands with the soldiers that bothered me. I couldn't see the coin slipping from palm to palm, but there was no mistaking what was happening. I tried not to hate the tilk who paid to protect their lives and goods. But I wondered how much better it would be if one of them were brave enough to slip a knife into a soldier's stomach instead of silver into his pocket.

I forced a pleasant expression onto my face when it was our turn at the gate.

"What's your business in the city?" one of the soldiers asked.

He kept his hand on the hilt of his sword, as though he suspected someone might decide he deserved a knife more than a coin.

"Looking for a warm bed for the night," Liam said. "We're heading south, and I don't fancy spending a night in the snow."

"Why are your traveling south?" the soldier asked. "What business do you have that can't wait until spring?"

"I'm ashamed to admit it," Liam said, "but I've got a distant uncle who isn't doing so well. He's got no children of his own, and I was hoping meeting my lovely new bride might be enough to convince him I deserve an inheritance."

"And the rest?" the soldier asked. "Are they all your brides?"

"Protection," Liam said. "I've heard rumors of nasty people plaguing the mountain road, and I won't put my wife at risk."

"And that one?" The guard raised an eyebrow at Cati.

My heart stuttered for a moment. Ilbrean women never wore pants, not unless they were bold enough to try and join the Soldiers Guild, or become a sailor, or a dozen other possibilities that made mothers' hearts crumble. But Cati had insisted, and Liam had agreed.

Do not let us die for lack of a chivving skirt. I sent my plea to the gods and stars, whoever would have sympathy for such a frivolous reason to chance execution.

"I'm here in case the men need help defending themselves." Cati winked. "I'm not wife material, but I am useful in my own way. I'm hoping that Demon's Torch comes after us. I'd like to try my sword against him. It could be fun."

The chivving soldier actually smiled. Flat out grinned like a young lad who's just seen tits for the first time.

"That's something I'd like to watch," the soldier said.

"Maybe if you're lucky, you'll be around to see it," Cati said. "But I won't get to shove my sword through any deserving bastards if we can't get in and find a room."

"I'm sure you'll find a warm place to polish your blade." The soldier began to step out of the way before stopping. "But be warned, the use of any weapons within the city walls carries the penalty of death."

"I'll be careful," Cati said.

The soldier gave us a nod and let us pass.

We rode through the tunnel in the twelve-foot thick stone wall and into the city proper.

Even though night had fallen, there were still plenty of people on the streets.

A passing cart sold pastries, another sweetmeats. Couples in fine clothes strode arm in arm, and a few tired-looking tilk shambled home from their day's labor.

Liam led us to the public stable. The horse painted on the front had received a fresh coat of white since the last time I'd been in Frason's Glenn.

"Anyone in there?" Liam called.

I jumped down from my horse without waiting for his help. There was something about being in the city that made me feel safer on foot than on horseback.

I recognized the gangly stable boy who ran out onto the street. He'd grown a patchy scruff on his chin.

"Sorry about that." The boy saw me and blushed. The red of it peeked through the patchy hair. "Hello." He bowed to me.

"Do you have room for five horses?" I asked.

"I…" The stable boy nodded and reached for the reins of my horse. "I'll find a place for them."

"Thank you." I gave the boy a smile along with the reins of my horse.

"Will you be staying in Frason's Glenn long?" the boy asked. "When you were here before, you left so quickly."

"I didn't think you'd remember." I tried to make myself blush. The effect must have been pleasing, because the boy turned a shade of red healthy people should not be able to manage.

"I never forget a good customer," the boy said.

"Just see that you pay as much attention to the horses as you do pretty girls." Emmet smacked his reins down into the boy's hand.

"Yes, of course." The boy gave Emmet a bow. "Absolutely."

The boy stammered and bowed as he took all our horses, then Emmet led the way toward Mave's.

We passed the paun's towering white building, but there weren't healers and sorcerers standing together on the carved stone steps. Only a flock of soldiers. All holding spears. All with swords at their hips.

"Emmet"—I let go of Liam's arm and stepped up to walk beside my brother—"when you went on a rampage searching for me, did you happen to take any of your worry and wrath out on Frason's Glenn?"

"I kept the flames clear of the city," Emmet said. "The buildings here are packed close together. There are too many tilk who could get caught in a blaze. That, and I didn't want to pull the Guilds' eye any closer to Mave."

We walked down a street filled with shops that sold all sorts of things people in towns and villages could never afford to buy.

"You did burn a sailors' office here last spring," I said.

"I didn't have much of a choice."

We moved on to rows of houses where the flickering lanterns only managed to light the corners of the streets.

"Why do you like fire so much?" I asked.

Emmet didn't answer.

"Are you going to make me ask how you ended up lighting Mave's square on fire while nude, or will you just tell me?" I poked Emmet in the ribs.

"It's better to leave old stories in the past," he said.

"I think that only applies to people who don't have younger sisters."

A few faint strings of well-played music made me forget my questions. I quickened my pace, walking in front of Emmet and straight to a cluster of tall stone buildings.

Light poured through the windows on the upper stories, and the loud laughter of drunken revelers carried from the square beyond.

A sense of joyful anticipation I couldn't quite explain filled my chest as I looked back toward the others.

Liam's eyes held joy as he met my gaze. Emmet walked somberly like we weren't heading toward a brothel. Cati gripped the hilt of her sword. Kely looked plain terrified.

I laughed through it all.

I don't know why I beckoned the others to walk faster as we cut through the alley.

I had been given my armor in Mave's house. I had kissed Liam for the first time on one of the little balconies. But those wonderful things did not change the true nature of Mave's business.

I ran back to take Liam's hand as we reached Mave's square.

The place was packed, despite the chill in the air.

Three fiddlers played on the platform in the center of the beautiful chaos. Men in matching orange coats poured from barrels of ale and frie. Patrons danced and drank and laughed as though the cold didn't exist.

There was a level of joy and frivolity that made it seem like, if I was only brave enough to join in, the demons of the world would forget I existed and I could just go on dancing forever.

The song ended, and the dancers gave a cheer that shook my ears. Before the roar had stopped, the fiddlers struck up a fresh tune, and the dance began again.

Emmet took the lead, heading over toward a wide porch filled with packed tables. Metal spheres with flames dancing inside hung around the edge of the overhang.

The men sat, drinking frie and leering at all the beautiful girls.

The girls, dressed in fine coats that still displayed their shoved-up breasts, prowled between the men. Some had already found their partners for the night. Those girls perched in the men's laps, flirting, giggling, and waiting for the men to be ready to head inside.

A girl with jet-black curls sat on an elderly man's lap. She tipped her head back as she laughed. The arch of her spine somehow pressed her tits all the way up to the man's chin.

I should learn that.

"Fresh ones!" A girl with auburn hair sauntered forward. "And here I thought I might be bored tonight."

"We're friends of Mave's," Emmet said. "Let her know we're here."

"Who's here?" The girl formed her lips into a scarlet-painted moue.

"Just go," Emmet said.

The girl turned on her heel and strutted through the pale blue door into the dining room.

"I'll have to tell Marta how quickly you dismissed a pretty girl with auburn hair," I said.

"I'm a married man with a child on the way," Emmet said.

"Being faithful is such a noble sacrifice," I said.

"I haven't touched another woman since I found Marta. And don't glare at me for letting women leer. You're ten times worse than I could ever be, little sister."

"Be careful, brother, or I might actually be grateful you slipped a child into my friend before you married her."

The door opened before Emmet could find the words to reply.

Mave stood in the doorway, her mass of dark curls surrounding her head like a living crown. Her dark complexion was perfect, and her fur-trimmed gown pristine. She looked from Emmet to the rest of us, though her crooked smile didn't appear until her gaze landed on Cati.

"How do I have the unbearable pleasure of welcoming Emmet Ryeland back so soon?" Mave held her hand out. The sapphire of her ring twinkled in the lamplight.

Emmet stepped forward and kissed the back of Mave's hand. "I've come to see an old friend and was hoping for a bit of shelter from the cold."

"Then welcome to my home." Mave nodded. "May you find all the joys your hearts long for."

38

Sitting by the fire in Mave's parlor was comforting and strange all at the same time. The girl I'd been the last time we'd come to Mave's hadn't had blood on her hands. She hadn't even known how to properly defend herself. She'd been frightened and innocent. I was amazed that girl had managed to stay alive.

Despite all the things I'd seen, I was still in awe of the rich, blue, flower-patterned fabric that covered the walls and furniture in Mave's parlor. The music and raucous cheering from the revelers in the square drifted through the closed windows. Their chaos made the pristine room bearable.

A man in an orange coat delivered a tray of food, frie, and chamb.

I sat for a long while, sipping chamb and staring at the golden seven-pointed star that hung above the fireplace. The glow of the firelight flickered off the shining surface, like the star itself was trying to shine. I hated that it was beautiful.

"I…" Kely said once we'd all eaten our fill and fallen into silence.

"Yes?" I looked to Kely, grateful to have something to pay attention to besides the golden star.

"I didn't think coming into Ilbrea would involve visiting a place like this." Kely gripped the stem of his chamb glass.

"It's a brothel, not a demon's lair," I said.

"I know, miss." Kely stared down at the bubbles in his glass. "But…but could you be sure this is never mentioned in Lygan Hall?"

Cati leaned forward. "You're a Black Blood who's doing his duty to his clan. Are you ashamed of our work?"

"Not at all," Kely said. "I'm proud to be working to protect the Black Bloods, but I've got a girl in Lygan Hall. I want to marry her next winter. If she thinks I've been rolling around with bought women—"

"We'll keep it between us," Emmet said. "The fewer people who know about Mave's, the better."

"Good." Kely downed the rest of his chamb. "That's very good."

A knock on the door sounded just before Mave pushed it open.

"I trust you've all had a chance to warm up and refresh yourselves." Mave's skirts rustled as she made her way to the blue-covered fainting couch. For some reason, I hated the starched sound less when her skirts were to blame.

"Thank you for the food and drink," Emmet said.

"I hope I don't come to regret my hospitality." Mave sat and smoothed out the skirt of her deep blue gown. Tiny black beads had been sewn in a spattered pattern around the hem. Each small speck shone in the firelight.

I gripped my chamb glass tighter, resisting the temptation to reach out and touch the beads to see if they actually held the heat of the flames.

"As much as I always adore a visit from Emmet Ryeland," Mave said, "the fact that you've come in the winter makes me wonder what horrors have led you to my door."

"We've been betrayed," Emmet said. "The monster that attacked our camp was only a small part of it. One of our own was sending information to another clan. The Hayes. The Hayes Clan was sending this information into Ilbrea to be handed over to the Guilds."

Mave stood and poured herself a large glass of frie.

"And who was this traitor in your ranks?" Mave asked. "Please tell me it was not Finn. If information about my family—"

"It wasn't Finn." I downed the rest of my chamb, took the bottle from Mave, and poured frie into my glass. "Finn's dead. The traitor is to blame." I sipped the frie. The burning as it raced down my throat did not singe my grief.

"Before they executed the one who betrayed us," Liam said, "he told us the Hayes contact is probably in Frason's Glenn."

"It would make sense," Mave said. "We have so many people, so many soldiers, so many goods going in and out. But if the Duwead traitor is dead, it seems you've sealed the leak from the inside."

"We're here to find the Hayes contact," Emmet said.

"And you think it might be me?" Mave sat back down.

"No," Liam said.

"Why?" Mave narrowed her perfectly kohl-lined eyes at him.

"Because I can't consider it," Liam said. "If you had chosen to abandon the cause we both fight for to work on behalf of the Guilds, we'd all be lost."

"If there is someone in Frason's Glenn who's aiding the paun, we need to find them," Emmet said. "Find out what they've told the Guilds and make sure they never talk again."

"Sounds wonderful." Mave raised her glass. "What's it got to do with me?"

"We need your help," Liam said. "You know this city. You know who might be willing to sell out."

"I also know that having a Black Blood in my home is dangerous at the best of times," Mave said. "Knowing that someone's been spilling secrets to the paun only makes it worse."

"If the Black Bloods' secrets are being handed to the paun, are your secrets any safer?" I said. "As long as there's a traitor in Frason's Glenn, your family isn't safe."

Mave studied the golden star above the fire. "Did the traitor come from the eastern mountains?"

"I have no idea." Liam ran his hands over his face. "The one we caught had never had any contact with the fiend in Ilbrea. The fiend could have already been told to go to ground when we found the spy in our own camp. They might never have been in Frason's Glenn at all."

"How kind of you to bring me such helpful information," Mave said.

"I wish we had more," Liam said.

"If anyone can root the spying bastard out, it's you, Mave." Emmet knelt in front of her. "Point us in their direction, and we'll do the rest."

"I could have my own people take them," Mave said.

"No," I said.

"We have questions we need answered," Liam said. "The clans are at war. Any information we can find could save Black Bloods' lives."

"Hmm." Mave looked to Cati. "Did they bring you along to do the dirty work of questioning?"

"I'm just here in case it comes to a fight," Cati said. "Though I don't mind using a knife to get answers."

"I think I might like you." Mave smiled.

"Just don't try to paint me up like you did Ena, and we'll be great friends," Cati said.

"It always is exciting when Emmet comes around." Mave laughed. "We should get you all settled in for the night. It might take some time for my little shadows to sneak into the corners where secrets like to hide. But if the paun have been buying information from someone in my city, I'll find them."

"Do you think someone's actually been selling the information the Hayes sent them?" I dug my fingers into the fancy blue fabric that covered my chair.

"Everything in Frason's Glenn costs coin." Mave stood and walked to the door. "Information of that value wouldn't be trusted if freely given. Someone's been making a tidy profit. I look forward to taking it all from them."

"Thank you, Mave," Liam said.

She opened the door to the hall.

A man in an orange jacket waited outside.

"See them all settled," Mave said.

The man bowed us down the hall toward the narrow door at the far end.

"Emmet," Mave said, "stay with me a little longer."

"Of course, Mave." Emmet stepped to the side while the rest of us filed out into the corridor.

I didn't like leaving him behind, but Liam didn't look worried.

"Don't forget to tell her your happy news." I gave Emmet a broad smile before following the others.

I tried my best to focus on the laughter drifting up from the dining room and not the sounds leaking through the doors that lined the long hall.

Kely gasped and leapt away as the door to one of the rooms flung open and a man who hadn't bothered buttoning his pants stumbled into the hall with a wide smile on his sweaty face. A naked girl lay on the bed, not bothering to hide her laughter as her customer lurched away from our group and hit the wall with a thud.

"If you would, sir." The man in the orange jacket raised an eyebrow at the patron's drooping pants. "House rules." He closed the bedroom door.

The girl laughed harder. The sound of it only managed to compete with the other noises in the corridor for a moment.

"This way." Mave's man led us farther down the hall.

"Isleen will never agree to marry me." Kely shook his head. "Her mother will forbid it. Her father will forbid it. Chivving gods and stars, if I were her father I'd forbid it myself."

"Just breathe." I patted Kely on the back. "No one is going to tell Isleen you were here."

The sound of two bodies thumping against the wall came from the last room in the hall.

Kely's face turned white.

"Just pretend it's the sound of swords smashing together on the practice field," I said.

Mave's man opened the door at the end of the hall. "Close the door tightly behind you. And don't roam while you're here. You won't be able to get back through this door."

"Of course," I said.

The man nodded and led us up the brightly painted steps.

I listened for any voices drifting from above but didn't hear anything.

"The women will stay on this level." Mave's man bowed Cati and me out on the landing of the third floor. "There are open rooms at the end of the hall. Feel free to enjoy our baths."

"Thank you," I said.

I met Liam's gaze as he followed the man up the next flight of stairs. He gave me a little smile.

I wanted to cling to him. But soon he disappeared, and Cati and I were left alone.

"This is quite the place," Cati said.

"It is." I looked around the big common room the stairs had dropped us into.

There was no one in the room. Not even a lone girl snoozing in front of the fire.

"You all right?" Cati asked.

"Of course," I said. "I guess all the girls are still working."

I led Cati down the long corridor of bedrooms.

There were eight empty rooms at the end of the hall. I chose the one at the very end, dropped my pack onto the ground, and went for a bath.

There weren't even any girls bathing in the four big copper tubs.

The hot water made it almost possible to forget how cold it was outside. I scrubbed myself clean and lingered until the water had lost its warmth.

There were still no girls upstairs by the time I slipped back into my borrowed room.

39

Morning light streamed through the window and into my eyes.

I rolled over, searching for Liam's warmth beneath the blankets, but I was alone.

My heart leapt into my throat. I'd already grabbed the hilt of my knife before opening my eyes and realizing where I was.

I lay back on my pillow, panting.

The room was cheerfully painted and immaculately clean. My fancy boots even looked out of place since they had mud from the road on them.

I took my time combing out my hair and putting on just enough paint that I wouldn't feel like a lost child who'd come to beg for scraps at Mave's door.

Once I'd finished dressing, I sat on the edge of the bed, trying to think through what to do. I hated the stillness.

Hiding somewhere in the city was a slitch who'd sold our camp's secrets to the paun. I wanted to stab him through the throat, not sit in a clean room waiting to be useful.

I wished I could convince Cati to give me a bit of training, but I didn't think Mave would like us playing with swords or even knives in her home.

I stood and paced the room as the feeling of being trapped in a cage made my heart race.

Knock, knock, knock.

"Yes." My hand slid to the knife at my hip.

"Ena," a voice called through the door, "it's Nora."

I raced the few steps to the door and threw it open.

"Ena!" Nora beamed at me. Her bright blond hair was still twisted up with little ringlets framing her perfectly painted face. Her pale purple dress barely covered enough of her chest to be worth wearing, and her jeweled pendant would have caused even a paun envy.

"It's so good to see you," I said. "I looked for you last night—"

"I had a private client." Nora took my hands and held them out to my sides, first examining my clothes, then my face and hair. "You wear your armor well, little bird."

"Thank you." I smiled.

"Come on." Nora kept hold of my hand and led me into the hall. "Mave's down in the kitchen with your men. I came in exhausted this morning. I'm glad she caught me before I tumbled into bed."

"We should bring Cati, too," I said.

"Cati?" Nora turned to me.

"Another friend." I knocked on Cati's door.

She opened it a breath later, her hand on the hilt of her sword.

"We're going to the kitchen," I said. "Fancy joining us?"

"Sure," Cati said. "It's either that or go mad."

"Come on." Nora bustled down the hall. "I don't want Mave to think I fell asleep on the steps on my way to collect you."

"How have you been?" I asked.

"Well." Nora turned around and trailed her fingers over her pendant. "My time on the floor is coming to an end."

"You're going to do it?" I asked. "You're going to leave Ilbrea?"

Nora winked. "My clients have been very generous lately. A few more months, and I'll be ready to book passage on a ship."

"I'm happy for you," I said.

"You could sail away, too." Nora continued down the hall. "A girl like you wouldn't have to work long to earn enough coin to retire."

"I don't think Liam would fancy that," Cati said.

"Liam?" Nora spun around at the top of the stairs. "Did you finally manage to fall into each other's arms?"

"They did," Cati said. "Which made life much more pleasant for the rest of us."

Nora laughed.

"I can't say I mind it myself," I said. "Besides, I can't leave Ilbrea. I've work to do."

"Right." Nora's mirth faded a bit. "I don't suppose that will ever be done."

"Not until we finish it," I said.

"We should hurry then," Nora said. "Can't let the men eat all the good pastries."

The house was quiet as we followed Nora down the stairs and to the second story corridor.

All the doors along the hall were open, and cleaning women bustled silently about, scrubbing everything down and remaking the beds to be ready for another night's worth of customers.

Downstairs, a man in an orange jacket polished the metal sconces around the fancy dining room. He hummed softly to himself as he worked, as though he were genuinely enjoying the peace of the morning.

Nora led us through the dining room and into the massive kitchen.

Mave sat at the giant wooden table in the center of the room, sipping from a mug. Emmet, Liam, and Kely sat with her, though they paid more attention to the sheets of paper on the table than to the breakfast in front of them.

"Thank you, Nora," Mave said.

Liam turned around. A bit of relief touched his eyes when he saw me.

"Is there anything else you need, Mave?" Nora gave a little curtsy.

"I'll take you to the safe." Mave stood. "I'll be right back." The skirt of her sapphire day dress rustled as she ushered Nora out of the kitchen.

"So the necklace is real then?" Cati asked.

"Probably," I said.

Liam reached for me.

I slipped my hand into his. A bit of worry I hadn't even realized I felt melted away from my heart.

"What are all the papers?" I took a seat beside Liam.

"Something else I asked Mave about." Emmet pushed the tray of pastries toward me.

As if the sound of the metal scraping the wood had been a cue, an older gentleman in an orange jacket appeared with a tray bearing a kettle and mugs.

I pressed my hands to my legs to keep from snatching the papers out of the man's view as he poured tea for Cati and me and forced myself to study the kitchen as he refilled the men's mugs.

The place was bigger than most tilk-owned houses. Five iron stoves stood along the back wall, with a massive fireplace on one end of the room and a sink a person could bathe in on the other.

I kept my gaze fixed on the sink as the man walked away.

"Do you think it's safe to be looking at anything in a place like this?" Cati whispered after the door closed behind him. "If it's to do with our people, shouldn't we be more careful with the information?"

"We have to trust Mave's judgment," Liam said.

"And none of this can be tracked to us." Emmet spread out the line of papers.

They were all names of towns and columns of numbers.

"What is it?" I asked.

"More manifests," Liam said. "Tracking shipments of supplies to troops."

"The Guilds have to keep their soldiers fed," Emmet said. "That means shipping provisions to their camps."

"How did Mave get these?" I pulled the papers closer to study the numbers.

"She wasn't very clear on how she'd been stealing them," Emmet said. "I convinced her it would be worth keeping an eye on the manifests before I started for Lygan Hall in the fall. How she's been doing it is her own business."

"And has it been worth Mave's trouble?" Cati sipped her tea.

"I'm not sure yet," Liam said. "There are more supplies going south than what we've seen before."

"Not surprising for this time of year," Emmet said. "Winter is kinder down there. The soldiers will fare better, and the taxes will be collected sooner."

"It's also closer to Brien territory," I said. "I've never even heard of some of these towns. I've no chivving clue where in Ilbrea they might be."

"Neither do I," Emmet said. "We need a more detailed map."

"Does Mave have one?" Cati pushed the tray of pastries toward me.

"Mave's concerns rarely move past the walls of Frason's Glenn," Emmet said.

My fingers hovered over a berry-filled pastry before I chose a fluffy, glazed roll.

"I can go find a map today," Emmet said.

"Do you really think anyone is going to believe that's a brilliant plan?" I asked.

689

"I know the city," Emmet said.

"You also have a chivving awful temper and a habit of setting things on fire." I bit into my sweet breakfast. "Let's not hand the Guilds the Demon's Torch."

"Can Mave get a map for us?" Kely asked. "It wouldn't be too odd a thing for her to want."

"The sort of map we'd need would have to come from the Guilds," Emmet said. "Someone of Mave's standing might get looked at twice for wanting such a thing."

"I can go," Liam said. "I've got the coin. I'll just buy one."

"If it shouldn't be me, it shouldn't be you," Emmet said. "Not after the way we left Frason's Glenn last time we were here."

"Nora could do it." I set my pastry down. "She's planning on sailing off soon. Mave's girls are known to leave Frason's Glenn once they've earned enough coin. No one would bat an eye at Nora wanting a decent map if she's choosing where she wants to go once her time here is done."

"It's better than them wondering how a random tilk would have enough coin to buy a map as detailed as the one we'll need," Emmet said.

"Should I stop her before she goes to sleep?" I asked.

"Let her rest," Liam said. "Mave's girls aren't known for being out in the morning hours."

"Is all of Ilbrea like this?" Kely asked.

"Most of it's farms and places where people barely survive," Liam said. "Most tilk spend their lives avoiding the Guilds' notice. There are a lot of towns like Lenton and a handful of cities like Frason's Glenn."

"But as for places like this"—Emmet pointed to the row of stoves along the wall—"most brothels are pits where no human should be forced to survive."

"Do the girls…" Kely said. "Do they want to be here?"

"The allure of a woman can drive a king to his knees," Mave said. "There is power in beauty. There are fortunes to be made by women bold enough to use their natural born gifts on men. And vengeance can be won with a smile if you know how to draw a man's attention away from the blade at his throat."

"I meant no offense." Kely's face turned a bright scarlet.

"Of course not," Mave said. "But a man who would kill to protect his domain should not be so willing to judge a woman who spreads her legs to defend hers."

"We need a small favor, Mave." Emmet stood, blocking Kely from Mave's view.

"I thought I was already doing you several large favors," Mave said.

"I'd like Nora to come out for an errand with me when she wakes up." I stood beside Emmet.

"And what does this errand involve, little bird?" Mave asked.

"Nothing much," I said. "I've only got to find a map."

40

We spent the morning in Mave's parlor.

It seemed strange that there wasn't anything for us to be doing. But we had to let Mave's shadows do their work, and keeping quiet was the best thing for all of us.

I sat beside Liam in the parlor, enjoying the feel of his leg against mine as we pored through months of odd papers. Kely copied things out onto pages we could keep. Cati prowled by the door, as though hoping paun would burst through and she might get to stab them.

Emmet had disappeared with Mave again.

Lunch had come and gone by the time Nora woke up, heard about our errand, and declared me unfit to be seen walking through town with her.

It took a full two hours of her primping and prodding before she considered me a decent walking companion.

She twisted my black hair into a fancy knot on the back of my head and dressed me in a deep purple gown that looked too much like Regan's colors for my comfort.

I didn't like my neck being so exposed. It felt too vulnerable, like teeth might tear through my throat at any moment.

The normal paints weren't good enough either. Apparently, if one had to deal with paun during daylight hours, deeper hues had to be used for the eyes and lips.

She gave me a coat that buttoned tightly around my waist so the thick fabric didn't obscure the curves of my body.

Finally, Nora circled me for a few minutes, judging everything from my newly polished boots to my freshly twisted hair.

"I think you'll pass." Nora bit her bottom lip. "We'll tell them you're new. Just joined Mave's family."

"Is anyone going to ask?" I said. "We're going out for a map."

"Oh, little bird, I forget how innocent you are sometimes." Nora took my hands in hers. "I'm rather notorious in Frason's Glenn, and I always dress the part. A girl as pretty as you would already be known to our regular customers. The only way they wouldn't recognize the stunning beauty with the raven hair would be if she were new, or an imposter."

"Then a new member of Mave's family it is." I pressed my face into an easy smile like Nora's.

"Come on, then." Nora led me out of her room and down the hall.

There were ten girls in the room by the stairs. Some reading, some eating. None of them had painted on their armor for the night.

"Where are you going?" a girl with chestnut ringlets asked.

"None of your business, Lolli." Nora winked and led me down the stairs.

The women had finished cleaning the bedrooms on the second floor. The scent of fresh lavender filled the air.

I wondered how long the scent would last before being consumed by the night.

Cold air cut through my borrowed coat as we stepped outside. The debris of the previous evening's frivolities had been cleared out of Mave's square. Men in orange coats were already rolling out fresh barrels of ale for the new night of merriment.

"Do people ever get tired of it?" I asked.

"Of working for Mave?" Nora said. "Absolutely."

"Of being a customer," I said. "Of coming here and drinking and dancing and paying for a place in someone's bed."

Nora didn't answer until she'd led me out of Mave's square.

"Some do." She steered me down a street I'd never followed before. "The young ones get married. The old ones can't manage it anymore. Some spend all their coin and can't afford to come back. But we're trained to keep them addicted to Mave's. The pleasure. The noise. We make it irresistible."

"Mave's a very smart woman."

"Why do you think the Guilds have never tried to shut her down?" Nora winked. "Imagine what she might get up to if the brothel weren't occupying her mind."

Pride burst through my chest as I followed Nora past the shops selling lace and gold finery.

Mave was doing more than running her business. She was working against the Guilds, and they didn't know it. A bit of beauty and seduction, and the paun had missed the rebellion right under their noses.

"Mave's chivving brilliant," I whispered to myself.

Nora led me through smaller, sleepy streets and thoroughfares packed with people. The closer we got to the Guilded part of the city, the more people recognized her. Or if not Nora herself, then at least the life she represented.

Women whispered behind their hands. Men stopped and bowed or gawked. Mothers pulled their little ones away from our path, and children openly stared.

"Is it always like this?" I asked.

Nora took a moment, smiling at one of the gawking men and waving at two of the whispering women. "It is. I suppose it should bother me. Maybe in another lifetime, it would have. But really, it's all just an excellent advertisement for Mave. That man won't be able to think about anything but me for the rest of the day. The women will complain to their husbands about me parading on the streets—"

"—and their husbands will find their way to Mave's before the end of the night." A strange sense of power filled me as a man nearly tipped over as he bowed to me.

"Exactly," Nora said. "Sometimes, I go out for things I don't even need just to make sure I do a speedy night's business."

"You are rather brilliant, you know."

"I do know." Nora grinned.

We turned onto a street filled with paun, and every bit of my joy and curiosity vanished.

A newly built office stood on the corner. The golden star of the Guilds hung above the twisting symbol of the sailors' wind.

A pack of healers in red robes streamed out of their building. None of them hurried like they were actually going to care for the tilk of the city, who paid taxes for the privilege of being able to pay coin they couldn't afford for the healers' services.

Soldiers in black uniforms patrolled the streets, but the few tilk I could see didn't seem afraid of them. It was like they trusted the soldiers. Like they believed the soldiers' swords and spears were meant to protect them.

Hatred mixed with revulsion in my gut.

Nora looped her arm through mine. "Smile, darling. A sour face does not win men's hearts."

I let out a shuddering breath and smiled.

"Good girl," Nora said. "Do not give in to your anger. All it does is take a bit of your power and hand it to your enemies. Our battle will be won with sweet whispers, not violence or shouting."

We passed a shop selling the colorful robes each of the Guilds wore. And a proper tea shop where the paun sat at pretty tables, nibbling on sweets.

I wondered how hard it would be to light the tea shop on fire.

I am Emmet's sister.

Finally, at the far end of the road, a white building with a golden seven-pointed star came into view.

There were more tilk waiting outside the scribes' shop than there had been at any of the other businesses. I studied each of the patrons, trying to reason through what they were there for.

The older man with tears on his face probably wanted funeral papers so he could be allowed to bury a relative. Maybe even his wife.

The young man who shifted his weight like he wanted nothing more than to bolt probably needed marriage papers. Sweat slicked his brow. I couldn't tell if he was just nervous about getting married or if he was terrified the scribe might reject his request. If the girl he hoped to wed was already pregnant, the scribe's rejection would be as good as a death sentence for her and the child.

There were a few women with newborns in their arms. They'd probably come to pay for the right to name their children.

If I had been on my own, if I hadn't needed to get the map for Liam, I might have stood in the street, screaming at the people to save their coins. The scribes had no right to demand the tilks' hard-earned money for the most basic of rights. Getting the dead into the ground should not take food out of the mouths of the living.

I would have been whipped for it. Maybe even hanged.

But seeing that line of sheep waiting to walk into the wolves' den and pay the beasts for allowing them to live made me ill.

"You've forgotten your smile, darling." Nora squeezed my arm as we breezed past the tilk to the front of the line.

"I hope you don't mind." Nora spoke to no one in particular. "I am in a bit of a hurry."

No one argued as she pushed open the door and led me into the scribes' shop.

It was not what I'd expected.

I'd never been in the proper selling part of a scribes' shop. The place seemed too clean and cheerful to cause so much harm to the common folk of Ilbrea.

Six scribes sat at desks flanking the center of the room. Each scribe wore a pristine white robe. Each had a tilk in front of them.

"I understand your neighbor wants to sell you their land," the nearest scribe spoke to an older woman, "but it's for the Guilds to decide if that land can actually be for sale."

"But he can't pay his taxes," the older woman said. "I can pay. I'll pay for the land, and I'll pay for his taxes. Doesn't that work out best for everyone?"

Not when the Guilds could steal the land and sell it to you themselves.

"Can I help you?" A young girl in white robes hurried up to us. "I'm afraid you'll have to wait for scribes' services. We're rather busy today."

"I don't need papers drawn." Nora's gaze slid up and down the girl, as though she were creating a list of all the things the girl should do to be prettier.

Nora gave a tight smile, and the girl blushed, her shoulders drawing up to her ears as though her greatest wish was to be able to hide from Nora's appraising gaze.

"I'm here to buy a map," Nora said.

"Right," the girl said. "We have plenty of maps straight from the Map Makers Guild." She gestured toward a rack on the wall that had been packed with scrolls.

"I need a better map than those apprentice-made copies," Nora laughed.

"They are serviceable," the girl said.

"I want a real map," Nora said. "One with all the villages and backwater holes drawn out in exquisite detail. Now fetch your head scribe, and I'll have him find one for me."

"What would you want with a map that grand?" A man walked through a door in the back of the shop. He had a spattering of gray in his hair but hardly any lines on his face.

"Owen." Nora beamed as she swept toward him. "I was hoping I'd see you today."

"There is that possibility when coming to my office," Owen said.

"As there is a possibility of seeing me if you come to mine." Nora held her hand out to Owen.

He took her hand and kissed it.

"I need a map," Nora said. "A wonderfully detailed map of Ilbrea."

"This way then." Owen placed Nora's hand on his elbow. "And your friend may come as well."

"Thank you," Nora said. "Ena is very new. I want to be sure she meets all the best people in Frason's Glenn."

Owen took a moment, staring at my face, then my waist, then my chest. "I am always pleased to make the acquaintance of such a beautiful woman."

"Thank you, scribe." I gave him a nod.

"Follow me." Owen led us through a door off to the side of the front room and into a space filled with golden sunlight.

A tilted worktable took up the center of the space. Rows of shelves lined the wall, books and scrolls filling every inch. A smaller shelf filled with bottles of ink stood beside the table. I squinted at the colors, at the way the light filtered through the pigments. Half were decently made. The other half were a cheap chivving mess that weren't worth writing with.

I bit back my laugh.

"You haven't told me why you'd want such a map," Owen said.

"Does it matter?" Nora asked.

"This sort of product is usually bought by traders plotting out new routes through Ilbrea or collectors who want something to delight their guests." Owen went to a shelf filled with scrolls.

"Are those the only people allowed to purchase such things?" Nora asked.

"Of course not." Owen selected a scroll from the stack. "But I wouldn't be doing my duty to the Guilds if I didn't ask why one of Mave's girls would spend her hard-earned coin on such a thing."

"Can you keep a secret?" Nora leaned forward against the table. Her breasts looked like they might spill out of her coat if she took too deep a breath.

Owen didn't hide his delight at seeing the tops of her tits. "Of course."

"I'm leaving Mave's," Nora said.

"What?" Owen wrinkled his brow.

"Not right now," Nora said. "But hopefully within the year. I want to go someplace else. Somewhere I've never been. I want the map so I can see what my choices are."

"You can't really mean to leave Frason's Glenn," Owen said.

Nora bit her bottom lip and looked up at him through the thick veil of her lashes. "I want to build a real life before I grow old. I don't think that's possible in this city. Please, don't tell anyone. If all my visitors abandon me, I'll never have the coin to go. But I think it would be nice, to have a home. To meet a man and not ask for coin before he comes to my bed."

Owen tipped her chin up and looked straight into her eyes. "Your departure will be a great loss for Frason's Glenn. But I promise, I will keep my grief to myself."

"Thank you," Nora whispered.

Their gaze stayed locked for a moment before Owen looked to the scroll in his hand.

"I believe this should suit your needs." He carefully unrolled the parchment on his worktable.

It was less a map and more a work of art.

All of Ilbrea had been laid out in exquisite detail. The rivers had been drawn in perfect blue, with variations in the ink that seemed to imply how quickly the current would run. The capital city of Ilara had the waves of the Arion Sea to one side and a towering cliff face to the other. The King's palace had been drawn in gold that seemed to glitter in the sunlight.

I followed the line of the mountain road south toward Harane. It wasn't just dots marking each of the small villages along the way. Each place had its own tiny image.

For Harane, a cluster of shadows had been drawn packed together with barely any shading outside the village, like whoever had drawn the map had known the people of Harane had built their homes close together as though they believed being near their fellow tilk would somehow keep them safe.

"What do you think of it?" Owen looked to me.

"I…" I swallowed my need to scream and pressed a smile onto my face. "I didn't know a map could be so beautiful. Did you draw it?"

Owen gave a little chuckle and stepped forward to take my hand.

Revulsion wound up my spine as his skin touched mine.

"The maps are created solely by the Map Makers Guild," Owen said. "They are not drawn by hand, but through the magic granted them by the Sorcerers Guild."

"They're drawn by magic?" A shiver shook my shoulders.

Owen kissed the back of my hand. "There is no other way for such exquisite detail to be obtained."

"Of course," I said. "I suppose I must seem a bit naïve to you."

"A bit." Owen smiled. The expression wasn't cheerful, more like the slitch had spotted his prey. "You're new at Mave's?"

"Yes," I said. "I've only just arrived. Nora is being very kind, showing me around the city."

Owen stepped closer to me. "And have you begun your work on the floor?" He trailed his fingers down the side of my neck.

My fingers burned as they longed to reach the knife hidden in my boot.

"Not yet," Nora said. "Mave has a bit more training to do with Ena before she's ready for the floor."

"Pity." Owen ran his thumb along the line of my chin. "I've been meaning to stop by and have no plans for this evening."

"Are you saying I'm not good enough for you?" Nora asked. "You've never seemed displeased with my services before."

"No." Owen let go of me and turned to Nora with a lust in his eyes that brought bile to my throat. "But it's hard to find an evening with someone so coveted."

"What if I were to set aside a whole night just for you?" Nora ran her finger along Owen's chin just as he had done to me. "I wonder what we might get up to if we had so much time to ourselves."

Owen took a shaky breath. "I'll be there as soon as the sun begins to fade."

"Prefect." Nora kissed his cheek and lingered for a moment, as though enjoying his masculine scent.

"Now, how much for my map, Owen?" She asked. "Even a night with you won't stop me from planning my future."

"Consider it a gift," Owen said. "In anticipation of our time together."

"I can't accept." Nora blushed and looked at the beautiful map. "You know Mave's rules, you'll have to pay her."

"I'll pay her." Owen kissed the side of Nora's neck. "I only hope that your owning such a beautiful thing will make you consider me when you're filling the nights you have left in Frason's Glenn."

"Oh, Owen." Nora grazed her lips against his. "You're too kind."

"And perhaps Ena will see the good that comes from having friends in high positions when she begins her time on the floor," Owen said.

"I have learned so much from Nora. I promise, I will not forget my lessons." That smile I did not have to fake.

41

There was a certain beauty to daily life in Mave's home. The quiet of the morning, the peace of the afternoon, the railing frivolity of the nighttime. I could see how a girl could spend years of her life under Mave's protection. Safe from their family, sheltered from the Guilds. In a constant trance of beauty and music, where the worries of the tilk could not touch them.

I saw Owen arrive at Mave's the night after he gave Nora the map. I watched him from the window of Mave's parlor. He'd traded his white robes for a fine coat only a paun could afford, like leaving his Guilded uniform behind would somehow keep him from staining his station by rolling about with a whore.

I burrowed deep into Liam's arms as Owen disappeared into the house, and I tried not to picture him running his paun hands all over my friend.

We spent four days at Mave's, studying the beautiful chaos, trying to plan our next step, waiting for Mave's shadows to bring us any news of the traitor.

I'd started to lose hope of ever finding the filth.

But one of the shadows managed to dive deep enough to drag me into the darkness.

42

I'm not sure how long I'd been staring at the place on the map where I knew Marten should be.

The road we'd traveled to reach Marten was still on the map. Towns farther west of Marten proved that section of Ilbrea hadn't just been overlooked.

But Marten itself was missing.

Liam, Emmet, Mave—none of them had a decent explanation for why the town had been erased. But it had. The paun had wiped away the place, just as they'd wiped out the people.

I did not believe the Guilds cared enough about the Massacre of Marten to feel guilt. But hiding the atrocity was the only reason I could find for the paun to pretend the place did not exist.

A knock sounded on the study door.

"Just a moment." Liam didn't hurry as he carefully re-rolled the map and slid the parchment back into its leather tube.

Cati slid the tube out of sight as Kely and Emmet stacked up all our papers and tucked them into a leather satchel.

I sat on the fainting couch and watched them work.

"Come in," Liam said.

Mave entered.

I'd opened my mouth to ask why she'd bothered knocking before I saw the young boy trailing behind her.

"What a lovely afternoon." Mave walked to the window and looked out over the square.

"It is," Liam said. "Thank you for allowing us to enjoy it from your study."

"This is Coll." Mave gestured for the boy to step forward.

Coll bowed to us. His clothes and face were clean, his cheeks didn't have the look of a boy who hadn't been fed, but there was something about him that felt neglected. Like the child truly had been left in the shadows to fend for himself.

"Coll has been listening in all sorts of corners," Mave said. "Tell them what you found for me."

"Yes, ma'am." Coll bowed again. "I was tailing Lolli—"

"Tailing?" I said. "Lolli is one of the girls here."

"I always send a shadow after my girls when they travel to private clients' homes," Mave said. "If something goes wrong and one of my girls is in danger, I don't want to wait until morning to find out. Isn't that right, Coll?"

"Yes, ma'am." Coll bowed for a third time. "I was following Lolli. Climbed up on the kitchen roof to stay out of the way and watch for trouble. I heard the cooks talking when they went out back to sneak a drink. The man Lolli visited has been getting in good with the Guilds. Feeding them information about where the bandits in the east are. He'll be sitting with the city heads soon if he keeps it up. The cooks were complaining about how much more fancy company he's been seeing. They don't like having to prepare for that many guests."

"What's the man's name?" Liam asked.

"Edgar Coburn," the boy said.

"Thank you, Coll," Mave said. "Now go to the kitchen and tell them I said you could have two pieces of cake and a portion of meat."

The boy's eyes lit up as he gave a quick bow and dodged out of the room like he hadn't had a meal in weeks.

Mave gave a soft laugh as the boy's footsteps faded away. "I pay the children to watch my girls. I give them treats if they bring me any decent information. I find it works better that way with children. The immediacy of cake makes their ears sharper than the promise of extra coin."

"It'll be worth a lot more than a basket of treats if this information is good," Emmet said.

"What do you know about Edgar Coburn?" Liam asked.

"He's rich in money and poor in friends," Mave said. "The man is abrasive to the point that most avoid him when they can. Coburn runs a booming shipping trade. He'd have gotten a seat on the city council already if he were better at dealing with his peers."

"The city council?" I sat forward on the couch. "Are the people in Frason's Glenn allowed to rule themselves?"

"Of course not." Mave sat beside me. "The council is only a pack of rich men sitting around trying to seem important. They decide things like what to request the Guilds undertake with the tax money—maintaining the city wall, building a new dock by the river. They write up requests and send them to the Guilds. The Guilds are still in control. They just let the council pretend to have a bit of a say to keep the rich from trying to stand against them."

"And Coburn is trying to win his place by feeding them information about us," Cati said. "I think a nice knife to the gut is in order for him."

"We need to know where he's been getting his information first," Liam said.

"You don't think he's the Hayes contact?" I asked.

"I don't see how he could be," Mave said. "A man like Coburn isn't easy to access. It would take time to earn his trust. There's a step between the Hayes and him. I would guess the intermediary is the greater danger to the clans."

"What's the best way to get to him?" Emmet asked.

"Get to him?" Mave smoothed out her skirt.

"I need a quiet place for a quick word," Emmet said. "Does he have an office he travels to regularly? Any odd habits that might leave him vulnerable?"

"Coburn has no regular schedule I know of," Mave said. "He has yet to be placed on the council, so he doesn't attend their meetings. He maintains his fortune by shipping goods to the south, but I doubt he really knows much about the day-to-day running of his business. I certainly can't see him going to the river docks."

"Any chance of our nabbing him at a gathering?" Liam asked.

"He would have to be invited to one," Mave said. "The man isn't popular. If he were, he wouldn't have had to resort to buying Black Blood secrets to impress the Guilds. Passing information to the paun is risky at the best of times. There is always the chance of the Guilds deciding you know too much for your own good. Then a quick visit from a sorcerer and you'll never be heard from again. Or worse, he could pass on bad information and face the pauns' ire."

"How many of our people could have been saved if Coburn knew how to smile and make friends?" Cati said.

"The traitor would have found someone else willing to take the Hayes' information," Liam said. "As long as the Hayes were willing to betray the clans, the outcome would have been the same."

"But the one buying the information might have been easier to get to." Cati paced in front of the fireplace.

"We'll have to go into his home," Emmet said. "If Coll could get onto the kitchen roof without being noticed, it shouldn't be too difficult to sneak in."

"I can do it," I said.

"No—"

"I'm the best climber," I said. "If someone's got to try and get through a window, it should be me."

"And what would you do when you got in?" Emmet said. "I doubt you'd be able to trick Coburn into giving you information."

"I could teach her a few knife tricks," Cati said.

"I don't think climbing in the window and trying to take Coburn by surprise would be the best idea, no matter who made the attempt." Mave held up a hand to silence us all. "If Coburn managed to escape or caused a stir and called for his staff, you'd risk getting caught."

"And risk Coburn slipping away and going into hiding," Liam said. "If he warned his source we were hunting for them, we'd be left with nothing."

"Then what do you suggest?" Emmet asked.

"I've spent years prying information from the laxe of this city," Mave said. "There is no need to reinvent the method now. I'll send Coburn a message. I have a new girl I think he'd like to meet. He'll accept. Edgar has never been one to resist temptations of the flesh. We send Ena in."

"Absolutely not," Emmet said.

"Once she has Coburn in a position he cannot flee," Mave pressed on, "you and Liam can join her for the questioning."

"This is how you normally do things?" Kely's face had gone a sallow white.

"When discretion is necessary. If I don't mind rumors of disappearances sweeping through the city, I take my marks from their homes and they never return." Mave smiled placidly at Kely. "But until we know who has been feeding Coburn information, we can't risk anyone knowing he's been questioned. Unless I'm wrong in thinking Coburn is the less important of the two links."

"And once we've questioned him," I said, "we can't just let him walk around the city. He'll know you sent me."

"You can't actually be considering going," Emmet said. "Liam, put an end to this madness."

Liam stared down at his hands for a long moment. I was jealous of his palms. I wanted to be able to look into his eyes and try to riddle through where his thoughts were leading him.

"You won't send one of your own girls?" Liam asked.

"I'm already allowing you to be tied to me." Mave stood. "My hospitality can't be stretched much further."

"I can do it," I said. "It's just a matter of trapping him so it's safe for you to join me."

"I'll go," Cati said.

"As much as I admire your ferocity, you'd never make it past Coburn's front door," Mave said. "You reek of predator."

"Liam, please," I said. "I want to help. I need to be useful. Do not let your fear for me diminish my worth."

"Ena will go in." Liam looked to Emmet. "You and I will both be ready to join her."

43

The rustling of my own skirt drove me mad as I made my way through the darkened streets of Frason's Glenn. The sound seemed as though it might call the paun toward me just the same as if I had been ringing a chivving dinner bell. Only the hope that Coburn might find the sound as threatening as I did made all the layers of fancy fabric seem worth wearing.

I turned down a narrow alley. The stench that clung to the sides of the stone houses burned my nose. I hovered a gloved hand over my mouth, trying to keep sour from springing up into my throat.

The street beyond the alley was well lit and packed with houses that all seemed too large to be meant for one family.

I had traveled the path to Coburn's earlier that day to be sure I would know my way in the dark.

In the bright afternoon light, there had been children running between houses as they played and proud mothers tutting at their disobedient babes while gossiping with their neighbors.

The night had shooed all those people away.

Now, men walked alone, some stumbling home, others hurrying away, as though eager to begin their night of debauchery. The women all walked on the arm of a man. Most of them glared at me as I passed.

I smiled back at them.

I do not need a man's protection to survive an Ilbrean city.

There had been a time not long before when I wouldn't have been able to defend myself. I had Cati to thank for my lack of fear as I turned down another alley and onto a street where the stenches of normal life would not have been welcome.

The fancy laxe homes all had wide stone staircases sweeping up to their front doors. Trees and flowers had been planted in front of the houses, as though the owners wanted to imply the grounds of an estate even though they were packed into a city. Lampposts with metal swirls arching around their flames made sure the grandeur of the street was not lost to the shadows.

My aim was a house built of pale stone. Reaching four stories high, there were even windows peeking out from the roof. An iron gate stood between the street and the low bushes that ran along the front of the house.

Lanterns flanked the front door, and lights beamed into the night, pouring out of every window. I couldn't even begin to imagine having so much coin I'd be willing to waste it on keeping empty rooms lit.

My feet stopped moving when I reached the front gate. Just froze, like they'd decided they didn't fancy our plan. I searched myself for fear. I listened to the sounds carrying through the darkness for any hint of attack.

There was nothing that should have made me stop. Only my loathing for the fancy house and the man who lived inside.

I took a deep breath and forced my feet to carry me to the front door, my chivving skirts rustling around me all the while.

The polished wooden door swung open before I had time to knock.

An older woman in a gray dress locked her gaze right onto my eyes. "Good evening. Mister Coburn has been waiting for your arrival."

"I'm sure he has." I gave the woman a knowing smile.

Her eyes widened, but she kept them locked on mine. "He's waiting for you in the upstairs parlor. This way."

She looked away from me, and her shoulders relaxed, as though she'd just completed a dreaded task.

A set of polished wooden stairs that matched the front door led up to the second story.

"This is a beautiful house," I said. "You must be very proud to care for it."

The woman's shoulders tensed right back up. "I am honored to serve as the Coburn family's housekeeper."

"Family?" I said. "Mister Coburn doesn't live here alone?"

"His wife and children will be kept to the third floor for the evening," the housekeeper said. "You will have no dealings with them. As far as you're concerned, Mister Coburn is alone."

"Of course." Anger wrapped its way from my stomach to my throat. "I am capable of being discreet."

"I'm sure that's a requirement in your profession."

"Yours as well," I said as we reached the second story and turned down a corridor lined with paintings. "We're not so different, you and I. We both tend to things that rightfully belong to others."

The housekeeper's shoulders crept even higher.

"I'm capable of doing my job without blushing," I said. "Can the same be said of you?"

The housekeeper said nothing as she stopped in front of a set of double doors. She took a deep breath before raising her hand to knock.

"Best to keep everyone as far from here as you can," I whispered. "I'm not known for being quiet as I go about my duties. I wouldn't want to startle anyone with modest sensibilities."

The housekeeper swayed as the door opened. "Mister Coburn, your guest has arrived." Her voice nigh on squeaked as she spoke.

Coburn stepped into view.

He might have been handsome if there were a good heart inside his broad chest. His sandy blond hair and beard had been exquisitely groomed, as though he'd tried to don his own sort of armor before greeting me.

"Thank you." Coburn's words were clipped. "You're dismissed."

The housekeeper hurried down the corridor and out of sight.

I looked up at Coburn.

He was nearly as tall as Emmet. His height made it quite obvious when he peeked down at the tops of my breasts.

"Please do come in." Coburn bowed me into his study.

Flames crackled in the fireplace. That was where the homey feel of the space ended.

In the center of the room, a table had been laid out with two unopened bottles of frie, a bottle of chamb, and berries that had no business being fresh outside of summer. An ornately carved wooden desk sat on one side of the room, with bookcases tucked behind, surrounding the window that looked out over the alley behind the house. On the other side of the room, a four-poster bed with deep red blankets waited for Coburn's evening vices.

I hate this man.

"Please, make yourself comfortable." Coburn bowed me to a chair beside the table.

I stared into the fire as I pulled off my gloves and unfastened the few buttons on the front of my coat. I laid my things across the back of the chair before turning to Coburn.

He drank in every curve of my body before smiling. "What's your name?"

"Ena." I turned away from him before he could ask me any more questions. "The other girls have told me about you." I wandered toward the fireplace.

"And what warnings have they given?"

"No warnings. Just interesting little things a new girl ought to know."

Glass clinked behind me.

I took a deep breath, straining against the laces that kept my chest pressed up near my chin.

"Why don't you visit us at Mave's?"

"I prefer to keep my business private." He reached in front of me with a glass of chamb. "And I don't like sharing. I've bought you for a whole night. I don't want to spend the time I've paid good money for in a tiny room they'll be trying to get me out of so the next poor bastard can have a run at you."

I sipped my chamb. "I suppose it's good you can afford such a luxury then."

"You're very new, aren't you?" Coburn trailed his fingers along my neck and across the tops of my breasts.

"Does it show?"

He stuck his thumb down the front of my bodice, running it across the skin I'd kept hidden.

I kept my gaze locked on his, refusing to allow my anger to betray me.

"Most girls would either go straight for the frie on the table or try to lead me right to the bed." Coburn stepped closer, moving his hand from my chest to my waist.

"Let's just say I'm new enough to Mave's not to have seen a bed in a study before."

"As I said, I like to keep my business private."

I rose up on my toes and let my cheek graze his as I whispered in his ear. "It's a good thing I like keeping secrets."

Coburn kissed the side of my neck and pressed his hips against me.

"Are the doors locked?" I gave a shuddering sigh.

"No one will bother us." He licked the tops of my breasts.

"I'll feel safer." I took a little step away from him.

He took a step toward me.

I let him wrap his arms around me and gripped his hair as I pulled him down so I could kiss him. I kept my lips close to his as I whispered, "Please. I don't want our time to be interrupted."

He kissed me again, plunging the tip of his tongue into my mouth before stepping away. "I want you to be reckless. If locking a door will let you enjoy our time, then so be it."

He set his glass on the table and walked to the door.

I picked up a bottle of frie and followed behind him, my skirt rustling like a chivving banshee.

"You had better be worth all this trouble." He turned the lock on the doors.

I swung the bottle for the back of his head. Pain shot up my arm as the glass made contact with his skull.

He swayed as the bottle cracked and frie dripped onto the floor.

I dropped the bottle and pulled my knife from my boot, ready to stab the slitch rather than let him touch me again.

He fell to the floor with a thud.

I held my breath, waiting for the housekeeper to come running to see what the noise had been. Or worse, for one of Coburn's children to come looking for their father.

But the house stayed silent.

I checked the lock on the doors before running to the window that faced the back of the house.

The disuse of winter had jammed the window in place.

"Come on, you stupid, chivving wood."

The window slid up, letting a wave of cold air sweep into the study.

I ran quietly back to Coburn. He lay still on the floor, blood leaking from his head where I'd hit him.

I pulled a length of thin rope from my pocket and tied his wrists behind him before even checking to see if he was alive. I snatched a fancy napkin from the table and shoved it into his mouth. Then I pulled up my chair and sat beside him, staring down at him with my knife still gripped in my hand.

My heart thumped against my ribs as I waited. It would have been so much simpler to just slice his throat and be done with it. If I left some of my petticoats behind, I'd even be able to slip out the window and climb to the alley below.

A faint scraping came from the back wall.

I didn't glance behind until I heard the soft thumps of boots on the floor.

Emmet reached into his bag and pulled out a coil of thick rope. He looped a hook over the windowsill and lowered the rope outside.

"Are you hurt?" Emmet glanced to me before looking back to the hook.

The metal dug into the wood as Liam began to climb.

"No. A little disgusted that a laxe who brings women into the house with his wife and children touched me, but that's all."

Liam climbed through the window and was beside me in a moment. He took my hands and drew me to my feet. "What happened? Are you all right?"

"I'm fine," I said.

"What went—"

"I didn't want him touching me," I said. "So I hit him over the head instead of waiting to corner him."

Liam kissed my forehead. "I'm sorry I sent you in here."

"Don't be." I nestled my nose next to Liam's neck and breathed in his scent. "Let's just get the information we need so we can get out of this lair."

Emmet moved a chair by the fire. It was a mark of how large Coburn was that Emmet actually had to work to carry the unconscious man. He pulled more rope from his bag and tied Coburn to the seat.

"Can I have my pouch?" I held my hand out to Emmet.

He pulled a padded leather pouch from his bag.

The smaller of the two vials I'd stored away didn't seem like it should be able to do us much good. But even just pulling the stopper wafted enough of the sharp aroma to knock away all traces of Coburn's and Liam's scents.

I held the vial beneath Coburn's nose.

Nothing happened.

I held the vial closer and gave him a hard slap on the back.

He gasped through his gag and woke with a start.

"Don't scream." Emmet held his knife right in front of Coburn's eyes. "Don't fight. If you do everything we say, you may well make it through this night alive. If you fight us, I will slit your throat." Emmet shifted his blade to Coburn's neck. "Nod if you understand."

Coburn gave a stiff nod and winced as though the pain from his skull still plagued him.

I wasn't sorry.

"I'm going pull the gag from your mouth," Liam said. "You're going to answer my questions honestly."

Coburn nodded again.

Liam removed the gag.

Coburn spat on his own floor before speaking. "However much gold you want, just tell me your price and get it over with."

"We're not here for gold," Liam said. "We're here for information. Tell me the truth, and it'll go quickly. Dare to lie, and we'll have to hurt you."

"What do you want to know?" Coburn asked.

"Who's been selling you information about the eastern mountains?" Liam said.

"What?"

"The information you've been passing to the Guilds," Liam said. "Tell me your source."

"You're out of your—"

Emmet clapped a hand over Coburn's mouth and stabbed him in the thigh.

Coburn screamed against Emmet's palm.

"Answer truthfully, and I won't hurt you again." Emmet pulled his knife from Coburn's leg before letting go of his mouth.

"My people will have heard me scream," Coburn said. "They're coming now. Run while you can."

I let out a loud, joyful laugh. "After what you paid me to come here for? Scream louder. They'll think you're having the best night of your chivving life."

"Who has been feeding you information?" Liam said. "Tell me, and we'll go."

"I've seen your faces," Coburn said. "I know you were sent by Mave. I'm not fool enough to think you'll let me live."

"I don't care who you think sent us," I said. "I don't care if you live or die. But you should care about the amount of pain you'll have to endure if you don't just tell us who you've been paying. I want to know what you've told the Guilds. You are going to tell us, even if I have to chop off your favorite plaything to make it clear how deadly serious we are."

"Look to your own house," Coburn said. "I never asked to be a part of any of this. She brought the information to me. She offered to sell it."

"Who?" I tightened my grip on the hilt of my knife.

"That chivving whore Lolli."

44

"How did she approach you?" Liam's voice was completely calm.

My mind was not.

It raced back through every chivving thing I'd said where Lolli might have been able to hear. I'd never mentioned the Black Bloods or traveling from the eastern mountains. But Emmet...we had spoken about Emmet. About him burning the square outside Mave's.

"Answer his question." Emmet lowered the tip of his knife toward Coburn's thigh.

"The girl told me someone was giving her information," Coburn said. "Things she thought it would be better for the Guilds to know, but she didn't want to get tangled up with the paun. She laid in my bed with chivving tears in her eyes and told me she knew the information was very valuable but that a girl in her position couldn't risk pulling the soldiers' notice in her direction."

"And you generously offered to take the information off her hands," Liam said.

"I offered to pay her what she deserved and take the risk of interacting with the Guilds on myself." Coburn glared at me. "Lolli knows her place and was very grateful."

"Was she grateful?" I pulled over a chair and sat opposite the filth. "Or is Lolli smarter than you give her credit for? Was she playing you like a letch of a fiddle the whole time?"

"Lolli is the only decent one among all you whores," Coburn said. "The only one with an ounce of character—"

"She played you very well." I laughed.

"What information has she given you?" Liam asked.

"I didn't keep a written chivving list."

"Pity," I said.

"You want the information," Coburn said, "torture the chivving whore."

I pointed the tip of my knife between Coburn's legs. "How we deal with Lolli and what I do to you are two separate matters. You've been asked a question. Answer, or I'll do worse than stab you in the thigh."

"There were all sorts of things." Coburn kept his gaze locked on my blade as he spoke. "Towns where bandits were going to try and steal children who belong to the Sorcerers Guild. That the children were being taken to the eastern mountains by rebels who want to overthrow the Guilds. She gave me a list of places where the rebels were getting supplies."

"And that's all?" I leaned closer to him.

The slitch's gaze actually flicked up to my breasts for a moment.

"There were other strange things." Sweat beaded on Coburn's brow. "I only passed bits of it on. I wasn't sure all of it was true."

"Tell us anyway," Liam said.

"There are sorcerers hiding in the southern end of the eastern mountains," Coburn said. "A whole horde of them, growing in strength like they're planning on fighting the Sorcerers Guild. And there are two assassins from the mountains working in Ilbrea."

"Who are they?" Emmet pressed the tip of his blade to Coburn's uninjured thigh.

"A man and a woman." Coburn raced through the words. "The man is the one they call the Demon's Torch. He tortures members of the Guilds and burns them alive. The woman poisoned soldiers, slaughtering them in the safety of their own camp. The whore said they'd both joined with the bandits and were plotting to destroy the Guilds."

"That's all she said about them?" Liam asked.

"She said they were brother and sister. That they'd come from Ilbrea and fled into the mountains to plot alongside the rebels hiding in the woods."

"Did she say where in Ilbrea the assassins had come from?" My voice came out even. I don't know how I managed it.

"Some small cact of a village, I don't know." Coburn whimpered as I slid my knife farther between his legs.

"And you told the Guilds all of this?" Liam asked.

"No," Coburn said. "I paid the whore the money for the information, but I wasn't fool enough to pass on such fairy stories. Magic does not exist outside the control of the Sorcerers Guild. If the rebels had magic of their own, they wouldn't be stealing children from Ilbrea. All that rot is lies being spread to cause trouble."

"And the assassins?" Emmet dug his knife into Coburn's thigh.

Coburn hissed in pain before speaking. "I let the Guilds know they were related and working together."

"Did you tell the Guilds where they were from?" Emmet asked.

"Give them a village but not the names of the assassins or a chivving thing about what they look like?" Coburn gave a rough laugh. "I'm not the monster you think I am. I don't want an entire village torn apart based on my actions. I'm a businessman, not a murderer. I'll not have innocent blood on my hands."

"It's too late for that." Fury and rage filled me as I leaned closer to the filth.

"When was the last time you were given information?" Liam laid a hand on my shoulder, anchoring me to something beyond my desire to gut Coburn.

"Not for months," Coburn said. "It's been wearing on my position. If the whore hadn't brought me something decent soon, I was going to have to stop paying her. The last thing she brought me was a warning to watch for the rebels near the Lir Valley. The Guilds sent an entire company there based on my word, and not a chivving thing has come of it. I can't keep risking my future if her sources have dried up."

Liam pulled on my shoulder, drawing me away from Coburn.

"Thank you for cooperating," Liam said.

Emmet didn't lift his blade from Coburn's thigh.

"I have money," Coburn said. "I will happily pay you for my safety."

"We don't want your chivving money." I stood and leveled my blade at Coburn's throat.

"I am a good man," Coburn said. "I have given information to the Guilds to protect Ilbrea. Tell me I have done wrong."

"You offered gold for your own life and never once tried to bargain for the safety of your wife and children." I pushed the words past the knot in my throat. "That would make you a beast even if I didn't know anything else about you."

I slid my blade back into the sheath hidden in the ankle of my boot.

Coburn let out a shaky breath like I had decided his fate even though Emmet still had his own knife pressed to Coburn's thigh.

I opened my little pouch and pulled out the second vial. "You're going to drink this without fighting."

"I won't." Coburn leaned as far away from me as being bound to the chair would allow.

"It'll make you sleep," I said. "When you wake up, we'll be gone. If you don't drink it so we can leave quietly, I'll have to hurt you to make you drink it. If you still refuse, I'll slit your throat."

"You're going to poison me."

"If it were poison, it would still be a better way to go than making me pick you apart with a knife." I uncorked the vial. "Hold his head."

Liam stepped behind Coburn to stand beside Emmet. He wrapped one arm around Coburn's forehead and pinned his jaw down with his free hand.

"Drink it all, and you'll never have to think of us again." I tipped the brew into Coburn's mouth.

Liam clamped Coburn's jaw shut, holding fast even as he struggled.

"Keep holding him," I said.

"Swallow." Emmet dug his blade into Coburn's thigh. "Swallow."

Coburn obeyed.

"Good," I said. "You're going to get quite sleepy. Give in to it. Fighting might make you nauseous. You wouldn't want to choke to death on your own sick."

Liam let go of Coburn's jaw, and I shoved the napkin into his mouth before the filth could speak.

None of us said anything as I pulled on my gloves and fancy coat. By the time I'd fastened my buttons, Coburn had already passed out.

"Toss him in the bed," I said.

"We can leave him in the chair," Emmet said.

"His housekeeper is a bother." I pulled back the deep red blankets that covered the bed, grateful it was my gloves and not my skin that touched the fabric. "Toss him in here, and she'll be too shy to go near him."

Emmet untied Coburn and, with Liam's help, carried him to the bed.

I tucked the slitch in so it looked like he'd passed out.

"What will Mave do to him?" I asked.

"No more than he deserves," Emmet said.

"I hope she isn't gentle," I said.

"That's never been a problem for Mave." Emmet headed back toward the window.

"Should I close it behind you?" I asked.

"Leave it open a crack," Liam said. "It might save Mave's people some time."

I tidied up the room as the men climbed out the window. Putting the chairs where they had been, placing the broken bottle of frie onto a napkin on the table, as though it had been dropped by accident and set aside for the servants to handle.

Once Emmet was down the rope, I lifted the metal hook, tossed it to him, and slid the window almost shut.

I stood quietly for a moment. I wasn't waiting for anything. I just wasn't sure what to do.

We hadn't lied to Coburn. He would live until morning. It would take Mave longer than one evening to decide what punishment he deserved. But he would be killed.

I didn't regret my part in it, but it still seemed wrong to leave him sleeping and vulnerable as the shadows came to take him away.

"It's the paun who make monsters of us all." I pressed my hand to my stone pendant hidden inside my bodice, letting the warmth of it comfort me. "It's their fault he can't be left alive."

I unlocked the doors and slipped into the hall, shutting them quietly behind me.

There was no one in the corridor.

I squared my shoulders and didn't try to quiet the rustling of my skirt as I made my way to the stairs leading down to the main entrance of the house.

I didn't hear a hint of another person until I'd reached the bottom of the steps.

"Where are you going?" The housekeeper stepped out of the shadows like she had been chivving lurking to make sure I didn't steal a painting on my way out.

"I thought you'd be happy to see me go." I gave her a coy smile. "It didn't seem like you approved of my services taking place in the house you tend to."

"The other girls don't leave so early. Is Mister Coburn"—her cheeks turned a splotchy red—"is he well?"

I tipped my head back and laughed. "He is as well as any man could hope to be and sleeping like a babe. I don't want to speak ill of the girls I work with, but it seems they've been missing a few tricks sweet Edgar truly enjoys." I sauntered close enough to the housekeeper to whisper, "I can teach you if you like."

"Out." She pointed toward the door. "Get back to your cesspit."

"Try not to wake the poor man," I said. "Or he'll be searching for another round, and I don't think his wife would fancy my particular method."

The housekeeper swayed.

I laughed as I opened the door and stepped out into the bitter cold of the night.

A few men still strolled by, but the stumblers outnumbered the sober ones.

I let out a long breath, watching the fog of it twist and grow as it whisked away the scent of Coburn's house.

I waited until the fog had faded before stepping out onto the street.

"Are you done for the night?" A man who reeked of frie lurched toward me. "I've plenty of coin if you'd like to make another house call."

I took the man's chin in my hand, keeping him from getting close enough to kiss me. "I promise you, sir, no matter how much gold you have, you can't afford me."

He stumbled as I let go of him and started on my path back to Mave's.

"I think I might have just fallen in love with you!" the man shouted after me.

"Just don't drown your heartache in any more frie," I called back.

Three men who were walking together laughed and bowed me past.

I gave them a nod and a smile, like we were all enjoying the same joke.

I didn't know if the three were actually Mave's men come to take Coburn away, or simply friends trying to fill the dark hours with secret delights.

Or perhaps it was whoever made the shadows flicker in the alley down the way. Maybe those were Mave's men, waiting for me to be well clear of the house before attacking their prey.

I searched every shadow I passed for a hint of danger or a glimpse of Emmet and Liam.

But I found no trace of anyone who knew I was more than just a girl walking alone in the darkness.

45

There are times I wish I had not trusted so easily, and a thousand mistakes I wish I could undo.

If I had never been foolish enough to tumble into a trap hidden by pretty lies, maybe I could have the comfort of blaming those who unknowingly sped our doom.

But I've used beauty to aid in murder. I know how dangerous an enemy lust can be.

I only wish that we had tumbled into the trap all at once and the fire could have consumed us in one, massive blaze.

It would have been easier to endure the flames if I had not watched others fall before me.

46

The frivolity outside Mave's was still in full force when I made it back to the square.

The dancers whirled through each other as the musicians flew from one tune to the next with barely a pause. The orange-coated men doled out ale and frie to the revelers without a hint of there being any danger or secrets lurking inside Mave's home.

I caught the eye of a few of the dancers—men winked and nodded my way—but it wasn't until I stepped up onto Mave's porch that the leering truly began.

I could feel the men's eyes on me. Feel them wondering how much a place in my bed would cost. Wondering how much joy they would find in exploring what hid beneath my clothes.

"You're new." A man wrapped his arm around my waist, pulling me onto his lap before I could make it to the door.

"I am." I forced my voice to stay cheerful even as my hands curled into fists.

"It's a wonder the beauty Mave manages to cultivate." He slid his cold hand over the tops of my breasts.

Without even thinking, I pulled my fist back to punch him.

"I thought you wanted to spend your evening with me?" The girl with the auburn hair caught my arm and wrenched me off the man's lap, sending me stumbling toward the door. "If you abandon me now, you know I'll never allow you to join me in my bed again." She sat on the man's lap and tipped his face down, planting it between her breasts. "Is that what you want, darling?"

I hurried through the door and into the dining room without listening to the man's muffled reply.

Inside, men in green vests prowled between the customers as the women outside had.

For a moment, relief flooded me, as though I'd made it out of the wolf's den and into a safe pasture. But then another arm looped around my waist.

"I'm not available for the—"

"Of course you are." A man in a green vest led me toward the stairs. "All of us are available when Mave tells us to be."

He didn't loosen his grip as he dragged me up the steps.

"If you think I'm going to strip off my clothes, you'll end up with a knife in your gut," I whispered.

"Well, Emmet Ryeland already threatened me with worse if I didn't get you straight to him as soon as I spotted you. So smile and don't make this harder on me."

I relaxed in his grip as we made it to the second floor, but he didn't stop at the door to Mave's parlor.

"Where am I supposed to meet Emmet?" I asked. "I'm happy to go on my own."

"I'll escort you," the green-vested man said.

He led me to the very end of the hall but turned just before the narrow door that led to the upper floors, stopping in front of one of the bedrooms used by guests.

"My brother would not ask me to meet him in there." I wriggled free of the man's grip.

"You don't know enough to be sure where I'm leading you," the man said. "Mave's secrets aren't to be bandied about, so come quietly before I have to toss you over my shoulder and play the brut."

"You could try. I doubt you'd survive it."

"Don't count too much on your own skill." He opened the door to the bedroom. "Emmet has asked me to bring you to him. Do you think I'm foolish enough to anger Emmet Ryeland?"

I stepped into the doorway and peeked inside the room. The bed was still made, the two lanterns glowed brightly, and the long mirror on the sidewall was perfectly polished. Music and laughter poured in through the lace-curtained window that overlooked the square. A cheer pounded through the glass as the musicians began a new song.

I checked all the corners before stepping inside and letting the man close the door behind us.

"Where's my brother?" I pulled my knife from my boot before the man could answer me.

"You're worse than the other girl." He stomped a strange rhythm on the floor.

"What other girl?" I tightened my grip on my knife.

"The one who wears pants and threatened me with a sword." He stepped away from the patch of ground he'd stomped on. "I would do anything to help Mave in her work, but I can't honestly say I like being threatened with gutting in Mave's own home. Back up a bit."

"What?" The front of my skirt shifted as a section of the floor began to rise. I leapt away, pressing my back against the wall.

"I was just trying to preserve your modesty." The man shrugged.

The oddly shaped bit of floor continued to tilt, swinging slowly open like a trapdoor. Only the hatch wasn't cut into a normal square. Instead, the planks were all different lengths, making a jagged pattern on two of the edges that had blended in perfectly with the rest of the floor.

"I couldn't see the door at all," I said.

"That's the point."

Another man, this one dressed in normal tilk clothes, carefully lifted the door the rest of the way open and leaned it gently against the side of the bed, as though trying not to make a sound.

"Down you get." The man in the green vest pointed into the hole.

"Are Emmet and Liam down there?" I asked the man who'd opened the door.

The man nodded.

"Right." I squared my shoulders, trying to convince myself that Mave would not have enemies hiding in her own home.

Lolli's been living here, telling the Guilds our secrets.

"We don't have a lot of time," the man in the green vest said. "My lingering with a woman might raise some eyebrows."

I took a step toward the trapdoor.

"Knife away." The man on the stairs pointed to my blade.

Tap.

Tap. Tap. Tap.

The sound against the window kept me from arguing.

The man on the stairs planted his hands on the floor and vaulted up into the room, reaching the window before I could.

He pulled a long dagger from a sheath at his hip before shifting the lace curtain to the side.

Tap. Tap. Tap.

The sharp noise carried over the music in the square.

"What is it?" the vested man asked.

"A chivving bird," the other one answered. "Get away." He rapped his knuckles on the glass.

The bird tapped harder against the windowpane.

"Just go down. I'll deal with the chivving bird," the vested man said.

I skirted around the gaping hole in the floor to reach the window.

"I have to get back downstairs," the vested man said.

I held my hand up, blocking the lamps' reflection on the window.

A black bird tapped its black beak against the glass.

I reached down to open the window.

"What are you doing?" The man from below pressed his hand to the top of the window, stopping me from opening it.

"That isn't a normal bird," I said. "Now, you will let me open this window. Once I have the bird, maybe I'll consider climbing through your chivving trapdoor. But if you try to make me leave this room before I've gotten that bird, I will scream such bloody murder, I promise you both, my brother will come to protect me. Do either of you want to face the true wrath of Emmet Ryeland?"

"Let her get the chivving bird," the vested man said.

The other one stepped back and let me slide the window open.

I didn't know if the cleaning women opened the windows to air out the rooms or if the customers liked to clearly hear the music from the square, but the window slid easily up without any sticking from disuse. I'd only raised it six inches before the bird flew into the room and dove through the trapdoor.

"Liam." I leaned over the trapdoor and watched the bird plummet out of sight.

The stairs leading down had been built in a tight spiral. There was no way for me to know how far down they went or what might wait at the bottom.

I gathered my skirt in my free hand and jumped across the gap to the first step.

"What are you doing?" the man from below said.

"Exactly what you wanted me to." I took a deep breath, tightened my grip on my knife, and started down the stairs.

47

It took me two twists around the spiral before I was sure the steps were leading me farther down than the first floor.

A soft thud came from above as the man closed the trapdoor, dampening the noise from the square. The thumping of his footsteps followed behind me.

Part of me wanted to fight my way back up the stairs and into Mave's house. But the bird had gone down the steps. If it wasn't a message for Liam, it had to have been sent by a trueborn. If Orla or Regan had sent news, I didn't want to wait to hear it.

I didn't care if the bird had been sent to Mave or Emmet or whoever else might be below, I had to know what the message said. Word of the war, a message from the Hayes to their spy, it didn't matter.

I picked up my pace and let the stairs lead me farther down. Small lanterns had been attached to the wall, but their light did little more than make the shadows sway. The sounds from outside faded from a dull thrum to silence as the stairs dove deeper into the ground.

"Where are you, Emmet?" I whispered.

Tap. Tap. Tap. Tap.

A wooden door blocked the bottom of the steps. The bird pecked at the wood, trying to get through.

"Who have you come for?" I tried to grab the bird, but it soared up out of my reach, then dove toward the top of the door to begin tapping again.

"Let's see if we can get you to your goal." I twisted the doorknob, but the metal didn't move.

"If you had stopped long enough to listen to me at the top of the stairs"—the man descended into view—"I would have told you it's easier for everyone if I go first. Now plaster your back to the wall and let me get around you."

I leaned against the wall as the man squeezed by.

He pulled a set of keys from his pocket.

"What is this place?" I asked as he fitted a key into the lock.

The bird dove through the gap at the top of the door as soon as the man began to open it.

"Does it matter?" he asked.

"I've been trapped underground enough times to know that where I am most definitely matters."

He led me into the hall beyond the door, letting me squeeze past him before turning to lock us in.

Even in the dim lantern light, the stone sections of the hall's walls seemed to have been roughly put together, as though the builder had been chosen for their secrecy, not skill. The corridor twisted out of sight, and the low sounds of voices carried from farther ahead.

"Mave's business gives a lot of people joy," the man said, "but it also keeps a lot of people around. This is where Mave conducts her business that's better done away from crowds."

I let the man get back in front of me this time, allowing him to lead me to whatever waited for us out of sight.

There was a tone to one of the voices that carried over the rustling of my skirt, an anger that seemed to promise that unexpected guests would not be welcome.

"Who's tapping on the door?" Emmet's voice reached me before I could actually hear the bird trying to get through the wood.

The dull thunk of a lock turning came right before light splashed into the corridor.

I tried to move faster, but the man lumbered steadily onward in front of me.

"Might as well leave it open," he called. "I've got the girl."

"Ena." Footsteps thumped toward us as we turned the corner.

I peered over the man's shoulder to find my brother, sword drawn and eyes filled with anger.

"Nice to see you, Emmet." I sidled around the man to stand in front of my brother. "Next time you plan on asking someone to bring me through a trapdoor, warn me first. I nearly gutted the sap you had waiting for me."

"Well, I didn't know the one who'd betrayed the Black Bloods would be living in Mave's own house." The anger left my brother's face, replaced by sadness for a slim moment before coming back as his familiar, fiery wrath.

"Did you find her?" I didn't say Lolli's name. I wasn't sure how much my escort knew.

"Come on." Emmet led me toward the bright room.

"Should I be expecting any more coming to join the mob down here?" the man asked.

"Chivving gods and stars, I hope not," Emmet said.

The bright room at the end of the hall had been more carefully built than the tunnel leading to it. The walls weren't covered in fancy fabric, but the place screamed of Mave's work.

Lamps hung from the ceiling, and mirrors set into the brightly painted walls reflected their light.

A long table with enough food and chamb to satisfy twenty sat to one side. A shelf with books, papers, and maps sat along the back wall near a small desk. There was even a fainting couch covered in fine red upholstery.

But all the people in the room were gathered around a wooden seat, which had been fitted with leather straps to bind a person in place. I didn't need anyone to lift the sack off her head to know it was Lolli who'd been tied down and left to struggle against her bonds.

"Liam," I said.

He looked up, the stone bird still in his hand.

"You're safe." He tucked the bird into his pocket and reached for me.

"What did the letter say?" I leaned against his chest as he wrapped his arm around my waist, grateful for the familiar feel of his solid strength surrounding me.

"Later." He kissed my forehead.

"Good to see you back," Cati said.

Kely gave me a nod.

Nora shot me a strained smile.

The only one in the group I didn't recognize was the man who stood beside Mave.

"I never dreamed it would be one of my own." Mave wore a black dress without any of her usual beads and trimming.

"I never dreamed Case would betray me either," Liam said.

"Did she…" I swallowed the anger that made me want to scream. "Did she know about your real work?"

"She was never a part of my inner circle," Mave said. "I don't know if she suspected anything or went digging."

"It seems hard to believe she ended up here by chance," Emmet said.

"This is the only respectable brothel in Frason's Glenn," Mave said. "A girl like her wouldn't have any other decent choices."

"Unless she only started taking coin for her body to be close to you," I said.

"Stepping into this life to gain a bit of information would be an awfully big sacrifice." Nora looked to Liam. "Would any of your people even agree to that?"

"I'd never ask it of them," Liam said.

"But some would gladly volunteer." I held tight to Liam's hand. "Your people are willing to die for you and kill for you. They would do anything to help your cause."

"But what cause is Lolli even working for?" Nora asked.

"Shall we?" Mave nodded to the man.

He reached forward and pulled the bag off Lolli's head.

Her eyes were wide, and her top lip leaked blood onto her gag.

"Scream all you like. There is absolutely no one who can hear you." Mave nodded again, and the man pulled the gag from Lolli's mouth.

Lolli didn't scream.

"How refreshing," Mave said.

"I don't know what you think I did," Lolli said, "but I swear I've done nothing wrong."

"You passed information on to Edgar Coburn," Mave said. "Do you deny it?"

"Are you mad I made a little extra coin from the man?" Lolli said. "I'll pay you a share if you like, but I promise I haven't been sent here by anyone."

"Where did you get the information?" Mave asked.

"Why does it matter?" Fat tears formed in the corners of Lolli's eyes. "I've just said I'll pay you."

"No amount of theatrics will help you," Mave said. "A girl like you does not come across information about rebellions by chance."

"But I didn't—"

"I cared for you Lolli, really I did." Mave pulled a cloth from her pocket and dabbed away the blood on Lolli's lip. "I care for all my girls. I want them to have a safe place to live. Money of their own so they can choose a future that doesn't involve relying on a man. A steady stream of customers that won't beat them and leave them for dead in an alley. I gave you a safe home, and you jeopardized my whole family."

"I didn't," Lolli said. "I only told a rich man things about the people in the mountains. I never said a word about anything in your house."

"I wish I could believe you. I truly wish you had ended up at my door by chance. But that sort of coincidence rarely happens where death and politics are concerned, and I can't risk my family based on a wish." Mave folded the cloth and tucked it back into her pocket. "Now, if you were sent here because of the true nature of my business, you'll know what happens next."

"No." Lolli strained against her bonds. "No! I didn't do anything wrong. Please don't hurt me!"

"I never mentioned pain." Mave smiled sadly.

"I'm bound to a chair. What else could you mean?" Tears slid down Lolli's face.

"You'll find out," Mave said. "Tell my friends what they want to know, and I may find some ill-placed sympathy for my lost little lamb."

"Who's been giving you information about the Black Bloods?" Liam asked.

"I don't—"

"Can I please just use my knife on her?" Cati asked.

"Who and how?" Liam said.

Cati pulled her knife from its sheath.

Lolli watched the light glint off the blade for a moment.

"Hurt me if you want. Kill me if you want." Lolli smiled. "The mountain will cherish those who sacrifice to protect the pact she holds with her beloved children. You'll get nothing from me, Liam Duwead."

I grabbed Liam's wrist as he reached for his sword.

"That's where you're wrong," Mave said. "I will extract tomes of information from you, Lolli. We have time and privacy. When I'm finished with you, I'll be able to record your whole life story. It's a pity. I really did like you."

"You're a chivving whore monger—"

The man smacked Lolli across the face and shoved the gag back into her mouth. "Hateful words aren't tolerated. You'll learn the rules."

"You should go," Mave said. "There are some things too private for friends to witness. I promise you'll receive a full account."

"Yes." Liam kept his grip on the hilt of his sword as he nodded. "Thank you, Mave."

"Thank you for finding the rat in my walls." Mave gave him a nod in return. "It seems our tally is even, Trueborn."

"This way." Nora opened the door with a key from her pocket.

The others filed out behind her, but I lingered, and Liam stayed beside me, holding my hand.

"Mave," I said. "Thank you for helping us. And protecting us."

"We're all fighting for the same thing," Mave said. "Even if we're looking at the battle from different angles."

"We are." I pressed down my pain and rage and gave Mave a smile before leading Liam out into the corridor.

.

48

We caught up to the others on the spiral staircase that wound up to the trapdoor.

Questions burned through my mind, but there was something in the way Liam kept silent that made me too afraid to ask.

As we climbed farther up, the noise from the square began filtering through the thick stone of the walls.

No one will ever hear Lolli scream.

"Going already?" the man's voice carried down.

"There's nothing more for us to do here," Emmet said.

"Don't all pile out at once," the man said. "Last thing we need is people poking around the bedroom."

"I'm not a chivving idiot," Emmet said.

There was no thump or squeak as the trapdoor opened, just more noise carrying from the square as our group started forward again.

The man stood to one side of the bedroom as the rest of us packed together against the opposite wall. Once Liam and I were both off the steps, he went back down and closed himself in.

And we were back in Mave's without a trace of there being a girl strapped to a chair far beneath us.

It seemed strange to step back up into the world so easily.

"Who knows about Mave's?" Liam asked Emmet as soon as the trapdoor had been shut.

"How do you mean?" Emmet asked.

"We know," Liam said. "Marta does. Case must have heard it from Finn."

"Then the bastard passed it on to the chivving Hayes," Cati said.

"But who else knows?" Liam said.

"I don't generally talk to people," Emmet said. "Especially not about those I care for.

The only people who know about Mave's from me are Marta and the ones who have been here. I haven't betrayed you, Liam."

"I know that. What I'm worried about is the Brien." Liam pulled the bird from his pocket.

The animal had returned to its solid stone form and lay lifeless in Liam's palm.

"Is it news from the war?" Kely asked. "Did Colm break the siege?"

"It's news from Tirra." Liam stroked the back of the bird's neck.

The bird ruffled its black stone wings and fluttered in the air for a moment before landing on Liam's palm.

Liam stroked the bird's neck again, and it lifted its chin to allow a scroll to push out through its throat.

"Regan slipped away from the others to come to Frason's Glenn." Liam passed the scroll to Emmet. "She thought we were taking too long to find the Hayes' contact and decided to come and search for herself."

"Fool of a worthless trueborn." Emmet's gaze darted across the note. "She brought her chivving sorcerers with her."

"Here?" The music from the square seemed to dull in my ears. "She brought sorcerers into Frason's Glenn?"

"Tirra sent the bird to warn us," Emmet said.

"What kind of chivving idiots have come out of the mountains with you?" Nora asked.

"There are Guilded sorcerers in Frason's Glenn." The room seemed to tip in front of me. "Sorcerers can sense magic. That's how they find the sorci children. Three full grown, powerful sorcerers—"

"Will be like lighting a chivving beacon." Liam placed his hand on the back of my waist, steadying me.

"We have to get out of here," Emmet said. "If Regan starts looking for us, we can't have her trailing us to Mave's door."

"Can we leave this late at night?" Cati asked. "Will they let us through the gate?"

"No." Emmet tore his fingers through his hair. "The chivving Brien make everything worse."

"We can find a tavern," I said. "Get rooms close to the gate and leave early tomorrow. We've done what we came here for. Mave will make sure Lolli never passes on another shred of information."

"The Hayes know about Mave. She won't be safe," Liam said. "They could send someone else once they realize Lolli's not helping them anymore."

"Mave can handle herself," Nora said. "Don't worry about us. You have battles enough of your own, Trueborn."

"We don't want to be the ones who lead the Guilds to her door," Emmet said. "Regan's sorcerers could bring more trouble than the Hayes."

"We'll pack up as quickly as we can and head for the gate," Liam said. "We'll figure out where to sleep once we're clear of here."

"We need to warn Mave," I said.

"I'll do it as soon as you're out the door," Nora said. "I'm glad to have you all here, but I agree with Emmet. The farther you are from Mave's home, the safer we'll be. I don't know this Regan, and I really don't think I'd like to meet her."

"You wouldn't," I said.

"We didn't mean to bring more trouble to Mave's door," Liam said. "I'm sorry."

"Don't be." Nora shook her head, sending her curls bouncing around her face. "This is the price we pay for helping the common folk." She stepped around Kely and opened the door. "Pretend you like me." She grabbed the front of his shirt and dragged him out into the hall.

Kely turned ash white and tripped over his own feet as Emmet shut the door behind them.

"We should find Regan before we leave Frason's Glenn," Cati said. "If she's caught, I don't know how hard it would be for the Guilds to break her or her lackey sorcerers."

"I can send her a message," Liam said. "Tell her it's done."

"And to meet us where?" Emmet said. "Back in the mountains sounds best to me."

"We might need Regan's pet sorcerers if there are still soldiers watching the Lir Valley. I don't know how else we'll make it to the mine," I said. "There's nowhere to hide near the entrance. Sneaking in wasn't possible even when it was just Finn and me. Evie knocked out the guards for us."

"We'll have to see how many soldiers there are and then work out a plan," Liam said. "The two of you go up." He nodded to Cati and Emmet.

"I'm not dragging you by your shirt," Cati said.

"It's all right." Emmet opened the door and bowed her out. "Not everyone has to flaunt what they do in the bedroom. Meet you at the backdoor."

He closed the door, and Liam and I were alone.

"Are you all right?" Liam took my hand in his.

"Wishing I had time for a bath, but I'll survive without."

"I'm sorry you had to be alone with that beast."

I tucked my knife into my boot and took Liam's face in my hands. "I asked to go into Coburn's, and I'm glad I did. Leaving Lolli here could have ruined everything we've been working for."

"How did the Hayes dig so deep into our work without me ever knowing?" An awful sadness filled Liam's dark eyes.

"You're a good man fighting for a just cause." I rose up on my toes and kissed Liam's forehead. "You have to keep hoping for a better tomorrow if you're going to keep fighting. The Hayes are snakes who slithered in beneath your faith in those who fight beside you. Case's betrayal is the Hayes' fault, not yours. The zealots in Lygan Hall were not made by you. Colm will fight the Hayes. Mave will deal with Lolli. We will fight the Guilds. Dwelling on the enemies we've already rooted out won't help us in the Lir Valley."

"How do I know I won't be foolish enough to let it happen again?"

I had no answer for him.

"If you want Tirra and the others in the Lir Valley, you should send her a message and have her meet us there," I said. "We'll all have to travel separately anyway."

"If it comes to a fight, we'll need every person we have." Liam wrapped his arms around me and held me close.

"We will find a way. We'll sort out the Lir Valley and build a nice little home in the cave with the waterfall. We'll ferry the sorcis away and keep pecking at the Guilds."

"Will that be enough?"

I laid my cheek against Liam's chest, reveling in the steady thumping of his heart.

"It's enough for now," I said. "It's the first step. Then we burn Ilara."

"Burn Ilara? And how do you propose we do that?"

I pulled away from him and brushed my lips against his cheek. "You have two assassins with you. Don't underestimate the Ryelands."

I winked at him and opened the door to the hall. I couldn't give him a chance to question how I wanted to attack Ilara. I didn't actually have a plan.

But I'd made a promise to Finn, and no matter what it took, I intended to keep it.

The door to the steps had been left slightly open, just enough so the lock hadn't bolted.

Liam pulled it all the way closed behind him.

"I don't know where the back door is," I said as we climbed to the women's floor.

"Go to the kitchen," Liam said. "I'll be down in a few minutes."

"Are you going to send a message to Regan?"

"I'm going to send her a warning." Liam continued up the stairs to the men's level.

I stepped out into the large room on the women's floor.

There were a few girls already up for the night, but they weren't lounging separately. They were all huddled together in a group.

I shot them a quick smile before hurrying off to my room.

Cati waited at the end of the hall, leaning against the wall with her pack already on her back.

"I won't be long." I ducked into my room.

"I've sorted your things."

I gasped as Nora spoke from the corner.

"And laid out the clothes you traveled here in," she continued without seeming to notice she'd nearly frightened me to death. "I'd make you keep the clothes you're wearing, but I don't think they'll fit in your bag."

"They won't." I pulled off the gloves and unbuttoned the coat. "Thank you for letting me borrow them."

"Thank you for finding a spider we didn't know existed." Nora loosened the laces on the front of my dress. "I thought Lolli was my friend. I never told her anything about Mave, I know better than that, but I wonder if she was only sweet to me hoping that I would let something slip."

"I'm sorry."

Nora held the shoulders of the dress while I wriggled free.

"I'm hardly innocent in all this." Nora passed me my shift. "I signed up for lying when I chose to help Mave. I can't even count the number of men I've sidled up to, trying to catch a bit of information. I'm just not used to being on this side of it."

She tossed me my skirt.

"How many of the girls know about Mave's work?" I asked.

"Three of us."

"What will Mave tell the others about Lolli?"

"Mave caught her trying to get into the safe." Nora tied the top of my pack shut. "All of the girls' money is kept in that safe. If someone were to steal it, we would all be destitute and right back where we were before we started here. If any of the girls saw Lolli on the street now, they'd scratch her eyes out."

"I didn't think Mave would be able to cover Lolli being taken away so quickly." I shimmied on my bodice and tied the laces.

"Mave's had to be quick to survive."

I snatched my coat off the bed.

"Will she be quick enough if the Brien accidentally lead the Guilds to her door?" I asked.

"What would the Guilds be looking for?" Nora passed me my pack. "We have no sorcerers here. No one living in the house who isn't an Ilbrean. And if some rebels came in looking for a bit of fun, there's no way for Mave to know what secrets lie in all her clients' lives."

"You're chivving well as brilliant as Mave."

"I know." Nora winked. "Now get away before I have to explain to the Guilds why you're here."

"Thank you for everything."

I'd already started for the door before Nora caught my hand. "May we meet again in a land of freedom."

"May we be strong enough to fight until Ilbrea is free." I squeezed her hand and walked out the door.

"Are we actually going to be able to find a place to wait for the gates to open?" Cati asked as I led her down the corridor and to the stairs.

"I'm sure we can," I said. "If we got into the city and went straight away to find some heavy drinks, we'd just now be settling in to sleep for the night. If anyone tries to ask questions, we'll just have one of the men play stumbling drunk and beg for a place to sober him up." I gave the whispering girls a quick wave before starting down the stairs.

"I think I like slipping through the shadows and stabbing people better than all this rot," Cati whispered.

"I have a horrible feeling you'll get plenty of use out of your sword in the Lir Valley. And I don't think there will be any tricks to be played."

I hurried along the second-floor corridor, trying not to think of the secrets and lies that might be whispered behind those locked doors, muffled by the sounds of human enjoyment.

I caught the eye of some of the people in the dining room as Cati and I skirted past men in orange jackets carrying trays of steaming hot food or glasses of bubbling chamb. They weren't the same sort of looks I'd gotten when I was dressed to go to Coburn's. It was more curiosity at who the pretty girl with the pack might be. I was beautiful enough to gain their attention even without fine feathers.

I liked being back to myself. I held power, just not riches.

"Coming out!" a voice called through the kitchen door before a man charged through, bearing a tray laden with food.

Cati and I leapt out of the way as he passed.

"Don't linger by the door." The man warned as he weaved his way into the crowd and across the packed dining room.

Cati peeked through the kitchen door before pushing it open and dodging inside. I stayed right behind her, wary of getting a tureen of boiling soup slopped down my front.

Liam and the others waited in the back corner. Liam's shoulders relaxed as he waved me toward him.

I'd never seen the kitchen outside of the morning hours when everything was quiet.

With her house packed with guests, Mave had people running all the stoves, two at the fireplace, and more working at the table.

"I've never seen this many people in a kitchen," I said.

"You should peek into the kitchen that feeds the crag and the keep when they're busy." Cati skirted around a woman brandishing a rolling pin with a bit too much vigor. "It's worse than this."

A pang cut through my chest. Just a tiny touch of missing Lygan Hall.

Emmet pushed open the door to the street behind Mave's before we'd reached them.

Liam held out his hand, waiting for me to join him.

I slipped my hand into his, and the bit of missing Lygan Hall drifted away. Lacing my fingers through Liam's made my heart hum, and when we stepped outside, I didn't mind the chill stinging my cheeks.

Even after Cati closed the kitchen door behind us, the chaos of Mave's still carried out onto the darkened street.

Empty crates and barrels were lined up against the stone wall, and a locked door led to a cellar below the kitchen. The music and laughter from the square echoed onto the empty street, and the balconies above us hosted couples willing to brave the cold night.

As Emmet led us away, I sent a plea up to the stars that Mave wouldn't find any other Black Bloods visiting her square.

49

Emmet found us rooms at a tavern a few streets away from the gate. The place smelled like week-old spilled ale and sweat, but the owner didn't give us any trouble about wanting rooms so late into the night. The only one who seemed at all unhappy about our finding beds was Emmet when I told the owner that Liam and I were married and would be sharing a room.

Then my brother looked like he might burn down the tavern rather than let Liam and me share a bed.

I didn't care about Emmet's anger. I just needed Liam to hold me. I needed to wake up in his arms and know there was at least one truth I could count on.

I was his, and he was mine.

When morning came, I lay in his arms long after the soft noises from the street had woken me. The sky had barely begun to lighten, but tilk were already heading toward their daily labors.

The clatter of wheels on cobblestone and the soft rumble of voices broke the stillness of the dawn.

I don't think Frason's Glenn could ever be quiet, not really. With Mave's being busy all night and the bakers starting before dawn, there was always some work to be done.

Liam sighed and pulled me closer to him.

I studied his face as he slept.

The short, dark beard that now covered his chin. The angle of his nose.

As the sun crept higher in the sky, I could even see the smooth skin next to his eyes. There were always worried wrinkles by his eyes when he was awake.

I waited until the sun had properly risen before kissing the side of his neck to wake him.

He gave a happy little mumble and held me even closer.

"We've got to get up and flee the city," I said.

"We do." He kissed my forehead.

"When we get back to camp or the cavern or wherever we end up after this, promise me we'll spend an entire day in bed."

"I'll ask Cati to stand guard." He brushed his lips gently against mine. His new beard tickled my chin. "I'll have her skewer anyone who dares try to disturb us."

I kissed him properly.

Longing flared through me, and for a moment, I forgot to worry about Regan's sorcerers luring the Guilds down upon us. I wanted nothing more than to slip away into a world where only Liam and I existed.

Only my fear for our friends at Mave's made me pull away from Liam and leave the comfort of our warm bed.

By the time we got down to the foul-scented dining room, the others were already waiting for us.

"It's not too burnt." Cati tossed me a roll. "Better than gruel at any rate."

"Thanks." I tried to brush some of the black off my breakfast.

"Come on, then." Emmet didn't look at Liam or me before leading our group out onto the street.

The bakery across the way already had people trickling through its door.

If we hadn't been in a hurry to get out of Frason's Glenn, I would have stopped in to replace my burnt meal.

A flock of children ran past, all shouting and laughing together, though I couldn't see any reason as to why. Men looking half-asleep and women carrying shopping baskets all went about their business in the beautiful way that everyday life carries thoughtlessly on.

"I can get the horses for us," I said after I'd managed to choke down my roll. "The stable boy will go quickly if I ask him to."

"If he's not too heartbroken that you're leaving." Liam gave me a little half-smile.

"I'll let him down gently."

There were already people at the gate, waiting for their chance to leave the city. Some riding, some on foot. A few had carts loaded with goods, and a few carts were still empty. All of them had packed into a line reaching past the stable with the white painted horse on the front.

I left the others near a cobbler's across the way and headed toward the stable, squeezing between a cart laden with barrels and a man on horseback.

"Hello," I called inside. "I've come to collect our horses."

I waited a moment for the stable boy to come trotting out.

"Sorry to come by so early." I stepped into the stable.

The scent of horses and their muck rammed into my nose. The long line of stalls reached back farther than I'd known the building went.

"Hello," I called more loudly.

The horses huffed and stomped their displeasure at my noise.

A figure appeared at the back of the stable, and the boy came loping toward me, his gangly arms swinging like they weren't sure how to manage their length.

"Good morning," I said. "Sorry to come in when the sun's barely up, but could we get our horses?"

"Right." The boy stopped in front of me. "I'd like to get you your horses."

"Thank you." I gave him a nice smile.

A hint of pink crept up his neck.

"We are in a bit of a hurry, so as quickly as you can saddle them—"

"I can't actually give you the horses." The pink changed to crimson as it climbed up the boy's face.

"What do you mean?" My hand drifted to the knife hidden at my hip. "Are the horses ill? Did you injure them?"

"No! I take good care of all my horses." The boy backed a step away from me. "But a woman came by and spotted your horses and said she knew you. She paid me two gold coins not to let you have the horses until you'd gone to see her."

"Was she blond?"

The boy took another step back as he nodded.

"Are my horses here?" I asked.

"Yes. But she's not far away, and she said she just wanted a word and she'll give me two more gold coins when she comes back, and—"

"That's close to a fortune for a boy like you." I pulled my knife free.

The boy's eyes went wide as he stared at the blade.

"You seem very nice," I said. "You treat the animals well, and I respect that. But I cannot allow you to hold my horses hostage."

"I'm not. I'm just—"

"I am asking you very nicely to saddle my horses and bring them to me. If you don't, I'll have to call for my friends outside."

"Ena, what's taking so long?"

I glanced over my shoulder to see Emmet striding toward me.

"Too late," I said to the boy. "It seems Regan paid this fool to keep our horses from us until we pay her a visit."

Emmet looked down at the knife in my hand. "And you've explained to him that he'll be getting us our horses now?"

"I have."

"But she only wants to talk to you." The stable boy stumbled away from us as Emmet drew his sword. "She said she's been trying to catch up to you."

"And where exactly is she?" I asked.

"At the River of Frie," the boy said. "I went over and got her and her companions rooms. There are only a few above the pub, and they don't let just anyone have them. Those are rooms for fine guests only."

"Get our horses saddled and ready," Emmet said. "Now."

The boy slipped and fell face first onto the filth-covered floor as he ran to obey. He scrambled to his feet and sprinted to the far end of the stable.

The horses fidgeted and snorted as he bolted by.

"Go tell Liam where Regan is," Emmet said. "I'll see to the horses."

"What kind of chivving fool stays right next to the gate?" I tucked my knife away and hurried back through the door.

The line to exit the city had shifted since I'd been inside. I had to weave through a pack of young couples to reach Liam.

"Is everything all right?" Liam leaned against the front of the cobbler's shop, casually watching the people going through the gate.

There weren't any more soldiers guarding the entrance than there had been when we'd arrived a few days before. I tried to let their numbers calm my nerves.

731

"Regan gave the stable boy a couple coins," I said. "Asked him not to give us our horses until we'd gone to see her—in her rooms at The River of Frie."

Liam's face turned to stone as he looked up at the sparkling silver sign above the pub's door.

"Emmet's getting our horses now?" Liam asked.

"He is."

"You three go through the gate and start riding north," Liam said. "Emmet and I will meet with Regan and catch up to you on the road."

"Absolutely not." I laid my hand on Liam's chest. "I am not riding out of this city without you. I've done it once before, and it was chivving awful."

"Ena—"

"Your path is mine, and we will walk it together to whatever end. Send Emmet with Cati and Kely. I'll stay with you."

"Or we could all just stay together," Cati said.

Liam looked back toward the soldiers at the gate.

"Our place is with you, Trueborn," Kely said.

Liam placed his hand over mine and met my gaze. "Wait for the horses while I go to Regan, all three of you. Keep them ready for us to go."

I had opened my mouth to argue that I didn't want him facing three sorcerers on his own, but a stream of men in black uniforms caught my eye before I could speak.

They didn't come through the gate, but marched up the road from the center of the city in three long lines.

Liam took my arm, pulling me behind him as the soldiers came nearer.

"We'll wait them out," Liam said. "Let the soldiers go through the gate. Then we'll worry about Regan and getting out of the city."

A flash of purple broke through the lines of black uniforms.

"I need to get to Emmet." I slipped out from behind Liam.

"Ena—"

"They aren't going through the gate, and I will not let my brother die for Regan's stupidity."

"Keep him out of their way," Liam said.

I felt Liam's fingers graze the back of my hand as I sprinted across the street and cut through the line of people before the soldiers could block my path.

Emmet stood in the shadows inside the stable door, peering out onto the street. He already held the reins of four of our horses.

"What's going on out there?" Emmet passed me two sets of reins.

"A sorcerer and a pack of soldiers." I stepped in front of my brother as he edged closer to the door. "You are not going outside. You are not lighting anything on chivving fire to distract them."

"If there's a sorcerer—"

"Then they are probably heading right for Regan. Do you think she slipped quietly into the pub? Or did she choose the chivving easiest-to-peg place and make a grand scene while towing unguilded sorcerers behind her? She brought this on her own head. I will not let you endanger yourself to protect her."

"And if they catch the Brien fools and torture them?"

"Torture?" The stable boy squeaked.

"Just give me the chivving horse." Emmet held out his empty hand.

"Is there a back way out of here?" I asked.

"Sure." The boy pointed to the far end of the stable.

"Go. Slip out the back and stay away from here."

"I can't." The boy balled his hands into fists and locked his arms by his sides. "I have to stay with the horses."

"There's a pack of soldiers and a sorcerer outside," Emmet said. "Are you smart enough to know what that means?"

"I am." The boy tipped his chin up. "But I will not leave my horses."

"At least keep to the back," I said.

"Clear the street!" a voice bellowed outside.

The people waiting in line to leave the city all surged toward the gate before realizing they wouldn't be allowed through. The shouts and chaos of them all pushing to go back the other way nearly covered the sorcerer's words.

"There is someone with magic hiding in our midst." The sorcerer's voice rang out louder than normal speech. "Perhaps more than one of you."

The people trapped by the gate all fell silent as they backed up as close to the city wall as they could manage.

"I can feel your magic. I felt it calling to me from all the way across the city," the sorcerer said. "Right now, I am picturing you as afraid. As a person who has never understood their power and does not know the great peril in which they place everyone around them every second they exist."

Frightened murmurs sprang up from the crowd.

"There is a very good reason all magic within Ilbrea is kept under the control of the Sorcerers Guild." The sorcerer stepped forward, out of the ranks of the soldiers, and stared up at the River of Frie. Her purple robes fluttered, as though some wind that could not bother with normal people danced around her. "Untrained magic is a danger to the innocent citizens of Ilbrea. I am willing to believe you did not understand the nature of your gift or the harm you were doing. Come to me, and I will help you. Resist me, and I will be forced to believe you are in Frason's Glenn with the intention of murdering the people of this city."

A child's wail cut through the frightened silence.

"Live or die," the sorcerer said. "I leave it up to you."

50

My heart seemed to beat slower in the quiet that followed the sorcerer's words. Or maybe time itself actually slowed down. I don't know if a sorcerer could manage such a thing.

I felt my heart beat, and beat, and beat again before a crack and a boom shook the street.

Rocks and dust burst out of the top floor of the River of Frie and rained down onto the street below.

The horses snorted and tried to yank their reins from my grip, fighting to back away from the noise.

"Surround the building," the sorcerer ordered.

The soldiers fanned out, darting through the alleys and making a line right in front of the pub.

The sorcerer stayed put in the middle of the street. The dust from above didn't touch her. It stayed hovering in the air, as though she'd surrounded herself with a bubble.

"We can't stay here," Emmet said.

"By order of the Sorcerers Guild, I command you to come out now," the sorcerer said.

Bright light flared from the gaping hole in the pub. A hiss shook my bones as liquid fire streamed down toward the sorcerer.

The sorcerer screamed as flames encased her like a cocoon.

The crowd shouted and backed closer to the city wall, crushing the people nearest the stone.

"Take these." I pressed the horses' reins into Emmet's hands.

"What are you doing?"

I'd already slipped out the door before Emmet had finished his question.

The young couples from the line, who'd seemed ready for a day of flirting just a few minutes before, had all bunched up at the front of the pack, tears streaming down the faces of the boys and girls alike.

"This way." I took one of the girl's hands. "There's a way out. Just come with me."

734

Her eyes were wide with horror, but she didn't fight me as I dragged her to the stable door.

"All the way at the back. Go through the door, and don't stop until you're far from here." I let go of the girl's wrist and slipped back out toward the crowd.

Blue streaks of lightning shot up from the sorcerer, striking the gap in the pub's wall. A painful wail came from inside.

I couldn't let myself think about who the wail might have come from.

The rest of the girl's group had followed her. All except one boy who seemed so frozen with fear, I didn't have much of a chance of making him move.

I took the shoulder of an older man instead. "Go into the stable, and cut out through the back."

The man nodded, grabbed the hand of an older woman, and bolted for the stable door.

A rumble shook the street, and the whole front of the River of Frie crumbled away, raining debris down onto the line of soldiers.

The screams of the wounded paun drove into my chest, freezing me in place.

A horrible scene of blood, and vicious claws, and falling earth stole my vision. The screams dug into my ears and all the way down my spine. I couldn't move. I couldn't breathe. My terror sent me back to that horrible place where the croilach surrounded me.

These are not your friends. Sharp claws are not tearing through the ones you care for.

I forced my lungs to accept air.

I sent a man on horseback to the stable.

Crack!

I turned around as a sheet of bright light flew toward the sorcerer on the street. The sheet shattered with a pop. Shimmering fragments fell to the ground.

One of Regan's sorcerers, the older man, stood alone on the top floor of the River of Frie. Blood trickled down his face as he swirled his hand through the air, forming a gleaming pike that shot toward the Guilded sorcerer.

The Guilded sorcerer batted the pike away from herself and toward the crowd.

I heard the scream of the tilk who'd been struck, but I couldn't see them through the mob of people.

I grabbed the shoulder of a woman who clutched a little girl in her arms. "Go into the stable. There's a path out through the back."

"Help us, please!" People who'd been trapped inside the pub with the Brien edged toward the front of the bottom story, as though hoping to bolt through the missing section of wall. They called out to the Guilded sorcerer like she might actually feel enough mercy to help them.

"Cut through the stable. Go out the back." I repeated the phrase over and over as I slogged my way deeper into the crowd.

A flash of blue came from behind, and a wave of warmth touched my skin.

A high-pitched scream carried from the pub. The crowd behind me had thinned out enough for me to be able to see the sorcerer on the street.

Blood covered her arm. She gripped her shoulder, as though trying to shield a wound.

Hatred burned in her eyes as she lifted her red-soaked hand to the sky.

I watched as tiny sparks of light gathered above her blood-slicked palm, sure that some horror would come with her magic but not knowing how to fight against her power.

A stone flew from the pub, shooting into the sorcerer's chest. Blood sprayed across the street as the sorcerer stumbled.

My breath hitched as I waited for her to fall.

But the light in her hand still grew, crackling as she let out one final scream.

Blood flew from her mouth as the spell soared from her hand to surround the pub.

"No!" I charged forward.

I only made it three steps.

A bright flash of light and terrible heat knocked me off my feet. I fell on my side, and my head hit something hard. I couldn't see anything beyond the bright spots dancing through my vision.

The rumble and cracking of falling stone shook the street as a fresh wave of terrified cries surrounded me.

"Ena."

I recognized the feel of Liam's hands as he lifted me to my feet.

"What happened?" I blinked, trying to see through the spots, but the world had turned a funny shade of red.

"Can you ride?" Liam asked.

"Here." Cati handed him a cloth.

He pressed it to my head.

Pain stole my sight again.

"How could this have happened?" Kely asked.

I fixed my eyes on him, blinking away the blood that blurred my vision.

"There were people in there. Innocent people." Kely looked like a terrified child with lines of worry pinched between his eyebrows.

"The Guilds don't care." Emmet appeared next to Kely. He had our horses with him. "Get her on a horse. We're leaving."

"I don't know if she can ride." Liam kept the cloth pressed to my head.

I reached up to touch it. The wet warmth of my own blood brought sour to my throat.

Emmet lifted me away from Liam and set me stomach-first on a horse. "I know my sister. As long as she can breathe, she can keep her seat on a chivving horse."

My head throbbed as I pulled myself up to sit on the saddle.

"It's not safe," Cati said.

"Anything is safer than being here," Emmet said.

Liam passed me the red-stained cloth he'd been holding to my head.

I pressed it to my scalp with one hand and gripped the reins with the other.

The crowd in front of the gate had thinned out. I'd managed to get more of them through the stable than I'd thought. I swayed as I smiled.

"Stay right behind me." Liam mounted his own horse. "We'll go nice and slow."

I didn't know how he thought we'd be able to go quickly. There were still people lined up to get out of the city.

Most of the soldiers minding the gate didn't seem to care that people wanted to leave. They stared wide-eyed at something behind me rather than search the ones who were fleeing.

I gripped the front of my saddle, trying to keep steady as I looked back.

The River of Frie was gone.

A pile of stone and dust was all that was left of the pub that only allowed in fancy folk.

Soldiers lay dead on the ground all around the awful pile. The sorcerer lay alone, set apart from the normal folk even in death.

"What's wrong with her?"

I looked forward when the soldier at the gate spoke. The world spun from the quick movement.

"She got knocked down as the brave sorcerer protected us from rogue magic." Liam pressed a coin into the soldier's hand. "My thanks to you and your brothers in arms for all the good you do for Ilbreans."

I pressed the cloth to my head as hard as I could, trying to make the pain drown out my rage.

"Safe journey." The soldier stepped away from Liam, clearing our path out of the city.

None of the other men in black uniforms looked our way.

Liam kept his pace slow as he led us north.

My head throbbed with every step my horse took.

By the time the sun was high, I couldn't tell if the pounding in my head was born of pain or anger.

51

I have long known the cruelty of the Guilds. There is no horror they could commit that would shock me.

But my anger is never dampened. Maybe if I had gone numb to my rage, I would have had the sense to stop fighting them.

I am not that wise.

The fire of my wrath burns constantly.

I try to hide it in the blackness alongside my fear and pain.

The flames still rise.

For brief moments, it is lost beneath the depths of my joy, but the inferno refuses to be buried.

I will never be able to stop the fire from burning. So I will pull the flames from my own chest and let them dance through the streets of Ilara.

5 2

It would take us three long days of riding to reach the Lir Valley.

For the first two, I kept looking over my shoulder, searching for a sign of either Regan coming to join us, or the soldiers coming to kill us.

Neither happened.

Liam sent a stone bird to Orla, telling her the traitor had been found and Regan had been killed.

Then there was nothing to do but ride. There were no plans to make. No tactics to discuss.

We just kept riding onward toward the Lir Valley.

The first night, I slept in Liam's arms in a tavern bed that made me miss the comfort of his cot in the camp. Emmet only argued with the arrangement by glaring at us in the morning.

The second night, we stopped in a village so near the eastern mountains, the temptation to run back into the safety of the forest tingled in my legs as I climbed down from my horse.

The village looked so much like Harane, I kept waiting for someone to call my name and ask where I'd been for most of a year.

But the buildings there had not been burned. That village had yet to be reduced to ashes and ghosts.

There was only one tavern in the place and one public stable right beside it.

Liam took my hand as Emmet gave the stable girl strict instructions for how to mind our horses.

"What's wrong?" Liam leaned down to ask, brushing his lips against my cheek, as though he knew I wouldn't want the others hearing.

"It feels like ghosts are going to pile out of the homes to smother me."

"They won't." Liam squeezed my hand. "I won't let them."

I let out a long breath and forced my body to relax. "Food and bit of frie, and I'll be fine."

Liam smiled at me, but I could tell he knew I was lying.

Cati was the first up the tavern's wooden front steps. She pushed open the door, and the scent of fresh baked bread wafted out onto the street.

"Come on in!" a cheerful voice called from inside. "Get yourselves out of the cold."

The warmth of the room surrounded me as I stepped into the tavern. The flames in the fireplace danced wildly, and the woman bustling toward us beamed in such a cheerful way, I couldn't help but smile back.

"It's getting late," the woman said. "I thought I was done seeing travelers tonight."

"Do you still have rooms?" I asked.

"I wouldn't leave anyone out in the snow, even if I was full up." The owner shooed us toward a table large enough for the five of us to share. "I've had people lay out blankets in the dining room before, but I don't think we'll come to that tonight. Have a seat, and I'll get you all a cup of hot tea to begin with."

"Thank you," I said as she bustled away into the kitchen.

"There are worse places to spend a night." Cati breathed onto her hands.

"In the snow, for one," Kely said.

We slipped into an easy patter of conversation that rubbed at my nerves. Chatting about the hope of spring coming soon, or the horses having made such a long journey, or anything but how we were going to make the Guilds pay for all the horrible things they'd done, seemed like a chivving worthless waste of words.

Liam gripped my leg under the table as the owner came back with a tray of steaming hot mugs.

"Where are you all heading on your travels?" She set the first mug in front of Emmet. "I assume you're not staying here. I would have heard if someone in the village were expecting so many guests."

"To Ilara," Emmet said. "On business."

"Ahh." The owner set mugs down in front of Liam and me. "Plan yourselves a bit of extra time heading through Carrickbeg. There's an entire flock of soldiers stationed there. The roads are a mess, and you've got to take time to cross through the Guilds' men."

"Carrickbeg," Emmet said. "What would soldiers be doing there? Last time I passed through, there wasn't much more to the place than this village."

"There still isn't," the owner said. "All I know is that everyone who comes to my tavern that's been through Carrickbeg complains to their teeth about hundreds of soldiers making their travel slower. Now, what can I get you to eat?"

"I'm actually not hungry." I pushed away from the table. "Could I get into a room now? The long day on horseback has me worn to the bone."

"You poor thing. I'll send up some bread for you at least." The owner kept smiling as she took coins from Liam and gave him keys. She chatted in such a familiar way, we might have been friends instead of customers.

Like Cal's mother.

I untied the leather tube from Liam's pack and took it upstairs with me.

The owner kept chattering as she led me to my room. "I haven't been very busy for the last few days. If you needed to stay another night and rest, I'd be more than happy to have you. We keep a fire burning in the dining room all day, and you can give yourself a chance to recover from being on the road."

"Thank you," I said. "I'll be fine once I've had some sleep."

"Here you are." She unlocked the last door in the hall. "This will be a nice, quiet room for you." She bustled into the room to light the lamp, then moved to kneel in front of the fireplace.

"I'll do it myself." I stepped into the room and laid my pack on the bed. "I find lighting fires to be a bit soothing."

"I understand." She smiled at me, a warm motherly smile that dug into my chest. "It makes a place feel homey when you fill it with your own warmth. I'll make sure that husband of yours brings bread up for you in case you wake up hungry."

"Thank you."

I stared at the closed door for a long while after she left. I'm not sure if I was waiting for disaster or testing my own self-restraint in not allowing myself to bolt for the frozen woods.

"There is work to do, Ena. And you've promised you'll see it through."

I knelt in front of the fireplace and lit the logs that had already been laid out.

There wasn't a table in the room. Only a bed and a chair, like the owner wanted to make sure you'd spend your time sitting in the dining room where she could speak to you.

I shifted my pack onto the floor and pulled the map from its tube. It seemed strange to unroll such a beautiful thing on top of a borrowed bed, but it was either that or the floor.

Squinting in the lamplight, I could just make out the marking for Carrickbeg.

Finn and I had passed through the village on our way to the Lir Valley. I tried to think through what I remembered of it. We'd seen soldiers in the village and slept in a barn. But it hadn't been a mob of paun, just enough to make me wary of going into a tavern.

I glanced over my shoulder to be sure the door was shut before pulling my lae stone from my pocket. In the blue glow, the map seemed even more detailed than it had in Mave's study.

There were tiny little rocks like a miniature cliff face drawn on the eastern side of Carrickbeg, behind the village if you were traveling on the mountain road. The buildings the map makers' magic had created were all wooden and spread apart, like the villagers hadn't been afraid to claim land.

"Why would the paun want so many soldiers there?" I ran my fingers across the image, as though some magic might tell me what the Guilds were doing putting so many men in a place with so few tilk.

Ilara was only two more days' ride northwest, not really far enough to warrant making men sleep in tents in the snow. I couldn't find a way to make sense of it, but Carrickbeg had been on the list of places the paun were shipping supplies.

Tap. Tap. Tap.

"Ena?" Liam called before I could speak.

"Come in." I tucked the lae stone back into my pocket.

Liam entered the room and locked the door behind him. "Are you ill?" He set a plate of bread down on the bed.

"I'm fine. I just didn't think I could hold my temper for a night's worth of blather about nonsense."

741

He knelt beside me and wrapped his arm around my waist.

"We should cut west through the woods before we reach Carrickbeg." I traced a line on the map. "There shouldn't be anything the horses can't make it through, and the time we'll lose being off the road won't be worse than what we'd lose making our way through the soldiers if what our host's heard is true."

"You're right."

"It'll probably be safer to come at the bridge before the Lir Valley from the woods anyway. Give us a chance to see any soldiers before they see us."

"We'll keep to the woods then."

"Are you just going to agree with everything I say?" I rolled the map up and shoved it back into its tube.

"As long as what you're saying is right, then I will."

"Good." I sat on the bed, pulled the knife and sheath from my boot, and tucked them under the pillow.

Liam sat in the chair, watching as I pulled off my shoes.

"What?" I laid my socks by the fire.

"I wish you would tell me what's wrong."

"What's wrong?" Icy rage rushed through my veins. "Regan and her pack of sorcerers are probably dead."

"I know. I can't honestly see how they could have survived."

"I don't feel sorry for them. I can't." I untied my bodice and tugged at the laces. "They were fools to go into Frason's Glenn with three sorcerers, and chivving slitches for staying near the gate where it was easy to find them."

"Regan didn't know anything about surviving in Ilbrea."

"And I hated her." I yanked my bodice over my head and chucked it by the fire. "She made me a killer. Whether or not she plotted to have that man touch me, it's her fault I had to go to the enclave. Her fault I can still remember the feel of his blood on my hand."

"You could also blame me for pulling you into working for the Black Bloods in the first place."

"Don't." I rounded on him. "Do not try and take the weight of my choices onto your shoulders."

"I'm sorry."

"My helping you did not give Regan the right to summon me. The Duweads and the Brien fighting together did not give her the right to chase us to Frason's Glenn. How dare Regan make us witness her death because she was too stubborn to follow the orders of someone who actually chivving knows how to survive in Ilbrea!"

"I'm so sorry." Liam stood.

"Stop chivving saying that."

"You are strong, Ena. And brave. I am grateful to have you by my side, but I am sorry there is so much pain on our path."

"It's not our path that got Regan killed. It was her own chivving arrogance."

"I know." Liam reached out, laying his hands on my shoulders.

I stepped closer to him, burying my face on his chest.

"I love you." Liam kissed the top of my head and wrapped his arms around me.

The feeling of being secure in his arms took the edge off my anger. I turned my head and looked up at him. "You are everything I want in this world. And if you'd gone in to see Regan before the sorcerer came, you'd have been stuck in there with her. You would have died because of…"

The words caught in my throat as tears threatened my eyes.

"I'm here. I'm right here, and I'm safe." Liam leaned down and kissed me.

He tasted of honey, sweet winds, and freedom. And fire. Flames that would burn through the evils that chased us until the demons were gone and the world was a safe and wonderful place where we could build a life together.

I didn't mind the foreign feel of his beard as I laced my fingers through his hair and deepened our kiss. Nothing mattered but that he was my Liam, and I would fight with everything I had to protect him.

I was a child born of ashes and filled with raging fire. I would defend the man who had claimed my heart.

The warmth of his hands as they trailed up my sides sent sparks of hope flying through my stomach.

The strength of his arms as he lifted me onto the bed made me believe we were strong enough to survive the path ahead.

As I twined my body around his, we fit together like the gods themselves had meant us to be one.

I slept peacefully that night. Warm and content as the darkness surrounded me.

53

There were six soldiers stationed at the bridge near the Lir Valley. Six of the most miserably cold-looking soldiers I'd ever seen.

If they hadn't been wearing Guild uniforms, I would have felt sorry for them as I peered out through the woods. As it was, I gripped the bark of the tree I hid behind, trying to convince myself not to run out onto the road and see how many of them I could stab.

I couldn't see the racing water of the river from where I hid, but I could hear it. And the sound was loud enough to block any chance of my catching a bit of the closest soldiers' conversation.

The two nearest me paced in front of the bridge, more like they were trying to keep warm than following orders.

On the far side of the river, two more soldiers stood watch while the last two huddled near the fire in front of their one, large tent.

I closed my eyes and pressed my forehead against the bark of the tree.

Six soldiers was nothing to be fussed about. If we had to fight our way through them to get across the river, we could.

But six soldiers here could mean many more lurking in the Lir Valley.

One trouble at a time. I clung to the sound of Lily's voice in my mind as I crept through the trees back toward where the others waited with our horses.

The snow in the woods was less than a foot high but still plenty deep enough to freeze my toes and dampen the hem of my skirt.

Liam waited for me halfway back to the others.

He didn't say anything as I reached him. Just joined me and walked by my side as we crunched carefully through the snow.

"How bad is it?" Cati asked when we reached the others.

Kely peeked out from behind the horses to listen.

Emmet leaned against a tree, knife in hand, as though he were expecting the soldiers to come tramping through the snow behind us.

"Six," I said. "Two on the near side, four on the far. They look like a sad bunch to be perfectly honest."

"Do we all go to take care of them?" Cati asked. "Or should Emmet and I nip ahead?"

"If people see dead soldiers on the side of the road, they'll know something's wrong," Emmet said.

"Then we throw them into the river." Cati shrugged.

"I think we should try and ride past," I said. "Tell them we're looking for jobs and heard Lir has land and houses he'll let out in exchange for labor."

"Maybe you and Emmet should stay here," Kely said, "as you are rumored assassins."

"I've never let anyone see my face," Emmet said.

"Of course you have," Cati said. "You just kill them after."

Emmet scowled at her.

"Sorry." Cati held up both hands. "I get antsy when there are people who deserve to be stabbed and I'm not allowed to just get on with it."

"They might recognize me in the valley," I said. "But the soldiers should be fine. I'll keep my hair covered and act meek."

"It's worth a try," Liam said. "If they start asking too many questions, we can fight them. I don't want to give the paun a hint we're here until we know what we're dealing with."

I pulled my scarf from my head and pressed back all the hairs that had fallen free from my braid.

"Cati and I will ride up front," Liam said. "Ena in the middle, Kely and Emmet in the back."

"Make sure you seem excited about the prospect of living in a proper home with a good man watching over you." I tucked my braid down the back of my coat and wrapped my scarf around my head tight enough to hide all my hair. "Lir is nigh on worshiped by the people who live in his valley, or at least they pretend to adore him."

"What turns people into such spineless saps?" Cati untied her horse.

"Fear," I said. "Lir owns the land and the houses. The people only live there at his will. If Lir kicks them out, they've got nothing. Evie told me most people who anger him just starve in the woods."

"Does that mean we get to go after Lir as well?" Cati climbed onto her horse.

"Let's hope it doesn't come to that." I untied my horse, trying not to wince as I climbed back into my saddle. "His house looks like he's chivving well waiting to be attacked. Add soldiers to that, and I don't fancy charging up the hill to his estate."

"Come on." Liam clicked to his horse and began leading us northeast, looping back to the road out of view of the soldiers. "We're here to find out if Lir really is mining mountain stone, or if there just happens to be a bit of the rock here and Finn found it by chance. We're looking for information. If we can avoid a fight, all the better."

There was a grimness in his tone, as though he'd already accepted the fact that there would probably be a fight.

I wanted to be the one to ride beside him, but I didn't argue as Cati took that place when we reached the road.

She was better with a sword than I was. Better than Emmet and Liam as well.

As we road up a long hill, I could hear the river again, rushing just out of sight. Soon, we would reach the soldiers, and then, whether it came to a fight or not, it would be time to cross to the far bank.

I gripped my reins as old fears surged through me.

"Panic has never helped anyone," I whispered the words and forced my body to relax, letting my shoulders round forward and loosening my grip on my reins, as though I were nothing but a mindless follower plodding along in Liam's wake.

Liam and Cati didn't pause at the top of the hill, but I suppose they had no reason to.

From the height of the slope, I could see the full width of the racing river and the dock on the far side.

My heart thundered in my chest, but my horse plodded steadily onward.

There were no boats tethered to the dock, and the soldiers' tent took up the place where wagons would have waited to load goods on and off the river.

"Stop where you are."

My heart shot into my throat at the soldier's words, and my hand began moving to the knife at my hip before I could stop it.

Don't be a chivving fool.

I laid my hands on top of my saddle as my horse stopped, and I turned my gaze up to the sky to keep my eyes from darting toward the dock.

The sun was still high enough for the sky to be a bright and cheerful blue. Little puffs of white clouds floated past with nothing but the gods capable of stopping them.

"What's your business in the Lir Valley?" the soldier's voice was gruff, as though he longed to unleash his displeasure at being left out in the snow on someone and Liam would suit him fine.

"We've heard Mister Lir is looking for some people to work in the valley," Liam said in a friendly tone.

He has to be kind. He has to be warm. He has donned his armor.

"What's your trade?" the soldier asked.

"We've got a smith, a farmer, a miner, an inker, and a cook," Liam said. "All good workers as well."

"Which one is she?" I glanced down at the soldier. He was pointing at Cati.

I held my breath, waiting for the rasp of Cati's sword clearing its sheath.

"I'm the cook," Cati said.

"You don't see many cooks armed with swords," the soldier said.

"The last tavern I worked in, my sword was necessary to make it through the night without a letch touching me," Cati said. "I'm an unmarried woman. I shouldn't be blamed for knowing how to defend myself."

"I don't think Lir will take to her," the soldier said.

"We're not set on all staying together," Liam said. "But with the rumors of trouble on the road, it seemed best to keep in a group for as long as we can."

"I'll head to Ilara if I can't find work here," Cati said. "I think I might like the opportunities the capital city has to offer."

"Ride on then." The soldiers stepped out of our path. "Don't cause any trouble in the valley. If you do, you won't be coming back across this bridge."

"We understand," Liam said. "We're here seeking honest work, that's all."

Liam clicked to his horse and rode onto the bridge.

746

I looked back up at the sky, trusting my horse to keep carrying me onward, not wanting to give the soldiers a better view of my face.

The hollow sound of our horses' hooves crossing the bridge felt ominous somehow. Like maybe the gods were trying to remind us how far we'd fall if the ground collapsed beneath us.

The sounds of Liam's and Cati's horses returned to the normal, frozen crunch, and then my horse stepped off the bridge and back onto solid ground.

The soldiers on the far side said nothing as we rode past.

We kept our pace steady until the road turned, twisting us out of view of the bridge.

"We should find a place to cut back into the trees." I rode as close to Cati and Liam as my horse would stand for.

"I don't like the snow," Liam said. "I hate leaving a trail that's so easy for the paun to follow."

"We don't have much of a choice," I said. "We need to get a view of the valley, and from the road, paun might see us before we see them."

"I can cut circles for a bit," Kely said.

"What do you mean?" Liam twisted in his saddle.

"Ride my horse in and out on the same path for a while," Kely said. "Leave enough tracks and it'll all just look like mush. I used to do it all the time when I'd sneak out of my mother's house. Once it's tamped down I'll follow along."

"I don't want anyone alone," Liam said.

"It'll be better if it's just one person," Kely said. "Me riding in and out is an eccentric man with a poor stomach for travel. More than one would look like plotting."

"He's right," Emmet said.

"Fine," Liam said.

It didn't take long to find a good place to cut into the trees. It looked like a cart had gotten trouble from one of the dips in the road and lost some of its goods. Bits of straw had been frozen into the mud, and hoofprints and footprints alike marked the snow where it looked as though the poor owner of the cart had tried to reclaim his belongings.

I trusted my horse to follow Cati and watched Kely over my shoulder as he cut far enough into the trees to be out of sight from the road, then back out along the same path, mucking through the single line of hoofprints our horses had left behind.

The woods were peaceful, and the sun streamed down through the winter bare trees, glistening off the snow. Even with the day fading, there was plenty of light to keep the woods from feeling ominous or ghostly.

I hated it.

I wanted the scent of smoke in the air and the shouts of people chasing us. I wanted these woods to be tainted forever.

It wasn't right that this valley had stolen Finn from me and the woods hadn't been cursed for their part in his fate.

Tucking my grief into the blackness didn't work. Casting it into the fire did nothing either.

Finn and I had laughed in these woods, joking about his legacy.

I will make sure they tell your story. And you will be glorious.

I waited for Finn's voice to creep into my mind. But he didn't come back to me.

Liam slowed as the trees in front of us thinned. He stopped and tethered his horse well before we'd reached the edge of the forest.

I climbed down from my horse, giving her a few pats on the neck as I led her to a tree to be tied up. I don't know what she thought when I wandered off without her for bits of time. She was a Black Blood horse, so I guessed she'd seen worse than caverns and forests.

Liam waited for me before creeping closer to the edge of the woods. This time, the others came with us as well.

Trying to stay hidden in the shadows of barren trees seemed a bit odd, but I did the best I could, moving from trunk to trunk, not leaving myself exposed for longer than necessary.

I heard the beasts braying before I could see the full valley.

The animals' pastures that reached up the near side of the valley had all been turned to brown muck. But on the far side of the valley, the snow leading up to the Lir Estate remained pristine with only the hint of the road slicing up through the white.

There was no trace of the ponds to the north or the flock of stone birds. The winter had covered those remnants of Cinni's magic.

The damage to the town could not be disguised by a bit of snow.

The outskirts of the woven, maze-like town were still whole, untouched by the fire Evie and Cinni had started to help us escape. But the center of the town was a strange mix of homes with new roofs peeking through the snow and burnt out shells of stone structures that had yet to be rebuilt.

"Lir's got to hate that." A vengeful little smile lifted my lips.

"What?" Emmet asked.

"The scars on his perfect town. His own children ruined his pristine order, and the rich man has yet to recover."

My smile slipped away as I looked farther south in the valley.

The miners' homes were still intact—three long buildings settled beside a road that only led to the mine—but the gaping black hole in the slope that marked the entrance to the mine looked even more dreadful surrounded by white, like a festering wound that would spread an infection and rot the valley.

The line of tents set up between the mine and the town didn't help the image.

"Seven large tents." Cati peered out from behind a tree to the south of us. "How many soldiers do we think that is?"

"One will be for the captain," Emmet said. "Another will be the kitchen. Best case about fifty. Worst case, seventy."

"I don't hate those odds," Cati said. "If we can take them by surprise and the others make it here, we should be able to get through seventy pretty quick."

"We need to know if there's a sorcerer in the valley before we can risk Allana coming down with us," I said.

"We need to know if there's anything worth fighting over in the valley before we do anything," Emmet said.

I looked to Liam, waiting for him to tell us what he wanted us to do, but he just stared down into the valley, his gaze locked on the mine.

"Liam?" I joined him behind his tree. "Liam." I laid a hand on his arm, and still he said nothing.

"Trueborn," Cati said, "what's wrong?"

"I can feel it." Liam looked to me, fear and wonder filling his eyes. "There is mountain stone in that mine. I can feel it calling to me."

I forced my heart to stay steady as I took Liam's face in my hands. "How much of the stone is down there?"

"A mountain's worth."

5 4

I had known there was mountain stone in the Lir Valley. I knew the stone could be used to forge horrible weapons. But I could not bring myself to match the dread on the others' faces.

Cati closed her eyes and tipped her face up to the sky.

"How much of it have they already mined?" Emmet narrowed his eyes and studied the frozen terrain of the valley.

"I don't think they've gotten much," I said. "Evie told me the miners are given frie to celebrate if they dig up even a small stone."

"It's buried deep," Liam said. "They might not have reached the heart of it yet. Without a trueborn, they probably don't know how much mountain stone is even down there, just waiting to be found."

"Or they've found it over the winter, and the Guilds are now rolling in stone magic." Cati opened her eyes and looked at Liam. "We need to know how their mining has been going. We need to know who takes the stone away and what they do with it. And we need to get the information before we risk an attack."

"Are we going to attack?" Kely hurried to join us, his face pink from cold and labor.

We all turned toward Liam.

This wasn't how we had ever worked. Liam's people didn't stage attacks. We snuck in quietly and did what good we could while avoiding the soldiers' notice. It was how we had managed to accomplish anything in Ilbrea.

If we hadn't been facing the prospect of the Guilds forging stone-made weapons, I don't think Liam would have considered forcing a real battle.

But his face was set and determined as he spoke. "We'll have to. We can't risk the Guilds gaining weapons that strong. Cati and I will go down into the valley. See what we can find out. Look for any weaknesses. You three stay up here. The others shouldn't be too far behind us. I don't want them to pass us on the road."

I swallowed my argument that I should be the one to go with Liam. I knew my going into the valley bore too many risks. There was little chance that no one would recognize the girl who'd stolen the children the night the town had caught fire. If I let the townsfolk see my face, it would surely be the start of a fight.

"Cati will need a skirt." I headed back toward my horse.

"Is that completely necessary?" Cati followed behind me.

"Yes. They're wary of strangers and have to keep to Lir's rules or risk being thrown out. A woman in pants wouldn't fit into Lir's perfect mold. You don't want them to see you as a threat. Don't bother asking questions in the tavern. They were suspicious of Finn and me. It will only be worse for you now."

I reached my horse and untied my pack. "The miners all live in the three houses on the southern end of the valley. I never spoke to any of them, but they live under Lir's thumb even more than the folks in town. I doubt they'll be willing to risk talking to strangers." I pulled my extra skirt from my pack and shook out the fabric. "This should fit you well enough, and you can keep your pants on underneath."

"From the way you talk, there's no point in asking anyone questions." Cati unfastened her sword belt and passed it to me.

"I don't know that there is," I said. "There's too much fear in the valley."

"Good thing I don't mind causing a little fear myself if it means getting answers." Cati pulled my skirt on and buttoned it in the back.

It was only a plain, gray traveling skirt, but it still looked absurd on Cati.

"I chivving hate these things." She stared down at the fabric. "Making it harder to move is somehow more feminine, and letting the world see I was born with legs will somehow tempt men. It's all a chivving load of rot."

"We will always have the harder fight. It's the curse of womanhood. So let them think you're soft, and surprise them with a knife between their ribs."

"And if I accidentally get blood on my borrowed skirt?"

"Don't worry. Blood's not too hard to wash out."

"Don't lose my sword." Cati walked toward the road.

"We'll be back before morning." Liam took my hand in his.

I wished I weren't wearing gloves. I wanted to feel his skin against mine.

"Be careful." I kissed him and pressed my forehead to his. "Promise me."

"I promise." He brushed his lips against mine and followed Cati through the trees.

"Should we all watch by the road?" Kely asked.

"We can't risk leaving the horses," Emmet said. "I don't know what beasts live in these woods."

"I'll go watch the road then," Kely said.

He tromped through the snow, following Cati and Liam's path.

"I don't like him being by himself," I said.

"He'll be fine," Emmet said. "Kely wasn't just allowed to come on this expedition because he needs to see what life in Ilbrea is actually like."

I followed the path in the snow the others had left behind.

"Are you going to go wait with him?" Emmet asked.

"No." I turned around and walked back the other direction. "I just want to get as little snow as possible in my boots while I pace."

"They'll be fine," Emmet said.

"You don't know Lir."

"Would you like me to go after them?"

I paused for a moment. "You're the last person I'd send down there until we're ready to start a fight." I paced back toward the road.

"What do you want me to do then?" Emmet asked.

"Nothing."

"Will you stop pacing?"

"No."

"You're driving me mad."

"Fine." I stopped and rounded on Emmet. "What are you and Marta going to name the baby?"

"What?"

"You don't want me to pace, then give me a chivving distraction."

"Marta will name the baby on her own." Emmet looked down at his gloved hands. "The baby will be born long before I make it back to Lygan Hall."

"But you've got to go back. You've got to be there for Marta during the birth."

"I've got to be out here protecting our child, making sure the Guilds don't creep any closer to Black Blood territory."

"We could manage without you for a bit." I walked closer to my brother. "Marta will want—"

"Marta understands."

"But—"

"You want to talk, pick something else to chatter about." My brother stared at me without any hint of being willing to be persuaded.

"Why did you light Mave's square on fire?"

"I'm not telling you that." Emmet crossed his arms.

"Then why do you think we couldn't manage without you for a month while you went home to your pregnant wife?"

"You're impossible."

"I'm your sister."

Emmet glared at me for a moment before speaking. "Before I met Liam, I'd already been around some people who stand against the Guilds. They'd come into the smith's shop more than once. Always looking for weapons to be made. They paid good money, just wanted the work kept secret. The smith had me do most of it. He liked to put his skill into fancy projects people would be able to coo at, not work that had to be hidden.

"The men who wanted the weapons taught me about proper fighting. I started by asking questions, like I was trying to forge them the exact tools they wanted. They figured out I just wanted to learn, and they were happy to teach me."

"And what did those lessons cost you, brother?"

"Nothing." Emmet ran his hands over his face. "A life in Ilbrea, I suppose. They asked for a load of things to be brought to Frason's Glenn. Maybe they really did need them delivered, maybe they were just trying to lure me further in, I don't know. I met them in one of the buildings at Mave's. They introduced me to her."

Emmet began pacing through the snow. The white crunched beneath his feet as he forged his own path.

"Mave wanted other things made, things that weren't plain weapons. Cuffs for prisoners, tools that shouldn't be used on human flesh. Things she didn't want forged in

Frason's Glenn where there are always soldiers roaming about. I didn't like the idea of it. Fighting the Guilds is one thing, but taking prisoners—"

"Implies more than just trying to survive."

Emmet met my gaze. "It does. We took too long talking. One of the orange vests raced in, saying there were soldiers coming. They'd heard about weapons being brought into the city. My friends wanted to stand and fight, Mave needed to protect her family, so I did the only thing I could think of."

I waited for him to continue.

Emmet cringed before speaking. "I stripped bare, snatched the bottle of frie from the table, and bolted out into the square."

I clapped my hands over my mouth to cover my laugh.

"Everyone froze to stare at the drunk, naked chivving fool, and no one listened to the soldiers telling them to clear a path. I grabbed one of the lampposts and crashed it into the wooden platform right between the musicians, smashed the frie beside it to make sure the wood would catch, then started screaming *fire* at the top of my chivving lungs. Everyone scattered, and the soldiers couldn't get through. I bolted into the brothel and hid in the kitchen while the paun tried to wade through the chaos."

"And by the time they found where your friends had been, they were gone."

Emmet nodded. "Mave forgave me for the burned platform and lost barrels of ale. One of the orange vests fetched my clothes for me, and I went back to Nantic."

"And the legend of Emmet Ryeland was born."

Emmet shook his head and started pacing again.

"I'm sorry," I said. "Should I call you the Demon's Torch?"

"Call me whatever you like. Just don't tell everyone about me sprinting through Frason's Glenn naked. I have a wife. I don't need people whispering about me."

"I'll keep your secret, brother."

We stayed silent for a long while, Emmet pacing his path in the snow. Me being kind enough not to tell him to stop.

"Why the fire?" I asked as the sky turned gray. "At Mave's, when you go after the paun, why the flames?"

"People are afraid of fire," Emmet said. "It's bigger than they are. Scared people are easier to fight, and they're hardly ever smart enough to look beyond the flames to see what enemy is really coming for their blood."

5 5

Tirra, Allana, and four of the others arrived in a cart just before dark. I recognized the cart. Finn and I had used it more than once on our sorci runs.

The sorcerer did something to the cart to make it blend in with the trees.

I didn't watch her work her magic. I had no desire to see any sorcery so soon after the River of Frie.

The rest of our party arrived on foot an hour later.

Allana used her magic to make a warm patch for us to sleep.

Emmet set up guards to watch through the night.

I knew I should curl up with the others and try to catch a bit of sleep, but I couldn't make myself stand still, let alone lie down while Liam was in the valley. I had to be on my feet and ready in case he needed me.

Emmet seemed to understand. At least he didn't try to force me to rest.

I circled the perimeter of our warmth, not allowing myself to count the number of times I'd looped my sleeping companions.

I don't know how long it had been dark before the crunching of footsteps caught my ears.

I pulled my knife from my boot before creeping through the center of our camp toward the sound, and the other knife from my belt before I'd reached the far side of our group.

Emmet and one of the other guards joined me, though none of us reached for our lae stones. We all stood together, peering into the dark, our weapons gripped in our hands.

"Ena, it's me."

The sound of Liam's voice washed over me, tossing away hours of worry and fear.

I resisted the urge to sprint toward him as his shadow appeared between the trees.

"Where's Cati?" I asked.

"Slogging behind him in a soaking wet skirt," Cati said.

When Liam reached me, he wrapped his arms around me and pressed his chilled lips to my forehead before I'd even tucked my knives away.

"The others all arrived," Emmet said. "Our friend didn't want to keep the cart anymore when he heard we couldn't confirm the deaths of four who'd been to his farm."

"I don't blame him." Liam looked into my eyes for a moment before leading us back to camp. "I wouldn't have trusted Regan and her sorcerers to keep my secrets either. We can sort out a new place to store the cart."

"What did you find?" I kept close on Liam's heels.

The people sleeping in our snowy camp had started to stir.

"Liam." I darted in front of him. "What did you find?"

Liam dragged his hands over his face. "Enough. The Guilds send a soldier to take the stone away. The runner comes on horseback, not with a wagon, so they haven't reached the mass of the stone."

"That's good," I said.

"No one knows where they take it," Liam said. "A soldier rides in and rides off."

"The sorcerer holed up on the Lir Estate might know." Cati took off her skirt and passed it to me. "But no one's actually seen her in weeks. They only think she's still there."

I looked down to where Allana slept on the ground. "Should we wake her? Does she need to run? If the Guilded sorcerer senses her, the paun could find us here."

"We'll need Allana," Liam said. "If there is a sorcerer lurking in Lir's manor, waiting for us to show up and go after the stone—"

"Then there's not a chivving chance of us surviving without magic," Emmet said.

"We should all rest here for what's left of the night," Liam said. "I'll lay out stones to protect us from attack. We'll keep people on watch until morning."

"And then?" Emmet said. "If we're going to go for the mine, Cati and I should head to the soldiers' camp tonight. Do as much damage as we can while the paun are sleeping."

"We can't let them know we're here," Liam said. "Not until we know what we're going to do."

"How did you get the information?" I asked.

"A man tried to flirt with me, and the rest I don't think you want to know," Cati said.

A terrified shiver shook my spine.

"The important thing is there's a massive amount of mountain stone in the mine, and the Guilds still don't seem to know how much of a cache they have," Cati said.

"Finn was right," I said. "The legends about the mountain can't be true."

"Sure they can," Cati said. "We just seem to be missing a very important chapter."

"I know the legends of the mountain are important to the Black Bloods, but this isn't the time to worry about stories," Emmet said.

"Finn died because the Hayes refused to believe him," I said.

"And Colm will make sure the Hayes pay," Emmet said. "Our work is here, in Ilbrea, dealing with the paun and men like Lir who don't even know the Black Bloods' stories. If the Guilds get their hands on that much mountain stone, the tilk would lose any slim chance of freedom they have."

I didn't know what a stone-made weapon could do, but the thought of any advantage being handed to the Guilds brought enough dread to my stomach to make me ill.

"We should collapse the mine," I said.

"What?" Liam asked.

"We have to tear the mine apart from the inside and make sure the paun can never reach the stone."

56

There is a certain calm before a fight. A time when blades are sharpened, plans are made, and bellies are full but there is not yet any enemy to face.

If I had been wiser, I would have taken better advantage of that time. I would have prodded my brother's nerves, or thanked Neil for somehow always finding a way to fill our bellies. I would have asked Cati for one more lesson.

I should have stared at Liam's face and made sure I etched every detail into my soul.

But I let nerves get the better of me.

I paced and rebraided my hair, painted my face to a mask of perfection, checked my pockets a hundred times.

And then, as though the whole day had taken only an instant, it was time for me to climb into the cart and hope the plan we'd built would be good enough to see us through the night alive.

I stood staring at the back of the cart, trying to remind myself that I had been the one to volunteer for the job.

"Ena."

I turned at the sound of Liam's voice and leaned against his chest without speaking.

I hated the thick layers of our coats between us. They shrouded his body, keeping his familiar form and comforting warmth from reaching my skin.

"You don't have to do this," Liam said.

"And who would you send in my place?" I kissed him, savoring his scent and the feel of his lips against mine.

"I love you, Ena." He kissed my forehead and held me tight, like he wanted to memorize the feel of me.

"I'll see you in the valley." I made myself let go of him and turn back to the cart.

I had to protect him. I had to make sure he could fight.

For Liam, I would face any fear.

I unfastened the latch on the back of the wagon and tipped up the center slats of wood.

The hollowed-out bottom was large enough for me to lie down comfortably. There were even blankets tucked inside so I could keep warm.

Still, my heart threatened to burst from my chest as I climbed up onto the ledge and down into the compartment.

"Stay calm." Emmet stepped up onto the wooden lip around the hollow and took the hinged slats from me. "We'll be there when it's time. Don't make a move without us."

"I can look out for myself." I knelt in the sunken-in section of the floor.

"Against seventy soldiers?" Emmet said. "I'm asking you to be smart, Ena."

"I will." I lay down on my back, pressing my palms against the wood beneath me to keep myself from trembling. Or worse, standing up and bolting into the woods never to be heard from again.

I tipped my head up far enough that I could see Liam standing at the back of the cart as Emmet closed me in.

Liam gave me a crooked smile just before the wood blocked him from view. The expression hadn't reached his eyes.

Do not panic. Panic has never helped anyone, Ena Ryeland.

The wooden slats that made the top of my prison were only a few inches above my face. I peeled my hands off the planks below me just to prove I hadn't been chained down. I pressed my palm to the stone pendant hidden beneath my layers of clothes.

The warmth of it comforted me. Like I wasn't trapped alone in the cart. Like Liam was lying beside me.

With a click from Neil, the cart started forward.

I tried to slow my breathing, but the need to break free surged through every bit of my body. I pressed the pendant to my chest, digging the stone against my bones.

"This is for Finn," I whispered to myself. "I can do this for Finn."

I tried to picture Finn lying beside me.

He'd make a joke and then grumble about not having been fed. He'd hold my hand and never mention my terror, only chatter enough that I'd forget to be afraid.

Bang.

The cart bounced, sending me flying. I hit the top of my cage and fell back to the bottom with a grunt.

"Sorry about that," Neil said. "The roads here leave much to be desired."

"It's not a problem," Kely said. "The wheels are still on, and I'm sure if anyone was hurt, they'd let us know."

I shut my eyes and tried to ignore the awful sensation of being tipped upside down as the cart started down the long hill into the valley.

The sounds of sheep bleating carried over the rumble and clacking of the wheels for a bit. Then my body leveled out and the road smoothed as we reached the bottom of the valley.

"By the gods, how are we to find our way through this town?" Kely asked.

I bit back my smile.

"Slowly would be my guess," Neil said.

The sound of the cart's wheels changed again as we entered the town.

Kely and Neil took turns asking directions through the weaving roads, Kely getting more flustered with every missed turn, Neil getting gruffer.

I hoped the others were faring better on their journeys. I wished I could be up front guiding the cart instead of hiding from the people who might want vengeance on the girl who'd caused the town to burn.

This was your idea. It's far too late to regret it now.

"We're looking for the road to the soldiers' camp," Kely said for the tenth time. "We've been hired to take a cart of goods from them to Carrickbeg."

"Are the soldiers leaving?" what sounded like a woman asked.

"No idea," Kely said. "We were just told to come here and take what they put on the wagon back to Carrickbeg."

"You're almost through the town," the woman said. "A right at the next street, straight for five-odd houses, and you should be able to see it from there."

"Thank you, ma'am," Kely said.

"It's getting dark," the woman said. "You can't mean to leave town tonight. You'll have to go to the tavern for a room."

"We'll get directions for that if we ever make it to the soldiers," Neil said. "At this point, I'm starting to think I'll die weaving through this place."

Neil had the horse moving before the woman's laugh faded.

I felt my pockets for the fifth time, trying to make sure I hadn't lost anything.

"And here we are at last," Neil said in a carrying voice. "I thought we'd never find our way to the place. Next time someone offers us coin for a run like this, I'm saying no."

The sound of the wheels changed again.

My heart picked up its pace as we neared the soldiers' camp.

I strained my ears, trying to hear past the thumping of my heart and the rumbling and clacking of the wheels.

"We'll be lucky if this cart makes it back to Carrickbeg," Kely said after a wheel banged into something.

"Stop right there," a voice called.

I slid the knife at my hip from its sheath.

"What do you think you're doing out this way?" the unfamiliar voice said.

"We're here to pick up the supplies," Neil said.

"What supplies?" the voice came from closer to the cart.

"I don't know," Neil said. "Whatever it is you hired us to haul."

"There was no cart hired," the voice said.

Be kind, Neil. For once, just be kind.

"Are you sure about that?" Neil asked. "The soldiers in Carrickbeg paid us half in advance to come here and bring a cartload of goods back with us. I don't know why they would have paid us if there weren't any goods to haul."

"Stay in your seats."

The cart bounced, and footfalls thumped on the wood above me as someone searched the back.

Bits of dirt sprinkled down onto my face, but I was too afraid to shut my eyes.

"And they didn't tell you what goods they wanted sent?" the voice asked.

The cart bounced again as the person jumped down.

"No," Neil said, "and as it was a Guilded soldier doing the paying, I didn't think it right to ask."

"We can't get the supplies we ask for, and then they send you to take things away," the voice said. "Come on then. I'll take you to the captain."

"Maybe you're packing up and can spend the rest of the winter in Ilara," Kely said.

"Don't try raising my hopes," the voice said. "It only makes it worse when you wake up in a tent again."

"Sorry about that," Kely said.

"Mind if I bring the cart closer?" Neil said. "I'm not one for walking distances, especially not after sitting so long in this cold."

"And you're going to load goods onto a cart?" the voice said.

"That's what I brought this one along for," Neil said as the cart began rumbling forward again. "I can drive a cart on my own"—he spoke over the clacking of the wheels—"this one is here for the heavy lifting."

I kept gripping the hilt of my knife even as the cart rattled to a stop.

"I'll come around and help you down," Kely said.

The cart shifted as he hopped off.

"The last thing we need is you falling over, old man."

There was a faint scraping from the back of the cart, then three thumps on the side as Kely walked around to Neil.

"I could come on my own next time," Kely said.

"The Guilds ask for a job to be done, they expect it done right." Neil gave a dramatic groan as he climbed down from the cart. "I'll send you on your own when I can be sure the job will be done properly without me. I'll never understand why people aren't grateful for the work I put in."

Neil's grumbling faded as their footsteps crunched away.

I took a deep breath, trying to convince myself I wasn't a chivving, death-bound fool, before beginning to scoot around to switch the positions of my head and feet.

I paused every other breath to listen for movement nearby. I could hear the rumble of voices, but that was all.

When I was finally twisted up properly and had run out of reasons to stall, I shifted my knees beneath me and pushed the slats up with my back, just enough to let me peek outside.

All I could see was a bunch of trampled down snow and the back corner of a tent.

I pushed up a little farther and stuck my head out to peer in either direction.

There was no one in sight.

"I am not afraid."

I lifted the slats just enough to be able to crawl out the back and hop down into the snow.

There was still no one nearby.

I let out a shaky breath and tucked my knife away. I hated having my hands empty. It felt wrong, like I was inviting doom to sweep out of the sky and snatch my life away.

I pulled my scarf down to let my braid show and gave my cheeks an extra pinch for good measure.

"You're a chivving fool, Ena Ryeland." I squared my shoulders and stalked away from the cart, following the path of trampled snow that led around toward the front of the tents.

I'd almost made it to the last tent in the line before seeing any of the soldiers.

Then two rounded the corner, nearly bumping into me.

"What are you doing out here?" one of the soldiers said. "Townsfolk aren't supposed to wander out this far."

"I...I..." I let my voice fade away as I looked to the second, younger soldier.

"Get back to your home," the younger soldier said. "And don't come this way again."

I took a deep breath and tipped my chin up. "I can't go back to my home. I don't live here."

"Then find a room at a tavern or sleep on the street." The older soldier laid his hand on the hilt of his sword. "Just get away from here."

"I can't. I've come here for a reason, and I won't be swayed."

The older soldier pulled his sword from its sheath.

I gave a squeak and leapt back a step.

"A wagon came this way," I said. "I saw it. I waited all day, trying to work up the nerve to come here, and if they can be here, so can I."

"Do not make me—"

"Just get back to town before we have to make a mess of things," the younger soldier cut off the older. "There are no common folk allowed by the mine."

"I'm here to see your captain," I said. "I've got important information for him that I'm sure he needs to hear."

"You've got to be joking," the older soldier said.

"What sort of information?" The younger one stepped closer to me, setting himself between me and the older man's blade.

"I can't tell you." I gripped the sides of my skirt. "I'm just trying to do my duty to the Guilds."

"You'd better be sure it's worth it," the younger man said. "If I take you to the captain and you're bothering him for no reason, it won't turn out well for you."

"He'll be interested in what I have to say." I stepped closer to the soldier, staring imploringly up into his eyes. "Please, I need you to believe me."

The younger soldier's shoulders sank, and he looked back at the older.

"He's going to be in a chivving mood now." The older slid his sword back into its sheath. "If I get an earful from our captain, you can bet you'll get a fist from me."

"Come on then," the younger said. "The captain's already speaking to some folks, but he'll see you soon."

"Thank you." I curtsied to the soldiers then followed them around to the front of the tents.

The sky had already turned the gray of evening. The time before dark was running out.

Chivving town just had to be a maze.

Dull sounds of life came from inside the canvas tents, and a few men prowled the wide, open space between the camp and the mine.

Most of the men I could see—at least twenty, maybe thirty—were across the packed-down snow, standing guard at the gaping void in the slope that led down into the darkness of the mine and to the treasure we hoped the Guilds hadn't understood.

"I don't know what goods I'm meant to bring back with me." Neil's voice carried from inside the middle tent. "It's as I've told you—the soldier came to my farm, gave me some coin, and told me to come here to pick up a load of goods."

"You are dealing with the Soldiers Guild," an unfamiliar voice spoke, "not some rotta, back alley traders. I have no orders telling me to send supplies, nor do I have supplies to send."

"I don't mind going back with an empty cart if you say you've got nothing," Neil said. "Last thing I'd want is to be a bother to the fine soldiers who protect Ilbrea. But what do you want me to say to the man who paid me to come here when I go back empty-handed?"

"Out. Now. I don't care if you're whipped or hanged in Carrickbeg. That is your problem, not mine. But if you do not leave my camp now, I will whip you myself."

"Yes, sir," Kely said. "We're so sorry for our mistake, sir."

The flap of the center tent was thrown open, and Kely and Neil came stumbling out, chins tucked and shoulders rounded as they hurried back to the cart.

Neither of them looked at me as they passed. They didn't have time. They had to get well out of the way.

"You tell him," the older soldier said to the younger. "You want her to see the captain, you can chivving well tell him."

"You're a slitching coward, you are." The younger soldier headed toward the tent Neil and Kely had just come out of.

I pulled off my gloves and tucked them into the waist of my skirt.

"There's a girl here to see you." The younger soldier spoke from inside the tent. "She says she has important information."

I reached into my pocket. The cold of the fragments hidden inside stung my fingers as I grabbed a pinch and scattered them across the ground behind me.

"Why are there rotta getting near our camp at all?" the captain said. "Has Lir lost control of his people? We were sent here to guard the mine, not deal with insolent townsfolk."

"I hope your captain is a patient man." I started pacing behind the older soldier. My fingers numbed to the cold of the fragments as I slipped another pinch out of my pocket.

"The captain isn't known for patience," the older soldier said. "You were warned not to waste his time."

"I won't." I paced a longer path in the other direction, following a line of dirt-caked snow the soldiers had already formed. "I'm not worried about his temper coming out at me."

"I'm sorry, sir," the younger soldier said. "But if she truly does have information that's important to our work here, it seemed wrong not to bring her to you."

I paced back past the older soldier, cutting an even longer line toward the edge of the tents, trusting the mud-stained snow to hide the darkness of the fragments as I sprinkled them onto the ground.

"Come here and hold still," the older soldier said.

"Sorry." I scampered back to him. "When I get nervous, it's either pace or cry, and I didn't want to bother you with blubbering."

"Shall I bring her in, sir?" the younger soldier said.

"This is a chivving waste of my time." The flap of the captain's tent burst open, and an angry looking man with silver hair and a golden seven-pointed star embroidered on his jacket stormed out. "Is this the girl?"

He pointed to me as though there were other girls standing in front of the soldiers' tents.

"It is, sir." The older soldier nodded to his captain and stepped well away from me, as though wanting to be clear of the beast's wrath.

"I've come with important information for you, Captain." I brushed my hand against the side of my skirt, cleaning away the leftover grit.

"And what information might that be?" the captain said. "What could a rotta girl possibly know that would justify her tramping into a Guilds' camp where rotta aren't supposed to be?"

I swallowed hard before speaking again. "I've come to report lechery among your men. I've come because one of your own is making a mockery of the laws of Ilbrea and abandoning women along the mountain road."

"There is no space for such nonsense in my camp." The captain stepped closer to me.

"I'm here to see Jesper," I said, "who left three girls in my village with nothing to do but be shipped to Ian Ayres with bastards in their bellies. I can't believe the Guilds would want such a beast carrying the honor of being called a Guilded soldier."

The muscles on the sides of the captain's neck tensed. "Jesper Collins!"

His shout echoed across the snow and all the way to the shadowy entrance of the mine.

A soldier turned and ran toward us.

My stomach dropped straight out of my body.

5 7

The sky was almost dark. Close enough that I don't think it mattered that my face must have turned sheet white as the soldier, Jesper Collins, ran across the packed snow to reach us.

I'd chosen the chivving name because I didn't know any chivving Jespers. But fate likes to laugh at our brilliant plans, so of course there had to be a paun named Jesper in the chivving camp.

I slipped my hand back into my pocket and pulled out another pinch of fragments. As Jesper ran toward us, I paced along the same worn line, letting the bits of stone slide down the side of my skirt to hit the ground.

"Stop moving," the captain said.

"It's best to let her, sir," the older soldier said.

"Yes, sir?" Jesper stopped in front of his captain, standing straight and proud, as though he were genuinely honored to be wearing a black paun uniform.

"This girl has come to tell me about you leaving a string of bastards in your wake," the captain said.

Jesper's eyes went wide.

"According to her, you're shipping girls to Ian Ayres because you can't keep your pants up." The captain stepped in front of me to loom over Jesper. "What do you have to say for yourself?"

"I have received no word of such a problem, sir." Jesper's gaze darted to me. He studied my face, as though trying to remember if we'd had a roll in some barn. The slitch was handsome enough, he might have had trouble remembering what girls he'd abandoned.

"It's not as though you're easy to find." I reached my hand into my other pocket and started pacing again. "I had to beg a scribe for help to figure out where you might be. A stain on the honor of the Guilds, that's what you are. How are common folk supposed to feel protected by the Soldiers Guild if the sight of a black uniform might mean having their daughters snatched away to Ian Ayres because a foul man like you abandoned them?"

"I didn't—" Jesper sputtered. "I never—"

"Are you saying this girl is lying?" the captain asked.

"I'm not entirely sure, Captain," Jesper said. "I spent the early part of winter marching up and down the mountain road."

"I am not lying." I paced a longer path and forced tears down my cheeks. "Why would I travel in the winter to tell such a lie?"

"This behavior is a disgrace to the uniform we all wear," the captain said. "Guilded soldiers should not leave messes in their wake that others have to clean up."

"What do you mean clean up?" I gripped the sides of my skirt. My pockets were empty.

"Wasting my time with fallen girls like you tramping into my camp." The captain stepped away from Jesper, coming closer to me. "Using scribe resources to record the girls who have to be shipped to Ian Ayres. Taking sailors away from important duties to haul a bunch of pregnant whores to an island where the Guilds will be expected to feed them."

"That's what matters?" I shouted. "Not the girls whose lives are ruined. Not the children who will be born on that demon's island. The waste of resources the Guilds have to use to hide whatever twisted shame some Guilded slitch decided we should feel?"

Pain sparked across my face as the captain slapped me.

I stumbled back, blinking to try and rid the dim dusk of the bright spots dancing before my eyes.

More men had come out of the tents, and the soldiers guarding the mine had crept closer to watch the scene.

A flicker of light on the hillside did not disappear as my vision cleared.

"Speak again, and I'll have you whipped," the captain said.

I pressed my cold hand to my cheek, wincing at the pressure. "I'm sorry, sir," I mumbled the words.

"You'll learn respect on Ian Ayres even if it is too late to save you from a life of indecency." The captain turned back to Jesper but stayed close to me, on the near side of the long line I'd been pacing.

"I'll not be going to Ian Ayres," I said.

"I told you to be quiet." The captain raised his hand again.

"If you want me to marry you..." Jesper said. "I mean, I don't even remember you, but—"

"And the other girls you've left in your wake?" I tipped my head back and laughed.

The captain stepped away from me, as though I'd gone mad and he was afraid the madness might be catching.

"My village was destroyed because a boy loved a girl and tried to save her from being sent to Ian Ayres. Every soldier who even thinks of snatching a girl to ship her off deserves far worse than a whipping."

"You bastard-bearing—"

"No reason to ship me off, Captain. Do you need to peer between my legs to check?" I winked at him.

He took another step back, crossing the path I had paced.

765

"I'll have you—" The captain never got to finish his threat.

A sound like fine sand scattering against polished marble whooshed through the air as a wave of black stone fragments rose from the ground and flew toward the mine, tearing into the soldiers that stood in the way.

Pain sliced through the sides of my legs as the remnants from my pockets soared away with the rest of the fragments.

The screaming of the soldiers began before the stone tore all the way to the mine.

This time, the sound did not bring back horrible memories of the people I cared for being ripped apart by vicious claws.

I was glad for the pain the soldiers felt. They deserved every ounce of agony.

I watched as the captain covered his face, trying to shield his eyes, though the flecks of stone had already torn through them.

The men behind me, the soldiers who hadn't been hit by the fragments, charged toward their wounded fellows.

"What have you done?" An arm wrapped around me, and a blade pressed to my throat.

"I don't know what's happening," I cried. "Please, you have to protect me!"

The hold around my waist loosened.

I slid my knife from the sheath at my hip and stabbed backward, sinking my blade into the side of my captor's stomach. As he cried out, I dug my heel into his toe and twisted away from him, tearing my blade free.

The younger soldier blinked at me and pressed his hand to the wound on his side.

"Do not touch me." I tightened my grip on my knife.

Before the soldier could even try to swing his sword, the sound of shattering glass cut through the screams, and flames burst from the soldiers' tents on either end. The inferno engulfed the canvas before I could blink.

The soldier looked toward the blaze.

I brought my forearm down on the hand that grasped his sword while stabbing up into his chin with my knife. I was glad the wails of the other wounded soldiers covered the sound of my blade wrenching free from his flesh.

I turned toward the mine as the fire spread to the other tents.

Some of the men who'd been struck by the storm of stone were still on their feet and charging either toward the mine or back toward the flaming tents. Others had fallen. Whether they were dead or only wounded, I didn't much care.

A few paun were still on their feet, though so wounded or stunned by the stone tearing through them, they didn't seem to know what to do.

The captain stood, still gripping his face as he shouted orders. "Defend the mine! By order of the Guilds, defend the mine!"

I ran toward him and sank my blade into his gut. The warmth of his blood touched my hand as I twisted the knife and pulled it free.

"Stop her!"

I heard the shout but didn't turn to see who had given the desperate call.

A line of men had formed in front of the mine.

I raced toward them, needing to be close, needing to be sure Liam would be protected.

Red peppered the snow, surrounding the bodies of the paun and sprinkling across the barren patches where the wounded hadn't fallen.

A dark figure appeared, standing on the hillside above the entrance to the mine.

I watched as stones flew from his hands and struck the men below.

Some soldiers fell to the ground, others dodged and managed to keep living a few moments more.

Footsteps pounded behind me.

I turned around, raising my knife to defend myself.

The soldier who bore down on me had a sword.

I was not Cati. I could not fight against a sword with only a knife. But I kept my knife raised, unwilling to die without trying to defend myself.

The soldier smiled as he swung his blade, but a bit of silver pierced his chest. He staggered and coughed blood onto the snow as the silver disappeared.

With a swing of a sword, the man's head broke free from his neck, and the paun toppled to the ground.

My brother stood over him, stone faced even as death surrounded him.

"Thanks for that." I yanked the sword from the dead man's grip.

A scream carried from the raging fire that had been the tents.

Cati and five other Black Bloods faced the soldiers.

Cati fought in the center of it all, sword in one hand, knife in the other.

She moved as though it were some sort of dance. The soldier whose throat she slit was her partner, aiding her in turning in to the pattern of steps where she sliced through a man's stomach and stabbed another in the chest.

I froze for a moment.

There were no soldiers to fight in the no man's land where Emmet and I stood. Liam battled by the mine, Cati and the others by the tents.

"You should help them," I said to Emmet.

"I should stay with my sister." Emmet took off running toward Liam.

I tucked my knife back into its sheath as I followed him.

Some of the soldiers by the mine had started trying to climb the hillside to reach Liam, ducking the stones that flew from his hands.

Four still stood on the ground.

Liam had turned his attention to the men climbing toward him, sending a stone into the chest of one and into the neck of another.

Emmet reached the soldiers on the ground first, running his sword through a paun's back before any of them had noticed him.

The other three rounded on my brother.

I raised my newly gained sword and charged the nearest man.

He looked like a demon as he leveled his own blade. He had blood smeared across his cheeks, and red still trickled from the wounds on his forehead. A loathing to match my own burned in his eyes as he lunged, reaching the tip of his blade for my stomach.

I spun to the side, dodging his attack, and slicing my own blade across his back.

He howled in pain and rage as he turned, arcing his sword toward my neck. But the wound on his back had slowed him.

I ducked low and blocked his sword with my own.

The clang of it dug into my ears.

He winced and staggered, drawing his sword back to attack again.

Keeping my blade low, I slashed through the front of his thigh.

I felt the tip of his sword graze my side, like fire searing my skin. I stumbled close to him and pulled my knife from its sheath, driving the tip up under his ribs before he could back far enough away from me to make use of his sword again.

My breath grated my throat as I stepped back and searched for the next enemy.

There were bodies scattered on the ground, but none of the soldiers were still standing.

"We should get back to the others," Emmet said.

"I won't leave him." I looked to the entrance of the mine in time to watch Liam jump to the ground.

There was no blood coating his skin, no sign at all that he had been fighting except for the sweat on his brow.

"Ena, you're bleeding." Liam reached for me.

A flash of horrible red light flared to life on the hill by the Lir Estate.

I raised my hand to shield my eyes. "Liam, just do it. I'm fine, I promise."

"Back up," Liam said, "both of you."

Emmet grabbed my arm, dragging me away from the mine.

"No." I fought against his grip.

"We have to defend him," Emmet said. "Getting crushed won't help anyone."

Crack.

I glanced behind.

Liam stood ten feet in front of the mine, both hands held out before him.

Crack!

I couldn't see what stone had shattered to make such a horrible noise.

Emmet let go of my arm. "Watch yourself."

Five soldiers had broken free from the fight by the burning tents and sprinted toward us, their weapons raised.

The fighting seemed like it should have lasted long enough for the flames to die down, but time moves strangely with blood on your blade. The fire still danced in the darkness, as though it had only just been lit.

I watched Cati's silhouette as she slid her sword into the chest of the last soldier she faced.

There were three other Black Bloods still standing. There were too many bodies on the ground for me to be sure of the fates of the other two.

Crack!

I stumbled forward as the ground shook beneath me.

The five who had broken free were almost to us.

He is mine, and I will not let you hurt him.

Ignoring the pain in my side, I raised my sword before the soldiers could reach us.

A rumble sounded deep within the earth, and the ground began to vibrate.

The fastest soldier ran straight for Emmet. The second came for me.

He screamed as he charged, like his rage was a weapon he could use to kill me.

A flash of silver soared through the air, flipping end over end.

The soldier's screaming stopped as he dropped to his knees and fell forward, Cati's knife sticking out of his back.

A groan, like a centuries-old beast had come back to life, echoed out of the entrance to the mine.

I wanted to look back, to be sure Liam hadn't been hurt, but another soldier had leapt over his fallen comrade to swing his sword at me.

I dodged to the side and away from his blade, bringing my own up to block his next blow.

A horrible scream came from near Emmet, but I couldn't spare even a glance as I lunged forward, sinking the tip of my sword into the soldier's hip.

Silver flashed in front of his neck, and blood spurted out as Cati slit his throat.

I swayed and looked toward Emmet, ready to try and help him, but there were no soldiers left to fight.

Lightning streaked down from the sky and struck the hill near the Lir Estate.

We were running out of time.

The earth shook again. I stumbled over the corpse of a soldier and fell to the ground.

"Liam." I spit blood-soaked snow from my mouth and struggled to my feet.

Blue light poured out of the mine.

Liam knelt near the entrance, the glow surrounding him, his hands still raised in front of him.

I didn't scream his name. I didn't know how much of a hold the stone magic had over him or what might happen if I distracted him.

Snatching up my newly claimed sword, I ran toward him. Not knowing how to help, only certain that I needed to be near him.

Crack!

The ground shook again.

Inside the tunnel, stones fell from the ceiling, sending dust flying through the air.

But the light only grew brighter.

The ground lurched and tipped beneath my feet, as though something below me were giving way.

Crack!

Light flared in the entrance of the mine as the snow from the hillside tumbled down.

"Ena!"

I fell to my knees as the rise in front of us crumbled and the ground shook as though the world might end.

"Ena!" Emmet wrapped an arm around me, dragging me to my feet.

Liam didn't move. He stayed kneeling on the ground as the tunnel collapsed and the light went out.

"We have to go," Emmet said.

"I won't leave Liam!"

I don't know if it was the sound of his name or if the magic had simply ended.

Liam looked to me—his face pale, his eyes red. "Run."

58

"Liam!" The ground seized again.

The earth in front of Liam shattered, splintering as rocks fell into the darkness far below.

I plunged my elbow into Emmet's stomach and broke free of his grip to sprint to Liam's side.

"You have to go." Liam's voice was hoarse, like he'd been ill and was lying beside his own grave.

"Get up." I dropped my sword to drag him to his feet.

"Run," he said again, even as I got my arm around him and made him stand.

The ground swayed, and Liam tipped to the side. He couldn't even keep his legs beneath him.

"Ena, go!" Emmet ducked under Liam's other arm and hoisted him across his shoulders.

"I'm staying with you." I reached down to snatch up my sword, but it had already slipped into a slit in the earth.

I started to run, leaping over the growing cracks in the ground. I didn't head back toward the still burning tents but went west toward the miners' houses, hoping it was the right path to choose and the earth wouldn't swallow us.

I could see Cati and the other three from our camp racing in the same direction. Lights glimmered in the distance as more figures charged toward us. There was no hint of horses or a cart coming to our rescue.

The rumbling from below grew louder.

"Go faster," Emmet shouted.

"Then you chivving run faster." I kept right by his side even as the snow began to tumble away through the widening cracks in the earth.

I would not lose them. I couldn't. Better to be buried beside them than to make it to safety alone.

There was shouting up ahead, but I couldn't make out the words over the final crashes of the layers of rock settling into place.

Cati drew her sword, and I pulled out my knife, not knowing who our enemy was but needing to be ready to meet them.

And then the sounds of the shattering stone stopped, leaving only shouts to fill the darkness.

"What's happening?" A man stood twelve feet in front of Cati, looking rightfully wary of getting any closer to her.

"Why is the ground shaking? Where are the soldiers?" A woman held her lantern high, as though hoping to be a beacon for the dead paun.

"Let me stand." Liam's voice rasped as he spoke.

I reached for him as Emmet set him on his feet.

Liam didn't fight me as I wrapped my arm around his waist to hold him steady.

He took a ragged breath before speaking.

"The mine is gone," Liam said. "Destroyed. The soldiers are gone. They no longer have a place in your valley."

"How did this happen?" a young woman asked.

She was pretty. I wondered how often Lir had visited her bed.

"How doesn't matter." Liam pulled himself up straighter. "What matters is that Lir doesn't own you. Not your lives, your bodies, or your land. You have been abused by Lir and the Guilds for too long. It is time to stop living in fear. This is your chance to seize your freedom."

Liam paused, but none of the miners made a sound.

"Without the mine, Lir has no hold over you and no sway with the Guilds. We are going to stop Lir. Fight with me tonight, stand up to Lir, and by morning, you will be free." Liam looked to the woman who held her lantern high. "He will not be able to hurt you or your children ever again. This is the only moment you will have. Take it, or live knowing you gave up your chance for freedom."

"We can't fight." A man stepped forward. "We don't have swords. We're miners."

"Grab a chopping knife," Cati said, "a pick, an axe, a shovel, a hammer. Get whatever you have and come with us. It's not always steel that wins. It's numbers."

A bright, gleaming sheet of purple light burst to life, surrounding Lir's grand house.

"Better hurry," Cati said. "We've got our sorcerer waiting on us."

"Sorcerer?" The man stumbled away from the light encasing the manor.

"We've come to fight the people who harm you. Join us, or live wondering what freedom would have tasted like." Cati didn't sheath her sword before weaving through the people.

"Was it you?" A girl near my age stepped in front of us before I could help Liam forward. "Did you destroy the mine?"

"It was the only way we could have a chance for freedom." Liam followed Cati's path.

I gripped his waist and stayed right by his side, terrified he might collapse.

"Put your arm around my shoulder," I said softly as we weaved through the people.

"I'm all right," Liam said.

"I can bear the weight," I said.

He draped his arm over my shoulder, letting me carry part of his burden.

The miners parted ways, giving us a wide berth as we cut through them. None of them ran to fetch weapons to join us.

"It's a long walk to the manor." Emmet stayed right behind us as we ventured beyond the lantern light and onto the dark road that led past the miners' houses and to Lir's estate.

"Where's Neil?" I peered into the shadows, hoping the gods would grant us a bit of luck.

"I can make it on foot," Liam said.

"We can fight without you," Emmet said.

"I just need a few more minutes," Liam said. "I've never moved that amount of stone."

"Liam!" a voice shouted in the distance.

Up ahead, Cati stopped in the middle of the path, her sword raised. The other Black Bloods stood right behind her, all of them ready to fight the shadow speeding toward us.

"Is Liam safe?" The rumble of wheels carried over the shout, and a blue glow shone as Kely pulled his lae stone from his pocket. He stood in the front of the cart, leaning forward and squinting into the darkness. "We saw you run this way—"

"Liam's here," Cati said. "Now get us to the fight."

We caught up to the others, and Liam sagged against me as Neil looped the cart around.

My heart stuttered as Liam let go of me to climb into the back of the cart on his own.

I leapt up and knelt beside him.

Emmet was the last to climb up. I don't know if he hated the undignified idea of riding into battle on the back of a cart or if he was afraid that more soldiers were hiding in the dark, waiting to slaughter us.

"Let me look at you," I said to Liam as Neil shouted the horse forward.

"I'm fine." Liam reached for my side. "You're bleeding."

I looked down. In the light of Kely's lae stone, the blood staining the side of my coat looked to be a sickening black.

"I'm not dizzy," I said, "and I can still move well enough. I'll be fine."

"I shouldn't have agreed to your being in the middle of the fight," Liam said. "I should have thought of another way to scatter the stone."

"It's done." I took Liam's face in my hands, neither of us caring that they'd been tainted with blood. "The mine is gone. The Guilds won't get the stone, and we're both still here. A scar will not hurt me, Liam."

He rested his forehead against mine. Neither of us mentioned the Black Bloods who had fallen. The time for mourning would come after Lir was dead.

Neil shouted at the horse, making the animal run faster as the light around the Lir manor began to pulse.

"Is that Allana's magic or the paun's?" Cati asked.

Emmet stood, holding on to the back of Neil's seat. "We'll find out when we see who's still standing."

The cart cut up the slope toward the Lir Estate.

The snow that had sparkled a bright white last time I'd seen the hillside had all been melted away and the ground beneath singed a terrible black.

The purple sheet of light that surrounded the massive stone manor pulsed like the heartbeat of a living thing. The horrible hue made every shape look like a nightmare broken free from sleep. Bodies lay scattered on the ground, but in the strange purple glow, I couldn't tell if they were fallen friends or defeated paun.

"There." Emmet pointed in front of us, not at the corpses on the singed ground, but at the entrance to the manor where three people stood staring up at the light.

"Can't get any closer," Neil said as the wheels of the cart stuck in the burned muck.

"We don't need you to." Liam pushed himself out of the back of the wagon.

I held my breath as his feet hit the ground, but he stayed standing.

He held his hands palms up as he walked toward the manor. Stones rose from the ground, gathering themselves in his hands.

I leapt out of the cart and followed behind him, wishing I had something bigger than a knife to fight with.

"Back the cart away and wait for us," Cati said as the rest of the group gathered around her.

"I can fight," Neil said. "I'm not just useful in the kitchen tent."

"We'll need someone ready to take us away if things go badly," Cati said. "Don't lie to yourself and say that's not chivving useful."

The horse huffed, and the sound of the cart's wheels faded away.

Lir's house might as well have been a palace or a castle for how large it was. And from the way it was built, Lir had been waiting for this night.

There was only one entrance that I could see, a door set into the thick stone wall, and the lowest of the windows were ten feet off the ground. Metal bars crossed the glass, blocking intruders from slipping in.

I kept scanning the darkness, searching for paun coming to attack, but the only living people in view were the three standing in front of the entrance.

"Liam?" one of the shadows called from near the door.

"What's happening here?" Liam's voice came out stronger than before, easing a tiny bit of the fear lodged in my chest.

Two of the people turned, relief filling their faces, like their Trueborn's presence promised salvation.

"I've locked Lir in." Allana didn't turn toward Liam as she spoke. "He does have a sorcerer hiding with him. He sent his guards out to die, but neither he nor his sorcerer were brave enough face us. The sorcerer killed our people while hiding like a coward."

"How long can your spell hold?" Liam stopped right behind the other Black Bloods.

"Not much longer," Allana said. "She's fighting me from the inside. If I push too hard, I risk burning out, and you wouldn't survive facing this magic without me. Shall I let the monsters loose?"

"Not yet." Liam tipped his head to the side, as though listening for something.

"What is it?" Emmet stepped up beside Liam, studying each of the windows as though trying to decide which he should break through.

"There's mountain stone in the house," Liam said.

"Not surprising since the man mined it," Cati said.

"There's something else. Something bright." Liam looked to me. "I can't be sure what it is."

A new wave of fear wrapped around my spine. "We can't just walk away from Lir. We can't let him take out his wrath on the people in this valley. We destroyed the mine. What will he do if he decides the townsfolk aren't useful?"

Liam held my gaze for a moment before looking to Allana. "Can you open a path to the door?"

"Just the door?" Allana said. "I will try to do as the Trueborn asks."

"Emmet, can you light it?" Liam asked.

"Not with a blaze, but it'll start." Emmet sheathed his sword and dug into his pockets.

"Once it's lit, I want all of you to clear away from the door," Liam said. "I'm taking the stone from Lir. We'll hope he follows his treasure out."

"If he doesn't follow the stone, he'll have to flee the smoke if it gets bad enough," Emmet said.

"I'll make it bad enough," Allana said. "Ready?"

I didn't want to step to the side. I wanted to stay next to Liam, but Emmet glared at me.

I stepped back between Kely and Cati.

"Do it," Liam said.

The purple around the manor gleamed brighter for a moment before a bit of blackness punctured the light right in front of the door. The dark spot grew, stretching out like a demon's mouth trying to swallow the world.

Emmet leapt into the darkness before the gap was half his height. He knelt in the entryway, scattering something from his pocket along the bottom of the door. He smashed a small vial against the wood before pulling two stones from his pocket and striking them together.

I had barely caught sight of a hint of a spark before flames lapped at the bottom of the door, popping and crackling as they spread.

Emmet leapt back through the purple of the spell before the blackness had stopped expanding.

A bang sounded from within the manor.

I looked to Liam, but he just tipped his head to listen, as though trying to sort out the source of the sound.

Bang.

Allana flinched as though she'd been slapped.

I made myself loosen my grip on my knife before my hand could go numb.

Bang.

Emerald light burst from the house, slicing through Allana's spell.

She gasped as all the windows in the manor shattered and the light of her magic vanished.

59

Shards of glass flew from the windows, raining down on the Black Bloods. I raised my hands to shield my eyes, but none of us backed away.

I heard a gasp of pain but didn't dare look to see who it had come from.

When the last of the glass had fallen, all our people were still standing.

I looked to the nearest window, searching for arrows ready to fly down and kill me.

Allana stumbled back, gasping for air as though she'd been struck in the chest.

"If you want freedom, I'll fill it with flames." She waved a hand through the air, and a rush of wind followed.

The gale shook the door and, for a moment, I thought the fire Emmet had lit would be blown out.

But the flames grew, burning bright blue as the wind whisked them under the door and into the house.

A high scream carried through the shattered windows.

"The workers from the estate," I said, "are they all inside?"

"We didn't see anyone but the ten-odd guards who charged out to fight," one of the Black Bloods said.

I didn't know his name. I should have known all their names. Every person I'd ever fought beside. But I was too weak to risk having the name of another fallen friend to add to my tally.

"Down!" Cati shouted.

I ducked, not even sure what I was meant to be dodging away from.

A flare of bright light shot out of one of the windows, striking the nameless Black Blood who'd been too slow to move.

Allana charged toward the source of the light.

The bars covering the window crackled and sparked, shining with a brilliant, silver light. Allana reached high over her head and wrenched her hand back, ripping the bars out of the stone.

"Stay down." Liam raised his hand, not toward the door that had been fully engulfed by blue flames, but toward a window on the top floor.

A crack sounded from inside the manor, and Allana stumbled back, though I could see no reason as to why.

I crouched, helplessly waiting, looking from the open windows to Liam, to Allana, trying to find a way I could aid in the fight.

Bits of black rained down toward Liam.

I started forward, desperate to protect him, but Emmet grabbed me, holding me back as six stones fell into Liam's hands.

"Is that it?" Cati glanced toward Liam before looking back up to the windows.

"There's something else," Liam said. "I can't tell where."

Boom!

The manor shook, though I still couldn't see what magic was making the awful noises.

Allana screamed in rage.

I spun toward her.

Blood marred her face, but she was still standing, still fighting.

Crack!

I spun toward the new sound.

Liam clawed through the air, tearing down the stones above the door, trapping whoever hid in the manor inside with the flames. He stood panting as the stones around the entryway began to collapse, tumbling away one by one without the center arch to support their weight.

A crackling came from Allana as her whole body seemed to tremble before a wave of darkness flew from her and into the window.

Boom!

The sound shook the house again, this time sending rocks cascading down.

I leapt forward, grabbing Liam's arm and yanking him back as the front of the manor crumbled away.

It was as though we'd gone back to Frason's Glenn and we were the Guilded sorcerer standing outside the pub ready to murder tilk. But this time, the people inside deserved a horrible death.

The splitting of stone carried around the sides of the manor as the place crumbled from the outside in.

A scream rent the night, and a figure in tattered purple robes flew from the window.

The Guilded sorcerer's feet barely touched the ground before she took off, sprinting toward the wooden barn behind the ruined grand house.

Allana didn't wipe the blood from her face before chasing after the paun. Black flew from her hand, stretching forward and wrapping around the sorcerer.

The paun screamed, whether in pain or fear I couldn't tell.

Allana's magic whipped the girl around to face us.

The paun was young, not much older than me, and pretty too. She had black hair that streamed behind her as Allana dragged her forward.

I didn't know if the girl was Lir's child or just another woman chosen to please his appetites.

"Let me go!" the girl screamed.

"I have no wish to harm anyone with magic in their blood," Allana said. "But I will not allow you to stand against us. Surrender and live."

The paun screamed. Light surrounded her face as she battled against her bonds.

But the sound didn't come just from her.

More shouts carried from the darkness as the doors of the wooden barn burst open and Lir's lackeys charged into the fray.

Two-dozen people ran to join the fight, most bearing swords, some with nothing better than axes and shovels.

We're trying to help you! I wanted to shout at the people charging toward us, but a blue light had begun to glow inside the barn.

Liam raced into the fray, Emmet and Cati close behind him.

Liam stayed steady as he met the fastest of Lir's people. Stones shot from his hands, downing three men at one.

Emmet sliced through two of Lir's people before even breaking his stride.

The clang of sword on sword rang over the paun sorcerer's scream.

Cati dove into the fight, moving her weapons so quickly, I didn't know who she had wounded and who had only stumbled away in fear.

I yanked my second knife from my boot before racing to join them.

The first man to come at me swung his sword so wide I barely had to lean to avoid the blade. He stumbled as the weight of his weapon pulled him sideways.

I kicked him in the hip, knocking him to the ground.

He wasn't trained to fight. His sword flew from his grip as he fell.

A strange wail filled the night, but I couldn't look away from the man to see what magic had made the sound.

I didn't want to hurt him, didn't want to kill a tilk who had only been scared into following Lir's orders.

Another wave of shouts filled the night.

This time, I did chance a glance toward the sound while my foe crawled across the singed earth toward his sword.

A dozen more people poured out of the barn.

The man on the ground seized his sword and tried to swing it at me.

I kicked him in the head and drove my knife into his back.

I left my knife in his flesh and slid my other blade into the sheath at my hip as I grabbed the sword from his hand and I turned to find my next opponent.

One of the Black Bloods staggered before me.

I swung for their attacker before my clansman hit the ground.

A new round of furious cries came, not from the barn, but from behind me.

I dodged around my foe to gain a view of the hillside.

A pack of thirty ran up the road from the miners' houses, armed with shovels, picks, hammers, and torches.

Pride filled my chest as I slashed through my foe's stomach.

The tilk did want freedom.

Ilbreans wanted freedom. All they needed was someone brave enough to offer them a chance to fight for themselves.

I rounded on Lir's men, sword raised and ready to fight. But a blinding blue light flared inside the barn, and a shadow stepped out into the night.

I squinted against the light, trying to make out more details of the silhouette.

A man with a shovel swung for my head.

I ducked low and kicked behind his ankles, knocking his feet out from under him.

The silhouette had one arm held high. Bright sapphire light flared from his raised hand.

The man with the shovel shot his hand out and grabbed my ankle, dragging me to the ground.

Liam ran toward the silhouette. He still didn't have a sword with him.

I swung my sword toward the man who had yanked me down, but he blocked the blow.

Pain shot up my arm from the impact of his shovel against my wrist. My hand went numb. I couldn't feel the hilt of my sword as it tumbled from my grip.

The man drove his knee into my chest and wrapped his hands around my neck.

Panic flew through me as my lungs shouted that I was about to die. I reached for the knife at my hip, though my fingers still buzzed.

Out of the corner of my eye, I saw Liam facing the silhouette. Rocks flew from Liam's palms, but the stone didn't seem to strike the figure hiding in the light.

The man on top of me slammed a knee down on my hand before I could grab my knife.

I kicked up, trying to knock him off me as spots blurred my vision.

The hands around my neck didn't move.

I punched with my free hand, catching the man in the ear.

His gripped slackened for a moment but tightened again before I could take a full breath.

I moved to punch again, but before my fist could strike his face, the man had tipped off of me.

Gasping in wonderful, crisp air, I blinked the spots from my eyes.

Kely stood above me. He reached down to take my hand, then tipped to the side as an axe struck him in the ribs.

60

"Kely!"

The woman with the axe swung for me.

I rolled to the side, grabbing my sword in my left hand as I fought to get back to my feet on the slick, black ground.

The weight of the sword felt foreign in my left hand, but the woman seemed less inclined to attack now that I was looking at her.

Flames flashed in front of me as a young girl from the miners' homes hit the woman in the head with a torch.

The axe woman screamed and fell to the ground.

The girl with the torch kept hitting her.

"Kely." I knelt beside him. "Kely, look at me."

His eyes had already gone blank.

"I'm so sorry," I whispered.

I forced my right hand to grip my sword and ran toward Liam.

Pop!

I didn't turn back as a hiss filled the air. If magic wanted to kill me, there wasn't a chivving thing I could do to stop it.

Liam stood before the silhouette, both arms raised in front of his face, as though he were pushing away a boulder with all his strength.

It wasn't until I neared Liam's side that I could see the features of the man hidden in the light.

Lir.

His black hair flew behind him. Hatred filled his dark eyes and twisted his face into an awful sneer. In the hand he held high, a crackling ball of sapphire blue shone with a dazzling light that was both glorious and terrifying.

"I will not let you hurt them." Sweat coated Liam's face, and the muscles in his neck strained as though Lir might crush him.

"This is my valley, and you will not take it," Lir said.

"It's already gone," I shouted over the buzzing crackle that came from the orb. "Your mine is gone. Your manor is gone."

"You." Lir looked from Liam to me. "I had hoped the child would have killed you."

"Which child?" I flexed my grip on my sword, testing the strength of my hand. "Or do you not even know their names?"

"They are mine," Lir spat.

"They are free." I stepped closer to Lir. A weight pressed on my shoulders, driving me back, though I couldn't see how. "Evie asked me to take them away. Dorran grumbles every day, but he's never once asked to be brought back to you. Gwen risked everything to get the others to safety. And Cinni—"

The weight doubled its pressure against my lungs.

"Cinni helped me get here." I coughed as I forced the words out. "Your children are free, and your people will be, too."

"I will burn them before I lose them."

I dove toward Lir, slashing my sword for his gut. But the weight of whatever magic filled the air pressed me down. My sword caught him in the leg, slicing through the front of his shin.

Lir shouted in pain and sagged back for a moment but kept hold of the light.

I curled in on myself, trying to convince my body I could keep breathing, despite the crushing weight bearing down on me.

"You are a thief," Lir said. "And I will kill you. Then I will find my children and take them back."

A thumping carried from above, as though my heart had decided to flee my body.

Twisting to the side, I pulled my knife free, hoping I could manage its weight.

A form appeared, standing on the roof just above Lir's light.

I coughed out a laugh. "You'll never see them again. He'd never let you take them from her."

I stabbed my knife into the top of Lir's foot.

He bowed his head forward, staring down at the blade sticking out of his fancy boot.

The form leapt down from above.

Silver flashed in the bright blue light as Emmet drove his sword down through Lir's back.

Lir coughed. Blood dripped from his mouth as he swayed. His grip on the sapphire orb loosened.

"No!" Liam dove forward, shooting his arm out toward the orb.

I thought he'd meant to catch it, but the orb soared away, flying high into the sky.

Liam held his hands close together, as though cradling the sphere, before wrenching them apart.

With a crack and a whoosh, fire filled the sky, blocking out the stars, raging through the night as though trying to burn the gods themselves.

Heat lapped at my skin as Liam dove toward me, sheltering me with his body.

Screams drowned out the crackling of the flames, and the light faded.

I lay panting on the ground, forcing my lungs to accept air with each breath.

"Ena?" Liam shifted, pulling away to look at me. "Ena, are you—"

I took his face in my hands and kissed him.

He sagged toward the ground even as his lips were pressed to mine.

"Liam." I scrambled up, trying to support him. "Where are you hurt?"

"Not hurt." He laced his fingers through mine. "Just tired. Very tired. I'd never felt the power of a stone-made weapon before. The clans were right to ban them."

I shoved aside my horror at what Lir might have done with such magic.

"We'll get you out of here." I looked toward the battle, but the fighting had ended.

I didn't know if all Lir's people had been killed, or if they'd just given up when their master had fallen.

Emmet took Liam's arm, hoisting him to his feet.

My brother bled from a gash on his leg, but his gaze was steady as his eyes met mine.

"We need to go," Liam panted the words. "We have to take our people and go. Others will have seen the flames in the sky. The Guilds will be coming."

"Emmet, get him to the cart." I ran toward the people standing on the singed earth, trying not to wonder what it would have looked like if the flames of the sphere had been unleashed on the ground.

I hadn't understood the horror of stone-made weapons, not until I watched the sky burn. I swallowed the sour that flew into my throat. If the Guilds decided to use those sorts of weapons against the tilk, they could burn whole villages without even using their soldiers to torment us.

I forced the thought from my mind. We had beaten Lir, destroyed the mine, and freed his people. The rest of the monsters would have to wait for another day.

There were more strangers than friends lying in the muck. I couldn't tell which side most of them had been fighting on.

I stopped beside Kely, making sure there was nothing I could do for him.

He'd long since fled his pain.

Helplessness pressed a knot into my throat. I couldn't even find any words to thank him for saving my life.

"I'm sorry," I whispered. "I'm sorry you didn't get to ask Isleen to marry you. I'll make sure she knows how much you loved her, and how well you fought. I'll make sure she never knows about Mave's."

I pulled my knife from the back of the man I'd killed before searching through more of the bodies.

"Is it over?" A young girl from the miners' homes limped toward me.

"It is," I said. "Lir's dead. And now we have to go."

I found another Black Blood on the ground. There was nothing I could do for him. Carrying the dead back to the mountains was too dangerous, too suspicious. It would slow us down too much.

Guilt joined the terrible helplessness.

"You're going to leave?" a man asked. Blood seeped from a slice along his jaw. "You can't do this and leave."

"Yes, we can," I said. "The Guilds will come to see what's happened. Soldiers will come. Sorcerers will come. And you can tell them we're responsible. We killed Lir. We destroyed the mine. You have to have someone to blame, or they will send swarms of soldiers to this valley that you cannot defeat. You have to plan for what you want to build here, for how you will keep the Guilds from making this valley worse than it was before.

But for you to survive long enough to do that, you have to blame us, and we have to leave."

"Thank you." The young girl reached for my hand.

I took a step back before I could stop myself. "Please don't thank me. Just bury our people before the Guilds get here. Hide the graves so the paun can't find them."

"We will," the girl said.

I gave her a nod and turned away, weaving between the bodies.

I hoped she would bury the Black Bloods properly. I hoped her life really would be better without Lir.

Allana knelt beside the fallen sorcerer. The girl looked even younger in death.

"This shouldn't have happened," Allana said. "She was strong. She was skilled. Her power shouldn't have been twisted by the Guilds."

"This is what the paun make of magic. It happens to every child the Sorcerers Guild claims."

Allana swallowed a sob.

I reached for her hand. "Convince Wyman that more Ilbrean sorcis should be brought to Lygan Hall. Evie could have ended up like this girl. Or Gwen. Or Cinni."

Tears streamed down Allana's cheeks.

"It's bring them to you or leave them to the Guilds. Which path will you fight for, sorcerer?"

Allana took my hand and stood. "The mountain works in ways that are not for us to understand, Solcha. But our path forward is clear."

She started for the cart while I kept working my way through the fallen. I hoped the path I had led them toward would matter, would give more meaning to the deaths of those who lay scattered on the singed and sodden ground.

"Ena."

I spun toward the voice.

Cati limped toward me, one hand pressed to her side.

"Cati." I leapt over corpses to reach her. "Are you all right?"

"I don't know. You're the healer, not me."

"Let's get you to the cart," I said. "Can you make it that far?"

"Sure," Cati said. "Bleeding never really hurt anyone."

I looped her arm around my shoulders and half-carried her across the bloodied lawn.

Neil sat in the front of the cart.

Allana had taken the seat beside him.

Liam and two of the others sat in the back, all barely conscious.

Emmet helped me get Cati into the cart and lying down.

"Some of us should run behind," Emmet said. "There's too much weight."

"We should all stay together, and you chivving well know it," Cati mumbled.

"Get in." I pointed my brother into the cart.

As soon as I'd clambered up, Neil had the horse running.

I scooted around to kneel beside Cati and gently peeled her shirt away from the wound.

The cart hit a rut in the road, sending all of us bouncing.

"If you tell me to lie still while this cart is tossing me around, I'll have to come up with new ways to torture you in training," Cati said.

I pulled my lae stone from my coat pocket. The familiar feel of the sphere in my hand sent a shiver down my spine. The same stone had nearly burned us all.

I shook away my fear and held the light close to Cati's side.

She sucked air in through her teeth as I pressed on the skin around the wound.

"It needs to be cleaned and stitched, but I think all the important bits should be all right," I said.

Cati grinned. "My mother always wanted me to pay more attention to needle work. I never thought I'd find sewing to be a useful skill."

I made myself laugh as I tore a bit of the lining from my coat.

"How did it happen anyway?" I pressed the poor bandage against the wound.

"Chivving glass sliced me when the windows exploded," Cati said.

"But you dove straight into the fight. I saw you. Why didn't you tell me you were hurt?"

"I didn't want to miss out." Cati laid her head back, not fighting as I kept pressure on her side.

As we neared the town, I could see people filling the road, all staring up at the ruins of the Lir Estate, but none of them seemed willing to venture toward it.

"Clear the road!" Neil bellowed at them.

They scattered like frightened rats.

I wished we could stop and Liam could tell them that, if they all stood together, there was hope for a beautiful future.

But we had to leave. Had to run away and be the bandits and myths Ilbrea had made of us.

May we meet again in a land of freedom.

The cost had been high. So few of us would be returning to the cavern with the waterfall, or the camp, or Lygan Hall.

But I'd proven Finn was right. There could be no denying he'd told the truth, and the Black Bloods would have to accept it. Liam had destroyed the stone the Guilds needed to make horrible weapons, and we had stopped Lir from terrorizing his people, too.

Nothing could be worth losing Finn, but at least there was meaning, purpose behind the heartbreak. And no one could pretend Finn's life hadn't made a difference.

When the Black Bloods told the tale of the triumph in the Lir Valley, Finn's name would begin the story. He would not be forgotten.

Kely would be in the story, too, and the others who'd fallen. The families who mourned in Lygan Hall would have something to cling on to, some change in the world that marked the importance of the loved ones they'd lost.

Tirra waited on the eastern side of the valley near the edge of the woods, pacing between the saddled horses.

Liam wasn't fit to ride, and I needed to stay in the cart to tend to Cati's side. Allana made no move to leave her seat beside Neil. The rest all gratefully claimed horses.

By the time I grabbed my pack and dug out the things I'd need to tend to Cati, the others were mounted.

Emmet led the way forward, Tirra followed the cart with the spare horse trailing behind, and we began our journey back to the safety of the eastern mountains.

We had not won a shining victory. Stitching Cati's side as we trundled along the rut-covered road brought me no bliss.

But after I'd bandaged her wound, I sat next to Liam.

He wrapped his arm around my waist and pulled me close to his side.

I leaned into the embrace, letting the joy of being near him surround me. I laced my fingers through his and knew I would gladly bear the pain and fear and fighting if it meant having a chance at a world where we could build a life together.

A bright spark of hope filled my chest.

I had found my home, and together we would defend it.

We would both fight for freedom, and I would walk that dangerous path by his side, to whatever end.

61

I wish my story ended there. Covered in blood and filled with hope, sitting by Liam's side.

I wish I could lie and tell you we raced away into a joyous peace earned by those who risk their lives so others may live freely.

The tilk rose up, Ilara burned, and the Guilds fell. There were summers of dancing and winters spent wrapped in Liam's arms.

But I will not lie.

I can't.

I am too broken. Even pretty lies cannot mend my shattered soul.

The bumps in the road got worse as we neared the bridge beyond the Lir Valley.

"Drop back, Neil," Emmet called from the front of the pack.

Neil slowed the horse as Emmet and two of the others charged forward.

I leaned around the side of the wagon, watching my brother disappear into the darkness.

"If he gets to kill those bridge troll soldiers without me, I'm going to be chivving furious," Cati said.

"You've lost too much blood." I leaned over and squeezed her shoulder. "If you rip your stitches and keep bleeding, you might not make it to the next battle."

I sat back and dug my nails into my palms as a pained cry carried from up ahead.

The clang of metal on metal came a moment later.

"I should take the last horse," I said. "Ride forward and join them."

"I'll go." Liam tried to push himself up, but his arms wouldn't hold his weight.

"You have to rest," I said. "I can fight."

I stood up, holding on to the back of Neil's seat as the cart bounced down the road.

We rounded the corner, and the shadowy shape of the bridge came into view.

The stars offered enough light to see two soldiers lying on the ground. One of our people had fallen as well. His horse still stood beside him, staring down at her rider as though wondering when he would move.

Emmet and the other Black Blood had charged across the bridge, where each of them fought another paun.

"The tent." I pointed over Neil's shoulder. "There might be more soldiers in the tent."

Allana held out her hand. A great gust of wind tore the white canvas away. Cots and a table tumbled toward the river. A few trunks withstood the gale, but there was no hint of a person.

Emmet killed his soldier and turned to quickly finish the other.

"We can't leave that horse," Tirra said.

"I'll take her."

Neil slowed the cart.

"Ena." Liam reached up and squeezed my hand. "Be safe."

"I'll be riding right in front of you." I kissed his forehead and jumped to the ground before the cart had properly stopped.

"Hello there." I spoke gently to the horse. "I'm going to ride you for a bit, all right?"

I knelt beside my fallen clansman. He had already drifted beyond all aid.

"What do we do with him?" I looked to the cart. "Allana, can you bury him?"

Allana's face was drawn and her eyes dark as she met my gaze.

I swallowed the bile in my throat and climbed onto the horse. I recognized the black mare. I'd ridden her before, through the tunnels to the Broinn. I kicked the horse forward, not looking back to see what magic Allana would work.

The hollow clopping of the horse's hooves on the bridge seemed obscenely loud, even over the rushing of the river. The rumbling of the cart's wheels was worse.

Emmet waited for us across the bridge, his horse pawing at the frozen ground.

"There were six before," I said as soon as I'd reached him. "Where are the other two soldiers?"

"Gone for help." Emmet pointed to one of the dead paun. "He promised me there would be an army of Guilded soldiers and sorcerers on us before dawn."

"How?" I searched the shadows of the trees, trying to find any murderers lurking in the darkness.

"With the way the Guilded soldiers are patrolling, I don't know," Emmet said. "But there's only one road for us to follow right now."

I stared at the dark road ahead of us. It would be twenty-five miles, maybe a bit more, to reach Carrickbeg and the shelter of the eastern mountains. The only other branch in the road led to Ilara, but no matter how many soldiers might be in Carrickbeg, there would be more in Ilbrea's capital.

I glanced behind to the dock reaching out into the roaring river. When we'd crossed the bridge to enter the valley, I'd been glad there were no boats that might hide vengeful ghosts out for my blood. Knowing the Guilds would be racing through the shadows with their dogs chasing our scent, I would have gladly faced a horde of ghosts in exchange for a boat that could carry us downriver and to the safety of the eastern mountains.

"We have to move to fast." Liam clung to the side of the cart, propping himself up as he spoke to his people. "Keep riding, no matter what happens. We will not let them corner us. Go."

The other Black Blood shouted to his horse and bolted down the road.

I kept close behind him while Emmet fell back to ride beside the cart. I couldn't hear the words he and Liam exchanged over the thunder of our racing horses.

I wanted to ride faster, cut into the woods and race through the trees until the Guilds couldn't hope to track us. But, even if Cati and Liam had been well enough to ride, there weren't enough horses for all of us, and the cart wouldn't make it through the woods. If we left anyone on foot, it would be as good as handing them to the paun and their dogs.

My horse wanted to run faster, too. I could feel her pulling against me, wanting to chase the winds and get out of Ilbrea.

Just reach the crossroad. Once you've made it that far, they won't know which way you've gone.

I kept repeating the hopeless thought to myself over and over.

The pounding of horses' hooves and the rumble and clatter of the cart's wheels were the only sounds in the dark woods.

I pressed my stone pendant to my chest, needing to feel its warmth as terror threatened to overwhelm me. I focused on the feel of Liam's magic against my skin as I promised myself that I was not slipping back into the old nightmare. This ride would not last forever, and I would not fail the people I loved.

We passed the crossroad.

The path to Ilara cut through the trees and into the darkness. There were no soldiers waiting in the shadows.

A slim shred of my fear dissolved. We'd left the Lir Valley so quickly and were traveling so fast. All we had to do was reach the forest of the eastern mountains without being caught. Allana could use her magic to cover our tracks in the snow, then we could find a way to hide from the soldiers and sorcerers and their dogs.

I leaned forward, patting the back of my horse's neck. "Just keep running. We'll make it if you can just keep running."

An odd twang caught my ears.

I peered into the darkness, trying to see where the sound had come from.

I heard it again.

The horse in front of me screamed.

My own mount reared back as the Black Blood fell from his horse, barely scrambling out of the way as the animal toppled to the ground. A pale arrow stuck out of the horse's chest.

"Keep riding!" Emmet shouted.

I didn't want to keep riding. I wanted to check on the horse and find the one who'd shot the arrow and slit their chivving throat, but there was nothing I could do.

Another twang sounded.

I ducked low and kicked my horse forward.

With nothing in front of her, she raced into the darkness.

I looked back, trusting my mount to keep to the road.

Cati reached over the side of the cart, catching the hand of the Black Blood who'd lost his horse. She screamed as she dragged him up. Her stitches would be torn. She needed my help.

I didn't hear the twang of the next arrow.

It struck Neil in the side. He toppled over in his seat.

"No." I tried to scream but couldn't find enough air.

Allana grabbed the reins of the cart's horse. She held her other hand up in the air, as though trying to create some magic to protect us, but there were no lights or sounds.

I didn't know if it was working.

My heart pummeled my throat as Liam stood in the back of the cart, swaying with its movement, barely staying on his feet.

He raised both hands, as though tearing up great chunks of earth, then flung them to the side.

The crashing of stone ripping through wood and flesh carried over the screams of the people hiding in the dark.

Liam fell to his knees.

Cati caught him.

"Liam!" I did manage to scream that time.

"Keep riding." Emmet rode in front of the wagon, racing right behind me. "He's fine, keep going."

I stayed bent over my horse's neck as we fled through the darkness. I kept glancing back every other breath, making sure I hadn't left Emmet and Liam behind.

One of Neil's feet hung over the edge of the wagon, bouncing lifelessly.

Heat burned in my eyes.

Keep riding. Just keep riding.

I don't know how far we'd gone when Liam finally gave the order to stop. A sob caught in my chest at hearing his ragged shout.

He is mine, and he is alive.

I closed my eyes and thanked the gods and stars before slowing my horse and looping her around to stop beside the cart.

Liam pushed himself to his feet. He had to grip the side of the wagon to manage it.

"Liam," I began.

"I'm fine." He reached out to me, touching my hand.

"Cati, your stitches. I need to—"

"Don't worry about me." Cati lay in the bottom of the cart. Someone had wrapped a fresh bandage around her side. "You can fuss about it later."

"We can't count on them not following us," Liam spoke to the few of his people who were still alive. He held the side of the cart as he made his way to the back and jumped down. He swallowed hard, gripping the wooden planks as he swayed. "Tirra, the horse."

"Yes, Liam." Tirra passed him the reins of the last horse.

"They'll bring sorcerers and dogs," Liam said. "We have to get past Carrickbeg and head south down the mountain road. We can't risk cutting into the forest before that. Our tracks and scent would be too easy to follow."

Liam dragged himself up onto the horse. "We will ride, and we will fight. But we will not lead them toward our home."

"Yes, Trueborn," Allana said.

"Yes, Trueborn," the others echoed.

Liam rode up to me and reached for my hand.

I laced my fingers through his, trying to find the words to tell him that I would fight by his side even as the world burned. I would not let the Guilds part us.

"I need you to ride into the forest," Liam said softly. "You have to cut around the north side of Carrickbeg to the eastern mountains."

"We're sticking to the road. You just said—"

"Ena, I need you to get to the cliffs east of Carrickbeg. Climb to the top."

"Liam, no—"

"I sent for help days ago. When we lost Regan." Liam pressed an ink-stained letter into my hand. "Gabe is coming, with more that he's recruited. I told him to meet us up there, but we won't have time to get to them. And I'm not sure enough of where they are to trust a stone bird."

"I'm staying with you."

"If it comes to a fight, we'll need Gabe's people." Liam squeezed my hand. "Get to him.

Tell him to come down to the road south of Carrickbeg. Tell him to be ready to run or fight. Tell him his Trueborn needs him."

"No." I forced the letter into Liam's hand. "Send Emmet. My place is with you."

"You're a lighter rider than I am," Emmet said.

I looked to him. I hadn't realized he was close enough to hear.

"You're a better climber than me, too," my brother said. "Liam's right, we need Gabe. You have to find him."

"I won't." I turned back to Liam, touching his cheek with my frozen hand. "Your path is mine, and we will walk side by side to whatever end."

Liam laid his hand over mine, pressing my palm to his cheek.

"I need you to do this. I'm asking you to save us, Ena." Liam lifted my hand away from his face and kissed my palm. "I need you to ride as fast as you can. Get to the cliff. Find Gabe. We won't survive a fight without his men."

Fear engulfed me. More fear than I could tuck into the blackness inside me.

"I'll find him." My voice echoed like I was speaking from far away.

I looked to Emmet. The pressure in my throat kept me from speaking.

He held my gaze for a moment, gave Liam a nod, and steered his horse to the front of the pack.

"Go." Liam pressed the ink-stained letter into my hand. "You are strong enough to burn the world."

Liam kicked his horse and rode up beside Emmet. The two of them raced into the darkness, taking the others with them.

Leaving me alone on the mountain road.

63

Branches tore at my hair and face. I didn't care.

Nothing mattered but reaching Gabe. I had to find him. I had to save Liam and Emmet. I would not fail the people who were counting on me.

I pushed my horse as hard as I could.

She embraced the challenge, leaping over downed trees, never hesitating as we weaved through the dark forest.

I didn't know if I was going the right way. I bit my lips together and begged the gods and stars to guide me.

I had to get to the cliff.

Reach the cliff. Climb the cliff.

Save Liam. Save my brother.

The pounding of my horse's hooves surrounded me, rattling into my chest until there was nothing else in the world. Just the horse and me and the people I needed to save.

When the sun finally started to rise, my breath caught in my chest, and tears threatened my eyes.

I steered my horse straight toward the glow.

Still, I didn't catch sight of the eastern mountains until I broke free of the forest and reached the northern edge of Carrickbeg.

Lines of soldiers' tents filled the fields, stretching all the way to the backs of the houses along the mountain road.

And I could see the cliff, towering above the village. I couldn't see a hint of Gabe, but he had lived as a Guilded soldier. He would know to stay hidden.

I wanted to cut south, to meet Liam on the road, but I had to find Gabe.

Cati needed fresh stitches, Liam needed rest, Emmet needed more fighters. I would lose them all if I didn't find help.

Their deaths would be my fault if I couldn't find help.

I aimed my horse north, cutting around the soldiers' tents, hoping the gray light of morning would hide me, not caring about being seen as long as I beat the soldiers to the cliff.

The sound of my horse's hooves pounding against the ground drove into my ears as I tried to listen for any trace of Liam. A bang of magic. The screams of battle. Any hint that he was near. That I was already too late.

I pressed my hand to my stone pendant. The warmth of Liam's magic filled my chest, and I pushed my horse to run faster. I could feel her labored breathing and see the sweat glistening on her neck.

"Please," I whispered. "Just a bit farther. Please."

Somewhere in the back of my mind, I heard a shout, like someone telling me to stop.

The voice wasn't Liam's, so I kept riding toward the cliff.

As I neared the rock face, I started searching the cracks for a path to the top. It was taller than anything I'd climbed before, but cutting around would take too much time. I had to go straight up.

I steered my horse to the bottom of the best route I could see and leapt off as soon she stopped.

She panted and huffed, but I didn't even stop to give a thank you. I just dried my frozen hands on my skirt and started climbing.

The rocks were colder than my skin and sent an icy sting through my fingers. I pulled myself up high enough to puff a bit of warm breath onto each hand, then kept climbing.

Heat flowed down my side where I had been sliced what seemed like a lifetime before. I hadn't even looked at the wound.

My arms shook every time I dragged myself up.

"I will not fail you." I pushed myself to climb faster.

The rocks slipped out from under my foot.

I clung to the cliff as my heart hammered in my chest.

I looked down to find a new foothold. The ground was far below, too far to survive a fall.

"I am not afraid. I cannot be afraid."

I climbed and climbed, not bothering to look to see how close I was to the top.

My legs trembled, my body screaming that it would be better to let go and just fall.

But I had to save Liam.

I reached up to find another handhold, and my fingers dug into the snow on the top of the cliff.

I dragged myself onto the flat surface.

Snow chilled my face and froze my hands.

"Gabe," I panted out his name.

The forest in front of me stayed silent.

I pushed myself to my feet, finding enough air to shout. "Gabe!"

A bird burst from the top of a tree, screaming its displeasure to the sky.

I tore through the snow, heading east, farther into the trees. There were animal prints, but no sign of people marked the white.

"Gabe!" My shout carried through the forest, but still, there was no answer.

I ran farther east, falling and pushing myself back up before I had time to spit the ice from my mouth.

"Gabe." I turned south.

If Gabe had wanted a view of the mountain road, he would have gone there, where he could watch more easily.

"Gabe!"

My foot caught on something hidden beneath the snow, and I fell, tumbling down the slope.

Pain shot through my ribs as I struck something hard.

A dark form flashed before my eyes, and I reached out, catching a low branch and stopping my fall. The sudden jolt sent pain throbbing through my shoulder.

"Gabe!"

I looked around, searching for any hint of salvation. Dots of my blood had stained the snow red. I turned away from the proof of my own weakness.

I'd fallen toward the cliff.

I stared out over the land below me. I could see it all.

The houses of Carrickbeg. The soldiers' tents. The mountain road.

Men in black uniforms had gathered at the edge of the trees where the road from the Lir Valley broke free of the woods to run in front of the village.

None of the soldiers entered the forest. They just stood. Waiting. As though their entire reason for creation was to block anyone from breaking free of the woods.

"Gabe! Where are you? Gabe, please!" I tried to make myself run back into the trees. But I couldn't. Helpless fear had frozen me.

"Please." The plea fell from my lips.

A flash of bright blue light flared from inside the woods. Then a boom so loud it shook the snow around my boots.

The soldiers stood their ground.

The trees in the woods trembled.

"Liam." I waited for him to charge out into the open.

The ranks of soldiers backed away from the road, fleeing something I was too distant to see or hear.

A light so bright it pained my eyes flared within the woods, devouring the trees, growing like it would swallow the world.

Without a sound, the light disappeared, leaving a circle of barren ground filled with pure white snow.

The trees had vanished. The muddy scar of the road was gone. There were no hints of life. The light had stolen it all.

I held my breath, waiting for the next round of magic.

But the world stayed still.

"Liam." I pressed my hand to my pendant.

The stone had gone cold.

No warmth. No magic. No life.

I didn't hear my scream, but I felt it tearing from my throat.

I fell to my knees. My legs couldn't hold me anymore, but my screaming didn't stop.

The noise flew from me like it was its own creature. A beast I was too frightened to name.

"Please, Liam." I looked back into the eastern mountains, waiting for Gabe to come running and tell me that he knew what to do. He knew how to save Liam.

No one came.

My sobs banged against my chest, stealing all words and reason.

The pendant turned to ice against my skin. The chill of it stabbed through me like a mortal wound.

My screaming echoed through the woods, and still, no one came.

The snow had numbed my legs before I remembered the letter Liam had given me.

My hands shook as I pulled the paper from my pocket, desperate to find the instructions for some magical trick to save Liam.

The letter hadn't been sealed. It was nothing more than hastily scrawled words on a stained bit of paper.

The first word banished all the air from the world.

Ena,

I'm sorry. I'm sorry I was not brave enough to keep you with me. I can face my end, but I am not strong enough to watch you die. I am not as brave as you.

I have to protect you. I have to keep you safe. It is an oath I will not break.

You are the weakness I cannot overcome.

I don't ask for your forgiveness, I know I won't find it, but I love you. Please believe that.

Fight. Live. Not for me. For the ones who are not strong enough to fight on their own.

I love you.

I would burn the stars to save you.

Liam

64

I don't remember tearing up the letter, but I remember the pieces fluttering in the wind as they fell from my hands. And the sound of my sobs crashing in my chest. And the horrible pain that should have split me in two.

I wanted it to split me in two.

The cold from the snow seeped into my clothes as I waited for the soldiers to come for me. To find me and execute me. To let me flee from the pain I should not have been made to bear.

They didn't come. The woods didn't swallow me.

The world has no mercy.

There was nothing left of me. I was broken beyond repair.

But my heart kept beating, too foolish to understand.

My whole body had gone numb by the time the sun began to set. Physical pain sprang back into being, searing my limbs as I pushed myself to my feet.

I left the girl who was Ena Ryeland in the snow. I cannot carry the grief of the orphan from Harane any longer.

Her story has ended, but my work is far from done.

I will never forgive the ones I had loved for robbing me of the death I had earned. I should have been with them. I should have been fighting by Liam's side when the end came.

Every promise has been broken.

I have been betrayed far past the point of redemption.

I will not do the same to Finn.

I will keep my promise to him. I will burn Ilara.

I headed north, trudging through the snow toward a place I had never been.

There is nothing left for me in this world. I will not leave it until the Guilds crumble to ash.

A NOTE FROM THE AUTHOR

Dear Reader,

I want to thank you for walking alongside Ena throughout her journey. While *Feather and Flame* is the final book in Ena's series, the story of the Guilds and Ilbrea does continue.

Inker and Crown is the first installment of the *Guilds of Ilbrea* series—where danger, treachery, and the fight for freedom continue.

And, of course, our beloved inker will not rest until the Guilds have crumbled to ash. So her part in the story is far from over.

Inker and Crown was actually written two years before I began work on the *Ena of Ilbrea* series. But when I first met our brave and fierce Ena in *Inker and Crown*, I knew she needed the chance to tell you her own story.

If you turn the page, you'll find a chapter of *Inker and Crown* and get a peek at what life is like for those who cherish their place in the Guilds.

Thank you for believing in the strength of an orphan from Harane,

Megan

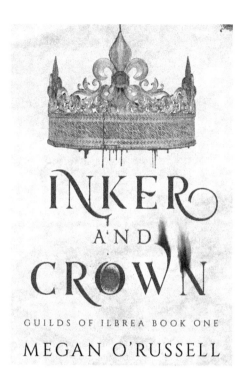

Continue reading for a preview of *Inker and Crown*, Book One in the *Guilds of Ilbrea* series.

ADRIAL

"Sorry," Adrial muttered as he slowly maneuvered his way through the crowd. "So sorry."

Servants carrying trays of bubbling chamb, sweetmeats, and rich cheeses weaved through the Guilded revelers.

The people in the ballroom weren't separated by Guild color anymore. It was all a confusing mass of mingling and laughing.

Paintings of beautiful landscapes and great lords lined the walls, their golden frames glinting in the light of the sparkling chandeliers. All the finery of the Gilded Hall, from crystal glasses to ornate bannisters, had been polished for the occasion.

A troupe of musicians had been brought in for the Winter's End Ball, and the center of the room had been taken over by dancing.

"Pardon me." Adrial sidestepped a girl in healer red as she dragged a soldier onto the floor.

Pain shot through Adrial's bad leg. He struggled to keep his gait even and face pleasant as he plunged deeper into the crowd.

Standing in the cathedral for hours had been torture, but he couldn't say it. Couldn't allow himself the luxury of going home to sleep. Weakness could not be accepted from Lord Gareth's second, not when so much responsibility fell on the head scribe. Not when Lord Gareth was counting on him.

Not when everyone in Ilara agreed Adrial was too young for the position.

"A faster tune!" Kai shouted from the center of the dancers as the song ended. The people around him cheered as Kai grabbed a girl in white, scooping her into his arms and twirling her around.

"Adrial"—a hand slipped into his—"come on."

Keeping his gaze on the dancers, Adrial let himself be led away.

"Kai's lucky the Sailors Guild has very loose expectations of their men." Allora nodded to the revelers who parted ways to grant her and Adrial a path. "Honestly, he shouldn't be making such a spectacle. And even if he seems to be getting away with terrible decorum, he ought to know better. I should know. I'm the one who worked for years trying to teach that boy manners."

"He's only having a good time," Adrial said when they reached the edge of the horde and the crowd swallowed the surging mass of dancers. "He's young. Let him enjoy himself."

"What am I, an old maid?" Allora tossed her long, blond hair over her shoulder. "Kai's barely younger than we are, and we know how to behave properly."

"Some of us are made older."

Allora stopped so quickly, Adrial nearly toppled over trying not to run into her.

"A limp and old age are two very different things, Adrial Ayres." She brushed imagined dust off the shoulders of his white robes. "Don't let a bad leg take credit for good manners."

"Thank you, Allora."

"Now come along." Allora smoothed the folds of her green and gold gown. "The others will be waiting for us."

A wide, stone staircase cut up from the corner of the room. A few people leaned over the railings, either watching the party below or trying to hide how much chamb they'd drunk.

A young man in healer red gripped a glass of frie as he dangled precariously over the crowd. The pungent smell of the strong liquor emanated from the man as much as from his glass.

Allora glared at the man as they climbed the stairs, keeping Adrial's hand firmly in hers as they weaved past a sorcerer trying to fend off the affections of a healer.

Adrial didn't need the help to dodge the couples on the stairs. He could manage the steps on his own, even make better speed than Allora allowed. But she'd been helping him for years. Shaking her off would have been a cruel slight at Winter's End.

And, if he really dared to be honest with himself, he enjoyed the comfort of having someone to walk with. He might not be dancing in the crowd below, but at least he wouldn't be spending his evening alone.

"Are you really hauling us all away from the dancing?" Kai bounded up the stairs to catch them.

Mara followed behind him at a statelier pace, her lips pursed as she hid her smile.

"I'm not hauling anyone away from anything," Allora said. "I'm merely trying to spend time with *my family* before they scatter to the winds on the King's command. If you'd rather cavort with someone you've never met before and will probably never see again—"

"There's nothing I would rather do than spend the evening with the lovely Allora Karron." Kai beat them to the top of the stairs, grabbed Allora's free hand, and gave it a dramatic kiss. "Just promise me there will still be dancing."

"I'll dance with you, you getch." Allora breezed past him. "But only out of pity."

"And you, Mara?" Kai caught her around the waist, twirling her down the hall. "Will you dance with me?"

"I will always dance with you, Kai." Mara laughed as he spun her under his arm.

"Do you want to see what I've planned for us or not?" Allora's severe tone did not match the glimmer in her eyes.

"Of course we do, Allora." Adrial bowed, unable to keep from laughing as Kai lifted Mara high overhead.

"Don't break her!" Allora squealed.

"Not everyone is as fragile as Lady Allora Karron." Kai set Mara back on her feet. "Please forgive me and show us your surprise, miss."

"I don't know why I bother trying to do anything nice for the lot of you." Allora poked Kai's nose and beckoned them all down the corridor.

One side of the hall was lined with doors, but the other was painted with a glorious mural of the southern countryside, an image broken only by one, wide double door set with glass panes.

Allora flung the glass doors open. "Welcome to the Karron clan party!"

A balcony looked out over the thousands of common revelers in the square and the shining white cathedral beyond. Shouts and cheers rose from the crowd below, but the balcony was empty.

"Allora," Mara breathed, stepping past her to take in the view, "what have you done?"

Tiered trays of cakes, fruits, and other delights sat on one round table. Bottles of chamb chilled in the spokes of a compass-shaped ice sculpture. Couches draped with warm blankets to guard against the night chill sat next to candelabras with brightly burning candles.

"And how did you do it?" Niko asked from the doorway.

Tham stood behind Niko's shoulder. While Niko radiated delight, Tham's brow furrowed as he took in the lavish display.

"I know all the best people." Allora grinned. "Sometimes being nice means people are thrilled to help you. You might consider trying it sometime."

"Having coin to pay doesn't hurt, I'm sure." Kai grabbed a bottle of chamb and began pouring a glass for each of the six.

"It's wonderful, Allora." Adrial moved toward the rail.

Torches on poles that reached high above the crowd shed light on the square.

"A toast then?" Kai pressed a glass into Adrial's hand.

"But of course!" Niko grabbed a glass. "A drink for everyone. Even Tham."

"I'm fine." Tham stood in the doorway, hovering on the edge of the group. There wasn't a hint of merriment on his face, but then his dark hair, complexion, and eyes had the effect of making him appear somber at the best of times.

"You must have a drink for the toast." Allora flitted over, glass in hand. "Adrial and I are about to be abandoned in Ilara while you all adventure yet again. Be kind and toast with us. Give me a perfect night to remember when I'm lonely all year."

Without a word, Tham accepted the glass.

"To the Karron clan." Allora held her glass high. "May we bring honor to Ilbrea and the name of Karron wherever we go!"

"To Lord Karron." Mara raised her glass.

"To Lord Karron!" Adrial joined in with the rest of the pack.

"It really is remarkable." Mara sipped her chamb, wrinkling her nose at the taste. "Lord Karron manages to collect one daughter—"

Allora curtsied.

"—two apprentices—"

Mara raised her glass to Niko.

"—and three wards—"

"To the motherless children!" Kai cheered.

"—and look how well each of us has done," Mara finished.

"I really thought one of us would have ended up in prison by now." Niko poured himself another glass of chamb.

"I really thought it would be me." Kai threw himself back onto a couch. "Or maybe Tham."

"I'm quiet about the trouble I make." Tham gave a rare smile. "It would have been you."

"And we always knew who would rise the highest." Mara pulled two sandwiches from the tray, passing one to Tham before biting into her own. "To Adrial, the future Lord Scribe of Ilbrea."

"I was always certain our sweet Adrial would achieve greatness." Allora leaned on the railing by his side. "From the day my father dragged a ragged boy from Ian Ayres into the Map Master's Palace, I was quite sure there was utter brilliance beneath those caked-on pounds of mud."

"To our brilliant prodigy, Adrial Ayres!" Kai raised his fresh glass of chamb.

"I'm not brilliant. I'm just the only one of us not to have caused any trouble." Adrial smiled. "And perhaps becoming a lord isn't what it should be." He sipped his chamb, letting the dry sweetness flood his mouth.

He could say it to them. They were his family. They'd all been raised by Lord Karron, though none but Allora shared Lord Karron's blood. They'd seen each other at their worst and best and still held fast to their little clan. "Master Gareth wants me to make the vellum. He thinks it will be a good way to show my worth. To prove to the Scribes Guild that he was right to name me as his heir."

"What vellum?" Niko asked as the rest of them looked somewhere between awed and sympathetic.

"Didn't you listen in the council?" Allora asked.

"Of course he didn't," Mara said. "I had to kick him to make him look in the right direction."

"The King wants a new vellum made." Tham finally stepped onto the balcony, joining the rest of the group. "A new, fully illuminated volume detailing the history of the royal Willoc family in Ilbrea. A wedding gift for Princess Illia to take with her to her new home in Wyrain."

"And you're to make it?" Allora clasped Adrial's hand. "That's wonderful, Adrial. Just fantastic!"

"A book like that will have to be a real work of art," Kai said.

"He'll be brilliant." Allora shot a glare at Kai.

"If I'm not, if I fail, all of Ilbrea will know." A lump formed somewhere between his lungs and throat as he said the words. "A project this large will take the full two years."

"The vellum will be magnificent." Mara set down her glass and pulled Adrial into a tight hug. "Lord Karron will be so proud of you. We're all so proud of you."

"To Adrial." Niko raised his glass.

"To Adrial!" the others chorused.

"What about the rest of you?" Allora asked. "Where are you going, and how soon are you abandoning us?"

"No idea," Kai said. "The King wants a fleet of new ships and a path plotted around the horn at the southern tip of the continent. Who knows where in that I'll fall? Though I do hope I'll get to sail around the horn. See the great southern storms, fight the wind herself."

"Don't talk like that, you terrify me," Allora chided.

"Like you've never been shipwrecked before," Kai laughed.

"Hush, you." Allora blushed and sipped her chamb.

"I've no idea where I'll be sent," Mara said. "We're meeting in the Map Makers' Hall tomorrow. I suppose your father will tell us where we're to be assigned then."

"And our stalwart Tham?" Allora asked.

"I don't know." Tham's eyes flitted to Mara for a moment. "I've experience guarding the map makers' journeys, and with the amount of work that needs done, they can't venture into uncharted lands with new blood who can't tell a compass from a sword."

"I'm sure my father will request you, as always." Allora raised her glass to Tham, giving a not so subtle wink to Mara.

"It takes time to organize a journey," Niko said. "No matter what the King wants, we won't be able to leave for a week at least, more likely two."

"Two weeks of company, Adrial," Allora cooed. "How very lucky are we?"

"Exceptionally." Adrial nodded.

"A lot can happen in two weeks." Niko sat forward on his couch. "You could plan a whole wedding in two weeks if a certain girl who knows all the right people set her mind to it."

"Are you planning on getting married, Nikolas? I must meet the lucky girl." Allora took a long drink of chamb.

"Oh, Allora." Mara poured herself another glass.

"For the love of Aximander's greatness, just marry me, Allora." Niko dropped to his knees. "I'll beg in front of those we like best, just marry me."

"Will he bark like a dog, too?" Kai whispered loudly.

"Marry you?" Allora laughed.

If he hadn't spent years with her, Adrial might not have noticed the hurt in Allora's tone.

"Marry you and spend two weeks in your grand company? Leave my father's magnificent palace on the cliffs to move into a small house where I can console myself in your long absences that at least I'm a wife? I'd rather not."

"You break my heart with every rejection." Niko slumped dramatically to the ground.

"Then stop asking." Allora tossed her hair over her shoulder and turned toward the square.

"And what will you do, my beautiful Allora? Marry a merchant? A commoner?" Niko asked.

"She'd never lower herself so," Kai said. "None but a Guilded man for Allora Karron."

"Perhaps I'll marry Adrial," Allora said. "Be the Lord Scribe's wife."

"Careful, Allora," Adrial said. "Tease one too many times, and poor Niko might believe you."

"No, I refuse." Niko ran to Allora, sweeping her into his arms, leading her in a dance to match the music coming from the square below. "I will have you or no one. You have held my heart for years, Allora Karron. I have learned patience none but Dudia can match."

"I will not have a husband whose breath smells of frie." Allora laughed, leaning into Niko's arms as he spun her.

"Tham, will you dance with Mara?" Kai asked.

"Not tonight," Tham said.

"Then it is my happy duty." Kai pulled Mara from her seat, leading her in a rather more athletic dance than the one Niko and Allora swayed to.

Adrial turned back out to the square, closing his eyes, trying to memorize the laughter of his friends.

Allora was right. It would be a long, lonely time before they were together again.

The music changed, and the crowd cheered as the new song began.

Adrial opened his eyes, wanting to bask in the joy of the people below.

A girl danced at the center of the throng, spinning as she flitted from partner to partner, never staying near one man long enough for him to wrap his arms around her, though most of them tried. Her hair shimmered in the torchlight, one moment seeming pale purple, the next deep blue, matching the tight bodice she wore. Tiers of fabric cut into slices, like fish scales of every color imaginable, made the layers of her skirt.

She twirled between two men, and her skirt swirled around her like a cloud.

It was as though a fairy had escaped a children's tale and landed in the middle of the cathedral square. She tipped her head back and laughed.

Adrial wished he could hear the sound over the music.

A man dressed in the dull brown and yellow of the Guilds' servants waved as he wound his way toward her, his gaze fixed on the fluttering of her hair.

Adrial gripped the rail, not letting go even when pain snuck into his bad shoulder. Surely, the girl hadn't done anything wrong. There was no reason for her to be in trouble with the Gilded Hall. There was no rule against dancing in the square on Winter's End.

The girl smiled as the man reached her, letting the servant lean in to speak in her ear.

Her eyes flicked up to the balcony, landing on Adrial.

Heat rose to Adrial's face. He shouldn't have been watching. Not that there was anything wrong with watching the dancers.

The girl cut through the crowd, keeping her gaze locked on Adrial, not pausing as a man offered her a drink, or as a child poked at her flowing skirt.

Adrial tried to pull his hands from the railing, tried to look away from the square. But there was an enchantment about the girl, an undeniable pull as she reached the front of the building.

She finally looked away, examining the columns that held up the stone balcony.

Air flooded back into Adrial's lungs. It was only a coincidence the girl had looked at him, nothing more. Still he couldn't pull his gaze away from her.

She was only twenty feet below him now, and the light from the front of the building showed her hair as it truly was—not one color that changed in the light, but a dozen beautiful colors spread haphazardly through the strands.

Adrial's heart stopped as the girl looked up at him and winked.

She grabbed on to the stone flowers that coated the column and began to climb. The movement was as easy as that of a cat scaling a tree. The girl pulled herself up, rose by rose, her toes finding purchase on the spirals cut deep into the stone.

"Adrial, what are you..." Allora began before gasping, "By Aximander's greatness," as the girl pulled herself over the railing and onto the balcony.

"Hello, scribe." The girl smiled.

Tham stepped forward, pulling his knife from its sheath.

"Going to stab a girl for climbing a balcony?" The girl raised an eyebrow at Tham. "Didn't know the soldiers had sunk so low."

"How dare—" Allora began, but the girl turned back to Adrial and pulled three glass vials from deep within the folds of her layered skirt.

"I'll be by in the morning to discuss your order, scribe." She pressed the vials into Adrial's hand and started toward the glass doors. "But fair warning, my work is very expensive."

Without a backwards glance, she strolled into the hall and out of sight.

"What?" Allora squeaked indignantly.

"Who was she?" Kai stared after her.

"More importantly, what did she give you?" Mara peered over Adrial's shoulder.

Adrial held the vials up to a glowing candelabra.

The first held a black so deep, the light couldn't pass through it. The second, a pale lilac to match the most prominent color woven through the girl's hair. And the third, a vibrant red that seemed to hold a spark of fire hidden just out of sight.

"Ink," Adrial said after a long moment. "She's brought me ink."

"An inker climbed the balcony to give you samples?" Allora shut the balcony doors. "Commoners can't seem to understand their place in the world these days."

"Marks for determination though," Niko said. "That was a bit of a climb."

"I suppose this will be your life from now on," Kai sighed. "Beautiful, technicolor women fighting to win your business. Perhaps I should have chosen a more scholarly path. Too late for me, I suppose. Ah, well. A toast to Adrial. May many women scale our beloved scribe's balcony."

Order your copy of Inker and Crown *to continue the story.*

ESCAPE INTO ADVENTURE

Thank you for reading Ena of Ilbrea: The Four Book Saga. If you enjoyed the book, please consider leaving a review to help other readers find Ena Ryeland's story.

As always, thanks for reading,

Megan O'Russell

Never miss a moment of the danger or romance.

Join the Megan O'Russell mailing list to stay up to date on all the action by visiting https://www.meganorussell.com/book-signup.

ABOUT THE AUTHOR

Megan O'Russell is the author of several Young Adult series that invite readers to escape into worlds of adventure. From *Girl of Glass*, which blends dystopian darkness with the heart-pounding danger of vampires, to *Ena of Ilbrea*, which draws readers into an epic world of magic and assassins.

With the *Girl of Glass* series, *The Tethering* series, *The Chronicles of Maggie Trent*, *The Tale of Bryant Adams*, the *Ena of Ilbrea* series, and several more projects planned for 2020, there are always exciting new books on the horizon. To be the first to hear about new releases, free short stories, and giveaways, sign up for Megan's newsletter by visiting the following:

https://www.meganorussell.com/book-signup.

Originally from Upstate New York, Megan is a professional musical theatre performer whose work has taken her across North America. Her chronic wanderlust has led her from Alaska to Thailand and many places in between. Wanting to travel has fostered Megan's love of books that allow her to visit countless new worlds from her favorite reading nook. Megan is also a lyricist and playwright. Information on her theatrical works can be found at RussellCompositions.com.

She would be thrilled to chat with you on Facebook or Twitter @MeganORussell, elated if you'd visit her website MeganORussell.com, and over the moon if you'd like the pictures of her adventures on Instagram @ORussellMegan.

ALSO BY MEGAN O'RUSSELL

The Girl of Glass Series
Girl of Glass

Boy of Blood

Night of Never

Son of Sun

The Tale of Bryant Adams
How I Magically Messed Up My Life in Four Freakin' Days

Seven Things Not to Do When Everyone's Trying to Kill You

Three Simple Steps to Wizarding Domination

Five Spellbinding Laws of International Larceny

The Tethering Series
The Tethering

The Siren's Realm

The Dragon Unbound

The Blood Heir

The Chronicles of Maggie Trent
The Girl Without Magic

The Girl Locked with Gold

The Girl Cloaked in Shadow

Ena of Ilbrea
Wrath and Wing

Ember and Stone

Mountain and Ash

Ice and Sky

Feather and Flame

Guilds of Ilbrea
Inker and Crown

Myth and Storm